NEW TOEIC
950

聽力＋閱讀
5回達標

全新完整試題

Hackers Academia ／著　　林建豪、陳宜慧／譯

suncolor
三采文化

國家圖書館出版品預行編目資料

NEW TOEIC 950 聽力＋閱讀 5 回達標：全新完整試題＋解析本【附線上 1000 單字記憶本＋聽力訓練筆記】/Hackers Academia 作；林建豪、陳宜慧譯 . -- 初版 . -- 臺北市：三采文化股份有限公司 , 2024.05　面；　公分
ISBN 978-626-358-334-4(平裝)

1.CST: 多益測驗

805.1895　　　　　　　　　　113003728

suncolor 三采文化

多益瘋狂拿分 02

NEW TOEIC 950 聽力+閱讀 5 回達標
全新完整試題＋解析本【附線上 1000 單字記憶本＋聽力訓練筆記】

作者｜ Hackers Academia　　譯者｜林建豪、陳宜慧
編輯三部 副總編輯｜喬郁珊　　編輯｜王惠民　　美術主編｜藍秀婷　　封面設計｜李蕙雲
內頁編排｜菩薩蠻電腦科技有限公司　　執行編輯｜劉兆婷　　版權選書｜孔奕涵

發行人｜張輝明　　總編輯長｜曾雅青
發行所｜三采文化股份有限公司　　地址｜台北市內湖區瑞光路 513 巷 33 號 8 樓
傳訊｜ TEL:（02）8797-1234　　FAX:（02）8797-1688　　網址｜ www.suncolor.com.tw
郵政劃撥｜帳號：14319060　　戶名：三采文化股份有限公司
本版發行｜ 2024 年 5 月 31 日　　定價｜ NT$699

一本就夠
提升「多益實戰能力」

想要有效準備多益測驗，
最重要的就是充分利用實戰練習，
提升「多益實戰能力」。

《NEW TOEIC 950 聽力+閱讀 5 回達標》
可讓你在短時間內熟悉多益題型，
憑一本書就能準備實戰。

利用多元的
學習資料補強！

翻譯、解析精準到位，
掌握判斷選項對錯的根據！

透過 5 回聽力+閱讀模擬測驗
提升實戰能力！

Contents

試題本

📖 解析本

📑 線上單字記憶本

📖 線上聽力訓練筆記

特色介紹

01 5 回聽力+閱讀模擬考，快速提升實戰力！

想提升多益測驗的實戰能力，就必須全面熟悉聽力和閱讀。本書收錄實戰模擬測驗共 5 回，一本解決聽力、閱讀的解題練習。

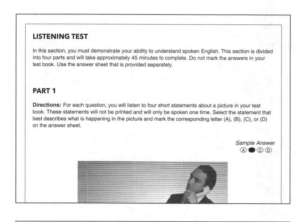

Listening Test

聽力實戰模擬測驗完整反映多益的出題趨勢，只要根據教材練習解題，就能在短時間內累積實戰能力。

Reading Test

閱讀實戰模擬測驗完整反映多益的出題趨勢，只要根據教材練習解題，就能在短時間內累積實戰能力。

Answer Sheet

運用本書附錄的 Answer Sheet 空白答案卡，比照實戰練習，熟悉管理時間的方法，讓臨場感更逼真。

02 精準翻譯，確實掌握選項對錯的原因！

本書包含所有題目的精準翻譯與解析，作答後加以對照再確實統整是很重要的，能幫助你掌握正確答案與錯誤選項的原因，補強自身弱點。

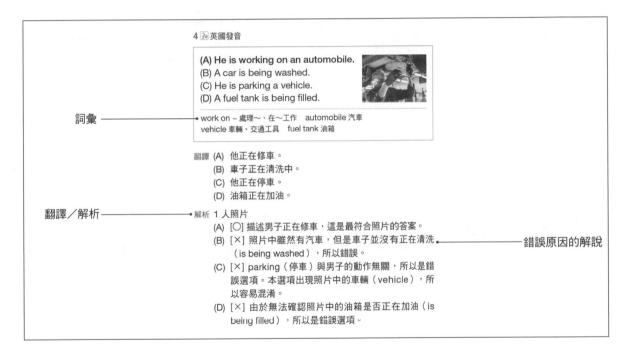

4 英國發音

(A) He is working on an automobile.
(B) A car is being washed.
(C) He is parking a vehicle.
(D) A fuel tank is being filled.

詞彙 → work on ~ 處理～、在～工作　automobile 汽車
vehicle 車輛、交通工具　fuel tank 油箱

翻譯 (A) 他正在修車。
(B) 車子正在清洗中。
(C) 他正在停車。
(D) 油箱正在加油。

翻譯／解析 → **解析** 1 人照片
(A) [○] 描述男子正在修車，這是最符合照片的答案。
(B) [×] 照片中雖然有汽車，但是車子並沒有正在清洗 ——— 錯誤原因的解說
（is being washed），所以錯誤。
(C) [×] parking（停車）與男子的動作無關，所以是錯誤選項。本選項出現照片中的車輛（vehicle），所以容易混淆。
(D) [×] 由於無法確認照片中的油箱是否正在加油（is being filled），所以是錯誤選項。

翻譯與解析

利用所有短文與問題的正確翻譯，可清楚了解不好懂的句子結構，透過解析則有助於思索如何選出正確答案。

錯誤選項的解說

詳細說明錯誤選項不是答案的理由，幫助你掌握錯誤的原因、加強自身觀念。

詞彙

同時收錄短文與問題中的單字與表達方式，省去複習題目時要一一查字典的不便。

特色介紹

03 多元化的附贈學習資源，著重加強弱點！

當你藉由解題掌握自身弱點之後，可運用本書附贈的多元化學習資源予以補強，這點相當重要。補強弱點，更容易達到目標分數。

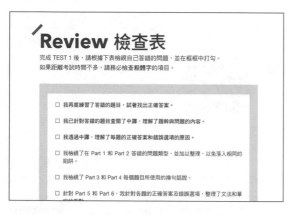

Review 檢查表

依照每回測驗後面的 Review 檢查表，可詳細檢視答錯的題目，補強自身弱點。

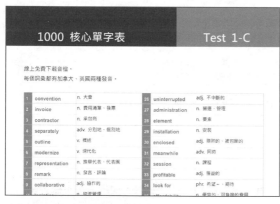

單字記憶本（PDF & MP3）

運用免費的線上單字記憶本，可複習、記憶本書收錄的測驗重要詞彙與表達方式。

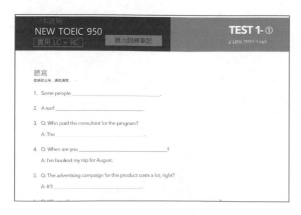

聽力訓練筆記（PDF & MP3）

運用免費的聽力訓練筆記，可複習測驗中的核心句子，培養基本實力，進而提升聽力的分數。

04 線上資源、多種版本的 MP3，掃 QR code 就能取得！

TEST 1~5 共 6 款音檔、單字記憶本、聽力訓練筆記都可線上聆聽或下載，檔案格式為 MP3。

步驟 1
掃描書中 QR code 進入網頁。

步驟 2
點選要使用的素材或音檔。

※TEST 1~5音檔，包含實戰版、練習版（分部、分題）、考場蟬聲版、考場雜音版、英澳發音版、高速版。

※單字記憶本、聽力訓練筆記之內容 PDF 可線上閱覽或下載使用。

多益測驗介紹

什麼是多益測驗？

TOEIC 由 Test Of English for International Communication 縮寫而成，這個測驗是以母語非英文的人為對象，著重於語言基本的「溝通」功能，用於評估日常生活或國際商務等需要的實用英文能力。多益是以上述需要之內容而研發的，主要涵蓋下列的實用性主題。

- 合作開發：研究、產品研發
- 財務計畫：貸款、投資、稅務會計、銀行業務
- 一般業務：契約、協商、行銷、販售
- 技術領域：電力、工業技術、電腦、實驗室
- 事務領域：會議、文件業務
- 物品購買：購物、訂購、付款

- 用餐：餐廳、聚餐、宴會
- 文化：電影、運動、野餐
- 健康：醫療保險、醫院診療、牙科
- 製造：生產裝配線、工廠經營
- 聘僱：僱用、退休、獎勵、升遷、工作機會
- 建築：不動產、搬家、辦公場所

多益各 PART 測驗內容

部分	內容		題數	時間	配分
Listening Test	Part 1｜	照片描述	6 題（1~6 題）	45 分鐘	495 分
	Part 2｜	應答問題	25 題（7~31 題）		
	Part 3｜	簡短對話	39 題，13 篇短文（32~70 題）		
	Part 4｜	簡短獨白	30 題，10 篇短文（71~100 題）		
Reading Test	Part 5｜	句子填空（文法／單字）	30 題（101~130 題）	75 分鐘	495 分
	Part 6｜	段落填空（文法／單字／句子）	16 題，4 篇短文（131~146 題）		
	Part 7｜	短文閱讀（解讀）	54 題，15 篇短文（147~200 題）		
		- 單篇短文（Single Passage）	- 29 題，10 篇短文（147~175 題）		
		- 雙篇短文（Double Passages）	- 10 題，2 篇短文（176~185 題）		
		- 三篇短文（Triple Passages）	- 15 題，3 篇短文（186~200 題）		
總計	7 個部分		200 題	120 分鐘	990 分

從報名到確認成績

1. 報名

查看報名時間	準備照片（jpg 圖檔）	網路／APP 報名
·詳細資訊請至「TOEIC 臺灣區官方網站上查詢。（https://www.toeic.com.tw/） ·經常會有追加考試，可上網確認。	·報名需要 jpg 格式的照片，請事先備妥。	·從 TOEIC 臺灣區官網或 APP 的考試報名視窗中，依照程序輸入資料。

2. 考試

相關用品

| 證件 | 2B 鉛筆與橡皮擦 | 指針式手錶 |

＊考試當天如果沒有攜帶證件，將無法參加考試。有效身分證件包括：「中華民國國民身分證正本」或「有效期限內之中華民國護照正本」；未滿 16 歲的考生可持「健保卡正本」入場。

測驗流程

時間	項目
AM 09:30 - 09:50	填寫基本資料及問卷
AM 09:50 - 10:10	確認身分證件與分發試題本
AM 10:10 - 10:55	聽力測驗（Listening Test）
AM 10:55 - 12:10	閱讀測驗（Reading Test）

＊考試時間約 150 分鐘，測驗中無休息時間。建議至少提早 30 分鐘抵達考場，測驗（含基本資料填寫）開始後即不得入場。
＊臺灣考區一般的測驗時間為上午，若遇到場地租借問題或其他原因，可能會更改測驗時間或同時有上、下午場次，因此確切時間請以考前上網查詢的應考資訊為準。

3. 確認成績

網路查詢	報名時有填寫 Email 的考生，可於成績開放查詢期間內進入測驗服務專區查詢。
成績單	測驗結束後 12 個工作天（不含假日）以平信方式寄出。

Part 1~7 題型解說 & 解題策略

Part 1 照片描述（6 題）

・Part 1 是要從 4 個選項中選出最符合照片情境的敘述。
・試題本上只會出現照片，語音則會唸出 4 個選項。

題型

<table>
<tr><td>

【試題本】

1.

</td><td>

【語音】

Number 1.

Look at the picture marked number one in your test book.

(A) A woman is serving a meal.
(B) A woman is washing a bowl.
(C) A woman is pouring some water.
(D) A woman is preparing some food.

</td></tr>
</table>

出題趨勢與應對策略

以人為主軸的照片最常出現！

事物與風景
的照片 28%

以人為主軸
的照片 72%

> Part 1 以人為主軸的照片最常出現，平均會有 4~5 題。

核心應對策略

聽選項前先確認照片類型，事先聯想相關的表達方式。
依照是否有人物、人數多少來確認照片類型，並事先聯想人物的動作／狀態或事物的狀態／位置與相關表達方式，就能把選項聽得更清楚，進而更容易選出正確答案。

練習標示 ○、×、△ 與過濾錯誤選項。
如果不標示 ○、×、△，就容易把不同選項搞混，因此解題時邊聽選項邊標示 ○、×、△，刪除容易混淆視聽的錯誤選項，以確保能選出正確答案。

Part 2 應答問題（25 題）

· Part 2 要根據問題或敘述選出最合適的答案。
· 試題本上沒有問題與選項，會由語音唸出問題與 3 個選項。

題型

【試題本】	【語音】
7. Mark your answer on your answer sheet.	Number 7. Where is the nearest park? **(A) There's one on Lincoln Avenue.** (B) No, I don't drive. (C) I'm nearly finished.

出題趨勢與應對策略

疑問詞疑問句最常出現！

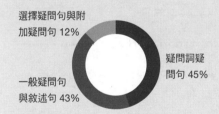

選擇疑問句與附加疑問句 12%

一般疑問句與敘述句 43%

疑問詞疑問句 45%

> Part 2 中的疑問詞疑問句平均為 11~12 題，最常出現；其次是一般疑問句和敘述句，平均 10~11 題；選擇疑問句和附加疑問句則平均為 3~4 題。

【核心應對策略】

務必留意問題的第一個字
Part 2 平均出現 11~12 題的疑問詞疑問句，大部分只聽句首的疑問詞就能選出正確答案；不過，附加疑問句是在句末加上 isn't it 或是 right，選擇疑問句則必須聽完中間的連接詞 or 後才能掌握其類型。

練習標示 ○、×、△ 與過濾錯誤選項。
如果不標示 ○、×、△，就容易把不同選項搞混，因此解題時邊聽選項邊標示 ○、×、△，刪除容易混淆視聽的錯誤選項，以確保能選出正確答案。

Part 1~7 題型解說 & 解題策略

Part 3 簡短對話（39 題）

- Part 3 的每段交談會有 2~3 個說話者，要先聽完，再為 3 個相關問題選出正確答案。
- 試題本上總共有 39 題，每一題都有 1 個提問與 4 個選項，部分問題也會搭配圖表資料。語音會先播放對話內容，再提出 3 個相關問題。

題型

【試題本】

32. What did the woman do during lunchtime?

(A) **Spoke with a supervisor**
(B) Called an important client
(C) Visited another company
(D) Finished a report

33. Why does the woman say, "But I have to meet with a Sorel representative on Friday"?

(A) To confirm an appointment
(B) To explain a mistake
(C) **To express concern**
(D) To change a deadline

34. What do the men suggest the woman do?

(A) Deal with a complaint
(B) Work on another project
(C) Review their proposals
(D) **Meet them after work**

【語音】

Questions 32 through 34 refer to the following conversation with three speakers.

W: George, Jerry . . . I'm sorry I couldn't make it for lunch today. My boss wanted to talk with me about the advertising campaign for Sorel Incorporated. This is a big project, and I'm a little nervous about it.

M1: Don't worry. You're a hard worker. And our clients never complain about your work.

W: But I have to meet with a Sorel representative on Friday. I'm not sure if I'll be able to create a proposal in time.

M2: Why don't we all go to a café after work? We can help you come up with some ideas.

M1: Yeah. We're happy to help.

Number 32. What did the woman do during lunchtime?

Number 33. Why does the woman say, "But I have to meet with a Sorel representative on Friday"?

Number 34. What do the men suggest the woman do?

出題趨勢與應對策略

每次都有 2 組 3 人的對話！

2 人對話 + 圖表
資料 23%

3 人對話
15%

2 人對話 62%

> Part 3 每次都有 2 組 3 人對話，2 人對話則最多有 8 組，也會有 3 組 2 人對話搭配圖表資料。

核心應對策略

聆聽對話前一定要先讀問題。
先讀問題的關鍵字句，才能擬定對策，找出要著重的部分；如果是有圖表資料的問題，則要同時確認問題與圖表資料，掌握資料的類型與內容。如果是判斷意圖的問題，先確認提示中的引述句，事先預測可使用該引述句的語境。

邊聽對話，邊選出正確答案。
讀問題時，必須根據擬定的對策邊聽對話邊回答 3 個問題。換句話說，每次一聽完對話內容，就必須選出問題的答案。

一定要聽清楚對話初期的內容。
Part 3 在對話一開始談到的內容，80% 以上都會出題，特別是詢問對話的主題、目的、說話者或場所的問題，答題線索都會在對話前面出現。因此，如果沒有聽清楚，很可能會把後面出現的特定表達方式誤認為答案，所以必須多加留意。

注意 3 人登場的對話內容。
在 3 人對話中，2 名相同性別的說話者會用不同國籍的發音來區分，因此需要練習聆聽美國、英國、澳洲、加拿大的發音，以辨別說話者，精準掌握語境。

Part 1~7 題型解說 & 解題策略

Part 4 簡短獨白（30 題）

· Part 4 的題型是要聽完獨白，再為 3 個相關問題選出正確答案。
· 試題本上共有 30 題，每一題都是 1 個提問搭配 4 個選項，部分題目也會有圖表資料，而每次說完獨白之後，就會提出 3 個問題。

題型

【試題本】

Lunch Specials	
Item	**Price**
Panini Sandwich	$7
Spaghetti	$6
Dinner Specials	
Item	**Price**
Lasagna	$9
Grilled Chicken	$11

71. What did the speaker do yesterday?

(A) Raised dish prices
(B) Attended a staff gathering
(C) Met with customers
(D) Sent menu information

72. Look at the graphic. Which meal will come with a complimentary beverage?

(A) Panini Sandwich
(B) Spaghetti
(C) Lasagna
(D) Grilled Chicken

73. What will the speaker probably do next?

(A) Arrange some tables
(B) Stock some ingredients
(C) Hand out a list
(D) Print a coupon

【語音】

Questions 71 through 73 refer to the following talk and menu.

As many of you already know, our restaurant's menu will be updated soon. I sent everyone an e-mail with the details yesterday, but I'll go over the main changes quickly now. First, the prices of our dinner menu items have been reduced by 10 percent to attract more evening customers. Also, we will provide a complimentary coffee or soft drink with one of our lunch specials . . . uh, the cheaper one. Some new dishes will be offered as well. I will now pass around a list of these dishes and the ingredients they will contain. Please study it so you'll be able to answer diners' questions.

Number 71. What did the speaker do yesterday?

Number 72. Look at the graphic. Which meal will come with a complimentary beverage?

Number 73. What will the speaker probably do next?

出題趨勢與應對策略

詢問獨白細節的問題最常出現！

關於整段獨白
的問題 23%

關於具體細節的
問題 77%

Part 4 會出現詢問獨白細節的問題，平均有 22~23 題，是最常
見的類型。其中會有 2 題需要對照圖片或表格等資料。

核心應對策略

聆聽獨白前一定要先閱讀問題，並掌握圖表資料的內容。
先讀問題的關鍵字句，才能擬定對策，找出要著重的部分；如果是有圖表資料的問題，則要同時確認問題與圖表資料，掌握
資料的類型與內容。如果是判斷意圖的問題，先確認提示中的引述句，事先預測可使用該引述句的語境。

邊聽對話，邊選出正確答案。
讀問題時，必須根據擬定的對策邊聽對話邊回答 3 個問題。換句話說，每次一聽完對話內容，就必須選出問題的答案。

一定要聽清楚對話初期的內容。
Part 4 在對話一開始談到的內容，80% 以上都會出題，特別是詢問對話的主題、目的、說話者或場所的問題，答題線索都
會在對話前面出現。因此，如果沒有聽清楚，很可能會把後面出現的特定表達方式誤認為答案，所以必須多加留意。

Part 1~7 題型解說 & 解題策略

Part 5 句子填空（30 題）

・Part 5 是要從 4 個選項中選出適合空格的文法或詞彙。
・如果想保留充裕時間回答 Part 7 的問題，則每題都要在 20~22 秒內完成，才能在 11 分鐘內完成 30 題。

題型

1. 文法

> **101.** Kathleen Wilson is a recent graduate who ------- three months ago to help the marketing team with graphic design.
>
> (A) hired   (B) hiring   **(C) was hired**   (D) is hiring

2. 詞彙

> **102.** In spite of the bad weather and traffic delays, Mr. Chandra showed up ------- for his coworker's housewarming party.
>
> (A) gradually   (B) intensely   (C) considerably   **(D) punctually**

出題趨勢與應對策略

文法問題最常出現！

詞彙問題 33%

文法問題 67%

在 Part 5 中，詢問文法構成要素和用途的問題平均有 20~21 個，而從語境中選出合適詞彙的問題平均有 9~10 個。

核心應對策略

先看選項，辨別是文法或詞彙問題。
出現像 hired、hiring、was hired、is hiring 這種都是由相同單字演變的不同型態，那就是文法問題；如果是像 gradually、intensely、considerably、punctually 這樣包含相同詞性的不同詞彙，則屬於詞彙問題。

辨別問題類型後，利用空格前後文、句子整體結構或語境選出正確答案。
文法問題可利用空格前後文或句子的整體結構，選擇適合填入的文法元素當作正確答案。如果單單只靠結構無法解題，請確認語境再答題。若是詞彙問題，則要選擇最適合其語境的詞彙。

Part 6 段落填空（16 題）

- Part 6 中，每個段落有 4 個空格，每個空格需要從 4 個選項中選出合適的文法或句子。
- 如果想保留充裕的時間回答 Part 7 的問題，則每個問題都要在 25~30 秒內完成，才能在 8 分鐘內完成 16 題。

題型

Questions 131-134 refer to the following e-mail.

-------. As you know, you are in charge of driving our visitor from Fennel Corporation, Mr. Palmer. He will be
131.
here as scheduled from May 16 to 20. However, his arrival time from Dublin has been moved back four hours
because he ------- a quick stop in New York. This means you do not need to be at the airport until 2 P.M. on
132.
the 16th. Also, the factory tour ------- he was supposed to take on Monday morning has been canceled. He'll
133.
have a breakfast meeting with the plant manager instead at the Oberlin Hotel. Attached is a revised -------.
134.
Please let me know as soon as you've confirmed these adjustments.

Helen Cho, Client relations Ctrek Apparel

---

131. (A) Regretfully, Mr. Palmer will no longer be needing our services.
    (B) I'm writing to inform you of a few changes concerning our client.
    (C) The following are some details about the new factory manager.
    (D) Finally, I have received the new schedule for your flight to Dublin.

132. (A) will be made   **(B) is making**
    (C) had made   (D) has been making

133. (A) this   (B) what
    (C) when   **(D) that**

134. **(A) itinerary**   (B) estimate
    (C) transcript   (D) inventory

出題趨勢與應對策略

選擇句子填空的問題共有 4 題！

詞彙問題 29%

選擇合適
的句子 25%

文法問題 46%

> Part 6 中，挑選適合填入空格之句子的題型，每次會出 4 題；詢問文法要素和用途的問題平均有 7~8 題，最為常見；而選擇符合語境之詞彙，平均會出現 4~5 題。

核心應對策略

利用包含空格的句子、前後文或整篇短文的結構和語境來選出正確答案。
先看包含空格的句子，假如這麼做還是很難答題，則務必了解前後文、整篇短文的結構和語境，再選擇最適合的選項。

Part 1~7 題型解說 & 解題策略

Part 7 閱讀理解（54 題）

· Part 7 會出現和短文相關的問題，每題都要從 4 個選項中選出最合適的答案。
· 閱讀短文分成單篇（Single Passage）、雙篇短文（Double Passages）和三篇短文（Triple Passages）。單篇短文有 29 題，雙篇短文有 10 題，三篇短文有 15 題。
· 如果想在有限時間內完成 Part 7 的所有問題，每題都必須在 1 分鐘內完成。

題型

1. 單篇短文（Single Passage）

Questions 149-150 refer to the following text message chain.

Natasha Lee	4:08 P.M.

Robert, about the sponsorship packages for the Shoreland Music Festival, do you want to go for the Platinum package? It allows us to broadcast commercials during the event.

Robert Brown	4:09 P.M.

That would give us good exposure. Plus, we can put up company banners at the venue.

Natasha Lee	4:10 P.M.

That's right. So, should I go ahead and sign us up? The deadline is this Friday.

Robert Brown	4:10 P.M.

Well, we can't spend any more than $6,000 on this. How much is it?

Natasha Lee	4:12 P.M.

More than that. How about the Gold sponsorship package then? It costs $5,250, and festival announcers will mention our company over the loudspeakers throughout the day.

Robert Brown	4:13 P.M.

That sounds OK to me. Send me all the details once you're done.

---

149. In which department do the writers most likely work?

(A) Accounting
(B) Marketing
(C) Customer service
(D) Human resources

150. At 4:12 P.M., what does Ms. Lee most likely mean when she writes, "More than that"?

(A) She believes that registering after the deadline is acceptable.
(B) She acknowledges that a cost exceeds a budgeted amount.
(C) She would like to receive some additional sponsorship benefits.
(D) She doubts that $6,000 is their maximum spending allowance.

2. 雙篇短文（Double Passages）

Questions 176-180 refer to the following e-mail and online form.

To	Jennifer Ellis <jenniferellis@jagmail.com>
From	Travis Whitman <traviswhitman@mywebpress.com>
Date	November 1
Subject	Action Needed on Your Account

Dear Ms. Ellis,

Your MyWebPress account is due for renewal in 10 days. You have the option to pay for another year at the rate of $29.99, or you may choose the three-year option at $79.99. We also offer a premium version of MyWebPress that enables many more features and design templates. One year of the higher level software costs $49.99 while the three-year package price is $129.99.

These special prices are only available if your renewal form is received by November 10.

Thank you,

Travis Whitman

MyWebPress Subscription Renewal Form   Date: November 8

Please fill out all information to process your renewal request and payment.

Account Name	Jennifer Ellis		Account Number	83402839

Please choose your renewal option:

	One Year	Three Years
MyWebPress Standard	☐ $29.99	☐ $79.99
MyWebPress Premium	☐ $49.99	☐ $129.99
Pre-made Forms Add-On	☐ $5.99	☐ $8.99
Graphic Design Add-On	☐ $12.99	☐ $18.99

Payment Information:

Credit Card Type	☐ Bankster	☐ SureCredit	☐ YPay	Card Number	2934 4992 0041
Expiration Date	November 30			Security Code	557

176. What is indicated about Ms. Ellis?

(A) She is using a new credit card for payment.
(B) She failed to meet a deadline set by MyWebPress.
(C) She chose an upgraded version of her original plan.
(D) She added some security features to her package.

...

3. 三篇短文（Triple Passages）

Questions 186-190 refer to the following Web page, form, and e-mail.

Laurel Art Center

Upcoming Events

Summer Sounds Fest	**Spectacular Vistas**
• Concert featuring local musicians • June 5, from noon to 10 P.M. • Tickets go on sale May 15	• Exhibit of watercolor paintings by local landscape artist Samantha Davey • Opens 6 P.M., July 3, at the Campbell Gallery • Refreshments provided by Gordon's Café
Exploring Wood	**Annual Craft Show**
• Seminar conducted by Paula Sue • Thursday July 6 from 10:00 P.M. to 4 P.M. • $25 for eight classes (participants must bring safety glasses and a pair of work gloves)	• Our biggest event of the year, featuring handicrafts made by talented local artists • August 5, 10 A.M. to 4 P.M. • Admission is $5 for adults and $2 for seniors • Includes a buffet lunch from Kostas Mediterranean Kitchen

To join our mailing list, click here.

Laurel Art Center

Registration Form

Name	Ella Chung	Date	June 12
Telephone	555-3205	Address	108 Spruce Drive Hendersonville, TN 37075
E-mail	ellachung@mymail.net		

Event title	Exploring Wood
Payment method	

☐ Cash (Please pay two weeks in advance to reserve your slot)
☐ Credit card: Liberty Bancard 2347-8624-5098-5728

To	Melissa Hamada <m.hamada@laurelart.org>
From	Hector Villa <h.villa@laurelart.org>
Subject	Catering
Date	June 21

Dear Melissa,

As we discussed yesterday afternoon, Kostas Mediterranean Kitchen had to back out of catering our August 5 event due to a scheduling conflict. However, I've received confirmation that Asian Flavors can take their place. Please update our website to reflect this change.

Hector Villa
Activities director, Laurel Art Center

186. What is suggested about Ms. Chung?

    (A) She is a member of the Laurel Art Center.

    (B) She will be attending an upcoming exhibit.

    (C) She is expected to bring gear to an activity.

    (D) She will be charged $5 for admission to an event.

187. Which event will Asian Flavors be catering?

    (A) Summer Sounds Fest

    (B) Spectacular Vistas

    (C) Exploring Wood

    (D) Annual Craft Show

...

出題趨勢與應對策略

多篇短文每次會出現 5 題！

雙篇短文 13%

三篇短文 20%

單篇短文 67%

> Part 7 中，雙篇短文每次會有 2 組，三篇短文會有 3 組，單篇短文最多，每次會有 10 組。

核心應對策略

先確認短文的種類、開頭句和標題，推測大概的內容。

利用短文最開頭介紹的句子確認短文的種類，並看過標題，推測短文內容，再開始解題。

先閱讀問題，從短文中找出攸關答案核心詞句的線索。

看過問題後，掌握其核心詞句，再從短文中找出相關內容，當成答題的線索。如果是雙篇短文或三篇短文，無法只憑一個線索便選出正確答案，就該從其他短文中找出和前面線索相關的第二個線索。

答案會是直接談到線索或換句話說的選項。

務必選擇直接談到答案線索或改述的選項，當作正確答案，如果是雙篇短文或三篇短文，則先綜合兩篇短文都談到的線索再答題。

不同程度的學習計畫

完成 TEST 1 後，請用本書的分數換算表（p. 244）推算自己的分數，再選擇符合推算分數的學習計畫。每天都確認學習進度，運用解析和附贈學習資源仔細複習各回測驗。

800 分以上的學習計畫　2 星期內輪流解題和複習，快速提升實戰能力

- 為了挑選適合自己的學習計畫，第一天要先進行 TEST 1。
- 利用 2 週的時間，每兩天一回合，一天進行模擬考、隔天複習。
- 完成各回測驗後，運用測驗後面的 Review 檢查表更仔細地複習。

	1st Day	2nd Day	3rd Day	4th Day	5th Day
1st week	TEST 1 解題	TEST 1 複習	TEST 2 解題	TEST 2 複習	TEST 3 解題
2nd week	TEST 3 複習	TEST 4 解題	TEST 4 複習	TEST 5 解題	TEST 5 複習

＊如果要在 2 週內完成，請根據上表進行。如果要在 1 週內完成，就要每天完成兩天的份量。

600 分 ~ **795** 分學習計畫　利用 3 週的深度學習加強弱點

- 為了挑選適合自己的學習計畫，第一天要先進行 TEST 1。
- 利用 3 週的時間，每三天一回合，第一天進行模擬考，第二天以答錯的問題為主，搭配解析本來複習，第三天再搭配各回測驗的附贈學習資源進行深度學習。
- 完成各回測驗後，運用測驗後面的 Review 檢查表更仔細地複習。

	1st Day	2nd Day	3rd Day	4th Day	5th Day
1st week	TEST 1 解題	TEST 1 複習	TEST 1 深度學習	TEST2 解題	TEST 2 複習
2nd week	TEST 2 深度學習	TEST 3 解題	TEST 3 複習	TEST 3 深度學習	TEST 4 解題
3rd week	TEST 4 複習	TEST 4 深度學習	TEST 5 解題	TEST 5 複習	TEST 5 深度學習

595 分以下學習計畫　利用 4 週仔細複習聽力、閱讀，培養實力

· 為了挑選適合自己的學習計畫，第一天要先進行 TEST 1。

· 利用 4 週的時間，每四天一回合，第一天進行聽力模擬考，第二天複習，第三天進行閱讀模擬考，第四天複習。在學習計畫最後一天，針對這段時間的學習內容進行總複習。

· 完成各回測驗後，運用測驗後面的 Review 檢查表更仔細地複習。

	1st Day	2nd Day	3rd Day	4th Day	5th Day
1st week	TEST 1 解題	TEST 1 LC 複習	TEST 1 RC 複習	TEST 2 LC 解題	TEST 2 LC 複習
2nd week	TEST 2 RC 解題	TEST 2 RC 複習	TEST 3 LC 解題	TEST 3 LC 複習	TEST 3 RC 解題
3rd week	TEST 3 RC 複習	TEST 4 LC 解題	TEST 4 LC 複習	TEST 4 RC 解題	TEST 4 RC 複習
4th week	TEST 5 LC 解題	TEST 5 LC 複習	TEST 5 RC 解題	TEST 5 RC 複習	總複習

NEW TOEIC 950

聽力+閱讀 5 回達標

TEST 1

LISTENING TEST

Part 1
Part 2
Part 3
Part 4

READING TEST

Part 5
Part 6
Part 7

Review 檢查表

注意！測驗前請務必檢查下列事項。

手機是否關機？
Answer Sheet（p. 247）、鉛筆、橡皮擦和手錶是否準備好了？
準備好聆聽音檔了嗎？

準備就緒後，想著你的目標分數，開始測驗。
測驗完畢後，請務必查看 Review 檢查表（p. 68），複習答錯的題目。

※ 透過 TEST 1 自我評估英文程度後，選擇適合自己的學習計畫（p. 24~p. 25），高效複習。

🎧 Test 1.mp3
可免費下載、播放 MP3，用於答題訓練和複習

MP3 音檔

LISTENING TEST

In this section, you must demonstrate your ability to understand spoken English. This section is divided into four parts and will take approximately 45 minutes to complete. Do not mark the answers in your test book. Use the answer sheet that is provided separately.

PART 1

Directions: For each question, you will listen to four short statements about a picture in your test book. These statements will not be printed and will only be spoken one time. Select the statement that best describes what is happening in the picture and mark the corresponding letter (A), (B), (C), or (D) on the answer sheet.

Sample Answer
(A) ● (C) (D)

The statement that best describes the picture is (B), "The man is sitting at the desk." So, you should mark letter (B) on the answer sheet.

1.

2.

GO ON TO THE NEXT PAGE

3.

4.

5.

6.

GO ON TO THE NEXT PAGE

PART 2

Directions: For each question, you will listen to a statement or question followed by three possible responses spoken in English. They will not be printed and will only be spoken one time. Select the best response and mark the corresponding letter (A), (B), or (C) on your answer sheet.

7. Mark your answer on your answer sheet.

8. Mark your answer on your answer sheet.

9. Mark your answer on your answer sheet.

10. Mark your answer on your answer sheet.

11. Mark your answer on your answer sheet.

12. Mark your answer on your answer sheet.

13. Mark your answer on your answer sheet.

14. Mark your answer on your answer sheet.

15. Mark your answer on your answer sheet.

16. Mark your answer on your answer sheet.

17. Mark your answer on your answer sheet.

18. Mark your answer on your answer sheet.

19. Mark your answer on your answer sheet.

20. Mark your answer on your answer sheet.

21. Mark your answer on your answer sheet.

22. Mark your answer on your answer sheet.

23. Mark your answer on your answer sheet.

24. Mark your answer on your answer sheet.

25. Mark your answer on your answer sheet.

26. Mark your answer on your answer sheet.

27. Mark your answer on your answer sheet.

28. Mark your answer on your answer sheet.

29. Mark your answer on your answer sheet.

30. Mark your answer on your answer sheet.

31. Mark your answer on your answer sheet.

PART 3

Directions: In this part, you will listen to several conversations between two or more speakers. These conversations will not be printed and will only be spoken one time. For each conversation, you will be asked to answer three questions. Select the best response and mark the corresponding letter (A), (B), (C), or (D) on your answer sheet.

32. Why is the woman calling?

   (A) To inquire about a job's requirements
   (B) To postpone a job interview
   (C) To ask whether her résumé was received
   (D) To accept an offer of a position

33. What experience does the woman have?

   (A) She worked as a research assistant.
   (B) She studied business in college.
   (C) She was employed as an intern.
   (D) She volunteered for a charitable event.

34. What does the man suggest that the woman do?

   (A) Read the description of a job online
   (B) Come to the office for an in-person interview
   (C) Obtain a reference letter from an employer
   (D) Send in an application by a due date

35. Where most likely does the conversation take place?

   (A) On a bus
   (B) On an airplane
   (C) On a train
   (D) On a boat

36. What problem does the man mention?

   (A) A password is incorrect.
   (B) A lamp is not working.
   (C) A connection is slow.
   (D) A service is unavailable.

37. What does the man say he will do?

   (A) Read a magazine
   (B) Watch a show
   (C) Reenter a password
   (D) Move to another location

38. Why is making a survey necessary?

   (A) A new advertisement was released.
   (B) Some workers have quit.
   (C) Customers have complained about a service.
   (D) Cafeteria menu items will be added.

39. What does the woman offer to do?

   (A) Take over an assignment
   (B) Assist with an interview
   (C) Talk to a supervisor
   (D) Send a document

40. What does the woman remind Mark to do?

   (A) Change some information
   (B) Submit an evaluation
   (C) Review an opinion
   (D) Inquire about a facility

41. What is the conversation mainly about?

   (A) The process for ordering a book
   (B) An upcoming literary reading
   (C) The shift schedule at a bookstore
   (D) An award ceremony for writers

42. What does the woman mean when she says, "You can read yours last"?

   (A) There will not be a long wait.
   (B) There will be a time for questions.
   (C) There will not be a schedule issue.
   (D) There will be enough time for dinner.

43. According to the woman, what will the participants do after an event?

   (A) Receive some refreshments
   (B) Read a new issue of a journal
   (C) Take a group photo
   (D) Purchase books at a discount

GO ON TO THE NEXT PAGE

44. Why is the man visiting?

(A) To inquire about renting a building
(B) To perform a repair
(C) To reset an alarm
(D) To set up a boiler system

45. What does the woman thank the man for?

(A) Opening up a basement
(B) Identifying a problem
(C) Responding very rapidly
(D) Giving her free service

46. What does the woman say the man will receive?

(A) A floor plan
(B) Some contact information
(C) Pictures of some equipment
(D) A security pass

47. Where does the conversation most likely take place?

(A) At a clothing shop
(B) At a hair salon
(C) At a car wash
(D) At an appliance store

48. What is the man's main priority?

(A) Finding a cost-effective option
(B) Using his gift card
(C) Purchasing from a specific brand
(D) Utilizing some eco-friendly materials

49. What is mentioned about the Lexpro?

(A) It features personalized settings.
(B) It has been discontinued.
(C) It requires more energy.
(D) It was recently released.

50. What problem does the man mention?

(A) He did not receive a statement.
(B) A bank application is unavailable.
(C) An unusual purchase was made with his card.
(D) He cannot use his credit card.

51. What information does the woman request from the man?

(A) His date of birth
(B) His telephone number
(C) His address
(D) His credit card number

52. According to the woman, what will happen later today?

(A) A website will be updated.
(B) A card will become usable.
(C) A purchase will be canceled.
(D) A new card will arrive in the mail.

53. What is the man surprised by?

(A) The reduced sales of merchandise
(B) The reputation established by a company
(C) The success of a marketing strategy
(D) The price for a service

54. What does the man agree about?

(A) Creating a plan for a new project
(B) Employing an expert
(C) Contacting another company
(D) Increasing the advertising budget

55. Why does the woman say, "He has been working in that field for five years"?

(A) To highlight the need for experience
(B) To justify a candidate recommendation
(C) To explain the reason for a salary increase
(D) To suggest a transfer to another branch

56. What will happen tomorrow morning?

(A) A fashion show will be held.
(B) A store will be reopened.
(C) A magazine will be published.
(D) A work shift schedule will be posted.

57. What industry do the speakers most likely work in?

(A) Advertising
(B) Journalism
(C) Manufacturing
(D) Education

58. What does the woman reassure the man about?

(A) Assignments will not be delayed.
(B) Hard work will not be ignored.
(C) There will not be a crowd.
(D) A busy period will not last long.

---

59. What does the man inquire about?

(A) A mobile phone service plan
(B) The location of a product
(C) The features of a device
(D) A current sales promotion

60. Why was the man unaware of a situation?

(A) He was visiting other stores.
(B) He did not work in the morning.
(C) He had been waiting in line.
(D) He took the day off.

61. What does the woman give the man information about?

(A) A repair service
(B) A store's return policy
(C) A sales tax increase
(D) A recycling program

Café	Building 1	Grocery store	Building 2	Convenience store
		Western Ave.		
Restaurant	Building 4	Bicycle shop		Building 3

62. Look at the graphic. Where will the barber shop be located?

(A) Building 1
(B) Building 2
(C) Building 3
(D) Building 4

63. According to the man, what is an advantage of the building?

(A) It does not require utility payments.
(B) It contains a large back room.
(C) It does not cost much per month.
(D) It is near public transportation.

64. How will the man recruit employees?

(A) By speaking to acquaintances
(B) By posting a sign on the building
(C) By contacting a staffing agency
(D) By putting ads in publications

GO ON TO THE NEXT PAGE

Friday			
	8 A.M.	9 A.M.	10 A.M.	11 A.M.
Carter	Conference call		Sales Meeting	HR Training
Delilah	Out of office			HR Training
Edgar		Conference call		
Frances			Out of office	

65. What does the man ask the woman to do?

(A) Approve a merger
(B) Create a new schedule
(C) Notify some employees
(D) Proofread an announcement

66. Look at the graphic. When will the department heads participate in a meeting?

(A) At 8 A.M.
(B) At 9 A.M.
(C) At 10 A.M.
(D) At 11 A.M.

67. Why is the woman's assistant unavailable right now?

(A) He is on a break.
(B) He only works part time.
(C) He is writing an e-mail.
(D) He is undergoing training.

Coupon

10% off purchases over $50
Valid June 1-30

Excludes gift card purchases
Only accepted at the Cordoba Mall location

68. Where most likely does the conversation take place?

(A) At a clothing store
(B) At a dry cleaner
(C) At a gift shop
(D) At a tailoring business

69. What does the woman ask the man about?

(A) His favorite color
(B) His preferred size
(C) His shopping budget
(D) His membership card

70. Look at the graphic. Why isn't this coupon valid for a purchase?

(A) It does not meet the minimum purchase.
(B) It has already expired.
(C) It cannot be used with gift cards.
(D) It is for another location.

PART 4

Directions: In this part, you will listen to several short talks by a single speaker. These talks will not be printed and will only be spoken one time. For each talk, you will be asked to answer three questions. Select the best response and mark the corresponding letter (A), (B), (C), or (D) on your answer sheet.

71. What problem does the speaker mention?
    (A) A distribution system is causing complaints.
    (B) A product's quality is inconsistent.
    (C) A manufacturing plant is too small.
    (D) A store has discontinued a brand.

72. What solution does the speaker suggest?
    (A) Establishing a new factory
    (B) Rethinking a packaging design
    (C) Switching out some ingredients
    (D) Changing an affiliated company

73. What does the speaker ask the listeners to do?
    (A) Taste a new yogurt flavor
    (B) Look up information
    (C) Visit a store location
    (D) Clear a production floor

74. What caused the park project to take longer than planned?
    (A) Lack of materials
    (B) Insufficient funding
    (C) Additional work
    (D) Inclement weather

75. What does the mayor expect to happen?
    (A) Some economic activities will increase.
    (B) Some people will move to a neighborhood.
    (C) Some areas will become more expensive.
    (D) Some tourist attractions will be rebuilt.

76. What will happen next week?
    (A) An installation will be finished.
    (B) A ceremony will take place.
    (C) Invitations will be sent out.
    (D) Residents' opinions will be heard.

77. What promotion is the company currently offering?
    (A) Free installation
    (B) Upgraded battery packs
    (C) A coupon for 50 percent off
    (D) An extended warranty

78. Who is the advertisement intended for?
    (A) Battery manufacturers
    (B) Homeowners
    (C) Utility providers
    (D) Energy professionals

79. Why should the listeners contact the company?
    (A) To get tips on reducing electricity usage
    (B) To cancel a utility account
    (C) To receive a discount code
    (D) To talk about some options

80. Where does the speaker most likely work?
    (A) At a repair shop
    (B) At an electronics retailer
    (C) At an office supply store
    (D) At a manufacturing facility

81. Why does the speaker say, "It's a popular item"?
    (A) To recommend a product
    (B) To turn down an additional discount
    (C) To apologize for a delay
    (D) To encourage a quick decision

82. What should the listener do to buy a product?
    (A) Phone an employee
    (B) Make a reservation
    (C) Visit the customer service desk
    (D) Go to another branch

GO ON TO THE NEXT PAGE

83. What event is most likely taking place?

(A) A movie premier
(B) A theater opening
(C) A film festival
(D) A fundraiser

84. Who is Robert Willis?

(A) A festival organizer
(B) An investor
(C) A critic
(D) A crew member

85. What is *Off the Highway* about?

(A) Wildlife in the Midwest
(B) The history of an event
(C) A recent musical collaboration
(D) Living in a small town

---

86. What is being announced?

(A) A new album
(B) A special guest
(C) A contest result
(D) A tour schedule

87. What does the speaker mean when she says, "Ultima Records was surprised by the response"?

(A) Record sales increased significantly.
(B) Many people participated in an event.
(C) A website crashed due to increased traffic.
(D) Tickets sold out immediately.

88. What should the listeners do to learn about an upcoming promotion?

(A) Subscribe to a podcast
(B) Visit a website
(C) Send a text message
(D) Join a fan club

---

89. Who most likely is the speaker?

(A) A business owner
(B) A sales manager
(C) A landscape architect
(D) A maintenance worker

90. What will the listeners receive in a few minutes?

(A) A catalog of cleaning supplies
(B) A list of places to work
(C) A sign for a park
(D) An inventory of goods

91. What does the speaker ask Mr. Sandoval to do?

(A) Check a weather forecast
(B) Oversee a planting project
(C) Create a schedule for employees
(D) Confirm the stock of materials

---

92. Where is the tour taking place?

(A) At a hotel lobby
(B) At a university campus
(C) At a research facility
(D) At a photography museum

93. What will happen during the tour?

(A) A movie will be screened.
(B) Some scientists will be interviewed.
(C) The professor will give a speech.
(D) An instrument will be demonstrated.

94. What does the speaker imply when he says, "A recording of the tour will be available on our website"?

(A) Participation in the tour is not mandatory.
(B) There is an online forum for exchanging comments.
(C) The listeners do not have to take notes.
(D) Registration on the website is recommended.

Item	Quantity
Airway Headset (IB875747)	10
Blockland Paper Box (IB374665)	4
Officepro Pen, black (IB323722)	40
Blockland Pad, large	20

95. Look at the graphic. Which is the best-selling item in the company's new line?

(A) Item 1
(B) Item 2
(C) Item 3
(D) Item 4

96. What does the speaker say customers like most about the bag?

(A) The fabric
(B) The sizes
(C) The design
(D) The color

97. What most likely will the listeners do next?

(A) Review some proposals
(B) Look at competing products
(C) Compare product materials
(D) Check sales figures

98. Why is the speaker calling?

(A) To request a payment
(B) To accept a change
(C) To point out an opportunity
(D) To inquire about shipping

99. Look at the graphic. Which quantity number needs to change to get a discount?

(A) 10
(B) 4
(C) 40
(D) 20

100. What does the speaker say about the business?

(A) It is running low on stock.
(B) It specializes in electronics.
(C) It is introducing a new product.
(D) It can offer expedited delivery.

This is the end of the Listening test. Turn to PART 5 in your test book.

GO ON TO THE NEXT PAGE

READING TEST

In this section, you must demonstrate your ability to read and comprehend English. You will be given a variety of texts and asked to answer questions about these texts. This section is divided into three parts and will take 75 minutes to complete.

Do not mark the answers in your test book. Use the answer sheet that is separately provided.

PART 5

Directions: In each question, you will be asked to review a statement that is missing a word or phrase. Four answer choices will be provided for each statement. Select the best answer and mark the corresponding letter (A), (B), (C), or (D) on the answer sheet.

🕐 **PART 5** 建議作答時間 **11 分鐘**

---

101. The Ballas sneaker company was ------- known as Ballas Athletics but rebranded itself a few years ago.

(A) currently
(B) so
(C) formerly
(D) aside

102. The factory employees ------- to reread the operating system handbook.

(A) had directed
(B) were directed
(C) direct
(D) directed

103. The science convention will be held in September ------- the event's major sponsor has withdrawn its support.

(A) if only
(B) so that
(C) above all
(D) even though

104. The invoices from contractors are copied and filed separately ------- tax purposes.

(A) for
(B) at
(C) like
(D) in

105. *The Rock Creek Times* encourages readers to ------- feedback by writing letters to the editor.

(A) submit
(B) determine
(C) teach
(D) accept

106. Mr. Holly was the first salesperson hired by the firm and had to develop ------- own methods for selling.

(A) himself
(B) he
(C) his
(D) him

107. Fox Books sells a wide ------- of genres, ranging from fiction and poetry to history and philosophy.

(A) variety
(B) version
(C) knowledge
(D) position

108. The mayor of London outlined plans ------- some of the city's older metro lines.

(A) to modernize
(B) modernized
(C) have been modernized
(D) should have modernized

109. Gage National Park recommends that hikers bring food and water ------- a compass.

(A) such as
(B) in case of
(C) along with
(D) seeing as

110. The company's project was announced by a marketing ------- at yesterday's press conference.

(A) representative
(B) representing
(C) representation
(D) represented

111. The invited speaker will have five minutes to give ------- remarks at the start of the seminar.

(A) most
(B) equal
(C) brief
(D) busy

112. The teams at Stranton Tech work ------- to identify problems and find appropriate solutions.

(A) collaborator
(B) collaborative
(C) collaboration
(D) collaboratively

113. The airline will be adding several new routes to South America to meet passengers' growing -------.

(A) cost
(B) demand
(C) attempt
(D) insight

114. ------- the elevator is fixed, residents of 110 Halpert Street will have to use the stairs.

(A) Then
(B) Only
(C) Since
(D) Until

115. Kemper Shipping is in ------- with a major US retailer to handle all of its logistics in the Middle East.

(A) negotiated
(B) negotiation
(C) negotiate
(D) negotiator

116. The institute will be unable to advance its research without obtaining ------- support from a funding agency.

(A) plain
(B) compact
(C) mere
(D) external

117. ------- extensive rainfall in Memphis, the city is dealing with widespread flood damage.

(A) Between
(B) After
(C) Aboard
(D) Except

118. Across the board, ------- personnel are required to wear identification badges issued by the company while working on the premises.

(A) all
(B) every
(C) each
(D) both

119. An investigation by the company's engineers ------- that the equipment's automatic control system had failed.

(A) chose
(B) requested
(C) revealed
(D) revised

120. Starting next week, Donald Peters will assume a ------- role at Zwingli Bank.

(A) supervises
(B) supervise
(C) supervisors
(D) supervisory

GO ON TO THE NEXT PAGE

121. The website gives recommendations to help people decide ------- smartphone will best suit their needs.

(A) whom
(B) whether
(C) which
(D) another

122. ------- production challenges earlier this year, the launch of the new Ecroon laptop was on schedule.

(A) With
(B) Owing to
(C) In spite of
(D) Because of

123. Dynaline has the ------- rating of any photo-editing application based on thousands of user reviews.

(A) high
(B) highest
(C) highly
(D) higher

124. Mr. Stewart was not allowed to return the items because he did not bring a -------.

(A) receipt
(B) guidance
(C) report
(D) procedure

125. Everyone who saw the film in a theater was ------- impressed with its spectacular special effects.

(A) ever
(B) quite
(C) last
(D) same

126. Anuman Foods opened its second international location in Hanoi this year, ------- its presence in Southeast Asia.

(A) expand
(B) expands
(C) expanding
(D) had expanded

127. ------- Mr. Hill nor Ms. Jackson had the qualifications to become head of regional sales.

(A) Not only
(B) Either
(C) Neither
(D) Other

128. The supermarket regularly issues coupons offering generous ------- on selected items.

(A) deals
(B) excuses
(C) shares
(D) chances

129. Ms. Chung dropped her car off at the repair shop and was asked to pick it up one week -------.

(A) left
(B) later
(C) more
(D) nowadays

130. ------- the recession is over, the travel industry is expected to recover.

(A) Despite
(B) Rather than
(C) In order that
(D) Now that

PART 6

Directions: In this part, you will be asked to read four English texts. Each text is missing a word, phrase, or sentence. Select the answer choice that correctly completes the text and mark the corresponding letter (A), (B), (C), or (D) on the answer sheet.

🕐 **PART 6** 建議作答時間 **8 分鐘**

Questions 131-134 refer to the following article.

Martindale's Celebrates Anniversary

December 12—This week, Martindale's celebrates its 20th year as a fine dining restaurant.

Trained in France, chef and owner Joyce Martindale had always dreamed of having a

restaurant in downtown Elkhart, but it took several long years to realize her dream. She

------- opened her restaurant with the help of family and friends who believed in her vision.
  131.
Today, Martindale's has become one of the best restaurants in Elkhart. -------.
                                                                          132.

The restaurant ------- a selection of familiar French and American dishes, and these are
                  133.
prepared using only the freshest ingredients. First-time visitors should make it a point to try

the restaurant's -------. These include the steak dinner and roast chicken, which are among
                 134.
the favorite dishes of longtime customers.

---

131. (A) instead
　　　(B) likewise
　　　(C) frequently
　　　(D) finally

132. (A) She has several favorite restaurants that she visits often.
　　　(B) It has even been recognized with various prestigious awards.
　　　(C) Reservations for groups can also be made through the application.
　　　(D) Visitors who are early can take a seat near the entrance while they wait.

133. (A) features
　　　(B) featured
　　　(C) has featured
　　　(D) will feature

134. (A) diversions
　　　(B) activities
　　　(C) specialties
　　　(D) performances

GO ON TO THE NEXT PAGE ➡

Questions 135-138 refer to the following notice.

AC Ambrose Farms Notice

AC Ambrose has decided to adopt a new ------- this year on its farms. We will be using the
                       135.
new HT509 robots made by Larkin Tech to speed up the packing process. Currently, it

takes our teams an average of one hour to pack 1,000 pounds of produce for shipment.

The robots can complete the same job in 30 minutes. Thus, we expect the robots to -------
                                                       136.
our productivity.

The robots will be delivered by the end of this month. ------- will be set up over a two-day
                                             137.
period at all of our locations. Workers will be temporarily relocated so that our packing

operations can continue uninterrupted. Once the robots are ready, the manufacturer will be

sending over some people to train selected staff members on using the robots. -------.
                                                             138.

---

135. (A) approach
    (B) approaching
    (C) approachable
    (D) approaches

136. (A) involve
    (B) double
    (C) repeat
    (D) measure

137. (A) Mine
    (B) That
    (C) Other
    (D) These

138. (A) The orientation for new employees will take place in the conference room.
    (B) We may experience some delays in shipping the requested items.
    (C) You will be notified if you are chosen as one of the participants.
    (D) The group's work performance has improved significantly last year.

To: All Staff <staff@brandesson.com>
From: Beverly Castro <b.castro@brandesson.com>
Subject: Software update
Date: October 8

Dear Staff,

We've upgraded our Torrino administration software. The program has some elements that

you may find -------. For instance, it makes organizing work schedules and arranging
          139.

meetings easier.

Now, the software must be installed on your individual computers, which could take time.

-------, I've asked the IT staff to perform the installations over the weekend. They will start
140.

on Friday after 6 P.M. -------. When you return on Monday, just let me know if you're unable
                   141.

------- the program for any reason.
  142.

Beverly Castro
Office Manager

---

139. (A) confusing
     (B) useful
     (C) enclosed
     (D) unfamiliar

140. (A) Similarly
     (B) Meanwhile
     (C) On the other hand
     (D) For this reason

141. (A) Always remember to sign in when you arrive at work in the morning.
     (B) You can sign up for the training session by contacting the administrator.
     (C) Please leave your computers on for them at the end of the day.
     (D) It should not take you more than a few minutes to find your password.

142. (A) to access
     (B) access
     (C) accessing
     (D) having accessed

GO ON TO THE NEXT PAGE

Questions 143-146 refer to the following press release.

LISBON (May 7)—Flores Leather Goods will begin ------- shoes and handbags this
143.
summer. The 50-year-old company is in the process of adding to the types of products it
sells. It currently only offers wallets and belts. The move comes as the company ------- a
144.
shift in consumer tastes and preferences over the last few years. "Revenues from our
wallets and belts have been significantly -------," explains CEO and founder Mario Flores.
145.
"We need to adjust to changes in the market if we want to become profitable." -------.
146.
Watch straps and backpacks are some of the products that the company is developing.

143. (A) sale
(B) sold
(C) sell
(D) selling

144. (A) seeing
(B) has seen
(C) seen
(D) will see

145. (A) enhanced
(B) boosted
(C) canceled
(D) diminished

146. (A) The new location will be opening
sometime in the fall.
(B) Users voted for their favorite one in an
online poll.
(C) The company hopes to offer even
more products in the future.
(D) Items without a proof of purchase may
not be returned or exchanged.

PART 7

Directions: In this part, you will be asked to read several texts, such as advertisements, articles, instant messages, or examples of business correspondence. Each text is followed by several questions. Select the best answer and mark the corresponding letter (A), (B), (C), or (D) on your answer sheet.

🕐 **PART 7** 建議作答時間 **54 分鐘**

Questions 147-148 refer to the following advertisement.

Fleetz Office Warehouse

At Fleetz Office Warehouse, we carry a full range of office furniture suitable for every budget and style. Choose from our extensive lineup of products made by top manufacturers from around the world. Looking for great savings? Then you may be interested in our own brand of office furniture, EZwerks, which includes everything from chairs and desks to conference tables and filing cabinets. Ever since our CEO introduced the brand on a television program, EZwerks has been popular with business owners throughout San Antonio.

Stop by any of our four locations in the city to see why Fleetz Office Warehouse ranks high among customers for quality, affordability, and convenience. Visit www.fleetzoffice.com for a complete catalog of products. This month only, enjoy a 20-percent discount on single or bulk purchases when you sign up as a member in our Fleetz Rewards loyalty program.

---

147. What made EZwerks popular with business owners?

(A) It uses high-quality materials.
(B) It was featured on a television show.
(C) It gives discounts on large orders.
(D) It could be purchased in installments.

148. What is NOT true about Fleetz Office Warehouse?

(A) It has several branches in a city.
(B) It sells its own brand of products.
(C) It receives new items every month.
(D) It operates a membership program.

GO ON TO THE NEXT PAGE ➤

Questions 149-150 refer to the following text-message chain.

Petra Bellamy   3:14 P.M.

Hi, Brian. Is your meeting over? I hope it went well. I'm wondering if you could help me with a problem. I've been trying to print a report for a client. However, the printer keeps rejecting my file. Is it because I'm using a new software program?

Brian Allman   3:16 P.M.

I just finished up, actually, and it went great. Thanks for asking. As for your problem, I don't think it's the software. This has happened to me before. You should check if the printer is out of ink.

Petra Bellamy   3:20 P.M.

I checked the printer, and you were right. Unfortunately, we seem to be out of ink. Can I order some more?

Brian Allman   3:21 P.M.

Let me call the manager. I'll get back to you, and let you know when you can proceed. You may have to wait until tomorrow morning, though, if she's busy.

---

149. What is Ms. Bellamy's problem?

(A) She is unable to print out a document.
(B) Her proposal was rejected by a client.
(C) She is not familiar with a program.
(D) Her manager left unclear instructions.

150. At 3:21 P.M., what does Mr. Allman most likely mean when he writes, "Let me call the manager"?

(A) A product's availability must be confirmed.
(B) Access to a storeroom is restricted.
(C) A supplier has not replied to a message.
(D) Approval is needed to order an item.

Questions 151-152 refer to the following announcement.

Announcement for Riverbend Apartments Tenants

We are pleased to announce that Riverbend Apartments will be conducting work on the tenant parking lot. This will involve making necessary repairs, repaving the surface of the lot, and upgrading lighting and security features. Work will commence next week on April 11 and is expected to last until the end of the month. To ensure everyone's safety, the entire parking lot will be closed while work is in progress. We recommend that those with vehicles park at the Center Street Parking Garage until the renovations are complete. We apologize for any inconvenience this may cause. In compensation for fees that may be incurred, Riverbend Apartments will waive the $50 parking fee that is normally included with the rent for next month. For inquiries, please contact the building management team at 555-7731. Thank you for your patience and understanding.

151. What is the purpose of the announcement?

(A) To apologize for noise caused by construction work
(B) To provide information about upcoming improvements
(C) To thank residents for contributing funds to a project
(D) To inform tenants of increased parking lot rates

152. What can be inferred about tenants?

(A) They should expect to receive a statement in the mail.
(B) Some of them will pay less than usual in May.
(C) They have complained about the condition of the parking lot.
(D) Some of them will need to apply for new parking permits.

GO ON TO THE NEXT PAGE

Questions 153-154 refer to the following advertisement.

StatBook
Make your dream project a reality

StatBook can help you turn your creative idea for a book project into a reality. Whether you want to print a personalized photo book to share with family and friends or publish a written work and sell it to the public, StatBook can help you realize your goal at an affordable price.

StatBook gives you complete control of your project from start to finish. Moreover, we offer software-based editing tools and assistance with design. When your book is ready to print, StatBook guarantees quick production and delivery of the finished work. Visit our website at www.statbook.com to view pricing or to get a quote based on your number of copies.

*Special November deal: Print a minimum of 2,000 copies, and we will upgrade the paper at no extra charge to the highest quality that we offer.

153. What is stated about StatBook?

(A) It specializes in producing audio books.
(B) It has an online application for smartphones.
(C) It offers discounts for students.
(D) It allows customers to publish their own work.

154. What is being offered in November?

(A) A discount on membership
(B) An upgrade on some paper
(C) A free set of holiday cards
(D) A limited trial of a service

MIDDLETON BANK WIRE TRANSFER REQUEST FORM

Please note that the wire transfer cutoff time is 3:00 P.M.

Customer Information	
Customer Name	Antoine Ducharme
Account Number	118825622042
Address	1432 Rue de Phare, Quebec, Canada

Wire Transfer Information					
Amount	$3,800 USD	Date		July 7	

Purpose of Wire Transfer: To pay for the purchase of a painting
*The beneficiary will receive the amount in their local currency.

Beneficiary Information	
Beneficiary Name	Salles Gallery
Bank and Account Number	Carrousel Credit Union — 227722662243
Address	8 Rue de Moulinet, Paris, France

Customer Authorization

I acknowledge that all information provided is correct and authorize Middleton Bank to transfer funds. Furthermore, I understand that if any details provided are incorrect, the transfer may be delayed or rejected.

Signature: *Antoine Ducharme*
Phone Number: 555-6012

Wire Transfer Fee

___ $15 Domestic ___ $25 International X Waived*

*Wire fees are waived for VIP customers.

---

155. What is indicated about Salles Gallery?

(A) It will cover the transfer fees.
(B) It opened a location in Canada.
(C) It sold a painting to Mr. Ducharme.
(D) It will ship an artwork to France.

156. What is true about Mr. Ducharme's transaction?

(A) It will require a change of currency.
(B) It will be completed the following day.
(C) It will be repeated every month.
(D) It will need a manager's signature.

157. What is mentioned about Mr. Ducharme?

(A) He recently attended an event in Paris.
(B) He sent money on behalf of a business.
(C) He is a VIP customer of Middleton Bank.
(D) He has an account with Carrousel Credit Union.

GO ON TO THE NEXT PAGE

Questions 158-160 refer to the following e-mail.

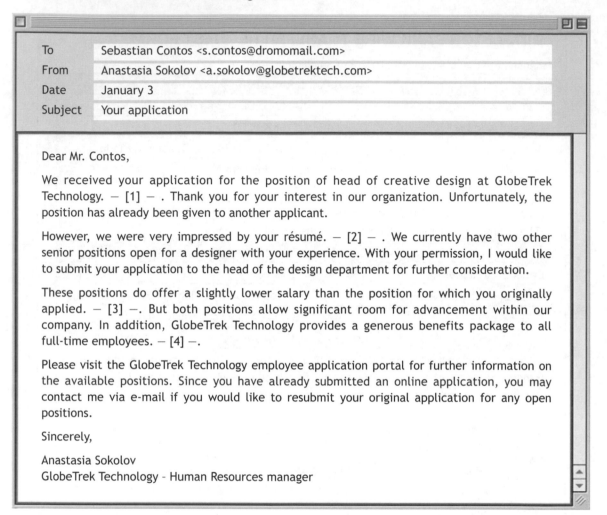

To: Sebastian Contos <s.contos@dromomail.com>
From: Anastasia Sokolov <a.sokolov@globetrektech.com>
Date: January 3
Subject: Your application

Dear Mr. Contos,

We received your application for the position of head of creative design at GlobeTrek Technology. — [1] — . Thank you for your interest in our organization. Unfortunately, the position has already been given to another applicant.

However, we were very impressed by your résumé. — [2] — . We currently have two other senior positions open for a designer with your experience. With your permission, I would like to submit your application to the head of the design department for further consideration.

These positions do offer a slightly lower salary than the position for which you originally applied. — [3] —. But both positions allow significant room for advancement within our company. In addition, GlobeTrek Technology provides a generous benefits package to all full-time employees. — [4] —.

Please visit the GlobeTrek Technology employee application portal for further information on the available positions. Since you have already submitted an online application, you may contact me via e-mail if you would like to resubmit your original application for any open positions.

Sincerely,

Anastasia Sokolov
GlobeTrek Technology – Human Resources manager

---

158. What is true about Mr. Contos?

(A) He worked at GlobeTrek Technology before.
(B) He has an advanced degree in business.
(C) He has no experience in the field of technology.
(D) He recently applied to be a department head.

159. What information can be found on the website?

(A) A list of openings
(B) An interview schedule
(C) A map of company facilities
(D) A team member's e-mail address

160. In which of the positions marked [1], [2], [3], and [4] does the following sentence best belong?

"We provide comprehensive health care and three weeks of paid vacation each year."

(A) [1]
(B) [2]
(C) [3]
(D) [4]

Questions 161-163 refer to the following Web page.

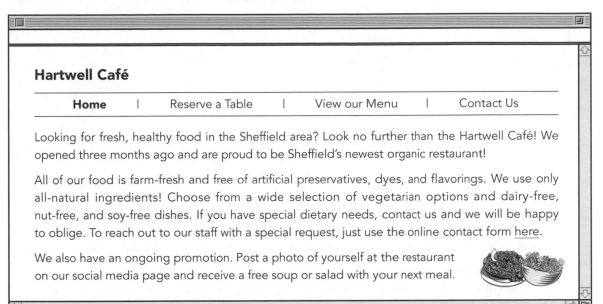

Hartwell Café

| **Home** | Reserve a Table | View our Menu | Contact Us |

Looking for fresh, healthy food in the Sheffield area? Look no further than the Hartwell Café! We opened three months ago and are proud to be Sheffield's newest organic restaurant!

All of our food is farm-fresh and free of artificial preservatives, dyes, and flavorings. We use only all-natural ingredients! Choose from a wide selection of vegetarian options and dairy-free, nut-free, and soy-free dishes. If you have special dietary needs, contact us and we will be happy to oblige. To reach out to our staff with a special request, just use the online contact form <u>here</u>.

We also have an ongoing promotion. Post a photo of yourself at the restaurant on our social media page and receive a free soup or salad with your next meal.

---

161. What is mentioned about Hartwell Café?

(A) It used to be known by another name.
(B) It does not offer custom meals.
(C) It has recently opened another branch.
(D) It does not use artificial dyes in its food.

162. The word "just" in paragraph 2, line 4, is closest in meaning to

(A) fairly
(B) carefully
(C) simply
(D) accurately

163. What will customers get if they participate in a promotion?

(A) A choice of side dish
(B) A complimentary beverage
(C) A discount on an entrée
(D) A gift card for future use

GO ON TO THE NEXT PAGE

To: Eliza Kemper <e.kemper@usgrandtours.us>
From: David Sims <david.sims@bridgeporttravelexpo.com>
Subject: Expo
Date: August 1

Dear Ms. Kemper,

I'm writing to confirm that we received the $300 deposit you submitted to participate as a vendor at the Bridgeport Travel Expo on September 1 and 2. I apologize for the delay. We attracted a record number of applicants, so contacting everyone took longer than normal. Your tour company will be a great addition to this year's lineup.

The deposit will cover any damage that may occur at the venue as a result of negligence. Any repair or cleaning costs will be deducted from it. Otherwise, it will be returned within five business days after the end of the event. The payment of $1,200 for the booth rental is due on August 28.

Please note the following requirements:
- Uniform exterior signs will be provided for each booth, but vendors may display other signs within the booth itself.
- Every item or service for sale must be preapproved by the organizers. No food or beverages are permitted to be sold.
- Never leave personal belongings unattended. You must leave these items in your assigned storage lockers.
- Vendors are responsible for cleaning inside and around the booth.

If you have questions or additional material to submit, please e-mail me directly.

Sincerely,

David Sims
Event Coordinator
Bridgeport Travel Expo

---

164. What is the purpose of the e-mail?

(A) To inform organizers of a sponsorship proposal
(B) To affirm participation in an event
(C) To request payment of a deposit
(D) To advertise a promotional opportunity

165. What is implied about the expo?

(A) The number of applicants reached an all-time high.
(B) The exhibition has been extended by three days.
(C) The vendors represent different industries.
(D) The venue was moved to a larger location.

166. What is indicated about the deposit?

(A) It must be paid on September 1.
(B) It costs half as much as a booth rental.
(C) It could be used to pay for damage.
(D) It will be returned on the last day of the event.

167. What is Ms. Kemper NOT required to do?

(A) Maintain her area's cleanliness
(B) Obtain approval for items sold
(C) Create a design for exterior booth's sign
(D) Place personal items in a locker

Keptics Envisions a Plastic-Free Future

February 8—Keptics, the global consumer goods corporation headquartered in Seattle, has just announced the launch of a pilot program to evaluate the market for a new line of eco-friendly cleaning products. — [1] —. The products will use sustainable packaging designed to reduce plastic waste and pollution. The three-month program will begin in Seattle on March 1.

To participate, customers must sign up online for the Keptics Up program. — [2] —. Participants will receive a shipment from Keptics that includes samples of its home cleaning products packaged in refillable containers. Once a container's contents are consumed, customers can order a refill from Keptics or visit one of several planned locations to refill it themselves. — [3] —.

According to Keptics CEO Fiona Simpleton, the program will be limited to Seattle so that the company can keep a close watch on costs. — [4] —. However, if it succeeds, it could be introduced to other cities across the US by early next year.

168. What is Keptics planning to do?

(A) Test a new product line
(B) Start an environmental group
(C) Update its brand design
(D) Introduce a rewards program

169. What will some Keptics customers receive?

(A) An event invitation
(B) An online voucher
(C) A set of samples
(D) A regular pickup service

170. Why is Keptics only launching a program in Seattle?

(A) It needs to get permission from other cities.
(B) It wants to monitor associated costs.
(C) It is using ingredients only found locally.
(D) It is trying to avoid competing with other firms.

171. In which of the positions marked [1], [2], [3], and [4] does the following sentence best belong?

"These locations will be announced in the coming weeks."

(A) [1]
(B) [2]
(C) [3]
(D) [4]

GO ON TO THE NEXT PAGE

Questions 172-175 refer to the following online chat discussion.

Jang-mi Bae	[2:09 P.M.]	Any news regarding a new office location? We have to extend our lease here next month if we don't find something.
Paul Knox	[2:11 P.M.]	I saw one yesterday that I think would work perfectly. It's in a building called Janus Tower.
Edward Watts	[2:12 P.M.]	What are the amenities like? Does it have a gym? Assigned parking?
Paul Knox	[2:15 P.M.]	It has those things and more. It also has a brand-new heating and cooling system, so that should save us on renovation costs. The only potential issue is that it's above our budget at $6,500 a month. That's $700 more than we pay now.
Barbara Thompkins	[2:16 P.M.]	We've had a good year. If utilities are included and it has everything we need, I say we should definitely consider it.
Jang-mi Bae	[2:16 P.M.]	Valid point. Still, I'd like to see it. Could you schedule a visit, Paul? I'm free on Friday.
Paul Knox	[2:18 P.M.]	Sure thing. Let me check the real estate agency's mobile app for a phone number.
Paul Knox	[2:20 P.M.]	OK. I called the realtor and she confirmed she can meet us on Friday at 11 A.M. We can all go to Janus Tower together in my car.
Edward Watts	[2:21 P.M.]	Great. I'm available at that time, too.
Barbara Thompkins	[2:21 P.M.]	I'm going to be out all day visiting a client.
Paul Knox	[2:24 P.M.]	You can also see the office on video through the mobile application. Anyone who can't come can do that instead.

172. What is true about Janus Tower?

(A) It includes a workout facility.
(B) It contains inexpensive units.
(C) It is located near public transportation.
(D) It is owned by the city.

173. At 2:16 P.M., what does Ms. Bae most likely mean when she writes, "Valid point"?

(A) She agrees that the company can accommodate a higher budget.
(B) She thinks that a group should consider a potential problem.
(C) She feels that other employees should be consulted about a decision.
(D) She believes that asking for a realtor's help would be wise.

174. How many people will be accompanying the realtor on Friday?

(A) One
(B) Two
(C) Three
(D) Four

175. According to the online chat discussion, what can people do on a mobile application?

(A) Get directions to a building
(B) See video of an office space
(C) Find alternatives within a price range
(D) Schedule a visit to a location

GO ON TO THE NEXT PAGE

Come to Surf Shack

Located on Malibu Beach, Surf Shack invites travelers and locals alike to come and enjoy spectacular views of the ocean. What started as a surfers' paradise for a few friends has developed into a surfing school, equipment shop, and restaurant. Surf Shack serves excellent cuisine and drinks while you enjoy the sunset and listen to the waves. This is truly a special experience that is not to be missed. It is why radio station Malibu 102.5 has named us the top attraction in the area.

Surf Shack has a tradition of offering fresh smoothies daily with ingredients that have been sustainably sourced. We are currently running a two-for-one special on the following combinations.
- Monday & Tuesday: Banana and Strawberry
- Wednesday & Thursday: Pineapple and Coconut
- Friday & Saturday: Apple and Pear
- Sunday: Tropical Mix

Call us at 555-9691 to reserve a beach table today.

Surf Shack

About	Restaurant	Surfing	Shop	Location	**Reviews**

Name: Katerina Stokov
Rating: 2/5

I went to Surf Shack recently while visiting Los Angeles on vacation. I visited with some local friends who had never been there before. We didn't think that the place was well-known to tourists, so we were looking forward to enjoying a relatively quiet afternoon at a lovely beachside location. We even chose to go on a Tuesday as that is supposedly when they are least busy.

When we arrived, we were shocked to find that the place was crowded with tourists. We were lucky to get a beach table at the restaurant considering we hadn't reserved one. I ordered the smoothie that was on special offer, and it turned out to be delicious. Still, the service was slow, and the tables were not very clean. Overall, especially because of the crowds, my experience was not very good, and I cannot recommend the place to anyone.

176. In the advertisement, the word "serves" in paragraph 1, line 3, is closest in meaning to

(A) tests
(B) performs
(C) provides
(D) accepts

177. What is stated about Surf Shack?

(A) It merged with a local sports school.
(B) It was recommended by a radio station.
(C) It changes the menu seasonally.
(D) It is owned by former surf champions.

178. According to the advertisement, how can customers reserve a table?

(A) By sending an e-mail
(B) By making a phone call
(C) By using a mobile app
(D) By visiting a website

179. Which smoothie special did Ms. Stokov most likely order?

(A) Banana and Strawberry
(B) Pineapple and Coconut
(C) Apple and Pear
(D) Tropical Mix

180. Why was Ms. Stokov dissatisfied with Surf Shack?

(A) The servers were unfriendly.
(B) The food was flavorless.
(C) The view was not as advertised.
(D) The location was crowded.

GO ON TO THE NEXT PAGE

Questions 181-185 refer to the following notice and article.

NOTICE from Holton Centre

The Holton Centre will be closed on September 19 for the annual Stafford Literary Festival. Over 200 publishers and 350 writers from around the UK are expected to attend. It will feature talks by the best of today's British authors. Among those invited are the authors of *East Kingdom* and *The Gate*, both of which were released to spectacular critical acclaim.

Throughout the day, writers will also be giving lectures and participating in group discussions. In the main lobby, publishing houses will have booths set up where visitors can buy the latest titles at a discount. Once the festival concludes, an after-party will be held in the Lewistown Hotel, during which attendees will have the opportunity to mingle with noted writers and get their books signed. General admission is $40, including the after-party, and author lectures cost an additional $10 to attend.

Margaret Davidson, a Bold New Literary Voice
By Charles Hagan

With *The Gate*, Margaret Davidson has become one of my favourite young writers. A 30-year-old correspondent at *New Music Monthly* magazine, Ms. Davidson has been a well-known journalist for some time, but I wasn't inclined to read her book until I heard her give a hilarious talk at the Stafford Literary Festival. I'm happy to report that she's as good a writer as she is a speaker. In *The Gate*, she writes about the experiences that drew her to music journalism in the first place, hearing R&B at the age of five and beginning to play bass at 12. The book is divided into three sections, one focusing on her early years, the second focusing on her time playing in a band as a teenager, and the final section on her career as a music journalist. At the end of the book are excerpts from her writings at *New Music Monthly*, ranging from incisive reviews of new hip-hop albums to a humorous account of travelling with the punk group Stone Age.

181. What is suggested about the Stafford Literary Festival?

(A) It takes place twice a year.
(B) It focuses on authors from one country.
(C) It is geared mostly towards fiction writers.
(D) It has not received much publicity.

182. What can people NOT do at the festival?

(A) Receive free copies of certain titles
(B) Listen to authors' lectures
(C) Interact with writers in attendance
(D) Collect authors' signatures

183. What is mentioned about Ms. Davidson?

(A) She has written two novels.
(B) She signed a book for Mr. Hagan.
(C) Her work was well received by critics.
(D) Her career has changed many times.

184. What can be inferred about Mr. Hagan?

(A) He is a well-known music journalist.
(B) He paid an extra fee to see Ms. Davidson speak.
(C) He used to play in a band.
(D) He stayed at the Lewistown Hotel.

185. In the article, the word "drew" in paragraph 1, line 5 is closest in meaning to

(A) attracted
(B) presented
(C) created
(D) allowed

GO ON TO THE NEXT PAGE

Rick Houseman
119 Willow Drive
Queensland, NZ 0600

Dear Mr. Houseman,

My name is Matilda Gleeson, and I am writing on behalf of the Alumni Office at Queensland University. We are reaching out to selected graduates of Queensland University to see if they would be willing to contribute short professional biographies for our website. Given that you are a high-profile conservationist, we think that you would be a good example of a successful Queensland University graduate.

If you are interested, please send us a short biography of 100 words or less describing your career. In addition, we would appreciate it if you sent samples of papers you have published, newspaper articles written about you, and a photograph of yourself taken in the last five years. Please submit these to gleeson22@qland.nz. Thank you, and I look forward to hearing from you.

Sincerely,

Matilda Gleeson
Alumni Office, Queensland University

TO: Matilda Gleeson <gleeson22@qland.nz>
FROM: Rick Houseman <rick.houseman@qlandwildlife.nz>
SUBJECT: Alumni bio
DATE: May 29
ATTACHMENTS: file1, file2, file3

Dear Ms. Gleeson,

Thank you for contacting me regarding the alumni biographies. I've attached all of the items you requested except for the last one. I will send this to you tomorrow. I've also made a small donation to the Alumni Fund for the maintenance of the school library.

When you add my biography to the website, could you let me know by sending me a link to the page? I'd like to share it with some friends and family. Also, I may need to update the biography soon. I am currently in talks with the New Zealand Conservation Commission to serve as their assistant chair. All that is left is to undergo a panel interview. I will let you know in the following days whether I get the position so that you can update my biography on your website.

Best regards,

Rick Houseman

QUEENSLAND UNIVERSITY

Home | Admissions | Campus Life | **Alumni** | Announcements | Help

ALUMNI PROFILES

<u>Rick Houseman</u>

Since graduating from Queensland University's undergraduate program 10 years ago, Rick Houseman has worked to advance the world's body of knowledge about science. He has a doctorate from the prestigious National Academy of Natural Sciences and has published extensive research on New Zealand's wildlife. Most recently, he worked to ensure the passage of new legislation that designated parts of the country as protected wildlife areas to help preserve the habitats of unique animals like the kiwi bird. Presently, he is the assistant chair of the New Zealand Conservation Commission.

186. Why did Ms. Gleeson write Mr. Houseman the letter?

(A) To ask him for a donation
(B) To offer him a position
(C) To remind him about an event
(D) To request some information

187. What will Mr. Houseman send tomorrow?

(A) A short article
(B) A photograph
(C) A personal profile
(D) A research paper

188. What does Mr. Houseman ask Ms. Gleeson to do?

(A) Add a link to his personal web page in his biography
(B) Give him an update on the school's operations
(C) Notify him when a post is made
(D) Add him to an alumni e-mail list

189. According to the post on the web page, what did Mr. Houseman do most recently?

(A) Appeared in a TV program
(B) Joined a university faculty
(C) Helped pass a new law
(D) Applied for a doctorate program

190. What is indicated about Mr. Houseman?

(A) He dropped out of a graduate program at Queensland University.
(B) He has worked at a library in the Queensland area.
(C) He wrote a college thesis on the kiwi bird.
(D) He passed a panel interview for a new position.

GO ON TO THE NEXT PAGE

Questions 191-195 refer to the following memo, survey, and report.

TO: Customer Relations Staff
FROM: Nick Christman, Customer Relations Manager
SUBJECT: YourPage at Three Years
DATE: March 22

As of today, YourPage has been operating for three straight years. Over the course of that period, our user base has grown exponentially. In just the past two months, in fact, we have experienced a 500-percent increase in users, making us the fastest-growing social networking site. That means it's time we conducted a survey of our customers to see how their experience with our site has been. We want to hear from people who have been using it for a while, so let's send survey requests to users who made YourPage profiles over a year ago. These should also be people whose activity is fairly regular. As an incentive for taking the survey, we could offer to enter their names into a raffle for prizes. The prizes could be brand-new electronic devices from one of the companies we are affiliated with.

YourPage: Survey

Name: Pauline Carson
Date: April 12

On a scale of 1 to 5, with 5 being the best, how would you rank your experience with YourPage?

☐ 1 ☐ 2 ☐ 3 ☑ 4 ☐ 5

How frequently do you check YourPage?

 I usually check it repeatedly throughout the day. I do this whenever I am bored or want to catch up on what my friends are doing.

How often do you post messages, pictures, or other content on your page?

 I don't post that frequently. I would say I post maybe once or twice a week. However, I do like to comment on other people's posts.

How did you hear about YourPage?

 Through some friends

What would you like YourPage to improve?

 I think the design of the profile pages is a little cluttered, with a lot of different information mixed up together.

YourPage: Survey Results

Throughout the month of April, we sent over 5,000 survey requests to various active users of YourPage. Those who took the survey were entered into a raffle for Silver Plus smartphones, which were distributed to 10 winners. Roughly 1,000 people responded to our requests. The vast majority (88 percent) ranked their experience with the site as either a 4 or 5 on a scale of 1 to 5, with 5 being the highest. However, there were some common criticisms, including that the site shut down fairly frequently and that profile pages were difficult to navigate because of the confusing layout. Going forward, it is important we address these problems by fixing errors in the computer code that cause pages to shut down and reformatting the pages with the convenience of users in mind.

191. What is the purpose of the memo?

(A) To praise employees for their work
(B) To report a change in leadership
(C) To ask for suggestions for improvements
(D) To make a proposal to gather information

192. What does Mr. Christman indicate about YourPage?

(A) It is used mainly by teenagers.
(B) It attracted 100 new users in the past few months.
(C) It is rapidly becoming more popular.
(D) It was launched a year ago.

193. What can be inferred about Ms. Carson?

(A) She has used YourPage for over a year.
(B) She finds YourPage very easy to use.
(C) She is not eligible to win a raffle prize.
(D) She did not submit the survey on time.

194. What is implied about Silver Plus?

(A) It produces software for companies.
(B) It has been having technical issues.
(C) It created a survey for YourPage.
(D) It has a partnership with YourPage.

195. What does the report recommend doing?

(A) Advertising the site in foreign countries
(B) Fixing a website's persistent problems
(C) Offering additional rewards for more feedback
(D) Conducting a more in-depth survey

GO ON TO THE NEXT PAGE

The 4th Boston Leadership Summit Is Going Live

Jefferson Bank is proud to announce that it has secured the participation of two keynote speakers for its fourth annual summit, which is scheduled for January 17 and 18. The CEO of SpitalGround, Susanne Coerver, will talk about how her innovative company is changing the health-care sector and how she manages her company in a competitive environment. Henry Moss, chief executive of Moss Tech, will close the summit with insights into what it takes to become a successful entrepreneur.

For the first time, the Boston Leadership Summit will also be streamed live through an online application, enabling it to reach a wider audience. A ticket to participate online is $220 for both days. However, customers of Jefferson Bank are invited to virtually join the event to learn about leadership skills, partake in workshops, and interact with other online visitors free of charge. Find the nearest Jefferson Bank branch, and become a customer in time for the summit.

To	Allison Cruise <a.cruise@jeffersonbank.com>
From	Preston Ali <p.ali@mosstechorg.com>
Subject	Summit
Date	December 28

Dear Ms. Cruise,

I am sorry to inform you that Mr. Moss will not be able to attend the summit as planned due to an unforeseen business matter. He asked me to send his regrets, especially since he had such an enjoyable time speaking at last year's event.

That said, Mr. Moss can recommend someone to take his place. She is the CEO of Galacomms, a software services company that she and Mr. Moss started together some years ago. I can send you her contact details once we receive confirmation of her availability. You can expect an update before the end of the week. Once again, please accept our apologies for this inconvenience.

Sincerely,

Preston Ali
Executive Assistant
Moss Tech

To: Leonard Vega <l.vega@jeffersonbank.com>
From: Allison Cruise <a.cruise@jeffersonbank.com>
Subject: Summit
Date: January 9

Leonard,

I need you to go to the summit location two days earlier than originally planned. Please go ahead and book a new flight if you have to.

As you know, there has been a change to our speaker lineup, and this change must be reflected in all printed materials posted at the venue. For your reference, the new speaker's name is Fiona Murphy, and she is the CEO of Galacomms. While you're at the venue, please test the setup for the live stream to ensure that everything runs smoothly.

Thanks for your help, and let me know if you have any questions.

Alison

196. What is NOT true about a summit?

(A) It has been put on before.
(B) It is expanding its audience reach.
(C) It is being hosted by a financial institution.
(D) It will focus on the health-care industry.

197. What are Jefferson Bank customers encouraged to do?

(A) Stream some content for free
(B) Take advantage of higher savings interest rates
(C) Enter a contest to win a cash prize
(D) Visit a branch location for some merchandise

198. What does Mr. Ali suggest about Mr. Moss?

(A) He was invited to speak at another event.
(B) He was in Boston the year before.
(C) He will be watching a speech online.
(D) He plans to retire from his company.

199. What is mentioned about Fiona Murphy?

(A) She requested a change of schedule.
(B) She is a customer of Jefferson Bank.
(C) She needs confirmation of a flight booking.
(D) She started a company with Mr. Moss.

200. What does Ms. Cruise ask Mr. Vega to do?

(A) Test a live stream connection
(B) Revise a speaker contract
(C) Find a new event venue
(D) Prepare an internal newsletter

This is the end of the test. You may review Parts 5, 6, and 7 if you finish the test early.

分數換算表 p. 244 / 正確答案、翻譯、解析〔解析本〕p. 2

▌請根據下一頁的 Review 檢查表複習答錯的題目

Review 檢查表

完成 TEST 1 後，請根據下表檢視自己答錯的問題，並在框框中打勾。
如果距離考試時間不多，請務必檢查**粗體字**的項目。

☐ **我再度練習了答錯的題目，試著找出正確答案。**

☐ **我已針對答錯的題目查閱了翻譯，理解了題幹與問題的內容。**

☐ **我透過翻譯，理解了每題各個選項正確或錯誤的原因。**

☐ 我檢視了在 Part 1 和 Part 2 答錯的問題類型，並加以整理，以免落入相同的陷阱。

☐ 我檢視了 Part 3 和 Part 4 每個題目所使用的換句話說。

☐ 在 Part 5 和 Part 6，我針對各題的正確答案及錯誤選項，整理了文法和單字的重點。

☐ 針對 Part 6「選擇合適句子」的題目，我正確理解了整個段落及空格前後文的語意。

☐ 在 Part 7，我找出了短文和題目中的重點，包含正確答題所需的句子和片語，並加以標示，也檢查了題目使用的換句話說。

☐ 針對 Part 1~Part 4，我使用線上的聽力訓練筆記，針對考試的重點語句練習聽寫、閱讀和複習。

☐ 針對 Part 1~Part 4，我使用單字記憶本來記下考試的關鍵詞彙和表達用語。

大量練習題目固然重要，但好好檢視自己答錯的問題也同樣關鍵。
只要仔細複習一遍答錯的題目，就能在短時間內有效達到目標分數。

TEST 2

LISTENING TEST

Part 1
Part 2
Part 3
Part 4

READING TEST

Part 5
Part 6
Part 7

Review 檢查表

注意！測驗前請務必檢查下列事項。

手機是否關機？
Answer Sheet（p. 249）、鉛筆、橡皮擦和手錶是否準備好了？
準備好聆聽音檔了嗎？

準備就緒後，想著你的目標分數，開始測驗。
測驗完畢後，請務必查看 Review 檢查表（p. 110），複習答錯的題目。

🎧 Test 2.mp3
可免費下載、播放 MP3，用於答題訓練和複習

MP3 音檔

LISTENING TEST

In this section, you must demonstrate your ability to understand spoken English. This section is divided into four parts and will take approximately 45 minutes to complete. Do not mark the answers in your test book. Use the answer sheet that is provided separately.

PART 1

Directions: For each question, you will listen to four short statements about a picture in your test book. These statements will not be printed and will only be spoken one time. Select the statement that best describes what is happening in the picture and mark the corresponding letter (A), (B), (C), or (D) on the answer sheet.

Sample Answer
Ⓐ ● Ⓒ Ⓓ

The statement that best describes the picture is (B), "The man is sitting at the desk." So, you should mark letter (B) on the answer sheet.

1.

2.

GO ON TO THE NEXT PAGE

3.

4.

5.

6.

GO ON TO THE NEXT PAGE →

PART 2

Directions: For each question, you will listen to a statement or question followed by three possible responses spoken in English. They will not be printed and will only be spoken one time. Select the best response and mark the corresponding letter (A), (B), or (C) on your answer sheet.

7. Mark your answer on your answer sheet.

8. Mark your answer on your answer sheet.

9. Mark your answer on your answer sheet.

10. Mark your answer on your answer sheet.

11. Mark your answer on your answer sheet.

12. Mark your answer on your answer sheet.

13. Mark your answer on your answer sheet.

14. Mark your answer on your answer sheet.

15. Mark your answer on your answer sheet.

16. Mark your answer on your answer sheet.

17. Mark your answer on your answer sheet.

18. Mark your answer on your answer sheet.

19. Mark your answer on your answer sheet.

20. Mark your answer on your answer sheet.

21. Mark your answer on your answer sheet.

22. Mark your answer on your answer sheet.

23. Mark your answer on your answer sheet.

24. Mark your answer on your answer sheet.

25. Mark your answer on your answer sheet.

26. Mark your answer on your answer sheet.

27. Mark your answer on your answer sheet.

28. Mark your answer on your answer sheet.

29. Mark your answer on your answer sheet.

30. Mark your answer on your answer sheet.

31. Mark your answer on your answer sheet.

PART 3

Directions: In this part, you will listen to several conversations between two or more speakers. These conversations will not be printed and will only be spoken one time. For each conversation, you will be asked to answer three questions. Select the best response and mark the corresponding letter (A), (B), (C), or (D) on your answer sheet.

32. Why did the man call?

   (A) To ask about an interview
   (B) To accept a job offer
   (C) To arrange a meeting
   (D) To discuss a project

33. Why has there been a delay?

   (A) An application form was not submitted.
   (B) Some team members are on vacation.
   (C) A hiring committee has yet to meet.
   (D) Some documents are being reviewed.

34. What will a human resources staff member probably do tomorrow morning?

   (A) Give candidates a tour
   (B) Contact applicants
   (C) Look over a résumé
   (D) Advertise a position

---

35. What most likely is the woman's profession?

   (A) Author
   (B) Publisher
   (C) Photographer
   (D) Performer

36. What does the man mean when he says, "I'm free today and tomorrow"?

   (A) He will perform a task.
   (B) He will extend a deadline.
   (C) He will update a schedule.
   (D) He will take a day off.

37. What will the woman do in the afternoon?

   (A) Attend a workshop
   (B) Give a presentation
   (C) Visit an office
   (D) Join an online meeting

---

38. What is the problem?

   (A) Customers have decreased.
   (B) A business has closed.
   (C) Guests have complained.
   (D) Food quality has gone down.

39. What does the man suggest?

   (A) Introducing new entrées
   (B) Reducing prices
   (C) Hiring more staff
   (D) Offering free appetizers

40. What do the women say about their restaurant?

   (A) It just moved to the neighborhood.
   (B) It recently changed its recipes.
   (C) It offers inexpensive dishes.
   (D) It plans to open a second location.

---

41. What will take place next week?

   (A) A travel fair
   (B) A store opening
   (C) A hotel convention
   (D) A trade show

42. What are the speakers mainly discussing?

   (A) Flight schedules
   (B) Accommodation options
   (C) Event venues
   (D) Exhibit dates

43. Why does the man say, "The company will reimburse me up to $250 per night"?

   (A) To reject a suggestion
   (B) To address a concern
   (C) To make an offer
   (D) To respond to a complaint

GO ON TO THE NEXT PAGE

44. What is the man's problem?

(A) An employee is not available.
(B) A highway is not accessible.
(C) A vehicle is not functioning.
(D) A garage is not open.

45. What does the woman agree to do?

(A) Forward a message
(B) Clear some snow
(C) Send a worker
(D) Contact emergency personnel

46. What does the woman inquire about?

(A) If a truck can be towed
(B) Whether the traffic has been blocked
(C) What caused a delay
(D) When the man must be picked up

47. What does the man ask the woman to do?

(A) Provide transportation
(B) Select a destination
(C) Make a purchase
(D) Verify information

48. What happened this morning?

(A) A bus was damaged.
(B) An event was rescheduled.
(C) A mechanic was hired.
(D) An appointment was confirmed.

49. What is mentioned about Bob Granger?

(A) He is a professional driver.
(B) He has a large automobile.
(C) He is an event organizer.
(D) He knows a retreat location well.

50. What problem does the man mention?

(A) An assignment was not completed.
(B) A document has been lost.
(C) A device is not working.
(D) An office is currently in use.

51. What did the woman do earlier today?

(A) Tested a projector
(B) Charged a battery
(C) Lost a phone
(D) Joined a conference

52. What does the man ask the woman about?

(A) The location of an outlet
(B) The length of a power cord
(C) The size of a room
(D) The height of a table

53. According to the woman, what is prepared every year?

(A) Some financial documents
(B) An industry conference
(C) Some training programs
(D) An investment plan

54. What is mentioned about Opus Investments?

(A) It is a well-known firm.
(B) It is on the ninth floor.
(C) It is a new company.
(D) It is relocating employees.

55. What does the woman offer to do?

(A) Set up a meeting with supervisors
(B) Guide a colleague to a work space
(C) Arrange seats for an office gathering
(D) Give a tour of a production facility

56. What is the woman's problem?

(A) She cannot watch a presentation.
(B) She is unable to attend a function.
(C) She cannot rent some equipment.
(D) She is unfamiliar with a venue.

57. Why is the Dumont Conference Center closed this week?

(A) It is being renovated.
(B) Its lobby is being cleaned.
(C) It is being prepared for an event.
(D) Its audio system is being upgraded.

58. How can the woman get the information she requires?

(A) By meeting with an investor
(B) By attending a workshop
(C) By calling a coworker
(D) By visiting a website

---

59. What does the man need assistance with?

(A) Finding a seat
(B) Returning a purchase
(C) Booking a trip
(D) Selecting a product

60. Who most likely is the woman?

(A) A tour guide
(B) A boat captain
(C) A customer
(D) A salesperson

61. What will the man most likely do next?

(A) Examine some vehicles
(B) Visit another store
(C) Watch a demonstration
(D) Order some food

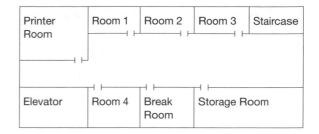

Printer Room	Room 1	Room 2	Room 3	Staircase
Elevator	Room 4	Break Room	Storage Room	

62. Who most likely is Mr. Zimmerman?

(A) A department head
(B) An intern
(C) A receptionist
(D) A sales manager

63. Look at the graphic. Where will a meeting be held?

(A) Room 1
(B) Room 2
(C) Room 3
(D) Room 4

64. What will the woman receive shortly?

(A) A beverage
(B) A document
(C) A room key
(D) A pass code

GO ON TO THE NEXT PAGE

Room Type	Regular Price
Standard	$250
Premium	$270
Deluxe	$300
Regal	$350

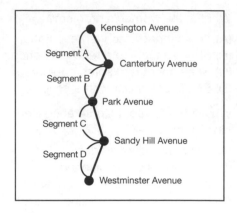

65. What does the man ask the woman for?

(A) A refund
(B) A statement
(C) A new room
(D) A discount

66. Why is the man surprised?

(A) He was expecting a different price.
(B) His room was in bad condition.
(C) His credit card was declined.
(D) He is being charged for late check-out.

67. Look at the graphic. Which type of room did the man stay in?

(A) Standard
(B) Premium
(C) Deluxe
(D) Regal

68. What did the woman recently do?

(A) Relocated to a new city
(B) Accepted a job offer
(C) Visited a government office
(D) Purchased a transit pass

69. Look at the graphic. Which segment is temporarily closed?

(A) Segment A
(B) Segment B
(C) Segment C
(D) Segment D

70. What will the woman most likely do next?

(A) Go to a bus stop
(B) Inspect a construction site
(C) Take a taxi
(D) Reschedule an appointment

PART 4

Directions: In this part, you will listen to several short talks by a single speaker. These talks will not be printed and will only be spoken one time. For each talk, you will be asked to answer three questions. Select the best response and mark the corresponding letter (A), (B), (C), or (D) on your answer sheet.

71. What type of business is being advertised?

(A) An interior design firm
(B) A cleaning company
(C) A real estate agency
(D) A home appliance retailer

72. What can the listeners receive until May 12?

(A) A product sample
(B) A free consultation
(C) A gift certificate
(D) A discounted service

73. Why should the listeners visit the website?

(A) To make a payment
(B) To schedule an appointment
(C) To download a coupon
(D) To complete a questionnaire

74. What is the speaker mainly discussing?

(A) An updated policy
(B) A refunded ticket
(C) A misplaced item
(D) A canceled flight

75. What should Ms. Freeman do to receive compensation?

(A) Submit some paperwork
(B) Provide a ticket
(C) Speak with a baggage handler
(D) Return a damaged product

76. What will the speaker most likely do next?

(A) Inspect a suitcase
(B) Go to an office
(C) Confirm a payment
(D) Send an e-mail

77. Where most likely are the listeners?

(A) At a retirement party
(B) At a writing workshop
(C) At an art exhibit
(D) At an award ceremony

78. What does the speaker imply when he says, "You've probably heard her name"?

(A) Jill Holloway was mentioned before.
(B) Jill Holloway has attended previous events.
(C) Jill Holloway won an award recently.
(D) Jill Holloway is famous.

79. What will the listeners most likely do next?

(A) Discuss a book
(B) Register for a seminar
(C) Take a brief break
(D) Listen to a speech

80. What is the speaker mainly talking about?

(A) A product review
(B) A marketing strategy
(C) A job opening
(D) A work schedule

81. Who most likely is Mindy Lineman?

(A) A company executive
(B) A business consultant
(C) A job applicant
(D) A recent hire

82. Why does the speaker say, "our time is almost up"?

(A) A gathering has to be rescheduled.
(B) A deadline is quickly approaching.
(C) A meeting is about to finish.
(D) A task has yet to be completed.

GO ON TO THE NEXT PAGE

83. According to the speaker, what should be done first?

(A) Make a delivery
(B) Examine a product
(C) Confirm a date
(D) Issue a refund

84. Why should the listeners contact a supervisor?

(A) To report that an item is damaged
(B) To check if a request was processed
(C) To receive some paperwork
(D) To provide a reason for a return

85. What should the listeners ask customers to do?

(A) Complete a form
(B) Make a purchase
(C) Cancel a payment
(D) Sign a contract

---

86. What is the broadcast mainly about?

(A) A traffic jam
(B) A local event
(C) A new restaurant
(D) A school competition

87. What are the listeners advised to do?

(A) Use public transportation
(B) Avoid a major highway
(C) Sign up early for an event
(D) Make a charitable donation

88. Who will the listeners hear from next?

(A) A weather forecaster
(B) A business owner
(C) A local politician
(D) A popular chef

---

89. Why did the speaker call?

(A) To place an order for products
(B) To continue a conversation
(C) To extend a deadline
(D) To ask for some advice

90. What has the speaker already done?

(A) Delivered some samples
(B) Turned down a business offer
(C) Contacted some retailers
(D) Reviewed a price list

91. Why should a presentation be prepared?

(A) To share information about products
(B) To introduce a recent hire
(C) To describe a new service
(D) To explain a shipping process

---

92. Who most likely is Judith Frost?

(A) A literary critic
(B) A novelist
(C) A program host
(D) A film director

93. What is mentioned about *Bright Lights*?

(A) It is part of a collection.
(B) It will be made into a movie.
(C) It has been featured in an article.
(D) It has not been published yet.

94. What does the speaker mean when he says, "Many people will likely be disappointed"?

(A) A guest has canceled an interview.
(B) Availability of tickets to a book signing is limited.
(C) A recent movie has received poor reviews.
(D) Some events will take place at a later time.

**Horgen Cultural Center
Lecture Series**

Time	Topic
9 A.M.	Salary negotiations
11 A.M.	Corporate branding
4 P.M.	Financial crimes
6 P.M.	Panel discussions

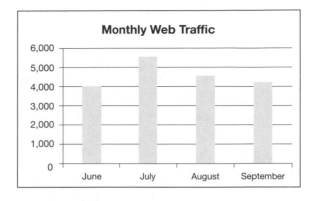

Monthly Web Traffic

95. Look at the graphic. When will Ms. Parkerson most likely speak?

(A) At 9 A.M.
(B) At 11 A.M.
(C) At 4 P.M.
(D) At 6 P.M.

96. What does the speaker say about Ms. Parkerson?

(A) She has not signed a contract.
(B) Her lecture will be recorded.
(C) Her payment will not change.
(D) She is the event's keynote speaker.

97. What are the listeners asked to do?

(A) Review a lecture
(B) Post a notice
(C) Print some handouts
(D) Open a ticket booth

98. What kind of business does the speaker most likely work for?

(A) A research firm
(B) A travel agency
(C) An online retailer
(D) A shipping company

99. Look at the graphic. When did the company run a television advertisement?

(A) In June
(B) In July
(C) In August
(D) In September

100. What does the speaker ask the listeners to do?

(A) Reduce costs
(B) Provide suggestions
(C) Review feedback
(D) Contact customers

This is the end of the Listening test. Turn to PART 5 in your test book.

GO ON TO THE NEXT PAGE

READING TEST

In this section, you must demonstrate your ability to read and comprehend English. You will be given a variety of texts and asked to answer questions about these texts. This section is divided into three parts and will take 75 minutes to complete.

Do not mark the answers in your test book. Use the answer sheet that is separately provided.

PART 5

Directions: In each question, you will be asked to review a statement that is missing a word or phrase. Four answer choices will be provided for each statement. Select the best answer and mark the corresponding letter (A), (B), (C), or (D) on the answer sheet.

🕐 **PART 5** 建議作答時間 **11 分鐘**

101. To attract young consumers, promoting new products online is more ------- than advertising on television.

(A) effects
(B) effectively
(C) effecting
(D) effective

102. Twins Excursions employs licensed guides who ------- tours in five different languages.

(A) conduct
(B) receive
(C) inspect
(D) distribute

103. The employee handbook provides information on how personnel may take advantage of ------- medical benefits.

(A) they
(B) their
(C) them
(D) themselves

104. Upon request, official receipts can be issued for all ------- to the Global Awareness Foundation.

(A) contributions
(B) contributed
(C) contributes
(D) contribute

105. Director Phillip Anderson's movie *Silent Moon* received a ------- for the Best Film Award this year.

(A) nomination
(B) subscription
(C) destination
(D) creation

106. The Seattle Food Convention was a success, attracting over 1,000 chefs ------- a large number of amateur cooks.

(A) nor
(B) and
(C) but
(D) only

107. During peak shopping seasons, Johnson's Sportswear provides additional staff training to ensure an ------- workforce.

(A) experienced
(B) experiencing
(C) experiences
(D) experience

108. Only staff employed for more than 15 years are ------- to receive an Excellent Worker Award.

(A) accountable
(B) modified
(C) entitled
(D) important

109. The new recruitment process ------- all
future job candidates to submit their
résumés via e-mail.

(A) requirement
(B) requires
(C) require
(D) requiring

110. The recent economic downturn does not
------- mean that the unemployment rate
will increase.

(A) necessarily
(B) expectedly
(C) hesitantly
(D) consciously

111. As a result of ------- from environmentally
conscious residents, the local government
is constructing bicycle lanes throughout the
town.

(A) encouragingly
(B) encourages
(C) encouraged
(D) encouragement

112. Foley Dental Clinic requests that patients
reconfirm an appointment at least two
days ------- its scheduled date.

(A) prior to
(B) provided that
(C) among
(D) since

113. After sending her manuscript to dozens
of publishers, Susan James was finally
------- a contract by Spring Books.

(A) offered
(B) offer
(C) offers
(D) offering

114. Peramo Co.'s management was ------- to
upgrade its computer systems because
of the high cost.

(A) reluctant
(B) unanticipated
(C) acceptable
(D) vulnerable

115. After Telestar Computing secures funding,
it ------- a large team of developers to
carry out its expansion plans.

(A) is recruited
(B) recruited
(C) will recruit
(D) was recruiting

116. Passengers on the canceled flight
received a full refund and a $500 voucher
as ------- for their inconvenience.

(A) compensation
(B) presentation
(C) motivation
(D) admiration

117. The ------- reason for the negative
reviews of the Central Highland Gym is
the poor condition of the pool.

(A) principal
(B) considerate
(C) secure
(D) beneficial

118. A recent poll indicates that residents are
------- of City Council's plan to raise taxes
for a new park.

(A) supporting
(B) supportive
(C) supported
(D) supports

119. Mr. Cruise ------- apologized for having
misspoken during his speech to the
company shareholders.

(A) quickness
(B) quickly
(C) quicken
(D) quickened

120. Killiam Public Library will be hosting a ----
--- of lectures by local authors over the
summer.

(A) gathering
(B) means
(C) series
(D) conclusion

GO ON TO THE NEXT PAGE

121. ------- an agreement is reached, representatives from both corporations will sign the contract.

(A) Not only
(B) In order to
(C) Due to
(D) As soon as

122. As a regional manager, Ms. Nissim reports ------- to the company's board of directors.

(A) directly
(B) directed
(C) directs
(D) directing

123. Bolton Enterprises decided to rent office space for its new branch ------- purchasing a building.

(A) about
(B) on behalf of
(C) regarding
(D) instead of

124. For the best results, give ------- time to recover between workouts.

(A) your
(B) yours
(C) yourself
(D) itself

125. Northpoint Cellular is investing heavily in new wireless technologies to ------- other well-established firms.

(A) surpassing
(B) surpass
(C) surpassed
(D) surpasses

126. Renewable energy has grown more affordable in recent years, and ------- more consumers are choosing to try it.

(A) otherwise
(B) therefore
(C) once
(D) instead

127. Joel Hardwick's second novel received ------- reviews from critics, who praised its realistic dialog and believable characters.

(A) defective
(B) renewable
(C) artificial
(D) favorable

128. The number of subscribers to *Edible Magazine* has increased steadily, ------- that of all other culinary publications.

(A) exceeds
(B) exceedingly
(C) exceeded
(D) exceeding

129. Sales ------- weeks three and four of the promotion will be monitored to determine whether it should be extended.

(A) above
(B) next
(C) during
(D) beside

130. CanAir's frequent flyer program is designed ------- passengers who regularly fly with the airline.

(A) reward
(B) rewarding
(C) to reward
(D) rewards

PART 6

Directions: In this part, you will be asked to read four English texts. Each text is missing a word, phrase, or sentence. Select the answer choice that correctly completes the text and mark the corresponding letter (A), (B), (C), or (D) on the answer sheet.

🕐 **PART 6** 建議作答時間 **8 分鐘**

Questions 131-134 refer to the following letter.

Ms. Victoria Collins
645 Keystone Avenue
Bellevue, WA 98007

Dear Ms. Collins,

When you were in our shop for a consultation last week, you ------- that you will need a
131.
unique outfit for the Bellevue Fine Art Society's charity dinner.

We just received an ------- of pieces from designer Eleanor Harris's summer collection. In
132.
particular, we have a blue evening dress that you might be interested in. This item is

exclusive to our shop, but it is a size small. -------.
133.

You said that the dinner is being ------- in May. The weather will be warm by then, so a light
134.
dress such as this one will be perfect for the event. Please let me know when you are

available to stop by.

Miranda Hudson
The Dot Boutique

131. (A) mentioning
(B) mentionable
(C) mentioned
(D) mentions

132. (A) assortment
(B) estimate
(C) invitation
(D) announcement

133. (A) We are concerned that the dress is too formal.
(B) Clothes can sometimes shrink when placed in a dryer.
(C) Minor alterations can be done to ensure a great fit.
(D) It is sold at popular retail stores around the country.

134. (A) represented
(B) discussed
(C) canceled
(D) held

GO ON TO THE NEXT PAGE

Questions 135-138 refer to the following memo.

Date: December 10
To: All staff
From: Jonathan Carter, COO
Subject: Policy change

To encourage greater efficiency, management has decided to change how staff ------- are
135.
carried out next year. Beginning in January, team members must participate in a -------
136.
assessment every year. This process will involve examining all aspects of their

performance. Employees ------- bonuses based on the results. Additional information about
137.
the new system has been included in the updated version of the employee manual. -------.
138.

If you have any questions, please contact Director of Personnel Dave Stewart.

135. (A) interviews
(B) assignments
(C) registrations
(D) evaluations

136. (A) thorough
(B) temporary
(C) voluntary
(D) selective

137. (A) have been receiving
(B) received
(C) will receive
(D) were receiving

138. (A) This process has already improved
performance.
(B) This document will be distributed next
week.
(C) Some members have not yet been
assessed.
(D) However, these results were not very
surprising.

Questions 139-142 refer to the following advertisement.

Vacancies for Cooks at Quinn Grill

We are a fine dining establishment with an excellent reputation, and we have been in business for over five years. Our customer base ------- rapidly during this period due to
139.
word of mouth and positive reviews from critics. ------- we are expanding our main dining
140.
room, we are in need of experienced cooks. All applicants must have at least two years of

experience working in a restaurant. This should include cooking a broad range of dishes.

-------. Our ideal candidate will be able to handle a high-pressure environment, collaborate
141.
with other members of a team, and work ------- hours, including weekends and holidays.
142.
Please send your application letter, résumé, and reference letters to Sophia Quinn at

squinn@quinngrill.com.

---

139. (A) grows
(B) had grown
(C) has grown
(D) will grow

140. (A) Because
(B) Then
(C) As if
(D) Unless

141. (A) Everyone passed the mandatory food safety course.
(B) We also have several other specific requirements.
(C) The results of the interview will be posted soon.
(D) Guests must be shown to their tables immediately.

142. (A) flexibility
(B) flexibleness
(C) flexible
(D) flexibly

GO ON TO THE NEXT PAGE

Questions 143-146 refer to the following letter.

Sandra Ericta
Landlord, Bristol Apartments
355 Main Street
San Francisco, CA 95125

Dear Ms. Ericta,

This letter serves as notice that I will be vacating Unit 307 of Bristol Apartments on

September 30. I am giving you the ------- 30 days' notice according to my rental contract.
                                    143.

I realize that I have an ------- to leave the apartment in good condition. Otherwise, I will lose
                         144.

my security deposit. Please let me know when you are available to inspect the unit and

confirm that everything is -------. I would like my deposit returned to me on September 30
                           145.

after I move out and hand you the key. -------.
                                       146.

Thank you.

Sincerely,
John Schroeder

---

143. (A) requesting
(B) request
(C) requests
(D) requested

144. (A) occupation
(B) obligation
(C) inquiry
(D) option

145. (A) capable
(B) challenging
(C) satisfactory
(D) appreciative

146. (A) Tenants are prohibited from making copies of the key.
(B) An incorrect amount must have been transferred.
(C) I will provide my bank account details on the same day.
(D) It will not be possible for me to move my furniture today.

PART 7

Directions: In this part, you will be asked to read several texts, such as advertisements, articles, instant messages, or examples of business correspondence. Each text is followed by several questions. Select the best answer and mark the corresponding letter (A), (B), (C), or (D) on your answer sheet.

🕐 **PART 7** 建議作答時間 **54 分鐘**

Questions 147-148 refer to the following advertisement.

Have you just moved into a new apartment or house? Do you need some help fixing up your home? If so, then you are in luck as you can just call:

Harold and Sons
Serving the greater Centerville area
555-2398

We provide a wide range of services, including:
Basic home repairs
Appliance, lighting, and fixture installation
Wallpaper pasting and wall painting
Furniture arrangement
Tile laying

Harold Clark started his business 25 years ago, and now his sons Robert and William work with him to provide their home services to local residents. The family's experience and professionalism is beyond comparison. If you call in the month of June, Harold and Sons will install a ceiling fan or light fixture for free with the purchase of any service.

147. What most likely does Harold and Sons do?

(A) Designs wallpaper patterns for home interiors
(B) Moves furniture from one house to another
(C) Conducts residential maintenance tasks
(D) Specializes in installing office lighting

148. What can customers receive in June?

(A) A gift certificate
(B) A complimentary service
(C) A product sample
(D) A new company catalog

GO ON TO THE NEXT PAGE

Questions 149-150 refer to the following text message chain.

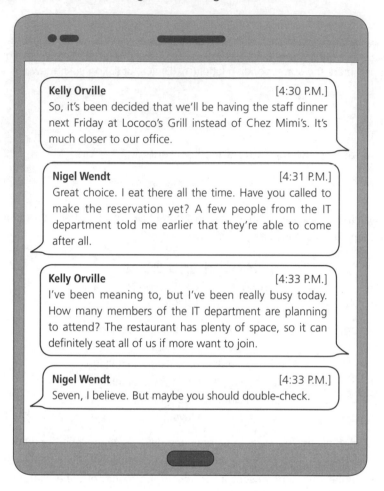

Kelly Orville [4:30 P.M.]
So, it's been decided that we'll be having the staff dinner next Friday at Lococo's Grill instead of Chez Mimi's. It's much closer to our office.

Nigel Wendt [4:31 P.M.]
Great choice. I eat there all the time. Have you called to make the reservation yet? A few people from the IT department told me earlier that they're able to come after all.

Kelly Orville [4:33 P.M.]
I've been meaning to, but I've been really busy today. How many members of the IT department are planning to attend? The restaurant has plenty of space, so it can definitely seat all of us if more want to join.

Nigel Wendt [4:33 P.M.]
Seven, I believe. But maybe you should double-check.

149. What is NOT true about Lococo's Grill?

(A) It can host corporate gatherings.
(B) It is frequently visited by Mr. Wendt.
(C) It is nearer to a workplace than Chez Mimi's.
(D) It requires reservations on weekends.

150. At 4:33 P.M., what does Ms. Orville most likely mean when she writes, "I've been meaning to"?

(A) She plans to invite members of another department.
(B) She does not know how many staff will attend.
(C) She intends to let employees know about a change.
(D) She has not contacted a restaurant.

Questions 151-153 refer to the following article.

Medallion Helps New Employees Adapt

Earlier this year, Medallion Corporation created a staff mentoring program to develop the skills of its employees. — [1] —. The program, called Medallion Mentoring, pairs newly hired workers with senior-level managers, who provide advice about day-to-day tasks as well as career growth strategies. — [2] —. Human resources coordinators assign mentors to new workers and schedule two one-hour sessions per week. — [3] —. Additionally, all mentors in the program must fulfill this time requirement.

Although it took a while to get this program off the ground, participation is gradually increasing. This year, human resources coordinators aim to have 200 mentors companywide. — [4] —. Medallion Corporation Chairperson Sally Kay said, "There is a lot more interest in this program now, so there will be no problem finding enough supervisors to volunteer as mentors."

151. What is suggested about the Medallion Mentoring program?

(A) It was featured on a business website.
(B) It requires quarterly recruiting efforts.
(C) It is not supported by upper management.
(D) It was established less than 12 months ago.

152. What are mentors required to do?

(A) Meet a minimum number of necessary hours
(B) Volunteer for two hours a day after work
(C) Get together with family members of mentored staff
(D) Have regular counseling sessions with a coordinator

153. In which of the positions marked [1], [2], [3], and [4] does the following sentence best belong?

"This goal is expected to be achieved by October."

(A) [1]
(B) [2]
(C) [3]
(D) [4]

Questions 154-155 refer to the following e-mail.

To: Leah Young <leahyoung@journeyon.com>
From: Evan Harris <evanharris@smartmail.com>
Date: May 9
Subject: Travel insurance
Attachment: Receipt, Police Report

Dear Ms. Young,

I am writing to request reimbursement for an unexpected expense. Recently, I traveled to Mexico on vacation. I insured my trip through Journey on Travel Insurance. My policy number is 4533906.

I booked a room at Hotel Fiesta in Cozumel for five nights. On the second day of my visit, someone gained access to my room and took my laptop computer. The hotel manager gave me a refund for the remaining three nights, but this doesn't come close to covering the cost of purchasing a replacement computer.

From my understanding, I am entitled to up to $5,000 of insurance coverage from your company in this type of situation. The total cost of my laptop was $2,300. I have attached copies of my receipt for the computer and the police report.

Sincerely,
Evan Harris

154. Why did Mr. Harris write the e-mail?

(A) To ask for compensation
(B) To make a reservation
(C) To criticize a hotel
(D) To cancel a payment

155. According to the e-mail, what happened at Hotel Fiesta?

(A) A guest was overcharged for a room.
(B) An electronic device was stolen.
(C) A personal computer was damaged.
(D) A refund request was denied.

Great Deals of Delta
Your source for special deals at area businesses

We work with shops, restaurants, travel companies, salons, spas, and home service businesses to create a one-stop shop for Delta area consumers. You won't find this many deals in any other place. Find a great deal today!

Product or Service SEARCH

Business SEARCH

This website has been provided by *The Delta Times* Newspaper.

Home	Shopping	**Home Services**	Personal Services

Great Deal #1:
Hammerhead Window Washing
-$40 off your first residential window cleaning service

Great Deal #2:
Scrub Masters Tile and Air Vent Cleaning
-Order both services and receive 20 percent off the regular price

Great Deal #3:
Bloom's Yards
-Six months of weekly lawn care services, prepaid, at 25 percent off

Great Deal #4:
Swift Swipe Carpet Cleaning
-Receive a one-time cleaning service for rugs in up to five rooms for 10 percent off

More on the next page. Click here! >>>

156. What is the purpose of the web page?

(A) To compare the costs of similar services
(B) To provide reviews of local services
(C) To introduce new enterprises
(D) To advertise business discount offers

157. How much of a discount is being offered on landscaping services?

(A) 10 percent
(B) 20 percent
(C) 25 percent
(D) 40 percent

GO ON TO THE NEXT PAGE

TEST 2   NEW TOEIC 950 聽力+閱讀 5 回試題

Questions 158-160 refer to the following letter.

April 12

Chad Steiner
1420 Elm Street, Suite 32
Madison, WI 53705

Dear Mr. Steiner,

This letter has been sent to all residents of Singing Vines Apartments. As you know, the spaces in this building's parking lot are reserved for tenants. However, we have received several complaints about visitors ignoring this regulation. Starting next week, we will be checking all automobiles parked in our lot. If a resident parking pass is not displayed in the window, we will have the vehicle removed.

Please inform your guests that they can park on Elm Street in front of the building for free at any time of the day. Parking is also allowed on Boulder Avenue and Park Road, but there is an hourly charge. Note that a city rule prohibits parking on Devon Boulevard, which runs along the west side of the building.

If you have any questions or concerns, please feel free to contact me.

Sincerely,
Rachel Solomon
Building manager, Singing Vines Apartments

158. What problem does Ms. Solomon mention?

(A) A building is not being cleaned.
(B) A fee has been increased.
(C) An automobile has been scratched.
(D) A rule is not being followed.

159. What will happen next week?

(A) Passes will be issued.
(B) Vehicles will be examined.
(C) Tenants will be contacted.
(D) Apartments will be renovated.

160. Where are visitors not allowed to park?

(A) On Elm Street
(B) On Boulder Avenue
(C) On Park Road
(D) On Devon Boulevard

Questions 161-163 refer to the following e-mail.

To:	Marcy Sizemore <marcysizemore@fullerchemical.com>
From:	Shane Ellis <shaneellis@quantumlaboratories.com>
Date:	January 14
Subject:	Congratulations
Attachment:	Résumé

Hi Marcy,

It has been nearly 10 years since we last worked together, but when I recently saw an article in *Science News Monthly* about your promotion to vice president of research and development at Fuller Chemical, I remembered our early days working together as research assistants for LabSure Corporation. I knew that with your talent and work ethic, you would be successful. Congratulations on your promotion.

As you may know, I am the director of quality assurance for Quantum Laboratories. We have a very talented researcher that will be leaving our company to seek out other employment opportunities. While we are sad to lose her, I would like to recommend her to you in case you have a suitable opening at your company. You will find that she has an impressive educational background and a great deal of experience in the field of biological research. I have attached her résumé for you to review.

Even if you don't have a position open, would you mind meeting her to offer career advice? If you are willing to help, please let me know. Thank you, and I wish you all the best at your new position.

Regards,

Shane Ellis

161. Why did Mr. Ellis write the e-mail?

(A) To request help with a research project
(B) To announce his promotion
(C) To offer an investment opportunity
(D) To recommend a potential employee

162. How do Ms. Sizemore and Mr. Ellis know each other?

(A) They attended the same conference.
(B) They used to be coworkers.
(C) They met through a shared acquaintance.
(D) They went to the same school.

163. What does Mr. Ellis suggest that Ms. Sizemore do?

(A) Apply for a position
(B) Propose a candidate
(C) Have a meeting
(D) Contact a client

GO ON TO THE NEXT PAGE

Questions 164-167 refer to the following online chat discussion.

Joy Saunders [2:15 P.M.] Have any of you had difficulties getting reimbursed for travel expenses? There have been some complaints lately.

Maurice Watts [2:17 P.M.] I ran into a problem. I was only reimbursed for a small portion of what I spent when I went to San Francisco for the trade exhibition last month. I'm not sure why, though. I didn't exceed the $1,000 limit, and I submitted my receipts before the first Friday of the month. That's the deadline, right?

Joy Saunders [2:18 P.M.] That's correct. Did you ask the accounting team what the issue was?

Maurice Watts [2:19 P.M.] Yes, but I haven't gotten a reply yet.

Jennifer Cole [2:20 P.M.] I had to wait almost three months to get the $600 I paid for a hotel in January. When I asked for an explanation, I was told that expenses over $400 have to be approved by the accounting team in advance. Otherwise, it can take several weeks for the request to be processed.

Charlie Pearson [2:22 P.M.] I spent over $500 on transportation and can't afford to wait that long for reimbursement.

Joy Saunders [2:25 P.M.] Let me call the accounting manager and see what I can do to speed things up.

Send

---

164. What is mentioned about Mr. Watts?

(A) He is a member of the accounting team.
(B) He will transfer to another branch soon.
(C) He helped organize a trade show.
(D) He went on a business trip recently.

165. At 2:18 P.M., what does Ms. Saunders most likely mean when she writes, "That's correct"?

(A) The accounting department usually copies receipts.
(B) A deadline falls on the first Friday of every month.
(C) The $1,000 limit cannot be exceeded for any reason.
(D) A team member explained her expenses properly.

166. How much did Ms. Cole spend on accommodations in January?

(A) $400
(B) $500
(C) $600
(D) $1,000

167. What can be inferred about Ms. Saunders?

(A) She will purchase some airline tickets.
(B) She approved a reimbursement request.
(C) She will contact a department manager.
(D) She submitted a complaint to management.

Questions 168-171 refer to the following letter.

January 28

Eugene Lee
66 Westing Road
Wilmington, DE 19801

Dear Mr. Lee,

At the Hoyle Community Theater, we strive to provide the best performing arts experience possible. As a nonprofit organization, we depend on the support of the community. Therefore, we ask that our patrons periodically make donations. — [1] —.

Enclosed is an envelope into which you can place your donation. — [2] —. Any amount would be greatly appreciated. Substantial benefits are available to those who contribute $100 or more. — [3] —.

And to show gratitude to our loyal patrons, we're planning on staging some of our most ambitious performances yet this year. — [4] —. In March, we'll be putting on a play by the famed Kenyan playwright David Kobo called *Searching for the Homeland*. And in June, we'll be holding a three-week-long performance of a new play by local playwright Steve Weller. Then, this autumn we're going to be performing a series of classical Greek tragedies.

As the only theater in Wilmington that offers free performances, we are supported by people like you. So, thank you for your continued dedication.

Sincerely,

Kathryn Little
Director, Hoyle Community Theater

---

168. What is the purpose of the letter?

(A) To solicit money from a patron
(B) To advertise a new theater
(C) To announce a schedule change
(D) To seek actors for a performance

169. What is mentioned about *Searching for the Homeland*?

(A) It will run for three weeks.
(B) It is based on a Greek tragedy.
(C) It is being directed by Steve Weller.
(D) It was written by a well-known artist.

170. What is indicated about the Hoyle Community Theater?

(A) It is located outside of Wilmington.
(B) It hires student actors for performances.
(C) It does not charge money for admission.
(D) It is closed on weekends and national holidays.

171. In which of the positions marked [1], [2], [3], and [4] does the following sentence best belong?

"These include gift cards to restaurants in the area and tickets to local concerts."

(A) [1]
(B) [2]
(C) [3]
(D) [4]

GO ON TO THE NEXT PAGE

Questions 172-175 refer to the following information.

Road Closures

Please note that certain sections of King Street, Queen Street, and Dundas Avenue will be closed in March and April. These closures are necessary to perform required work on parts of these roads that were damaged during the long winter. The roads are all major routes through the city, and they should not be left in their current condition.

Please note the following schedule:

- March 6 to March 20 – King Street will be closed between Bathurst Street and University Avenue.
- March 21 to April 3 – Queen Street will be closed between Ossington Avenue and Kensington Avenue.
- April 4 to April 18 – Dundas Avenue will be closed between University Avenue and Young Street.

We suggest using Royce Avenue and Church Street as detours for all of the routes listed above. If you decide to use smaller residential streets, please remember to observe the reduced speed limit at all times.

Thank you for your patience and understanding.

The Toronto Public Works Committee

172. Why are some roads being closed?

    (A) To allow a festival to take place
    (B) To repair them after the winter
    (C) To construct new sidewalks
    (D) To expand them by adding lanes

173. The word "condition" in paragraph 1, line 5, is closest in meaning to

    (A) requirement
    (B) district
    (C) state
    (D) task

174. Which road will NOT be closed?

    (A) Queen Street
    (B) King Street
    (C) Dundas Avenue
    (D) Royce Avenue

175. What are some drivers asked to do?

    (A) Follow the speed limit
    (B) Only travel along main roads
    (C) Contact a committee for information
    (D) Use a toll booth to access a road

GO ON TO THE NEXT PAGE ➤

Questions 176-180 refer to the following memo and form.

To: All employees
From: Chase Milton
Date: December 3
Subject: Employee holiday gift
Attachment: Gift choice card

Dear employees,

As you know, the holidays are fast approaching. To thank everyone for their hard work this year, Carrigan Foods will provide each employee with a turkey, ham, or basket of vegetarian food. The meat products will be available on December 12, while the baskets will be ready on December 16.

Please keep in mind that each employee is allowed to select only one gift. To indicate your choice, fill out the attached card and turn it in to your manager before December 6. We have also included the option of sending one of these items to a local food bank that provides meals to the homeless in case you do not wish to receive anything.

We hope you enjoy your gift and the coming holiday.

Sincerely,
Chase Milton
President, Carrigan Foods

Carrigan Foods
Employee Gift Choice Card

Check the label on the food product you receive for storage instructions. All items must be kept refrigerated or frozen. It is recommended that you pick up your gift from the administration office when your shift ends so that you do not have to leave it in your office or car for a long period of time.

If you will not be working on the day your gift is scheduled to be distributed, please arrange to have a coworker get it for you. Note that we cannot hold food items past their designated pickup days. Those that are not taken will be given to the food bank.

- -

Name: Selena Kim
Employee ID Number: 1002532
Division: Marketing
Phone Extension: 7457

Please pick one of the following options:
☐ Frozen turkey
☐ Frozen ham
☐ Vegetarian basket

I would like to give my gift to a food bank: Yes ☐ No ☐

176. What is Carrigan Foods planning to do?

(A) Organize a holiday dinner
(B) Show appreciation to its employees
(C) Offer a class on cooking techniques
(D) Send gift cards to some customers

177. In the memo, the word "select" in paragraph 2, line 1, is closest in meaning to

(A) vote
(B) choose
(C) assign
(D) prefer

178. According to the form, what are employees advised to do?

(A) Contact a local food bank
(B) Go to a storage area immediately
(C) Claim an item after finishing work
(D) Schedule a pickup time in advance

179. When will Ms. Kim most likely receive her gift?

(A) December 3
(B) December 6
(C) December 12
(D) December 16

180. What information is NOT requested on the form?

(A) Item preference
(B) Phone number
(C) Pickup time
(D) Department name

15TH ANNUAL BOOK SALE

The Carlton Library on Ferris Street is holding its 15th Annual Book Sale on Friday, August 2. Bring any books you have lying around to the staff at the front desk. Our staff will check these books to make sure that they don't have any torn pages, water damage, or writing in the margins. And if they are in good condition, we'll buy them at reasonable prices.

Also, we have a huge selection of used books on sale on the library's second floor. These include everything from translations of ancient poetry to contemporary bestsellers. All paperbacks are $5, and all hardcover books are $12. In addition, we are selling a variety of library merchandise, including tote bags for $8, backpacks for $20, and planners for $11.

The proceeds from all sales will be donated to the Appleton Institute, a charitable organization that provides tutoring to children. For more information about the Book Sale event, visit www.carltonsale.org.

TO: <questions@appleton.org>
FROM: Sally Fisher <sallyfisher44@fastmail.com>
SUBJECT: Volunteer opportunities
DATE: August 4
ATTACHMENT: Résumé

To Whom It May Concern,

Two days ago, I bought a $5 item at the Carlton Library's book sale event and received a flyer for the Appleton Institute. I had never heard of your organization before, but after reading over the flyer, I became very interested in the services you provide.

I am a former high school English teacher who has recently retired. However, I am looking to continue doing educational work in some capacity. I have extensive experience mentoring people who struggle with reading and writing, and I highly enjoy that kind of work. Therefore, I was wondering if your organization has any volunteer or part-time work opportunities.

I am available on most days of the week, although on Thursdays I perform charity work at a community center. I have attached my résumé to this e-mail. I look forward to hearing from you soon.

Sincerely,

Sally Fisher

181. According to the notice, what will library staff NOT check used books for?

(A) Damage from moisture
(B) Ripped pages
(C) Notes next to the text
(D) A missing cover

182. What will the money raised by the book sale be used for?

(A) Supporting a nonprofit organization
(B) Renovating a reading room
(C) Funding public schools
(D) Marketing new magazines

183. What did Ms. Fisher purchase at the Carlton Library?

(A) A backpack
(B) A paperback
(C) A hardcover
(D) A planner

184. What does Ms. Fisher say about her professional experience?

(A) She has worked at the Appleton Institute before.
(B) She published books to help struggling readers.
(C) She was employed as an educator.
(D) She has provided English tutoring at a library.

185. Why is Ms. Fisher not available on Thursdays?

(A) Because her language class was rescheduled
(B) Because she works at a bookstore
(C) Because her book club has weekly meetings
(D) Because she has a volunteer position

GO ON TO THE NEXT PAGE

RB BANK

Open an investment account with RB Bank and take advantage of our special offer. Get 60 days of free trading and a cash incentive when you deposit $2,500 or more.*

- $100 incentive + free trades with deposit of $2,500 to $49,999
- $250 incentive + free trades with deposit of $50,000 to $99,999
- $500 incentive + free trades with deposit of $100,000 to $249,999
- $750 incentive + free trades with deposit of $250,000 or more

Why choose RB Bank?
- Fair pricing with no hidden fees
- Educational resources for every investor
- Various investment types to choose from
- Round-the-clock support from financial advisers
- Easy-to-use trading software for desktop and mobile devices

* Offer is valid until April 30. Standard trading fee is $9.99. For inquiries, call 555-2975, e-mail info@rbbank.com, or visit one of our 60 branches nationwide.

To: Beth Viola <b.viola@ambercrafts.com>
From: Ron Campbell <r.campbell@rbbank.com>
Subject: Your account
Date: April 21

Dear Ms. Viola,

Thank you for opening an investment account with RB Bank. Your deposit of $50,000 was received yesterday. Please note that it will take approximately 60 days for your cash bonus to be released.

Regarding your other inquiry, there are a couple of options available for business owners who wish to borrow money. The first is the SBA Loan. This is for companies with fewer than 50 employees. Up to $100,000 may be borrowed at a 4.9-percent interest rate. The other option is the CTA Loan. It can only be applied for by firms with 50 employees or more. For this loan, up to $500,000 is available to the borrower at a 3.9-percent interest rate. Please visit our website for additional information about these loan programs and instructions on how to apply.

Sincerely,

Ron Campbell
Financial adviser

Loan Application Form

Company Information
Company Name: Amber Crafts
Owner: Beth Viola
Address: 527 Fairfax Avenue, Roanoke, VA 24016
Telephone: 555-2308
E-mail: b.viola@ambercrafts.com

Loan Type: SBA Loan
☑ Check here if you have read the RB Bank Privacy Agreement.

Please note that you must include a copy of your company's business license with your application.

186. What is NOT mentioned about RB Bank?

(A) It charges the lowest fees in the industry.
(B) It has a range of investment options.
(C) It offers 24-hour financial support.
(D) It provides learning materials for investors.

187. How much cash will Ms. Viola receive for opening an investment account?

(A) $100
(B) $250
(C) $500
(D) $750

188. According to the e-mail, what is an advantage of the CTA Loan over the SBA Loan?

(A) A more generous signup bonus
(B) A lower interest rate
(C) A longer borrowing period
(D) A less complex application process

189. What is implied about Amber Crafts?

(A) Its owner is looking for investors.
(B) It recently opened another branch.
(C) Its products are sold in multiple countries.
(D) It employs fewer than 50 workers.

190. What has Ms. Viola been asked to provide?

(A) Personnel records
(B) Financial statements
(C) An operating permit
(D) A legal contract

GO ON TO THE NEXT PAGE

About Empire Group

Within just 25 years, Empire Group has become a leader in property development, with experience in construction and financing.

Currently, Empire Group carries out commercial and residential construction projects in 45 cities, including New York, San Francisco, and Los Angeles. Over the past two years, it has established an international presence with offices and residential buildings in Malaysia, Canada, and Germany. Furthermore, the group has built 32 hotels in the US that are run by major operators like Blackwood and Le Clare.

Empire Group's most recent expansion has been into Australia. As in other places, its initial aim in Australia is to increase its workforce in cities that have a large population of upper-income residents.

Empire Group Australia is seeking qualified candidates to fill several full-time positions. To apply, e-mail your résumé to jobs@empiregroup.au.

Executive assistant
• Two positions (Brisbane and Melbourne)
• Duties involve providing administrative support
• Must be willing to travel
• College graduates preferred with 2+ years of experience in a business organization

Human resources worker
• Two positions (Melbourne and Perth)
• Duties include handling employee-related matters and assisting with recruiting
• Must hold a degree in human resources management with 3+ years of related experience
• Priority given to candidates with professional certification

Contracts specialist
• Four positions (Sydney and Perth)
• Duties include managing supplier relationships and negotiating commercial contracts
• Must have a business degree with 5+ years of real estate experience

Marketing associate
• Two positions (Brisbane and Perth)
• Duties include conducting research and developing advertising campaigns
• Must be proficient in office software and adept at presentations
• Must be college graduates with 3+ years of real estate work experience

Empire Group Australia

www.empiregroup.au

July 14

Dear Ms. Chen,

Thank you for your application and for participating in the interview. Unfortunately, we have decided to give the job to another applicant. Although you met our basic requirements in terms of experience and education, the applicant we selected has several certificates that you have not yet received.

We wish you well in your continued job search and encourage you to apply for other positions at Empire Group in the future. The company is still in its early stages in Australia and has further plans for growth, particularly in your city of Melbourne.

Warmly,

Leonora Mitchell
Recruiting specialist

---

191. What is indicated about Empire Group?

(A) It began as a financial services firm.
(B) Most of its offices are in Europe.
(C) It builds commercial and residential structures.
(D) Some of hotels it built will open next month.

192. What can be inferred about the city of Brisbane?

(A) It has the highest number of available job openings.
(B) It is the site of Empire Group's Australian headquarters.
(C) It has many residents with high incomes.
(D) It is the location of an upcoming real estate exposition.

193. What is true about the advertised marketing positions?

(A) They feature incentives for exceeding sales goals.
(B) They are only open to candidates with marketing degrees.
(C) They involve occasional overseas travel.
(D) They require good computer skills.

194. Why did Ms. Mitchell write the letter?

(A) To congratulate a successful applicant
(B) To invite a candidate to an interview
(C) To reject a job applicant
(D) To request details about work history

195. Which position did Ms. Chen most likely apply for?

(A) Executive assistant
(B) Human resources worker
(C) Contracts specialist
(D) Marketing associate

GO ON TO THE NEXT PAGE

Questions 196-200 refer to the following Web page, e-mail, and brochure.

www.pps.org

Support the Philadelphia Preservation Society (PPS)

Thanks to the work of the Philadelphia Preservation Society, Philadelphia boasts one of the largest ongoing collections of public art in the country. People from all backgrounds can enjoy access to these works at any time for free.

Here are some ways that you can support our mission to preserve public art for everyone:
- Join as a **PPS individual member** and receive advance invitations to PPS special events.
- Become a **PPS corporate partner** and attend our semiannual banquets at no cost to your business.
- Make a one-time donation for any amount by clicking <u>here</u>. Get a free PPS coffee mug when you donate.

To	Marilyn Johnson <m.johnson@pps.org>
From	Dixie Piper <d.piper@solomon.edu>
Subject	Class activity
Date	May 2

Dear Ms. Johnson,

I recently signed up as an individual member of the Philadelphia Preservation Society and am interested in bringing my 6th grade art class on one of the self-guided tours listed in your brochure. Ideally, I'd like to lead the students on a tour near a lake or river, where they can make sketches of what they see. We could do the activity on a Friday from 9 A.M. to 12 P.M. and end with a picnic lunch. Also, I'd prefer to rent bikes for this activity since one of your self-guided tours seemed to have that option. Please let me know what you think so that I can draw up a concrete plan.

Thank you,

Dixie Piper

Self-Guided Tours at the Philadelphia Preservation Society

Self-guided tours are a great way to experience Philadelphia's public art! Try one of the tours organized by the Philadelphia Preservation Society below.

Nature Center
2-hour trip
View fascinating works of contemporary public art set amid 28,000 square meters of well-tended greenery. (Grounds are open on weekdays only from 9 A.M. to 3 P.M.)

Philadelphia Museum of Art
1-hour trip
The area around the museum is home to a large collection of sculptures. For more art, stop in at the museum itself. (The area outside the museum is closed to the public on Mondays.)

Kelly Drive

2.5-hour trip

Take a leisurely trip along the Schuylkill River, passing a number of outdoor sculptures on the way. (Bike rentals available at Floyd Hall.)

Visit www.pps.org for details.

Rittenhouse Square

1-hour trip

See several historic sculptures in Rittenhouse Square, a lovely park dating back to Philadelphia's founding.

196. What most likely does the Philadelphia Preservation Society do?

(A) Offers art lessons to local students
(B) Manages a city's tourist industry
(C) Funds the maintenance of modern buildings
(D) Maintains artwork for public enjoyment

197. What is being offered to those who give a donation?

(A) A membership discount
(B) A complimentary item
(C) An information booklet
(D) A free trial class

198. What is suggested about Ms. Piper?

(A) She will receive invitations to PPS events.
(B) She recently participated in a field trip.
(C) She secured some funding for her organization.
(D) She will make a one-time donation to PPS.

199. Which tour is Ms. Piper interested in?

(A) Nature Center
(B) Kelly Drive
(C) Philadelphia Museum of Art
(D) Rittenhouse Square

200. What is indicated about the self-guided tours?

(A) Each one takes an hour to complete.
(B) They are discounted for students and groups.
(C) All of them are suitable for bikers.
(D) Some of them are unavailable on certain days of the week.

This is the end of the test. You may review Parts 5, 6, and 7 if you finish the test early.

分數換算表 p. 244 / 正確答案、翻譯、解析〔解析本〕p. 47

▌請根據下一頁的 Review 檢查表複習答錯的題目

/Review 檢查表

完成 TEST 2 後，請根據下表檢視自己答錯的問題，並在框框中打勾。
如果距離考試時間不多，請務必檢查**粗體字**的項目。

☐ **我再度練習了答錯的題目，試著找出正確答案。**

☐ **我已針對答錯的題目查閱了翻譯，理解了題幹與問題的內容。**

☐ **我透過翻譯，理解了每題各個選項正確或錯誤的原因。**

☐ 我檢視了在 Part 1 和 Part 2 答錯的問題類型，並加以整理，以免落入相同的陷阱。

☐ 我檢視了 Part 3 和 Part 4 每個題目所使用的換句話說。

☐ 在 Part 5 和 Part 6，我針對各題的正確答案及錯誤選項，整理了文法和單字的重點。

☐ 針對 Part 6「選擇合適句子」的題目，我正確理解了整個段落及空格前後文的語意。

☐ 在 Part 7，我找出了短文和題目中的重點，包含正確答題所需的句子和片語，並加以標示，也檢查了題目使用的換句話說。

☐ 針對 Part 1~Part 4，我使用線上的聽力訓練筆記，針對考試的重點語句練習聽寫、閱讀和複習。

☐ 針對 Part 1~Part 4，我使用單字記憶本來記下考試的關鍵詞彙和表達用語。

大量練習題目固然重要，但好好檢視自己答錯的問題也同樣關鍵。
只要仔細複習一遍答錯的題目，就能在短時間內有效達到目標分數。

TEST 3

LISTENING TEST

Part 1
Part 2
Part 3
Part 4

READING TEST

Part 5
Part 6
Part 7

Review 檢查表

注意！測驗前請務必檢查下列事項。

手機是否關機？
Answer Sheet（p. 251）、鉛筆、橡皮擦和手錶是否準備好了？
準備好聆聽音檔了嗎？

準備就緒後，想著你的目標分數，開始測驗。
測驗完畢後，請務必查看 Review 檢查表（p. 152），複習答錯的題目。

🎧 Test 3.mp3
可免費下載、播放 MP3，用於答題訓練和複習

MP3 音檔

LISTENING TEST

In this section, you must demonstrate your ability to understand spoken English. This section is divided into four parts and will take approximately 45 minutes to complete. Do not mark the answers in your test book. Use the answer sheet that is provided separately.

PART 1

Directions: For each question, you will listen to four short statements about a picture in your test book. These statements will not be printed and will only be spoken one time. Select the statement that best describes what is happening in the picture and mark the corresponding letter (A), (B), (C), or (D) on the answer sheet.

Sample Answer

The statement that best describes the picture is (B), "The man is sitting at the desk." So, you should mark letter (B) on the answer sheet.

1.

2.

GO ON TO THE NEXT PAGE

3.

4.

5.

6.

GO ON TO THE NEXT PAGE ➤

PART 2

Directions: For each question, you will listen to a statement or question followed by three possible responses spoken in English. They will not be printed and will only be spoken one time. Select the best response and mark the corresponding letter (A), (B), or (C) on your answer sheet.

7. Mark your answer on your answer sheet.

8. Mark your answer on your answer sheet.

9. Mark your answer on your answer sheet.

10. Mark your answer on your answer sheet.

11. Mark your answer on your answer sheet.

12. Mark your answer on your answer sheet.

13. Mark your answer on your answer sheet.

14. Mark your answer on your answer sheet.

15. Mark your answer on your answer sheet.

16. Mark your answer on your answer sheet.

17. Mark your answer on your answer sheet.

18. Mark your answer on your answer sheet.

19. Mark your answer on your answer sheet.

20. Mark your answer on your answer sheet.

21. Mark your answer on your answer sheet.

22. Mark your answer on your answer sheet.

23. Mark your answer on your answer sheet.

24. Mark your answer on your answer sheet.

25. Mark your answer on your answer sheet.

26. Mark your answer on your answer sheet.

27. Mark your answer on your answer sheet.

28. Mark your answer on your answer sheet.

29. Mark your answer on your answer sheet.

30. Mark your answer on your answer sheet.

31. Mark your answer on your answer sheet.

PART 3

Directions: In this part, you will listen to several conversations between two or more speakers. These conversations will not be printed and will only be spoken one time. For each conversation, you will be asked to answer three questions. Select the best response and mark the corresponding letter (A), (B), (C), or (D) on your answer sheet.

32. What are the speakers working on?

(A) A vehicle design
(B) A window display
(C) A publication cover
(D) A business website

33. What does the woman ask the man about?

(A) When a document should be printed
(B) Why an image must be removed
(C) Whether a draft requires more changes
(D) Who will attend a meeting

34. What will the speakers most likely do next?

(A) Select a design
(B) Visit an office
(C) Purchase a car
(D) Examine a vehicle

35. Where do the speakers most likely work?

(A) At an office supplies store
(B) At a dining venue
(C) At a grocery store
(D) At a flower shop

36. Why is the man behind schedule?

(A) A coworker is unavailable.
(B) An order was changed.
(C) An event was moved ahead.
(D) A delivery is late.

37. What does the woman offer to do?

(A) Get some supplies
(B) Talk to a client
(C) Set up an appointment
(D) Remove some packages

38. What did the woman do this morning?

(A) Read a message
(B) Visited another department
(C) Reviewed some receipts
(D) Sent an e-mail

39. What is mentioned about the company?

(A) It will move to another building.
(B) It will expand its parking lot.
(C) It will reimburse employees for a fee.
(D) It will hold a special event for clients.

40. What is the woman concerned about?

(A) The cost of a pass
(B) The location of a facility
(C) The amount of a fine
(D) The size of a garage

41. Where does the woman work?

(A) At a clothing shop
(B) At a fitness facility
(C) At a furniture store
(D) At a magazine company

42. What does the man want to know?

(A) The price of a product
(B) The location of a shop
(C) The reason for a call
(D) The purpose for a project

43. According to the woman, what will expire soon?

(A) A coupon
(B) A publication subscription
(C) A membership
(D) A lease contract

GO ON TO THE NEXT PAGE

44. What does the man say about the seminar?

(A) It took place at a hotel.
(B) It was attended by few people.
(C) It was sponsored by Actercorp.
(D) It focused on digital publishing.

45. What does the man want the woman to give to him?

(A) Some contact details
(B) A registration form
(C) Some directions
(D) A media file

46. What does the man ask for?

(A) Creating a new account
(B) Going to a lecture series
(C) Using another e-mail address
(D) Delivering an item in person

47. What does the man mean when he says, "I've always been interested in exotic cuisine"?

(A) He wants another option.
(B) He is not worried about cost.
(C) He has never tasted Thai food.
(D) He prefers an advertised deal.

48. What does the woman give to the man?

(A) Coupons
(B) Schedules
(C) Brochures
(D) Tickets

49. What most likely will the woman do next?

(A) Check a reservation system
(B) Update a tour timetable
(C) Reboot a computer
(D) Send out a book

50. What problem does the woman mention?

(A) A facility is short on supplies.
(B) A hotel reservation was lost.
(C) A room location is noisy.
(D) A bill is inaccurate.

51. What is suggested about Room 240?

(A) It has been reserved for tonight.
(B) It is the only available room.
(C) It has been recently renovated.
(D) It is located at the end of the hall.

52. What does the man offer to do?

(A) File a formal complaint
(B) Request a repair
(C) Find a supervisor
(D) Provide a free upgrade

53. Where is the conversation most likely taking place?

(A) At a production facility
(B) At a retail outlet
(C) At a financial institution
(D) At a travel agency

54. Why does the man say, "That program was just launched last week"?

(A) To express concern about a request
(B) To explain a mistake
(C) To promote a new service
(D) To apologize for a delay

55. What does the man ask the woman to do?

(A) Provide a credit card
(B) Return at a later time
(C) Try on other merchandise
(D) Complete a document

56. Where does the conversation most likely take place?

(A) At a manufacturing facility
(B) At a coffee shop
(C) At an exposition center
(D) At a fitness center

57. What does the man's new assignment consist of?

(A) Demonstrating a new tool
(B) Erecting a booth
(C) Organizing some drinks
(D) Checking the temperature

58. What will Ms. Jones do next?

(A) Provide some work clothes
(B) Print some manuals
(C) Prepare a payment
(D) Taste a new beverage

---

59. What does the woman say about the report?

(A) It was created by her supervisor.
(B) It should be submitted this week.
(C) It includes inaccurate information.
(D) It must be printed for a gathering.

60. What does the woman want to do?

(A) Make some copies
(B) Do some calculations
(C) Post a file to a website
(D) Rearrange some figures

61. According to the man, what can the woman find online?

(A) Registration forms
(B) Assistance with a program
(C) Information about an order
(D) Sample software

Presentation Schedule	
Speakers	**Time**
John Foreman	9:00 A.M. – 10:30 A.M.
Harry Garcia	10:30 A.M. – 12:00 P.M.
Fred Jones	1:30 P.M. – 3:00 P.M.
Peter Wright	3:00 P.M. – 4:30 P.M.

62. What are the speakers mainly discussing?

(A) Event venues
(B) Presentation schedules
(C) A deadline for an application
(D) A topic for a conference

63. Look at the graphic. Who will arrive from Boston?

(A) John Foreman
(B) Harry Garcia
(C) Fred Jones
(D) Peter Wright

64. What does the woman ask the man to do?

(A) Send out extra invitations
(B) Contact speakers
(C) Meet with a venue manager
(D) Extend a deadline

GO ON TO THE NEXT PAGE

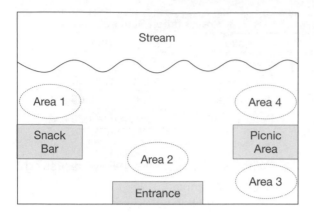

65. What did the woman recently do?

    (A) Installed a new door
    (B) Read a notification
    (C) Requested a lawn care service
    (D) Called the maintenance person

66. Why is the man worried?

    (A) Officials have rejected a request.
    (B) A city plan could have a negative impact.
    (C) A play area has been closed down.
    (D) Maintenance work has not been completed.

67. Look at the graphic. Where do the children usually play?

    (A) Area 1
    (B) Area 2
    (C) Area 3
    (D) Area 4

68. Why was the woman surprised?

    (A) A company stopped production of a device.
    (B) A speaker system is too expensive.
    (C) A product is relatively unpopular.
    (D) A business announced a recall.

69. Look at the graphic. What aspect will most likely be addressed immediately?

    (A) Price
    (B) Sound quality
    (C) Portability
    (D) Design

70. What will the man probably do this afternoon?

    (A) Meet with a director
    (B) Talk with some customers
    (C) Copy some charts
    (D) Test a new product

PART 4

Directions: In this part, you will listen to several short talks by a single speaker. These talks will not be printed and will only be spoken one time. For each talk, you will be asked to answer three questions. Select the best response and mark the corresponding letter (A), (B), (C), or (D) on your answer sheet.

71. Where most likely are the listeners?

   (A) At a community center
   (B) At an employment agency
   (C) At a financial institution
   (D) At a government office

72. What did Mr. Hernandez do in New York?

   (A) Interviewed an employee
   (B) Conducted a workshop
   (C) Received an award
   (D) Founded a business

73. What will the listeners probably do this evening?

   (A) Attend an employee orientation
   (B) Meet at a dining establishment
   (C) Drive to a convention center
   (D) Take a training course

74. Why has there been a flight cancellation?

   (A) The aircraft has a mechanical issue.
   (B) The weather conditions are too severe.
   (C) A security problem has occurred.
   (D) An airport has lost power.

75. What will be provided to certain passengers?

   (A) Accommodation vouchers
   (B) Discounted fares
   (C) Seat upgrades
   (D) Full refunds

76. According to the speaker, where is a service desk located?

   (A) By a check-in counter
   (B) Near a gate
   (C) Across from a cafeteria
   (D) Next to a ticketing office

77. What type of business is Spark?

   (A) A real estate office
   (B) An instrument store
   (C) A music academy
   (D) A consulting firm

78. What does the speaker say about Spark's staff?

   (A) They are familiar with different kinds of music.
   (B) They have 10 years of experience.
   (C) They are on site seven days a week.
   (D) They offer individual lessons.

79. How can the listeners receive a discount?

   (A) By calling a hotline
   (B) By visiting a facility
   (C) By going to a web page
   (D) By e-mailing a salesperson

80. Who most likely is Gregory Smyth?

   (A) A company executive
   (B) A government official
   (C) A medical professional
   (D) A university professor

81. Why does the speaker say, "The city cut our funding by 30 percent"?

   (A) To request some donations
   (B) To announce a schedule change
   (C) To provide the reason for a closure
   (D) To suggest some savings methods

82. What will happen next?

   (A) A speaker will take the stage.
   (B) A fitness class will begin.
   (C) A budget will be released.
   (D) A charity drive will be discussed.

GO ON TO THE NEXT PAGE

83. What is the speaker mainly discussing?

(A) A design flaw
(B) Sales performance
(C) Advertising strategies
(D) A department expansion

84. According to the speaker, what did On Point Solutions do?

(A) Manufactured parts
(B) Managed some funding
(C) Distributed some goods
(D) Developed a campaign

85. Why will a meeting be held this afternoon?

(A) To discuss customer feedback
(B) To test a device feature
(C) To plan a new product line
(D) To review financial analyses

86. What is the main purpose of the talk?

(A) To request that employees work late
(B) To explain a store policy
(C) To inform staff about an outing
(D) To describe a task

87. What happened yesterday?

(A) A promotion ended.
(B) A misplaced item was found.
(C) An employee was hired.
(D) A storage area was organized.

88. What does the speaker imply when he says, "You've all done this before"?

(A) A mistake has been made.
(B) A procedure should be familiar.
(C) A project will be completed quickly.
(D) A change is about to be announced.

89. Who is Philip Calandra?

(A) A corporate board member
(B) A departmental manager
(C) A training instructor
(D) A computer technician

90. What does the speaker ask the listeners to do first?

(A) Pass out some brochures
(B) Sign an attendance sheet
(C) Download an employee manual
(D) Visit a website

91. What does the speaker recommend?

(A) Deleting an account
(B) Registering for a seminar
(C) Watching a video
(D) Completing a survey

92. Where does the speaker probably work?

(A) At a call center
(B) At an employment agency
(C) At a chemical plant
(D) At a beauty shop

93. Why does the speaker say, "The person who provided you the service is no longer working here"?

(A) To suggest more staff members need to be hired
(B) To guarantee a problem will not occur again
(C) To show some services are no longer available
(D) To recommend an appointment be rescheduled

94. What will the listener most likely receive?

(A) Financial compensation
(B) Additional training
(C) A complimentary item
(D) In-home services

Mountain Music Festival - Schedule	
Saturday	9:00 P.M. – The Early Birds 11:00 P.M. – Open Source
Sunday	7:00 P.M. – Green Wave 9:00 P.M. – The Black Hats 11:00 P.M. – Cherry Blossom

Chicago Continental Suites	
Room	Type of bed(s)
Master Room	1 single regular-sized bed
Deluxe Room	1 king-sized bed
Premium Room	2 regular-sized beds
Gold Room	2 king-sized beds

95. What does the speaker say about the festival?

(A) It was organized by a musician.
(B) It is a charity event.
(C) It is held every year.
(D) It was moved to a new site.

96. What did the listener most likely ask about?

(A) Equipment
(B) Accommodations
(C) Fees
(D) Transportation

97. Look at the graphic. Which band will perform first on Saturday night?

(A) Open Source
(B) Green Wave
(C) The Black Hats
(D) Cherry Blossom

98. What does the speaker say about the Chicago Restaurant Convention?

(A) It provides a good chance to market a product.
(B) It requires attendees to pay a large admission fee.
(C) It is becoming more popular each year.
(D) It attracts attendees from around the world.

99. In which field does the speaker most likely work?

(A) Hospitality
(B) Commercial real estate
(C) Appliance manufacturing
(D) Restaurant management

100. Look at the graphic. Which type of suite are employees staying in?

(A) Master Room
(B) Deluxe Room
(C) Premium Room
(D) Gold Room

This is the end of the Listening test. Turn to PART 5 in your test book.

GO ON TO THE NEXT PAGE

READING TEST

In this section, you must demonstrate your ability to read and comprehend English. You will be given a variety of texts and asked to answer questions about these texts. This section is divided into three parts and will take 75 minutes to complete.

Do not mark the answers in your test book. Use the answer sheet that is separately provided.

PART 5

Directions: In each question, you will be asked to review a statement that is missing a word or phrase. Four answer choices will be provided for each statement. Select the best answer and mark the corresponding letter (A), (B), (C), or (D) on the answer sheet.

🕐 **PART 5 建議作答時間　11 分鐘**

---

101. MYK Inc. ------- opposed the government's plan to regulate the opening hours of restaurants and cafés.

(A) strongest
(B) stronger
(C) strength
(D) strongly

102. No one ------- the manager can deactivate the store's alarm system.

(A) within
(B) except
(C) across
(D) since

103. The researchers experienced some minor difficulties with the new program, but ------- were able to complete their projects.

(A) most
(B) no
(C) each
(D) another

104. Staff members are required to obtain ------- before ordering additional office supplies.

(A) distribution
(B) confession
(C) situation
(D) permission

105. Investors complained that ------- could not access information about the company's financial status.

(A) they
(B) their
(C) them
(D) themselves

106. Parker and Dean is the only local law firm ------- attorneys deal with both civil and criminal legal cases.

(A) what
(B) whose
(C) whom
(D) which

107. The patient asked Dr. Marple for a ------- to an eye specialist.

(A) referral
(B) refers
(C) refer
(D) referred

108. With its spectacular scenery and mild climate, Santa Rosa is a very ------- location for a resort.

(A) contributing
(B) promising
(C) proposing
(D) collecting

109. Southwest College ------- degrees in a wide variety of fields, from engineering to philosophy.

(A) grants
(B) will be granted
(C) granting
(D) is granted

110. Please submit the expense report to the accounting department ------- meeting with Ms. Thompson.

(A) before
(B) around
(C) in front of
(D) along

111. The prolonged drought caused the water level in the reservoir to fall ------- than it ever had before.

(A) low
(B) lower
(C) lowly
(D) lowest

112. Peter Lee spent the past year ------- searching for new ways to market his software to young consumers.

(A) continually
(B) continuous
(C) continue
(D) continual

113. The main role of the department supervisor is to ------- employees toward achieving the company's stated goals.

(A) adopt
(B) guide
(C) initiate
(D) establish

114. Please note that applicants will be notified of the company's decision ------- approximately two weeks.

(A) at
(B) to
(C) in
(D) on

115. As you requested, your website's design will be ------- to include brighter colors and larger images.

(A) partnered
(B) practiced
(C) altered
(D) relieved

116. Perot Petrochemicals signed a contract ------- oil and natural gas to the utility company.

(A) supply
(B) supplied
(C) to supply
(D) be supplied

117. Our latest television's product manual ------- to print by the end of next week.

(A) is ready
(B) will be ready
(C) has been ready
(D) was being ready

118. We will ------- send marketing team members to our stores to assist with promotional events.

(A) periodically
(B) absently
(C) mistakenly
(D) formerly

119. At the campaign event, the politician was busy meeting local citizens and ------- her policies.

(A) explain
(B) is explained
(C) explaining
(D) to explain

120. All fees must be received no more than one month ------- a bill has been issued for a course.

(A) even if
(B) over
(C) after
(D) soon

GO ON TO THE NEXT PAGE

121. The city council is relocating bus stops throughout the region to make them more ------- to local residents.

(A) increased
(B) adverse
(C) constructive
(D) accessible

122. The keynote speaker at the Detroit Accounting Convention discussed ------- the new tax regulations would affect the automobile industry.

(A) who
(B) whatever
(C) then
(D) how

123. ------- animals is prohibited in all of the country's national parks and conservation areas.

(A) Feed
(B) Fed
(C) Feeding
(D) Feeds

124. Factories constructed near residential areas must comply ------- strict environmental rules.

(A) into
(B) for
(C) on
(D) with

125. The company ------- the new Italian restaurant is known for its high-quality work.

(A) built
(B) build
(C) building
(D) builds

126. Once the financial assessment is -------, it will be sent to the legal department at Newfield Electronics.

(A) nominated
(B) consumed
(C) finalized
(D) misplaced

127. ------- the merger between Corus Corporation and Overland Resources is expected to take government officials several weeks.

(A) Approve
(B) Approved
(C) Approving
(D) Approval

128. The renovations of the Portman Building will be carried out on the weekend to ------- their effect on office operations.

(A) subtract
(B) minimize
(C) disturb
(D) consider

129. Record low temperatures were reported ------- the country during the severe winter storm.

(A) across
(B) under
(C) upon
(D) wide

130. Although Steven Harris has published books on a variety of topics, his ------- focus is European history.

(A) main
(B) cooperative
(C) convenient
(D) previous

PART 6

Directions: In this part, you will be asked to read four English texts. Each text is missing a word, phrase, or sentence. Select the answer choice that correctly completes the text and mark the corresponding letter (A), (B), (C), or (D) on the answer sheet.

🕐 **PART 6 建議作答時間 8 分鐘**

Questions 131-134 refer to the following e-mail.

To: Linda Shute <lshute@plustech.com>
From: Stanley Robinson <srobinson@midwayexhibitions.com>
Subject: Office Supplies Trade Show
Date: April 23

Hello Ms. Shute,

I am writing to inform you that ------- a recent cancellation, we have room for one more
        131.
exhibition booth at our Office Supplies Trade Show. I recall how disappointed you were

about missing last month's application deadline, but you now have a second chance to

register. However, you must indicate your interest as quickly as possible. You ------- to pay
                                                                        132.
a fee of $250 to participate. -------.
                        133.
I strongly encourage you to participate. This is an event ------- a growing following over the
                                                    134.
years and should draw a record number of visitors again this year.

Stanley Robinson
Customer Relations

---

131. (A) in spite of
(B) opposite
(C) due to
(D) as long as

132. (A) will need
(B) needing
(C) needed
(D) to need

133. (A) This can be done either by bank transfer or by visiting our office.
(B) The booth was widely visited throughout the show.
(C) There are several openings available for exhibitors.
(D) The deadline for registration has been adjusted significantly.

134. (A) will attract
(B) is attracting
(C) being attracted
(D) which has attracted

GO ON TO THE NEXT PAGE

Questions 135-138 refer to the following article.

A Flextime System for Edge Technologies
By Sarah Peterson

June 11—CEO of Edge Technologies Gerald McCarthy announced that his company will be

adopting a flextime system. Once ------- fully puts this system into practice, all employees
                                135.

will have the option of adjusting their daily work schedules. For example, a staff member

who comes in at 7:00 A.M. instead of 9:00 A.M. will be able to leave two hours earlier.

-------. Everyone must continue to work an eight-hour day at the office.
  136.

The stated goal of the new system is to have all employees develop a better work-life

balance. -------, Mr. McCarthy hopes that his company will experience improved morale.
        137.

The policy ------- as a response to increased competitiveness among technology
          138.

companies in terms of employee work benefits.

---

135. (A) it
(B) they
(C) someone
(D) him

136. (A) Employees are free to make up the missing hours from home.
(B) The store will still be open on weekends.
(C) Schedules will no longer change on a weekly basis.
(D) The total hours worked each day will remain the same.

137. (A) Instead
(B) Nevertheless
(C) In this way
(D) Despite that

138. (A) is creating
(B) was created
(C) creates
(D) has created

Tree Doctor

A tree can live a long time if it is taken care of well. ------- the life of your trees, you need to
139.
give them proper care. The staff members at Tree Doctor have ------- knowledge of tree
140.
management. This is because they are all certified professionals with a great deal of

experience. Our experts can visit your property to evaluate the condition of your trees.

-------. And if you are considering planting new trees, they can advise you on which ones
141.
you plan to add ------- in your soil well. To learn more about our services and to book an
142.
appointment, visit www.treedoctor.com.

139. (A) Prolonged
(B) To prolong
(C) Prolonging
(D) Prolong

140. (A) prior
(B) clever
(C) extensive
(D) partial

141. (A) As a result, they were familiar with a
variety of treatments.
(B) Certain trees have already been
removed from the yard.
(C) Some fertilizers are harmful to many
species.
(D) Specifically, they will check for
diseased branches and roots.

142. (A) will grow
(B) are growing
(C) grew
(D) have been growing

GO ON TO THE NEXT PAGE

Questions 143-146 refer to the following e-mail.

To: Belle Rogers <brogers@smail.com>
From: Aaron Cooper <aaroncooper@moneyphase.com>
Subject: Welcome!
Date: January 31

Dear Ms. Rogers,

On behalf of our entire company, I would like to welcome you as a new ------- . We are
143.
thrilled that you have chosen our company for assistance with managing your investment

portfolio.

We know that ------- your finances takes time, patience, and effort. There are a wide variety
144.
of investment options to choose from, and selecting the right ones requires guidance. You

can be assured that we will provide you with expert advice.

Please let me know when it would be convenient to hold our first meeting. ------- . Please
145.
either contact me at 555-1221 ------- reply to this e-mail. Once again, we welcome you and
146.
hope that our relationship will be a successful one!

Sincerely yours,

Aaron Cooper

Investment Analyst

---

143. (A) customer
(B) owner
(C) vendor
(D) student

144. (A) transferring
(B) decreasing
(C) planning
(D) canceling

145. (A) We are sure that these suggestions
will increase your profits.
(B) We appreciate the financial advice you
have e-mailed to us.
(C) We will discuss your short- and
long-term financial goals at that time.
(D) We think it is necessary to reschedule
our appointment.

146. (A) for
(B) and
(C) or
(D) but

PART 7

Directions: In this part, you will be asked to read several texts, such as advertisements, articles, instant messages, or examples of business correspondence. Each text is followed by several questions. Select the best answer and mark the corresponding letter (A), (B), (C), or (D) on your answer sheet.

PART 7 建議作答時間 **54 分鐘**

Questions 147-148 refer to the following notice.

Brandenburg's Third Annual Winter Festival Ceremony will be held on December 2. Decorations will be placed along Muller Way, ice sculptures will appear along Hastings Avenue, and the ice rink at the intersection of Rossellini Drive and Peters Street will be open to skaters from 8 A.M. to 6 P.M. The main event of the night will be the lighting of the large pine tree on Sterner Way, which will take place at 10 P.M. Afterward, the Brandenburg Brass Band will play a variety of holiday songs. The lights will stay up until New Year's Day, and they will be removed the next day by employees of the city park service.

147. What is NOT a feature of the Winter Festival Ceremony?

(A) The performance of some music
(B) The decoration of Peters Street
(C) The operation of a skating rink
(D) The lighting of a tree

148. What will happen immediately after New Year's Day?

(A) Some ice sculptures will be removed.
(B) A city park will reopen.
(C) Some lights will be taken down.
(D) A ceremony will be held.

GO ON TO THE NEXT PAGE

Questions 149-150 refer to the following letter.

May 12

John Simon
772 North Avenue
Tucson, AZ 85701

Dear Mr. Simon,

Thank you for agreeing to speak at the dinner in Flagstaff organized by the Foundation for World Cultures. Everyone is excited to hear about the studies you've conducted about the ancient cultures of the Andes Mountains region. Because you're the keynote speaker at the event, you'll be giving your speech right after our organization's president, Ernesto Paramo. Following that, Will Meyer, a university student, will show a video he made about a recent trip to Colombia, and then dinner will be served. The closing speech will be given by Robert Shelling, who runs the Flagstaff Cultural Institute.

Your name has been added to our guest list, so all you need to do is show up at the door. We look forward to having you.

Sincerely,
Roberto Marquez

149. Who most likely is Mr. Simon?

(A) The head of an organization
(B) A workshop organizer
(C) A filmmaker
(D) A researcher

150. Who will precede Mr. Simon?

(A) Ernesto Paramo
(B) Will Meyer
(C) Robert Shelling
(D) Roberto Marquez

Questions 151-152 refer to the following text messages.

Tony Webb	[1:15 P.M.]
Did you hear that Dave Jonson is leaving next week?	
Laura Hughes	[1:17 P.M.]
Yeah. When he and I were out for lunch earlier today, he mentioned that he had accepted an offer of a new job.	
Tony Webb	[1:19 P.M.]
He's not the only one. Will the company hire more staff soon?	
Laura Hughes	[1:21 P.M.]
Yeah. Human resources will interview applicants for our department next week. I've agreed to help with the training for newly hired employees.	
Tony Webb	[1:21 P.M.]
Good. It's about time. It's been really hard to meet all of our marketing deadlines with so few people.	
Laura Hughes	[1:22 P.M.]
I know. Everyone on my staff has been worried about that. Anyway, I'll let you know if I hear more.	

151. What is NOT true about Ms. Hughes?

(A) She recently went to eat with a colleague.
(B) She will prepare new employees for a job.
(C) She was offered a position at another company.
(D) She is a member of the marketing department.

152. At 1:19 P.M., what does Mr. Webb most likely mean when he writes, "He's not the only one"?

(A) A task will be assigned to someone else.
(B) A training document must be updated.
(C) Several applicants have been selected.
(D) Other team members have resigned.

GO ON TO THE NEXT PAGE

Questions 153-154 refer to the following e-mail.

TO: Mitchell O'Connor <moconnor@fastmail.com>
FROM: Playback Streaming <support@playback.com>
SUBJECT: *Secrets of Paris*
DATE: September 19

Dear Mr. O'Connor,

Thank you for using Playback Streaming, the number one streaming service for media content. Our records indicate that you recently watched the documentary *Secrets of Paris*, directed by Sam Marshall and first aired on the HistoryNow Channel. We always encourage our customers to write reviews of what they've watched. To do this, simply click the button beneath the video you want to comment on. As a special incentive, those who review 100 items or more are awarded the status of "premium user," making them eligible to receive $50 worth of complimentary movies and TV shows.

Once again, thank you for using our service.

Sincerely,

Playback Streaming Customer Support

153. What is indicated about *Secrets of Paris*?

(A) It is based on a famous book.
(B) It received an award for best director.
(C) It was first shown on a history channel.
(D) It is available to buy at an additional cost.

154. What can customers receive if they write 100 reviews?

(A) A DVD copy of a movie
(B) Extra membership points
(C) A yearlong subscription
(D) Free media content

Questions 155-157 refer to the following web page.

EXPLORE THE BRINKLEY SCIENCE CENTER

You don't need an excuse to visit the Brinkley Science Center, a three-story museum dedicated to sharing the wonders of science with the public. At our facility, you can view exhibits on everything from sound waves and tornadoes to soil and distant planets. So, bring all of your friends and family members!

MUSEUM HOURS
Tuesday-Friday: 9 A.M. to 5 P.M.
Saturday-Sunday: 9 A.M. to 6 P.M.
Closed on Mondays

TICKET PRICES
$10 general admission
$8 for students
$6 for people over 65 years old
Free admission for students attending Brinkley College
Free admission for children under age six
On the first Tuesday of every month, all residents of Brinkley are admitted for free. Proof of residence required.

DIRECTIONS
By car: From Interstate 20, take Exit 60 onto Grant Road. Then, turn left onto Lessing Way. The center will be on your left.
By subway: From Exit 2 of Havel Street Station, turn right onto Wallace Avenue. Continue for 100 meters and then turn right onto Lessing Way. The center will be on your right.
By bus: Buses 80 and 125 both stop right outside the center.

155. What is stated about the Brinkley Science Center?

(A) It has a special area for children.
(B) It attracts lots of international visitors.
(C) It has a weather-related exhibit.
(D) It is closed on holidays.

156. Who is never charged for admission?

(A) Senior citizens
(B) Parents of children under age six
(C) Students at Brinkley College
(D) Residents of Brinkley

157. Where is the Brinkley Science Center most likely located?

(A) On Grant Road
(B) On Havel Street
(C) On Wallace Avenue
(D) On Lessing Way

GO ON TO THE NEXT PAGE

Questions 158-160 refer to the following job advertisement.

Heimart Seeking Full-time Store Associate

Heimart is a leading European retailer that specializes in offering home goods and appliances at affordable prices. — [1] —. After the success of our first American stores in New York, Chicago, and Los Angeles, we are looking to fill positions at new locations in other major US cities.

As a store associate, you will be responsible for carrying out routine tasks, such as unloading new stock, filling shelves, and keeping the store clean and orderly at all times. — [2] —. Depending on performance, opportunities to try other roles may be offered. You could learn how to handle the register, work in customer service, and more. — [3] —.

Applicants must be 21 or older and have previous experience in a similar role. Employees should be willing to work on a flexible schedule. — [4] —. Successful candidates will receive a competitive hourly wage, health benefits, regular bonuses, and continuous job training.

To apply, e-mail jobs@heimart.com.

158. What is stated about Heimart?

(A) It is launching its first American store.
(B) It carries a variety of office furniture.
(C) It is offering a home delivery service.
(D) It has job openings in several cities.

159. What is the responsibility of a store associate?

(A) Arranging schedules
(B) Finding product suppliers
(C) Maintaining cleanliness
(D) Delivering orders

160. In which of the positions marked [1], [2], [3], and [4] does the following sentence best belong?

"This includes early morning and night shifts on occasion."

(A) [1]
(B) [2]
(C) [3]
(D) [4]

Questions 161-163 refer to the following memo.

To: All Brumfield Co. employees
From: Fred Sears, human resources manager
Date: May 10
Subject: Renovations

As you may be aware, Brumfield Co. will be undergoing a month-long renovation of its fourth floor starting next week. This creates a space problem for the marketing department employees currently working there. We initially looked into seating them in various available workstations on the other floors of the building. However, after some consideration, we concluded that this was not a good idea. Our marketers are required to do a lot of speaking over the telephone, so arranging them in this way would be bothersome to other department members whose jobs require silence.

Therefore, we have decided to create a temporary work area for the team in the main conference room on the second floor of the building. The IT department will set up the necessary computers and printers there tomorrow. The smaller meeting room on the third floor next to the employee break room will be the only one available for members of other departments to use for the next month or so.

Thank you.

161. What is mentioned about Brumfield Co.?

(A) It is expanding its marketing team.
(B) It will remodel its office.
(C) It will relocate its IT department.
(D) It is upgrading its computers.

162. Why will marketing staff not be spread out over several floors?

(A) They must work together on most assignments.
(B) They are preparing an important presentation.
(C) They would be disruptive to other workers.
(D) They need to discuss projects with one another.

163. What can be inferred about the main conference room?

(A) It will be unavailable to some staff members.
(B) It is located next to the printer room.
(C) It was refurbished last month.
(D) It has been used as an employee lounge.

GO ON TO THE NEXT PAGE

Questions 164-167 refer to the following text message chain.

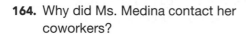

Carol Medina	[11:41 A.M.]	I'm planning the company's annual year-end party. I could really use some help.
Annie Sanders	[11:42 A.M.]	I'd be happy to lend a hand. What would you like me to do?
Carol Medina	[11:43 A.M.]	I still haven't found a place to hold the party. Could you look for a suitable banquet hall? We need to book one for December 22.
Annie Sanders	[11:43 A.M.]	Sure. How many people will be attending this year?
Carol Medina	[11:44 A.M.]	It's hard to say. Each employee is allowed to invite a guest. So, we should contact all of the employees and ask them whether they intend to bring someone to the party.
Vincent Bryce	[11:45 A.M.]	I can do that now. I'll just send an e-mail to everyone in the company. I'll let both of you know the number of guests to expect by lunch tomorrow.
Annie Sanders	[11:46 A.M.]	Perfect. What about food? Would you like me to look for catering companies as well?
Carol Medina	[11:47 A.M.]	No need. Bellwood Fine Foods has excellent menu options and reasonable prices. We've used them often over the past six years.

164. Why did Ms. Medina contact her coworkers?

(A) To announce an upcoming event
(B) To ask for advice on food
(C) To request assistance with a task
(D) To express interest in a project

165. What does Ms. Sanders agree to do?

(A) Confirm attendance
(B) Contact a caterer
(C) Find a venue
(D) Send invitations

166. At 11:47 A.M., what does Ms. Medina most likely mean when she writes, "No need"?

(A) She will ask about changing a menu.
(B) She is aware of the number of guests.
(C) She has already checked a hall's availability.
(D) She will use a particular catering company.

167. What is suggested about Bellwood Fine Foods?

(A) It specializes in parties for small groups.
(B) It has been in business for several years.
(C) It offers a limited number of menu options.
(D) It recently reduced its prices.

Questions 168-171 refer to the following article.

Construction News

East Parsons, June 3—At a press conference today, Transportation Commissioner Claudia Rittora announced that a new subway line—the Green Line—will be undergoing construction beginning in September. The line will provide service to the suburban neighborhoods of Peterson and Forest Falls. It will include stops at Pew Street, Jackson Avenue, and Crispin Boulevard, after which it will merge with the Red Line that runs downtown. — [1] —.

Ms. Rittora said that the decision to build a subway line in the suburbs was made in response to the many complaints that have been made by people who must commute to the city. — [2] —. There are only a few buses that go to the outlying neighborhoods, and they all run at infrequent intervals. There used to be a tram line that extended to the outer suburbs, with stops along Jackson Avenue and Wellford Street. However, it was very costly to operate, and not many people used it. — [3] —.

The new subway line should be more successful because the population of the suburban areas has greatly increased. — [4] —. The Green Line will operate 24 hours a day, seven days a week, and trains will reach stations every 10 minutes. Those wishing to learn more can go to www.eastparsonscity.gov.

---

168. The word "merge" in paragraph 1, line 5, is closest in meaning to

(A) join
(B) pile
(C) return
(D) trade

169. Why will the new subway line be constructed?

(A) To reduce commuting times for people living downtown
(B) To address some dissatisfaction from outlying areas
(C) To accommodate residents in a newly built community
(D) To compensate for the cancellation of bus services

170. What is stated about the tram line?

(A) It was operational 24 hours per day.
(B) It was owned by a private company.
(C) It was expensive to build.
(D) It was used by few people.

171. In which of the positions marked [1], [2], [3], and [4] does the following sentence best belong?

"As a result, the city decided to end this service 20 years ago."

(A) [1]
(B) [2]
(C) [3]
(D) [4]

GO ON TO THE NEXT PAGE

THE NORTHWEST LEDGER

NAME: Mohammed Abbar
SUBSCRIPTION: ☐ Daily   ☐ Weekly   ☐ Semiweekly
ADDRESS: 155 Winateka Lane, Tacoma, WA 98401

I WOULD LIKE TO:
☐ Change my subscription   ☐ Cancel my subscription

IF CHANGING YOUR SUBSCRIPTION, PLEASE SELECT A PLAN:
☐ Daily   ☐ Weekly   ☐ Semiweekly

IF CANCELING, PLEASE PROVIDE A REASON:
☐ I am moving to a different address.
☐ I cannot afford the subscription fee.
☐ I am dissatisfied with the quality of the content.
☐ Other

IF OTHER, PLEASE SPECIFY:

I used to rely on *The Northwest Ledger* for my daily local news. But in recent years, I have been getting news from TacomaToday.com and other websites instead. In addition, I'm busier than before, so I'm less likely to sit down and read a large newspaper.

SUGGESTIONS FOR IMPROVING *THE NORTHWEST LEDGER*:

Your paper mostly provides coverage of national sports leagues. I think there should be more stories devoted to our local league baseball and hockey teams. There should also be more restaurant reviews.

Once you submit this form, your service will be changed or discontinued. To confirm that this has been done, you will receive a letter at the address you have indicated above. If you do not receive this letter, please contact us at subscriptions@northwestledger.com.

---

172. Why did Mr. Abbar fill out the form?

(A) To sign up for a weekly mailing
(B) To stop getting a newspaper
(C) To change his mailing address
(D) To complain about some articles

173. What can be inferred about Mr. Abbar?

(A) He recently moved to Tacoma.
(B) He enjoys reading fiction publications.
(C) He wants to renew a subscription.
(D) He prefers online news sources.

174. What is implied about *The Northwest Ledger*?

(A) It does not have a reviews section.
(B) It has limited local sports sections.
(C) It is not published on a daily basis.
(D) It has an online version.

175. What will Mr. Abbar most likely receive?

(A) A confirmation letter
(B) A gift card
(C) A full refund
(D) A complimentary book

GO ON TO THE NEXT PAGE

Questions 176-180 refer to the following e-mail and product description.

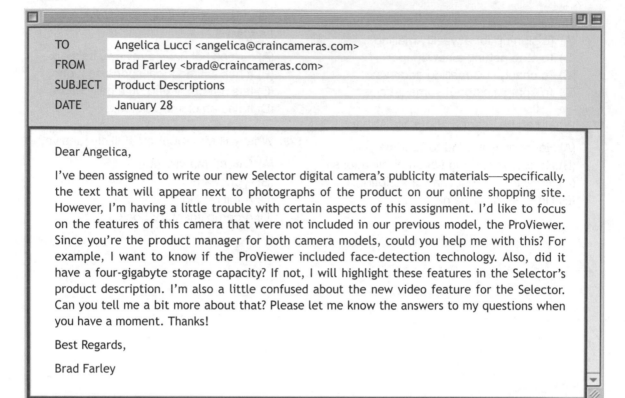

TO   Angelica Lucci <angelica@craincameras.com>

FROM   Brad Farley <brad@craincameras.com>

SUBJECT   Product Descriptions

DATE   January 28

Dear Angelica,

I've been assigned to write our new Selector digital camera's publicity materials—specifically, the text that will appear next to photographs of the product on our online shopping site. However, I'm having a little trouble with certain aspects of this assignment. I'd like to focus on the features of this that were not included in our previous model, the ProViewer. Since you're the product manager for both camera models, could you help me with this? For example, I want to know if the ProViewer included face-detection technology. Also, did it have a four-gigabyte storage capacity? If not, I will highlight these features in the Selector's product description. I'm also a little confused about the new video feature for the Selector. Can you tell me a bit more about that? Please let me know the answers to my questions when you have a moment. Thanks!

Best Regards,

Brad Farley

THE NEW SELECTOR DIGITAL CAMERA FROM CRAIN CAMERAS

Perfect for professional and amateur photographers alike, the new Selector camera is outstanding in every way. As with our earlier models, the Selector can store up to four gigabytes of photographs and be used in a variety of lighting conditions. However, we've added many new features to make it more versatile, accessible, and sophisticated.

■ The Selector has face-detection technology that automatically adjusts the focus to produce the clearest images of human faces.

■ We've upgraded the battery life so that the Selector can last for up to 20 hours without needing to be recharged.

■ The Selector can shoot videos of up to 30 minutes in length. Because these videos have a high resolution, they are very detailed. They can also be converted into various formats using almost any video-editing software.

Moreover, all units come with a foldout tripod on which the camera can be mounted. The tripod is adjustable, allowing you to shoot from both low and high angles.

176. Why did Mr. Farley write the e-mail?

(A) To ask for information about a product
(B) To follow up on a customer inquiry
(C) To request that a document be proofread
(D) To suggest a marketing strategy

177. In the product description, the word "outstanding" in paragraph 1, line 1, is closest in meaning to

(A) obvious
(B) overdue
(C) superior
(D) meaningful

178. What is suggested about the ProViewer?

(A) It can store up to four gigabytes of data.
(B) It is highly popular among professionals.
(C) It was released about one year ago.
(D) It automatically focuses on objects.

179. What does the product description say about the Selector's video feature?

(A) It can be added for an extra charge.
(B) It requires a certain software program.
(C) It sends footage to an online account.
(D) It allows for filming of half-hour videos.

180. According to the product description, what does the Selector come with?

(A) An extra battery
(B) An adjustable tripod
(C) A carrying case
(D) A selection of lenses

GO ON TO THE NEXT PAGE

Questions 181-185 refer to the following notice and e-mail.

NOTICE to Residents of West Carver

This week, several streets will be closed for the three-day Puerto Rican Culture Festival:

■ **The 100 to 800 blocks of Madeline Street** will be closed **from 8 A.M. to 12 P.M. on Friday, July 2,** for a Puerto Rican parade with dancers and a marching band.

■ **The 200 to 500 blocks of MacDunn Avenue** will be closed **from 11 A.M. to 5 P.M. on Saturday, July 3,** for a performance of traditional music.

■ **The 300 to 600 blocks of Harrison Street** will be closed **from 2 P.M. to 10 P.M. on Sunday, July 4,** for a day of fun and games featuring a waterslide and other carnival rides.

More activities, including singing, dancing, and a raffle for gifts, will be held in **Carver Park on July 3 and 4 between 9 A.M. and 11 P.M.**

If you have any disabilities that make it difficult to walk around town, we encourage you to contact a government representative at services@sanmiguel.gov. Arrangements will be made to bring you to the event that you are interested in.

TO: Lucy Garcia <lgarcia@puertoricanfestival.com>
FROM: Michael Gomez <mgomez@fastmail.com>
SUBJECT: Some questions
DATE: July 3

Dear Ms. Garcia,

My name is Michael Gomez, and I'm a resident of the West Carver neighborhood. Yesterday, I heard a large parade passing down the street my house is situated on and searched online to find out what it was. As I am a former resident of Puerto Rico, I'm interested in helping local residents celebrate my heritage. Are you still accepting volunteers? I can put up posters around the neighborhood, guide attendees to certain events, or set up tents for activities. I also have a truck, so I can pick up and drop off supplies. Please let me know if there's any way I can assist with this event.

I look forward to hearing from you.

Sincerely,

Michael Gomez

---

181. What is NOT an attraction listed on the notice?

(A) A musical performance
(B) A water ride
(C) A prize drawing
(D) A food tasting event

182. When should residents contact a government official?

(A) When they cannot purchase a ticket
(B) When they cannot get to a location on foot
(C) When they want to learn more about a party
(D) When they want to see videos of an event

183. What is indicated about Mr. Gomez?

(A) He has given a performance before.
(B) His family members are visiting West Carver.
(C) His house is located on Madeline Street.
(D) He will move to a new neighborhood.

184. Why does Mr. Gomez want to volunteer at the festival?

(A) He previously lived in Puerto Rico.
(B) He has some extra decorations in storage.
(C) He enjoys cooking traditional cuisine.
(D) He wants to work for a nonprofit organization.

185. What does Mr. Gomez offer to do?

(A) Transport items in his vehicle
(B) Post advertisements online
(C) Block off certain streets
(D) Clean up trash in a park

GO ON TO THE NEXT PAGE

Opal Museum of Art
Visitor Notice

Visitors to the Opal Museum of Art have three parking options: the Fairfield Lot, the Morrison Lot, and the Gosling Garage. The Morrison Lot offers the closest access to the museum's front entrance, while the Gosling Garage is nearest to our event hall.

Make sure to take a parking ticket from an automated machine. Fees are payable by credit card or cash at one of these machines upon leaving. To receive a discount as a museum member, scan your Opal Museum of Art membership card at a machine in the Gosling Garage.

Period	Non-member Fee	Member Fee
Less than 1 hour	$10	$8
1-2 hours	$12	$10
2-3 hours	$14	$12
3-4 hours	$16	$14
4 or more hours	$20	$18

For any inquiries, please call the museum's administrative office at 555-6698.

Ms. Kerry Fulton,
As a longtime member of the Opal Museum of Art
You are formally invited to
Dinner with the Artist
A quarterly event hosted at Crystal Hall
On Friday, June 5, 5-10 P.M.

This spring, our museum will hold a five-hour dinner event introducing internationally acclaimed sculptor Alexandra Galanos and her latest exhibit, *Crossing the Road*, which will be unveiled in the Alabaster Wing on June 12. Dinner will be brought out promptly at 8 P.M., followed by a speech from Ms. Galanos and then announcements from museum director Darrell Finn.

As Gosling Garage will be painted during the first week of June, guests should park at either of our other lots.

June 12

Darrell Finn
Opal Museum of Art, Director's Office
400 Morrison Avenue
Trenton, NJ 08618

Dear Mr. Finn,

I want to commend you on the success of last week's event. Your speech was inspiring and made me proud to be a member of your organization.

Also, I want to mention that I attended the opening of Ms. Galanos's exhibit today. I was impressed with not only the sculptural pieces but also the renovations that were made in the area where the exhibition was held.

Thank you, and I look forward to future museum events.

Sincerely,

Kerry Fulton

186. What is the purpose of the information?

(A) To present options for parking
(B) To announce some new charges
(C) To give some safety reminders
(D) To promote museum memberships

187. What is indicated about Gosling Garage?

(A) It is the most expensive parking option.
(B) It has a device for scanning cards.
(C) It is closest to the museum's entrance.
(D) It was recently closed for a city event.

188. What is mentioned about Ms. Galanos?

(A) She has visited the Opal Museum of Art before.
(B) She will conduct some classes on sculpture.
(C) She has signed a contract with Mr. Finn.
(D) She will make some remarks at a gathering.

189. How much must Ms. Fulton pay for parking if she stays for the entire event?

(A) $10
(B) $14
(C) $18
(D) $20

190. According to the letter, what was Ms. Fulton impressed with on June 12?

(A) Ms. Galanos's informative lecture
(B) The repainted Crystal Hall
(C) Mr. Finn's tour of the facility
(D) The improved Alabaster Wing

GO ON TO THE NEXT PAGE

Questions 191-195 refer to the following Web page, e-mail, and review.

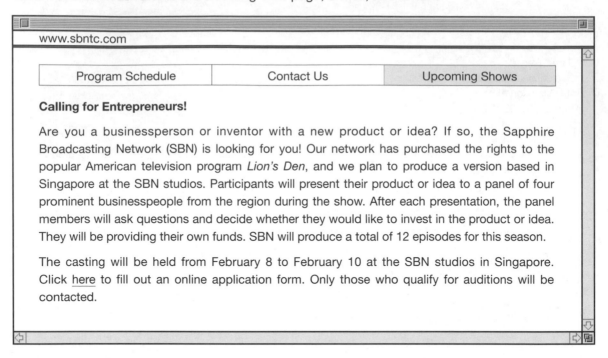

www.sbntc.com

| Program Schedule | Contact Us | Upcoming Shows |

Calling for Entrepreneurs!

Are you a businessperson or inventor with a new product or idea? If so, the Sapphire Broadcasting Network (SBN) is looking for you! Our network has purchased the rights to the popular American television program *Lion's Den*, and we plan to produce a version based in Singapore at the SBN studios. Participants will present their product or idea to a panel of four prominent businesspeople from the region during the show. After each presentation, the panel members will ask questions and decide whether they would like to invest in the product or idea. They will be providing their own funds. SBN will produce a total of 12 episodes for this season.

The casting will be held from February 8 to February 10 at the SBN studios in Singapore. Click here to fill out an online application form. Only those who qualify for auditions will be contacted.

TO   Susan Tsang <susantsang@rubydevelopments.com>
FROM   Dennis Ping <dping@sbntc.com>
SUBJECT *Lion's Den Asia*
DATE   January 29

Dear Ms. Tsang,

I am so pleased that you are interested in appearing on our program as an investor. We have already hired company presidents Chanchai Akkarat and Deepa Sidhu for the show. Mi-young Choi, the CEO of Trinity Manufacturing, is considering taking the fourth spot but still has to see if her work schedule can be adjusted to join the show.

Production starts at the beginning of April, but I would like to meet with you and the other members of our panel before then to discuss your responsibilities in more detail. Therefore, I will require you to attend a meeting with us at our downtown Singapore office on March 28.

Thanks so much again for agreeing to be part of our program!

Regards,

Dennis Ping
Producer, *Lion's Den Asia*

http://www.couchtvreviewer.com/realitytv/lionsdenasia/

TELEVISION PROGRAM: *Lion's Den Asia*　**NETWORK:** SBN
BROADCAST TIME: 8 P.M. on Wednesdays　**REVIEWER:** Abdul Hassan

I am a big fan of the original *Lion's Den* show. So, when I heard an Asian edition was being produced, I was very excited. I have watched the first six episodes of the show, and they have not disappointed me. Host Rajiv Sunder is very charming, and all the panel members are really interesting. Mi-young Choi is especially clever, often asking presenters unexpected questions. And Chanchai Akkarat adds some humor to the otherwise serious program. I also appreciate that Susan Tsang makes frequent offers to the show's entrepreneur participants. In contrast, I'm a bit worried that panel member Deepa Sidhu has only offered to be an investor for three of the entrepreneurs so far. I think she should be more open to investing her money. But overall, I find this version of the show to be as satisfying as the American one.

191. What is NOT true about *Lion's Den*?

(A) It features regional entrepreneurs.
(B) It was first broadcast in Singapore.
(C) It holds auditions for show participants.
(D) It involves presentations by contestants.

192. Why did Mr. Ping arrange a meeting for March 28?

(A) To secure approval for some ideas
(B) To negotiate compensation for presenters
(C) To introduce investors to a production team
(D) To discuss the obligations of panel members

193. What did Ms. Choi probably do?

(A) Made schedule changes to appear on a show
(B) Interviewed some businesspeople for panel positions
(C) Negotiated the purchase of a local television network
(D) Partnered with an associate in a manufacturing firm

194. What is indicated about Mr. Hassan?

(A) He was contacted by e-mail for an audition.
(B) He has not seen half of the episodes of *Lion's Den Asia*.
(C) He thinks *Lion's Den Asia* was less entertaining than the original.
(D) He personally met with one of participating investors before.

195. Which panel member does Mr. Hassan express concern about?

(A) Chanchai Akkarat
(B) Susan Tsang
(C) Mi-young Choi
(D) Deepa Sidhu

GO ON TO THE NEXT PAGE ➡

The Richmond Sun

Healthy Fast Food is On Its Way

Fredericksburg, July 9—The country's first organic fast food restaurant, Fresh Goods, opens next month on Interstate 95. Proprietor Libby Hawkins hopes it will be the first of several hundred to serve quick, healthy, and affordable meals to travelers.

Ms. Hawkins has been a supporter of organic products since she started running her own farm 20 years ago. Today, her farm is one of Virginia's biggest producers of milk and cheese. A frequent traveler herself, she decided to open Fresh Goods when she noticed the lack of healthy dishes sold at rest stops.

Currently, she is working on establishing a network of farms that will supply organic ingredients for Fresh Goods. Participating farmers can expect to receive organic certification and fair prices for their products. However, to ensure the freshness of ingredients, farms that will be part of this network can be no farther than 50 miles from the restaurant.

Fourth Annual Culpeper Harvest Festival
Friday, September 8, to Sunday, September 10

SEPTEMBER 8: DISCUSSION
5 P.M. • Spotswood Inn Coffeehouse, 215 Davis Street
With Emmett Ashby, Director for the Virginia Food Cooperative (VFC)
More details at www.vfc.org

SEPTEMBER 9: FARM TOURS
11 A.M. - 1 P.M. • Westover Farms, 15384 Mill Road
1 - 3 P.M. • Whisper Hill Field, 899 Yowell Drive
3 - 5 P.M. • Salt Cedar Hatchery, 11452 Maple Lane

SEPTEMBER 10: FARMER'S MARKET
Followed by the Great Meal, a community meal prepared with locally grown ingredients
Anyone can bring dishes to share (optional)
2 - 4:30 P.M. • Farmer's Market
5 P.M. • Great Meal
Both the Farmer's Market and the Great Meal will be held
at Kingsbrook Park, 308 Chandler Street

To	Marvin Cooper <m.cooper@harrisonburg.net>
From	Libby Hawkins <l.hawkins@freshgoods.com>
Subject	Meeting
Date	August 29

Dear Mr. Cooper,

Thank you for recently becoming a member of my network of farms and deciding to supply chicken for my restaurant. Also, regarding the inquiry you e-mailed me about, I would be happy to meet with you at the upcoming Culpeper Harvest Festival. I won't be able to join the tour of your farm, the Salt Cedar Hatchery, but I can spare some time the following day before the Great Meal to stop by your booth at the Farmer's Market. If there is a problem, you can call me at 555-2498. Thanks, and I'll see you soon!

Sincerely,

Libby Hawkins

196. What is stated about Ms. Hawkins's farm?

(A) It is expected to expand next year.
(B) It is located near Interstate 95.
(C) It produces dairy products.
(D) It supplies restaurants nationwide.

197. What caused Ms. Hawkins to open her restaurant?

(A) An article published in a food industry magazine
(B) The unavailability of healthy food options at some locations
(C) A recommendation from one of her former colleagues
(D) The need to find a market for her products

198. What is true about the Culpeper Harvest Festival?

(A) It is usually held twice a year.
(B) It will last for one week.
(C) It is sponsored by the government.
(D) It will feature local food.

199. Where does Ms. Hawkins want to meet Mr. Cooper?

(A) At the Spotswood Inn
(B) At Kingsbrook Park
(C) At Salt Cedar Hatchery
(D) At Westover Farms

200. What can be inferred about Mr. Cooper?

(A) He will serve some dishes at the Great Meal.
(B) His facility has been operating for more than 10 years.
(C) He is participating in a festival for the first time.
(D) His farm is within 50 miles of Fresh Goods.

This is the end of the test. You may review Parts 5, 6, and 7 if you finish the test early.

分數換算表 p. 244 / 正確答案、翻譯、解析〔解析本〕p. 90

▌缺請根據下一頁的 Review 檢查表複習答錯的題目

ˊ**Review** 檢查表

完成 TEST 3 後，請根據下表檢視自己答錯的問題，並在框框中打勾。
如果距離考試時間不多，請務必檢查**粗體字**的項目。

☐ **我再度練習了答錯的題目，試著找出正確答案。**

☐ **我已針對答錯的題目查閱了翻譯，理解了題幹與問題的內容。**

☐ **我透過翻譯，理解了每題各個選項正確或錯誤的原因。**

☐ 我檢視了在 Part 1 和 Part 2 答錯的問題類型，並加以整理，以免落入相同的陷阱。

☐ 我檢視了 Part 3 和 Part 4 每個題目所使用的換句話說。

☐ 在 Part 5 和 Part 6，我針對各題的正確答案及錯誤選項，整理了文法和單字的重點。

☐ 針對 Part 6「選擇合適句子」的題目，我正確理解了整個段落及空格前後文的語意。

☐ 在 Part 7，我找出了短文和題目中的重點，包含正確答題所需的句子和片語，並加以標示，也檢查了題目使用的換句話說。

☐ 針對 Part 1~Part 4，我使用線上的聽力訓練筆記，針對考試的重點語句練習聽寫、閱讀和複習。

☐ 針對 Part 1~Part 4，我使用單字記憶本來記下考試的關鍵詞彙和表達用語。

大量練習題目固然重要，但好好檢視自己答錯的問題也同樣關鍵。
只要仔細複習一遍答錯的題目，就能在短時間內有效達到目標分數。

TEST 4

LISTENING TEST

Part 1
Part 2
Part 3
Part 4

READING TEST

Part 5
Part 6
Part 7

Review 檢查表

注意！測驗前請務必檢查下列事項。

手機是否關機？
Answer Sheet（p. 253）、鉛筆、橡皮擦和手錶是否準備好了？
準備好聆聽音檔了嗎？

準備就緒後，想著你的目標分數，開始測驗。
測驗完畢後，請務必查看 Review 檢查表（p. 194），複習答錯的題目。

🎧 Test 4.mp3
可免費下載、播放 MP3，用於答題訓練和複習

MP3 音檔

LISTENING TEST

In this section, you must demonstrate your ability to understand spoken English. This section is divided into four parts and will take approximately 45 minutes to complete. Do not mark the answers in your test book. Use the answer sheet that is provided separately.

PART 1

Directions: For each question, you will listen to four short statements about a picture in your test book. These statements will not be printed and will only be spoken one time. Select the statement that best describes what is happening in the picture and mark the corresponding letter (A), (B), (C), or (D) on the answer sheet.

Sample Answer
Ⓐ ● Ⓒ Ⓓ

The statement that best describes the picture is (B), "The man is sitting at the desk." So, you should mark letter (B) on the answer sheet.

1.

2.

GO ON TO THE NEXT PAGE

3.

4.

5.

6.

GO ON TO THE NEXT PAGE

PART 2

Directions: For each question, you will listen to a statement or question followed by three possible responses spoken in English. They will not be printed and will only be spoken one time. Select the best response and mark the corresponding letter (A), (B), or (C) on your answer sheet.

7. Mark your answer on your answer sheet.

8. Mark your answer on your answer sheet.

9. Mark your answer on your answer sheet.

10. Mark your answer on your answer sheet.

11. Mark your answer on your answer sheet.

12. Mark your answer on your answer sheet.

13. Mark your answer on your answer sheet.

14. Mark your answer on your answer sheet.

15. Mark your answer on your answer sheet.

16. Mark your answer on your answer sheet.

17. Mark your answer on your answer sheet.

18. Mark your answer on your answer sheet.

19. Mark your answer on your answer sheet.

20. Mark your answer on your answer sheet.

21. Mark your answer on your answer sheet.

22. Mark your answer on your answer sheet.

23. Mark your answer on your answer sheet.

24. Mark your answer on your answer sheet.

25. Mark your answer on your answer sheet.

26. Mark your answer on your answer sheet.

27. Mark your answer on your answer sheet.

28. Mark your answer on your answer sheet.

29. Mark your answer on your answer sheet.

30. Mark your answer on your answer sheet.

31. Mark your answer on your answer sheet.

PART 3

Directions: In this part, you will listen to several conversations between two or more speakers. These conversations will not be printed and will only be spoken one time. For each conversation, you will be asked to answer three questions. Select the best response and mark the corresponding letter (A), (B), (C), or (D) on your answer sheet.

32. Who most likely is the man?

(A) A cashier
(B) A receptionist
(C) A pharmacist
(D) A doctor

33. What does the man offer to do?

(A) Write a note
(B) Send a text message
(C) Prescribe a medicine
(D) Postpone an appointment

34. What is mentioned about the woman?

(A) She expects to arrive late.
(B) She hurt her back last month.
(C) Her condition has improved.
(D) Her payment was not received.

35. Where does the man most likely work?

(A) At a law office
(B) At a financial institution
(C) At a retail outlet
(D) At a security firm

36. What is mentioned about the woman's credit card?

(A) It has a regular fee.
(B) It offers cash back rewards.
(C) It was charged for a hotel stay.
(D) It is valid for one year.

37. Why does the woman say, "I've had this card for over a year"?

(A) To request a replacement
(B) To express satisfaction with a service
(C) To question a charge
(D) To ask for a free gift

38. What are the speakers mainly discussing?

(A) A software upgrade
(B) A productivity decline
(C) A product launch
(D) An office improvement

39. What does the woman say about the office lights?

(A) They are too strong.
(B) They use too much electricity.
(C) They were poorly installed.
(D) They are out of date.

40. What will happen next Thursday?

(A) A light will be repaired.
(B) A new space will be opened.
(C) A regular meeting will be held.
(D) A budget cut will be announced.

41. What was delivered yesterday?

(A) A replacement part
(B) An electronic device
(C) A personal letter
(D) A product list

42. What does the woman ask the man about?

(A) The date of a product launch
(B) The price of a publication
(C) The size of an item
(D) The weight of a tablet

43. What does the man offer to do?

(A) Share some financial details
(B) Call back at a later time
(C) Check with a supervisor
(D) Propose other model options

GO ON TO THE NEXT PAGE

44. According to the man, what must the speakers do?

(A) Write a report
(B) Give a presentation
(C) Review an account
(D) Set up a projector

45. Why is the woman concerned?

(A) She is not confident about a task.
(B) She is not able to attend a meeting.
(C) She misplaced a document.
(D) She made a calculation error.

46. What will the speakers do this evening?

(A) Look over some figures
(B) Meet with supervisors
(C) Stay late at work
(D) Reserve seats for a seminar

47. What is the conversation mainly about?

(A) A company dinner
(B) A house showing
(C) A volunteer event
(D) A private gathering

48. According to the man, what is located on Folgers Drive?

(A) A department store
(B) A workplace
(C) A residence
(D) A supermarket

49. What does the man ask Kelly to bring?

(A) Books
(B) Gifts
(C) Dessert
(D) Beverages

50. Why is the woman traveling to Frankfurt?

(A) To visit a relative
(B) To inspect a facility
(C) To meet a designer
(D) To attend a conference

51. What does the man ask the woman to do?

(A) Speak with a manager
(B) Go to another branch
(C) Remove a protective tag
(D) Provide proof of purchase

52. What will the woman most likely do in half an hour?

(A) Schedule an appointment
(B) Get on a shuttle bus
(C) Return to a retail outlet
(D) Board a plane

53. What is the woman considering?

(A) Accepting a summer job
(B) Working as a tour guide
(C) Taking a trip overseas
(D) Changing travel plans

54. Why does the man recommend the Peru Adventure package?

(A) It includes a luxury hotel room.
(B) It will save her some money.
(C) It offers more flexibility.
(D) It will come with a complimentary gift.

55. According to the man, what benefit does a membership provide?

(A) Travel insurance
(B) Reduced rates
(C) Free guidebooks
(D) Additional destinations

56. Who most likely is the man?

(A) A delivery person
(B) A personal assistant
(C) A computer programmer
(D) An office manager

57. What does the woman tell the man to do?

(A) Send a package to a new address
(B) Check the contents of a box
(C) Stop by a service counter
(D) Put a shipment on a desk

58. What will the woman most likely do next?

(A) Write her signature on a document
(B) Look over a list of purchased goods
(C) Contact the original sender
(D) Place another hardware order

---

59. What did the man do earlier in the week?

(A) Talked with a team leader
(B) Went on a business trip
(C) Participated in a workshop
(D) Requested a promotion

60. Why were interviews conducted?

(A) A manager will resign.
(B) A branch will expand.
(C) A department is understaffed.
(D) A job offer was turned down.

61. Why does the man say, "she has requested a transfer to our Vancouver office"?

(A) To explain why an option is unavailable
(B) To stress the importance of a position
(C) To recommend another location
(D) To encourage the woman to make a decision

62. Look at the graphic. Which model was most recently released?

(A) XD26
(B) CY16
(C) UW07
(D) DR13

63. What problem does the woman mention?

(A) Reviews of new watches were negative.
(B) Inventory of an item is running low.
(C) Production in the factory has been shut down.
(D) A supervisor is having trouble finding staff.

64. Why does the man expect sales to increase?

(A) Some items have been put on sale.
(B) Watches are becoming more popular.
(C) An outside marketing firm was hired.
(D) The holiday season is approaching.

GO ON TO THE NEXT PAGE

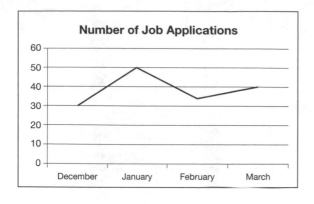

Number of Job Applications

60
50
40
30
20
10
0

December   January   February   March

Cot Area

| Window | A-1 | A-2 | Aisle | A-3 | A-4 | Window |

65. What does the man still need to do?

(A) Post an advertisement
(B) Prepare for an interview
(C) Contact recent applicants
(D) Train new employees

66. According to the woman, why is a hiring decision urgent?

(A) A meeting is approaching.
(B) A project is on hold.
(C) A key staff member quit.
(D) A team was reorganized.

67. Look at the graphic. When were job openings advertised on the website?

(A) In December
(B) In January
(C) In February
(D) In March

68. Where most likely are the speakers?

(A) At a ferry port
(B) At an airport
(C) At a train station
(D) At a bus stop

69. What does the man give to the woman?

(A) A credit card
(B) A missing-item form
(C) Some luggage
(D) Some identification

70. Look at the graphic. Which seat will the man be given?

(A) A-1
(B) A-2
(C) A-3
(D) A-4

PART 4

Directions: In this part, you will listen to several short talks by a single speaker. These talks will not be printed and will only be spoken one time. For each talk, you will be asked to answer three questions. Select the best response and mark the corresponding letter (A), (B), (C), or (D) on your answer sheet.

71. Why is the facility closed?

    (A) A holiday is being celebrated.
    (B) A building is being repaired.
    (C) A device needs to be inspected.
    (D) A system needs to be updated.

72. According to the speaker, what can the listeners do during a closure?

    (A) Return books
    (B) Pick up materials
    (C) Renew library cards
    (D) Go to other branches

73. How should the listeners address urgent issues?

    (A) By meeting with an employee
    (B) By dialing a number
    (C) By filling out an online form
    (D) By sending an e-mail

74. Who most likely is the speaker?

    (A) A computer repairperson
    (B) A research analyst
    (C) A corporate trainer
    (D) A sales representative

75. What does the speaker say about NextBook?

    (A) It was updated several months ago.
    (B) It takes a while to load on computers.
    (C) It was approved by a president.
    (D) It requires a special code to access.

76. What will an assistant pass out?

    (A) Application forms
    (B) Training materials
    (C) Office equipment
    (D) Electronic devices

77. Who most likely is John Harris?

    (A) A journalist
    (B) A weather forecaster
    (C) A snow plow operator
    (D) A public official

78. What is mentioned about the Harborview Bridge?

    (A) It is the site of an accident.
    (B) It is frozen over.
    (C) It is the only way to get to downtown.
    (D) It is completely clear of snow.

79. What does the speaker imply when she says, "you may want to reconsider"?

    (A) An event might be postponed.
    (B) A traffic light is not working properly.
    (C) An alternative route should be taken.
    (D) A recent report has not been confirmed.

80. What does the speaker say will happen next week?

    (A) A manufacturing plant will open.
    (B) A beverage line will be released.
    (C) A TV commercial will be completed.
    (D) A client will come to an office.

81. What did the speaker ask the research team to do?

    (A) Begin surveying customers
    (B) Make corrections to a report
    (C) Share some results online
    (D) Prepare a brief presentation

82. Why should the listeners contact the speaker?

    (A) To ask questions
    (B) To coordinate schedules
    (C) To confirm attendance
    (D) To volunteer for a job

GO ON TO THE NEXT PAGE

NEW TOEIC 950 聽力+閱讀 5 回達標

83. What does Mr. Kramer have a lot of experience doing?

(A) Selling insurance products
(B) Managing employees
(C) Addressing customer complaints
(D) Handling business mergers

84. What does the speaker mention about Mr. Kramer?

(A) He would like to give a talk.
(B) He has lived in another country.
(C) He refused other offers.
(D) He will hire an assistant.

85. What will probably take place next Friday?

(A) A language class
(B) A trade fair
(C) A sales meeting
(D) An informal gathering

86. Who most likely are the listeners?

(A) Corporate presidents
(B) Bank tellers
(C) Company stakeholders
(D) Magazine editors

87. What is inferred about *BizSurprise*?

(A) It publishes monthly issues.
(B) It wants to interview a CEO.
(C) It sponsors business fairs.
(D) It has to hire more writers.

88. What does the speaker ask Ms. Harvey to do?

(A) Present an award
(B) Make a speech
(C) Applaud for a winner
(D) Take her seat

89. Who most likely is the speaker?

(A) A radio host
(B) A city employee
(C) A tour guide
(D) An advertising executive

90. Why does the speaker say, "It is tourist season, after all"?

(A) To indicate why there are many tour buses near a park
(B) To note that repairs must be finished by a certain date
(C) To explain why there is a lot of trash in parks
(D) To recommend holding a promotional event

91. What does the speaker suggest?

(A) Handing out trash bags
(B) Running some advertisements
(C) Recruiting temporary staff
(D) Speaking to a cleaning company

92. According to the speaker, what has to be approved?

(A) Time off
(B) Additional work hours
(C) A product design
(D) Management changes

93. Who most likely is Brittany Jacobs?

(A) A personnel employee
(B) A sales representative
(C) A photography expert
(D) A training instructor

94. What does the speaker mean when he says, "we have only five people"?

(A) An important decision cannot be agreed upon.
(B) A company will hire more workers soon.
(C) Some help is needed to complete a task.
(D) Some employees should work overtime.

Viva Rentals

Type	Capacity	Daily Rate
Sports car	2 people	$32.00
Sedan	4 people	$22.00
SUV	6 people	$28.00
Minivan	8 people	$34.00

	Building A		City Library
Building B	City Hall	Ocean Avenue	Building C
Oak Street			
Department Store	Building D		Subway Station

95. Why is the speaker calling?

(A) To confirm a reservation
(B) To offer a special deal
(C) To reply to some questions
(D) To give a store location

96. Look at the graphic. Which vehicle will the listener most likely choose?

(A) Sports car
(B) Sedan
(C) SUV
(D) Minivan

97. What is the listener instructed to do?

(A) Return a vehicle on time
(B) Make an online booking
(C) Verify some travel dates
(D) Submit a form in person

98. What is the broadcast mainly about?

(A) A corporate acquisition
(B) A property purchase
(C) An event place
(D) A land development

99. What will happen on June 3?

(A) A company will relocate.
(B) A project will start.
(C) An executive will retire.
(D) An office will reopen.

100. Look at the graphic. Which building did Western Development rent?

(A) Building A
(B) Building B
(C) Building C
(D) Building D

This is the end of the Listening test. Turn to PART 5 in your test book.

READING TEST

In this section, you must demonstrate your ability to read and comprehend English. You will be given a variety of texts and asked to answer questions about these texts. This section is divided into three parts and will take 75 minutes to complete.

Do not mark the answers in your test book. Use the answer sheet that is separately provided.

PART 5

Directions: In each question, you will be asked to review a statement that is missing a word or phrase. Four answer choices will be provided for each statement. Select the best answer and mark the corresponding letter (A), (B), (C), or (D) on the answer sheet.

🕐 **PART 5** 建議作答時間　**11 分鐘**

101. Sanders Industries recently ------- high-tech machinery that will allow it to double its output.

(A) to purchase
(B) purchase
(C) purchased
(D) purchases

102. ------- of the staff members surveyed is pleased with the expansion of the retirement program.

(A) Each
(B) All
(C) Other
(D) Their own

103. The heavy snowfall delayed the train's ------- by more than four hours.

(A) depart
(B) departed
(C) departs
(D) departure

104. The Shoreline Restaurant is ------- busy, as the area is filled with tourists year-round.

(A) less
(B) always
(C) exactly
(D) soon

105. Most new businesses fail within five years, but ------- go on to become very successful.

(A) any
(B) these
(C) some
(D) every

106. Ms. Wang had her home ------- by a real estate agent before offering it for sale.

(A) performed
(B) appeared
(C) assessed
(D) outlined

107. There are 30 seats ------- for the recipients' family and coworkers at the awards ceremony.

(A) reserve
(B) reserved
(C) reserving
(D) reservation

108. In order to maintain your account security, ------- at least one number and one letter in your password.

(A) include
(B) included
(C) including
(D) to include

109. Findera Construction took advantage of ------- growth in Vietnam's housing market to raise its international profile.

(A) best
(B) rapid
(C) original
(D) adverse

110. Many critics praised director John Parker for the ------- ending to his most recent action movie.

(A) thrilled
(B) thrillers
(C) thrilling
(D) thrills

111. The upcoming sale at Westside Electronics ------- shoppers a great deal of money on televisions.

(A) save
(B) saved
(C) saving
(D) will save

112. RubioTech recalled the new computer model after discovering that it contained ------- components.

(A) functional
(B) adjustable
(C) portable
(D) defective

113. Before ------- Carla Evans to schedule an interview, Mr. Harris verified the information on her résumé.

(A) contact
(B) contacts
(C) contacted
(D) contacting

114. Those planning to attend the conference need ------- at least seven days in advance.

(A) register
(B) to register
(C) registering
(D) registered

115. TriGem Chemicals admitted that it had ------- shipped the client's order to the wrong address.

(A) generously
(B) mutually
(C) productively
(D) accidentally

116. Product deliveries must be completed within three days according to the terms of the -------.

(A) figure
(B) contract
(C) research
(D) concept

117. Sales of the XL550 Tablet increased ------- 15 percent after a new version of the operating system was released.

(A) for
(B) on
(C) along
(D) by

118. The number of visitors to Ice River National Park in October was ------- higher than in the previous month.

(A) very
(B) much
(C) more
(D) so

119. The company's executive cafeteria will be ------- into an employee lounge during the renovations.

(A) converted
(B) convinced
(C) consented
(D) concealed

120. It is ------- whether countries can continue increasing the size of their economies while limiting fossil fuel use.

(A) debate
(B) debates
(C) debating
(D) debatable

GO ON TO THE NEXT PAGE

121. Poole Automotive ------- planned to expand overseas but decided to focus on increasing domestic sales instead.

(A) negatively
(B) currently
(C) initially
(D) rarely

122. At only $50 per night, the Warren Inn is considered a bargain ------- the many hotels in the area.

(A) before
(B) toward
(C) onto
(D) among

123. Applicants who are ------- in finding out more about the firm's benefits package should visit our website.

(A) obsessed
(B) displayed
(C) interested
(D) stimulated

124. To ------- its latest microwave from previous models, Langford Appliances launched a major marketing campaign.

(A) concentrate
(B) handle
(C) designate
(D) differentiate

125. The retailers' association selected the Debran Center for the meeting based on its members' ------- for a central location.

(A) performance
(B) preference
(C) collection
(D) exception

126. ------- he had decided to find a new job, Mr. Cooper made appointments with several recruitment agencies.

(A) Once
(B) During
(C) Soon
(D) Next

127. Pacer Industries purchased a factory in China ------- produces a wide range of electronic components.

(A) it
(B) that
(C) what
(D) whether

128. Recent polls suggest that most employees would take a pay cut if they could work ------- hours.

(A) shortly
(B) shorter
(C) shorten
(D) shortest

129. The Paxton Hotel offers a 20-percent discount to anyone ------- stays there more than four nights per month.

(A) who
(B) whom
(C) which
(D) whose

130. Donations from the Lumour Corporation ------- funding for the National Museum of Ancient Art.

(A) notify
(B) interpret
(C) provide
(D) confront

PART 6

Directions: In this part, you will be asked to read four English texts. Each text is missing a word, phrase, or sentence. Select the answer choice that correctly completes the text and mark the corresponding letter (A), (B), (C), or (D) on the answer sheet.

PART 6 建議作答時間 **8 分鐘**

Questions 131-134 refer to the following article.

A Franchise or an Independent Business?

April 11—A difficult decision that an entrepreneur faces is whether to open a franchise or

an independent business. -------. A franchise owner does not have to spend years
                                   131.
developing brand recognition and receives support from the headquarters. On the other

hand, people who open an independent business have more freedom to select products

and can decide how to set ------- prices. Another factor to consider is the initial investment.
                            132.
------- running a franchise only requires a small initial investment, some profits must be
133.
paid to the corporate headquarters. In contrast, an independent business owner will have

high startup costs but ------- all the profits.
                       134.

---

131. (A) Most people prefer to shop at international chains.
(B) Many companies lose money in their first year of operation.
(C) Some brands on the market are significantly overpriced.
(D) Both choices have advantages and disadvantages.

132. (A) themselves
(B) them
(C) they
(D) their

133. (A) Except
(B) Just as
(C) Although
(D) Even

134. (A) estimate
(B) waste
(C) eliminate
(D) keep

GO ON TO THE NEXT PAGE

Questions 135-138 refer to the following announcement.

To all customers:

We are pleased to announce that Hamby-Russ has merged with Carmona Incorporated.

------- the start of the month, our headquarters in Seattle began operating under the name
135.
Hamby-Russ & Carmona.

-------. During this time, both companies negotiated extensively to develop a strategy for
136.
providing shoppers with the best recreational products available. As for our organizational

structure, it is being adjusted. However, we will ------- all our original employees. As a
137.
result, you will be able to work with the same salespeople that you had before. Our phone

numbers will also remain unchanged. Do not ------- to contact our administrative team at
138.
555-3438 with any questions.

135. (A) While
(B) At
(C) Down
(D) Into

136. (A) We determined it would be best to
cease operations entirely.
(B) The spring shopping season is our
busiest time of the year.
(C) This merger had been planned for
nearly 10 months.
(D) An announcement will be made when
an agreement is finalized.

137. (A) maintain
(B) transfer
(C) replace
(D) dismiss

138. (A) hesitate
(B) be hesitated
(C) to hesitate
(D) hesitating

Questions 139-142 refer to the following customer review.

For a recent trip to Miami, I arranged a car ------- through EZ Auto. I chose this company
　　　　　　　　　　　　　　　　　　　　　　139.
because it has lower daily rates for travelers than its competitors. However, when I arrived

at the EZ Auto branch near the airport, the SUV I had reserved was unavailable. -------.
　　　　　　　　　　　　　　　　　　　　　　　　　　　　　　　　　　　140.
As there was a truck on the lot, I asked to rent it instead. But I ------- that I would have to
　　　　　　　　　　　　　　　　　　　　　　　　141.
pay the full price for the larger vehicle, which was higher than that of the SUV. The EZ Auto

staff should have provided me with an upgrade at no additional charge to compensate for

their mistake. Therefore, I have decided not ------- this company's services again in the future.
　　　　　　　　　　　　　　　　　　　142.

139. (A) repair
　　　(B) rental
　　　(C) inspection
　　　(D) delivery

140. (A) They had no record of my request for
　　　　　a navigation system.
　　　(B) Unfortunately, there were no other
　　　　　vehicles.
　　　(C) Apparently, there was a mistake with
　　　　　the date.
　　　(D) I had already asked for a refund.

141. (A) was informed
　　　(B) informed
　　　(C) informing
　　　(D) was informing

142. (A) to use
　　　(B) using
　　　(C) used
　　　(D) use

GO ON TO THE NEXT PAGE

Questions 143-146 refer to the following memo.

From: Diane Langston, Sales Manager
To: All Employees
Date: September 23
Subject: Fall Marathon Street Closures

The annual Renfield Fall Marathon takes place this Friday. Be aware that some ------- **143.** streets may be closed during the event. Both Sandy Brook Road and the parking garage next to our building will be ------- from 9 A.M. to 2 P.M. So if you normally drive to work, you **144.** should make other plans. -------. It is only a five-minute walk from the office. You can also **145.** take the bus to Davis Lane, which is two blocks from here. You can look up all the bus routes online. ------- more assistance, you can let me know. **146.**

143. (A) neighborly
     (B) neighbors
     (C) neighborhood
     (D) neighborliness

144. (A) safe
     (B) vulnerable
     (C) inaccessible
     (D) acceptable

145. (A) If you can telecommute, I recommend doing so.
     (B) Luckily, we only experienced a temporary inconvenience.
     (C) The office will open after the marathon is finished.
     (D) For instance, there is a garage on 29th Street you can use.

146. (A) Do you need
     (B) Should you need
     (C) As you are needed
     (D) When you are needed

PART 7

Directions: In this part, you will be asked to read several texts, such as advertisements, articles, instant messages, or examples of business correspondence. Each text is followed by several questions. Select the best answer and mark the corresponding letter (A), (B), (C), or (D) on your answer sheet.

🕐 **PART 7** 建議作答時間 **54 分鐘**

Questions 147-148 refer to the following online review.

---

https://www.oakridge.com/customerreviews

Customer Name: Ruth Bell
Rating: ★
Date: April 3
Product: Lucas Coffee Table

I ordered a coffee table from Oakridge Furniture on February 10. Overall, I am happy with this piece of furniture. The design is very stylish and modern, and the table is just the right size for the living room of my new apartment. It was also very easy to assemble. The reason that I am giving this company only one star out of a possible five is that my order took much longer than expected to arrive. I was originally told it would be delivered on March 8, but it wasn't dropped off at my house until March 26. I guess there was a technical error with the company's distribution system that resulted in the table being shipped to the wrong address. I should have been offered an apology for this mistake and maybe even a discount, but I never was. Therefore, I don't think I'll be shopping at Oakridge Furniture again.

---

147. What is indicated about Ms. Bell?

(A) She was unable to assemble a table.
(B) She will return a piece of furniture.
(C) She moved into a new residence.
(D) She is looking for a new apartment.

148. Why did Ms. Bell give the company a poor review?

(A) An item is no longer in stock.
(B) An apology letter was sent too late.
(C) A package was damaged in transit.
(D) A delivery did not arrive on schedule.

GO ON TO THE NEXT PAGE ➤

Questions 149-150 refer to the following text messages.

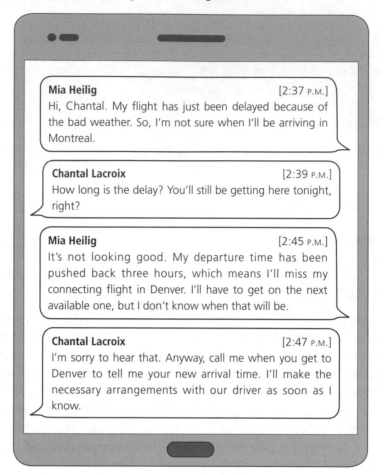

Mia Heilig [2:37 P.M.]
Hi, Chantal. My flight has just been delayed because of the bad weather. So, I'm not sure when I'll be arriving in Montreal.

Chantal Lacroix [2:39 P.M.]
How long is the delay? You'll still be getting here tonight, right?

Mia Heilig [2:45 P.M.]
It's not looking good. My departure time has been pushed back three hours, which means I'll miss my connecting flight in Denver. I'll have to get on the next available one, but I don't know when that will be.

Chantal Lacroix [2:47 P.M.]
I'm sorry to hear that. Anyway, call me when you get to Denver to tell me your new arrival time. I'll make the necessary arrangements with our driver as soon as I know.

149. What is true about Ms. Heilig?

(A) She departed from Montreal.
(B) She will pick up Ms. Lacroix.
(C) She will take multiple flights.
(D) She contacted Ms. Lacroix from Denver.

150. At 2:45 P.M., what does Ms. Heilig most likely mean when she writes, "It's not looking good"?

(A) She cannot exchange a ticket.
(B) She may not receive a refund.
(C) She cannot contact a driver.
(D) She may not arrive tonight.

Questions 151-152 refer to the following flyer.

Video Marketing Enterprise
372 Highland Avenue
Mobile, AL 36575
555-8230

At Video Marketing Enterprise, we offer various video production services for your business, including idea generation, script writing, casting, directing, filming, and editing.

We produce videos for organizations of all types and sizes. Contact us if you need videos for marketing campaigns, product demonstrations, or training workshops. We employ a variety of professionals who are knowledgeable about all steps of the video-making process. Not to mention, our filming equipment and stage props are of the highest quality available.

From November 1 to December 31, we are offering a special winter deal for small business owners. For just $2,000, we will create a 30-second video for your company. Then, our online marketing team will give you tips on how to promote your video on social media sites. This will ensure that your advertisement is viewed by a large audience without your having to pay for costly airtime on television networks. For more information about this deal or our company in general, visit our website at www.videomarketingenterprise.com.

151. What is indicated about Video Marketing Enterprise?

(A) It has only a few staff members.
(B) It conducts workshops for filmmakers.
(C) It provides a wide range of services.
(D) It sells video production equipment.

152. What will happen from November 1 to December 31?

(A) A website will be updated.
(B) A business will be expanded.
(C) A promotion will be held.
(D) A social media platform will be launched.

GO ON TO THE NEXT PAGE

Questions 153-154 refer to the following e-mail.

TO All Instructors
FROM Adam Fitzpatrick <afitzpatrick@hardingbusinessinstitute.com>
SUBJECT Update
DATE June 17

Hello everybody,

As you probably know, the basement of the Farley Building was flooded last night as a result of yesterday's typhoon. Therefore, we are temporarily moving all classes that meet in the basement to the Sherman Center next door. Here is a list of temporary room assignments:

CLASS	INSTRUCTOR	ROOM
Attracting Investors to Your Start-up	Mark Helling	200
Branding 101	Jesse Weiner	205
Advanced Financial Accounting	Helen Boucher	207
Marketing with Social Media	Megan Davis	210

Your class times will remain the same, and your students will be notified of the situation by e-mail this afternoon. Alfred King, the Farley Building's manager, informed me that the flooded rooms will be cleaned out and repaired over the next three days. He said they will be available for use again next Monday.

Please contact me if you have any questions.

Best regards,

Adam Fitzpatrick
President, Harding Business Institute

---

153. According to the memo, what happened on June 16?

(A) A storm took place.
(B) Some classes were canceled.
(C) Some exams were corrected.
(D) A lecturer went on vacation.

154. What did Mr. King tell Mr. Fitzpatrick?

(A) The second floor of the Sherman Center is open.
(B) A class on marketing can meet as scheduled.
(C) The water damage is too expensive to repair.
(D) The Farley Building basement will be usable next week.

NOTICE

The Bristol City Council, in support of Mayor Thomas Anderson's recycling initiative, has agreed to conclude its contract with Sanders Waste Management by the end of the year. From that point on, all waste will be handled by Perry Waste and Recycling.

As a result of this recycling initiative, Bristol residents will be asked to separate their trash beginning on January 1. Regular trash will be placed in black bins, while metal, glass, and paper will be placed in green bins. The new bins will be delivered this week, along with a detailed pamphlet. Residents are advised to review the printed guidelines carefully.

155. What is the purpose of the notice?

(A) To call for a council meeting
(B) To express support for a project
(C) To announce a service change
(D) To report on a program's success

156. What is stated about the recycling initiative?

(A) It will take effect the following year.
(B) It was proposed by the previous mayor.
(C) It will be managed by a council member.
(D) It is part of a larger campaign.

157. What are Bristol residents encouraged to do?

(A) Dispose of trash more often
(B) Use one type of bin
(C) Attend a city council meeting
(D) Read a document

GO ON TO THE NEXT PAGE

Questions 158-161 refer to the following article.

On the Loose Again Set to Premiere at Goldwin Theater

On the Loose Again, the sequel to the popular comedy *On the Loose*, will premiere at Goldwin Theater on May 16. The stars of both films—Max Walter and Elena Marconi—will be in attendance, and a brief photo shoot will take place before the movie screens. The red carpet event will begin as soon as the theater opens, and the film will be shown one hour later, from 6 P.M. to 8 P.M. Immediately following the film will be a question-and-answer session with the cast and crew. Finally, an autograph signing will take place at 8:30 P.M.

On the Loose Again continues where the previous film ended. It features an escaped criminal and his wife as they travel across the American South attempting to avoid the police. Director Jamie Moya, who has also produced numerous popular television series, including *Above Ground* and *Special Investigations*, replaced Richard Weber, the director of the original movie. As the first movie did quite well, *On the Loose Again* is expected to draw large crowds. Those wishing to obtain tickets to the premiere should buy them well in advance by going to www.goldwintheater.com/tickets or calling 555-3716.

158. What is true about *On the Loose Again*?

(A) It is the third film in a series.
(B) It is especially popular among teenagers.
(C) It features the same actors as the first movie.
(D) It has received positive reviews.

159. The word "shown" in paragraph 1, line 6, is closest in meaning to

(A) exposed
(B) reported
(C) performed
(D) presented

160. What is mentioned about Mr. Moya?

(A) He was the director of *On the Loose.*
(B) He is known for his work in television.
(C) He is a friend of Ms. Marconi.
(D) He wrote the script for *On the Loose Again.*

161. What does the article advise people to do?

(A) Get to the theater by 8 P.M.
(B) Purchase tickets early
(C) Participate in a photo shoot
(D) Enter a raffle online

Questions 162-165 refer to the following online chat discussion.

Robin Underwood [8:30 P.M.] Hi, everyone. I think I've come up with a way to attract new gym members.

Franklin Bates [8:31 P.M.] I'm glad. We've lost a lot of customers to the fitness center that recently opened down the street. What's your plan?

Robin Underwood [8:33 P.M.] We can waive one month's fee for new members who sign up for a six-month membership and two months' fees if it's an annual membership.

Norma Flores [8:34 P.M.] Lots of other gyms have similar promotions. Maybe we need to do more.

Robin Underwood [8:35 P.M.] That's why I'm also planning to encourage our existing members to recommend us to their friends. Members who get someone else to sign up here will receive a free gym bag as a gift.

Franklin Bates [8:37 P.M.] That will probably work. Would you like me to add this information to our website? The first exercise class I teach isn't until 1:00 P.M. tomorrow, so I'll have time to do it before lunch.

Robin Underwood [8:38 P.M.] That would be great. Norma, could you put up some notices in the gym about this new policy?

Norma Flores [8:38 P.M.] Sure. I'll also notify the other employees so that they can tell our customers.

162. What is mentioned about the gym where Ms. Underwood works?

(A) It opened a second branch.
(B) It has a new competitor.
(C) It will move to another location.
(D) It offers two-month memberships.

163. At 8:34 P.M., what does Ms. Flores most likely mean when she writes, "Lots of other gyms have similar promotions"?

(A) She wants to imitate an offer.
(B) She agrees with a suggestion.
(C) She is doubtful about a plan.
(D) She needs to check on some details.

164. What will some existing members be eligible to receive?

(A) A gift certificate
(B) A fee reduction
(C) A membership upgrade
(D) A complimentary item

165. What will Mr. Bates most likely do tomorrow morning?

(A) Print some notices
(B) Lead a fitness class
(C) Update a website
(D) Meet with employees

GO ON TO THE NEXT PAGE

Questions 166-168 refer to the following information.

Workplace Health Research Association

www.whra.org

The Workplace Health Research Association (WHRA) is holding its Fifth Annual Workplace Health Conference on October 10 and 11 at the WHRA Institute. An alliance of research groups, WHRA has made the well-being of employees its primary goal.

This year's conference will offer participants the latest information on how sleep, nutrition, and exercise affect productivity in the workplace. Additional details about lecture topics and presenters will be finalized and posted on www.whra.org/events on August 7.

To register, please fill out the online registration form. If you are a member of WHRA, you will receive 30 percent off the total cost of attending on both days. Please be prepared to provide your membership number at the time of registration. If you would like to apply for membership, please visit the site's membership page.

Registration begins on August 1 and ends on September 15. Should you need to cancel your registration, please send an e-mail to rebecca.smith@whra.org by September 21. After this date, no refunds will be granted. For questions and inquiries, you may write to fifthconference@whra.org.

166. What is suggested about the WHRA?

(A) It will start a new research project.
(B) It was established recently.
(C) It operates offices overseas.
(D) It has hosted conferences before.

167. What is NOT mentioned about the event?

(A) Attendees may qualify for a discount.
(B) A program will be posted online.
(C) A membership is required to attend.
(D) Participants can register on a website.

168. By what date should participants register?

(A) August 1
(B) August 7
(C) September 15
(D) September 21

Questions 169-171 refer to the following article.

Stanton Rental Property Demand Continues to Rise

As the job market in Stanton has been good for the past 10 years, the need for rental housing has climbed steadily upward. — [1] —. People who work in the downtown business district want to live in the city, and a market survey has shown that they would rather rent apartments than take out large loans to own expensive downtown real estate. — [2] —. Developers have taken advantage of this trend, constructing high-rise apartment buildings in and around the district. — [3] —. Although many new apartment complexes have been built, monthly rental fees continue to rise due to high demand for units in Stanton. — [4] —. Real estate experts predict that the pattern will continue for a few more years before demand is satisfied.

169. What is the article mainly about?

(A) The popularity of multi-story buildings
(B) High rental housing demand in an area
(C) The declining price of urban real estate
(D) Forecasted patterns of growth in the suburbs

170. What is suggested about Stanton's rental housing market?

(A) It has already reached its peak.
(B) It is expected to slow down considerably.
(C) It will maintain its current growth for a while.
(D) It is being affected by high unemployment.

171. In which of the positions marked [1], [2], [3], and [4] does the following sentence best belong?

"However, the rising costs have not prevented people from renting."

(A) [1]
(B) [2]
(C) [3]
(D) [4]

GO ON TO THE NEXT PAGE

Questions 172-175 refer to the following memo.

Date: May 5
To: All staff
From: Joel Smith, Human Resources Director
Subject: Employee benefits

Hello everyone,

There has been much discussion among the managers about the company's benefits package. When Smartech first opened, we could only provide basic health insurance to employees. — [1] —.

Since the company was founded three years ago, however, we have experienced significant revenue growth. — [2] —. Therefore, we have decided to improve our staff benefits package. Starting July 1, basic dental care will be provided. — [3] —. Employees will also have the option of paying extra for more dental insurance coverage. To take advantage of this, simply fill out an application and bring it to the human resources department.

An updated employee manual with information about this benefit change will be sent to all staff members next week. — [4] —. If you have any questions, please feel free to e-mail me at j.smith@smartech.com or to stop by my office. Thank you.

Best wishes,

Joel Smith

172. What is NOT mentioned about Smartech?

(A) Its revenues have increased.
(B) It has provided health insurance since its founding.
(C) Its employees receive annual bonuses.
(D) It was established three years ago.

173. How can employees acquire additional insurance coverage?

(A) By contacting a supervisor
(B) By choosing an option online
(C) By submitting a medical report
(D) By paying an additional charge

174. What will happen next week?

(A) A policy will be implemented.
(B) A document will be distributed.
(C) A contract will be negotiated.
(D) A staff meeting will be scheduled.

175. In which of the positions marked [1], [2], [3], and [4] does the following sentence best belong?

"This will cover the costs of regular checkups and cleaning but not major dental work."

(A) [1]
(B) [2]
(C) [3]
(D) [4]

Launch Technologies Recalls Laptops

At a press conference on May 13, Launch Technologies CEO Jasmine Hong stated that the company has issued a recall for two of its laptops—the Edge XL and the Glide 780. Over 750,000 units of these models have been sold over the past year, making this recall larger than any others the company has ever had before.

According to Ms. Hong, the Edge XL has a defective power cable. This component is prone to overheating when the computer is running, in some cases causing the laptop to catch on fire. "Although there have been only a few reported instances of this, we take the safety of our customers very seriously. That is why we are asking everyone who purchased this laptop to return it immediately," said Ms. Hong. The company decided to recall the Glide 780 at the same time because it has a faulty hard drive that causes it to shut down unexpectedly.

Customers who own either model are eligible to receive a full refund and a $200 voucher that can be used for any Launch Technologies product.

Product Return Form
Launch Technologies
2839 Cumberland Road
Wheeling, WV 26003

■**Customer Information**   **Date:** May 14

Name: Garret Brewer   **E-mail:** gbrewer@breweraccounting.com
Phone Number: 555-4119   **Home address:** 990 Park Road, Suite 314, Columbus, OH 43203

Product Name	Quantity	Reason
Edge XL	7	Product recalled by manufacturer

■**Comments**

I purchased these computers to be used by the staff working at the company I own. Obviously, having to return them is a significant inconvenience. I would like my refund request to be processed by May 16 so that I can order replacements immediately. The amount owed to me should be refunded to the corporate credit card that I used to make the original purchase. If you require additional information, you can reach me at the number provided above. Thank you.

176. In the article, the word "issued" in paragraph 1, line 3, is closest in meaning to

(A) decided
(B) distributed
(C) recognized
(D) announced

177. What can be inferred about Launch Technologies?

(A) It has released a laptop within the past month.
(B) It has recalled products previously.
(C) It was established over a decade ago.
(D) It has recently hired a new CEO.

178. What will buyers of the Edge XL and the Glide 780 receive?

(A) A free software program
(B) A discount on a computer accessory
(C) Complimentary repair services
(D) Credit for a future purchase

179. Who most likely is Mr. Brewer?

(A) A product inspector
(B) A business owner
(C) A computer technician
(D) A factory worker

180. What is indicated about the devices purchased by Mr. Brewer?

(A) They came with replacement components.
(B) They turn off without warning.
(C) They become hot while being operated.
(D) They require hard drive upgrades.

GO ON TO THE NEXT PAGE

Questions 181-185 refer to the following Web page and online review.

Captain Jack's Seafood

About	Menu	Location	Reviews

Located on Bridgeport Beach, Captain Jack's Seafood was founded over a decade ago by Jack Hoult, a local fisherman who dreamed of opening his own seafood restaurant. This restaurant faced a lot of competition from nearby seafood establishments in its early years. However, Mr. Hoult's dedication to providing fresh, well-prepared dishes has made Captain Jack's Seafood a popular eatery. In fact, *Food & Drink Magazine* has named Captain Jack's Seafood in many of its articles as the best seafood restaurant in Bridgeport.

Captain Jack's Seafood is known for its signature seafood dishes like lobster and crab cakes. And its delicious drinks are favorites among locals. Try one of several daily specials offered at reasonable prices:

Thursdays – Crab Cakes	**Fridays** – Fish and Chips
Saturdays – Fried Squid	**Sundays** – Lobster

Arrive before 6 P.M., and you will also receive a coupon for your next visit. Reservations are recommended. To book a table, call 555-2243.

Captain Jack's Seafood

About	Menu	Location	Reviews

Name: Carmen Vasquez
Rating: ★★★☆☆

I went to Captain Jack's Seafood last week expecting to be amazed. My friends had told me it was the greatest seafood place in town and that there was a large selection of items on the menu. When I got there, however, there was a 30-minute wait, despite it being only 5 P.M. on Thursday. After standing outside the restaurant for a while, I was finally seated. But it took another 10 minutes for a waiter to give me a menu. I ordered a cocktail and the special of the day, and then the waiter disappeared for another 40 minutes before bringing me my food.

Overall, I would give Captain Jack's Seafood three stars. The food and beverages were excellent, and the atmosphere was very welcoming. But the staff members need to learn how to address their customers' needs more quickly and efficiently.

181. What is stated about Captain Jack's Seafood?

(A) Its menu was changed recently.
(B) It has been recognized by a publication.
(C) Its chefs are mostly fishermen.
(D) It has multiple locations.

182. According to the web page, what do locals especially enjoy at Captain Jack's Seafood?

(A) Nice surrounding views
(B) Tasty beverages
(C) Polite waiters
(D) Healthy food choices

183. What dish did Ms. Vasquez most likely order?

(A) Crab Cakes
(B) Fish and Chips
(C) Fried Squid
(D) Lobster

184. What can be inferred about Ms. Vasquez?

(A) She subscribes to a food magazine.
(B) She sat at an outdoor table.
(C) She recently moved to Bridgeport.
(D) She received a coupon for future use.

185. In the online review, the word "address" in paragraph 2, line 3, is closest in meaning to

(A) comply
(B) record
(C) talk to
(D) deal with

GO ON TO THE NEXT PAGE

Questions 186-190 refer to the following e-mails and schedule.

To	Tom Gonzales <t.gonzales@gomail.com>
From	Cecilia Wiggins <c.wiggins@topsmile.net>
Subject	Sudden change
Date	May 25

Dear Mr. Gonzales,

I regret to inform you that Dr. Makata will not be available on the date you requested for your oral health checkup. I realize that you made this appointment on April 12. However, Dr. Makata was asked to fill in for a colleague and will be at a conference in El Paso on the day scheduled for you. She is not due back in the office until June 16. Could we possibly move your appointment to the following week? I could schedule an appointment for your preferred time of 10 A.M. Please let me know.

Sincerely,

Cecilia Wiggins

15th Southern Regional Dental Conference
June 12 to 14, Bamba Hotel, El Paso, Texas

Schedule for Saturday, June 14

Time	Event	Location	Speaker
8:00 – 11:30 A.M.	Workshop: Dental Photography and Digital Processing	Javelina Hall	Dr. Stephen Gentry
9:00 – 11:30 A.M.	Lecture: Material Selection for Dental Surgery	Oryx Room	Dr. Warren Francis
11:30 A.M. – 1:30 P.M.	Lunch Break		
1:30 – 2:30 P.M.	Workshop: Excellence in Patient Customer Service	Javelina Hall	Dr. Janine Kirst
1:30 – 3:00 P.M.	Meeting: Financial Strategies for New Dentists	Oryx Room	Dr. Heather Wallace
2:00 – 4:30 P.M.	Lecture: Issues Surrounding Patient Insurance	Finch Room	Dr. Noemi Makata

Note: Members may attend any lecture or meeting free of charge. However, a fee may be charged for attending a workshop. All fees may be refunded in the event of cancellation.

To: Kyle Green <k.green@srdc.org>
From: Larry Ayala <l.ayala@bamba.com>
Subject: Your concern
Date: June 13

Dear Mr. Green,

We asked our engineers to check the air conditioner in Javelina Hall. Unfortunately, it will need repairs, and the earliest these can be done is tomorrow morning. I apologize for the inconvenience, but this means we will have to cancel the event for the Southern Regional Dental Conference being held in that hall before lunchtime tomorrow. By the way, I spoke to Ms. Lopez regarding your concern about the temperature of the buffet food. She will make sure that any dishes left out are kept warm until the lunch break ends. If you need further assistance, you may contact me at my mobile phone number, 555-4106.

Warmly,

Larry Ayala
Bamba Hotel

186. Who most likely is Ms. Wiggins?

(A) A facility owner
(B) An event coordinator
(C) A conference speaker
(D) A clinic receptionist

187. When was Mr. Gonzales supposed to meet with Dr. Makata?

(A) On April 12
(B) On May 25
(C) On June 14
(D) On June 16

188. What is NOT mentioned about Dr. Makata?

(A) She will return to work on June 16.
(B) She will be present at a morning workshop.
(C) She will be filling in for an associate.
(D) She will speak at an event.

189. What can be inferred about the Southern Regional Dental Conference?

(A) Dr. Francis' lecture will be canceled.
(B) Its lunch will have additional meal options.
(C) Dr. Kirst's event might be delayed.
(D) Some of its workshop participants will be refunded.

190. What is Mr. Green's concern?

(A) A room might be too crowded.
(B) Some food will become cold.
(C) A manager will be unreachable.
(D) Some materials might be distributed late.

GO ON TO THE NEXT PAGE

Thumping Thursdays at the Billings Hotel

Join us after work at Gordon's Grill for great music, food, and wine! Grab a chair on the veranda or take a seat on the lawn while enjoying live music. We are open for dinner from 5 P.M. to 10 P.M. The dates and musicians for live music performances are noted below. All performances will run from 6 P.M. to 8 P.M., if the weather permits. Per city regulations, alcoholic beverages are not allowed on the lawn. Go to www.billingshotel.com for more details.

July 10: Mister Misty	August 14: Roxy Blues
July 17: Elder Lake	August 21: Terry Crank
July 24: Roxy Blues	August 28: Mister Misty
July 31: Mister Misty	September 4: Roxy Blues
August 7: Elder Lake	September 11: Mister Misty

To	Walt Galvin <galvinw@stompmail.com>
From	Pauline Eagan <eaganp@bluemail.com>
Subject	Possible shows
Date	July 4

Walt,

Do you remember when I left my business card with Dena Harris, the event director at the Billings Hotel? Well, she contacted me today to ask if you and your fellow members of Deacon Delta would be willing to play at a hotel event called Thumping Thursdays. Apparently, she had originally booked Roxy Blues, but they backed out when they were invited to play at a blues festival in Edinburgh. She'd like you to cover all of their time slots. Currently, I only have your band scheduled to perform on Friday nights at the Cowhead Lounge, so you'll have plenty of time for these performances. I've already told Ms. Harris that Deacon Delta is available for the event, so please confirm that you can take the job.

Pauline

TRIP TALES
www.triptales.com

Home > Accommodations Reviews > Billings Hotel Reviews

Mississippi Dreaming ★★★★☆
Posted on September 20 by Isabel Calhoun

I stayed at this hotel earlier this month for three nights and four days while attending a friend's wedding that was held there. The rooms were basic but comfortable and included free Wi-Fi. The breakfast buffet at the Polk Room was decent, though I much preferred the food at the hotel's other restaurant, Gordon's Grill. The hotel also had a great blues band called Mister Misty on the first night I ate there. Nearby, there was plenty to do and see. My only complaint about this entire trip was getting woken up at 8 A.M. by construction noise outside my window. I discovered later that this happened because the hotel is building a new wing. Overall, the hotel offered good value and great fun, and I highly recommend it to other travelers, particularly those who enjoy blues music.

191. According to the flyer, what could cause organizers to cancel a musical event?

(A) City regulations
(B) Inclement weather
(C) Ongoing renovations
(D) Another event reservation

192. Who most likely is Ms. Eagan?

(A) An event director
(B) A restaurant owner
(C) A band manager
(D) An amateur musician

193. What is indicated about Deacon Delta?

(A) It may have to reschedule a concert in Edinburgh.
(B) It has performed with Roxy Blues in the past.
(C) It auditioned for a spot at a music festival.
(D) It might be scheduled for three shows at the Billings Hotel.

194. When did Ms. Calhoun probably see Mister Misty's performance?

(A) On July 10
(B) On August 28
(C) On September 4
(D) On September 11

195. What did Ms. Calhoun dislike about the Billings Hotel?

(A) The way her room was decorated
(B) The small selection of food items on offer
(C) The disturbances caused by some work
(D) The distance from tourist attractions

GO ON TO THE NEXT PAGE

Improve Your Self-Care with the Glider

The Glider is a multifunctional massage tool that works on all body parts. High-frequency vibrations release stress and pain and assist with physical recovery. The Glider is also a smart device, recording statistics on its use and providing live information and program suggestions. The Glider syncs with the Glider online application, which functions as your daily wellness tracker.

The Glider is already being used by professional athletes and in sports clinics. Order your device today, and become one of the thousands of satisfied customers. If you are a first-time customer, you will receive 10 percent off the Glider. Check out www.gliderdevice.net. We also welcome wholesale accounts. This September, become a wholesale partner and receive 20 percent off your order.

Glider
www.gliderdevice.net

| Home | | Shop | | About | | **Partnerships** | | Help |

Wholesale Information
The Glider is available for wholesale orders. Use and promote the device at your health clinic, workout studio, or sports organization. Apart from promoting the device on-site, we recommend that you feature it on your social media page. Uploading a promotional post about the device will entitle you to receive free accessories.

For inquiries, please contact Brianna Perez directly at b.perez@gliderdevice.net. You will be instructed by her personally on how to use the device correctly. This is a free service offered to any new wholesale account.

Pursuit Pilates Employee Notice
Week of September 14

Pursuit Pilates became an official wholesale partner of the Glider massage device last week. Through personal experience, I can say that this machine is highly effective and that our clients would benefit from using it regularly.

In connection with this development, each instructor is being asked to attend a workshop on September 30 at 7 P.M. A Glider representative will instruct us directly on the correct use of the device. Please download the accompanying Glider software application before the workshop. Lastly, I would like everyone to encourage our clients to purchase a Glider device from our studio directly. We will have a display model at reception that they can try before buying.

196. What is true about the Glider?

(A) It is the latest model in a series.
(B) It was designed by a fitness professional.
(C) It provides live feedback to users.
(D) It comes with a 30-day money-back warranty.

197. What are wholesale customers encouraged to do?

(A) Promote a device on social media
(B) Place an order on a regular basis
(C) Obtain an official certificate
(D) Sign a two-year commitment

198. What can be inferred about Pursuit Pilates?

(A) It holds online classes.
(B) It has purchased other massage tools before.
(C) It received a 20-percent discount.
(D) It had an increase in membership.

199. What is suggested about Brianna Perez?

(A) She has a degree in software engineering.
(B) She is one of the cofounders of Glider.
(C) She agreed to a meeting on September 30.
(D) She regularly works out at Pursuit Pilates.

200. What are employees at Pursuit Pilates asked to do?

(A) Download a program
(B) Install a device
(C) Attend a sales meeting
(D) Instruct a new team member

This is the end of the test. You may review Parts 5, 6, and 7 if you finish the test early.

分數換算表 p. 244 / 正確答案、翻譯、解析〔解析本〕p. 133

▌請根據下一頁的 Review 檢查表複習答錯的題目

/Review 檢查表

完成 TEST 4 後，請根據下表檢視自己答錯的問題，並在框框中打勾。
如果距離考試時間不多，請務必檢查**粗體字**的項目。

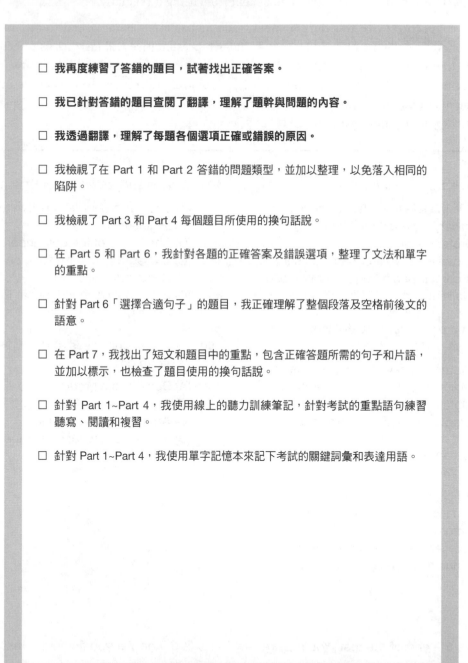

☐ **我再度練習了答錯的題目，試著找出正確答案。**

☐ **我已針對答錯的題目查閱了翻譯，理解了題幹與問題的內容。**

☐ **我透過翻譯，理解了每題各個選項正確或錯誤的原因。**

☐ 我檢視了在 Part 1 和 Part 2 答錯的問題類型，並加以整理，以免落入相同的陷阱。

☐ 我檢視了 Part 3 和 Part 4 每個題目所使用的換句話說。

☐ 在 Part 5 和 Part 6，我針對各題的正確答案及錯誤選項，整理了文法和單字的重點。

☐ 針對 Part 6「選擇合適句子」的題目，我正確理解了整個段落及空格前後文的語意。

☐ 在 Part 7，我找出了短文和題目中的重點，包含正確答題所需的句子和片語，並加以標示，也檢查了題目使用的換句話說。

☐ 針對 Part 1~Part 4，我使用線上的聽力訓練筆記，針對考試的重點語句練習聽寫、閱讀和複習。

☐ 針對 Part 1~Part 4，我使用單字記憶本來記下考試的關鍵詞彙和表達用語。

大量練習題目固然重要，但好好檢視自己答錯的問題也同樣關鍵。
只要仔細複習一遍答錯的題目，就能在短時間內有效達到目標分數。

NEW TOEIC 950
聽力+閱讀 5 回達標

TEST 5

LISTENING TEST

Part 1
Part 2
Part 3
Part 4

READING TEST

Part 5
Part 6
Part 7

Review 檢查表

注意！ 測驗前請務必檢查下列事項。

手機是否關機？
Answer Sheet（p. 255）、鉛筆、橡皮擦和手錶是否準備好了？
準備好聆聽音檔了嗎？

準備就緒後，想著你的目標分數，開始測驗。
測驗完畢後，請務必查看 Review 檢查表（p. 236），複習答錯的題目。

🎧 Test 5.mp3
可免費下載、播放 MP3，用於答題訓練和複習

MP3 音檔

LISTENING TEST

In this section, you must demonstrate your ability to understand spoken English. This section is divided into four parts and will take approximately 45 minutes to complete. Do not mark the answers in your test book. Use the answer sheet that is provided separately.

PART 1

Directions: For each question, you will listen to four short statements about a picture in your test book. These statements will not be printed and will only be spoken one time. Select the statement that best describes what is happening in the picture and mark the corresponding letter (A), (B), (C), or (D) on the answer sheet.

Sample Answer

The statement that best describes the picture is (B), "The man is sitting at the desk." So, you should mark letter (B) on the answer sheet.

1.

2.

GO ON TO THE NEXT PAGE

3.

4.

5.

6.

GO ON TO THE NEXT PAGE ➤

PART 2

Directions: For each question, you will listen to a statement or question followed by three possible responses spoken in English. They will not be printed and will only be spoken one time. Select the best response and mark the corresponding letter (A), (B), or (C) on your answer sheet.

7. Mark your answer on your answer sheet.

8. Mark your answer on your answer sheet.

9. Mark your answer on your answer sheet.

10. Mark your answer on your answer sheet.

11. Mark your answer on your answer sheet.

12. Mark your answer on your answer sheet.

13. Mark your answer on your answer sheet.

14. Mark your answer on your answer sheet.

15. Mark your answer on your answer sheet.

16. Mark your answer on your answer sheet.

17. Mark your answer on your answer sheet.

18. Mark your answer on your answer sheet.

19. Mark your answer on your answer sheet.

20. Mark your answer on your answer sheet.

21. Mark your answer on your answer sheet.

22. Mark your answer on your answer sheet.

23. Mark your answer on your answer sheet.

24. Mark your answer on your answer sheet.

25. Mark your answer on your answer sheet.

26. Mark your answer on your answer sheet.

27. Mark your answer on your answer sheet.

28. Mark your answer on your answer sheet.

29. Mark your answer on your answer sheet.

30. Mark your answer on your answer sheet.

31. Mark your answer on your answer sheet.

PART 3

Directions: In this part, you will listen to several conversations between two or more speakers. These conversations will not be printed and will only be spoken one time. For each conversation, you will be asked to answer three questions. Select the best response and mark the corresponding letter (A), (B), (C), or (D) on your answer sheet.

32. What is the woman's problem?

    (A) She forgot to make a reservation.
    (B) She lost a personal belonging.
    (C) She left her wallet at home.
    (D) She is unhappy with a meal.

33. What does the woman want the man to do?

    (A) Move her to another table
    (B) Talk to some workers
    (C) Remove a charge from a bill
    (D) Bring her a lunch menu

34. What will the woman most likely do next?

    (A) Take a seat
    (B) Return to work
    (C) Describe an item
    (D) Place an order

35. What has been replaced?

    (A) Some seating
    (B) A reception desk
    (C) Some lobby tables
    (D) A filing cabinet

36. What did the company recently do?

    (A) Applied for a loan
    (B) Sent back merchandise
    (C) Increased profits
    (D) Hired employees

37. What does the woman agree to do?

    (A) Summarize a meeting
    (B) Contact some clients
    (C) Suggest some ideas
    (D) Look over a budget

38. What is the man's problem?

    (A) He cannot contact a client.
    (B) He has a scheduling conflict.
    (C) He forgot about an appointment.
    (D) He missed a deadline.

39. Why does the man say, "Your team created it"?

    (A) To remind her that she agreed to help
    (B) To indicate that she is familiar with a project
    (C) To commend her for being a valued employee
    (D) To show her that there is a problem

40. What will the woman most likely do next?

    (A) Meet with a CEO
    (B) Cancel a project
    (C) Visit a factory
    (D) Review a document

41. What are the speakers mainly discussing?

    (A) Expenses for a retreat
    (B) Parking spaces for vans
    (C) Directions to a camp
    (D) Transportation to an event

42. What does the woman want to know about?

    (A) How much a shuttle bus will cost
    (B) Whether an employee has a van
    (C) Who will drive a rental vehicle
    (D) Where a parking garage is located

43. What will the man most likely do next?

    (A) Take a bus ride
    (B) Make a phone call
    (C) Register for an event
    (D) Compare some prices

GO ON TO THE NEXT PAGE

44. What is the conversation mainly about?

(A) Selecting a hotel room
(B) Preparing for a vacation
(C) Choosing an activity
(D) Paying for a trip

45. What is mentioned about Rachel?

(A) She went to the spa.
(B) She is interested in surfing lessons.
(C) She lives in Hawaii.
(D) She has a meeting at 11 o'clock.

46. What does the man give to the woman?

(A) A suitcase
(B) A souvenir
(C) A key
(D) A brochure

---

47. Who most likely is the man?

(A) A cleaning business owner
(B) A store bookkeeper
(C) A delivery truck driver
(D) A café manager

48. What was sent with a shipment?

(A) Sample goods
(B) A revised bill
(C) Office supplies
(D) A special coupon

49. What does the man ask the woman to do?

(A) Write an e-mail
(B) Send some packages
(C) Use a voucher
(D) Return some products

---

50. Where most likely is the conversation taking place?

(A) At a bookstore
(B) At a library
(C) At a publishing expo
(D) At a broadcasting studio

51. What does the woman say about *Voting for Peanuts*?

(A) It was released after *The Old Bride*.
(B) It is shelved behind the help desk.
(C) It was publicized in the media.
(D) It was written by a talk show host.

52. Why does the man say, "I heard it was popular"?

(A) To express excitement
(B) To indicate a lack of surprise
(C) To explain a decision
(D) To recommend a new book

---

53. What does the man say about *Help Yourself*?

(A) It was filmed this year.
(B) It is playing at a local theater.
(C) It features a well-known actor.
(D) It deals with food choices.

54. What type of service do the speakers most likely offer?

(A) Product advertising
(B) Nutritional consulting
(C) Video sales
(D) Career advice

55. What does the man suggest?

(A) Viewing a documentary
(B) Waiting in another room
(C) Filming a commercial
(D) Uploading materials online

56. What is the conversation mainly about?

(A) Launching a campaign
(B) Saving money on utilities
(C) Preventing environmental pollution
(D) Trying a new water source

57. In which department does the man work?

(A) Accounting
(B) Shipping
(C) Human Resources
(D) Maintenance

58. What do the women decide to do?

(A) Reschedule a meeting
(B) Collect some deliveries
(C) Order a new system
(D) Get some price quotes

59. What is the woman trying to do?

(A) Plan some entertainment
(B) Convince a friend to join her
(C) Promote a community event
(D) Get tickets to a museum

60. What does the man recommend?

(A) Having a picnic in the park
(B) Visiting a shopping center
(C) Watching a performance
(D) Taking a countryside tour

61. What does the man say he will do?

(A) Inquire about a building address
(B) Share an online link
(C) Confirm performance times
(D) List some attractions

> ### Helga's Dry Cleaning
> Helga Kim, Facility Owner
>
> **Phone Number**: 555-6922
> **Daily Hours**: 9 A.M.–7 P.M.
> **Street Address**: 37 Pine Road
> **E-mail Address**: helga@cleanwiz.net

62. Why is the woman visiting the shop?

(A) To verify an amount
(B) To make a complaint
(C) To select some materials
(D) To collect some items

63. Look at the graphic. What information contains an error?

(A) Phone Number
(B) Street Address
(C) Daily Hours
(D) E-mail Address

64. What will take 10 minutes to be completed?

(A) Cleaning some garments
(B) Fixing a photocopier
(C) Filling out a form
(D) Printing new cards

GO ON TO THE NEXT PAGE

TEST 5 NEW TOEIC 950 聽力＋閱讀 5 回達標

Room	Maximum Capacity
Majesty Hall	100 people
Throne Hall	150 people
Scepter Hall	200 people
Royalty Hall	250 people

	Bronze Plan	Silver Plan	Gold Plan	Platinum Plan
free domestic calls	v	v	v	v
free international calls				v
unlimited texts		v	v	v
unlimited internet			v	v

65. Why is the woman calling?

(A) To sign up for an event
(B) To inquire about a conference speaker
(C) To ask about a facility's location
(D) To update a reservation

66. Look at the graphic. Which room did the woman originally book?

(A) Majesty Hall
(B) Throne Hall
(C) Scepter Hall
(D) Royalty Hall

67. What does the woman request?

(A) Additional food
(B) Presentation equipment
(C) An updated list of rooms
(D) Extra guest passes

68. Why does the woman want to change her service plan?

(A) She has established new business relationships.
(B) She needs an additional phone line.
(C) She wants to upgrade to a smart phone.
(D) She is going on an international business trip.

69. Look at the graphic. Which plan does the man recommend?

(A) Bronze Plan
(B) Silver Plan
(C) Gold Plan
(D) Platinum Plan

70. What will the man probably do next?

(A) Provide a free gift
(B) Collect a payment
(C) Update an account
(D) Make a telephone call

PART 4

Directions: In this part, you will listen to several short talks by a single speaker. These talks will not be printed and will only be spoken one time. For each talk, you will be asked to answer three questions. Select the best response and mark the corresponding letter (A), (B), (C), or (D) on your answer sheet.

71. What was supposed to be discussed tomorrow?

(A) A work schedule
(B) A project cancellation
(C) A job opportunity
(D) A sales proposition

72. Why must a meeting be postponed?

(A) A family matter needs to be handled.
(B) A flight was overbooked.
(C) A worker is traveling overseas.
(D) An office manager is feeling ill.

73. What does the speaker ask the listener to do?

(A) Stop by her office
(B) Contact her assistant
(C) Call her mobile phone
(D) Send her an e-mail

74. What is still taking place?

(A) A running race
(B) A sign installation
(C) Building construction
(D) Bridge repairs

75. What will probably happen within the hour?

(A) A further update will be provided.
(B) A community event will begin.
(C) Cars will be moved from an area.
(D) A hospital will reopen.

76. What does the speaker recommend?

(A) Using a different route
(B) Starting a commute early
(C) Taking public transport
(D) Avoiding an intersection

77. What is the company planning to do?

(A) Relocate its headquarters
(B) Order some chemicals
(C) Open a new plant
(D) Transfer some employees

78. Why does the speaker say, "Actually, it's near a residential area"?

(A) To dismiss a potential concern
(B) To highlight a convenient location
(C) To suggest moving a facility
(D) To point out a complicating factor

79. What is the speaker concerned about?

(A) Financial costs
(B) Environmental pollution
(C) A production schedule
(D) A government policy

80. What is the speaker mainly discussing?

(A) Advice on working relationships
(B) Guidance for job seekers
(C) Selecting a career path
(D) Pursuing job training

81. What does the speaker imply when he says, "You'd be surprised"?

(A) A document includes few errors.
(B) A process has become more complicated.
(C) A requirement is relatively new.
(D) A problem can easily occur.

82. According to the speaker, what can leave a bad impression?

(A) Long cover letters
(B) Insufficient experience
(C) Spelling mistakes
(D) Inappropriate attire

GO ON TO THE NEXT PAGE

83. Who most likely is the speaker?

(A) A facility manager
(B) A government official
(C) A professional athlete
(D) A corporate investor

84. What will the CRT Center be used for?

(A) Charity auctions
(B) Sporting events
(C) Industry conventions
(D) Community gatherings

85. What is mentioned about Kent Berkley?

(A) He oversaw some construction.
(B) He recently met with a mayor.
(C) He supported a project.
(D) He plans to give a talk.

---

86. Who most likely is the listener?

(A) A concert organizer
(B) A music instructor
(C) A school secretary
(D) A store owner

87. What is the main purpose of the message?

(A) To respond to a question
(B) To book a performer
(C) To sign up for a class
(D) To get a suggestion

88. Why does the speaker say, "I'm flexible"?

(A) He has an open schedule.
(B) He has no brand preference.
(C) He is available to take a course.
(D) He is a fan of different performers.

---

89. Where most likely are the listeners?

(A) At a recruitment interview
(B) At a trade show
(C) At a retirement celebration
(D) At a holiday party

90. According to the speaker, why was a campaign significant?

(A) It attracted foreign media attention.
(B) It won an award.
(C) It used new technology.
(D) It helped grow a business.

91. What does the speaker say she values the most?

(A) The dedication of her employees
(B) The purpose of her project
(C) Her overseas experience
(D) Her relationships with coworkers

---

92. What is the report mainly about?

(A) Establishing an additional school
(B) Training some teachers
(C) Appointing a new principal
(D) Expanding current curriculum

93. What did Yolanda Moya announce yesterday?

(A) The location of an office
(B) The size of a program
(C) The cost of a development
(D) The length of a project

94. What is mentioned about some parents?

(A) They do not want kids to be relocated.
(B) They voted on an issue last week.
(C) They accept a government plan.
(D) They think expenses should be lowered.

Product Specification	
Product Weight	**Price**
20 lbs	$2,000
25 lbs	$1,750
28 lbs	$1,000
35 lbs	$2,200

PRODUCTION LINE

95. What kind of product is being demonstrated?

(A) A cleaning appliance
(B) A digital printer
(C) A musical instrument
(D) A flat screen television

96. According to the speaker, what is on the front panel?

(A) A display screen
(B) Control buttons
(C) A power switch
(D) Warning indicators

97. Look at the graphic. How much does the TouchFone 1000 cost?

(A) $2,000
(B) $1,750
(C) $1,000
(D) $2,200

98. What is the characteristic of Dwyers' Sweets?

(A) It produces 100 types of candy.
(B) It has opened a second location.
(C) It operates a century-old facility.
(D) It has remained a family-owned business.

99. Look at the graphic. Where will the tour group go next?

(A) Area 1
(B) Area 2
(C) Area 3
(D) Area 4

100. What will the listeners receive after the tour?

(A) Samples of candy
(B) A list of best sellers
(C) Locations of international stores
(D) A set of gift vouchers

This is the end of the Listening test. Turn to PART 5 in your test book.

READING TEST

In this section, you must demonstrate your ability to read and comprehend English. You will be given a variety of texts and asked to answer questions about these texts. This section is divided into three parts and will take 75 minutes to complete.

Do not mark the answers in your test book. Use the answer sheet that is separately provided.

PART 5

Directions: In each question, you will be asked to review a statement that is missing a word or phrase. Four answer choices will be provided for each statement. Select the best answer and mark the corresponding letter (A), (B), (C), or (D) on the answer sheet.

🕐 **PART 5** 建議作答時間 **11 分鐘**

101. Visitors must present ------- when entering the research facility or accessing sensitive areas.

    (A) identification
    (B) identity
    (C) identified
    (D) identifying

102. Orex Enterprises' ------- focus is still fashion, although it has expanded into the restaurant business.

    (A) high
    (B) multiple
    (C) primary
    (D) outside

103. Mr. Kurtz was extremely ------- with the contract negotiations, which resulted in a 15-percent salary increase.

    (A) pleased
    (B) pleasing
    (C) please
    (D) pleasure

104. Only ------- who submit a résumé through the company's website will be considered for the intern position.

    (A) neither
    (B) that
    (C) those
    (D) which

105. Pete's Produce is well-known for ------- selling organic fruit and vegetables.

    (A) exclusively
    (B) exclusion
    (C) exclude
    (D) exclusive

106. By the time SolarTech opened its first factory in Europe, it ------- facilities in America and Asia already.

    (A) is establishing
    (B) has established
    (C) establishes
    (D) had established

107. Staff members at Flemwell Department Store ------- work overtime during the busy holiday season.

    (A) routed
    (B) routine
    (C) routines
    (D) routinely

108. Air East passengers are advised to use the automated check-in machines ------- the airport.

    (A) upon
    (B) throughout
    (C) between
    (D) almost

109. Customers can ------- unexpected fees by applying for a cellular plan that provides unlimited texting and data usage.

(A) prepare
(B) shorten
(C) comply
(D) avoid

110. Employees must contact the human resources department ------- request a leave of absence.

(A) after all
(B) in order to
(C) as for
(D) just

111. Under the ------- of the lease agreement, the tenant must give a month's notice before moving out.

(A) terms
(B) rights
(C) causes
(D) signs

112. This Wednesday is ------- the name of Zoltek Engineering's new CEO will be announced.

(A) when
(B) what
(C) why
(D) who

113. Athletes ------- more than 50 countries participated in the World Tennis Tournament held last year in Guangzhou.

(A) representing
(B) represented
(C) represents
(D) representation

114. The continued ------- of residents from rural to urban areas has created a housing shortage in Manila.

(A) arrangement
(B) relocation
(C) environment
(D) discovery

115. Details about the upcoming training workshop will begin to ------- following the announcement.

(A) compile
(B) include
(C) appoint
(D) emerge

116. All discussions regarding the potential company merger have been put on hold ------- the first week of February.

(A) about
(B) towards
(C) until
(D) except

117. Mr. Ross was considered an ------- candidate for the marketing position because he lacked professional experience.

(A) inadequately
(B) inadequacy
(C) inadequate
(D) inadequateness

118. Although participation in HPS Company's social responsibility committee is purely -------, employee involvement is very high.

(A) precise
(B) voluntary
(C) significant
(D) persistent

119. New boxes placed by the library's main entrance allow patrons ------- materials even after the facility has closed.

(A) return
(B) returned
(C) returning
(D) to return

120. Because *SharpBiz* Magazine is published -------, readers get updates on essential business news four times per year.

(A) quarterly
(B) properly
(C) constantly
(D) recently

GO ON TO THE NEXT PAGE

121. According to recent surveys, advertisements on television have a greater ------- on consumers than those found in newspapers and magazines.

(A) influence
(B) influential
(C) influenced
(D) have influenced

122. Edgecom will issue a statement today ------- the status of the company's overseas expansion.

(A) behind
(B) beyond
(C) regarding
(D) within

123. Customers who exceed the monthly mobile data allocation will ------- additional charges.

(A) replace
(B) incur
(C) switch
(D) possess

124. Mayfield Footwear's summer sale will be a good ------- for shoppers to purchase a variety of new shoes.

(A) opportunity
(B) contribution
(C) appearance
(D) restoration

125. Software products from Digital Age can be refunded within one month of purchase ------- they are accompanied by an original receipt.

(A) on behalf of
(B) although
(C) so that
(D) as long as

126. The revised environmental regulations ------- at reducing the amount of greenhouse gases emitted by local factories.

(A) aims
(B) aiming
(C) to aim
(D) are aimed

127. ------- did the buyers like the price of the house, but they also appreciated its location.

(A) Neither
(B) Not only
(C) Either
(D) Such as

128. To qualify for financial -------, students must submit a funding request each term.

(A) assistance
(B) assisted
(C) to assist
(D) assistant

129. Nesbit Software ------- its sales projections as it expects revenues to decrease this year.

(A) overtook
(B) connected
(C) reduced
(D) complimented

130. The ------- laptop model released by Core Electronics was much more popular with customers than its latest one.

(A) various
(B) relative
(C) customary
(D) previous

PART 6

Directions: In this part, you will be asked to read four English texts. Each text is missing a word, phrase, or sentence. Select the answer choice that correctly completes the text and mark the corresponding letter (A), (B), (C), or (D) on the answer sheet.

PART 6 建議作答時間 **8 分鐘**

Questions 131-134 refer to the following e-mail.

To: Allan White <a.white@trytek.com>
From: Joseph Winfield <j.winfield@trytek.com>
Date: March 12
Subject: Orientation Seminar

Dear Allan,

I'm glad to report that the planning of our orientation seminar for new interns is proceeding smoothly. However, one important detail remains unresolved. We still need to schedule a short presentation by someone from the marketing department, but I have not heard from anyone who would ------- in the seminar. -------. So, please let everyone know that the

131. **132.**

presenter will talk about the interns' ------- duties for only 10 minutes. -------, you should

133. **134.**

remind everyone that contributors to the seminar will receive $200 as compensation for their time and effort.

Thank you very much,

Joe

---

131. (A) have liked participating
(B) have liked to participate
(C) like participating
(D) like to participate

132. (A) Presenters have already begun rehearsing their speeches.
(B) Staff members might think that it will take too much time.
(C) New members have also joined to talk about their experiences.
(D) Participation is mandatory for specified employees.

133. (A) anxious
(B) momentary
(C) regular
(D) ongoing

134. (A) Unfortunately
(B) In addition
(C) Namely
(D) Nevertheless

GO ON TO THE NEXT PAGE

Questions 135-138 refer to the following advertisement.

Madison Woodworks
Established 1987

Planning to ------- your home or office? Complement your new interior with finely crafted
                135.
items from Madison Woodworks. For over 30 years, we have supplied quality handmade

goods to homes and businesses throughout Chesterfield County. Whether you like

traditional or contemporary styles, you are sure to find something in our store to enjoy for

years to come. If you prefer more ------- items, consult one of our in-house designers about
                               136.
creating a unique table, desk, or chair. Stop by our store today at 627 Stockport Lane in

Manchester. Take advantage of discounts on all ready-made ------- until the end of July.
                                                            137.
You can also view our catalog online. -------.
                                      138.

135. (A) leave
     (B) renovate
     (C) finance
     (D) promote

136. (A) personalize
     (B) personalizes
     (C) personalizing
     (D) personalized

137. (A) fabric
     (B) gadgets
     (C) furniture
     (D) structures

138. (A) A team of technicians has been
         scheduled to inspect the product in
         your home.
     (B) The items can be replaced if you
         provide us with this warranty card.
     (C) Use the included instruction manual
         and a few simple tools to assemble it.
     (D) Go to www.madisonwoodworks.com
         to browse our entire collection.

Questions 139-142 refer to the following memo.

To: All staff
From: Jason Fraser, Human resources
Date: August 5
Subject: Professional development classes

Management is happy to announce that, beginning this fall, staff members of Hearthstone

Appliances will be ------- to receive financial support for academic courses related to their
                       139.
areas of responsibility. Participating employees will be reimbursed for 50 percent of their

total tuition fees. -------.
                   140.
Only employees ------- a class delivered by an approved educational institution may
              141.
receive funding. In addition, there are some other restrictions that may prevent certain

individuals from participating. -------, we strongly recommend scheduling a meeting with a
                              142.
human resources representative before registering for a class.

139. (A) eligible
(B) prominent
(C) social
(D) preferable

140. (A) This amount will be paid upon
successful completion of their chosen
programs.
(B) District managers are required to lead
at least 20 hours of instruction.
(C) Employees of the school will receive
discounts on textbooks and other
materials.
(D) Applications for the job opening will
be collected by the human resources
department.

141. (A) take
(B) takes
(C) taking
(D) taken

142. (A) Likewise
(B) Afterward
(C) Consequently
(D) For instance

GO ON TO THE NEXT PAGE

Questions 143-146 refer to the following announcement.

PEN AND PAPER: ANNOUNCING OUR OPENING DAY

Come and celebrate our grand opening with us on November 1. Pen and Paper is a retail

------- supplying all kinds of business equipment, stationery, and other office supplies.
  143.

We are certain that whatever you require for your workspace, you will be able to ------- at
  144.

our store. Just tell our staff members what you are looking for, and they'll provide you with

a range of options to choose from. In addition to binding services, we also perform a

variety of print jobs, such as brochures and business cards.

We'll have all kinds of giveaways for any customer who ------- our store on that day. Plus,
  145.

the 100th customer will receive a $100 gift card. -------. So, make sure to join us at 550
  146.

Emerald Avenue for this special event!

---

143. (A) establish
(B) establishes
(C) established
(D) establishment

144. (A) find
(B) deliver
(C) repair
(D) exchange

145. (A) was entered
(B) enters
(C) enter
(D) entering

146. (A) It can be used for anything inside our store.
(B) The opening will be attended by our company's CEO.
(C) Our store's renovations have been completed.
(D) We will announce the winner of the prize tomorrow.

PART 7

Directions: In this part, you will be asked to read several texts, such as advertisements, articles, instant messages, or examples of business correspondence. Each text is followed by several questions. Select the best answer and mark the corresponding letter (A), (B), (C), or (D) on your answer sheet.

PART 7 建議作答時間 **54 分鐘**

Questions 147-148 refer to the following questionnaire.

Petra's Grill

It is our mission to provide you with the best dining experience possible, so we welcome customer feedback. Please fill out this short questionnaire and place it in the box beside the exit. Thank you!

Were you provided with prompt service?
---Yes   -**X**-No

How would you rate the quality of your meal?
---Excellent   -**X**-Very good   ---Satisfactory   ---Terrible

What was your main meal?
Roast chicken and a green salad with Italian dressing

Was the food worth the price?
-**X**-Yes   ---No

How frequently do you visit Petra's Grill?
---Often   ---Occasionally   ---Rarely   -**X**-This was my first visit

Comments
I think my next visit here will be better as I'll make sure to come when it's less busy. My server was dealing with a number of other tables and, although she was friendly and polite, it took a very long time for her to notice me and bring over a menu.

---

147. What can be inferred from the questionnaire?

(A) The restaurant primarily serves Italian cuisine.
(B) The customer intends to eat at Petra's Grill a second time.
(C) The dining area was recently remodeled.
(D) The menu was changed to reflect customer feedback.

148. What problem did the customer have at the restaurant?

(A) The food was cold when it arrived.
(B) There were no tables immediately available.
(C) It took a while to be acknowledged by a server.
(D) The items listed on the menu were overpriced.

GO ON TO THE NEXT PAGE

TEST 5   Part 7   **215**

Questions 149-151 refer to the following notice.

June 4 marks 50 years since Millington State Park first opened to the public. In honor of this milestone and to thank people for supporting our efforts to protect the region's wildlife, our regular entry fees of $55 per recreational vehicle, $35 per car, $25 per motorcycle, and $10 per pedestrian or cyclist will be waived from June 4 until June 10. Please note that this exemption applies only to entrance fees and not to those for organized tours, camping sites, and the rental of equipment such as boats or fishing gear. Furthermore, if you enter the park during this period but stay until June 11 or later, you will be charged the fee when you leave.

149. What is the topic of the notice?

(A) Changes to a facility's parking regulations
(B) An organization's environmental efforts
(C) Temporary free admission to a recreational area
(D) An anniversary banquet held at a state park

150. How much does it cost to enter the park on a bicycle?

(A) $10
(B) $25
(C) $35
(D) $55

151. What is suggested about Millington State Park?

(A) It charges guests based on the number of people in a car.
(B) Its organized tours are discounted for large groups.
(C) It regularly asks for financial support from the public.
(D) Its visitors can stay for multiple days.

Questions 152-153 refer to the following text message chain.

Brad Lee   9:34 A.M.
I just received a call from a tenant in one of the properties we manage. She's in Unit 202 of the Plaza Tower on Fifth Street.

Sara Godfrey   9:35 A.M.
Is she upset about the noise from the renovation work in the lobby? I've gotten a lot of complaints from the residents of that building this week.

Brad Lee   9:36 A.M.
No, that's not it. She was offered a position with a firm in Seattle. The job starts next week, so she will have to move out of the apartment this month. But she signed a one-year lease agreement. She wants to know if she will have to pay a penalty.

Sara Godfrey   9:38 A.M.
That depends She has until the end of the month to find a new tenant. Otherwise, she will have to pay.

Brad Lee   9:39 A.M.
Actually, she mentioned that her brother was interested in the apartment. I'll tell him to fill out an application this week. Then, I'll speak with the owner.

---

152. What is indicated about the Plaza Tower?

(A) It is owned by a company in Seattle.
(B) It was built less than a year ago.
(C) It has several vacant apartments.
(D) It is currently being remodeled.

153. At 9:38 A.M., what does Ms. Godfrey most likely mean when she writes, "That depends"?

(A) An agreement has not yet been signed.
(B) A building owner has been difficult to reach.
(C) A penalty will be waived if a new tenant is found.
(D) A unit might not be available after a certain date.

GO ON TO THE NEXT PAGE

Questions 154-156 refer to the following e-mail.

To: Diana Mansfield <dmans@timemail.com>
From: Herbal Greens Customer Support <cs@herbalgreens.com>
Date: August 2
Subject: Membership

Dear Ms. Mansfield,

We noticed that you have placed several orders with us over the last few months, but you have not yet signed up for a membership on our website. — [1] —. While it is still possible to buy our products without registering, there are numerous reasons to become a member.

First of all, you will no longer be required to enter your shipping address, telephone number, and credit card details each time you make a purchase. — [2] —. You will also receive updates on our weekly promotions, allowing you to see great deals you would otherwise not know about. — [3] —. Furthermore, only members can build up loyalty credit. If you join, you will earn 10 percent of the total amount you spend whenever you place an order. You can put this credit toward the cost of your next purchase or let it accumulate to use at a later time. — [4] —.

Creating an account takes less than two minutes and costs nothing. We encourage you to take advantage of Herbal Greens' membership benefits by signing up today.

Clay Lewis
Herbal Greens Customer Support

---

154. What is the purpose of the e-mail?

(A) To explain how to set up an online account
(B) To convince a customer to become a member
(C) To ask a client to change a password
(D) To describe a membership upgrade benefit

155. What is NOT mentioned about loyalty credit?

(A) It can be used to purchase items.
(B) It can only be earned by members of a website.
(C) It expires after a certain amount of time.
(D) It is acquired each time an order is paid for.

156. In which of the positions marked [1], [2], [3], and [4] does the following sentence best belong?

"This information will be automatically inputted into the necessary fields when you are ready to check out."

(A) [1]
(B) [2]
(C) [3]
(D) [4]

Questions 157-158 refer to the following advertisement.

Tam Bakery – The Best Cakes in Town!

Are you planning a birthday, wedding, or other important event? If you want the perfect cake to celebrate your special occasion, visit Tam Bakery on the corner of Harbor Street and Elm Avenue. Our talented cake designers can create works of art that are both affordable and delicious. They will work closely with you to ensure that the cake you receive is the one you envisioned. What's more, we use only the best ingredients and offer both vegan and low-fat options as well. From May 15 to June 15, we are reducing the prices of all custom cakes by 10 percent to celebrate our 10th anniversary. So, don't delay—stop by soon to begin planning your perfect cake.

For more information about Tam Bakery and the products we offer, visit our website at www.tambakery.com.

157. What is NOT mentioned about Tam Bakery's cakes?

(A) They can be made with high-quality ingredients.
(B) They can be planned by a customer.
(C) They can be purchased at a discount.
(D) They can be delivered to an event venue.

158. What is indicated about Tam Bakery?

(A) It sells merchandise online.
(B) It will be opening another branch.
(C) It has been in business for a number of years.
(D) It includes recipes on its website.

GO ON TO THE NEXT PAGE

September 7—A spokesperson for Brytwells Department Store announced today that, for the first time in 31 years, the company will change its logo. The classic red and yellow design that customers are so familiar with is being replaced by a more modern one. This is part of a wider effort to update the company's image by CEO Marcus Cathwell, who moved up into his position when Jackson Stevens retired two months ago.

For more than two decades now, Brytwells has faced stiff competition from new department stores offering more variety at cheaper prices. Several store closures have resulted each year, and another five are set to cease operations within the next 12 months. Mr. Cathwell acknowledges that the Brytwells brand is long overdue for an update and says he feels confident that the new logo will fit in well with the other changes being made to the company. These include a new contemporary store layout and the introduction of 15 clothing brands for young people.

Brytwells locations in the northeastern region of the nation, where Brytwells opened its initial store, will be the first to begin using the logo in October. Other Brytwells stores across the country will adopt the new corporate image before the end of autumn.

159. What is the article mainly about?

(A) An idea for a new store's logo
(B) The closure of a national chain
(C) Changes to a corporate symbol
(D) Competition among retailers

160. What is mentioned about Mr. Cathwell?

(A) He created a floor plan.
(B) He was hired in March.
(C) He was recently promoted.
(D) He founded a company.

161. What will most likely happen next year?

(A) Brytwells will launch a new website.
(B) Brytwells will lower prices at all locations.
(C) A number of Brytwells stores will close down.
(D) The CEO of Brytwells will resign from his position.

162. What is NOT mentioned about Brytwells?

(A) It will begin selling more products for young people.
(B) Its original branch will relocate.
(C) It opened its first store in the northeast.
(D) It has branches throughout the country.

NOTICE

Hopewell Productions will be filming a scene from *A New Life* on July 8. This feature-length film stars Christina Harvey and Mike Mann and is being directed by Herbert Mercer.

Anyone over the age of 18 is invited to audition as an extra. The casting call for extras will take place at West Newton High School on July 1 from noon until 8 P.M., and all participants must bring a driver's license, a passport, or some other type of official photo identification.

Extras will be used primarily as crowd members for a short sequence that takes place in a mall. The shoot will take 10 to 12 hours and involve a lot of standing and waiting around. Food will be provided, and a raffle for small prizes will be held at the end. The pay will be $9 an hour.

163. According to the notice, what is Hopewell Productions encouraging people to do?

(A) Work on a catering crew
(B) Set up equipment
(C) Conduct tours of a set
(D) Appear in a scene

164. What should participants bring to West Newton High School?

(A) A bank statement
(B) A résumé and cover letter
(C) A form of identification
(D) A recording of a performance

165. What is mentioned about the shoot?

(A) It will last for several days.
(B) It will include a prize drawing.
(C) It will mostly take place outside.
(D) It will start at noon.

GO ON TO THE NEXT PAGE

Questions 166-169 refer to the following e-mail.

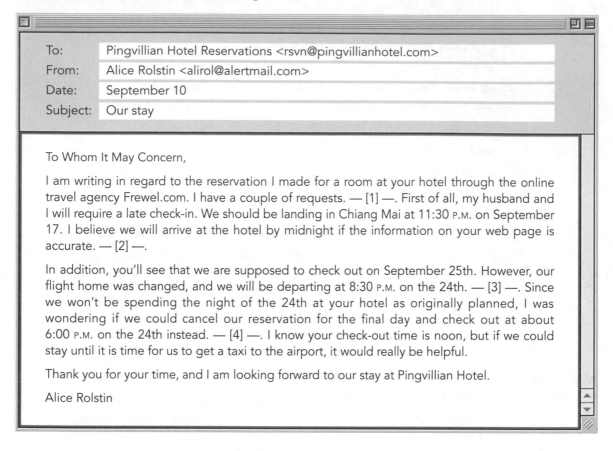

To: Pingvillian Hotel Reservations <rsvn@pingvillianhotel.com>

From: Alice Rolstin <alirol@alertmail.com>

Date: September 10

Subject: Our stay

To Whom It May Concern,

I am writing in regard to the reservation I made for a room at your hotel through the online travel agency Frewel.com. I have a couple of requests. — [1] —. First of all, my husband and I will require a late check-in. We should be landing in Chiang Mai at 11:30 P.M. on September 17. I believe we will arrive at the hotel by midnight if the information on your web page is accurate. — [2] —.

In addition, you'll see that we are supposed to check out on September 25th. However, our flight home was changed, and we will be departing at 8:30 P.M. on the 24th. — [3] —. Since we won't be spending the night of the 24th at your hotel as originally planned, I was wondering if we could cancel our reservation for the final day and check out at about 6:00 P.M. on the 24th instead. — [4] —. I know your check-out time is noon, but if we could stay until it is time for us to get a taxi to the airport, it would really be helpful.

Thank you for your time, and I am looking forward to our stay at Pingvillian Hotel.

Alice Rolstin

---

166. What is true about Ms. Rolstin?

(A) She made a reservation through a website.

(B) She will arrive at the hotel earlier than scheduled.

(C) She will be staying in Chiang Mai until next month.

(D) She has booked two rooms at the Pingvillian Hotel.

167. The word "originally" in paragraph 2, line 3, is closest in meaning to

(A) uniquely

(B) completely

(C) differently

(D) initially

168. What does Ms. Rolstin ask for?

(A) A compensation voucher

(B) A late check-out time

(C) A drive to the airport

(D) An additional night

169. In which of the positions marked [1], [2], [3], and [4] does the following sentence best belong?

"It says getting a taxi from the airport only takes about 15 to 20 minutes."

(A) [1]

(B) [2]

(C) [3]

(D) [4]

Construction of Wastewater Treatment Center Still in Doubt

A proposal by the local government to build a wastewater treatment center in Komlossy has been met with some uncertainty from the public. If municipal water-quality officials approve this construction project, residential and commercial property owners in the area will have to pay higher taxes to cover the cost. It is estimated that the system will cost $52 million to construct and a subsequent $420,000 a month to operate and maintain. Although some taxpayers are reluctant to stop using the far cheaper system currently in use, the majority feel that the new one is worth the added cost. At the very least, it will not permit any contaminants to enter nearby rivers and lakes, as the old one does. The issue will be discussed in depth at Komlossy's Water Quality Control Board meeting on November 6.

170. What is suggested about the current wastewater system?

(A) It contributes to water pollution.
(B) It is very expensive to operate.
(C) It was installed last year.
(D) It is preferred by most residents.

171. According to the article, what will occur in November?

(A) Construction of a new city facility will begin.
(B) Citizens will vote on whether to build a sewage system.
(C) A municipal matter will be examined at a gathering.
(D) A new citywide tax will be implemented.

GO ON TO THE NEXT PAGE

Questions 172-175 refer to the following online chat discussion.

Soomin Park	[6:38 P.M.]	There has been a change of plans. Ms. Lawson just texted me to say she will no longer be requiring our services on June 4. Her wedding date has been moved to September 16, and she wants our studio to do the photography for her ceremony and reception on that day instead.
Lauren Jean	[6:41 P.M.]	That is going to be a problem. I am covering another client's event all day then. Also, we don't have any jobs booked for June 4 now.
Taylor Morgan	[6:43 P.M.]	Is her wedding still going to be at the same place and time on September 16? If so, I can do it. I'll be free all afternoon.
Soomin Park	[6:44 P.M.]	Thanks, Taylor. The time and venue are the same as previously requested. I told Ms. Lawson that if we get another booking for June 4, we will transfer her deposit to her bill for September 16. If not, she will lose the deposit.
Lauren Jean	[6:45 P.M.]	That makes sense. We turned down several other prospective clients who wanted to hire us for that day. Now that I think about it, a few of them may still need a photographer.
Soomin Park	[6:45 P.M.]	Really? If you have any time, please get in touch with them.

Send

172. Why did Ms. Lawson contact Ms. Park?

(A) To arrange a photo shoot at a studio
(B) To negotiate a reduced rate
(C) To notify her of a location change
(D) To reschedule an appointment

173. What can be inferred about Ms. Lawson's wedding?

(A) It will be held at an outdoor venue.
(B) It will be photographed by Mr. Morgan.
(C) It has been paid for in full.
(D) It will occur a month from now.

174. What will happen if the studio cannot make a booking for June 4?

(A) Ms. Park will draft a new contract.
(B) Ms. Jean will be free to attend a wedding.
(C) Ms. Lawson will lose some money she paid.
(D) Mr. Morgan will be unable to access a venue.

175. At 6:45 P.M., what does Ms. Jean most likely mean when she writes, "That makes sense"?

(A) She wants to complain about other clients.
(B) She plans to check an account.
(C) She thinks a decision is reasonable.
(D) She feels a deposit should be refunded.

TEST

5

NEW TOEIC 950 聽力+閱讀 5 回達標

Watertown Music Festival

From Saturday, June 5 through Sunday, June 6, the city of Watertown is hosting an event that every music lover will surely enjoy! The Watertown Music Festival will be a two-day celebration featuring vocalists from the surrounding region, including Kayla Swank, Sienna Hanson, and Tristan Woodlawn. Performances will be given on multiple stages that have been set up both outside and within the Morton Arena. Tickets will grant access to all performance areas and dining facilities. Adults will be charged $30 for entry, and children under the age of 10 can come for free.

The festival is sponsored by New Wave, a music and book retailer that has been in business for nearly 30 years. Be sure not to miss New Wave's booth next to the complex's entrance for a chance to win backstage passes to a concert on Darrell Lane's nationwide tour. For more information and to purchase tickets, visit www.watertownmusicfest.com.

Local Festival a Major Hit

By Marcus Cooper

June 10—The Watertown Music Festival, which occurred earlier this month, was a major event for the city. This year, musical artists drew in more than 20,000 audience members over two days. What helped make this possible was the change of venue. This June's location allowed more space for additional stages to be installed than Westfield Arena did last year.

Local restaurant owner, Nancy Welsh, said that the festival was incredibly popular with her entire family. "There was plenty of space for my three young kids to run around, and I had lots of fun enjoying all of the great music," Ms. Welsh noted. "I even took part in a prize giveaway sponsored by New Wave, which resulted in me winning backstage passes to a concert I was already planning on attending in August!"

For those who did not make it this June, keep up to date with information on next year's event by downloading the festival's smartphone application.

176. What is mentioned about the Watertown Music Festival?

(A) It has been held for more than a decade.
(B) It will have indoor and outdoor performance areas.
(C) It will feature international celebrities.
(D) It has been delayed due to another event.

177. In the advertisement, the word "grant" in paragraph 1, line 8, is closest in meaning to

(A) permit
(B) sign
(C) research
(D) request

178. What is indicated about the Westfield Arena?

(A) It is used as a festival venue every year.
(B) It will be closed down for the summer.
(C) It is less spacious than Morton Arena.
(D) It will be renovated to include a dining area.

179. Which performer does Ms. Welsh plan to see in August?

(A) Kayla Swank
(B) Darrell Lane
(C) Sienna Hanson
(D) Tristan Woodlawn

180. What is stated about the smartphone application?

(A) It will undergo some design changes this June.
(B) It was downloaded by Ms. Welsh's kids.
(C) It will include details about a subsequent festival.
(D) It was introduced in a local magazine last year.

GO ON TO THE NEXT PAGE

Sales Contract

This contract represents the sale of a used car by City Street Motors of Danville (represented by Blaine Ritter) to Grace Huang on November 5. All parties have agreed to the sale as outlined in this agreement. The contract remains valid unless terminated by both the buyer and the seller.

Make and Model: <u>Merriton Motors, Juniper</u>
Exterior and Interior Colors: <u>Blue, Gray</u>
Vehicle Identification Number: <u>XCN138004832738</u>
Sales Price: <u>$14,000</u>
Payment Method: ■ Cash   ☐ Check   ☐ Credit card

The seller has released all information regarding the car's accident and repair history. The buyer has agreed to purchase the car as is and, once the agreement is signed, will not be able to cancel the deal due to any defect found. The seller will provide two keys for the car and recent automobile inspection records to the buyer at the time of signing, along with an official receipt for the sale of the automobile.

Signature of Seller's Representative _____
Signature of Buyer _____

To:	Blaine Ritter <blaineritter@citystreetmotors.com>
From:	Grace Huang <gracehuang@huangdesign.com>
Date:	November 2
Subject:	Contract Review

Dear Mr. Ritter,

Thank you for writing the contract for the Juniper sedan. I am excited to purchase such a nice car. My old car cannot be repaired, making me especially eager to have the new one. I have a question to ask about the contract. When we talked yesterday, we agreed to meet on November 6. But the contract says that the sale date is November 5. Shouldn't this date be corrected? Please make the change and have the corrected document ready before I arrive.

I plan to visit your location at 10:00 A.M. A friend of mine is dropping me off there, so I do not need a ride from you, although I appreciate your offer. I will stop by the bank on the way to City Street Motors so that I'll be prepared to make the payment when I arrive.

Thank you for your assistance, and I look forward to meeting with you on November 6.

Sincerely,
Grace Huang

181. Where does Blaine Ritter most likely work?

(A) At a car dealership
(B) At a rental agency
(C) At a law office
(D) At a vehicle parts store

182. According to the form, what will the seller NOT provide?

(A) An insurance form
(B) Inspection results
(C) A set of keys
(D) Proof of payment

183. What is indicated about Ms. Huang's current vehicle?

(A) It needs to be painted.
(B) It requires a new component.
(C) It is unfixable.
(D) It is too small.

184. What problem does Ms. Huang have with the contract?

(A) A name is misspelled.
(B) A signature is missing.
(C) A date is incorrect.
(D) A price is inaccurate.

185. Why most likely will Ms. Huang visit a bank on November 6?

(A) To pick up some checks
(B) To send a wire transfer
(C) To withdraw some money
(D) To apply for a credit card

GO ON TO THE NEXT PAGE

TEST

5

NEW TOEIC 950 聽力+閱讀 5 回達標

Questions 186-190 refer to the following Web page, e-mail, and text message.

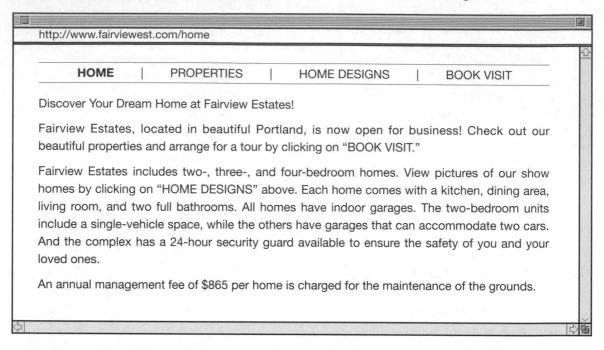

http://www.fairviewest.com/home

| **HOME** | PROPERTIES | HOME DESIGNS | BOOK VISIT |

Discover Your Dream Home at Fairview Estates!

Fairview Estates, located in beautiful Portland, is now open for business! Check out our beautiful properties and arrange for a tour by clicking on "BOOK VISIT."

Fairview Estates includes two-, three-, and four-bedroom homes. View pictures of our show homes by clicking on "HOME DESIGNS" above. Each home comes with a kitchen, dining area, living room, and two full bathrooms. All homes have indoor garages. The two-bedroom units include a single-vehicle space, while the others have garages that can accommodate two cars. And the complex has a 24-hour security guard available to ensure the safety of you and your loved ones.

An annual management fee of $865 per home is charged for the maintenance of the grounds.

TO   Fairview Estates Management Office <inquiries@fairviewest.com>
FROM   Mona Sawyer <monasawyer@genmail.com>
SUBJECT   Visit booking
DATE   March 2

Hello,

I have been offered a new position and I have to move from my current place here in Chicago. I have just completed the sale of my house, and I am looking to purchase a new one. I will be arriving on March 8, and I am interested in seeing your property and touring your show homes. My husband and I have two children, so we require three bedrooms. But please show us the four-bedroom unit as well because we are considering turning the extra bedroom into a home office. I do hope to hear from you soon as we need to find a place quickly. You can reply to this e-mail or send me a text message at 555-2833.

Regards,

Mona Sawyer

From: Andrew Kraft (555-5121)

To: Mona Sawyer (555-2833)

Received: March 10, 2:10 P.M.

I just want to let you know some of the details for our appointment tomorrow. I'll meet with you at the administrative office at 10 A.M. I think this time will be OK for you since you mentioned you need to stop by your accounting office at 8 A.M. After we go through the paperwork, I'll provide you with the keys and security codes to your new four-bedroom home. To ensure there is no delay, could you please make sure to bring a copy of your bank loan agreement with you? Thanks.

186. What is NOT true about Fairview Estates?

(A) Its units all have indoor spaces for parking.
(B) It allows visitors to make reservations to view homes.
(C) Its grounds are only protected by a security guard at night.
(D) It requires tenants to pay for the cost of maintenance.

187. Why will Ms. Sawyer relocate?

(A) Her family has outgrown their current residence.
(B) She recently accepted an accounting job.
(C) Her husband requires a larger home office.
(D) She is overpaying for her residence in Chicago.

188. Why does Ms. Sawyer wish to see the four-bedroom show home?

(A) She needs an additional parking spot.
(B) She is thinking about setting up a work space.
(C) She is planning to have many guests.
(D) She wants a large play area for her children.

189. What is indicated about Ms. Sawyer's chosen home?

(A) It includes a garage for multiple vehicles.
(B) It currently has tenants living in it.
(C) It is situated next to the complex's main entrance.
(D) It comes with a small storage closet.

190. What does Mr. Kraft request?

(A) A signed housing contract
(B) An initial deposit
(C) A financial document copy
(D) An apartment access code

GO ON TO THE NEXT PAGE

New Leaf Grocers: Natural Produce at Affordable Prices!

Maintaining a healthy diet that is low in processed or genetically modified foods, and free of pesticides can be a challenge! Reading all the information on labels is time-consuming, and researching which products are natural and organic can be tedious. Well, that is a problem of the past now that New Leaf Grocers is here in Kingston. We operate a full-service grocery store with one major difference—we guarantee that only natural, organic products are sold in our establishment. Our strict requirements for products allow you to rest assured that whatever you buy in our store is safe for you and your family. Check out our weekly specials and other offers at www.newleafgrocers.com! Or visit us from 8 A.M. through 8 P.M. Mondays through Fridays, and 11 A.M. to 6 P.M. on weekends at 694 Victoria Street.

TO	Rob Dawson <robdawson@selectcereals.com>
FROM	Ariana Septus <arianas@newleafgrocers.com>
SUBJECT	Order
DATE	May 2
ATTACHMENT	Order form

Dear Mr. Dawson,

I very much enjoyed meeting with you at your company booth during the Eco-Food Fair in Las Vegas. I have shared some of the samples of the Select Cereals products you gave me with my colleagues, and they enjoyed them as well. As food items from Select Cereals meet all the criteria for merchandise sold at New Leaf Grocers, we would like to test out your cereals with customers and place an initial order. We are interested in regular delivery of the product we requested the greatest amount of on the attached order form. Future shipments will be for the same amount, and we'd like them to arrive during the last week of each month. And should your other products prove popular with our shoppers, we would be open to placing regular orders for them also.

Thanks for your time, and let me know if you require any further information.

Regards,

Ariana Septus

SELECT CEREALS
Order Form

Customer Name: Ariana Septus   **Phone**: (613) 555-2039
Company: New Leaf Grocers   **E-mail**: arianas@newleafgrocers.com
Payment method: Company Check   **Shipping address**: 694 Victoria Street, Kingston ON

ITEM	COST PER CASE*	QUANTITY OF CASES	TOTAL COST
Bran Cereal with Blueberries	$24.00	2	$48.00
Oat Cereal with Honey	$20.00	3	$60.00
Corn Cereal with Fruit and Nuts	$24.00	2	$48.00
Multigrain Cereal with Raisins	$22.00	4	$88.00

SUBTOTAL: $244.00
SALES TAX: $24.40
SHIPPING AND HANDLING: $56.00
TOTAL AMOUNT DUE: $324.40

*Each case contains 5 boxes of cereal. You may pay with a credit card or by bank transfer. Payment by company check is also acceptable, but the order will not be shipped until the check has been cleared by your bank and the money has been deposited in our account.

191. According to the advertisement, what can be found on the store's website?

(A) Directions to the establishment
(B) A calendar of holiday closures
(C) Details on special promotions
(D) A list of product ingredients

192. What is suggested about Select Cereals?

(A) It hopes to expand its range of organic products.
(B) Its food items are only sold in specialty stores.
(C) It participates in a Las Vegas food fair every year.
(D) Its products are made from naturally grown ingredients.

193. What is indicated about Mr. Dawson?

(A) He represented his company at a food industry event.
(B) He mailed some product samples to his colleagues.
(C) He filled out purchase forms during a business trip.
(D) He is a regular supplier for New Leaf Grocers.

194. Which product will Select Cereals deliver to New Leaf Grocers regularly?

(A) Bran Cereal with Blueberries
(B) Oat Cereal with Honey
(C) Corn Cereal with Fruit and Nuts
(D) Multigrain Cereal with Raisins

195. According to the order form, what is implied about New Leaf Grocers?

(A) It wants more corn cereals than oat cereals.
(B) Its receipts are delivered to customers by e-mail.
(C) It will not have to pay for shipping fees on its next order.
(D) Its order will be sent after a payment has been processed.

GO ON TO THE NEXT PAGE

Government Considering Incentive Plan

By Evan Proust
January 3

Several New South Wales government officials held discussions yesterday and proposed a new tax incentive program. They said that if it is authorised, this program will exempt residential building and manufacturing facility owners from paying taxes on repair costs for solar panels. However, a 12-percent tax will continue to be charged for the sale of any unused energy generated by the panels.

The program will be voted on by the department of environmental protection before the end of January. Should the program be approved, residence and business owners will be able to apply for enrollment on the department's website.

TO: Patty Kindale <patkin@eastonmanufacturing.co.au>
FROM: Rich Ward <richward@eastonmanufacturing.co.au>
SUBJECT: New assignment
DATE: February 10

Patty,

I'm writing regarding the matter we discussed last week. I'd like you to prepare the documentation we need to apply for the recently approved tax incentive program for each of our properties using solar power panels. The requirements for application may differ according to the type of facility, so please double-check those details on the department of environmental protection's Web page. I understand this is potentially a lot of work, but it really is important that we enroll in this program as soon as possible. I have also asked Jerry Headley and Brianne O'Neil to assist you with these preparations. I would like to have all of the application documents ready by the end of Friday, if possible. If that simply isn't enough time, please indicate a more reasonable deadline for this work. And should you need extra help with this task, I can have my assistant Vera Santos help you out as well.

Thanks,

Rich

March 28

Rich Ward
Accounting Division Manager
Easton Manufacturing
44 Grahame Street
Blaxland, NSW 2774

Dear Mr. Ward,

This letter serves to verify that your company's applications for the government's newly implemented solar energy tax benefit program have been approved. You will qualify for tax benefits for each of your manufacturing facilities from April 1.

I did notice, however, that three of your buildings have an excess amount of energy generated by solar panels, which you have been selling to local firms. Please keep in mind that the tax incentive program's policy regarding this practise has not changed.

Thank you for taking part in this program and for helping New South Wales in its clean and safe production of energy.

Sincerely yours,

Fred Dionne
Department of environmental protection

---

196. According to the article, what did government officials do yesterday?

(A) Created new guidelines for government offices
(B) Rejected a proposal to remove taxes on solar panels
(C) Proposed a deal to purchase solar panels for a community
(D) Discussed a plan that benefits some property owners

197. What is indicated about the tax incentive program?

(A) It was authorised by the government in January.
(B) It only applies to privately owned businesses.
(C) It has attracted foreign manufacturers to the region.
(D) It can be applied for starting next year.

198. What does Mr. Ward offer to do for Ms. Kindale?

(A) Provide additional funding for a project
(B) Assign Vera Santos to a task
(C) Send some helpful documents
(D) Ask Jerry Headley to inspect a facility

199. Why was the letter written?

(A) To announce the results of a study
(B) To approve a construction proposal
(C) To confirm eligibility for a program
(D) To verify receipt of a tax payment

200. What is suggested about some of Easton Manufacturing's facilities?

(A) They may be charged a 12-percent tax.
(B) They are in need of more electricity than anticipated.
(C) They cut back on production levels on February 10.
(D) They require renovation before resuming operations.

This is the end of the test. You may review Parts 5, 6, and 7 if you finish the test early.

/Review 檢查表

完成 TEST 5 後，請根據下表檢視自己答錯的問題，並在框框中打勾。
如果距離考試時間不多，請務必檢查**粗體字**的項目。

☐ **我再度練習了答錯的題目，試著找出正確答案。**

☐ **我已針對答錯的題目查閱了翻譯，理解了題幹與問題的內容。**

☐ **我透過翻譯，理解了每題各個選項正確或錯誤的原因。**

☐ 我檢視了在 Part 1 和 Part 2 答錯的問題類型，並加以整理，以免落入相同的陷阱。

☐ 我檢視了 Part 3 和 Part 4 每個題目所使用的換句話說。

☐ 在 Part 5 和 Part 6，我針對各題的正確答案及錯誤選項，整理了文法和單字的重點。

☐ 針對 Part 6「選擇合適句子」的題目，我正確理解了整個段落及空格前後文的語意。

☐ 在 Part 7，我找出了短文和題目中的重點，包含正確答題所需的句子和片語，並加以標示，也檢查了題目使用的換句話說。

☐ 針對 Part 1~Part 4，我使用線上的聽力訓練筆記，針對考試的重點語句練習聽寫、閱讀和複習。

☐ 針對 Part 1~Part 4，我使用單字記憶本來記下考試的關鍵詞彙和表達用語。

大量練習題目固然重要，但好好檢視自己答錯的問題也同樣關鍵。
只要仔細複習一遍答錯的題目，就能在短時間內有效達到目標分數。

NEW TOEIC 950
聽力+閱讀 5 回達標

解答
分數換算表
ANSWER SHEET

解答 ANSWER KEYS

▍TEST 1

LISTENING TEST				
1 (B)	**2** (A)	**3** (D)	**4** (A)	**5** (D)
6 (C)	**7** (C)	**8** (B)	**9** (C)	**10** (C)
11 (A)	**12** (A)	**13** (C)	**14** (A)	**15** (A)
16 (A)	**17** (A)	**18** (B)	**19** (B)	**20** (C)
21 (C)	**22** (A)	**23** (A)	**24** (C)	**25** (C)
26 (A)	**27** (C)	**28** (B)	**29** (B)	**30** (B)
31 (C)	**32** (A)	**33** (C)	**34** (D)	**35** (B)
36 (D)	**37** (B)	**38** (B)	**39** (D)	**40** (A)
41 (B)	**42** (C)	**43** (A)	**44** (B)	**45** (C)
46 (D)	**47** (D)	**48** (A)	**49** (D)	**50** (D)
51 (C)	**52** (B)	**53** (C)	**54** (B)	**55** (B)
56 (A)	**57** (B)	**58** (D)	**59** (B)	**60** (B)
61 (D)	**62** (D)	**63** (C)	**64** (D)	**65** (C)
66 (B)	**67** (A)	**68** (A)	**69** (D)	**70** (C)
71 (A)	**72** (D)	**73** (B)	**74** (D)	**75** (A)
76 (B)	**77** (A)	**78** (B)	**79** (D)	**80** (B)
81 (D)	**82** (C)	**83** (C)	**84** (D)	**85** (D)
86 (C)	**87** (B)	**88** (A)	**89** (D)	**90** (B)
91 (D)	**92** (C)	**93** (D)	**94** (C)	**95** (B)
96 (C)	**97** (A)	**98** (C)	**99** (A)	**100** (D)

READING TEST				
101 (C)	**102** (B)	**103** (D)	**104** (A)	**105** (A)
106 (C)	**107** (A)	**108** (A)	**109** (C)	**110** (A)
111 (C)	**112** (D)	**113** (B)	**114** (D)	**115** (B)
116 (D)	**117** (B)	**118** (A)	**119** (C)	**120** (D)
121 (C)	**122** (C)	**123** (B)	**124** (A)	**125** (B)
126 (C)	**127** (C)	**128** (A)	**129** (B)	**130** (D)
131 (D)	**132** (B)	**133** (A)	**134** (C)	**135** (A)
136 (B)	**137** (D)	**138** (C)	**139** (B)	**140** (D)
141 (C)	**142** (A)	**143** (D)	**144** (B)	**145** (D)
146 (C)	**147** (B)	**148** (C)	**149** (A)	**150** (D)
151 (B)	**152** (B)	**153** (D)	**154** (B)	**155** (C)
156 (A)	**157** (C)	**158** (D)	**159** (A)	**160** (D)
161 (D)	**162** (C)	**163** (A)	**164** (B)	**165** (A)
166 (C)	**167** (C)	**168** (A)	**169** (C)	**170** (B)
171 (C)	**172** (A)	**173** (A)	**174** (C)	**175** (B)
176 (C)	**177** (B)	**178** (B)	**179** (A)	**180** (D)
181 (B)	**182** (A)	**183** (C)	**184** (B)	**185** (A)
186 (D)	**187** (B)	**188** (C)	**189** (C)	**190** (D)
191 (D)	**192** (C)	**193** (A)	**194** (D)	**195** (B)
196 (D)	**197** (A)	**198** (B)	**199** (D)	**200** (A)

TEST 2

LISTENING TEST

1 (D)	**2** (D)	**3** (B)	**4** (C)	**5** (A)
6 (B)	**7** (B)	**8** (A)	**9** (B)	**10** (C)
11 (C)	**12** (C)	**13** (A)	**14** (C)	**15** (B)
16 (C)	**17** (A)	**18** (C)	**19** (B)	**20** (A)
21 (A)	**22** (A)	**23** (C)	**24** (B)	**25** (A)
26 (B)	**27** (A)	**28** (B)	**29** (A)	**30** (C)
31 (A)	**32** (A)	**33** (D)	**34** (B)	**35** (A)
36 (A)	**37** (D)	**38** (A)	**39** (B)	**40** (C)
41 (D)	**42** (B)	**43** (B)	**44** (C)	**45** (C)
46 (B)	**47** (A)	**48** (A)	**49** (B)	**50** (C)
51 (B)	**52** (A)	**53** (A)	**54** (A)	**55** (B)
56 (D)	**57** (A)	**58** (C)	**59** (D)	**60** (D)
61 (A)	**62** (A)	**63** (D)	**64** (A)	**65** (B)
66 (A)	**67** (B)	**68** (A)	**69** (A)	**70** (C)
71 (B)	**72** (D)	**73** (B)	**74** (C)	**75** (A)
76 (D)	**77** (B)	**78** (D)	**79** (D)	**80** (B)
81 (D)	**82** (C)	**83** (C)	**84** (A)	**85** (A)
86 (B)	**87** (A)	**88** (B)	**89** (B)	**90** (C)
91 (A)	**92** (B)	**93** (A)	**94** (D)	**95** (D)
96 (C)	**97** (B)	**98** (B)	**99** (A)	**100** (B)

READING TEST

101 (D)	**102** (A)	**103** (B)	**104** (A)	**105** (A)
106 (B)	**107** (A)	**108** (C)	**109** (B)	**110** (A)
111 (D)	**112** (A)	**113** (A)	**114** (A)	**115** (C)
116 (A)	**117** (A)	**118** (B)	**119** (B)	**120** (C)
121 (D)	**122** (A)	**123** (D)	**124** (C)	**125** (B)
126 (B)	**127** (D)	**128** (D)	**129** (C)	**130** (C)
131 (C)	**132** (A)	**133** (C)	**134** (D)	**135** (D)
136 (A)	**137** (C)	**138** (B)	**139** (C)	**140** (A)
141 (B)	**142** (C)	**143** (D)	**144** (B)	**145** (C)
146 (C)	**147** (C)	**148** (B)	**149** (D)	**150** (D)
151 (D)	**152** (A)	**153** (D)	**154** (A)	**155** (B)
156 (D)	**157** (C)	**158** (D)	**159** (B)	**160** (D)
161 (D)	**162** (B)	**163** (C)	**164** (D)	**165** (B)
166 (C)	**167** (C)	**168** (A)	**169** (D)	**170** (C)
171 (C)	**172** (B)	**173** (C)	**174** (D)	**175** (A)
176 (B)	**177** (B)	**178** (C)	**179** (C)	**180** (C)
181 (D)	**182** (A)	**183** (B)	**184** (C)	**185** (D)
186 (A)	**187** (B)	**188** (B)	**189** (D)	**190** (C)
191 (C)	**192** (C)	**193** (D)	**194** (C)	**195** (B)
196 (D)	**197** (B)	**198** (A)	**199** (B)	**200** (D)

解答 ANSWER KEYS

▌TEST 3

LISTENING TEST				
1 (D)	**2** (D)	**3** (A)	**4** (D)	**5** (A)
6 (B)	**7** (A)	**8** (A)	**9** (C)	**10** (B)
11 (A)	**12** (C)	**13** (B)	**14** (C)	**15** (B)
16 (B)	**17** (C)	**18** (A)	**19** (A)	**20** (C)
21 (B)	**22** (C)	**23** (B)	**24** (C)	**25** (C)
26 (B)	**27** (A)	**28** (C)	**29** (C)	**30** (A)
31 (A)	**32** (C)	**33** (C)	**34** (B)	**35** (D)
36 (A)	**37** (A)	**38** (A)	**39** (C)	**40** (B)
41 (A)	**42** (C)	**43** (C)	**44** (A)	**45** (D)
46 (C)	**47** (A)	**48** (C)	**49** (A)	**50** (C)
51 (B)	**52** (D)	**53** (B)	**54** (B)	**55** (D)
56 (C)	**57** (C)	**58** (A)	**59** (B)	**60** (D)
61 (B)	**62** (B)	**63** (A)	**64** (B)	**65** (B)
66 (B)	**67** (D)	**68** (C)	**69** (B)	**70** (A)
71 (C)	**72** (B)	**73** (B)	**74** (A)	**75** (A)
76 (B)	**77** (B)	**78** (A)	**79** (B)	**80** (A)
81 (A)	**82** (A)	**83** (B)	**84** (D)	**85** (A)
86 (D)	**87** (D)	**88** (B)	**89** (B)	**90** (D)
91 (C)	**92** (D)	**93** (B)	**94** (A)	**95** (B)
96 (B)	**97** (B)	**98** (A)	**99** (C)	**100** (B)

READING TEST				
101 (D)	**102** (B)	**103** (A)	**104** (D)	**105** (A)
106 (B)	**107** (A)	**108** (B)	**109** (A)	**110** (A)
111 (B)	**112** (A)	**113** (B)	**114** (C)	**115** (C)
116 (C)	**117** (B)	**118** (A)	**119** (C)	**120** (C)
121 (D)	**122** (D)	**123** (C)	**124** (D)	**125** (C)
126 (C)	**127** (C)	**128** (B)	**129** (A)	**130** (A)
131 (C)	**132** (A)	**133** (A)	**134** (D)	**135** (A)
136 (D)	**137** (C)	**138** (B)	**139** (B)	**140** (C)
141 (D)	**142** (A)	**143** (A)	**144** (C)	**145** (C)
146 (C)	**147** (B)	**148** (C)	**149** (D)	**150** (A)
151 (C)	**152** (D)	**153** (C)	**154** (D)	**155** (C)
156 (C)	**157** (D)	**158** (D)	**159** (C)	**160** (D)
161 (B)	**162** (C)	**163** (A)	**164** (C)	**165** (C)
166 (D)	**167** (B)	**168** (A)	**169** (B)	**170** (D)
171 (C)	**172** (B)	**173** (D)	**174** (B)	**175** (A)
176 (A)	**177** (C)	**178** (A)	**179** (D)	**180** (B)
181 (D)	**182** (B)	**183** (C)	**184** (A)	**185** (A)
186 (A)	**187** (B)	**188** (D)	**189** (C)	**190** (D)
191 (B)	**192** (D)	**193** (A)	**194** (B)	**195** (D)
196 (C)	**197** (B)	**198** (D)	**199** (B)	**200** (D)

▌TEST 4

LISTENING TEST

1 (D)	2 (A)	3 (C)	4 (A)	5 (B)
6 (C)	7 (C)	8 (C)	9 (A)	10 (C)
11 (A)	12 (B)	13 (A)	14 (C)	15 (C)
16 (C)	17 (C)	18 (B)	19 (C)	20 (B)
21 (A)	22 (A)	23 (A)	24 (B)	25 (B)
26 (B)	27 (B)	28 (B)	29 (A)	30 (B)
31 (B)	32 (B)	33 (A)	34 (C)	35 (B)
36 (A)	37 (C)	38 (D)	39 (A)	40 (C)
41 (D)	42 (C)	43 (B)	44 (B)	45 (A)
46 (C)	47 (D)	48 (C)	49 (D)	50 (D)
51 (D)	52 (B)	53 (C)	54 (C)	55 (B)
56 (A)	57 (D)	58 (A)	59 (B)	60 (A)
61 (A)	62 (D)	63 (B)	64 (D)	65 (A)
66 (B)	67 (B)	68 (B)	69 (D)	70 (D)
71 (B)	72 (A)	73 (B)	74 (C)	75 (D)
76 (B)	77 (D)	78 (B)	79 (C)	80 (D)
81 (D)	82 (A)	83 (B)	84 (B)	85 (D)
86 (C)	87 (A)	88 (B)	89 (B)	90 (C)
91 (B)	92 (B)	93 (A)	94 (C)	95 (C)
96 (C)	97 (B)	98 (A)	99 (B)	100 (B)

READING TEST

101 (C)	102 (A)	103 (D)	104 (B)	105 (C)
106 (C)	107 (B)	108 (A)	109 (B)	110 (C)
111 (D)	112 (D)	113 (D)	114 (B)	115 (D)
116 (B)	117 (D)	118 (B)	119 (A)	120 (D)
121 (C)	122 (D)	123 (C)	124 (D)	125 (B)
126 (A)	127 (B)	128 (B)	129 (A)	130 (C)
131 (D)	132 (D)	133 (C)	134 (D)	135 (B)
136 (C)	137 (A)	138 (A)	139 (B)	140 (C)
141 (A)	142 (A)	143 (C)	144 (C)	145 (D)
146 (B)	147 (C)	148 (D)	149 (C)	150 (D)
151 (C)	152 (C)	153 (A)	154 (D)	155 (C)
156 (A)	157 (D)	158 (C)	159 (D)	160 (B)
161 (B)	162 (B)	163 (C)	164 (D)	165 (C)
166 (D)	167 (C)	168 (C)	169 (B)	170 (C)
171 (D)	172 (C)	173 (D)	174 (B)	175 (C)
176 (D)	177 (B)	178 (D)	179 (B)	180 (C)
181 (B)	182 (B)	183 (A)	184 (D)	185 (D)
186 (D)	187 (C)	188 (B)	189 (D)	190 (B)
191 (B)	192 (C)	193 (D)	194 (D)	195 (C)
196 (C)	197 (A)	198 (C)	199 (C)	200 (A)

解答 ANSWER KEYS

▌TEST 5

LISTENING TEST

1 (D)	**2** (A)	**3** (D)	**4** (B)	**5** (A)
6 (B)	**7** (C)	**8** (B)	**9** (B)	**10** (B)
11 (C)	**12** (C)	**13** (A)	**14** (B)	**15** (B)
16 (A)	**17** (A)	**18** (C)	**19** (C)	**20** (B)
21 (C)	**22** (C)	**23** (C)	**24** (B)	**25** (B)
26 (A)	**27** (B)	**28** (C)	**29** (A)	**30** (A)
31 (B)	**32** (B)	**33** (B)	**34** (C)	**35** (A)
36 (C)	**37** (A)	**38** (B)	**39** (B)	**40** (D)
41 (D)	**42** (B)	**43** (B)	**44** (C)	**45** (A)
46 (D)	**47** (D)	**48** (A)	**49** (B)	**50** (A)
51 (C)	**52** (B)	**53** (D)	**54** (B)	**55** (A)
56 (D)	**57** (A)	**58** (D)	**59** (A)	**60** (C)
61 (B)	**62** (D)	**63** (B)	**64** (D)	**65** (D)
66 (A)	**67** (A)	**68** (A)	**69** (D)	**70** (C)
71 (D)	**72** (A)	**73** (B)	**74** (D)	**75** (C)
76 (A)	**77** (C)	**78** (D)	**79** (B)	**80** (B)
81 (D)	**82** (C)	**83** (A)	**84** (B)	**85** (C)
86 (B)	**87** (D)	**88** (B)	**89** (C)	**90** (D)
91 (D)	**92** (A)	**93** (D)	**94** (C)	**95** (C)
96 (B)	**97** (A)	**98** (C)	**99** (B)	**100** (A)

READING TEST

101 (A)	**102** (C)	**103** (A)	**104** (C)	**105** (A)
106 (D)	**107** (D)	**108** (B)	**109** (D)	**110** (B)
111 (A)	**112** (A)	**113** (A)	**114** (B)	**115** (D)
116 (C)	**117** (C)	**118** (B)	**119** (D)	**120** (A)
121 (A)	**122** (C)	**123** (B)	**124** (A)	**125** (D)
126 (D)	**127** (B)	**128** (A)	**129** (C)	**130** (D)
131 (D)	**132** (B)	**133** (C)	**134** (B)	**135** (B)
136 (D)	**137** (C)	**138** (D)	**139** (A)	**140** (A)
141 (C)	**142** (C)	**143** (D)	**144** (A)	**145** (B)
146 (A)	**147** (B)	**148** (C)	**149** (C)	**150** (A)
151 (D)	**152** (D)	**153** (C)	**154** (B)	**155** (C)
156 (B)	**157** (D)	**158** (C)	**159** (C)	**160** (C)
161 (C)	**162** (B)	**163** (D)	**164** (C)	**165** (B)
166 (A)	**167** (D)	**168** (B)	**169** (B)	**170** (A)
171 (C)	**172** (D)	**173** (B)	**174** (C)	**175** (C)
176 (B)	**177** (A)	**178** (C)	**179** (B)	**180** (C)
181 (A)	**182** (A)	**183** (C)	**184** (C)	**185** (C)
186 (C)	**187** (B)	**188** (B)	**189** (A)	**190** (C)
191 (C)	**192** (D)	**193** (A)	**194** (D)	**195** (D)
196 (D)	**197** (A)	**198** (B)	**199** (C)	**200** (A)

分數換算表

※分數換算表是根據 Hackers 網站的使用者資料製作而成，並定期更新。請留意，這是推測值，不是百分百 準確的計算方式。

LISTENING

請使用以下分數換算表來估算自己的多益聽力分數。

正確答題數量	換算分數	正確答題數量	換算分數	正確答題數量	換算分數
100	495	66	305	32	135
99	495	65	300	31	130
98	495	64	295	30	125
97	495	63	290	29	120
96	490	62	285	28	115
95	485	61	280	27	110
94	480	60	275	26	105
93	475	59	270	25	100
92	470	58	265	24	95
91	465	57	260	23	90
90	460	56	255	22	85
89	455	55	250	21	80
88	450	54	245	20	75
87	445	53	240	19	70
86	435	52	235	18	65
85	430	51	230	17	60
84	425	50	225	16	55
83	415	49	220	15	50
82	410	48	215	14	45
81	400	47	210	13	40
80	395	46	205	12	35
79	390	45	200	11	30
78	385	44	195	10	25
77	375	43	190	9	20
76	370	42	185	8	15
75	365	41	180	7	10
74	355	40	175	6	5
73	350	39	170	5	5
72	340	38	165	4	5
71	335	37	160	3	5
70	330	36	155	2	5
69	325	35	150	1	5
68	315	34	145	0	5
67	310	33	140		

READING

請使用以下分數換算表來估算自己的多益閱讀分數。

正確答題數量	換算分數	正確答題數量	換算分數	正確答題數量	換算分數
100	495	66	305	32	125
99	495	65	300	31	120
98	495	64	295	30	115
97	485	63	290	29	110
96	480	62	280	28	105
95	475	61	275	27	100
94	470	60	270	26	95
93	465	59	265	25	90
92	460	58	260	24	85
91	450	57	255	23	80
90	445	56	250	22	75
89	440	55	245	21	70
88	435	54	240	20	70
87	430	53	235	19	65
86	420	52	230	18	60
85	415	51	220	17	60
84	410	50	215	16	55
83	405	49	210	15	50
82	400	48	205	14	45
81	390	47	200	13	40
80	385	46	195	12	35
79	380	45	190	11	30
78	375	44	185	10	30
77	370	43	180	9	25
76	360	42	175	8	20
75	355	41	170	7	20
74	350	40	165	6	15
73	345	39	160	5	15
72	340	38	155	4	10
71	335	37	150	3	5
70	330	36	145	2	5
69	320	35	140	1	5
68	315	34	135	0	5
67	310	33	130		

Answer Sheet

TEST 1

LISTENING (PART I~IV)

	A	B	C	D		A	B	C	D		A	B	C	D		A	B	C	D		A	B	C	D
1	Ⓐ	Ⓑ	Ⓒ	Ⓓ	21	Ⓐ	Ⓑ	Ⓒ	Ⓓ	41	Ⓐ	Ⓑ	Ⓒ	Ⓓ	61	Ⓐ	Ⓑ	Ⓒ	Ⓓ	81	Ⓐ	Ⓑ	Ⓒ	Ⓓ
2	Ⓐ	Ⓑ	Ⓒ	Ⓓ	22	Ⓐ	Ⓑ	Ⓒ	Ⓓ	42	Ⓐ	Ⓑ	Ⓒ	Ⓓ	62	Ⓐ	Ⓑ	Ⓒ	Ⓓ	82	Ⓐ	Ⓑ	Ⓒ	Ⓓ
3	Ⓐ	Ⓑ	Ⓒ	Ⓓ	23	Ⓐ	Ⓑ	Ⓒ	Ⓓ	43	Ⓐ	Ⓑ	Ⓒ	Ⓓ	63	Ⓐ	Ⓑ	Ⓒ	Ⓓ	83	Ⓐ	Ⓑ	Ⓒ	Ⓓ
4	Ⓐ	Ⓑ	Ⓒ	Ⓓ	24	Ⓐ	Ⓑ	Ⓒ	Ⓓ	44	Ⓐ	Ⓑ	Ⓒ	Ⓓ	64	Ⓐ	Ⓑ	Ⓒ	Ⓓ	84	Ⓐ	Ⓑ	Ⓒ	Ⓓ
5	Ⓐ	Ⓑ	Ⓒ	Ⓓ	25	Ⓐ	Ⓑ	Ⓒ	Ⓓ	45	Ⓐ	Ⓑ	Ⓒ	Ⓓ	65	Ⓐ	Ⓑ	Ⓒ	Ⓓ	85	Ⓐ	Ⓑ	Ⓒ	Ⓓ
6	Ⓐ	Ⓑ	Ⓒ	Ⓓ	26	Ⓐ	Ⓑ	Ⓒ	Ⓓ	46	Ⓐ	Ⓑ	Ⓒ	Ⓓ	66	Ⓐ	Ⓑ	Ⓒ	Ⓓ	86	Ⓐ	Ⓑ	Ⓒ	Ⓓ
7	Ⓐ	Ⓑ	Ⓒ	Ⓓ	27	Ⓐ	Ⓑ	Ⓒ	Ⓓ	47	Ⓐ	Ⓑ	Ⓒ	Ⓓ	67	Ⓐ	Ⓑ	Ⓒ	Ⓓ	87	Ⓐ	Ⓑ	Ⓒ	Ⓓ
8	Ⓐ	Ⓑ	Ⓒ	Ⓓ	28	Ⓐ	Ⓑ	Ⓒ	Ⓓ	48	Ⓐ	Ⓑ	Ⓒ	Ⓓ	68	Ⓐ	Ⓑ	Ⓒ	Ⓓ	88	Ⓐ	Ⓑ	Ⓒ	Ⓓ
9	Ⓐ	Ⓑ	Ⓒ	Ⓓ	29	Ⓐ	Ⓑ	Ⓒ	Ⓓ	49	Ⓐ	Ⓑ	Ⓒ	Ⓓ	69	Ⓐ	Ⓑ	Ⓒ	Ⓓ	89	Ⓐ	Ⓑ	Ⓒ	Ⓓ
10	Ⓐ	Ⓑ	Ⓒ	Ⓓ	30	Ⓐ	Ⓑ	Ⓒ	Ⓓ	50	Ⓐ	Ⓑ	Ⓒ	Ⓓ	70	Ⓐ	Ⓑ	Ⓒ	Ⓓ	90	Ⓐ	Ⓑ	Ⓒ	Ⓓ
11	Ⓐ	Ⓑ	Ⓒ	Ⓓ	31	Ⓐ	Ⓑ	Ⓒ	Ⓓ	51	Ⓐ	Ⓑ	Ⓒ	Ⓓ	71	Ⓐ	Ⓑ	Ⓒ	Ⓓ	91	Ⓐ	Ⓑ	Ⓒ	Ⓓ
12	Ⓐ	Ⓑ	Ⓒ	Ⓓ	32	Ⓐ	Ⓑ	Ⓒ	Ⓓ	52	Ⓐ	Ⓑ	Ⓒ	Ⓓ	72	Ⓐ	Ⓑ	Ⓒ	Ⓓ	92	Ⓐ	Ⓑ	Ⓒ	Ⓓ
13	Ⓐ	Ⓑ	Ⓒ	Ⓓ	33	Ⓐ	Ⓑ	Ⓒ	Ⓓ	53	Ⓐ	Ⓑ	Ⓒ	Ⓓ	73	Ⓐ	Ⓑ	Ⓒ	Ⓓ	93	Ⓐ	Ⓑ	Ⓒ	Ⓓ
14	Ⓐ	Ⓑ	Ⓒ	Ⓓ	34	Ⓐ	Ⓑ	Ⓒ	Ⓓ	54	Ⓐ	Ⓑ	Ⓒ	Ⓓ	74	Ⓐ	Ⓑ	Ⓒ	Ⓓ	94	Ⓐ	Ⓑ	Ⓒ	Ⓓ
15	Ⓐ	Ⓑ	Ⓒ	Ⓓ	35	Ⓐ	Ⓑ	Ⓒ	Ⓓ	55	Ⓐ	Ⓑ	Ⓒ	Ⓓ	75	Ⓐ	Ⓑ	Ⓒ	Ⓓ	95	Ⓐ	Ⓑ	Ⓒ	Ⓓ
16	Ⓐ	Ⓑ	Ⓒ	Ⓓ	36	Ⓐ	Ⓑ	Ⓒ	Ⓓ	56	Ⓐ	Ⓑ	Ⓒ	Ⓓ	76	Ⓐ	Ⓑ	Ⓒ	Ⓓ	96	Ⓐ	Ⓑ	Ⓒ	Ⓓ
17	Ⓐ	Ⓑ	Ⓒ	Ⓓ	37	Ⓐ	Ⓑ	Ⓒ	Ⓓ	57	Ⓐ	Ⓑ	Ⓒ	Ⓓ	77	Ⓐ	Ⓑ	Ⓒ	Ⓓ	97	Ⓐ	Ⓑ	Ⓒ	Ⓓ
18	Ⓐ	Ⓑ	Ⓒ	Ⓓ	38	Ⓐ	Ⓑ	Ⓒ	Ⓓ	58	Ⓐ	Ⓑ	Ⓒ	Ⓓ	78	Ⓐ	Ⓑ	Ⓒ	Ⓓ	98	Ⓐ	Ⓑ	Ⓒ	Ⓓ
19	Ⓐ	Ⓑ	Ⓒ	Ⓓ	39	Ⓐ	Ⓑ	Ⓒ	Ⓓ	59	Ⓐ	Ⓑ	Ⓒ	Ⓓ	79	Ⓐ	Ⓑ	Ⓒ	Ⓓ	99	Ⓐ	Ⓑ	Ⓒ	Ⓓ
20	Ⓐ	Ⓑ	Ⓒ	Ⓓ	40	Ⓐ	Ⓑ	Ⓒ	Ⓓ	60	Ⓐ	Ⓑ	Ⓒ	Ⓓ	80	Ⓐ	Ⓑ	Ⓒ	Ⓓ	100	Ⓐ	Ⓑ	Ⓒ	Ⓓ

測驗時間：120 分鐘（聽力 45 分鐘，閱讀 75 分鐘）

READING (PART V~VII)

	A	B	C	D		A	B	C	D		A	B	C	D		A	B	C	D		A	B	C	D
101	Ⓐ	Ⓑ	Ⓒ	Ⓓ	121	Ⓐ	Ⓑ	Ⓒ	Ⓓ	141	Ⓐ	Ⓑ	Ⓒ	Ⓓ	161	Ⓐ	Ⓑ	Ⓒ	Ⓓ	181	Ⓐ	Ⓑ	Ⓒ	Ⓓ
102	Ⓐ	Ⓑ	Ⓒ	Ⓓ	122	Ⓐ	Ⓑ	Ⓒ	Ⓓ	142	Ⓐ	Ⓑ	Ⓒ	Ⓓ	162	Ⓐ	Ⓑ	Ⓒ	Ⓓ	182	Ⓐ	Ⓑ	Ⓒ	Ⓓ
103	Ⓐ	Ⓑ	Ⓒ	Ⓓ	123	Ⓐ	Ⓑ	Ⓒ	Ⓓ	143	Ⓐ	Ⓑ	Ⓒ	Ⓓ	163	Ⓐ	Ⓑ	Ⓒ	Ⓓ	183	Ⓐ	Ⓑ	Ⓒ	Ⓓ
104	Ⓐ	Ⓑ	Ⓒ	Ⓓ	124	Ⓐ	Ⓑ	Ⓒ	Ⓓ	144	Ⓐ	Ⓑ	Ⓒ	Ⓓ	164	Ⓐ	Ⓑ	Ⓒ	Ⓓ	184	Ⓐ	Ⓑ	Ⓒ	Ⓓ
105	Ⓐ	Ⓑ	Ⓒ	Ⓓ	125	Ⓐ	Ⓑ	Ⓒ	Ⓓ	145	Ⓐ	Ⓑ	Ⓒ	Ⓓ	165	Ⓐ	Ⓑ	Ⓒ	Ⓓ	185	Ⓐ	Ⓑ	Ⓒ	Ⓓ
106	Ⓐ	Ⓑ	Ⓒ	Ⓓ	126	Ⓐ	Ⓑ	Ⓒ	Ⓓ	146	Ⓐ	Ⓑ	Ⓒ	Ⓓ	166	Ⓐ	Ⓑ	Ⓒ	Ⓓ	186	Ⓐ	Ⓑ	Ⓒ	Ⓓ
107	Ⓐ	Ⓑ	Ⓒ	Ⓓ	127	Ⓐ	Ⓑ	Ⓒ	Ⓓ	147	Ⓐ	Ⓑ	Ⓒ	Ⓓ	167	Ⓐ	Ⓑ	Ⓒ	Ⓓ	187	Ⓐ	Ⓑ	Ⓒ	Ⓓ
108	Ⓐ	Ⓑ	Ⓒ	Ⓓ	128	Ⓐ	Ⓑ	Ⓒ	Ⓓ	148	Ⓐ	Ⓑ	Ⓒ	Ⓓ	168	Ⓐ	Ⓑ	Ⓒ	Ⓓ	188	Ⓐ	Ⓑ	Ⓒ	Ⓓ
109	Ⓐ	Ⓑ	Ⓒ	Ⓓ	129	Ⓐ	Ⓑ	Ⓒ	Ⓓ	149	Ⓐ	Ⓑ	Ⓒ	Ⓓ	169	Ⓐ	Ⓑ	Ⓒ	Ⓓ	189	Ⓐ	Ⓑ	Ⓒ	Ⓓ
110	Ⓐ	Ⓑ	Ⓒ	Ⓓ	130	Ⓐ	Ⓑ	Ⓒ	Ⓓ	150	Ⓐ	Ⓑ	Ⓒ	Ⓓ	170	Ⓐ	Ⓑ	Ⓒ	Ⓓ	190	Ⓐ	Ⓑ	Ⓒ	Ⓓ
111	Ⓐ	Ⓑ	Ⓒ	Ⓓ	131	Ⓐ	Ⓑ	Ⓒ	Ⓓ	151	Ⓐ	Ⓑ	Ⓒ	Ⓓ	171	Ⓐ	Ⓑ	Ⓒ	Ⓓ	191	Ⓐ	Ⓑ	Ⓒ	Ⓓ
112	Ⓐ	Ⓑ	Ⓒ	Ⓓ	132	Ⓐ	Ⓑ	Ⓒ	Ⓓ	152	Ⓐ	Ⓑ	Ⓒ	Ⓓ	172	Ⓐ	Ⓑ	Ⓒ	Ⓓ	192	Ⓐ	Ⓑ	Ⓒ	Ⓓ
113	Ⓐ	Ⓑ	Ⓒ	Ⓓ	133	Ⓐ	Ⓑ	Ⓒ	Ⓓ	153	Ⓐ	Ⓑ	Ⓒ	Ⓓ	173	Ⓐ	Ⓑ	Ⓒ	Ⓓ	193	Ⓐ	Ⓑ	Ⓒ	Ⓓ
114	Ⓐ	Ⓑ	Ⓒ	Ⓓ	134	Ⓐ	Ⓑ	Ⓒ	Ⓓ	154	Ⓐ	Ⓑ	Ⓒ	Ⓓ	174	Ⓐ	Ⓑ	Ⓒ	Ⓓ	194	Ⓐ	Ⓑ	Ⓒ	Ⓓ
115	Ⓐ	Ⓑ	Ⓒ	Ⓓ	135	Ⓐ	Ⓑ	Ⓒ	Ⓓ	155	Ⓐ	Ⓑ	Ⓒ	Ⓓ	175	Ⓐ	Ⓑ	Ⓒ	Ⓓ	195	Ⓐ	Ⓑ	Ⓒ	Ⓓ
116	Ⓐ	Ⓑ	Ⓒ	Ⓓ	136	Ⓐ	Ⓑ	Ⓒ	Ⓓ	156	Ⓐ	Ⓑ	Ⓒ	Ⓓ	176	Ⓐ	Ⓑ	Ⓒ	Ⓓ	196	Ⓐ	Ⓑ	Ⓒ	Ⓓ
117	Ⓐ	Ⓑ	Ⓒ	Ⓓ	137	Ⓐ	Ⓑ	Ⓒ	Ⓓ	157	Ⓐ	Ⓑ	Ⓒ	Ⓓ	177	Ⓐ	Ⓑ	Ⓒ	Ⓓ	197	Ⓐ	Ⓑ	Ⓒ	Ⓓ
118	Ⓐ	Ⓑ	Ⓒ	Ⓓ	138	Ⓐ	Ⓑ	Ⓒ	Ⓓ	158	Ⓐ	Ⓑ	Ⓒ	Ⓓ	178	Ⓐ	Ⓑ	Ⓒ	Ⓓ	198	Ⓐ	Ⓑ	Ⓒ	Ⓓ
119	Ⓐ	Ⓑ	Ⓒ	Ⓓ	139	Ⓐ	Ⓑ	Ⓒ	Ⓓ	159	Ⓐ	Ⓑ	Ⓒ	Ⓓ	179	Ⓐ	Ⓑ	Ⓒ	Ⓓ	199	Ⓐ	Ⓑ	Ⓒ	Ⓓ
120	Ⓐ	Ⓑ	Ⓒ	Ⓓ	140	Ⓐ	Ⓑ	Ⓒ	Ⓓ	160	Ⓐ	Ⓑ	Ⓒ	Ⓓ	180	Ⓐ	Ⓑ	Ⓒ	Ⓓ	200	Ⓐ	Ⓑ	Ⓒ	Ⓓ

請用鉛筆在答案卡上畫記。

正確題數：_____ /200

裁切線 ✂

Answer Sheet

TEST 2

LISTENING (PART I~IV)

#	A	B	C	D		#	A	B	C	D		#	A	B	C	D		#	A	B	C	D
1	A	B	C	D		21	A	B	C	D		41	A	B	C	D		61	A	B	C	D
2	A	B	C	D		22	A	B	C	D		42	A	B	C	D		62	A	B	C	D
3	A	B	C	D		23	A	B	C	D		43	A	B	C	D		63	A	B	C	D
4	A	B	C	D		24	A	B	C	D		44	A	B	C	D		64	A	B	C	D
5	A	B	C	D		25	A	B	C	D		45	A	B	C	D		65	A	B	C	D
6	A	B	C	D		26	A	B	C	D		46	A	B	C	D		66	A	B	C	D
7	A	B	C	D		27	A	B	C	D		47	A	B	C	D		67	A	B	C	D
8	A	B	C	D		28	A	B	C	D		48	A	B	C	D		68	A	B	C	D
9	A	B	C	D		29	A	B	C	D		49	A	B	C	D		69	A	B	C	D
10	A	B	C	D		30	A	B	C	D		50	A	B	C	D		70	A	B	C	D
11	A	B	C	D		31	A	B	C	D		51	A	B	C	D		71	A	B	C	D
12	A	B	C	D		32	A	B	C	D		52	A	B	C	D		72	A	B	C	D
13	A	B	C	D		33	A	B	C	D		53	A	B	C	D		73	A	B	C	D
14	A	B	C	D		34	A	B	C	D		54	A	B	C	D		74	A	B	C	D
15	A	B	C	D		35	A	B	C	D		55	A	B	C	D		75	A	B	C	D
16	A	B	C	D		36	A	B	C	D		56	A	B	C	D		76	A	B	C	D
17	A	B	C	D		37	A	B	C	D		57	A	B	C	D		77	A	B	C	D
18	A	B	C	D		38	A	B	C	D		58	A	B	C	D		78	A	B	C	D
19	A	B	C	D		39	A	B	C	D		59	A	B	C	D		79	A	B	C	D
20	A	B	C	D		40	A	B	C	D		60	A	B	C	D		80	A	B	C	D
																	81	A	B	C	D
																	82	A	B	C	D
																	83	A	B	C	D
																	84	A	B	C	D
																	85	A	B	C	D
																	86	A	B	C	D
																	87	A	B	C	D
																	88	A	B	C	D
																	89	A	B	C	D
																	90	A	B	C	D
																	91	A	B	C	D
																	92	A	B	C	D
																	93	A	B	C	D
																	94	A	B	C	D
																	95	A	B	C	D
																	96	A	B	C	D
																	97	A	B	C	D
																	98	A	B	C	D
																	99	A	B	C	D
																	100	A	B	C	D

測驗時間：120 分鐘（聽力 45 分鐘，閱讀 75 分鐘）

READING (PART V~VII)

#	A	B	C	D		#	A	B	C	D		#	A	B	C	D		#	A	B	C	D
101	A	B	C	D		121	A	B	C	D		141	A	B	C	D		181	A	B	C	D
102	A	B	C	D		122	A	B	C	D		142	A	B	C	D		182	A	B	C	D
103	A	B	C	D		123	A	B	C	D		143	A	B	C	D		183	A	B	C	D
104	A	B	C	D		124	A	B	C	D		144	A	B	C	D		184	A	B	C	D
105	A	B	C	D		125	A	B	C	D		145	A	B	C	D		185	A	B	C	D
106	A	B	C	D		126	A	B	C	D		146	A	B	C	D		186	A	B	C	D
107	A	B	C	D		127	A	B	C	D		147	A	B	C	D		187	A	B	C	D
108	A	B	C	D		128	A	B	C	D		148	A	B	C	D		188	A	B	C	D
109	A	B	C	D		129	A	B	C	D		149	A	B	C	D		189	A	B	C	D
110	A	B	C	D		130	A	B	C	D		150	A	B	C	D		190	A	B	C	D
111	A	B	C	D		131	A	B	C	D		151	A	B	C	D		191	A	B	C	D
112	A	B	C	D		132	A	B	C	D		152	A	B	C	D		192	A	B	C	D
113	A	B	C	D		133	A	B	C	D		153	A	B	C	D		193	A	B	C	D
114	A	B	C	D		134	A	B	C	D		154	A	B	C	D		194	A	B	C	D
115	A	B	C	D		135	A	B	C	D		155	A	B	C	D		195	A	B	C	D
116	A	B	C	D		136	A	B	C	D		156	A	B	C	D		196	A	B	C	D
117	A	B	C	D		137	A	B	C	D		157	A	B	C	D		197	A	B	C	D
118	A	B	C	D		138	A	B	C	D		158	A	B	C	D		198	A	B	C	D
119	A	B	C	D		139	A	B	C	D		159	A	B	C	D		199	A	B	C	D
120	A	B	C	D		140	A	B	C	D		160	A	B	C	D		200	A	B	C	D
											161	A	B	C	D						
											162	A	B	C	D						
											163	A	B	C	D						
											164	A	B	C	D						
											165	A	B	C	D						
											166	A	B	C	D						
											167	A	B	C	D						
											168	A	B	C	D						
											169	A	B	C	D						
											170	A	B	C	D						
											171	A	B	C	D						
											172	A	B	C	D						
											173	A	B	C	D						
											174	A	B	C	D						
											175	A	B	C	D						
											176	A	B	C	D						
											177	A	B	C	D						
											178	A	B	C	D						
											179	A	B	C	D						
											180	A	B	C	D						

請用鉛筆在答案卡上畫記。

正確題數：_____ /200

裁切線 ✂

Answer Sheet

TEST 3

裁切線

測驗時間：120 分鐘（聽力 45 分鐘，閱讀 75 分鐘）

請用鉛筆在答案卡上畫記。

正確題數：_____ /200

LISTENING (PART I~IV)

A multiple-choice answer grid for questions 1–100, each with options (A)(B)(C)(D).

READING (PART V~VII)

A multiple-choice answer grid for questions 101–200, each with options (A)(B)(C)(D).

Answer Sheet

TEST 4

LISTENING (PART I~IV)

READING (PART V~VII)

測驗時間：120 分鐘（聽力 45 分鐘，閱讀 75 分鐘）

請用鉛筆在答案卡上畫記。

正確題數：_____ / 200

裁切線

Answer Sheet

TEST 5

LISTENING (PART I~IV)

#					#					#					#				
1	Ⓐ Ⓑ Ⓒ Ⓓ				21	Ⓐ Ⓑ Ⓒ Ⓓ				41	Ⓐ Ⓑ Ⓒ Ⓓ				61	Ⓐ Ⓑ Ⓒ Ⓓ			
2	Ⓐ Ⓑ Ⓒ Ⓓ				22	Ⓐ Ⓑ Ⓒ Ⓓ				42	Ⓐ Ⓑ Ⓒ Ⓓ				62	Ⓐ Ⓑ Ⓒ Ⓓ			
3	Ⓐ Ⓑ Ⓒ Ⓓ				23	Ⓐ Ⓑ Ⓒ Ⓓ				43	Ⓐ Ⓑ Ⓒ Ⓓ				63	Ⓐ Ⓑ Ⓒ Ⓓ			
4	Ⓐ Ⓑ Ⓒ Ⓓ				24	Ⓐ Ⓑ Ⓒ Ⓓ				44	Ⓐ Ⓑ Ⓒ Ⓓ				64	Ⓐ Ⓑ Ⓒ Ⓓ			
5	Ⓐ Ⓑ Ⓒ Ⓓ				25	Ⓐ Ⓑ Ⓒ Ⓓ				45	Ⓐ Ⓑ Ⓒ Ⓓ				65	Ⓐ Ⓑ Ⓒ Ⓓ			
6	Ⓐ Ⓑ Ⓒ Ⓓ				26	Ⓐ Ⓑ Ⓒ Ⓓ				46	Ⓐ Ⓑ Ⓒ Ⓓ				66	Ⓐ Ⓑ Ⓒ Ⓓ			
7	Ⓐ Ⓑ Ⓒ Ⓓ				27	Ⓐ Ⓑ Ⓒ Ⓓ				47	Ⓐ Ⓑ Ⓒ Ⓓ				67	Ⓐ Ⓑ Ⓒ Ⓓ			
8	Ⓐ Ⓑ Ⓒ Ⓓ				28	Ⓐ Ⓑ Ⓒ Ⓓ				48	Ⓐ Ⓑ Ⓒ Ⓓ				68	Ⓐ Ⓑ Ⓒ Ⓓ			
9	Ⓐ Ⓑ Ⓒ Ⓓ				29	Ⓐ Ⓑ Ⓒ Ⓓ				49	Ⓐ Ⓑ Ⓒ Ⓓ				69	Ⓐ Ⓑ Ⓒ Ⓓ			
10	Ⓐ Ⓑ Ⓒ Ⓓ				30	Ⓐ Ⓑ Ⓒ Ⓓ				50	Ⓐ Ⓑ Ⓒ Ⓓ				70	Ⓐ Ⓑ Ⓒ Ⓓ			
11	Ⓐ Ⓑ Ⓒ Ⓓ				31	Ⓐ Ⓑ Ⓒ Ⓓ				51	Ⓐ Ⓑ Ⓒ Ⓓ				71	Ⓐ Ⓑ Ⓒ Ⓓ			
12	Ⓐ Ⓑ Ⓒ Ⓓ				32	Ⓐ Ⓑ Ⓒ Ⓓ				52	Ⓐ Ⓑ Ⓒ Ⓓ				72	Ⓐ Ⓑ Ⓒ Ⓓ			
13	Ⓐ Ⓑ Ⓒ Ⓓ				33	Ⓐ Ⓑ Ⓒ Ⓓ				53	Ⓐ Ⓑ Ⓒ Ⓓ				73	Ⓐ Ⓑ Ⓒ Ⓓ			
14	Ⓐ Ⓑ Ⓒ Ⓓ				34	Ⓐ Ⓑ Ⓒ Ⓓ				54	Ⓐ Ⓑ Ⓒ Ⓓ				74	Ⓐ Ⓑ Ⓒ Ⓓ			
15	Ⓐ Ⓑ Ⓒ Ⓓ				35	Ⓐ Ⓑ Ⓒ Ⓓ				55	Ⓐ Ⓑ Ⓒ Ⓓ				75	Ⓐ Ⓑ Ⓒ Ⓓ			
16	Ⓐ Ⓑ Ⓒ Ⓓ				36	Ⓐ Ⓑ Ⓒ Ⓓ				56	Ⓐ Ⓑ Ⓒ Ⓓ				76	Ⓐ Ⓑ Ⓒ Ⓓ			
17	Ⓐ Ⓑ Ⓒ Ⓓ				37	Ⓐ Ⓑ Ⓒ Ⓓ				57	Ⓐ Ⓑ Ⓒ Ⓓ				77	Ⓐ Ⓑ Ⓒ Ⓓ			
18	Ⓐ Ⓑ Ⓒ Ⓓ				38	Ⓐ Ⓑ Ⓒ Ⓓ				58	Ⓐ Ⓑ Ⓒ Ⓓ				78	Ⓐ Ⓑ Ⓒ Ⓓ			
19	Ⓐ Ⓑ Ⓒ Ⓓ				39	Ⓐ Ⓑ Ⓒ Ⓓ				59	Ⓐ Ⓑ Ⓒ Ⓓ				79	Ⓐ Ⓑ Ⓒ Ⓓ			
20	Ⓐ Ⓑ Ⓒ Ⓓ				40	Ⓐ Ⓑ Ⓒ Ⓓ				60	Ⓐ Ⓑ Ⓒ Ⓓ				80	Ⓐ Ⓑ Ⓒ Ⓓ			

#				
81	Ⓐ Ⓑ Ⓒ Ⓓ			
82	Ⓐ Ⓑ Ⓒ Ⓓ			
83	Ⓐ Ⓑ Ⓒ Ⓓ			
84	Ⓐ Ⓑ Ⓒ Ⓓ			
85	Ⓐ Ⓑ Ⓒ Ⓓ			
86	Ⓐ Ⓑ Ⓒ Ⓓ			
87	Ⓐ Ⓑ Ⓒ Ⓓ			
88	Ⓐ Ⓑ Ⓒ Ⓓ			
89	Ⓐ Ⓑ Ⓒ Ⓓ			
90	Ⓐ Ⓑ Ⓒ Ⓓ			
91	Ⓐ Ⓑ Ⓒ Ⓓ			
92	Ⓐ Ⓑ Ⓒ Ⓓ			
93	Ⓐ Ⓑ Ⓒ Ⓓ			
94	Ⓐ Ⓑ Ⓒ Ⓓ			
95	Ⓐ Ⓑ Ⓒ Ⓓ			
96	Ⓐ Ⓑ Ⓒ Ⓓ			
97	Ⓐ Ⓑ Ⓒ Ⓓ			
98	Ⓐ Ⓑ Ⓒ Ⓓ			
99	Ⓐ Ⓑ Ⓒ Ⓓ			
100	Ⓐ Ⓑ Ⓒ Ⓓ			

測驗時間：120 分鐘（聽力 45 分鐘，閱讀 75 分鐘）

READING (PART V~VII)

#					#					#					#				
101	Ⓐ Ⓑ Ⓒ Ⓓ				121	Ⓐ Ⓑ Ⓒ Ⓓ				141	Ⓐ Ⓑ Ⓒ Ⓓ				161	Ⓐ Ⓑ Ⓒ Ⓓ			
102	Ⓐ Ⓑ Ⓒ Ⓓ				122	Ⓐ Ⓑ Ⓒ Ⓓ				142	Ⓐ Ⓑ Ⓒ Ⓓ				162	Ⓐ Ⓑ Ⓒ Ⓓ			
103	Ⓐ Ⓑ Ⓒ Ⓓ				123	Ⓐ Ⓑ Ⓒ Ⓓ				143	Ⓐ Ⓑ Ⓒ Ⓓ				163	Ⓐ Ⓑ Ⓒ Ⓓ			
104	Ⓐ Ⓑ Ⓒ Ⓓ				124	Ⓐ Ⓑ Ⓒ Ⓓ				144	Ⓐ Ⓑ Ⓒ Ⓓ				164	Ⓐ Ⓑ Ⓒ Ⓓ			
105	Ⓐ Ⓑ Ⓒ Ⓓ				125	Ⓐ Ⓑ Ⓒ Ⓓ				145	Ⓐ Ⓑ Ⓒ Ⓓ				165	Ⓐ Ⓑ Ⓒ Ⓓ			
106	Ⓐ Ⓑ Ⓒ Ⓓ				126	Ⓐ Ⓑ Ⓒ Ⓓ				146	Ⓐ Ⓑ Ⓒ Ⓓ				166	Ⓐ Ⓑ Ⓒ Ⓓ			
107	Ⓐ Ⓑ Ⓒ Ⓓ				127	Ⓐ Ⓑ Ⓒ Ⓓ				147	Ⓐ Ⓑ Ⓒ Ⓓ				167	Ⓐ Ⓑ Ⓒ Ⓓ			
108	Ⓐ Ⓑ Ⓒ Ⓓ				128	Ⓐ Ⓑ Ⓒ Ⓓ				148	Ⓐ Ⓑ Ⓒ Ⓓ				168	Ⓐ Ⓑ Ⓒ Ⓓ			
109	Ⓐ Ⓑ Ⓒ Ⓓ				129	Ⓐ Ⓑ Ⓒ Ⓓ				149	Ⓐ Ⓑ Ⓒ Ⓓ				169	Ⓐ Ⓑ Ⓒ Ⓓ			
110	Ⓐ Ⓑ Ⓒ Ⓓ				130	Ⓐ Ⓑ Ⓒ Ⓓ				150	Ⓐ Ⓑ Ⓒ Ⓓ				170	Ⓐ Ⓑ Ⓒ Ⓓ			
111	Ⓐ Ⓑ Ⓒ Ⓓ				131	Ⓐ Ⓑ Ⓒ Ⓓ				151	Ⓐ Ⓑ Ⓒ Ⓓ				171	Ⓐ Ⓑ Ⓒ Ⓓ			
112	Ⓐ Ⓑ Ⓒ Ⓓ				132	Ⓐ Ⓑ Ⓒ Ⓓ				152	Ⓐ Ⓑ Ⓒ Ⓓ				172	Ⓐ Ⓑ Ⓒ Ⓓ			
113	Ⓐ Ⓑ Ⓒ Ⓓ				133	Ⓐ Ⓑ Ⓒ Ⓓ				153	Ⓐ Ⓑ Ⓒ Ⓓ				173	Ⓐ Ⓑ Ⓒ Ⓓ			
114	Ⓐ Ⓑ Ⓒ Ⓓ				134	Ⓐ Ⓑ Ⓒ Ⓓ				154	Ⓐ Ⓑ Ⓒ Ⓓ				174	Ⓐ Ⓑ Ⓒ Ⓓ			
115	Ⓐ Ⓑ Ⓒ Ⓓ				135	Ⓐ Ⓑ Ⓒ Ⓓ				155	Ⓐ Ⓑ Ⓒ Ⓓ				175	Ⓐ Ⓑ Ⓒ Ⓓ			
116	Ⓐ Ⓑ Ⓒ Ⓓ				136	Ⓐ Ⓑ Ⓒ Ⓓ				156	Ⓐ Ⓑ Ⓒ Ⓓ				176	Ⓐ Ⓑ Ⓒ Ⓓ			
117	Ⓐ Ⓑ Ⓒ Ⓓ				137	Ⓐ Ⓑ Ⓒ Ⓓ				157	Ⓐ Ⓑ Ⓒ Ⓓ				177	Ⓐ Ⓑ Ⓒ Ⓓ			
118	Ⓐ Ⓑ Ⓒ Ⓓ				138	Ⓐ Ⓑ Ⓒ Ⓓ				158	Ⓐ Ⓑ Ⓒ Ⓓ				178	Ⓐ Ⓑ Ⓒ Ⓓ			
119	Ⓐ Ⓑ Ⓒ Ⓓ				139	Ⓐ Ⓑ Ⓒ Ⓓ				159	Ⓐ Ⓑ Ⓒ Ⓓ				179	Ⓐ Ⓑ Ⓒ Ⓓ			
120	Ⓐ Ⓑ Ⓒ Ⓓ				140	Ⓐ Ⓑ Ⓒ Ⓓ				160	Ⓐ Ⓑ Ⓒ Ⓓ				180	Ⓐ Ⓑ Ⓒ Ⓓ			

#				
181	Ⓐ Ⓑ Ⓒ Ⓓ			
182	Ⓐ Ⓑ Ⓒ Ⓓ			
183	Ⓐ Ⓑ Ⓒ Ⓓ			
184	Ⓐ Ⓑ Ⓒ Ⓓ			
185	Ⓐ Ⓑ Ⓒ Ⓓ			
186	Ⓐ Ⓑ Ⓒ Ⓓ			
187	Ⓐ Ⓑ Ⓒ Ⓓ			
188	Ⓐ Ⓑ Ⓒ Ⓓ			
189	Ⓐ Ⓑ Ⓒ Ⓓ			
190	Ⓐ Ⓑ Ⓒ Ⓓ			
191	Ⓐ Ⓑ Ⓒ Ⓓ			
192	Ⓐ Ⓑ Ⓒ Ⓓ			
193	Ⓐ Ⓑ Ⓒ Ⓓ			
194	Ⓐ Ⓑ Ⓒ Ⓓ			
195	Ⓐ Ⓑ Ⓒ Ⓓ			
196	Ⓐ Ⓑ Ⓒ Ⓓ			
197	Ⓐ Ⓑ Ⓒ Ⓓ			
198	Ⓐ Ⓑ Ⓒ Ⓓ			
199	Ⓐ Ⓑ Ⓒ Ⓓ			
200	Ⓐ Ⓑ Ⓒ Ⓓ			

正確題數：_____ /200

請用鉛筆在答案卡上畫記。

NEW TOEIC
950
聽力＋閱讀
5 回達標

$$\boxed{\text{解析本}}$$

Hackers Academia ／著　林建豪、陳宜慧／譯

suncolor
三采文化

LISTENING TEST
p.28

1 (B)	2 (A)	3 (D)	4 (A)	5 (D)
6 (C)	7 (C)	8 (B)	9 (C)	10 (C)
11 (A)	12 (A)	13 (C)	14 (A)	15 (A)
16 (A)	17 (A)	18 (B)	19 (B)	20 (C)
21 (C)	22 (A)	23 (A)	24 (C)	25 (C)
26 (A)	27 (C)	28 (B)	29 (B)	30 (B)
31 (C)	32 (A)	33 (C)	34 (D)	35 (B)
36 (D)	37 (B)	38 (B)	39 (D)	40 (A)
41 (B)	42 (C)	43 (A)	44 (B)	45 (C)
46 (D)	47 (D)	48 (A)	49 (D)	50 (D)
51 (C)	52 (B)	53 (C)	54 (D)	55 (B)
56 (A)	57 (B)	58 (D)	59 (B)	60 (B)
61 (D)	62 (D)	63 (D)	64 (D)	65 (C)
66 (B)	67 (C)	68 (D)	69 (D)	70 (C)
71 (A)	72 (D)	73 (D)	74 (D)	75 (A)
76 (B)	77 (A)	78 (D)	79 (D)	80 (B)
81 (D)	82 (C)	83 (C)	84 (D)	85 (D)
86 (C)	87 (B)	88 (A)	89 (D)	90 (B)
91 (D)	92 (C)	93 (D)	94 (C)	95 (B)
96 (C)	97 (A)	98 (C)	99 (A)	100 (D)

READING TEST
p.40

101 (C)	102 (B)	103 (D)	104 (A)	105 (A)
106 (C)	107 (A)	108 (A)	109 (C)	110 (A)
111 (C)	112 (D)	113 (B)	114 (D)	115 (B)
116 (D)	117 (B)	118 (A)	119 (C)	120 (D)
121 (C)	122 (C)	123 (B)	124 (A)	125 (B)
126 (C)	127 (C)	128 (B)	129 (B)	130 (D)
131 (C)	132 (B)	133 (A)	134 (C)	135 (A)
136 (B)	137 (D)	138 (C)	139 (B)	140 (D)
141 (C)	142 (A)	143 (D)	144 (B)	145 (D)
146 (D)	147 (B)	148 (C)	149 (A)	150 (D)
151 (B)	152 (B)	153 (D)	154 (B)	155 (C)
156 (A)	157 (C)	158 (D)	159 (A)	160 (D)
161 (D)	162 (C)	163 (A)	164 (B)	165 (A)
166 (C)	167 (C)	168 (A)	169 (C)	170 (B)
171 (C)	172 (A)	173 (A)	174 (C)	175 (B)
176 (C)	177 (B)	178 (B)	179 (A)	180 (D)
181 (B)	182 (A)	183 (C)	184 (B)	185 (A)
186 (D)	187 (B)	188 (C)	189 (C)	190 (D)
191 (D)	192 (C)	193 (A)	194 (D)	195 (B)
196 (D)	197 (A)	198 (B)	199 (D)	200 (A)

PART 1

1 ᴺ加拿大發音

(A) The man is putting on a scarf.
(B) The man is sitting on a bike.
(C) The man is wearing a helmet.
(D) The man is using a bicycle rack.

bicycle rack 腳踏車駐車架

翻譯 (A) 男子正在圍圍巾。
　　 (B) 男子正坐在腳踏車上。
　　 (C) 男子戴著安全帽。
　　 (D) 男子正在使用腳踏車駐車架。

解析 1 人照片
(A) [✕] putting on（穿上）與男子的動作無關，因此是錯誤選項。wearing 表達的是已經穿著衣服、帽子、鞋子等的狀態，與表達「正在穿」這個動作的 putting on 不同。
(B) [○] 描述男子坐在腳踏車上的樣子，這是最符合照片的正確答案。
(C) [✕] 因為照片中沒有安全帽（helmet），男子也沒戴安全帽，所以是錯誤選項。
(D) [✕] 因為照片中沒有腳踏車駐車架（bicycle rack），所以是錯誤選項。本選項出現了照片中的腳踏車（bicycle），所以容易混淆。

2 ᴺ澳洲發音

(A) She is cleaning a room.
(B) She is watching television.
(C) She is wiping a countertop.
(D) There is a flowerpot on the floor.

wipe 擦拭　countertop 廚房流理臺
flowerpot 花盆

翻譯 **(A) 她正在打掃房間。**
　　 (B) 她正在看電視。
　　 (C) 她正在擦拭廚房流理臺。
　　 (D) 地上有一個花盆。

解析 1 人照片
(A) [○] 描述女子正在打掃房間，這是最符合照片的正確答案。
(B) [✕] watching television（正在看電視）與女子的動作無關，因此是錯誤選項。本選項出現照片中的 television（電視），所以容易混淆。
(C) [✕] 照片中沒有廚房流理臺（countertop），所以錯誤。請注意不要一聽到 She is wiping（她正在擦拭）就選擇這個選項。

(D) [×] 花盆不在地上，而是在架子上，所以是錯誤選項。本選項出現照片中的 flowerpot（花盆），所以容易混淆。

3 美國發音

(A) A man is pushing a cart.
(B) Some people are putting items in a bag.
(C) A woman is paying for some groceries.
(D) Two men are on opposite sides of a register.

pay for 付款　grocery 雜貨
be on opposite sides of ~ 在～的兩側　register 收銀機

翻譯 (A) 一名男子正推著購物車。
　　 (B) 有幾個人正把東西放進包包。
　　 (C) 一名女子正在付雜貨的錢。
　　 (D) 兩名男子站在收銀機的兩側。

解析 2 人以上照片
　　 (A) [×] 照片中沒有推著購物車（pushing a cart）的男子，所以錯誤。
　　 (B) [×] putting items in a bag（正把東西放進包包）與照片人物的動作無關，所以錯誤。
　　 (C) [×] 因為照片中沒有正在付錢（paying for）的女子，所以錯誤。
　　 (D) [○] 描述兩名男子站在收銀機的兩側，這是最符合照片的正確答案。

4 英國發音

(A) He is working on an automobile.
(B) A car is being washed.
(C) He is parking a vehicle.
(D) A fuel tank is being filled.

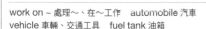

work on ~ 處理～、在～工作　automobile 汽車
vehicle 車輛、交通工具　fuel tank 油箱

翻譯 **(A) 他正在修車。**
　　 (B) 車子正在清洗中。
　　 (C) 他正在停車。
　　 (D) 油箱正在加油。

解析 1 人照片
　　 (A) [○] 描述男子正在修車，這是最符合照片的答案。
　　 (B) [×] 照片中雖然有汽車，但是車子並沒有正在清洗（is being washed），所以錯誤。
　　 (C) [×] parking（停車）與男子的動作無關，所以是錯誤選項。本選項出現照片中的車輛（vehicle），所以容易混淆。
　　 (D) [×] 由於無法確認照片中的油箱是否正在加油（is being filled），所以是錯誤選項。

5 澳洲發音

(A) They are carrying a toolbox.
(B) An antenna is being installed.
(C) They are painting some boards.
(D) A roof is being constructed.

toolbox 工具箱　antenna 天線、尖塔　install 安裝
construct 建設

翻譯 (A) 他們正在搬工具箱。
　　 (B) 天線正在安裝。
　　 (C) 他們正在油漆一些板子。
　　 (D) 屋頂正在建造。

解析 2 人以上照片
　　 (A) [×] carrying（搬動）與照片人物的動作無關，所以錯誤。本選項出現照片中的工具（tool），所以容易混淆。
　　 (B) [×] 由於無法從照片中確認天線是否正在安裝（is being installed），所以是錯誤選項。
　　 (C) [×] painting（油漆）與照片人物的動作無關，所以錯誤。
　　 (D) [○] 描述屋頂正在建造，這是最符合照片的正確答案。

6 美國發音

(A) Food has been set out on a patio.
(B) Some chairs have been stacked up.
(C) Some pictures are mounted on the wall.
(D) A window has been left open.

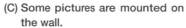

set out 準備好（食物、食材等）　patio 露臺、陽臺　stack 堆放
mount 固定、安裝

翻譯 (A) 飯菜擺好在陽臺上。
　　 (B) 幾把椅子堆疊在一起。
　　 (C) 一些畫被固定在牆上。
　　 (D) 窗戶開著。

解析 物品及風景照
　　 (A) [×] 因為照片中的場所不是陽臺（patio），所以錯誤。
　　 (B) [×] 照片中雖然有椅子，但不是堆疊在一起（have been stacked up），所以錯誤。
　　 (C) [○] 描述幾幅畫固定在牆上的樣子，這是最符合照片的正確答案。
　　 (D) [×] 雖然照片中有窗戶，但並不是敞開的（has been left open），所以錯誤。

PART 2

7 加拿大發音→澳洲發音

Which spreadsheet software are you using?
(A) To manage financial data.
(B) Sure, you can use it.
(C) It's called Organizer Plus.

financial data 財務資料

翻譯 你正在用什麼電子表單軟體？
    (A) 為了管理財務資料。
    (B) 當然，你可以用。
    (C) 它叫做 Organizer Plus。

解析 Which 疑問句
    (A) [×] 使用與問題中出現的 software（軟體）有關的 data（資料），所以容易造成混淆。
    (B) [×] 本選項出現 use，是容易與題目中的 using 混淆的錯誤選項。
    (C) [○] 提到了正在使用的軟體名稱是 Organizer Plus，所以是正確答案。

8 英國發音→加拿大發音

Who paid the consultant for the program?
(A) A visit was scheduled for 2 P.M.
(B) The manager of our department.
(C) They'll take place next Tuesday.

pay for 付～的錢　　be scheduled for 為～訂行程
take place 舉行、發生

翻譯 誰付了錢給該計劃的顧問？
    (A) 拜訪行程訂在下午 2 點。
    (B) 我們部門的經理。
    (C) 它們將於下週二舉行。

解析 Who 疑問句
    (A) [×] 題目問的是誰支付費用給計劃的顧問，但本選項回答拜訪行程訂在下午 2 點，與題目無關，所以錯誤。
    (B) [○] 提到了支付費用的人，也就是部門的經理，所以是正確答案。
    (C) [×] 回答它們將在下週二舉行，與詢問誰支付費用給計劃的顧問的問題無關，所以是錯誤選項。

9 美國發音→澳洲發音

I placed an order for baked chicken about 20 minutes ago.
(A) Just place it on the table over there.
(B) Do you need help cooking it?
(C) Unfortunately, it's not ready yet.

bake 烤　　unfortunately 遺憾地

翻譯 我大約 20 分鐘前點了烤雞。
    (A) 就把它放在那邊的桌子上吧。
    (B) 你需要我幫忙料理它嗎？
    (C) 很遺憾，現在還沒好。

解析 直述句
    (A) [×] 將題目中的 placed 改為 place，是容易混淆的錯誤選項。
    (B) [×] 出現與題目中的 chicken（烤雞）發音相似的 cooking（料理），是容易讓人混淆的錯誤選項。
    (C) [○] 本選項以「很遺憾，還沒好」來回答訂單的情況，所以是正確答案。

10 加拿大發音→英國發音

Have you ever been to the Bridgeport Museum of Art?
(A) The sculpture in the main hall.
(B) Museum hours are listed online.
(C) Yes. I go at least twice a year.

sculpture 雕塑品　　list 記載、列出　　at least 至少、最少

翻譯 你曾經去過 Bridgeport 藝術館嗎？
    (A) 主廳內的雕塑品。
    (B) 藝術館的開放時間列在網站上。
    (C) 是的，我每年至少去兩次。

解析 助動詞疑問句
    (A) [×] 出現與題目中的 Museum of Art（藝術館）相關的 sculpture（雕塑品），所以是容易混淆的錯誤選項。
    (B) [×] 出現題目中的 Museum，所以是容易混淆的錯誤選項。
    (C) [○] 透過 Yes 表達去過藝術館後，補充說明一年至少去兩次，所以是正確答案。

11 澳洲發音→英國發音

Didn't your sales surpass those of Uvic Inc. last quarter?
(A) Yes. We came out on top.
(B) At the quarterly report meeting.
(C) All items are 20 percent off.

sales 賣出、銷售額　　surpass 超越、優於　　quarter 季
come out on top（從競爭中）勝出　　quarterly 每季的

翻譯 上一季你們的銷售額不是超越了 Uvic 公司嗎？
    (A) 是的，我們贏了。
    (B) 在季度報告會議上。
    (C) 所有品項都打八折。

解析 否定疑問句
    (A) [○] 透過 Yes 表達超越 Uvic 公司的銷售額後，補充說明自己贏了，所以是正確答案。
    (B) [×] 出現與題目中的 quarter 發音相似的詞彙 quarterly，是容易讓人混淆的錯誤選項。

(C) [×] 出現與題目中的 sales（銷售額、銷售量）相關的詞彙 items（品項），也是容易讓人混淆的錯誤選項。

12 ᵃⁿ 加拿大發音→澳洲發音

Where will the annual retreat for employees be held next month?
(A) The same resort we went to last year.
(B) More than 300 employees will attend.
(C) I'll hold on to that for you.

annual 年度的、每年的　retreat 郊遊　the same 就是那個、相同的　hold on to（為他人）負責、保管

翻譯 下個月為員工們舉辦的年度郊遊會在哪裡舉行？
(A) 就在我們去年去過的那個度假村。
(B) 超過 300 名員工會參加。
(C) 我會為你保管它。

解析 Where 疑問句
(A) [○] 回答我們去年去過的那個度假村，間接傳達了舉行年度郊遊的場所，所以是正確答案。
(B) [×] 出現題目中的 employees，所以是容易混淆的錯誤選項。
(C) [×] 將題目中的 held 改為 hold，是容易讓人混淆的錯誤選項。

13 ᵃⁿ 美國發音→英國發音

Could you send me an update on the current state of the market?
(A) Inside the supermarket.
(B) Sure, send it to me later.
(C) I'll get that to you in a minute.

state 狀態、情況　in a minute 馬上、立刻

翻譯 你能把目前市場狀態的最新情況寄給我嗎？
(A) 在超市裡。
(B) 當然可以，待會請寄給我。
(C) 我馬上拿給你。

解析 請求疑問句
(A) [×] 使用與題目中的 market 發音相似的詞彙 supermarket，是容易混淆的錯誤選項。
(B) [×] 出現題目中的 send，是容易讓人混淆的錯誤選項。
(C) [○] 回答馬上拿給你，表達可以寄送市場狀態的最新情況，所以是正確答案。

14 ᵃⁿ 澳洲發音→美國發音

When are you planning to take your vacation?
(A) I've booked my trip for August.
(B) A luxurious spa.
(C) The train ticket for Barcelona.

book 預約　luxurious 華麗的、奢侈的

翻譯 你計劃何時去休假？
(A) 我已經預約了 8 月的旅行。
(B) 奢侈的水療。
(C) 往巴塞隆納的火車票。

解析 When 疑問句
(A) [○] 回答預約了 8 月的旅行，因為題目提到了休假時間，所以是正確答案。
(B) [×] 出現與題目中的 vacation（休假）相關的 spa（水療），所以是容易混淆的錯誤選項。
(C) [×] 出現與題目中的 vacation（休假）相關的 train ticket（火車票），所以是容易混淆的錯誤選項。

15 ᵃⁿ 澳洲發音→英國發音

Mark ran the marathon this year, didn't he?
(A) He skipped it due to an injury.
(B) I don't like running long races.
(C) The course has many hills.

skip 略過　injury 受傷

翻譯 Mark 今年有跑馬拉松，不是嗎？
(A) 他因為受傷，所以略過了。
(B) 我不喜歡長跑比賽。
(C) 那條路線有許多山丘。

解析 否定疑問句
(A) [○] 藉由回答他因為受傷而略過比賽，表達 Mark 今年沒參加馬拉松，所以是正確答案。
(B) [×] 將題目中的 ran 改為 running，是容易造成混淆的錯誤選項。
(C) [×] 出現與題目中的 marathon（馬拉松）有關的 course（路線），是容易混淆的錯誤選項。

16 ᵃⁿ 加拿大發音→澳洲發音

We should buy a microwave for the apartment.
(A) I'll search online for cheap ones.
(B) I usually cook for my family.
(C) The apartment is out of our price range.

microwave 微波爐　price range 價格範圍、預算範圍

翻譯 我們應該為公寓買臺微波爐。
(A) 我會在網路上找臺便宜的。
(B) 我常常為家人煮飯。
(C) 這間公寓已經超出我們的預算了。

解析 直述句
(A) [○] 回答要在網路上找便宜的東西，表達同意了應該買微波爐的意見，所以是正確答案。
(B) [×] 出現與題目中的 microwave（微波爐）有關的 cook（煮飯），所以是容易混淆的錯誤選項。
(C) [×] 出現題目中的 apartment，所以是容易讓人混淆的錯誤選項。

17 英國發音→加拿大發音

How much will the construction of an additional manufacturing facility cost?
(A) We are waiting for a quote.
(B) It will take weeks to manufacture.
(C) Due to a large tax incentive.

---

construction 建造、建築　additional 額外的
manufacturing 製造的　facility 設施、設備
quote 報價、估價　incentive 優惠、獎勵措施

翻譯　建造額外的製造設備須花費多少錢？
　　　(A) 我們正在等待報價。
　　　(B) 須花幾週的時間製造。
　　　(C) 因為有很大的稅金優惠。

解析　How 疑問句
　　　(A) [○] 用「等待報價」間接回答還不知道工程可能需要的花費，所以是正確答案。
　　　(B) [×] 出現與題目中的 manufacturing 發音相似的 manufacture，所以是容易混淆的錯誤選項。
　　　(C) [×] 出現與題目中的 cost（費用）相關的 tax incentive（稅金優惠），所以是容易混淆的錯誤選項。

18 美國發音→加拿大發音

When will the new network system be installed?
(A) Don't forget to install the update.
(B) No later than next Friday.
(C) This weekend's networking event was canceled.

---

no later than 不晚於

翻譯　何時安裝新的網路系統？
　　　(A) 別忘了安裝更新版本。
　　　(B) 不晚於下週五。
　　　(C) 本週末的社交活動取消了。

解析　When 疑問句
　　　(A) [×] 將題目中的 installed 改為 install，所以是容易造成混淆的錯誤選項。
　　　(B) [○] 回答最晚不會超過下週五，因為題目詢問新網路系統的安裝時間，所以是正確答案。
　　　(C) [×] 出現與題目中的 network 發音相似的詞彙 networking，所以是容易混淆的錯誤選項。

19 英國發音→澳洲發音

Anna's wedding is on Saturday morning at the Renaissance Hotel.
(A) Two double rooms.
(B) Are you planning to attend the ceremony?
(C) It had many guests.

---

attend 參與　ceremony 儀式、典禮

翻譯　Anna 的結婚典禮週六早上在萬麗飯店舉行。
　　　(A) 兩間雙人房。
　　　(B) 你打算參加典禮嗎？
　　　(C) 有很多賓客。

解析　直述句
　　　(A) [×] 出現與題目中的 Hotel（飯店）相關的 double rooms（雙人房），所以是容易混淆的錯誤選項。
　　　(B) [○] 藉由反問是否打算參加典禮，回應對方對於婚禮時間的敘述，所以是正確答案。
　　　(C) [×] 出現與題目中的 wedding（婚禮）相關的詞彙 guests（客人），所以是容易造成混淆的錯誤選項。

20 澳洲發音→英國發音

The advertising campaign for this product costs a lot, right?
(A) They make great quality products.
(B) Yes, she's an advertising manager.
(C) It'll be worth it in the long run.

---

quality 高級的、出色的　worth 值得的　in the long run 長期地

翻譯　這個產品的廣告活動花了很多錢，對吧？
　　　(A) 他們製作出色的產品。
　　　(B) 是的，她是廣告的負責人。
　　　(C) 從長遠來看，這是值得的。

解析　附加疑問句
　　　(A) [×] 出現題目中的 products，所以是容易混淆的錯誤選項。
　　　(B) [×] 出現題目中的 advertising，所以是容易混淆的錯誤選項。
　　　(C) [○] 藉由「從長遠來看，這是值得的」，間接回應對廣告活動花了很多錢的疑問，所以是正確答案。

21 加拿大發音→美國發音

Didn't Rachel submit her monthly plan already?
(A) I'm going to be away for a month.
(B) I've already checked your submission.
(C) No. I'll send an e-mail to remind her.

---

be away 不在　submission 提交　remind 提醒

翻譯　Rachel 不是已經提交了每月計劃書嗎？
　　　(A) 我將會有一個月不在。
　　　(B) 我已經確認了你提交的內容。
　　　(C) 還沒，我會寄一封電子郵件提醒她。

解析　否定疑問句
　　　(A) [×] 出現與題目中的 monthly 發音相似的 month，所以是容易混淆的錯誤選項。
　　　(B) [×] 出現題目中的 already，以及與題目中的 submit 發音相似的 submission，所以是容易混淆的錯誤選項。

(C) [○] 用 No 傳達 Rachel 沒有提交每月計劃書後，補充說明會寄電子郵件提醒她，所以是正確答案。

22 🎧 加拿大發音→英國發音

Should we stay for the award ceremony or leave after your speech?
(A) It's entirely up to you.
(B) Two speakers were placed on stage.
(C) Let's leave it as it is.

speech 演說　entirely 完全地

翻譯 我們應該留下來參加頒獎典禮還是在你演講結束後離開？
(A) 這完全取決於你們。
(B) 臺上安排了兩位演講者。
(C) 讓我們保持原樣。

解析 選擇疑問句
(A) [○] 回答完全取決於對方，間接傳達留下來參加頒獎典禮與演講後離開這兩件事都行，所以是正確答案。
(B) [×] 出現與題目中的 speech（演講）有關的 speakers（演講者），所以是容易混淆的錯誤選項。
(C) [×] 出現題目中的 leave，所以是容易造成混淆的錯誤選項。

23 🎧 加拿大發音→英國發音

The rent for this unit is only $400 per month.
(A) That's quite affordable for the area.
(B) Yes, we can just go to a rental car place.
(C) Payment is due on the first of the month.

rent 租金　unit 一戶、單位　affordable 便宜的
payment 付款、支付　due 應付（錢）的

翻譯 該戶的租金每月僅 400 美元。
(A) 這在該地區相當便宜。
(B) 是的，我們可以去租車地點。
(C) 付款日期為當月第一天。

解析 直述句
(A) [○] 藉由回答這在該地相當便宜，對租金提出意見，所以是正確答案。
(B) [×] 出現與題目中的 rent 發音相似的 rental，所以是容易混淆的錯誤選項。
(C) [×] 出現與題目中的 rent（租金）相關的 payment（支付），所以是容易混淆的錯誤選項。

24 🎧 美國發音→英國發音

How can I register for the management basics course?
(A) It's pretty easy to distinguish the material.
(B) A management position will open soon.
(C) I'll give you a hand with that.

register 註冊　distinguish 區別、分辨、分類
material 資料　open 公開的　give a hand 幫忙

翻譯 我如何註冊管理基礎課程？
(A) 很容易區分這些資料。
(B) 管理職即將開缺。
(C) 我會幫你的。

解析 How 疑問句
(A) [×] 出現與題目中的 course（課程）相關的 material（資料），所以是容易造成混淆的錯誤選項。
(B) [×] 出現題目中的 management，所以是容易混淆的錯誤選項。
(C) [○] 藉由要幫忙，間接回答將會告訴對方註冊管理基礎課程的方法，所以是正確答案。

25 🎧 美國發音→澳洲發音

Would you mind bringing this package to Mr. Smith?
(A) Please don't mind the noise.
(B) You can wrap it with this paper.
(C) He's not at his desk right now.

package 包裹、宅配　wrap 包裝

翻譯 你介意把這個包裹帶給 Smith 先生嗎？
(A) 請不要理會噪音。
(B) 你可以用這張紙把它包起來。
(C) 他現在不在位子上。

解析 請求疑問句
(A) [×] 出現題目中的 mind，所以是容易混淆的錯誤選項。
(B) [×] 出現與題目中的 package（包裹）相關的 wrap（包裝），所以是容易造成混淆的錯誤選項。
(C) [○] 藉由回答他現在不在位子上，間接拒絕把包裹拿給 Smith 先生的請求。

26 🎧 加拿大發音→美國發音

Have you heard about the new hotel development across the street?
(A) It's all anyone is talking about.
(B) You can use the crosswalk.
(C) You have to develop your driving skills.

crosswalk 斑馬線　develop 發展、進展

翻譯 你聽說了這條街對面的新飯店開發案嗎？
(A) 這是大家都在談論的事情。
(B) 你可以使用斑馬線。

(C) 你必須提升你的駕駛技巧。

解析 助動詞疑問句
(A) [○] 藉由回答那是大家都在談論的事，間接傳達已經聽說這條街對面的新飯店開發案，所以是正確答案。
(B) [×] 出現與題目中的 across 發音相似的詞彙 crosswalk，所以是容易混淆的錯誤選項。
(C) [×] 出現與題目中的 development 發音相似的 develop，所以是容易混淆的錯誤選項。

27 美國發音→加拿大發音

Are you coming to my accounting seminar?
(A) I'll check the account.
(B) He's going with his colleagues.
(C) As long as I finish my work in time.

accounting 會計　account 帳戶　colleague 同事

翻譯 你要來參加我的會計研討會嗎？
(A) 我會檢查一下帳戶。
(B) 他要和他的同事一起去。
(C) 只要我能按時完成工作。

解析 Be 動詞疑問句
(A) [×] 出現與題目中的 accounting 發音相似的 account，所以是容易混淆的錯誤選項。
(B) [×] 出現與題目中的 coming（來）有關的 going（去），所以是容易造成混淆的錯誤選項。
(C) [○] 以「只要按時完成工作」間接回答也許去參加會計研討會，所以是正確答案。

28 美國發音→澳洲發音

Where did you place the document I gave you this morning?
(A) We replaced the printer.
(B) It must be on my desk.
(C) During the morning team meeting.

document 文件　replace 替換

翻譯 你把我今天早上給你的文件放在哪裡？
(A) 我們換了印表機。
(B) 它肯定在我的桌上。
(C) 在早上的團隊會議期間。

解析 Where 疑問句
(A) [×] 出現與題目中的 place 發音相似的 replaced，所以是容易混淆的錯誤選項。
(B) [○] 回答肯定在自己的桌子上，因為提到了文件的位置，所以是正確答案。
(C) [×] 出現題目中的 morning，所以是容易混淆的錯誤選項。

29 澳洲發音→美國發音

Andy, who owns the property on the corner?
(A) That's the proper way to do it.
(B) It's a city property.
(C) I live a few blocks down.

property 房地產、財產　proper 合適的、適當的

翻譯 Andy，街角的房地產是誰的？
(A) 這是適當的做法。
(B) 這是市政府的房地產。
(C) 我住在幾個街區之外。

解析 Who 疑問句
(A) [×] 出現與題目中的 property 發音相似的 proper，所以是容易混淆的錯誤選項。
(B) [○] 回答這是市政府的房地產，藉此提到街角房地產的所有者，所以是正確答案。
(C) [×] 出現與題目中的 corner（轉角）相關的 blocks（區），所以是容易混淆的錯誤選項。

30 英國發音→加拿大發音

Why are there maintenance workers in the lobby?
(A) We'll maintain the current deadline.
(B) The air-conditioning system broke down.
(C) We can work on it together.

maintenance 維護　maintain 維持
current 現在的　break down 故障

翻譯 為什麼大廳裡有維修人員？
(A) 我們將維持目前的截止期限。
(B) 空調系統壞了。
(C) 我們可以一起處理它。

解析 Why 疑問句
(A) [×] 出現與題目中的 maintenance 發音相似的 maintain，所以是容易混淆的錯誤選項。
(B) [○] 藉由回答空調系統故障，提出維修人員在大廳的理由，所以是正確答案。
(C) [×] 使用與題目中的 workers 發音相似的 work，所以是容易混淆的錯誤選項。

31 英國發音→美國發音

Did you find a suitable candidate for the marketing position?
(A) I voted for the other candidate.
(B) I don't think a suit is necessary.
(C) I e-mailed you a résumé.

suitable 合適的　candidate 應徵者、候選人
vote 投票　necessary 必要的

翻譯 你為行銷職位找到合適的應徵者了嗎？
(A) 我投給了另一位候選人。

(B) 我認為沒有必要穿西裝。
(C) 我透過電子郵件寄了一份履歷給你。

解析 助動詞疑問句
    (A) [×] 出現題目中的 candidate（應徵者、候選人），所以是容易混淆的錯誤選項。
    (B) [×] 出現與題目中的 suitable 發音相似的 suit，所以是容易混淆的錯誤選項。
    (C) [○] 回答用電子郵件將履歷寄給對方，間接傳達針對行銷職位找到了合適的應徵者，所以是正確答案。

PART 3

32-34 [3-1] 美國發音→加拿大發音

Questions 32-34 refer to the following conversation.

W: Hi. ³²I wanted to inquire about the job advertisement for a secretary you posted on your website. Does that require a college degree? It wasn't clear in the advertisement.
M: You don't have to be a college graduate, but we would prefer it if you were at least working towards a degree. We would also like you to have some experience in a secretarial role.
W: Well . . . I'm studying for a bachelor's now at Queen College. ³³I don't have any experience in a secretarial role, but I completed an internship at Artest Industries.
M: That's OK. We'd be happy to read your application. ³⁴Be sure to submit it by Tuesday, which is the deadline.

inquire 詢問　job advertisement 徵才廣告　secretary 秘書
graduate 畢業　work towards 向〜努力　secretarial 秘書職的
bachelor 學士（學位）　internship 實習期間
be happy to 很高興做〜　application 申請書
be sure to 一定要〜　submit 提交　deadline 截止日期、期限

翻譯 問題 32-34，請參考以下對話。
    女：嗨，³² 我想請問您在網站上發布的秘書招聘廣告，這需要大學學歷嗎？廣告中並沒有明確說明。
    男：您不需要是大學畢業生，但是如果您至少正在攻讀學位，我們會更為樂見。我們也希望您有一些擔任秘書職務的經驗。
    女：嗯……我現在正在 Queen 學院攻讀學士學位。³³ 我沒有任何擔任秘書的經驗，但我在 Artest Industries 完成了實習。
    男：沒關係。我們很樂意檢閱您的申請書。³⁴ 請務必在週二，也就是截止日期之前提交。

32 目的問題

翻譯 女子為什麼打電話？
    (A) 為了詢問職務的要求條件。
    (B) 為了延期面試。
    (C) 為了詢問對方是否收到她的履歷。
    (D) 為了接受工作職位。

解析 這題詢問打電話的目的，所以一定要聽對話的前半部。女子說：「I wanted to inquire about the job advertisement for a secretary you posted on your website. Does that require a college degree?」這是想詢問男子公布的秘書職缺是否需要大學學位，所以 (A) 是正確答案。

字彙 requirement 要求條件、資格　postpone 延期　résumé 履歷

33 特定細節問題

翻譯 女子有什麼經歷？
    (A) 當過研究助理。
    (B) 在大學學過商業經營。
    (C) 曾受僱擔任實習生。
    (D) 自願為慈善活動當志工。

解析 注意聽女子話中提到關鍵字 experience 前後的內容。女子表示：「I don't have any experience in a secretarial role, but I completed an internship at Artest Industries.」由此可知，她雖然沒有秘書工作經驗，但完成了 Artest Industries 的實習，表示她曾經實習過，所以 (C) 是正確答案。

換句話說
completed an internship 完成實習→
was employed as an intern 曾受僱擔任實習生

字彙 research assistant 研究助理
volunteer 自願
charitable 慈善的

34 提議問題

翻譯 男子建議女子做什麼？
    (A) 在網路上閱讀職務說明。
    (B) 來辦公室當面面試。
    (C) 從僱主那裡取得推薦信。
    (D) 在報名截止日期之前提交申請書。

解析 注意聽男子話中與提議相關的內容。男子說：「Be sure to submit it[application] by Tuesday, which is the deadline.」，要求必須在截止日期，也就是週二前提交申請書，所以 (D) 是正確答案。

換句話說
submit 提交 → Send in 提交
deadline 截止期限 → due date 截止日期

字彙 description 說明　in-person interview 當面面試
obtain 取得、獲得　reference letter 推薦信　due date 截止日期

35-37 [3-1] 英國發音→加拿大發音

Questions 35-37 refer to the following conversation.

W: Good morning, sir. ³⁵I'm the head flight attendant, Sarah. My colleague says you're having a problem.
M: Yes. ³⁵/³⁶I purchased the onboard Wi-Fi package, ³⁶but I can't get it working. I followed the instructions on the seat-back screen, and my phone connects after I enter the password. ³⁶But it says that there is no Internet service available.

W: Oh, I'm sorry. There are sometimes problems with the system right after departure, and then the Wi-Fi system needs to be rebooted. I'll go do that now. It should be back up and running in 10 minutes or so.

M: OK. That will be fine. ³⁷I'll just watch one of the shows on the screen in the meantime. Thank you so much for your help.

---

head 首席的、領導地位　flight attendant 空服員　colleague 同事
onboard 機艙上的　instruction 指示、說明　departure 出發
reboot 重新啟動　up and running（完全正常）運轉的、運轉中的
or so ～程度、～左右　in the meantime 在此期間

翻譯 問題 35-37，請參考以下對話。
　　女：早安，先生，³⁵ 我是座艙長 Sarah，我的同事說您遇到問題。
　　男：是的，^{35/36} 我購買了機上 Wi-Fi 方案，但無法使用。我按照座椅背螢幕上的指示操作，我在輸入密碼後手機連上了，³⁶ 但卻顯示沒有可用的網路服務。
　　女：哦，對不起。有時出發後系統會出現問題，需要重新啟動 Wi-Fi 系統。我現在就去處理，它應該會在 10 分鐘左右之後恢復運行。
　　男：好的。那就沒問題了。³⁷ 我就在這期間觀看螢幕上的其中一檔節目，非常感謝你的幫忙。

35 地點問題

翻譯 對話最可能在哪裡發生？
　(A) 在公車上
　(B) 在飛機上
　(C) 在火車上
　(D) 在船上

解析 不要錯過對話中有關地點的用語。女子說：「I'm the head flight attendant, Sarah.」，表示自己是座艙長，男子則說：「I purchased the onboard Wi-Fi package」。根據女子的話，以及男子買了機上 Wi-Fi 方案，可以看出這是在飛機上發生的對話，所以 (B) 是正確答案。

36 問題點問題

翻譯 男子提到什麼問題？
　(A) 密碼錯了。
　(B) 電燈壞了。
　(C) 連線緩慢。
　(D) 無法使用服務。

解析 注意聽男子話中提到否定用語時的內容。男子說：「I purchased the onboard Wi-Fi package, but I can't get it working.」，表達自己購買了機上 Wi-Fi 方案卻無法使用，並說：「But it says that there is no Internet service available.」表示螢幕顯示沒有可用的網路服務，所以 (D) 是正確答案。

字彙 connection 連線　unavailable 不可使用的

37 之後將發生的事

翻譯 男子說之後要做什麼？
　(A) 讀雜誌。

　(B) 觀看節目。
　(C) 重新輸入密碼。
　(D) 移動到其他位置。

解析 注意聽對話的最後部分，男子說：「I'll just watch one of the shows on the screen in the meantime.」，透過「在這段時間觀看螢幕上的其中一檔節目」，可以得知男子會看節目，所以 (B) 是正確答案。

字彙 magazine 雜誌　location 位置

38-40 🎧 加拿大發音→澳洲發音→英國發音

Questions 38-40 refer to the following conversation with three speakers.

M1: Tom and Marla, ³⁸I need to work on an employee satisfaction survey for management as several employees have resigned recently. But the problem is . . . I am not sure where I should start.

M2: Well, I've never made one, but Marla, you worked on an employee survey before, didn't you?

W: Yes. ³⁹I did the last one, and I still have it in my files. I can send it to you if you like.

M1: Great! That would be very helpful.

W: But . . . ⁴⁰Mark, you'll have to change the details in it. It only asked about satisfaction with our facilities.

---

satisfaction 滿意（度）　survey（問卷）調查
management 管理　resign 辭職　detail 細節　facility 設施

翻譯 問題 38-40，請參考以下三方對話。
　　男 1：Tom 和 Marla，³⁸ 我需要針對管理進行員工滿意度調查，因為最近有幾位員工辭職了。但問題是……我不知道該從哪裡開始。
　　男 2：嗯，我從來沒有做過，但是 Marla，你以前做過員工問卷調查，不是嗎？
　　女：是的，³⁹ 我之前做過，我的檔案中仍然保留著它。如果你想要的話我可以寄給你。
　　男 1：太好了！這會非常有幫助。
　　女：但是……⁴⁰Mark，你必須更改其中的細項，因為它只詢問對我們設施的滿意度。

38 理由問題

翻譯 為什麼需要做問卷調查？
　(A) 新的廣告推出了。
　(B) 一些員工離職了。
　(C) 顧客們抱怨某項服務。
　(D) 將要增加公司餐廳的菜單品項。

解析 注意聽題目關鍵字 survey 出現前後的內容。男子 1 說：「I need to work on an employee satisfaction survey for management as several employees have resigned recently.」，表示最近多名員工離職，為了管理需要進行員工滿意度問卷調查，所以 (B) 是正確答案。

換句話說
several employees have resigned 多名員工辭職 →

Some workers have quit 某些員工離職

字彙 release 釋出、發表　quit 離職　complain 抱怨

39 提議問題

翻譯 女子提議做什麼？
(A) 接手一項業務。
(B) 幫助面試。
(C) 跟主管談。
(D) 寄送文件。

解析 注意聽女子話中與提議相關的句子，女子說：「I did the last one[employee survey], and I still have it in my files. I can send it to you if you like.」，表示她做了上次的員工問卷調查，並且檔案中還留有資料，如果對方想要可以寄過去，所以 (D) 是正確答案。

字彙 take over 接手　assignment 業務　supervisor 主管
document 文件、資料

40 特定細節問題

翻譯 女子提醒 Mark 做什麼？
(A) 更改一些資訊。
(B) 提交評估書。
(C) 檢視一項意見。
(D) 打聽某項設施。

解析 仔細聽女子話中與關鍵句 remind Mark to do 相關的內容，女子說：「Mark, you'll have to change the details in it[employee survey].」，表示她建議 Mark 更改問卷調查內的細節，所以 (A) 是正確答案。

換句話說
details 細節 → information 資訊

字彙 evaluation 評估　review 檢視

40-43 🎧 英國發音→澳洲發音

Questions 41-43 refer to the following conversation.

W: Hey, Kevin. This is Mary from the Book Corner on Second Avenue. I really enjoyed your poems in *The Kentucky Quarterly* last month. ⁴¹Are you interested in reading them at our bookstore's poetry reading this Thursday?
M: That'd be great. ⁴²When does the reading start? I get off work at 6, and it will take about 30 minutes to get there.
W: ⁴²It starts at 5:30. But if you want to participate, I won't put you in an early time slot. You can read yours last. ⁴²Then, you'll have time to make it. ⁴³We'll have some snacks and drinks after the reading.

poem （一篇）詩、韻文　reading 朗讀（會）
poetry 詩、詩歌（的總稱）　participate 參與　time slot 時段

翻譯 問題 41-43，請參考以下對話。
女：嗨，Kevin。我是第二大道 Book Corner 的 Mary。我真的很喜歡你上個月在《The Kentucky

Quarterly》雜誌上發表的詩。⁴¹你有興趣在本週四我們書店的詩歌朗讀會上朗誦它們嗎？
男：太好了，⁴²朗讀會什麼時候開始？我 6 點下班，大約需要 30 分鐘才能到達。
女：⁴²5 點 30 分開始，但是如果你想參加，我不會安排你在太早的時段，你可以在最後時段朗讀你的詩，⁴²所以你將有足夠的時間來趕上，⁴³讀完後我們會吃一些零食和飲料。

41 主題問題

翻譯 對話主要是關於什麼？
(A) 訂書過程
(B) 即將舉行的文學朗讀會
(C) 書店輪班表
(D) 作家頒獎儀式

解析 這是詢問對話主題的問題，所以一定要聽對話的前半部。女子說：「Are you interested in reading them[poems] at our bookstore's poetry reading this Thursday?」，詢問男子是否有興趣在本週四書店的詩歌朗讀會上朗讀詩作，再開啟關於朗讀會的內容，所以 (B) 是正確答案。

換句話說
poetry reading 詩歌朗讀會 → literary reading 文學朗讀會

字彙 process 過程　upcoming 即將來臨的、即將到來的
literary 文學的　shift 輪班

42 意圖掌握問題

翻譯 女子說「你可以在最後時段朗讀你的詩」，她的意思是什麼？
(A) 不會有長久的等待。
(B) 會有時間提問。
(C) 行程不會出現問題。
(D) 晚餐會有足夠的時間。

解析 注意聽對話中的句子「You can read yours last」的前後內容，男子說：「When does the reading start? I get off work at 6, and it will take about 30 minutes to get there.」，詢問朗讀會何時開始，他在下班後抵達那裡需要 30 分鐘左右。女子說：「It starts at 5:30. But if you want to participate, I won't put you in an early time slot.」，表達會在 5 點 30 分開始，並表示如果男子想參加，她不會將男子安排在太早的時段，接著從「Then, you'll have enough time to make it.」，由此可知男子會有足夠的時間抵達，所以不會出現行程問題，因此 (C) 是正確答案。

43 之後將發生的事

翻譯 據女子所說，參加活動的人會在活動結束後做什麼？
(A) 吃點零食。
(B) 讀雜誌的新刊號。
(C) 合影留念。
(D) 折扣購書。

解析 仔細聽女子話中與題目核心語句（the participants do after an event）相關的內容。女子說：「We'll have some snacks and drinks after the reading.」，表示朗讀後會吃一些零食和飲料，所以 (A) 是正確答案。

換句話說
some snacks and drinks 一些零食和飲料 →
some refreshments 一些茶點

字彙 participant 參與者　refreshment 茶點、零食
journal （學會、專業機構等的）期刊　at a discount 打折

44-46 加拿大發音→美國發音

Questions 44-46 refer to the following conversation.

M: Hello, I'm Steven from Water Mates Services. [44]We received a call about a broken pipe in this building. I'm here to fix it.
W: Oh, yes. I called you earlier. [45]Thank you for coming so quickly. There's a problem with one of the pipes coming out of the boiler. Do you have any idea how long it will take to repair?
M: If the pipe is easy to access, it should take less than 30 minutes. However, I can't guarantee that because I don't know the actual situation.
W: OK. That is fine. Wait here for one second while I call the security guard. [46]He will give you an access card for the building.

---

pipe 管道　earlier 之前、早些時候　access 靠近　guarantee 保證
actual 實際的　security guard 警衛　access card 門禁卡

翻譯 問題 44-46，請參考以下對話。
男：你好，我是 Water Mates 服務的 Steven，[44] 我們接到電話表示這棟大樓的管道破裂，我是來修理的。
女：哦，是的。我之前打過電話給你，[45] 謝謝你這麼快就來了。有一根從鍋爐伸出的管道出現問題，你知道需要多長時間修理嗎？
男：如果管道容易接近，應該不會超過 30 分鐘，但是我不能保證這一點，因為我不知道實際情況。
女：好的，沒關係，請在這等一下，我打給警衛，[46] 他會給你一張大樓的通行證。

44 目的問題

翻譯 男子為什麼來訪？
(A) 為了諮詢租賃建築物的事情。
(B) 為了施行維修事務。
(C) 為了重新調好警報裝置。
(D) 為了設置鍋爐系統。

解析 這題問的是對話的目的，所以請注意聽對話的前半部。
男子說：「We received a call about a broken pipe in this building. I'm here to fix it.」，表示接到該建築有破裂管道的電話後前來修理，所以 (B) 是正確答案。

換句話說
fix 修理 → perform a repair 進行修復

字彙 rent 租賃　perform 施行
reset 重置　alarm 警報器　set up 設定

45 特定細節問題

翻譯 女子感謝男子什麼？
(A) 開放地下室。
(B) 發現問題。
(C) 快速回應。
(D) 為她提供免費服務。

解析 仔細聽關鍵字 thank 的前後內容，女子說：「Thank you for coming so quickly.」，感謝男子很快趕來，所以 (C) 是正確答案。

換句話說
quickly 快速 → rapidly 迅速地

字彙 basement 地下室　identify 發現、辨識出　respond 回應
rapidly 迅速地

46 特定細節問題

翻譯 女子說男子會得到什麼？
(A) 平面圖
(B) 一些聯絡資訊
(C) 一些設備的照片
(D) 門禁卡

解析 注意聽出現關鍵字 receive 前後的內容，女子說：「He[security guard] will give you an access card for the building.」，表示警衛將會給男子大樓的門禁卡，所以 (D) 是正確答案。

換句話說
access card 通行證 → security pass 門禁卡

字彙 floor plan 平面圖　security 保全的、警衛　pass 出入證、通行證

47-49 澳洲發音→英國發音→美國發音

Questions 47-49 refer to the following conversation with three speakers.

M: Excuse me. [47]I am interested in getting a new washing machine. Do you have any on sale at the moment?
W1: Yes, [47]we have several models discounted for a limited time. Do you also need a dryer?
M: Not necessarily. [48]My priority is getting the washer at a good price.
W1: OK, then I'll introduce you to my associate Laura. She can help you. Laura, could you point out some of our economical washers for this customer?
W2: Certainly, please follow me . . . [49]I personally have this Lexpro model, which the manufacturer recently launched. It is highly effective and also energy and water-efficient. It will save you time and money in the long run.

---

washing machine 洗衣機　on sale 打折中的
not necessarily ～不是必要的　priority 優先順位
associate 夥伴、朋友　point out 告知、指出
economical 實惠的、精打細算的　personally 個人地
launch 上市、問世

解析 問題 47-49，請參考以下三方對話。
男：不好意思，⁴⁷ 我有興趣購買一臺新洗衣機，現在有正在打折的嗎？
女 1：是的，⁴⁷ 我們有幾款限時折扣，您還需要烘衣機嗎？
男：不太必要，⁴⁸ 我的優先順位是以優惠的價格買到洗衣機。
女 1：好的，那我向您介紹我的同事 Laura，她可以幫助您。Laura，您能為這位顧客推薦一些經濟實惠的洗衣機嗎？
女 2：當然可以，請跟我來……⁴⁹ 我個人有這款 Lexpro 型號，是製造商最近推出的，它非常有效，而且節能省水，從長遠來看，它將節省您的時間和金錢。

47 地點問題

翻譯 對話可能發生在哪裡？
(A) 在服裝店
(B) 在美容院
(C) 在洗車場
(D) 在家電賣場裡

解析 不要錯過對話中任何有關地點的字句，男子說：「I am interested in getting a new washing machine. Do you have any on sale at the moment?」，表示想買洗衣機，並詢問是否有正在打折的型號，女子 1 說：「we have several models discounted for a limited time.」，表示有幾款型號限時打折，由此可見這是在家電賣場展開的對話，所以 (D) 是正確答案。

字彙 hair salon 美容院　appliance 家電

48 特定細節問題

翻譯 男子的主要優先順位是什麼？
(A) 尋找成本有效益高的品項。
(B) 使用他的禮券。
(C) 從特定品牌購買。
(D) 使用一些環保材質。

解析 注意聽出現關鍵字 priority 前後的內容，男子說：「My priority is getting the washer at a good price.」，表達自己的優先順位是找到價格優惠的洗衣機，所以 (A) 是正確答案。

換句話說
at a good price 以優惠的價格 → cost-effective 價格實惠的

字彙 cost-effective 價格實惠的　option 選項　gift card 禮券　specific 特定的、具體的　utilize 利用、運用　eco-friendly 環保的　material 物質、材料

49 提及何事的問題

翻譯 關於 Lexpro，何者被提及？
(A) 以客製化的設定為特徵。
(B) 生產中斷了。
(C) 消耗更多能源。
(D) 最近上市了。

解析 仔細聽關鍵字 Lexpro 前後的內容，女子 2 說：「I personally have this Lexpro model, which the

manufacturer recently launched.」，表示自己有 Lexpro 這個型號，這是最近推出的，所以 (D) 是正確答案。

換句話說
launched 上市 → was ~ released 問世

字彙 feature 作為特徵　personalized 客製化的　discontinue 中斷（生產）的

50-52 🔊英國發音→澳洲發音

Questions 50-52 refer to the following conversation.

W: Thank you for calling Sky Card. How may I help you?
M: Hi. My name is Aiden Sellers. ⁵⁰I'm calling because when I tried using my credit card today, the salesperson told me it was suspended. Can you tell me why?
W: Sure. I can check your account. ⁵¹To verify your identity, can you tell me where you live and the last four digits of your social security number?
M: 122 Oak Lane, Houston, and 5729.
W: OK, let's see. It looks like we suspended your account because there was an unusual purchase of $1,000.
M: Oh. Actually, I bought a television for my new house.
W: In that case, ⁵²I'll reactivate your account. It should be working again by the end of the day.

credit card 信用卡　salesperson 銷售員　suspend 終止、中斷　verify 確認、證明　identity 身分、認同　digit 數字　social security number 社會安全號碼　unusual 反常的、罕見的　in that case 那麼　reactivate 重新啟用

翻譯 問題 50-52，請參考以下三方對話。
女：感謝您致電 Sky Card，我能幫您什麼？
男：嗨，我是 Aiden Sellers，⁵⁰ 我打電話是因為今天我嘗試使用信用卡時，銷售人員告訴我已被停卡了，你能告訴我為什麼嗎？
女：當然，我可以查一下您的帳戶。⁵¹ 為了驗證您的身分，能告訴我您的住址以及您的社會安全號碼的後四碼嗎？
男：5729 休士頓，橡樹街 122 號。
女：好的，我來看看，我們似乎暫停了您的帳戶，因為有 1,000 美元的異常購物紀錄。
男：喔，事實上，我為我的新房子買了一臺電視。
女：這樣的話，⁵² 我會重新啟動您的帳號，今天結束前它應該會再次啟用。

50 問題點問題

翻譯 男子提到什麼問題？
(A) 沒有收到明細表。
(B) 無法使用銀行應用程式。
(C) 他的卡被用來進行了一次罕見的購物。
(D) 他的信用卡無法使用。

解析 注意聽男子話中的否定內容，男子說：「I'm calling because when I tried using my credit card today, the salesperson told me it was suspended.」，表示今天要用信用卡時，銷售員告訴自己被停卡了，所以才打電話詢問，因此 (D) 是正確答案。

字彙 statement 明細表、陳述

51 特定細節問題

翻譯 女子向男子要了什麼資訊？
(A) 他的出生年月日
(B) 他的電話號碼
(C) 他的住址
(D) 他的信用卡號碼

解析 這題須注意聽女子說的話，女子問男子：「To verify your identity, can you tell me where you live ~?」，詢問是否能告訴自己住址以便確認身分，所以 (C) 是正確答案。

換句話說
where ~ live 住的地方 → address 住址

52 之後將發生的事

翻譯 據女子所說，今天晚一點會發生什麼事？
(A) 網站會更新。
(B) 信用卡將可使用。
(C) 某一筆購物將被取消。
(D) 新卡將郵寄送達。

解析 這題須注意聽女子話中關鍵詞 later today 前後的內容，女子說：「I'll reactivate your account. It should be working again by the end of the day.」，表示會重新開啟男子的信用卡帳戶，帳戶在今天結束前會重新啟用，由此可知今天晚一點將可以使用信用卡，所以 (B) 是正確答案。

換句話說
later today 今天稍晚 → by the end of the day 今天結束前

字彙 usable 可以使用的

53-55 🔊 加拿大發音→英國發音

Questions 53-55 refer to the following conversation.

M: Our social media channels drove sales up by 20 percent last month. [53]I'm surprised that our advertising campaign was as effective as it was.
W: That makes me happy. I always thought we had to be more active on those platforms. [54]As we are getting more followers quickly, we should hire a professional to manage our accounts.
M: [54]I agree with you. Could you take care of that?
W: Well, [55]I know someone who is qualified. It's my former coworker Luke. He has been working in that field for five years.
M: That's great. Ask him if he'd be interested in the position.

drive up （價格等）上漲　advertising 廣告　effective 有效的
active 積極的　professional 專家　manage 管理
take care of ~ 處理～　qualify 有資格　former 之前的
coworker 同事　field 領域

翻譯 問題 53-55，請參考以下對話。
男：上個月我們的社群媒體管道推動銷售額成長了20%，[53] 我很驚訝我們的廣告活動如此有效。
女：這讓我很高興，我一直都認為我們必須在這些平臺上更加活躍，[54] 隨著我們快速獲得更多追蹤者，我們應該聘請專家來管理我們的帳戶。
男：[54] 我同意你的看法，你能處理這件事嗎？
女：嗯，[55] 我認識一個符合資格的人，是我以前的同事Luke，他已經在該領域工作了五年。
男：那太好了，請問問他是否對該職位有興趣。

53 特定細節問題

翻譯 男子對什麼感到驚訝？
(A) 商品縮減的銷量
(B) 公司確立的聲譽
(C) 行銷策略的成功
(D) 某項服務的價格

解析 注意聽出現關鍵字 surprised 的前後內容，男子說：「I'm surprised that our advertising campaign was as effective as it was.」，表示廣告活動如此有效令他驚訝，所以 (C) 是正確答案。

換句話說
advertising campaign was ~ effective 廣告活動有效 →
The success of a marketing strategy 行銷策略的成功

字彙 reputation 名譽、評價　establish 確立、設立　strategy 策略

54 特定細節問題

翻譯 男子同意什麼？
(A) 為新專案制定計劃
(B) 聘請專家
(C) 聯絡另一間公司
(D) 增加廣告預算

解析 注意聽出現關鍵字 agree 前後的內容，女子說：「As we are getting more followers quickly, we should hire a professional to manage our accounts.」，因為公司正迅速獲得更多粉絲，所以要聘僱管理帳號的專家，男子說：「I agree with you.」，同意了女子，所以 (B) 是正確答案。

換句話說
hire a professional 聘請專家 → Employing an expert 僱用專家

字彙 employ 聘僱　expert 專家　budget 預算

55 意圖掌握問題

翻譯 女子為什麼說「他在那個領域工作了五年」？
(A) 為了強調經驗的必要性
(B) 為了將應徵者推薦正當化
(C) 為了說明提高薪水的理由
(D) 為了提議調到其他分店

解析 注意聽題目中這句（He has been working in that field for five years）出現的部分，女子說：「I know someone who is qualified. It's my former coworker Luke.」，表示知道有資格勝任的人，那就是自己以前的同事 Luke，由此可以看出女子是為了佐證推薦人選的合

理性，所以 (B) 是正確答案。

字彙 highlight 強調　justify 正當化　recommendation 推薦
salary 薪水　transfer 傳遞、轉移　branch 分店

56-58 [3山] 美國發音→澳洲發音

Questions 56-58 refer to the following conversation.

W: I was just sent an invitation from a public relations firm. ⁵⁶There will be a Jack Farmer fashion show tomorrow morning.

M: ⁵⁷Do you want me to write about it? I could come with you and take some notes.

W: Yes. ⁵⁷It would be great if you could write something about the collection. I am expecting some colorful garments from Jack's new line. I also have to attend the opening of the Mara Flex store on 5th avenue after his show.

M: ⁵⁷/⁵⁸Fashion week is always the busiest time of year for our magazine.

W: Right. ⁵⁸But don't worry. Fashion week will end soon.

---

take notes 記錄、筆記　colorful 色彩繽紛的　garment 服裝、衣服
line 產品系列、商品系列　opening 開店、開幕
fashion week 時尚週（設計師發表作品的週）

翻譯 問題 56-58，請參考以下對話。
女：我剛收到公關公司的邀請。⁵⁶ 明天早上將有一場 Jack Farmer 時裝秀。
男：⁵⁷ 你希望我來寫嗎？我可以和你一起去做一些筆記。
女：是的，⁵⁷ 如果你能寫一些有關該系列的內容，那就太好了。我期待 Jack 新系列會有一些色彩繽紛的服裝。在他的秀結束後，我還必須參加第五大道 Mara Flex 商店的開幕典禮。
男：⁵⁷/⁵⁸ 時裝週一直是我們雜誌社一年中最繁忙的時期。
女：對，⁵⁸ 但不用擔心，時裝週很快就會結束了。

56 之後將發生的事

翻譯 明天早上會發生什麼事？
(A) 時裝秀即將舉行。
(B) 賣場將重新開張。
(C) 雜誌要發行了。
(D) 將公布輪班時間表。

解析 注意聽出現關鍵詞 tomorrow morning 前後的內容，女子說：「There will be a Jack Farmer fashion show tomorrow morning.」，透過明天早上會有 Jack Farmer 時裝秀的這句話，可以得知明天早上將舉行時裝秀，所以 (A) 是正確答案。

字彙 reopen 重新開幕、再次開始　publish 發行、出刊
post 刊載、記錄

57 說話者問題

翻譯 說話者們最可能在哪種產業工作？
(A) 廣告
(B) 媒體
(C) 製造
(D) 教育

解析 不要錯過題目中提到身分及職業相關的語句，男子說：「Do you want me to write about it[fashion show]？」，詢問女子是否希望自己寫關於時裝秀的文章，女子說：「It would be great if you could write something about the collection.」，回答如果男子能寫一些關於服裝系列的東西就好了，男子又說：「Fashion week is always the busiest time of year for our magazine.」，表示時裝週是雜誌社一年最忙碌的時期。透過這些對話可以得知說話者們是在媒體產業工作，所以 (B) 是正確答案。

字彙 industry 產業　journalism 媒體界　education 教育

58 特定細節問題

翻譯 女子請男子放心什麼？
(A) 工作不會延遲。
(B) 努力不會被忽視。
(C) 不會有人潮。
(D) 繁忙的時期不會持續很久。

解析 仔細聆聽關鍵字 reassure 前後的內容，男子說：「Fashion week is always the busiest time of year for our magazine.」，表示時裝週總是自家雜誌社一年中最忙的時期，女子則說：「But don't worry. Fashion week will end soon.」，請男子不用擔心，因為時裝週馬上就要結束了。由此可以看出女子認為忙碌的時期不會太久，請男子安心，因此 (D) 是正確答案。

換句話說
will end soon 即將結束 → will not last long 不會持續太久

字彙 reassure 使安心　hard work 努力付出　ignore 無視、忽略
crowd 人潮、群眾　period 時期　last 持續

59-61 [3山] 加拿大發音→英國發音

Questions 59-61 refer to the following conversation.

M: Rachel, ⁵⁹a customer is looking for the new Truna phone that was released today. Do you know where it is?

W: Oh, it is already sold out. There was a line of people waiting for it around the block this morning when we opened.

M: Ah, ⁶⁰I didn't know because my shift started at noon. I will tell him to visit another store.

W: It'll be the same thing elsewhere. You should put the customer on our wait list.

M: Good idea.

W: ⁶¹Don't forget to mention that if he has an older Truna phone, we can recycle that one for him. He will then get a discount on the new one.

---

look for 尋找～　be sold out 售罄　elsewhere 別處
wait list 等候名單　recycle 回收　discount on ～打折

翻譯 問題 59-61，請參考以下三方對話。

男：Rachel，⁵⁹ 一位客戶正在尋找今天推出的新款 Truna 手機，你知道在哪裡嗎？

女：喔，已經賣完了。今天早上我們開店時，街口周圍已經排起了長隊。

男：啊，⁶⁰ 我不知道，因為我今天中午才開始上班，我會告訴他去另一家店。

女：其他地方也是一樣的，你應該將這位顧客列入我們的等候名單。

男：好主意。

女：⁶¹ 別忘了提醒他，如果他有舊的 Truna 手機，我們可以幫他回收，這樣他買新手機就能獲得折扣。

59 特定細節問題

翻譯 男子詢問什麼？
(A) 手機服務收費制
(B) 產品的位置
(C) 設備特點
(D) 現在的行銷活動

解析 在對話中注意聽男子說的話，男子對女子說：「a customer is looking for the new Truna phone that was released today. Do you know where it is?」，表示一位顧客正在尋找今天上市的新款 Truna 手機，並詢問她是否知道在哪，所以 (B) 是正確答案。

字彙 plan 收費制、制度　feature 特徵　device 裝置　promotion 行銷

60 理由問題

翻譯 男子為什麼不知道情況？
(A) 他正在拜訪其他商店。
(B) 早上沒有排班。
(C) 一直在排隊等候。
(D) 他當天休假。

解析 注意聽題目中的關鍵語句（unaware of a situation）出現的部分，男子說：「I didn't know because my shift started at noon.」，表示自己的工作時間是從中午開始，由此可以看出男子早上沒有工作，所以 (B) 是正確答案。

換句話說
was ~ unaware 不知情 → didn't know 不知道

字彙 unaware of 對~不知情　wait in line 排隊等待　day off 休假日

61 特定細節問題

翻譯 女子給男子關於什麼的資訊？
(A) 維修服務
(B) 商店退貨政策
(C) 銷售稅提高
(D) 回收方案

解析 這題須注意聽女子說的話，她對男子說：「Don't forget to mention that if he has an older Truna phone, we can recycle that one for him.」，請男子不要忘了提醒顧客如果有舊的 Truna 手機，可以協助他回收，所以 (D) 是正確答案。

字彙 return policy 退貨政策　sales tax 銷售稅　recycling 回收

62-64 🎧 美國發音→澳洲發音

Questions 62-64 refer to the following conversation and map.

W: ⁶²Have you found a location for your new barber shop yet?

M: Actually, I have. ⁶²It's on Western Avenue, right between a restaurant and a bicycle shop. It meets all my needs. Here's a picture of the space.

W: Oh, that seems spacious. And it's in an excellent part of town. Have you signed the lease?

M: I'm signing it next Thursday. ⁶³The rent is pretty cheap. It's just $2,000 per month. ⁶⁴The problem will be finding employees, so I'm posting job ads in newspapers.

W: Good idea. I'm sure you'll get a lot of responses. Let me know how that goes.

barber shop 理髮店　meet 滿足　spacious 寬敞的　sign 簽名　lease 租賃合約書　response 反應、回應

翻譯 問題 62-64，請參考以下對話。

女：⁶² 你找到新理髮店的地點了嗎？

男：事實上，我找到了，⁶² 它位於 Western 街，就在一家餐廳和一家自行車店之間，它能滿足我所有的需求，這是那家店的照片。

女：哦，看起來很寬敞，而且它位於城鎮的絕佳地段，你簽約了嗎？

男：我下週四簽約，⁶³ 房租相當便宜，每個月只需要 2,000 美元。⁶⁴ 問題會是尋找員工，所以我在報紙上張貼了招聘廣告。

女：好主意，我相信你會收到很多回應。讓我知道接下來進展如何。

咖啡廳 ☕	大樓 1	雜貨店	大樓 2	便利商店
		Western 街		
餐廳	⁶² 大樓 4	腳踏車店 🚲	大樓 3	

62 地圖題

翻譯 請看地圖，理髮店將位於哪裡？
(A) 大樓 1
(B) 大樓 2
(C) 大樓 3
(D) 大樓 4

解析 請確認地圖上的資訊，仔細聽關鍵詞 barber shop 前後的內容。當女子以「Have you found a location for your new barber shop yet?」問男子是否已經找到新的理髮店地點時，男子回答：「It's on Western Avenue, right between a restaurant and a bicycle shop.」，表示位於 Western 街，並正好在餐廳和自行車店之間，從地圖上可以看出理髮店就是大樓 4，所以 (D) 是正確答案。

63 特定細節問題

翻譯 據男子所說，那棟大樓的優點是什麼？
(A) 不要求支付公共設施費用。
(B) 包括很大的內間。
(C) 一個月花不了多少費用。
(D) 靠近大眾運輸。

解析 這題須仔細聽男子話中出現關鍵句 advantage of the building 前後的內容，男子說：「The rent is pretty cheap.」，表達租金相當便宜，所以 (C) 是正確答案。

換句話說
is ~ cheap 便宜 → does not cost much 不花很多錢

字彙 advantage 優點　utility 公共設施　contain 包含
back room 內間；密室　public transportation 大眾運輸

64 方法問題

翻譯 男子將如何招募員工？
(A) 透過熟人介紹
(B) 透過在建築物上貼廣告
(C) 透過連絡招聘公司
(D) 在出版物上刊登廣告

解析 這題須注意聽與關鍵詞 recruit employees 相關的內容，男子說：「The problem will be finding employees, so I'm posting job ads in newspapers.」，表示在報紙上刊登招聘廣告，所以 (D) 是正確答案。

換句話說
posting job ads in newspapers 在報紙上刊登求才廣告 → putting ads in publications 在出版物上放廣告

字彙 recruit 募集、招聘　acquaintance 熟人
staffing agency 招聘公司　publication 出版物

65-67 🎧 澳洲發音→英國發音

Questions 65-67 refer to the following conversation and schedule.

M: Leslie, we are going to announce our merger on Friday afternoon. 65I'd like to have a meeting with all of our department heads to discuss it in the morning. Could you ask everyone to be present?
W: OK. 66What time do you think we should hold the meeting?
M: Hmm . . . Friday is usually pretty busy. 66It looks like Carter has the busiest schedule in the morning, so let's do it when he is available.
W: 67I'll ask my assistant to send out an e-mail this afternoon when he gets back to the office. He's having lunch in the cafeteria now.

announce 發表　merger 合併
discuss 探討、討論　present 參與

翻譯 問題 65-67，請參考以下對話。
男：Leslie，我們將於週五下午宣布合併。65 我想在早上與我們所有部門的負責人開會討論這個問題，你能請大家都到場嗎？

女：好的，66 你認為我們應該什麼時候開會？
男：嗯……星期五通常很忙，66 看起來 Carter 早上的行程最忙，所以在他有空的時候來開會。
女：67 我會請我的助理今天下午回到辦公室後寄一封電子郵件，他現在正在餐廳吃午餐。

星期五				
	早上 8 點	66 早上 9 點	早上 10 點	早上 11 點
Carter	電話會議		銷售會議	HR 培訓
Delilah	不在			
Edgar		電話會議		
Frances			不在	

65 請求問題

翻譯 男子要求女子做什麼？
(A) 批准合併。
(B) 制定新的行程表。
(C) 通知一些員工。
(D) 校對公告。

解析 這題須注意聽男子話中有關請求的內容，男子對女子說：「I'd like to have a meeting with all of our department heads to discuss it[merger] in the morning. Could you ask everyone to be present?」，表達自己為了在早上討論合併問題，想和所有部門負責人開會，並詢問女子能否邀請所有人參加，所以 (C) 是正確答案。

字彙 approve 批准　notify 通知、告知　proofread 校對

66 表格問題

翻譯 請看表格，各部門負責人將於什麼時候參加會議？
(A) 上午 8 時
(B) 上午 9 點
(C) 上午 10 時
(D) 上午 11 時

解析 先確認題目中的行程表後，仔細聽與關鍵句 department heads participate in a meeting 相關的內容。當女子詢問：「What time do you think we should hold the meeting?」，也就是應該幾點與部門負責人開會時，男子回答：「It looks like Carter has the busiest schedule in the morning, so let's do it when he is available.」，表示早上似乎是 Carter 最忙的時候，應該在他有空時開會，從行程表可以得知部門負責人可以在 9 點開會，所以 (B) 是正確答案。

67 理由問題

翻譯 女子的助理為什麼現在不在？
(A) 他正在休息。
(B) 他只是兼職員工。
(C) 他正在寫電子郵件。
(D) 他正在接受培訓。

解析 這題須仔細聽與關鍵句 assistant unavailable right now 相關的內容，女子說：「I'll ask my assistant to send out an e-mail this afternoon when he gets back to the office. He's having lunch in the cafeteria now.」，表示自己的助手回到辦公室後，會請他寄電子郵件，他現在正在公司餐廳吃午餐，所以 (A) 是正確答案。

字彙 be on a break 休息　undergo 遭受、經歷、經驗

68-70 🎧 加拿大發音→美國發音

Questions 68-70 refer to the following conversation and coupon.

> M: Hello. ⁶⁸I would like to buy that black sweater.
> W: Certainly. ⁶⁸However, that's actually our last one. You can buy the one on display if you don't mind.
> M: That doesn't matter to me. I'll take it.
> W: OK. It'll be $85. ⁶⁹Do you have a Centralix Clothes customer loyalty program card?
> M: Yes. Here it is. And ⁷⁰here is a gift card to pay for my purchase. Also, I'd like to use this coupon. It says it can be applied to purchases made in June at this location.
> W: I'm sorry. ⁷⁰This coupon can't be used for this purchase.
> M: Oh, OK. That's no problem.

on display 被陳列的、被展示的　matter 重要的、有問題的
loyalty 忠誠　gift card 禮品卡　apply 應用　location 分店、地點

翻譯 問題 68-70，請參考以下對話。
男：你好，⁶⁸ 我想買那件黑色毛衣。
女：當然，⁶⁸ 但事實上這是我們的最後一件，如果您不介意，可以購買展示的這一件。
男：我並不介意，我要買下它。
女：好的，價格為 85 美元，⁶⁹ 您有 Centralix Clothes 顧客忠誠度計劃卡嗎？
男：有的，在這裡，⁷⁰ 我還要用一張禮品卡來支付費用。另外，我想使用這張優惠券，上面寫著可以適用於 6 月在該分店購買的品項。
女：對不起，⁷⁰ 此優惠券無法用於本次購買。
男：喔，好的，沒關係。

> 優惠券
> 超過 50 美元優惠 10%
> 6 月 1 日至 30 日有效
> ⁷⁰ 禮品卡購買除外
> 只適用於 Cordoba Mall 分店

68 地點問題

翻譯 對話最可能發生在哪裡？
(A) 在服裝店
(B) 在乾洗店
(C) 在禮品店
(D) 在西裝店

解析 不要錯過對話中有關地點的語句，男子說：「I would like to buy that black sweater.」，表示想買黑色毛衣，女子回答：「However, that's actually our last one. You

can buy the one on display if you don't mind.」，表示那是最後一件，如果男子不介意可以買，由此可知這是在服裝店進行的對話，所以 (A) 是正確答案。

字彙 clothing store 服裝店　tailoring 西裝店、裁縫店

69 特定細節問題

翻譯 女子問男子什麼？
(A) 他最喜歡的顏色
(B) 他偏好的尺寸
(C) 他的購物預算
(D) 他的會員卡

解析 這題須注意聽對話中女子說的話，女子說：「Do you have a Centralix Clothes customer loyalty program card?」，詢問男子是否有 Centralix Clothes 顧客忠誠度計劃卡，所以 (D) 是正確答案。

換句話說
customer loyalty program card 顧客忠誠度計劃卡 →
membership card 會員卡

70 圖片題

翻譯 請看圖片，為何無法在這次購物使用這張優惠券？
(A) 未滿最低消費。
(B) 已過期。
(C) 不能與禮品卡一起使用。
(D) 這是用於其他分店的。

解析 先確認優惠券上的資訊後，仔細聽與關鍵句 isn't ~ valid for a purchase 相關的內容，男子說：「here is a gift card to pay for my purchase. Also, I'd like to use this coupon.」，表示想用禮品卡付款，同時使用優惠券，女子說：「This coupon can't be used for this purchase.」，回答該優惠券無法用於這次購買。我們從優惠券上的資訊可以得知不能與禮品卡並用，所以 (C) 是正確答案。

字彙 minimum 最低限度　expire 到期　for ～用的

PART 4

71-73 🎧 加拿大發音

Questions 71-73 refer to the following excerpt from a meeting.

> ⁷¹Let's discuss our distribution issue. Some of the stores that carry our yogurt have complained that they are not getting enough products. Therefore, they are faced with partially empty shelves. Our production facility is not the problem. We produce enough yogurt to consistently restock our wholesale partners. ⁷²I was thinking we should change our partner distribution company as it is the reason for the delays. ⁷³Please look into new companies and get estimates. And then share what you find later.

distribution 物流、分配　carry 經銷　complain 抱怨、抗議
partially 部分地　consistently 持續地　restock 補貨
wholesale 零售的、大量的　look into 調查　estimate 估價單

翻譯 問題 71-73，請參考以下會議摘要。

71 我們來討論一下我們的物流問題。一些銷售我們優格的商店抱怨他們沒有取得足夠的產品。因此，他們的貨架有部分閒置。我們的生產設施不是問題。我們能生產足夠的優格來持續為批發合作夥伴補充庫存。72 我認為我們應該更換的是合作的物流公司，因為這是延誤的原因。73 請調查新公司並進行估價，再分享你們找到的東西。

71 特定細節問題

翻譯 說話者談到什麼問題？
(A) 物流系統正在引起不滿。
(B) 產品品質參差不齊。
(C) 製造工廠太小。
(D) 店鋪中斷了某品牌的進貨。

解析 這題須注意聽與關鍵字 problem 相關的內容，說話者說：「Let's discuss our distribution issue. Some of the stores that carry our yogurt have complained that they are not getting enough products.」，表示要討論物流問題，並提出部分批發合作夥伴抱怨沒有得到充足的產品，所以 (A) 是正確答案。

字彙 inconsistent 不一致的　plant 工廠　discontinue 中斷

72 提議問題

翻譯 說話者提出什麼解決方案？
(A) 設立新工廠。
(B) 重新考慮包裝設計。
(C) 更改某些材料。
(D) 更換合作公司。

解析 注意聽中後段與提議相關的語句，說話者說：「I was thinking we should change our partner distribution company as it is the reason for the delays.」，提出物流是延遲的原因，所以認為應該更換合作的物流公司，因此 (D) 是正確答案。

換句話說
partner ~ company 合作公司 → affiliated company 關係企業

字彙 establish 設立、建立　rethink 再考慮　switch out 變更
ingredient 材料　affiliated 附屬的、聯合的

73 請求問題

翻譯 說話者請聽者們做什麼？
(A) 品嚐新的優格口味。
(B) 尋找資訊。
(C) 拜訪店鋪的地點。
(D) 整頓生產工廠。

解析 注意聽中後段與請求有關的用語，說話者說：「Please look into new companies and get estimates.」，要求調查新公司並取得報價，所以 (B) 是正確答案。

字彙 flavor 口味　look up 尋找　floor 工廠、樓層

74-76 🎧 美國發音

Questions 74-76 refer to the following news report.

This is KMIA, and I'm Lisa Barker. 74The mayor just announced the completion of the River East Park Project. After a two-month delay due to bad weather, the path along the riverfront is now open to pedestrians. However, the bike lanes will not be completed until later this month. The mayor has made projects like these a cornerstone of her city-improvement efforts. 75She insists that the park will create new economic opportunities for local vendors and provide more greenery in the area. 76The official ribbon cutting will be held at the park next Monday at 10 A.M. and everyone is welcome.

mayor 市長　completion 完成　delay 延遲、延期　path 路、小徑
riverfront 河邊　pedestrian 行人　cornerstone 基石　effort 努力
insist 主張　opportunity 機會　vendor 小販
greenery 綠地、綠化　ribbon cutting 開館儀式、剪綵儀式
welcome 歡迎～光臨

翻譯 問題 74-76，請參考以下新聞報導。

我是 KMIA 的 Lisa Barker，74 市長剛剛宣布 River East 公園工程竣工。由於惡劣天氣延遲了兩個月後，沿河的道路現已向行人開放。然而，自行車道要到本月月底才能完工。市長已經將此類工程作為其城市改善工作的基石。75 她堅信該公園將為當地商家創造新商機，並為該地區提供更多的綠化。76 正式剪綵儀式將於下週一上午 10 點在公園舉行，歡迎大家光臨。

74 特定細節問題

翻譯 是什麼原因使公園工程比原訂的施工時間更長？
(A) 材料不足
(B) 資金不足
(C) 額外的施工
(D) 惡劣天氣

解析 仔細聽與題目的關鍵句 take longer than planned 相關的內容，「The mayor just announced the completion of the River East Park Project. After a two-month delay due to bad weather」，說話者表示市長剛剛宣布完成 River East 公園工程，因為天氣不好而延遲了兩個月，所以 (D) 是正確答案。

換句話說
bad weather 不好的天氣 → Inclement weather 惡劣的天氣

字彙 lack 不足、缺乏　insufficient 不足的　funding 資金、財政資源
addition 增加、添加之物　inclement weather 惡劣天氣

75 特定細節問題

翻譯 市長預期會發生什麼事情？
(A) 一些經濟活動將會增加。
(B) 一些人將搬到附近。
(C) 部分地區會變得更貴。
(D) 一些旅遊景點將被重建。

解析 這題須注意聽與關鍵句 mayor expect to happen 相關的內容,「She[mayor] insists that the park will create new economic opportunities for local vendors.」,說話者表示市長主張該公園將為地區商販創造新的商機,所以 (A) 是正確答案。

字彙 neighborhood 鄰近、週邊
tourist attraction 觀光景點　rebuild 重建

76 之後將發生的事

翻譯 下週將發生什麼事情?
(A) 將完成某項安裝。
(B) 將舉行紀念儀式。
(C) 將發送邀請函。
(D) 將聽取居民們的意見。

解析 這題須注意聽與關鍵詞 next week 相關的內容,「The official ribbon cutting will be held at the park next Monday at 10 A.M.」,說話者表示正式剪綵儀式將於下週一早上 10 點在公園舉行,所以 (B) 是正確答案。

換句話說
The ~ ribbon cutting will be held 將舉行剪綵活動 →
A ceremony will take place 將舉辦慶祝儀式

字彙 installation 安裝　take place 舉行、發生　resident 居民

77-79 英國發音

Questions 77-79 refer to the following advertisement.

Do you want to save money and help the environment at the same time? Then contact Action Energy today. [77]We're currently offering a 20-percent discount and free installation on all orders of new solar power packages. [78]Our systems include everything that you need to power your home, from the rooftop solar panels to the batteries. With our help, you can cut your monthly electric bill by 50 percent or more and reduce your reliance on fossil fuels that are polluting the environment. [79]Call 555-8000 to discuss our products with a professional energy consultant and find the one that best suits your needs.

---

environment 環境　currently 現在　installation 安裝
solar power 太陽能發電　power 電力供給、能源　rooftop 屋頂
cut 減少、削減　reliance 依存、依賴　pollute 汙染
suit 匹配、適合

翻譯 問題 77-79,請參考以下廣告。
您想在省錢的同時保護環境嗎?那麼今天就聯絡 Action Energy 吧![77] 目前,我們對所有新太陽能發電系統訂單提供 20% 的折扣和免費安裝。[78] 我們的系統包括您為家庭供電所需的一切,從屋頂太陽能板到電池都可以。在我們的幫助下,您每月的電費可以減少 50% 或更多,並減少對汙染環境的化石燃料的依賴。[79] 請致電 555-8000 與專業能源顧問討論我們的產品,並找到最適合您需求的品項。

77 特定細節問題

翻譯 公司現在提供什麼促銷?
(A) 免費安裝
(B) 升級版電池組
(C) 五折優惠券
(D) 延長的保固

解析 這題須仔細聽與關鍵句 promotion ~ currently offering 相關的內容,「We're currently offering a 20-percent discount and free installation on all orders of new solar power packages.」,說話者表示目前對新太陽能發電套組的所有訂單提供 20% 的折扣和免費安裝,所以 (A) 是正確答案。

字彙 extend 延長　warranty 保固

78 聽者問題

翻譯 廣告是以誰為對象?
(A) 電池製造商
(B) 住宅擁有者
(C) 公共設施供應商
(D) 能源專家

解析 不要錯過與身分及職業相關的語句,「Our systems include everything that you need to power your home, from the rooftop solar panels to the batteries.」,說話者表示他們的系統包含為家庭電力供給所需的一切,從屋頂的太陽能板到電池等都有,由此可知廣告是以住宅擁有者為對象,所以 (B) 是正確答案。

字彙 be intended for 旨在用於~　homeowner 住宅擁有者
utility 公共設施　provider 供給者　professional 專家

79 理由問題

翻譯 聽者為什麼要聯絡該公司?
(A) 為了得到減少用電量的建議。
(B) 為了註銷公共服務的帳戶。
(C) 為了得到折扣代碼。
(D) 為了談論一些選項。

解析 這題須注意聽與關鍵句 contact the company 有關的內容,「Call 555-8000 to discuss our products with a professional energy consultant and find the one that best suits your needs.」,說話者請聽者打電話與專業能源諮詢師討論產品,並尋找最適合自己需求者,所以 (D) 是正確答案。

字彙 tip 訣竅　electricity 電力　usage 使用量

80-82 加拿大發音

Questions 80-82 refer to the following telephone message.

Hello, Ms. Johnson. This is Arthur calling from Technical Innovations. [80]I wanted to let you know that we now have the hard drive you requested last month in stock. The manufacturer was behind schedule. [81]I've put one aside for you in case they sell out again. However, we can only hold it for three days. It's a popular item. [82]To purchase it, just stop by the customer service desk at any time during store hours and tell them that you have an item on reserve. If you no longer need the item, please let us know so that we can put it back on the sales floor. Our number is 555-2840.

---

have ~ in stock 有～的庫存　behind schedule 進度落後
put aside for 將～放在一邊　in case 以防～　hold 擁有
stop by 順道過來　store hours 營業時間　sales floor 賣場

翻譯 問題 80-82，請參考以下電話留言。
　　您好，Johnson 女士，這是 Technical Innovations 的 Arthur 打來的電話。[80] 我想告訴您，我們庫存現在有您上個月要求的硬碟。製造進度落後了，[81] 但是我已經為您留了一份，以防它們再次賣完。然而，我們只能保留三天，因為這是一個熱銷品項。[82] 如果您要購買，只須在商店營業時間內隨時前往客戶服務臺，並告訴他們您有預訂商品即可。如果您不再需要該商品，請再告知，以便我們將其放回賣場。我們的電話號碼是 555-2840。

80 說話者問題

翻譯 說話者最可能在哪裡工作？
(A) 在維修店
(B) 在電子產品零售店
(C) 在辦公用品店
(D) 在製造工廠

解析 不要錯過對話中與身分和職業相關的語句，「I wanted to let you know that we now have the hard drive you requested last month in stock.」，透過「上個月要求的硬碟現在有庫存」這句話，可看出說話者在電子產品零售店工作，所以 (B) 是正確答案。

字彙 retailer 零售店、流通業者　office supply 辦公用品

81 意圖掌握問題

翻譯 說話者為什麼說「這是一個熱銷品項」？
(A) 為了推薦產品
(B) 為了拒絕額外的折扣
(C) 為了延遲而道歉
(D) 為了鼓勵快速的決定

解析 這題須注意聽出現關鍵句 It's a popular item 的內容，「I've put one[hard drive] aside for you in case they sell out again. However, we can only hold it for three days.」，說話者表示為了因應硬碟再次售完，所以為對方留了一份，但是只能保留三天，由此可看出這是為了鼓勵聽者快速做出決定，所以 (D) 是正確答案。

字彙 turn down 拒絕　apologize 道歉　encourage 獎勵、鼓勵

82 特定細節問題

翻譯 聽者需要做些什麼來購買產品？
(A) 打電話給員工。
(B) 預約。
(C) 拜訪顧客服務臺。

(D) 去別的分店。

解析 這題須仔細聽出現關鍵句 buy a product 的部分，「To purchase it[item], just stop by the customer service desk at any time during store hours.」，說話者表示如果想購買產品，在營業時間內可以隨時到顧客服務臺，所以 (C) 是正確答案。

換句話說
stop by 順道過來 → Visit 拜訪

83-85 [3w] 澳洲發音

Questions 83-85 refer to the following speech.

I would like to thank the judges for awarding *Off the Highway* the Best Documentary of the Year Award. I can't say how much this means to me. [83]I've been coming to this festival for over 20 years, and I consider it the most important film event of the year. [84]I also want to thank my amazing crew, especially Robert Willis, our sound engineer. He was a tireless, enthusiastic collaborator. Finally, [85]I want to thank all the amazing people of New Bridge, Iowa, who gave interviews to our crew about growing up in that little town. I couldn't be more grateful.

---

judge 評審、審查　award 頒獎、獎　crew 工作人員
tireless 不知疲倦的　enthusiastic 熱情的　collaborator 合作者
grateful 感激的

翻譯 問題 83-85，請參考以下演說。
　　我要感謝評審們授予《Off the Highway》年度最佳紀錄片獎。我無法以言語表達這對我有多重要，[83] 我參加這個影展已經有 20 多年了，我認為這是年度最重要的電影活動。[84] 我還要感謝我優秀的工作人員，尤其是我們的音響工程師 Robert Willis。他是一位不知疲倦又熱情的合作夥伴。最後，[85] 我要感謝愛荷華州 New Bridge 所有出色的人們，接受我們團隊針對他們在那個小鎮成長的採訪。我非常感激。

83 特定細節問題

翻譯 正在進行的最可能是什麼活動？
(A) 電影首映
(B) 劇場開館儀式
(C) 電影節
(D) 募捐活動

解析 這題須注意聽與關鍵字 event 相關的內容，「I've been coming to this festival for over 20 years, and I consider it the most important film event of the year.」，說話者表示自己參加該影展 20 多年了，並認為這是一年中最重要的電影活動，所以 (C) 是正確答案。

字彙 premier（電影的）首映、（戲劇的）首演　fundraiser 募款活動

84 特定細節問題

翻譯 Robert Willis 是誰？
(A) 活動主辦者

(B) 投資者
(C) 評論家
(D) 製作組成員

解析 不要錯過與 Robert Willis 的身分及職業相關的句子，「I also want to thank my amazing crew, especially Robert Willis, our sound engineer.」，說話者表示 Robert Willis 是團隊的音響工程師，所以 (D) 是正確答案。

字彙 organizer 主辦者、籌辦者　investor 投資者　critic 評論家

85 特定細節問題

翻譯 《Off the Highway》是關於什麼的作品？
(A) 中西部的野生動物
(B) 某個活動的歷史
(C) 最新的音樂合作
(D) 小鎮的生活

解析 這題須注意聽與關鍵詞 Off the Highway 相關的內容，「I want to thank all the amazing people of New Bridge, Iowa, who gave interviews to our crew about growing up in that little town.」，說話者想感謝愛荷華州 New Bridge 出色的人們，讓拍攝團隊能針對《Off the Highway》這部作品，對他們採訪在小鎮成長的事情，所以 (D) 是正確答案。

換句話說
growing up in ~ little town 在小鎮成長 → Living in a small town 在小鎮生活

字彙 wildlife 野生動物　collaboration 合作、一起工作

86-88 🔊美國發音

Questions 86-88 refer to the following podcast.

Welcome to the *Listening Together Podcast*. Today, our topic is modern jazz. Before we start, [86]we're going to announce the winner of the trip to the Greely Brothers concert. [87]More than 50,000 listeners registered for the special event. Our one lucky winner is June Sharp of Hamilton, Ontario. She and a guest will receive a fully paid trip to the concert, including tickets, airfare, and hotel, thanks to the generosity of our sponsor, Ultima Records. [87]Because of the great interest in the contest, we're already working together on another event. Actually, Ultima Records was surprised by the response. And [88]be sure to subscribe to the podcast, so you don't miss details about our next giveaway.

register 登記　airfare 機票　generosity 慷慨
sponsor 贊助企業、贊助者　interest 興趣　response 回應、回覆
subscribe 訂閱　giveaway 贈品

翻譯 問題 86-88，請參考以下廣播。
　　歡迎來到 Listening Together Podcast，今天我們的主題是現代爵士樂。在開始之前，[86] 我們將宣布 Greely Brothers 演唱會之旅的獲勝者。[87] 超過 50,000 名聽眾登記參加了這次特別活動。我們唯一的幸運獲獎者是來自安大略省漢密爾頓的 June Sharp，感謝我們的贊助

商 Ultima Records 的慷慨解囊，她和一位嘉賓將獲得全額付費的音樂會之旅，包括門票、機票和飯店。[87] 由於大家對活動的興趣濃厚，我們已經在合作舉辦另一項活動。事實上，Ultima Records 對這樣的反應感到驚訝。[88] 請務必訂閱我們的播客，這樣您就不會錯過有關我們下一個贈品的詳細資訊。

86 主題問題

翻譯 這是關於什麼的公告？
(A) 新專輯
(B) 特邀嘉賓
(C) 比賽結果
(D) 旅遊行程

解析 這是詢問主題的問題，所以一定要仔細聽前半部分。「we're going to announce the winner of the trip to the Greely Brothers concert.」，說話者表示將公布前往 Greely Brothers 演唱會之旅的獲獎者，所以 (C) 是正確答案。

字彙 contest 競賽、比賽

87 意圖掌握問題

翻譯 說話者說「Ultima Records 對這樣的反應感到驚訝」，她的意思是什麼？
(A) 唱片的銷售有了相當大的增長。
(B) 很多人參加活動。
(C) 由於流量增加，網站突然停止運作。
(D) 門票立即售罄。

解析 這題須注意聽關鍵句 Ultima Records was surprised by the response 前後的內容，「More than 50,000 listeners registered for the special event.」，說話者表示超過 50,000 名聽眾報名參加特別活動，並說：「Because of the great interest in the contest, we're already working together on another event.」，由此可知，由於大家對活動有極大的關注，他們已經著手準備其他活動，所以 (B) 是正確答案。

字彙 significantly 顯著地　crash（系統、程序）突然停止運作　traffic（通過電網的資訊）流量　immediately 立刻

88 特定細節問題

翻譯 聽者應該做些什麼來了解即將舉行的宣傳活動？
(A) 訂閱播客。
(B) 造訪網站。
(C) 發簡訊。
(D) 加入粉絲俱樂部。

解析 這題須注意聽與關鍵詞 upcoming promotion 相關的內容，「be sure to subscribe to the podcast, so you don't miss details about our next giveaway」，說話者表示如果大家不想錯過接下來攸關贈品的詳細資訊，請務必訂閱播客，所以 (A) 是正確答案。

換句話說
upcoming promotion 即將到來的宣傳活動 → next giveaway 接下來的贈品

字彙 join 加入

Questions 89-91 refer to the following announcement.

⁸⁹I've just come back from meeting with the community center manager, and she instructed me to get the park ready for visitors as soon as possible. People will be flocking to the park as the weather warms up over the coming weeks. So, this Friday, we will go around the park and check that everything is in order. ⁸⁹We will do minor repairs, replant where necessary, and clean up. To ensure a thorough job, each of you will be responsible for a specific area. ⁹⁰I will hand out a copy of location assignments in a few minutes. ⁹¹Mr. Sandoval, could you please check the storeroom to make sure we have enough supplies for the job?

---

flock 聚集、蜂擁而至　replant 移植　ensure 保證
thorough 徹底的　be responsible for 負責～
specific 特定的、具體的　hand out 分配　storeroom 儲藏室

翻譯 問題 89-91，請參考以下公告。
　　⁸⁹ 我剛與社區中心經理開會，她指示我盡快為遊客準備好公園。隨著未來幾週天氣變暖，人們將湧向公園，所以這個星期五，我們將繞公園一圈，檢查一切是否都井然有序。⁸⁹ 我們將進行小維修，必要處會重新植栽，並清理打掃。為了確保工作徹底全面，你們每個人都會負責一個特定領域。⁹⁰ 幾分鐘後我將分發一份位置分配副本。⁰¹ Sandoval 先生，您能檢查儲藏室，以確保我們有足夠的物資來完成這項工作嗎？

89 說話者問題

翻譯 說話者最可能是誰？
(A) 業主
(B) 業務經理
(C) 景觀設計師
(D) 維護人員

解析 不要錯過與身分和職業相關的語句，「I've just come back from meeting with the community center manager, and she instructed me to get the park ready for visitors as soon as possible.」。說話者表示剛剛和社區管理者開完會，她指示盡快為遊客們準備好公園，並表示「We will do minor repairs, replant where necessary, and clean up.」，透過「將進行小維修，必要處會重新植栽，並清理打掃」這句話可以得知，說話者是維護人員，所以 (D) 是正確答案。

字彙 landscape architect 景觀設計師

90 特定細節問題

翻譯 聽眾幾分鐘後會收到什麼？
(A) 清潔用品目錄
(B) 工作地點列表
(C) 公園標誌牌
(D) 庫存商品目錄

解析 這題須注意聽關鍵句 in a few minutes 前後的內容，「I will hand out a copy of location assignments in a few minutes.」，說話者表示稍後將分給大家位置分配的副本，所以 (B) 是正確答案。

字彙 inventory 庫存目錄　goods 商品

91 請求問題

翻譯 說話者請 Sandoval 先生做什麼？
(A) 確認天氣預報。
(B) 監督種植計劃。
(C) 制定員工班表。
(D) 確認用具庫存。

解析 這題須注意聽中後段與請求相關的句子，「Mr. Sandoval, could you please check the storeroom to make sure we have enough supplies for the job?」，說話者要求 Sandoval 先生確認儲藏室是否有足夠的用具進行作業，所以 (D) 是正確答案。

換句話說
supplies 物資 → materials 用具

字彙 weather forecast 天氣預報　oversee 監督　planting 種植

Questions 92-94 refer to the following tour information.

Hi, everyone. My name is Neil Cantwell, and ⁹²I'm the public relations manager here at Los Angeles Black Hill Observatory. I understand you're here for a class on astrophysics, so I'm going to go into more detail than usual about this place and how our instruments work. Our first stop will be the main lobby, where we have various pictures of the stars and planets our astronomers took. Then ⁹³we'll proceed to the main dome, where we'll demonstrate the telescope. We'll stay there for about 30 minutes and then finish the tour outside. Oh, ⁹⁴you won't need those pads and pens. A recording of the tour will be available on our website.

---

public relations 公關　observatory 天文臺、觀測站
astrophysics 天文物理學、宇宙物理學　go into detail 詳細說明
instrument 儀器　various 多樣的　planet 行星
astronomer 天文學家　proceed to 航向～、前往～
demonstrate 示範、說明　telescope 望遠鏡
recording 錄製、錄音、記錄

翻譯 問題 92-94，請參考以下觀光導覽。
　　大家好，我叫 Neil Cantwell，⁹² 是洛杉磯 Black Hill 天文臺的公關經理。我知道大家是來這裡參加天文物理學課程，所以我將比平常更詳細地介紹這個地方以及儀器如何運作。我們的第一站將是主廳，那裡有天文學家拍攝的各種恆星和行星的照片，⁹³ 接著我們將前往主穹頂，在那裡我們會示範望遠鏡。我們將在那裡停留約 30 分鐘，然後在外面結束導覽。哦，⁹⁴ 你們不需要帶那些筆記本和筆。我們的網站上將提供這次導覽的錄音。

92 地點問題

翻譯 導覽在哪裡舉行？
(A) 在飯店大廳
(B) 在大學校園
(C) 在研究設施
(D) 在攝影博物館

解析 不要錯過與地點相關的句子，「I'm the public relations manager here at Los Angeles Black Hill Observatory. I understand you're here for a class on astrophysics, so I'm going to go into more detail than usual about this place and how our instruments work.」，說話者自稱是洛杉磯 Black Hill 天文臺的公關經理後，並說「據我所知，你們是為了上天文物理學而來這裡，所以會比平時更詳細介紹此地點及儀器使用方法」，從這句話可以看出導覽正在研究設施中舉行，所以 (C) 是正確答案。

換句話說
Observatory 天文臺 → research facility 研究設施

字彙 university 大學　research facility 研究設施

93 特定細節問題

翻譯 導覽中將發生什麼事情？
(A) 電影將放映。
(B) 將會採訪一些科學家。
(C) 教授將發表演說。
(D) 將示範儀器的使用法。

解析 這題須注意聽與關鍵詞 during the tour 相關的內容「we'll proceed to the main dome, where we'll demonstrate the telescope」，說話者表示將前往主穹頂，並在那裡示範如何使用望遠鏡，所以 (D) 是正確答案。

換句話說
telescope 望遠鏡 → instrument 儀器

字彙 screen 放映　give a speech 演說

94 意圖掌握問題

翻譯 當說話者說「可以在我們的網站上使用導覽錄音」時，他的意思是什麼？
(A) 參加導覽並不是必要的。
(B) 有一個交流意見的線上論壇。
(C) 聽者不必記筆記。
(D) 建議登錄網站。

解析 這題須注意聽關鍵句 A recording of the tour will be available on our website 的前後內容。「You won't need those pads and pens」，說話者告訴聽者們不需要筆記本和筆，由這句話可以得知聽者們沒有必要做筆記，所以 (C) 是正確答案。

字彙 participation 參加、參與　mandatory 必須的　exchange 交換 comment 意見　registration 登記

95-97 美國發音

Questions 95-97 refer to the following talk and presentation slide.

We've received a lot of positive feedback about our new line of bags. While they've all sold well, [95]the backpack is clearly the star of the lineup. Its sales are nearly double those of all the other bags combined. It has also received the best customer reviews online. [96]They all mentioned that the bag's design made it perfect for both casual and formal settings. To build on its popularity, I'd like to offer some other varieties of it. [97]Let's look at some of my plans to modify it to increase its sales even further.

positive 正向的　feedback 意見、回應　star 主角、主演
double 兩倍的　combine 合併、結合　casual 隨意的
formal 正裝的、正式的　build on ~ 以～為基礎　popularity 人氣
variety 變形、多樣性　modify 變更、修改　further 更、進而

翻譯 我們收到了很多關於我們新系列包包的正面回饋。雖然它們都賣得很好，[96] 但背包顯然是該系列中的明星。它的銷量幾乎是所有其他款式銷量總和的兩倍。它還獲得了線上最佳客戶評價。[96] 大家都提到該包包的設計在休閒和正式這兩種場合都非常適合。以它的受歡迎程度為基礎，我想提供它的一些其他變化款式。[97] 讓我們看看我為了進一步增加其銷售量的一些修改計劃。

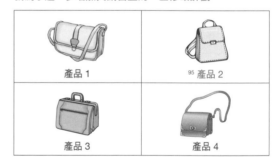

產品 1　[95] 產品 2
產品 3　產品 4

95 圖表題

翻譯 請看表格，公司的新產品中，最暢銷的產品是什麼？
(A) 產品 1
(B) 產品 2
(C) 產品 3
(D) 產品 4

解析 先確認題目的表格後，仔細聽與關鍵詞 best-selling item 相關的內容。「the backpack is clearly the star of the lineup. Its sales are nearly double those of all the other bags combined.」，從這句話可以得知背包明顯是這系列的主力，其銷售額幾乎是所有其他包包總和的兩倍，所以新產品中最暢銷的是產品 2，因此 (B) 是正確答案。

字彙 best-selling 最暢銷的

96 特定細節問題

翻譯 說話者表示顧客最喜歡那個包包的哪個部分？
(A) 材質
(B) 尺寸
(C) 設計
(D) 顏色

解析 這題須注意聽與關鍵句 customers like most about the bag 相關的內容，「They[customer reviews] all mentioned that the bag's design made it perfect for both casual and formal settings.」，顧客評價顯示該包包的設計使其在休閒和正式的場合都非常適合，因此 (C) 是正確答案。

字彙 fabric 材質、織品

97 之後將發生的事

翻譯 聽者接下來最可能會做什麼？
(A) 研究一些提案。
(B) 看看競品。
(C) 比較產品材質。
(D) 確認銷售數據。

解析 這題須注意聽最後一部分。「Let's look at some of my plans to modify it to increase its sales even further.」，說話者表示為了進一步增加銷售額，將研究幾個變化的方案，因此 (A) 是正確答案。

用法
look at some of ~ plans 看看幾個方案 → Review some proposals 研究幾個提案

字彙 review 檢視　proposal 提案　compare 比較
sales figures 銷售數據

98-100 澳洲發音

Questions 98-100 refer to the following telephone message and order form.

Hello, Ms. Reynolds. This is Brad Pressley calling from Officepro Wholesale regarding an order you just placed. While looking at your order, I noticed that it included some phone accessories. 98/99I wanted to let you know about a quantity discount on the Airway headsets. 99If you purchase two more, you will get one more for free. It might be useful to have some extra pairs on hand. Let me know if you would like to add those. 100We are ready to expedite the shipment, so you should receive everything within two business days.

regarding 與～有關　notice 察覺到　quantity 數量
useful 有用的　extra 其餘的　pair 一雙、一套
on hand 擁有的、手中的　expedite 迅速處理　shipment 運輸
business day 工作日

翻譯 您好，Reynolds 女士，我是 Brad Pressley，從 Officepro 批發打電話來詢問您剛剛下的訂單。在查看您的訂單時，我注意到其中包含一些手機配件。98/99 我想讓您知道 Airway 耳機的數量折扣。99 如果您再購買兩

副，將免費再獲得一副，身邊多備幾副可能會很有用。如果您想加購，請告訴我。100 我們已經準備好加快出貨速度，因此您應該會在兩個工作天內收到所有品項。

品項	數量
99 Airway 耳機（IB875747）	10
Blockland 紙箱（IB374665）	4
Officepro 筆，黑色（IB323722）	40
Blockland 記事本，大	20

98 目的問題

翻譯 說話者為什麼打電話？
(A) 為了請求付款
(B) 為了接受更改
(C) 為了提及機會
(D) 為了了解配送問題

解析 這題是詢問電話目的的問題，所以一定要聽前半部。「I wanted to let you know about a quantity discount on the Airway headsets.」，透過「想要告知 Airway 耳機數量折扣」這句話，可以看出說話者是為了提及機會而打電話，所以 (C) 是正確答案。

字彙 point out 提及、指出

99 表格題

翻譯 請看表格，為了得到折扣，需要更改以下哪個數量？
(A) 10
(B) 4
(C) 40
(D) 20

解析 先確認訂單資訊後，仔細聽關鍵字 discount 前後的內容，「I wanted to let you know about a quantity discount on the Airway headsets. If you purchase two more, you will get one more for free.」，說話者想告知 Airway 耳機的數量折扣，表示如果聽者再購買兩副，將免費獲得一副，因此為了得到折扣，需要更改 Airway 耳機的數量，也就是 10 副，因此 (A) 是正確答案。

100 提及何事的問題

翻譯 說話者說了關於這間公司的什麼事？
(A) 庫存正在枯竭。
(B) 專做電子產品。
(C) 正在引進新產品。
(D) 可以提供快速處理的配送。

解析 這題須注意與關鍵字 business 相關的內容，「We [Officepro Wholesale] are ready to expedite the shipment.」，說話者表示 Officepro 批發公司已準備好迅速處理配送，所以 (D) 是正確答案。

字彙 run low 枯竭　specialize in 擅長～

PART 5

101 選出副詞

解析 句子的意思是「Ballas 運動鞋公司以前稱為 Ballas Athletics」，所以 (C) formerly（以前、之前）是正確答案。(A) currently 是「現在、目前」；(B) so 是「非常」；(D) aside 是「另外、除此之外」。

翻譯 Ballas 運動鞋公司以前稱為 Ballas Athletics，但幾年前重新命名。

字彙 be known as 以～聞名　rebrand v. 重新打造品牌形象

102 填入符合時態的動詞

解析 句子裡沒有動詞，所以所有選項都可能是答案，主詞（The factory employees）和動詞（direct）形成「員工們接受指示」的被動意思，因此被動式動詞 (B) were directed 是正確答案。

翻譯 工廠員工被要求重新閱讀作業系統手冊。

字彙 operating system 作業系統　handbook n. 手冊　direct v. 指示

103 填入副詞子句連接詞

解析 這句話具備完整句子該有的元素（The science convention ~ in September），因此 the event's major sponsor ~ its support 應視為修飾語。該修飾語是具有動詞（has withdrawn）的子句，所以能夠引領子句的副詞子句連接詞 (A)、(B)、(D) 都可能是正確答案。因為句子的意思為「雖然活動的主要贊助商撤回了贊助，但是該科學大會將於 9 月舉行」，所以 (D) even though（雖然～）是正確答案。(A) if only 是「只要～做的話」；(B) so that 是「使～能做到」，所以不符合這句話的意思；副詞 (C) 不能連接子句和子句，因此不能成為答案。

翻譯 儘管活動主要贊助商已撤回贊助，但科學大會仍將於 9 月舉行。

字彙 convention n. 大會　sponsor n. 贊助商、贊助者　withdraw v. 撤回、棄權　support n. 贊助、支持

104 填入介係詞

解析 正確答案是 (A) for（～用意、～的對象），句子的意思是「承包商的發票被影印，並單獨歸檔，以用於稅務目的」。(B) at 是「在～」；(C) like 是「如同～、像～一樣」；(D) in 是「在～之中、在～裡」。

翻譯 承包商的發票被影印，並單獨歸檔，以用於稅務目的。

字彙 invoice n. 費用清單、發票　contractor n. 承包商　separately adv. 分別地、個別地　purpose n. 用途、意圖

105 選出動詞

解析 句子的意思是「《The Rock Creek Times》雜誌鼓勵讀者提出意見」，所以 (A) submit（提交）是正確答案。(B) determine 是「決定」；(C) teach 是「教導」；(D) accept 是「接受、答應」。

翻譯 《The Rock Creek Times》雜誌鼓勵讀者寫信向編輯提出意見。

字彙 encourage v. 鼓勵、獎勵　editor n. 編輯

106 填入符合格式的人稱代名詞

解析 可以像形容詞一樣放在其他名詞（own methods）前形容該名詞的人稱代名詞是所有格，因此 (C) his（他的）是正確答案。

翻譯 Holly 先生是公司僱用的第一位銷售人員，他必須開發自己的銷售方法。

字彙 salesperson n. 銷售員、推銷員　own adj. 擁有的　method n. 方式、方法

107 完成名詞片語

解析 句子的意思是「Fox Books 公司銷售多種類型的書籍」，可以與空格前的不定冠詞 (A) 和後面的介係詞（of）一起使用，構成「多種」意思的 (A) variety 是正確答案（a variety of：各種的）。(B) version 是「版本、變形」；(C) knowledge 是「知識」；(D) position 是「位置」。

翻譯 Fox Books 公司銷售各種類型的書籍，從小說和詩歌到歷史和哲學都有。

字彙 range from A to B 範圍從 A 到 B　fiction n. 小說　poetry n. 詩　philosophy n. 哲學

108 填入 to 不定詞

解析 可以在後面修飾名詞 plans 的 to 不定詞 (A) 和過去分詞 (B) 都可能是正確答案。從「計劃將該城市一些舊地鐵路線進行現代化」的句意來看，可以接受詞（some of ～ metro lines），並在後面裝飾名詞（plans）的 to 不定詞 (A) to modernize 是正確答案。過去分詞 (B) modernized 在後面不能接受詞，因此不能成為答案。另外，plan 後面要接 to 不定詞。

翻譯 倫敦市長概述了對該市一些舊地鐵線進行現代化改造的計劃。

字彙 mayor n. 市長　outline v. 概述　metro line 地下鐵路線　modernize v. 現代化

109 填入介係詞

解析 因為句子的意思為「攜帶食物、水以及指南針」，所以 (C) along with（和～一起）是正確答案。(A) such as 是「如同～」；(B) in case of 是「～的情況」。

翻譯 Gage 國家公園建議健行者攜帶食物、水以及指南針。

字彙 hiker n. 健行者　compass n. 指南針

110 分別填入可數名詞和不可數名詞

解析 空格前面有不定冠詞 (A)，句子的意思則是「公司的計劃由行銷代表發表」，因此可數名詞 (A) representative（代表人、代理人）是正確答案。不可數名詞 (C) 不能與不定冠詞 (A) 一起使用。即使分詞 (B) 和 (D) 可以修飾空格前名詞 marketing（行銷），marketing 也是不可數的名詞，因此不能與不定冠詞 (A) 一起使用。

翻譯 該公司的計劃是由行銷代表在昨天的記者會上宣布的。

字彙 press conference 記者會
representation n. 推舉代表、代表團

111 選出形容詞

解析 因為句意是「受邀演講者將在研討會開始時有五分鐘的時間進行簡短評論」，所以 (C) brief（短時間的、簡短的）是正確答案。(A) most 是「（數量、程度、金額）最多」；(B) equal 是「相同的、一樣的」；(D) busy 是「忙碌的」。

翻譯 受邀演講者將在研討會開始時有五分鐘的時間進行簡短評論。

字彙 remark n. 發言、評論

112 填入副詞

解析 為了修飾動詞（work），需要副詞，因此副詞 (D) collaboratively（合作地）是正確答案。名詞 (A)、(C) 以及形容詞 (B) 不能修飾動詞。即使名詞 (C) 能作為動詞（work）的受詞，也要以 work in collaboration with someone 的形式使用，因此不能成為答案。

翻譯 Stranton Tech 的團隊通力合作，發現問題，並找到適當的解決方案。

字彙 identify v. 發現、確認　appropriate adj. 合適的
solution n. 解決對策、解方　collaborator n. 共同研究者、合作者
collaborative adj. 協作的　collaboration n. 合作

113 填入搭配詞

解析 句子的意思是「為了滿足旅客增加的需求，將增加航線」，所以能和空格前的 meet 結合，並符合句意「滿足需求」meet demand 的名詞 (B) demand（需求）是正確答案。(A) cost 是「價格、費用」；(C) attempt 是「嘗試」；(D) insight 是「洞察力」。

翻譯 該航空公司將增加幾條飛往南美的新航線，以滿足旅客不斷增加的需求。

字彙 airline n. 航空公司　route n. 路線　passenger n. 旅客

114 填入副詞子句連接詞

解析 此句是具備所有句子必要元素（residents ～ the stairs）的完整句子，因此___the elevator is fixed 應視為修飾語。該修飾語是具有動詞（is fixed）的子句，因此能夠引領子句的副詞子句連接詞 (C) 和 (D) 可能是正確答案。因為句子的意思是「直到電梯修好為止，必須使用樓梯」，所以 (D) Until（～為止）是正確答案。(C) Since 的意思「從～以來、因為是～」，所以不適合此句意；副詞 (A) 和 (B) 不能連接兩個句子。

翻譯 在電梯修好之前，Halper 街 110 號的居民必須使用樓梯。

115 區分人物名詞和抽象名詞

解析 介係詞（in）和介係詞（with）之間能放入的是名詞，因此名詞 (B) 和 (D) 可能是正確答案。因為句意為「Kemper Shipping 正在和零售商進行交涉」，所以抽象名詞 (B) negotiation（交涉、協商）是正確答案。放入人物名詞 (D) negotiator（交涉者）句意不通，因此不能

成為答案。此外，negotiation 經常以 be in negotiation with（與～交涉中）的形式使用。

翻譯 Kemper Shipping 正在與美國大型零售商進行談判，以處理其在中東的所有物流。

字彙 retailer n. 零售商　handle v. 處理　logistics n. 物流管理

116 填入形容詞

解析 句子的意思是「如果沒有從資助機構獲得外部支援，就無法進行研究」，所以 (D) external（外部的）是正確答案。(A) plain 是「明顯的、原原本本的」；(B) compact 是「小型的、簡便的」；(C) mere 是「單純的、純粹的」。

翻譯 如果沒有資助機構的外部支援，該研究所將無法推進其研究。

字彙 advance v. 進行、進展　obtain v. 獲得、得到

117 填入介係詞

解析 句子的意思為「在大量降雨後，該城市正在應對大規模的水災毀損」，所以 (B) After（～之後）是正確答案。(A) Between 是「～之間」；(C) Aboard 是「搭乘～」；(D) Except 是「除了～」。

翻譯 曼菲斯在大量降雨後，該市正處理大規模的水災毀損。

字彙 extensive adj.（數量、規模、程度等）大量的、巨大的
rainfall n. 降雨（量）　deal with 處理～、應對
widespread adj. 大範圍的、大規模的　flood damage 水災毀損

118 填入數量用語

解析 可以修飾空格後的複數可數名詞（personnel）的 (A) 和 (D) 可能是正確答案。句子的意思是「要求整個公司所有員工都要佩戴身分識別證」，所以數量用語 (A) all（所有）是正確答案。(D) 如果使用 both（兩個），會變成「整個公司要求兩名員工都要佩戴身分識別證」的奇怪句意；(B) every 和 (C) each 必須與單數可數名詞一起使用。

翻譯 全面要求所有員工在工作場所工作時，必須佩戴公司發給的身分識別證。

字彙 across the board 整個（公司、企業等）
identification badge 身分識別證　issue v. 發給、交付
premise n. 區內、用地

119 填入動詞

解析 句子的意思是「調查揭露了設備的自動控制系統失靈」，因此 reveal 的過去式 (C) revealed（揭露）是正確答案。(A) choose 是「選擇、挑選」；(B) request 是「請求、要求」；(D) revise 是「變更」。

翻譯 該公司的工程師調查發現，設備的自動控制系統故障。

字彙 investigation n. 調查、搜查　automatic adj. 自動的

120 填入形容詞

解析 為了修飾名詞（role），必須填入形容詞，所以形容詞 (D) supervisory（指揮監督的）是正確答案。動詞 (A) 和

(B) 以及名詞 (C) 都不能放在形容詞的位置。

翻譯 從下週開始，Donald Peters 將負責 Zwingli 銀行的監管職務。

字彙 assume v. 擔負（責任、任務等）　supervisor n. 監督者、管理者

121 填入名詞子句連接詞

解析 能夠引領動詞（decide）的受詞，也就是名詞子句（smartphone~ their needs）的名詞子句連接詞 (A)、(B)、(C) 都可能是正確答案。空格後面有名詞（smartphone），句子的意思為「哪款智慧型手機最適合他們的需要」，因此與 smartphone 一起作為名詞子句主詞的疑問形容詞 (C) which 是正確答案。疑問代詞 (A) whom 引領名詞子句，可以做為名詞子句的主詞、受詞和補語，因此後面應該接沒有主詞、受詞或補語的不完整子句。名詞子句連接詞 (B) 可以連接子句（The website ~ decide）和子句（smartphone ~ their needs），但是 smartphone 是可數名詞，前面需要冠詞（a/the），因此不能成為答案；數量用語 (D) another 不能引領名詞子句。

翻譯 該網站提供建議，幫助人們決定哪款智慧型手機最適合他們的需求。

字彙 recommendation n. 推薦、建議

122 填入介係詞

解析 因為句子的意思為「儘管今年年初面臨生產問題」，所以 (C) In spite of（～不顧）是正確答案。(A) With 是「和～一起、帶著～」；(B) Owing to 和 (D) Because of 是「因為～」的意思。

翻譯 儘管今年稍早面臨生產挑戰，新款 Ecroon 筆記型電腦的推出還是如期進行。

字彙 challenge n. 問題、難題　on schedule 如期

123 填入最高級

解析 空格內應填入可以修飾空格後名詞（rating）的形容詞，因此形容詞 (A)、(B)、(D) 都可能是正確答案。句子的意思是「在所有照片編輯應用程式中擁有最高評價」，空格前有定冠詞（the），因此形容詞 high（高）的最高級 (B) highest 是正確答案。原級 (A) 和比較級 (D) 不能與最高級一起使用；副詞 (C) 不能放在形容詞的位置。

翻譯 根據數千名用戶的評論，Dynaline 在所有照片編輯應用程式中獲得最高評價。

字彙 rating n. 評分、評論　based on 根據～

124 選出名詞

解析 句子的意思是「因為沒帶收據，所以不允許退貨」，因此 (A) receipt（收據）是正確答案。(B) guidance 是「地圖、指南」；(C) report 是「報告」；(D) procedure 是「程序、方法」。

翻譯 Stewart 先生不被允許退貨，因為他沒有攜帶收據。

字彙 be allowed to 被允許做～

125 填入強調副詞

解析 句子的意思是「因為對壯觀的特效印象深刻」，所以副詞 (B) quite（相當地）是正確答案。(A) ever 是「無論何時、總是」；(C) last 是「最後、最近」；(D) same 主要搭配 the，一起以「the same」的形態使用，意思是「一模一樣」。

翻譯 每個在電影院看過這部電影的人都對其壯觀的特效印象深刻。

字彙 spectacular adj. 華麗的、壯觀的　special effect 特效

126 填入分詞構句

解析 這句話是具有主詞（Anuman Foods）、動詞（opened）、受詞（its second international location）的完整句子，所以＿＿its presence in Southeast Asia 應被視為修飾語。因此，有可能成為修飾語的現在分詞 (C) expanding 是正確答案。動詞 (A)、(B)、(D) 不能成為修飾語。

翻譯 Anuman Foods 公司今年在河內開設了第二家國際分店，擴大了在東南亞的業務。

字彙 presence n. 存在、實際存在　expand v. 擴張、擴大

127 填入相關連接詞

解析 正確答案是與連接詞 nor 一起使用的 (C) Neither。Neither A nor B 連接名詞（Mr. Hill）和名詞（Ms. Jackson）。

翻譯 Hill 先生和 Jackson 女士都沒有資格擔任區域銷售主管。

字彙 qualification n. 條件、資格　regional adj. 區域的、地方的

128 選出名詞

解析 因為句子的意思是「對精選商品給予豐厚的折扣優惠」，所以 (A) deals（折扣優惠）是正確答案。(B) excuse 是「辯解、藉口」；(C) share 是「份額、負擔」；(D) chance 是「機會」。

翻譯 超市定期發放優惠券，對精選商品提供豐厚優惠。

字彙 issue v. 發行、發給　generous adj. 豐厚的、很多的　selected adj. 嚴選的

129 填入時間副詞

解析 因為句子的意思是「被要求一週後來取回它」，所以 (B) later（～後、之後）是正確答案。(A) left 是「左側、左邊」；(C) more 是「（更）多」；(D) nowadays 是「最近」。

翻譯 Chung 女士被要求把車停在維修店，並在一週後取車。

字彙 repair shop 維修店

130 填入副詞子句連接詞

解析 這句話是具有所有句子必要要素（the travel industry ～ recover）的完整句子，因此＿＿the recession is over 應該視為修飾語。由於該修飾語是具有動詞（is）的子句，因此能夠引領子句的副詞子句連接詞 (B)、(C)、(D) 都可

能是正確答案。因為句子的意思是「經濟不景氣結束，期待旅遊業恢復」，所以表示理由的副詞子句連接詞 (D) Now that（～因此、～所以）是正確答案。如果使用 (B) Rather than（～比）和 (C) In order that（為了使～），句子的意思就會變成「比起／為了使經濟不景氣結束，期待旅遊產業能夠恢復」，因此不能成為答案。

翻譯 現在經濟衰退已經結束，旅遊業可望復甦。

字彙 recession n. 不景氣、蕭條　recover v. 恢復

PART 6

問題 131-134，請參考以下報導。

> Martindale's 慶祝週年紀念日
>
> 12 月 12 日——本週，Martindale's 慶祝其作為一家高級餐廳成立 20 週年。在法國接受培訓的主廚兼老闆 Joyce Martindale 一直夢想著在 Elkhart 市中心開一家餐廳，但她花了好幾年的時間才實現夢想。131 在相信她願景的家人和朋友的幫助下，她終於開設了自己的餐廳。如今，Martindale's 餐廳已成為 Elkhart 最好的餐廳之一。132 它甚至獲得了各種享有盛譽的獎項。
>
> 133 餐廳提供一系列常見的法國和美國料理，都是採用最新鮮的食材烹調而成。134 第一次來的客人一定要嚐嚐餐廳的招牌菜，包括牛排晚餐和烤雞，這些都是老顧客最喜歡的料理之一。

celebrate v. 適逢、慶祝　anniversary n. 紀念日
realize v. 實現、達成　vision n. 願景　a selection of 多樣的
ingredient n. 材料、成分　roast adj. 烤的　longtime adj. 很久的

131 選出副詞 掌握文意

解析 因為這句話的意思是「她在家人和朋友的幫助下開了餐廳」，所以所有的選項都可能是正確答案，也因此這題不能僅憑空格語句的句意來選擇答案，必須掌握上下文的脈絡。前一句話為「Joyce Martindale 一直夢想在 Elkhart 市中心開一家餐廳，但她花了好幾年的時間才實現夢想」（Joyce Martindale had always dreamed of having a restaurant in downtown Elkhart, but it took several long years to realize her dream），可見她最終在家人和朋友的幫助下開了餐廳。因此 (D) finally 是正確答案。

字彙 instead adv. 代替　likewise adv. 再加上、況且
frequently adv. 常常、頻繁地

132 選擇合適的句子

翻譯 (A) 有一些她經常光顧的熱門餐廳。
　　(B) 它甚至獲得了各種享有盛譽的獎項。
　　(C) 團體預約也可以透過應用程式進行。
　　(D) 早來的客人可以在等待期間坐在出入口周圍的位子上。

解析 這題須選擇適合放入空格的句子，所以要掌握上下文的脈絡，前一句「Today, Martindale's has become one of the best restaurants in Elkhart」表示今天 Martindale's

成為了 Elkhart 最好的餐廳之一，因此空格中應該填入它榮獲各種享有盛譽的獎項，所以 (B) 是正確答案。

字彙 recognize v. 認同、認可　prestigious adj. 享有盛譽的

133 填入時態正確的動詞

解析 那家餐廳以各種熟悉的法式和美國料理為特色，均只使用最新鮮的食材準備，這句話提到的是現在的情況，因此現在式 (A) features 是正確答案。

字彙 feature v. 為特色、特別包含

134 選出名詞 掌握上下文脈絡

解析 因為句子的意思是「第一次來的客人一定要嘗試一下餐廳的____」，所以所有的選項都可能是正確答案，因此這題不能僅憑空格所在語句的句意來選擇答案，而是必須掌握上下文的脈絡。後文中提到「包括牛排晚餐和烤雞，這些都是老顧客最喜歡的料理之一（These include the steak dinner and roast chicken, which are among the favorite dishes of longtime customers.）」，可見這是初次來的客人一定要嘗試的餐廳招牌菜。因此 (C) specialties（招牌菜）是正確答案。

字彙 diversion n. 轉換　activity n. 活動　performance n. 表演、演出

問題 135-138，請參考以下公告。

> AC Ambrose 農場公告
>
> 135AC Ambrose 決定今年在我們的農場採用新方法。我們將使用 Larkin Tech 製造的新型 HT509 機器人來加快包裝製程。目前，我們的團隊平均需要一個小時才能包裝完 1,000 磅的農產品進行配送。機器人則可以在 30 分鐘內完成相同的工作。136 因此，我們期望機器人能夠使我們的生產力翻倍。
>
> 這些機器人將於本月底交付。137 我們將於兩天內在所有的分店安裝。工人將被暫時重新配置，以便我們的包裝作業能夠不間斷地持續進行。一旦機器人準備就緒，製造商將派出一些人員來培訓被選出的工作人員如何使用機器人。138 如果你被選為參與者之一，將收到通知。

adopt v. 導入、採用　average n. 平均；adj. 平均的
produce n. 農產品　productivity n. 生產力
temporarily adv. 暫時地　relocate v. 重新配置
uninterrupted adj. 不中斷的

135 區分可數名詞和不可數名詞

解析 空格前的形容詞（new）修飾的是名詞，因此名詞 (A) 和 (D) 都可能是正確答案。空格前面有不定冠詞 a，因此單數名詞 (A) approach（方法）是正確答案。(B) 是動名詞，所以不能放在不定冠詞 a 之後，如果是現在分詞，就不能放到名詞的位置；形容詞 (C) 不能放在名詞的位置。

136 選出動詞 掌握整體文意

解析 因為句子的意思是「因此期待機器人能夠____生產力」，所以動詞 (B) double（翻倍）和 (D) measure（測

量）都可能是正確答案，因此這題不能僅憑空格所在語句的句意來選擇答案，必須掌握上下文的脈絡。前一句表示「現在的團隊平均需要一個小時才能包裝完 1,000 磅的農產品進行配送（Currently, it takes our teams an average of one hour to pack 1,000 pounds of produce for shipment.）」，後一句則表示「這些機器人可以在 30 分鐘內完成同樣的工作（The robots can complete the same job in 30 minutes）」，所以可以期待機器人使生產力翻倍，因此 (B) double 是正確答案。

字彙 involve v. 涉及、包括　repeat v. 重複

137 與名詞的數量／人稱一致的代名詞　掌握上下文脈絡

解析 句子的意思是「____在兩天時間內設置在所有分店」，所以 (A)、(B)、(D) 都可能是正確答案。因此這題不能僅憑空格所在語句的句意來選擇答案，必須掌握上下文的脈絡。前一句提到機器人（The robots）將在本月底之前交付，因此填入空格的代名詞指的是 robots，所以複數事物名詞（robots）的代名詞 (D) These 是正確答案。

138 選出合適的句子

翻譯 (A) 新員工的培訓將在會議室進行。
(B) 我們在配送下訂物品時可能會遇到一些延遲。
(C) 如果你被選為參與者之一，將收到通知。
(D) 那個團體的工作績效去年有了很大的提升。

解析 這題要選出適合放入空格的句子，所以要掌握上下文脈絡。前一句話「Once the robots are ready, the manufacturer will be sending over some people to train selected staff members on using the robots」表示機器人一旦準備就緒，製造商就會派遣部分人力培訓被選出的員工，所以空格中應該填入「如果你被選為參與者之一，將收到通知。」，因此 (C) 是正確答案。

字彙 performance n. 成果、績效　significantly adv. 相當地、大大地

問題 139-142，請參考以下電子郵件。

收件人：全體員工 <staff@brandesson.com>
寄件人：Beverly Castro <b.castro@brandesson.com>
主旨：軟體更新
日期：10 月 8 日

親愛的員工們：

我們升級了 Torrino 管理軟體。139 該程式包含一些你可能會覺得有用的元素。例如，它使整理工作行程和安排會議變得更加容易。

現在，軟體必須安裝在你的個人電腦上，這可能需要一些時間。140 為此，我要求 IT 人員在週末進行安裝。他們將於週五下午 6 點後開始作業。141 請協助他們，讓你的電腦在下班時保持開啟。142 當你週一回到公司時，如果因為任何原因而無法使用該程式，請聯絡我。

Beverly Castro
辦公室主管

administration n. 營運、管理　element n. 要素
organize v. 整理、組織　arrange v. 安排、配置
individual adj. 個人的、各自的　installation n. 安裝

139 選出形容詞　掌握上下文脈絡

解析 句子的意思是「該程式包含一些元素，可能讓你覺得____」，所以 (A) confusing（混亂的）、(B) useful（有用的）、(D) unfamiliar（不熟悉的）都可能是正確答案，因此這題不能僅憑空格語句的句意來選擇答案，必須掌握上下文的脈絡。後面提到這句話：「例如，它使整理工作行程和安排會議變得更加容易。（For instance, it makes organizing work schedules and arranging meetings easier.）」，由此可見，該程式具有一些有用的元素。因此，(B) useful 是正確答案。

字彙 enclosed adj. 隨附的、被包圍的

140 填入連接副詞　掌握上下文脈絡

解析 空格和逗號都位在句子最前面的連接副詞位置，因此要掌握前面句子和空格所在句子的意思關係，才能選擇正確答案。在前一句話中提到該軟體必須安裝在個人電腦上，但這可能需要時間，空格所在的句子則表示 IT 員工將在週末進行安裝，因此能承接前一句內容的 (D) For this reason（因上述原因）是正確答案。

字彙 similarly adv. 類似地、相似地　meanwhile adv. 同時
on the other hand 另一方面

141 選出合適的句子

翻譯 (A) 大家請記得早上到公司的時候一定要登錄。
(B) 大家可以透過聯絡管理員來註冊培訓課。
(C) 請協助他們，讓你的電腦在下班時保持開啟。
(D) 找到密碼不會多花大家太多時間。

解析 這題要選出適合填入空格的句子，所以要掌握上下文脈絡，前一句話「They[IT staff] will start on Friday after 6 P.M.」提到 IT 員工們將在週五下午 6 點以後開始安裝，因此空格中應該填入下班時為他們保留電腦的開啟狀態，所以 (C) 是正確答案。

字彙 session n. 課程　administrator n. 管理員

142 接 to 不定詞的形容詞

解析 空格前的形容詞 unable（～不能）是接 to 不定詞的形容詞，因此 to 不定詞 (A) to access 是正確答案。名詞或動詞 (B)、現在分詞 (C) 和 (D) 都不能放在 to 不定詞的位置。

字彙 access v. 使用

問題 143-146，請參考以下報導。

里斯本（5 月 7 日）—143 Flores 皮革製品公司將於今年夏天開始銷售鞋子和手提包。這家擁有 50 年歷史的公司正在增加其銷售的產品類型。目前僅提供錢包和皮帶。144 此變革的原因在於該公司發現過去幾年消費者品味和偏好發生了變化。145「我們的錢包和皮帶收益大幅減少，」執行長兼創始人 Mario Flores 解釋道：「如果我們想獲利，就需要適應市場的變化。」146 該公司希望今後提供更多的產品。錶帶和背包是該公司正在開發的產品之一。

shift n. 變化　taste n. 品味、喜好　preference n. 偏好、愛好
revenue n. 收益、收入　adjust v. 適應　profitable adj. 獲益的

143 填入動名詞

解析 名詞 (A) 和動詞 (D) 可以放在動詞（begin）的受詞位置。正確答案是取名詞（shoes and handbags）作為受詞，同時可以放在動詞受詞位置的動名詞 (D) selling。如果沒有介係詞，就不能在名詞前面直接連接其他名詞，因此名詞 (A) 不能成為答案。

144 填入與時間用語時態一致的動詞

解析 由於空格前是現在完成式「over the last few years」，所以正確答案是現在完成式 (B) has seen，表示過去開始的事情一直持續到現在。

145 選出動詞 掌握上下文脈絡

解析 句子的意思是「錢包和皮帶帶來的收益大大＿＿＿」，所以 (A) enhanced（強化）、(B) boosted（增加）、(D) diminished（減少）都可能是正確答案，因此這題不能僅憑空格所在語句的句意來選擇答案，必須掌握上下文的脈絡。後面的句子表示「如果想要獲利，就要適應市場的變化（We need to adjust to changes in the market if we want to become profitable.）」，由此可推斷錢包和皮帶帶來的收益大幅減少，所以 (D) diminished 是正確答案。

146 選出合適的句子

翻譯 (A) 新分店將在秋天的某個時候開放。
(B) 用戶在網路投票中投給他們最喜歡的東西。
(C) 該公司希望今後提供更多的產品。
(D) 沒有購買憑證的商品可能無法退貨或換貨。

解析 這題要選出適合填入空格的句子，所以要掌握上下文脈絡，後面的句子「Watch straps and backpacks are some of the products that the company is developing」表示錶帶和背包是該公司正在開發的產品之一，因此可以看出空格中應該填入公司今後想提供更多產品的內容，所以 (C) 是正確答案。

字彙 vote v. 投票　poll n. 投票、輿論調查　proof n. 憑證、證據

PART 7

問題 147-148，請參考以下廣告。

Fleetz Office Warehouse 公司

Fleetz Office Warehouse 公司提供適合各種預算和風格的全系列辦公家具。從我們由世界各地頂級製造商生產的廣泛產品種類中進行選擇。想省很多嗎？那麼您可能會對 148-B 我們自家的辦公家具品牌 EZwerks 感興趣，包括從椅子、桌子到會議桌和文件櫃等所有產品。147 自從我們的執行長在電視節目中介紹品牌以來，EZwerks 一直深受聖安東尼奧全區企業主們的歡迎。

148-A 請前往我們在該市四家分店中的任一分店，了解為什麼 Fleetz Office Warehouse 在品質、價格實惠和便利性方面的顧客評價名列前茅。請上 www.fleetzoffice.com 以取得完整的產品目錄。僅限本月，148-D 當您註冊加入我們的 Fleetz Rewards 忠誠度會員計劃時，可享有單次或大量購買的 20% 折扣。 ➡

---

a full range of 大幅的　extensive adj. 廣泛的
look for 希望〜、期待　rank high among 在〜之間取得高地位
affordability n. 便宜的、可負擔的費用　bulk adj. 大量的

147 5W1H 問題

翻譯 是什麼讓 EZwerks 受到企業主們的歡迎？
(A) 採用優質材料。
(B) 它出現在電視節目中。
(C) 對大訂單給予折扣。
(D) 可以分期付款。

解析 這題詢問是什麼（What）讓 EZWerks 受到企業主歡迎，因此屬於 5W1H 問題。題目的關鍵句是「EZwerks popular with business owners」，文章中提到「Ever since our CEO introduced the brand on a television program, EZwerks has been popular with business owners throughout San Antonio.」，指出公司執行長在電視節目中介紹品牌後，EZwerks 在聖安東尼奧全區的企業主們中人氣很高，因此正確答案是 (B)。

字彙 installment n. 分期付款

148 Not/True 問題

翻譯 關於 Fleetz Office Warehouse，下列何者不正確？
(A) 在一座城市有多家分店。
(B) 銷售自有品牌的產品。
(C) 每個月都會收到新品項。
(D) 它實行會員計劃。

解析 這是將題目的關鍵詞 Fleetz Office Warehouse 相關內容與選項對照，並找出答案的 Not/True 問題。在「Stop by any of our four locations in the city」這句中，請顧客造訪市內四家分店其中一家，因此與選項 (A) 的內容一致。在「our own brand of office furniture, EZwerks, which includes everything from chairs and desks to conference tables and filing cabinets」中提到，自家的辦公用家具品牌 EZwerks 包含了椅子、桌子乃至會議桌和文件櫃，因此與 (B) 的內容一致。(C) 是文章中沒有提及的內容，所以 (C) 是正確答案。在「enjoy a 20-percent discount ~ when you sign up as a member in our Fleetz Rewards loyalty program」中表示，如果加入 Fleetz Rewards 忠誠度會員計劃將享 20% 的折扣，因此與 (D) 的內容一致。

字彙 branch n. 分店　operate v. 營運

問題 149-150，請參考以下簡訊對話。

Petra Bellamy　　　　　　　　下午 3 點 14 分

嗨，Brian，你的會議結束了嗎？我希望一切順利。我想知道你是否可以幫我解決問題。149 我一直試著為客戶列印一份報告。但是，印表機不斷拒絕我的文件，是因為我正在使用新的軟體程式嗎？

Brian Allman　　　　　　　　下午 3 點 16 分

事實上，會議剛結束，一切都很順利。謝謝你的詢問。至於你的問題，我認為不是軟體的問題。我以前也遇過這種情況，你應該檢查印表機是否缺墨水。 ➡

Petra Bellamy	下午 3 點 20 分

我檢查了印表機，你是對的。不幸的是，[150] 我們的墨水似乎用完了。我可以再訂購一些嗎？

Brian Allman	下午 3 點 21 分

我來打電話給經理，[150] 之後再回覆你，並告知你何時可以進行。不過，如果她很忙，你可能要等到明天早上。

---

client n. 顧客　reject v. 拒絕　as for 說到～
get back to （之後）再聯絡～　proceed v. 進行

---

149 5W1H 問題

翻譯 Bellamy 女士的問題是什麼？
(A) 她無法列印文件。
(B) 她的建議被客戶拒絕了。
(C) 她不熟悉軟體。
(D) 她的主管留下了不明確的指示。

解析 題目詢問 Bellamy 女士的問題是什麼（What），因此是 5W1H 問題。題目的關鍵詞是「Ms. Bellamy's problem」，在「I've been trying to print a report for a client. However, the printer keeps rejecting my file.(3:14 P.M.)」中提到 Bellamy 女士嘗試為顧客列印報告書，但印表機一直拒絕文件，因此 (A) 是正確答案。

換句話說
report 報告書 → document 文件

字彙 proposal n. 提案　unclear adj. 不明確的
instruction n. 指示、命令

150 掌握意圖問題

翻譯 下午 3 點 21 分，Allman 先生寫道：「Let me call the manager」時，最有可能是什麼意思？
(A) 必須確認產品是否有貨。
(B) 進出儲藏室會受到管制。
(C) 供應商未回覆訊息。
(D) 訂購商品需要獲得批准。

解析 這題問的是 Allman 先生的意圖，所以應確認關鍵句 Let me call the manager 的上下文脈絡。在「we seem to be out of ink. Can I order some more? (3:20 P.M.)」中，Bellamy 女士說墨水用完了，詢問是否可以再訂購一些，Allman 先生表示「Let me call the manager（我打個電話給經理）」後，在「I'll get back to you, and let you know when you can proceed. (3:21 P.M.)」中表示會再次聯絡 Bellamy 女士告知可列印的時間，因此 (D) 是正確答案。

字彙 confirm v. 確認　access n. 使用　restrict v. 限制
reply v. 回應　approval n. 批准

問題 151-152，請參考以下公告。

Riverbend 公寓住戶公告

我們很高興地宣布 [151] Riverbend 公寓將進行住戶停車場施工。這將涉及進行必要的維修、重新鋪設地面以及升級照明和安全功能。[152] 工程將於下週 4 月 11 日開始，預計將持續到月底。為了確保每個人的安全，施工期間整個停車場將關閉。[152] 我們建議車主將車停在 Center Street 停車場，直到施工完成。對於由此造成的任何不便，我們深表歉意。[152] 為了補償可能產生的費用，Riverbend 公寓將免除通常包含在下個月租金中的 50 美元停車費。如有疑問，請致電 555-7731 聯絡大樓管理團隊。感謝您的耐心與體諒。

---

tenant n. 住戶、居民　conduct v. 進行、執行
involve v. 包含　repave v. 重新鋪設　surface n. 地面、表面
security n. 安全、保全　commence v. 開始　ensure v. 確保
compensation n. 補償　incur v. 發生、招致
waive v. 免除　patience n. 耐心

---

151 目的問題

翻譯 該公告的目的是什麼？
(A) 對建築工程造成的噪音致歉。
(B) 提供即將進行的改善工程的相關資訊。
(C) 感謝住戶為專案捐款。
(D) 通知房客停車場收費上漲。

解析 這題問的是公告的目的，在「Riverbend Apartments will be conducting work on the tenant parking lot. This will involve making necessary repairs, repaving the surface of the lot, and upgrading lighting and security features.」中提到 Riverbend 公寓將進行住戶停車場工程，這包括必要的維修、重新鋪設地面以及升級照明和安全功能等，所以 (B) 是正確答案。

換句話說
making ~ repairs, repaving the surface ~, and upgrading ~ features 維修、重新鋪設地面，以及功能升級
→ improvements 改善工程

字彙 improvement n. 改良（工程）、改善　contribute v. 捐助、貢獻

152 推論問題

翻譯 關於房客可以推斷出什麼？
(A) 他們應該會收到郵寄的聲明。
(B) 部分房客五月的租金會比平常少。
(C) 他們曾投訴停車場的狀況。
(D) 其中一些房客需要申請新的停車許可證。

解析 這題要針對關鍵字 tenants 做推論。「Work will commence next week on April 11 and is expected to last until the end of the month.」提到工程預定在下週 4 月 11 日開始，並持續到月底，「We recommend that those with vehicles park at the Center Street Parking Garage until the renovations are complete. In compensation for fees that may be incurred, Riverbend Apartments will waive the $50 parking fee that is normally included with the rent for next month.」則表示在修理完成之前，建議車主將車停在 Center Street 停

車場，並說明為了補償因此產生的費用，下個月將免除租金內含的 50 美元停車費，因此可以推論出部分房客在 5 月分的租金會比平時少，所以 (B) 是正確答案。

字彙 statement n. 明細　condition n. 狀態、環境
permit n. 許可（證）

問題 153-154，請參考以下廣告。

StatBook 公司
實現您的夢想專案

StatBook 公司可以幫助您實現圖書專案創意。[153-D] 無論您是想印製一本個人化相簿與家人和朋友分享，還是出版書面作品並向大眾出售，StatBook 公司都可以幫助您以實惠的價格實現目標。

StatBook 公司讓您能夠從頭到尾完全掌握您的專案。此外，我們也提供基本的軟體編輯工具和設計協助。當您的書籍準備印刷時，StatBook 公司保證快速產製並交付成品。請上我們的網站 www.statbook.com 查看定價，或依據您需要的份數取得報價。

*[154] 11 月特別優惠：列印至少 2,000 份，我們免費將紙張升級到我們提供的最高品質。

---

reality n. 現實　creative adj. 創意的、創造的
personalize v. 個人化　written work 著作
public n. 大眾、一般民眾　control n. 指揮（權）、控制力
assistance n. 協助　guarantee v. 保證　quote n. 報價
deal n. 交易　minimum n. 最低（限度）、最少量

---

153 Not/True 問題

翻譯 關於 StatBook 公司，下列何者被提及？
(A) 專門製作有聲書。
(B) 它有一個智慧型手機線上應用程式。
(C) 為學生提供折扣。
(D) 它協助客戶出版自己的作品。

解析 這是 Not/True 的問題，需要將與關鍵字 StatBook 相關的內容和選項對照，再找出答案。(A)、(B)、(C) 是文章中沒有提及的內容。「Whether you want to print a personalized photo book to share with family and friends or publish a written work and sell it to the public, StatBook can help you realize your goal~」中提到，不論是為了與家人和朋友分享而希望印刷個人化相簿，或者出版作品向大眾銷售，StatBook 公司都可以幫忙實現目標，所以 (D) 是正確答案。

字彙 specialize in 擅長～

---

154 5W1H 問題

翻譯 11 月將有什麼優惠？
(A) 會員折扣
(B) 用紙的升級
(C) 一套免費的節日賀卡
(D) 限量的服務試用

解析 這題是詢問 11 月將提供什麼（What）的 5W1H 問題。關於題目的關鍵字 November，在「Special November

---

deal: Print a minimum of 2000 copies, and we will upgrade the paper at no extra charge to the highest quality that we offer.」中提到，11 月透過特別優惠，只要印刷 2,000 本，則無需追加費用即可將紙張升級到最高品質，因此 (B) 是正確答案。

字彙 holiday card 節日賀卡　trial n. 體驗、試驗

問題 155-157，請參考以下表格。

MIDDLETON 銀行電匯申請表

[156-B] 請注意，電匯截止時間為下午 3 點

[156-A] 顧客資訊	
[155] 顧客姓名	Antoine Ducharme
帳號	118825622042
[156-A] 地址	加拿大，魁北克省，Phare 街 1432 號

電匯資訊			
金額	3,800 美元	日期	7 月 7 日

[155] 電匯目的：支付購買繪畫的費用
*[156-A] 受款人將以當地貨幣收到金額

[156-A] 受款人資訊	
[155/157-D] 受款人姓名	Salles 藝廊
[157-D] 銀行及帳號	Carrousel 信用社 — 227722662243
[156-A] 地址	法國，巴黎，Moulinet 街 8 號

客戶權限委任

我確認所提供的所有資訊均正確無誤，並授權 Middleton 銀行轉帳。此外，我了解如果提供的任何詳細資訊不正確，轉帳可能會被延遲或拒絕。

簽名：Antoine Ducharme
電話號碼：555-6012

電匯手續費

___ 國內 15 美元　　___ 國際 25 美元　　[157-C] X 免除*
[157-C] *VIP 顧客免收電匯手續費。

---

wire transfer 電匯　cutoff adj. 截止的　beneficiary n. 受款人
currency n. 貨幣　acknowledge v. 確認
authorize v. 授權

---

155 推論問題

翻譯 Salles 藝廊有什麼特色？
(A) 它將負擔轉帳手續費。
(B) 它在加拿大開設了分店。
(C) 它把一幅畫賣給了 Ducharme 先生。
(D) 它將運送一件藝術品到法國。

解析 這題須用題目的關鍵詞 Salles Gallery 作出推論。從「Customer Name, Antoine Ducharme」、「Purpose of Wire Transfer: To pay for the purchase of a painting」、「Beneficiary Name, Salles Gallery」可知，Ducharme 先生為了支付購畫款項，要求電匯

給 Salles 藝廊，因此可以推測 Salles 藝廊將畫賣給 Ducharme 先生，所以 (C) 是正確答案。

字彙 cover v. 負擔、負責　artwork n. 藝術作品、美術品

156 Not/True 問題

翻譯 有關 Ducharme 先生的交易，下列何者為真？
　(A) 需要兌換貨幣。
　(B) 將於隔天完成。
　(C) 每個月都會重複發生。
　(D) 需要經理簽名。

解析 這個 Not/True 的問題，需要將與題目的關鍵詞 Mr. Ducharme 相關的內容和選項對照，再找出答案。在「Customer Information」和「Address, 1432 Rue de Phare, Quebec, Canada」中提到，客戶的地址是加拿大魁北克，「The beneficiary will receive the amount in their local currency」則表示受款人將以當地貨幣收取金額，在「Beneficiary Information」、「Address, 8 Rue de Moulinet, Paris, France」中，受款人的地址是法國巴黎，所以 (A) 是正確答案。「the wire transfer cutoff time is 3:00 P.M.」提到，雖然電匯的截止時間是下午 3 點，但是由於無法知道顧客要求匯款的時間，所以 (B) 與文章內容不一致。(C) 和 (D) 則是文章中沒有提到的內容。

157 Not/True 問題

翻譯 關於 Ducharme 先生，下列何者被提及？
　(A) 他最近參加了在巴黎舉行的活動。
　(B) 他代表一家企業匯款。
　(C) 他是 Middleton 銀行的 VIP 客戶。
　(D) 他在 Carrousel 信用社有一個帳戶。

解析 這是 Not/True 問題，需要將與題目的關鍵詞 Mr. Ducharme 有關的內容和選項對照，再找出答案。(A) 和 (B) 是文章中沒有提到的內容。在「X Waived*」和「*Wire fees are waived for VIP customers」中提到 VIP 顧客免收電匯手續費，而 Ducharme 先生沒有收取電匯手續費，因此 (C) 與文章內容一致，所以是正確答案。「Beneficiary Name, Salles Gallery」、「Bank and Account Number, Carrousel Credit Union—227722662243」中提到，在 Carrousel 信用社擁有帳戶的是 Salles 藝廊，因此 (D) 與文章內容不一致。

字彙 on behalf of 代表～

問題 158-160，請參考以下電子郵件。

收件人：Sebastian Contos <s.contos@dromomail.com>
寄件人：Anastasia Sokolov <a.sokolov@globetrektech.com>
日期：1 月 3 日
主旨：您的申請

158-D 親愛的 Contos 先生：

158-D 我們收到了您對 GlobeTrek Technology 公司創意設計主管職位的申請。— [1] —. 感謝您對我們公司的興趣。不幸的是，該職位已被授予另一位應徵者。

不過，您的履歷使我們留下了深刻的印象。— [2] —. 目前，我們還有另外兩個高階職位正在招募有您這樣經驗的設計師。經您同意，我有意將您的申請提交給設計部負責人進一步考慮。

這些職位的薪水確實比您最初申請的職位略低。— [3] —. 但是我們公司提供這兩個職位巨大的晉升空間。此外，160 GlobeTrek Technology 也為所有全職員工提供豐厚的福利待遇。— [4] —.

159 請上 GlobeTrek Technology 公司員工應徵網站，以了解有關職缺的更多資訊。由於您已經提交了線上申請，如果您想針對任何職缺重新提出，可以透過電子郵件與我聯絡。

Anastasia Sokolov
GlobeTrek Technology – 人力資源經理

---

position n. 職位　organization n. 組織　open adj. 開缺的
permission n. 許可、批准　further adj. 額外的
consideration n. 考慮、深思熟慮　room n. 空間
advancement n. 升職、發展　benefits package 福利待遇

158 Not/True 問題

翻譯 有關 Contos 先生，下列何者為真？
　(A) 他曾在 GlobeTrek Technology 工作。
　(B) 他擁有管理學高階學位。
　(C) 他沒有技術領域的經驗。
　(D) 他最近申請擔任部門主管。

解析 這是 Not/True 問題，需要將與題目的關鍵詞 Mr. Contos 相關的內容和選項對照，再找出答案。(A)、(B)、(C) 是文章中沒有提及的內容。「Dear Mr. Contos」和「We received your application for the position of head of creative design at GlobeTrek Technology.」中表示，收到了 Contos 先生對 GlobeTrek Technology 公司創意設計主管職位的申請書，因此與文章內容一致，所以 (D) 是正確答案。

字彙 advanced degree （學士以上的）高階學位

159 5W1H 問題

翻譯 在網站上可以找到哪些資訊？
　(A) 空缺職位清單
　(B) 面試行程
　(C) 公司設施圖
　(D) 團隊成員的電子郵件地址

解析 這題是詢問在網站上可以找到什麼（What）的 5W1H 問題。題目的關鍵字是 website，「Please visit the GlobeTrek Technology employee application portal for further information on the available positions」中提到，可以上 GlobeTrek Technology 公司的員工應徵網站確認職缺額外資訊，所以 (A) 是正確答案。

換句話說
website 網站 → portal 入口網站
information on the available positions 有關可聘用職缺的資訊
→ A list of openings 空缺職位清單

字彙 opening n. 空缺、職缺

160 將句子放入合適的位置

翻譯 以下句子最適合放入 [1]、[2]、[3] 或 [4] 的哪個位置？
「我們提供全面的醫療保險和每年三週的有薪假。」
(A) [1]
(B) [2]
(C) [3]
(D) [4]

解析 本題須看文章脈絡，選擇最適合放入句子的位置。「We provide comprehensive health care and three weeks of paid vacation each year」的意思是「我們提供全面的醫療保險和每年三週的有薪假」，因此可以預期在這句前面會有與福利制度相關的內容。[4] 的前一句話為「GlobeTrek Technology provides a generous benefits package to all full-time employees」，意思是 GlobeTrek Technology 公司向所有正式員工提供豐厚的福利制度，如果將句子填入 [4]，即可知全面的醫療保險和每年三週有薪假是豐厚福利之一，所以 (D) 是正確答案。

字彙 comprehensive adj. 綜合的

問題 161-163，請參考以下網頁。

Hartwell 咖啡館

| 首頁 | 訂位 | 瀏覽菜單 | 詢問 |

您想在 Sheffield 地區尋找新鮮、健康的食物？Hartwell 咖啡館就是您的最佳選擇！我們三個月前開幕，很榮幸成為 Sheffield 最新的有機餐廳！

161-D 我們所有的食物都是農場直送的，不含人工防腐劑、色素和調味料。我們只使用純天然成分！有多種素食選項以及無乳製品、無堅果和無大豆料理供您選擇。161-B 如果您有特殊飲食需求，請聯絡我們，我們將很樂意為您服務。如需聯絡我們的員工提出特殊要求，162 只要使用此處的線上聯絡表單。

163 我們目前還有進行中的促銷活動，只要在我們的社群媒體網站上發布您在餐廳的照片，您就能在下一餐獲得免費的湯或沙拉。

---

organic adj. 有機的　farm-fresh adj. 農場直送的、產地直送的
artificial adj. 人工的　preservative n. 防腐劑　dye n. 色素
flavoring n. 調味料　all-natural adj. 只用純天然材料製作的
dietary adj. 飲食的　oblige v. 協助、給予（幫助等）
reach out 取得聯絡　ongoing adj. 持續進行的

---

161 Not/True 問題

翻譯 關於 Hartwell 咖啡館，下列何者被提及？
(A) 它曾經以另一個名字為人所知。
(B) 不提供客製化餐點。
(C) 最近又開設了另一家分店。
(D) 其料理不使用人工色素。

解析 這是 Not/True 問題，需要將與題目的關鍵詞 Hartwell Café 相關內容和選項對照，再找出答案。(A) 是文章中沒有提及的內容。「If you have special dietary needs, contact us and we will be happy to oblige.」提到，如

果有什麼特別的飲食要求，只要聯絡餐廳，餐廳就會欣然提供幫助，因此 (B) 與文章的內容不一致。(C) 是文章中沒有提及的內容。「All of our food is farm-fresh and free of artificial preservatives, dyes, and flavorings」中表示所有食品都是農場直送，沒有人工防腐劑、色素和調味料，因此 (D) 與文章的內容一致，所以是正確答案。

字彙 custom adj. 客製的

162 尋找同義詞

翻譯 第 2 段第 4 行的「just」，意思最接近下列何者？
(A) 相當地
(B) 仔細地
(C) 簡單地
(D) 準確地

解析 從 just 所在的句子「just use the online contact form here」可看出，just 在此的意思是「只是」，所以 (C) 是正確答案。

163 5W1H 問題

翻譯 如果顧客參加促銷活動，他們會得到什麼？
(A) 配菜選擇
(B) 免費飲料
(C) 主菜折扣
(D) 供將來使用的禮品卡

解析 這題詢問如果顧客參與促銷活動會得到什麼（What），所以是 5W1W 問題。題目的關鍵句「participate in a promotion」、「We also have an ongoing promotion. Post a photo of yourself at the restaurant on our social media page and receive a free soup or salad with your next meal.」提到，促銷活動將持續進行，只要將自己在餐廳的照片上傳到社群媒體網站，就能免費獲得湯或沙拉，所以 (A) 是正確答案。

換句話說
a free soup or salad 免費的湯或沙拉 → side dish 配菜

字彙 side dish 配菜　complimentary adj. 免費的　entrée n. 主菜

問題 164-167，請參考以下電子郵件。

收件人：Eliza Kemper <e.kemper@usgrandtours.us>
寄件人：David Sims <david.sims@bridgeporttravelexpo.com>
主旨：博覽會
日期：8 月 1 日

親愛的 Kemper 女士：

164 我寫這封信是為了通知您，我們已收到您欲以供應商身分參加 9 月 1 日至 2 日 Bridgeport 旅遊博覽會而提交的 300 美元押金。對於延誤，我深表歉意。165 我們吸引了創紀錄數量的申請者，因此聯絡每個人所需的時間比平常要長。您的旅行社將成為今年重要的陣容之一。

166-C 押金將用於支付可能因疏忽而導致活動場地發生的任何損壞。任何維修或清潔費用將從中扣除。166-D 否則，這筆錢將在活動結束後五個工作天內退回。166-B 1,200 美元的展位租金應於 8 月 28 日支付。　➡

請注意以下要求：

- 167-C 每個展位將提供統一的外部看板，但供應商可以在展位內展示其他看板。
- 167-B 每件待售商品或服務都必須獲得主辦單位預先批准。不允許販售食物或飲料。
- 167-D 切勿使個人物品無人看管。您必須將這些物品放在指定的置物櫃中。
- 167-A 供應商須負責展位內部和周圍的清潔。

如果您有疑問或需要提交其他資料，請直接寄電子郵件給我。

David Sims
活動負責人
Bridgeport 旅遊博覽會

---

confirm v. 確認　deposit n. 保證金　vendor n. 攤商
addition n. 補充、附加　cover v. 負擔、擔任
negligence n. 不慎的、疏忽　deduct v. 扣除
due adj. 應付款（錢）的　requirement n. 要件、要求
uniform adj. 同樣的、一致的　exterior adj. 外部的　sign n. 看板
organizer n. 主辦者　belonging n. 個人物品
unattended adj. 擱置的、放任不管的　assigned adj. 分配的
coordinator n.（計劃、活動等的）負責人

---

164 目的問題

翻譯 該電子郵件的目的為何？
　(A) 通知主辦單位贊助提案。
　(B) 確認參與某項活動。
　(C) 要求支付押金。
　(D) 宣傳促銷機會。

解析 因為這題問的是電子郵件的目的，所以要仔細確認文章的前半部。在「I'm writing to confirm that we received the $300 deposit you submitted to participate as a vendor at the Bridgeport Travel Expo」中提到，寫這封電子郵件是為了告知對方，已收到對方以攤商身分參加 Bridgeport 旅遊博覽會所提交的 300 美元押金，所以 (B) 是正確答案。

字彙 sponsorship n. 贊助、支援　affirm v. 確認

165 推論問題

翻譯 關於博覽會，下列何者被提及？
　(A) 報名人數創歷史新高。
　(B) 展覽延長三天。
　(C) 供應商代表不同的產業。
　(D) 場地搬到更大的地方。

解析 這是對題目的關鍵字 expo 進行推論的問題。「We [Bridgeport Travel Expo] attracted a record number of applicants, so contacting everyone took longer than normal」提到，Bridgeport 旅遊博覽會吸引了創紀錄數量的申請者，所以花了比之前更久的時間聯絡大家，因此 (A) 是正確答案。

字彙 represent v. 代表、表現

166 Not/True 問題

翻譯 關於保證金，下列何者被提及？
　(A) 必須在 9 月 1 日支付。
　(B) 費用是展位租金的一半。
　(C) 它可以用來支付損害賠償。
　(D) 將於活動最後一天返還。

解析 這是 Not/True 問題，需要將與題目關鍵字 deposit 相關的內容和選項對照，再找出答案。(A) 是文章中沒有提及的內容。「we received the $300 deposit you submitted」和「The payment of $1,200 for the booth rental is due on August 28」提到押金是展位租金的四分之一，因此 (B) 與文章的內容不一致。「The deposit will cover any damage that may occur at the venue as a result of negligence」則表示，押金將用於支付因疏忽而導致場地出現的任何損壞，所以 (C) 與文章的內容一致，因此是正確答案。「it[deposit] will be returned within five business days after the end of the event」提到押金將在活動結束之日起 5 個工作日內退回，因此 (D) 與文章的內容不一致。

換句話說
cover ~ damage 負責損害 → pay for damage 賠償損害

字彙 pay for 賠償～

167 Not/True 問題

翻譯 Kemper 女士不需要做什麼？
　(A) 保持區域整潔。
　(B) 針對所售商品取得批准。
　(C) 設計展位外部看板。
　(D) 將個人物品放入置物櫃中。

解析 這是 Not/True 問題，需要將與題目關鍵句 Ms. Kemper ~ required to do 相關的內容和選項對照，再找出答案。「Vendors are responsible for cleaning inside and around the booth」提到銷售者應負責清掃展位內部和周圍，所以 (A) 與文章的內容一致。「Every item or service for sale must be preapproved by the organizers」表示，所有銷售用商品或服務都必須事先得到主辦方的批准，因此 (B) 與文章的內容一致。「Uniform exterior signs will be provided for each booth」提到主辦方將提供同樣的外部看板給各展位，因此 (C) 與文章的內容不一致。「Never leave personal belongings unattended. You must leave these items in your assigned storage lockers.」中提到個人隨身物品不能放置不管，應該放在分配的置物櫃裡，因此 (D) 與文章的內容一致。

換句話說
leave ~ items in ~ lockers 將物品放在置物櫃裡 → Place ~ items in a locker 將物品放置在置物櫃

字彙 obtain v. 收到、得到

問題 168-171，請參考以下報導。

嚮往無塑未來的 Keptics

2 月 8 日——[168] 總部位於西雅圖的全球消費品公司 Keptics 剛剛宣布啟動一項示範計劃，以評估新系列環保清潔產品的市場。— [1] —. 這些產品將使用永續包裝，旨在減少塑膠廢棄物和汙染。這個為期三個月的計劃將於 3 月 1 日在西雅圖展開。

如想參與，客戶必須線上報名 Keptics Up 計劃。— [2] —. [169] 參與者將收到 Keptics 發來的一批商品，其中包括包裝在可再填容器中的家庭清潔用品樣本。一旦用完容器內的內容物，[171] 顧客可以向 Keptics 訂購補充品，或前往幾個計劃地點之一自行補充。— [3] —.

Keptics 執行長 Fiona Simpleton 表示，[170] 該計劃將僅限於西雅圖，以便公司能夠密切關注成本。— [4] —. 然而，若計劃成功，它可能會在明年初推廣到美國其他城市。

---

envision v. 預見、設想　pilot program 示範計劃
evaluate v. 評估　sustainable adj. 永續的
shipment n. 運輸品　refillable adj. 可補充的
container n. 容器　consume v. 消耗、用盡
keep a close watch on 密切關注～

---

168 5W1H 問題

翻譯 Keptics 打算做什麼？
　(A) 測試新產品系列。
　(B) 成立環保團體。
　(C) 更新品牌設計。
　(D) 推出獎勵計劃。

解析 這題是詢問 Keptics 計劃做什麼（What）的 5W1H 問題，題目的關鍵句「Keptics planning to do」和「Keptics ~ has just announced the launch of a pilot program to evaluate the market for a new line of eco-friendly cleaning products.」提到，Keptics 實施示範計劃是為了評估環保產品的新市場，所以 (A) 是正確答案。

　換句話說
　evaluate the market for a new line of ~ products 為了新產品系列評估市場 → Test a new product line 測試新產品系列

字彙 start v. 設立、開始

---

169 5W1H 問題

翻譯 部分 Keptics 的顧客將會收到什麼？
　(A) 活動邀請函
　(B) 網路優惠券
　(C) 一組樣品
　(D) 定期收件服務

解析 這題是詢問部分 Keptics 顧客會收到什麼（What）的 5W1H 問題，題目的關鍵句「some Keptics customers receive」和「Participants will receive a shipment from Keptics that includes samples of its home cleaning products」提到，參與者將從 Keptics 那裡收到包括家庭清潔用品在內的樣本，所以正確答案為 (C)。

字彙 pickup n. 回收、去取東西

---

170 5W1H 問題

翻譯 為什麼 Keptics 只在西雅圖展開此計劃？
　(A) 其他城市需要許可。
　(B) 它希望監控相關成本。
　(C) 它使用僅在當地找到的原材料。
　(D) 它試圖避免與其他公司競爭。

解析 這題問的是 Keptics 為什麼（Why）只在西雅圖實施計劃的 5W1H 問題。題目的關鍵句「Keptics only launching the program in Seattle」和「the program will be limited to Seattle so that the company can keep a close watch on costs」中提到，該計劃僅限西雅圖是因為該公司希望能密切關注成本，所以 (B) 是正確答案。

　換句話說
　is ~ only launching the program in Seattle 只在西雅圖展開計劃 → the program will be limited to Seattle 該計劃僅限西雅圖
　keep a close watch on costs 密切關注成本 → monitor ~ costs 監控成本

字彙 permission n. 許可　monitor v. 觀察、監控
　associated adj. 相關的　locally adv. 當地

---

171 將句子放入合適的位置

翻譯 以下句子最適合放入 [1]、[2]、[3] 或 [4] 的哪個位置？
　「這些地點將在未來幾週內公布。」
　(A) [1]
　(B) [2]
　(C) [3]
　(D) [4]

解析 本題須看文章脈絡，選擇最適合放入句子的位置。「These locations will be announced in the coming weeks」提到地點將在未來幾週內公布，所以可推測句子的前面會有與地點相關的內容。[3] 的前一句「customers can order a refill from Keptics or visit one of several planned locations to refill it themselves」表示顧客們可以在 Keptics 訂購補充用品，或直接造訪多個預定地點的其中一處自行補充，因此將句子放入 [3] 後，意思將變成「這幾個預定地點將在幾週內公布」，所以 (C) 是正確答案。

字彙 coming adj. 即將到來的

問題 172-175，請參考以下線上討論。

Jang-mi Bae [下午 2 點 9 分]
你有什麼關於新辦公地點的消息嗎？如果我們找不到新地點，我們下個月就要續簽這裡的租賃合約。

Paul Knox [下午 2 點 11 分]
我昨天看到一個很適合的地方，位在被稱為 Janus 大樓的建築物裡。

Edward Watts [下午 2 點 12 分]
裡面的設施如何？[172-A] 有體育館嗎？指定的停車場？

Paul Knox [下午 2 點 15 分]
172-A 你提到的都有，還有更多其他的。它配備了全新的冷暖系統，這可以讓我們節省改裝費用。173 唯一可能的問題是，這裡每月租金是 6,500 美元，高於我們的預算。我們將比現在多付 700 美元。

Barbara Thompkins [下午 2 點 16 分]
173 我們度過了美好的一年。如果租金包括水電費，還有我們需要的一切，我認為我們應該考慮。

Jang-mi Bae [下午 2 點 16 分]
你說得有道理，173 不過，我還是想看看。可以安排參觀嗎，Paul？174 我星期五有空。

Paul Knox [下午 2 點 18 分]
當然了。我來看看房地產仲介公司的手機應用程式，確認一下電話號碼。

Paul Knox [下午 2 點 20 分]
好了，174 我打電話給房地產經紀人，她確認星期五上午 11 點可以見我們。我們可以一起坐我的車去 Janus 大樓。

Edward Watts [下午 2 點 21 分]
好啊。174 我那個時間也有空。

Barbara Thompkins [下午 2 點 21 分]
174 我那天整天都要外出拜訪客戶。

Paul Knox [下午 2 點 24 分]
175 你可以透過手機應用程式看辦公室影片。不能來的人都可以這麼做。

---

regarding prep. 與～相關的、關於～　extend v. 延長
lease n. 租賃合約　amenity n. 便利設施
assign v. 指定、分配　brand-new adj. 全新的
definitely adv. 一定　real estate agency 房地產仲介公司
realtor n. 房地產經紀人

---

172 Not/True 問題

翻譯 關於 Janus 大樓，下列何者為真？
(A) 它有健身設施。
(B) 它包含便宜的家具。
(C) 它鄰近大眾運輸工具。
(D) 它歸市政府所有。

解析 這是 Not/True 問題，需要將與題目關鍵詞 Janus Tower 相關的內容和選項對照，再找出答案。在「Does it[Janus Tower] have a gym?(2:12 P.M.)」中，當 Watts 先生詢問 Janus 大樓是否有健身房時，Knox 先生在「It has those things and more.(2:15 P.M.)」中表示有，而且不只這些，所以與對話內容一致的 (A) 是正確答案。(B)、(C)、(D)都是沒有提的內容。

換句話說
gym 體育館 → workout facility 健身設施

173 掌握意圖問題

翻譯 下午 2 點 16 分，Bae 女士寫下「Valid point」時，最有可能是什麼意思？
(A) 她同意公司可以將預算調更高。

(B) 她認為團隊應該考慮一個潛在的問題。
(C) 她認為應該針對這項決定徵求其他員工的意見。
(D) 她認為尋求房地產經紀人的幫助是明智的。

解析 這題問的是 Bae 女士的意圖，所以應確題目的關鍵詞 Valid point 被提及的上下文脈絡。在「The only potential issue is that it's above our budget at $6,500 a month(2:15 P.M.)」中，Knox 先生表示唯一可能的問題是每個月租金 6,500 美元，高於公司的預算，「We've had a good year. If utilities are included and it has everything we need, I say we should definitely consider it.(2:16 P.M.)」中，Thompkins 女士則提到，如果租金包含水電費和需要的一切就應該考慮，Bae 女士說完「Valid point（你說得有道理）」後，接著以「Still, I'd like to see it.(2:16 P.M.)」表示想去看房，由此可知她同意公司提高預算，所以 (A) 是正確答案。

字彙 accommodate v. 調整、接受　consult v. 協議、協商

174 5W1H 問題

翻譯 星期五將有多少人會和房仲一起看房？
(A) 1
(B) 2
(C) 3
(D) 4

解析 這題問的是星期五會有多少人（How many）與房仲一起看房的 5W1H 問題。在題目的關鍵句 accompanying the realtor on Friday，「I'm free on Friday. (2:16 P.M.)」中，Bae 女士表示週五有空，在「I called the realtor and she confirmed she can meet us on Friday at 11 A.M. We can all go to Janus Tower together in my car. (2:20 P.M.)」中，Knox 先生表示已打電話給房仲，對方確認星期五早上 11 點可以看房，並提到大家可以搭他的車一起去 Janus 大樓。在「I'm available at that time, too.(2:21 P.M.)」中，Watts 先生說自己那個時間也有空；相反地，在「I'm going to be out all day visiting a client.(2:21 P.M.)」中，Thompkins 女士提到她那天一整天都要外出拜訪客戶，因此除了 Thompkins 女士之外，Bae 女士、Knox 先生、Watts 先生共三人，週五都將和房仲一起看房，所以 (C) 是正確答案。

字彙 accompany v. 同行、伴隨

175 5W1H 問題

翻譯 根據線上討論內容，人們可以在手機應用程式上做什麼？
(A) 取得前往建築物的路線。
(B) 觀看辦公空間的影片。
(C) 在價格範圍內尋找替代方案。
(D) 安排參觀地點。

解析 這題是詢問大家可以在手機應用程式中做什麼（What）的 5W1H 問題。在關於題目關鍵詞 mobile application 的句子「You can also see the office on video through the mobile application.(2:24 P.M.)」中，Knox 先生表示可以透過手機應用程式觀看辦公室影片，所以 (B) 是正確答案。

字彙 alternative n. 代替、替代方案　range n. 範圍

問題 176-180，請參考以下廣告和線上評論。

歡迎來到 Surf Shack

Surf Shack 位於馬里布海灘，誠摯邀請遊客和在地人前來欣賞壯麗的海景。這裡最初是幾個朋友的衝浪者天堂，現已發展成為衝浪學校、裝備商店和餐廳。[176] Surf Shack 供應一流的美食和飲品，您可以一邊欣賞日落，一邊聆聽海浪的聲音。這確實是一次不容錯過的特別體驗。[177-B] 這就是為什麼馬里布 102.5 廣播電臺將我們評為該地區的最佳景點。

Surf Shack 有著每天供應新鮮奶昔的傳統，均採用永續供給的食材。我們目前正在針對以下組合推出買一送一的特價活動。

· [179] 週一和週二：香蕉和草莓
· 週三和週四：鳳梨和椰子
· 週五和週六：蘋果和梨子
· 週日：熱帶風情飲品

[178] 請今天就來電 555-9691 預訂海灘座位。

---

alike adv. 所有　spectacular adj. 壯麗的
paradise n. 天堂、樂園　sunset n. 日落　truly adv. 真心地、真正地
name v. 指定、任命　attraction n. 名勝、觀光景點
sustainably adv. 長期地、永續地　source v. 供給、提供
two-for-one 買一送一（銷售方式）

Surf Shack

介紹	餐廳	衝浪	購物	地點	評論

姓名：Katerina Stokov
評分：2／5

我最近在洛杉磯度假時去了 Surf Shack。我和一些以前從未去過那裡的當地朋友一起造訪。我們以為這個地方並不為觀光客所熟知，所以我們期待在一個美麗的海邊享受一個相對安靜的下午。[179] 我們甚至選擇在星期二去，因為據說那是他們最不忙的時候。

當我們到達時，我們驚訝地發現那裡擠滿了遊客。雖然我們沒有預訂，還是很幸運在餐廳找到了一處海灘座位。[179] 我點了特價的奶昔，結果很好喝。儘管如此，服務還是很慢，而且桌子不是很乾淨。整體來說，[180] 因為人太多，我的體驗不是很好，我無法向任何人推薦這個地方。

---

look forward to 期待～　relatively adv. 比較地、相對地
supposedly adv. 也許　overall adv. 整體地

---

176 尋找同義詞問題

翻譯 在廣告中，第 1 段第 3 行中的「serves」，意思最接近下列何者？
(A) 測試
(B) 執行
(C) 提供
(D) 接受

解析 廣告中有 serves 的句子是「Surf Shack serves excellent cuisine and drinks while you enjoy the sunset and listen to the waves.」，在這句話中 serves 是「供應」的意思，所以 (C) 是正確答案。

---

177 Not/True 問題

翻譯 關於 Surf Shack，下列何者被提及？
(A) 與當地一所體育學校合併。
(B) 由廣播電臺推薦。
(C) 菜單隨季節變化。
(D) 它的擁有者是前衝浪冠軍。

解析 這題是關鍵詞為 Surf Shack 的 Not/True 問題，所以應在提到 Surf Shack 的第一篇文章（廣告）中確認相關內容。(A) 是文章中沒有提到的內容。「radio station Malibu 102.5 has named us the top attraction in the area」提到，馬里布廣播電臺 102.5 將自己評價為該地區最佳景點，所以 (B) 與文章內容一致，因此是正確答案。(C) 和 (D) 都是文章中沒有提到的內容。

字彙 seasonally adv. 依據季節地、季節性地

178 5W1H 問題

翻譯 根據廣告，顧客該如何預訂座位？
(A) 透過電子郵件
(B) 透過打電話
(C) 透過使用行動應用程式
(D) 透過網站

解析 這題是詢問顧客如何（How）預訂座位的 5W1H 問題，所以應在提到關鍵句 customers reserve a table 的廣告中確認相關內容。第一篇文章（廣告）中的「Call us at 555-9691 to reserve a beach table today.」提到請今天就撥打 555-9691 預訂海灘座位，所以 (B) 是正確答案。

換句話說
Call 致電 → making a phone call 打電話

179 推論問題 連結兩篇文章

翻譯 Stokov 女士最有可能點的是哪一種特色奶昔？
(A) 香蕉和草莓
(B) 鳳梨和椰子
(C) 蘋果和梨子
(D) 熱帶風情

解析 從題目的關鍵句「smoothie special ~ Ms. Stokov ~ order」可知，這題問的是 Stokov 女士點了什麼特色奶昔，所以要先確認 Stokov 女士所寫的線上評論。
線索1 第二篇文章（線上評論）的「We even chose to go on a Tuesday」和「I ordered the smoothie that was on special offer」提到 Stokov 女士決定週二前往，並點了特別活動菜單中的奶昔，但是評論中沒有提到是什麼樣的奶昔，所以必須從第一篇文章中尋找相關內容。
線索2 從第一篇文章（廣告）中的「Monday & Tuesday: Banana and Strawberry」可以看出週二的特色奶昔是香蕉和草莓。
綜合以上兩個線索，Stokov 女士點的是週二特別活動菜單中的香蕉和草莓奶昔，所以 (A) 是正確答案。

180 5W1H 問題

翻譯 Stokov 女士為何不滿意 Surf Shack？
(A) 服務生不友善。
(B) 食物沒有味道。

(C) 風景並不像宣傳的那樣。
(D) 場地很擁擠。

解析 這題是詢問 Stokov 女士為什麼（Why）不滿意 Surf Shack 的 5W1H 問題，所以應該在提到關鍵句「Ms. Stokov dissatisfied with Surf Shack」的線上評論中尋找答案。第二篇文章（線上評論）的「especially because of the crowds, my experience was not very good, and I cannot recommend the place to anyone」提到，因為人太多，體驗不太好，因此無法向任何人推薦該地點，所以 (D) 是正確答案。

換句話說
was ~ dissatisfied 不滿意 → experience was not very good 體驗不太好

字彙 dissatisfy v. 不滿意　flavorless adj. 沒味道的

問題 181-185，請參考以下廣告和報導。

Holton 中心公告

Holton 中心將於 9 月 19 日因一年一度的斯塔福文學節而關閉。181 預計來自英國各地的 200 多家出版社和 350 名作家將出席，文學節將有當今最優秀的英國作家的演講。183-C 受邀者包括《East Kingdom》和《The Gate》的作者，這兩本書的出版都獲得了廣泛的好評。

182-B 作家們一整天都會進行講座，並參與小組討論。在主廳，出版社設立攤位，遊客可以用折扣價購買最新的書籍。慶典結束後，Lewistown 飯店將舉辦一場餘興派對，182-C/D 與會者將有機會與著名作家交流，並請他們在書上簽名。一般遊客入場費為 40 美元，內含餘興派對，184 參加作家講座須額外支付 10 美元。

acclaim n. 讚譽、好評　set up 準備、設置　title n. 書、書籍
mingle v. 交織、混雜

Margaret Davidson，大膽的新文學之聲
Charles Hagan 文

183-C 憑藉《The Gate》，Margaret Davidson 成為我最喜歡的年輕作家之一。Davidson 女士是《New Music Monthly》雜誌的一名 30 歲記者，身為知名記者已經有一段時間了，184 但直到我聽到她在斯塔福文學節上發表了一場有趣的演講後，我才開始想讀她的書。我很高興地向大家報告，她既是一位出色的講者，也是一位優秀的作家。在《The Gate》中，185 她講述了最初吸引她從事音樂新聞工作的經歷，她 5 歲聽 R&B，12 歲開始彈貝斯。這本書分為三個部分，第一部分的重點是她的早年，第二部分介紹她青少年時期在樂團中演奏的時光，最後一部分介紹她作為音樂記者的職業生涯。書的最後摘錄了她在《New Music Monthly》上的文章，包含從對新嘻哈專輯的精闢評論到與龐克樂團 Stone Age 一起旅行的幽默故事。

bold adj. 大膽的　correspondent n. 記者、新聞記者
journalist n. 記者　be inclined to 想做~、打算做
hilarious adj. 愉快的、有趣的　excerpt n. 摘錄、引用
incisive adj. 銳利的　account n. 故事

---

181 推論問題

翻譯 關於斯塔福文學節，下列何者被提及？
(A) 每年舉行兩次。
(B) 它著重於一個國家的作者。
(C) 它主要針對小說作家。
(D) 它沒有得到太多的宣傳。

解析 這題需要針對關鍵詞 Stafford Literary Festival 進行推論，所以應在提到斯塔福文學節的公告中尋找相關內容。第一篇文章（公告）中的「Over 200 publishers and 350 writers from around the UK are expected to attend.」提到，預計全英國將有 200 多家出版社和 350 多名作家參加，所以可以推論出斯塔福文學節將焦點放在一個國家的作家上，因此 (B) 是正確答案。

字彙 gear v. 配合、適合　receive publicity 得到知名度

182 Not/True 問題

翻譯 參加者無法在文學節做什麼？
(A) 取得某些作品的免費贈書。
(B) 聆聽作家講座。
(C) 與到場作家互動。
(D) 收集作家們的簽名。

解析 這題是關鍵句為 people~ do at the festival 的 Not/True 問題，所以應在提到斯塔福文學節的第一篇文章（公告）中確認相關內容。(A) 是文章中沒有提到的內容，所以是正確答案。「writers will also be giving lectures」中提到作家們將進行講座，所以 (B) 與文章內容一致。「attendees will have the opportunity to mingle with noted writers and get their books signed」中提到，參與者將有機會與著名作家們互動，並請他們在書上簽名，所以 (C) 和 (D) 與文章的內容一致。

換句話說
mingle with ~ writers 與作家互動 → Interact with writers 與作家交流
get ~ signed 得到簽名 → Collect ~ signatures 收集簽名

字彙 interact with 與~交流、互動

183 Not/True 問題　連結兩篇文章

翻譯 關於 Davidson 女士，下列何者被提及？
(A) 她寫了兩本小說。
(B) 她為 Hagan 先生在一本書上簽名。
(C) 她的作品受到評論家的好評。
(D) 她的職涯已經轉變過很多次。

解析 這題須連結兩篇文章的資訊來解題。Not/True 問題應在文章中尋找與題目關鍵詞 Ms. Davidson 相關的內容，並逐一對照選項，所以要先找提到 Davidson 女士的文章。線索1 第二篇文章（報導）中的「With *The Gate*, Margaret Davidson has become one of my[Mr. Hagan] favourite young writers.」提到，Margaret Davidson 因為《The Gate》成為 Hagan 先生最喜歡的年輕作家之一。然而，由於報導中沒有提到與《The Gate》有關的資訊，所以應在公告中尋找相關內容。線索2 從第一篇文章（公告）的「Among those invited are the authors of East Kingdom and The Gate, both of which were released to spectacular critical acclaim.」中，可以得知被邀請的作家中，有人因為《East Kingdom》和《The Gate》的出版得到評論家的稱讀。

綜合這兩個線索可以看出 Davidson 女士的作品《The Gate》得到評論家的好評，所以 (C) 是正確答案。

換句話說
spectacular critical acclaim 評論家的稱讀 → was well received by critics 得到評論家的好評

字彙 well received 獲得好評

184 推論問題 連結兩篇文章

翻譯 關於 Hagan 先生，可以推論出什麼？
(A) 他是一位著名的音樂記者。
(B) 他支付了額外費用參加 Davidson 女士的演講。
(C) 他曾經在樂團中演奏。
(D) 他住在 Lewistown 飯店。

解析 題目的關鍵詞是 Mr. Hagan，所以應先在他寫的報導中尋找線索。
線索1 第二篇文章（報導）的「I wasn't inclined to read her[Ms. Davidson] book until I heard her give a hilarious talk at the Stafford Literary Festival」提到，Hagan 先生表示聽到 Davidson 女士在斯塔福文學節上的有趣演講後才想讀她的書。然而，由於報導中沒有與斯塔福文學節演講相關的資訊，所以需要在公告中尋找相關內容。
線索2 從第一篇文章（公告）的「author lectures cost an additional $10 to attend」可以確認想參加作家的演講需要額外付 10 美元。
綜合這兩條線索可以看出 Hagan 先生為了參加 Davidson 女士的演講，支付了 10 美元的額外費用，所以 (B) 是正確答案。

185 尋找同義字

翻譯 在報導中，第 1 段第 5 行中的「drew」，意思最接近下列何者？
(A) 吸引
(B) 提出
(C) 創造
(D) 允許

解析 報導中出現 drew 的句子為「she writes about the experiences that drew her to music journalism in the first place」，drew 在此句中的意思是「吸引」，所以 (A) 是正確答案。

問題 186-190，請參考以下信件、電子郵件及網站公告。

Rick Houseman
0600 紐西蘭，昆士蘭州
柳樹大道 119 號

親愛的 Houseman 先生：

我叫 Matilda Gleeson，我代表昆士蘭大學校友辦公室寫這封信。186 我們正在聯絡被選出的昆士蘭大學畢業生，詢問他們是否願意為我們的網站提供簡短的專業個人簡介。

⟳

鑑於您是一位備受矚目的環保主義者，我們認為您將成為昆士蘭大學成功畢業生的好典範。

如果您有興趣，186/187 請寄送一份 100 字以內描述您職業生涯的個人簡介給我們。187 此外，如果您能寄來您發表的論文範本、有關您的報導以及您在過去五年內拍攝的照片，我們將不勝感激。請將這些提交至 gleeson22@qland.nz。謝謝您，期待您的來信。

Matilda Gleeson
昆士蘭大學校友辦公室

on behalf of 代表～ alumni n. 校友
selected adj. 嚴選的 be willing to 有做～的意願、想做～
biography n. 傳記、個人簡介 high-profile adj. 受矚目的
conservationist n. 環保主義者

收件人：Matilda Gleeson<gleeson22@qland.nz>
寄件人：Rick Houseman <rick.houseman@qlandwildlife.nz>
主旨：校友個人簡介
日期：5 月 29 日
附件：文件 1、文件 2、文件 3

親愛的 Gleeson 女士：

感謝您與我聯絡校友個人簡介事宜。187 除了最後一項之外，我已附上您要求的所有項目。我明天會再把這一項寄給您。我還向校友基金捐贈了一小筆錢，用於維護學校圖書館。

188 當您將我的個人簡介新增至網站時，能否寄送該頁面的連結來通知我？我想與一些朋友和家人分享。另外，我可能很快又需要更新個人簡介。190 我為了擔任紐西蘭保育委員會的副主委正在與該委員會進行討論。接下來只剩下小組面試。我會在未來幾天內通知您我是否獲得該職位，以便您可以在網站上更新我的個人簡介。

Rick Houseman

maintenance n. 維持、維護 conservation n. 保存、保護
commission n. 委員會 serve as 擔任～
assistant chair 副主委 undergo v. 經歷、遭受

昆士蘭大學

首頁	招生	學校生活	校友	公告	協助

校友簡介
Rick Houseman

自 10 年前從昆士蘭大學學士畢業以來，Rick Houseman 一直致力於推動世界科學知識體系的發展。他擁有著名的國家自然科學院的博士學位，並發表了有關紐西蘭野生動物的廣泛研究。189 最近，他致力於確保新立法的通過，該法將紐西蘭部分地區指定為野生動物保育區，以協助保護奇異鳥等獨特動物的棲息地。190 目前，他是紐西蘭保育委員會的副主委。

profile n. 簡歷、個人簡介 undergraduate program 學士班
doctorate n. 博士學位 research n. 學術調查 passage n. 通過
legislation n. 法案 designate v. 指定 habitat n. 棲息地

186 目的問題

翻譯 Gleeson 女士為什麼要寫這封信給 Houseman 先生？
(A) 請他捐款。
(B) 為他提供一個職位。
(C) 提醒他某個活動。
(D) 索取一些資訊。

解析 這題問的是 Gleeson 女士寫信給 Houseman 先生的目的，所以應從 Gleeson 女士寫的信尋找相關線索。第一篇文章（信件）的「We are reaching out to selected graduates of Queensland University to see if they would be willing to contribute short professional biographies for our website」和「please send us a short biography of Queensland University of 100 words or less describing your career」提到，寫信是為了聯絡昆士蘭大學選出的畢業生，請他們為網站提供 100 字以下的個人簡介，所以 (D) 是正確答案。

字彙 donation n. 捐款、捐贈

187 5W1H 問題　連結兩篇文章

翻譯 Houseman 先生明天要寄什麼？
(A) 短新聞
(B) 照片
(C) 個人資料
(D) 研究論文

解析 這題是詢問 Houseman 先生明天要寄什麼（What）的問題，關鍵句則是 Mr. Houseman send tomorrow，所以應先確認 Houseman 先生寫的電子郵件。
線索1 第二篇文章（電子郵件）中的「I've attached all of the items you[Ms. Gleeson] requested except for the last one. I will send this to you tomorrow.」提到，除了最後一個項目要明天寄送之外，已經寄出了 Gleeson 女士要求的所有項目。然而，由於這裡沒有提到最後一項是什麼，所以要在 Gleeson 女士寫的信中尋找相關資訊。
線索2 第一篇文章（信件）中的「please send us a short biography of 100 words or less describing your career. In addition, we would appreciate it if you sent samples of papers you have published, newspaper articles written about you, and a photograph of yourself taken in the last five years.」提到，如果對方能寄來 100 字以內的個人簡介、發表的論文範本、相關報導以及過去五年內拍攝的照片，她會很感激。
綜合上述線索，Houseman 先生明天將寄送照片，因為這是 Gleeson 女士要求的所有項目中的最後一項，所以 (B) 是正確答案。

188 5W1H 問題

翻譯 Houseman 先生要求 Gleeson 女士做什麼？
(A) 在他的個人簡介中添加一個有他個人網頁的連接。
(B) 向他介紹學校運作的最新情況。
(C) 發文時通知他。
(D) 將他加入校友電子郵件清單中。

解析 這題是詢問 Houseman 先生要求 Gleeson 女士做什麼（What）的 5W1H 問題，所以要在有關鍵詞 Mr. Houseman 的文章，也就是他寫的電子郵件中尋找資訊。第二篇文章（電子郵件）中的「When you add my biography to the website, could you let me know by sending me a link to the page?」詢問在網站上發布他的個人簡介時，是否可以寄送網頁連結來通知他，所以 (C) 是正確答案。

換句話說
let ~ know 告知 → Notify 通知

字彙 operation n. 運作　notify v. 通知　post n. 發文

189 5W1H 問題

翻譯 根據網站上的發文，Houseman 先生最近做了什麼？
(A) 上了電視節目。
(B) 進入大學任教。
(C) 幫助通過一項新法律。
(D) 申請博士學位。

解析 這題問的是 Houseman 先生最近做了什麼（What）的 5W1H 問題，所以請在提到關鍵詞 most recently 的網站發文中確認相關資訊。在第三篇文章（網路發文）的「Most recently, he[Mr. Houseman] worked to ensure the passage of new legislation」中提到 Houseman 先生最近為保障新法案的通過付出了努力，所以 (C) 是正確答案。

換句話說
worked to ensure the passage of new legislation 為了保障通過新法案而努力 → Helped pass a new law 協助通過新法案

字彙 faculty n. 教職員工

190 推論問題　連結兩篇文章

翻譯 關於 Houseman 先生，下列何者被提及？
(A) 他從昆士蘭大學的研究生課程退學。
(B) 他曾在昆士蘭地區的圖書館工作。
(C) 他寫了一篇關於奇異鳥的大學論文。
(D) 他通過了新職位的小組面試。

解析 先看有關鍵詞 Mr. Houseman 的文章，也就是他寫的電子郵件。
線索1 在第二篇文章（電子郵件）的「I am currently in talks with the New Zealand Conservation Commission to serve as their assistant chair. All that is left is to undergo a panel interview.」中，Houseman 先生表示目前正在與紐西蘭保育委員會討論是否擔任他們的副主委，只剩小組面試。然而，由於電子郵件中沒有提到是否被選上，所以要在網站發文中確認相關資訊。
線索2 從第三篇文章（網路發文）中的「Presently, he[Mr. Houseman] is the assistant chair of the New Zealand Conservation Commission.」可以確認目前 Houseman 先生是紐西蘭保育委員會的副主委。
綜合以上兩個線索可以得知 Houseman 先生通過了紐西蘭保育委員會副主委的小組面試，所以 (D) 是正確答案。

字彙 drop out 退出　thesis n. 論文

問題 191-195，請參考以下備忘錄、問卷調查和報告。

收件人：客服部員工
寄件人：Nick Christman，客服經理
主旨：三年後的 YourPage
日期：3 月 22 日

[192-D] 截至今天，YourPage 已連續營運三年。在此期間，[192-C] 我們的用戶呈指數成長。事實上，在過去的兩個月裡，用戶成長了 500%，使我們成為成長最快的社群網站。[191] 這意味著是時候對客戶進行問卷調查，以了解他們對我們網站的體驗。我們希望聽到已經使用一段時間的用戶意見，[193] 因此讓我們向一年多前創建 YourPage 個人資料的用戶寄送調查請求，這些人也應該是使用相當規律的人。[194] 作為參與調查的獎勵措施，我們可以將他們的名字輸入抽獎活動中以獲得獎品。獎品可能是我們所屬公司之一的全新電子設備。

---

as of 做為～　exponentially adv. 指數地
social networking 社群網路　for a while 一段時間、一陣子
fairly adv. 相當地　raffle n. 抽獎　affiliate v. 附屬

---

[193]YourPage：問卷調查

[193] 姓名：Pauline Carson
日期：4 月 12 日

以 1 到 5 的評分標準（5 為最佳），您對 YourPage 的體驗有何評價？

□ 1　□ 2　□ 3　■ 4　□ 5

您多久登入一次 YourPage？
我通常會一整天反覆查看。每當我感到無聊或想了解朋友們在做什麼時，我就會這樣做。

您多久在頁面上發布訊息、圖片或其他內容？
我不常發文。我大概每週發一兩次。不過，我很喜歡評論別人的貼文。

您是如何得知 YourPage 的？
透過一些朋友的介紹

您希望 YourPage 能改進哪些面向？
我認為個人資料頁面的設計有點混亂，很多不同的資訊混合在一起。

---

scale n. 等級、規模　rank v. 評價　repeatedly adv. 反覆地
catch up on 了解（消息、資訊）　cluttered adj. 雜亂的

YourPage：調查結果

在整個 4 月分，我們向 YourPage 的各活躍用戶發送了 5,000 多份問卷調查邀請。[194] 參與調查的人可以參加 Silver Plus 智慧型手機抽獎活動，我們已將獎品發給 10 名獲獎者。大約 1,000 人回應了我們的調查。在 1 到 5 的等級中，絕大多數人（88%）將網站的體驗評為 4 或 5，其中 5 是最高分。然而，[195] 也存在一些常見的批評，包括網站相當頻繁地關閉，並且由於個人資料頁面設計混亂，所以難以瀏覽。關於未來，重點是我們要透過修改電腦程式碼中導致頁面關閉的錯誤，並重新格式化頁面來解決問題，讓使用者更便利。 ●

---

active user 活躍的用戶　enter into 參加～
common adj. 共同的、一般的　criticism n. 批判、批評
navigate v. 瀏覽（網站）　layout n. 設計
going forward 之後、將來　reformat v. 重新格式化

---

191 尋找目的

翻譯　備忘錄的目的是什麼？
(A) 表揚員工的工作。
(B) 報告領導階層的變動。
(C) 徵求改進意見。
(D) 提出收集資訊的建議。

解析　這題問的是備忘錄的目的，所以需要確認備忘錄的內容。第一篇文章（備忘錄）中的「it's time we conducted a survey of our customers to see how their experience with our site has been」提到，為了了解顧客使用網站的經驗而進行問卷調查，所以 (D) 是正確答案。

192 Not/True 問題　連結兩篇文章

翻譯　Christman 先生針對 YourPage 提到什麼？
(A) 主要由青少年使用。
(B) 過去幾個月吸引了 100 名新用戶。
(C) 它正在迅速變得越來越流行。
(D) 它是一年前推出的。

解析　這是詢問 Christman 先生針對 YourPage 提到什麼的 Not/True 問題，所以應從 Christman 先生所寫的第一篇文章（備忘錄）中確認相關內容。(A) 與 (B) 是文章中沒有提到的內容。「our[YourPage] user base has grown exponentially. In just the past two months, in fact, we have experienced a 500-percent increase in users, making us the fastest-growing social networking site.」提到 YourPage 的用戶呈指數增加，僅在過去兩個月就增加了 500%，成為成長最快的社群網站，所以 (C) 與文章的內容一致，因此是正確答案。「As of today, YourPage has been operating for three straight years.」中提到，YourPage 連續營運三年，所以 (D) 與文章的內容不一致。

換句話說
user base has grown exponentially 使用者呈指數增加 → rapidly becoming more popular 迅速變得更受歡迎

193 推論問題　連結兩篇文章

翻譯　關於 Carson 女士，可以推論出下列何者？
(A) 她使用 YourPage 已經一年多了。
(B) 她發現 YourPage 非常容易使用。
(C) 她沒有資格贏得抽獎。
(D) 她沒有按時提交問卷調查。

解析　先確認出現關鍵詞 Ms. Carson 的問卷調查。
[線索1] 第二篇文章（問卷調查）的「YourPage: Survey」和「Name: Pauline Carson」表示回答 YourPage 問卷調查的人是 Carson 女士。然而，問卷調查中沒有提出成為 YourPage 調查對象的條件，所以需要在備忘錄中確認相關內容。

線索 2 第一篇文章（備忘錄）的「let's send survey requests to users who made YourPage profiles over a year ago」表示要針對一年前創建 YourPage 帳戶的用戶進行問卷調查。

綜合這兩個線索，可以看出 Carson 女士已經使用 YourPage 一年多了，因此成為問卷調查的對象，所以 (A) 是正確答案。

字彙 eligible adj. 有資格的　on time 準時

194 推論問題　連結兩篇文章

翻譯 關於 Silver Plus，提到了什麼？
(A) 它為公司製作軟體。
(B) 一直存在技術問題。
(C) 它為 YourPage 建立了一項問卷調查。
(D) 它與 YourPage 建立了合作關係。

解析 先看提到關鍵詞 Silver Plus 的報告。

線索 1 第三篇文章（報告書）的「Those who took the survey were entered into a raffle for Silver Plus smartphones, which were distributed to 10 winners.」提到，接受問卷調查者可以參加 Silver Plus 公司智慧型手機的抽獎，將會有 10 人獲獎。然而，報告中沒有提供與 Silver Plus 公司有關的資訊，所以需要在備忘錄中確認相關內容。

線索 2 第一篇文章（備忘錄）的「As an incentive for taking the survey, we[YourPage] could offer to enter their names into a raffle for prizes. The prizes could be brand-new electronic devices from one of the companies we are affiliated with.」提到，YourPage 會將問卷調查參與者的名字輸入抽獎名單，做為問卷調查的獎勵，獎品將會是與 YourPage 合作公司中的新型電子產品。

綜合上述兩個線索，可以看出接受問卷調查的人中，有部分人獲得了與 YourPage 合作之 Silver Plus 公司的智慧型手機做為獎品，所以 (D) 是正確答案。

換句話說
are affiliated 有附屬關係 → has a partnership 有合作夥伴關係

195 5W1H 問題

翻譯 報告建議做什麼？
(A) 在國外為網站做廣告。
(B) 解決網站長期存在的問題。
(C) 為更多回饋提供額外獎勵。
(D) 進行更深入的調查。

解析 這題是詢問報告建議做什麼（What）的 5W1H 問題，所以要確認有 report recommend doing 相關內容的部分。第三篇文章（報告）中的「there were some common criticisms, including that the site shut down fairly frequently and that profile pages were difficult to navigate because of the confusing layout. Going forward, it is important we address these problems」提到普遍的批評，包含網站經常關閉、混亂的設計導致使用者很難瀏覽個人資料頁面等，並表示處理這些問題非常重要，所以 (B) 是正確答案。

字彙 persistent adj. 持續的　in-depth adj. 深入的、仔細的

問題 196-200，請參考以下公告及兩封電子郵件。

---

198 **第四屆波士頓領導力高峰會即將舉行**

196-C Jefferson 銀行自豪地宣布，196-A 其第四屆年度峰會 196-C 已獲得兩位主講嘉賓的參與，該峰會定於 1 月 17 日至 18 日舉行。SpitalGround 執行長 Susanne Coerver 將談論她的創新公司如何改變醫療服務業，以及她如何在競爭激烈的環境中管理公司。Moss Tech 執行長 Henry Moss 將以如何成為成功企業家的見解來結束高峰會。

197 波士頓領導力高峰會也將首次透過線上應用程式進行現場直播，196-B 使其能夠接觸到更廣泛的受眾。兩天線上參加的門票價格為 220 美元。然而，197 Jefferson 銀行的客戶將受邀虛擬參加該活動，免費了解領導技能、參加研討會並與其他線上訪客交流。請找到最近的 Jefferson 銀行分行，及時成為客戶以參加高峰會。

live adv. 直播地、即時地　secure v. 確保、獲得
innovative adj. 創新的　health-care n. 醫療服務
insight n. 洞察力　entrepreneur n. 企業家　enable v. 使可以做～
virtually adv. 虛擬地　in time for 準時做～

收件人：Allison Cruise<a.cruise@jeffersonbank.com>
寄件人：Preston Ali <p.ali@mosstechorg.com>
主旨：高峰會
日期：12 月 28 日

親愛的 Cruise 女士：

我很遺憾地通知您，Moss 先生因無法預期的業務因素無法按計劃參加高峰會。他請我轉達他的遺憾，特別是因為 198 他在去年的活動中發表演說，度過非常愉快的時光。

雖然如此，199-D Moss 先生可以推薦某人來接替他的位置。她是 Galacomms 的執行長，這是一家軟體服務公司，是她和 Moss 先生幾年前共同創辦的。一旦我確認她有空，我就會寄送她的聯絡資訊給您。您將會在本週末之前收到最新消息。對於由此帶來的不便，請再次接受我們的歉意。

Preston Ali
行政助理
Moss Tech 公司

unforeseen adj. 意想不到的　regret n. 遺憾、後悔
enjoyable adj. 愉快的　take one's place 取代某人的位置
contact detail 聯絡方式

收件人：Leonard Vega <l.vega@jeffersonbank.com>
寄件人：Allison Cruise <a.cruise@jeffersonbank.com>
主旨：高峰會
日期：1 月 9 日

Leonard：

我需要你比原計劃提前兩天到達高峰會會場。如有需要，請預訂新航班。

如你所知，我們的演講者陣容發生了變化，這一變化必須反映在會場張貼的所有印刷品中。以下資訊供你參考，

➡

190-D 新講者的名字是 Fiona Murphy，她是 Galacomms 公司的執行長。當你到達現場時，200 請測試直播的播放設定，以確保一切順利進行。

感謝你的幫助，如果你有任何疑問，請告訴我。

Alison

lineup n. 人員、陣容　reflect v. 反映、反射
smoothly adv. 順利地、順暢地

---

196 Not/True 問題

翻譯 關於高峰會，下列何者為非？
(A) 以前舉辦過。
(B) 正在擴大其受眾範圍。
(C) 由金融機構主辦。
(D) 聚焦在發展醫療健康產業。

解析 這是關鍵字為 summit 的 Not/True 問題，所以應確認與此相關的第一篇文章（公告）。「its fourth annual summit」中提到這是第四屆年度高峰會，所以 (A) 與文章內容一致。「enabling it[Summit] to reach a wider audience」表示高峰會將觸及更多聽眾，所以 (B) 與文章內容一致。「Jefferson Bank is proud to announce that it has secured the participation of two keynote speakers」中提到，Jefferson 銀行對於已獲得兩位主講嘉賓的參與感到自豪，所以 (C) 與文章內容一致。(D) 是文章中沒有提到的內容，所以是正確答案。

換句話說
reach a wider audience 接觸更多聽眾 → is expanding ~ audience reach 擴大聽眾的範圍
Bank 銀行 → a financial institution 金融機關

字彙 put on 舉辦　reach n. 範圍；v. 接觸、觸及　host v. 主辦　financial adj. 金融的、財政的　institution n. 機關、協會

---

197 5W1H 問題

翻譯 Jefferson 銀行的客戶被鼓勵做什麼？
(A) 免費串流一些內容。
(B) 利用較高的儲蓄利率。
(C) 參加競賽以贏得獎金。
(D) 前往分行購買部分商品。

解析 這題是詢問 Jefferson 銀行的客戶被鼓勵做什麼（What）的 5W1H 問題，所以要確認與題目的關鍵句「Jefferson Bank customers encouraged to do」相關的公告。第一篇文章（公告）的「the Boston Leadership Summit will also be streamed live through an online application」和「customers of Jefferson Bank are invited to virtually join the event to learn about leadership skills, partake in workshops, and interact with other online visitors free of charge」提到，波士頓領導力高峰會將透過線上應用程式直播，Jefferson 銀行的客戶將能免費學習領導能力技術、參加研討會，並與其他線上顧客交流，所以 (A) 是正確答案。

換句話說
free of charge 免費地 → for free 免費

字彙 interest n. 利息　merchandise n. 商品

---

198 推論問題　連結兩篇文章

翻譯 關於 Moss 先生，Ali 先生提到什麼？
(A) 他受邀在另一場活動中發言。
(B) 前一年他在波士頓。
(C) 他將線上觀看演講。
(D) 他計劃從公司退休。

解析 請先確認有題目關鍵詞 Mr. Ali 的第一封電子郵件。
線索1 第二篇文章（第一封電子郵件）的「he[Mr. Moss] had such an enjoyable time speaking at last year's event」提到，Moss 先生在去年的活動中進行演講，並度過了非常愉快的時光。然而，由於電子郵件中沒有提供與去年活動有關的資訊，所以應在提到活動的公告中確認相關內容。
線索2 在第一篇文章（公告）的「The 4th Boston Leadership Summit Is Going Live」中提到，第四屆波士頓領導力高峰會將現場直播，所以可以確認高峰會每年都在波士頓舉行。
綜合上述兩個線索，可以得知 Moss 先生去年參加了在波士頓舉行的高峰會，所以 (B) 是正確答案。

字彙 retire v. 退休

---

199 Not/True 問題　連結兩篇文章

翻譯 關於 Fiona Murphy，下列何者被提及？
(A) 她要求更改行程。
(B) 她是 Jefferson 銀行的客戶。
(C) 她需要確認預定的航班。
(D) 她和 Moss 先生創辦了一家公司。

解析 這題需要連結兩篇文章來解題，Not/True 問題必須在文章中找出與題目關鍵詞 Fiona Murphy 相關的內容，並對照每個選項，所以應先確認提到 Fiona Murphy 的第二封電子郵件。
線索1 第三篇文章（第二封電子郵件）的「the new speaker's name is Fiona Murphy, and she is the CEO of Galacomms」表示，新講者的名字是 Fiona Murphy，她是 Galacomms 公司的執行長，所以應在提到 Galacomms 公司的第一封電子郵件中確認相關內容。
線索2 從第二篇文章（第一封電子郵件）的「Mr. Moss can recommend someone to take his place. She is the CEO of Galacomms, a software services company that she and Mr. Moss started together some years ago.」可以確認，Moss 先生推薦某人來代替他，這個人現在是幾年前與 Moss 先生一起創立的軟體服務公司 Galacomms 公司的執行長。
綜合這兩個線索，可以看出 Fiona Murphy 與 Moss 先生共同創立了 Galacomms 公司，所以 (D) 是正確答案。

字彙 confirmation n. 確認

---

200 5W1H 問題

翻譯 Cruise 女士要求 Vega 先生做什麼？
(A) 測試直播連結。
(B) 修改演講者合約。
(C) 尋找新的活動場地。
(D) 準備內部通訊。

解析 這是詢問 Cruise 女士要求 Vega 先生做什麼（What）的 5W1H 問題，所以應在 Cruise 女士寫給 Vega 先生的電子郵件中尋找相關資訊。第三篇文章（第二封電子郵件）中的「please test the setup for the live stream」要求測試直播的播放設定，所以 (A) 是正確答案。

換句話說
test the setup for the live stream 測試直播播放設定 → Test a live stream connection 測試直播連結

字彙 newsletter n. 新聞報刊

TEST 2

LISTENING TEST

p.70

1 (D)	2 (D)	3 (B)	4 (C)	5 (A)
6 (B)	7 (B)	8 (A)	9 (B)	10 (C)
11 (C)	12 (C)	13 (A)	14 (C)	15 (B)
16 (C)	17 (A)	18 (C)	19 (B)	20 (A)
21 (A)	22 (A)	23 (C)	24 (B)	25 (A)
26 (B)	27 (A)	28 (B)	29 (A)	30 (C)
31 (A)	32 (A)	33 (D)	34 (B)	35 (A)
36 (A)	37 (D)	38 (A)	39 (B)	40 (C)
41 (D)	42 (B)	43 (B)	44 (C)	45 (C)
46 (B)	47 (A)	48 (A)	49 (B)	50 (C)
51 (B)	52 (A)	53 (A)	54 (A)	55 (B)
56 (D)	57 (A)	58 (C)	59 (D)	60 (D)
61 (A)	62 (A)	63 (B)	64 (A)	65 (B)
66 (A)	67 (B)	68 (A)	69 (A)	70 (C)
71 (B)	72 (D)	73 (B)	74 (C)	75 (A)
76 (D)	77 (B)	78 (D)	79 (D)	80 (B)
81 (D)	82 (C)	83 (C)	84 (A)	85 (A)
86 (B)	87 (A)	88 (B)	89 (B)	90 (C)
91 (A)	92 (B)	93 (A)	94 (C)	95 (D)
96 (C)	97 (B)	98 (B)	99 (A)	100 (B)

READING TEST

p.82

101 (D)	102 (A)	103 (B)	104 (A)	105 (A)
106 (B)	107 (A)	108 (C)	109 (B)	110 (A)
111 (D)	112 (A)	113 (A)	114 (A)	115 (C)
116 (A)	117 (A)	118 (B)	119 (B)	120 (C)
121 (D)	122 (A)	123 (D)	124 (C)	125 (B)
126 (B)	127 (D)	128 (D)	129 (C)	130 (C)
131 (C)	132 (A)	133 (C)	134 (D)	135 (D)
136 (A)	137 (C)	138 (B)	139 (C)	140 (A)
141 (B)	142 (C)	143 (D)	144 (B)	145 (C)
146 (C)	147 (C)	148 (D)	149 (D)	150 (D)
151 (D)	152 (A)	153 (B)	154 (A)	155 (B)
156 (D)	157 (B)	158 (C)	159 (B)	160 (D)
161 (A)	162 (B)	163 (C)	164 (D)	165 (B)
166 (C)	167 (C)	168 (A)	169 (D)	170 (C)
171 (B)	172 (C)	173 (C)	174 (D)	175 (A)
176 (B)	177 (B)	178 (C)	179 (C)	180 (C)
181 (D)	182 (A)	183 (B)	184 (C)	185 (D)
186 (A)	187 (B)	188 (B)	189 (D)	190 (C)
191 (C)	192 (C)	193 (D)	194 (C)	195 (B)
196 (D)	197 (B)	198 (A)	199 (B)	200 (D)

PART 1

1 🔊 澳洲發音

(A) He is wiping down a table.
(B) He is typing on a laptop.
(C) He is making a cup of coffee.
(D) He is wearing an apron.

wipe down 擦乾淨～　type 打字　apron 圍裙

翻譯 (A) 他正在擦桌子。
　　 (B) 他在使用筆電打字。
　　 (C) 他正在泡咖啡。
　　 (D) 他穿著圍裙。

解析 1 人照片
　　 (A) [×] wiping down（擦乾淨～）與男子的動作無關，是錯誤選項。因為照片中使用了桌子（table），所以會造成混淆。
　　 (B) [×] typing（打字）與男子的動作無關，是錯誤選項。因為照片中使用了筆電（laptop），所以會造成混淆。
　　 (C) [×] making a cup of coffee（正在泡咖啡）與男子的動作無關，是錯誤選項。因為照片中使用了杯子（cup），所以會造成混淆。
　　 (D) [○] 男子穿著圍裙的描述是正確答案。

2 🔊 英國發音

(A) The woman is swimming near a ship.
(B) The woman is waving her hand.
(C) The man is soaking his legs in the water.
(D) The man is pulling on a rope.

wave one's hand 揮手　soak 浸泡　pull on a rope 拉繩子

翻譯 (A) 女子在船隻附近游泳。
　　 (B) 女子在揮手。
　　 (C) 男子的腿浸泡在水中。
　　 (D) 男子在拉繩子。

解析 2 人以上的照片
　　 (A) [×] swimming（正在游泳）與女子的動作無關，是錯誤選項。
　　 (B) [×] waving her hand（正在揮手）與女子的動作無關，是錯誤選項。
　　 (C) [×] 男子的雙腳都在船上，浸泡在水中是錯誤選項。
　　 (D) [○] 男子拉著繩子的描述是正確答案。

3 加拿大發音

(A) Some trees are lined up along a trail.
(B) The ornate building has several awnings.
(C) Some tables are stacked near a door.
(D) A sign has fallen down.

---

line up 排成一列　trail 小徑　ornate 裝飾華麗的　awning 遮棚
stack 堆疊　fall down 倒下、摔倒

翻譯 (A) 樹木沿著小徑排成一列。
　　(B) 裝飾華麗的建築物有數個遮陽板。
　　(C) 門的附近有好幾張桌子堆疊在一起。
　　(D) 標示牌倒下了。

解析 事物與風景的照片
　　(A) [×] 照片中沒有小徑（trail），是錯誤選項。
　　(B) [○] 裝飾華麗的建築物有數個遮陽板的描述是正確答案。
　　(C) [×] 照片中沒有看見桌子，也沒有出現堆疊的（are stacked）狀態，是錯誤選項。
　　(D) [×] 標示牌是豎立的狀態，不是倒下的。

4 澳洲發音

(A) The woman is making a purchase.
(B) The woman is folding some clothes.
(C) The woman has a bag on her back.
(D) The woman is ironing a shirt.

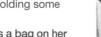

---

make a purchase 購買物品　fold 折疊、摺　iron 熨、熨燙

翻譯 (A) 女子正在購物。
　　(B) 女子正在摺衣服。
　　(C) 女子揹著背包。
　　(D) 女子在燙襯衫。

解析 1 人的照片
　　(A) [×] making a purchase（正在購買物品）與女子的動作無關，是錯誤選項。
　　(B) [×] folding（摺疊）與女子動作無關，是錯誤選項。
　　(C) [○] 女子揹著背包是最正確的描述，因此是答案。
　　(D) [×] ironing（熨燙）與女子的動作無關，是錯誤選項。照片中使用了襯衫（shirt），所以會造成混淆。

5 英國發音

(A) A man is giving a lecture.
(B) Some seats are unoccupied.
(C) Desks are arranged in a circle.
(D) A lecturer is pointing toward a student.

---

give a lecture 演講　unoccupied 空的　arrange 排列
point toward 指向～

翻譯 **(A) 男子在演講。**
　　(B) 有幾個空位。
　　(C) 書桌排成圓形。
　　(D) 講師指著一個學生。

解析 2 人以上的照片
　　(A) [○] 男子在演講是最正確的描述，因此是答案。
　　(B) [×] 從照片中無法確認還有沒有座位是空置的（unoccupied），所以是錯誤選項。
　　(C) [×] 桌子排成一列，因此排成圓形是錯誤的描述。
　　(D) [×] 講師不是指著學生，而是指著白板，因此是錯誤選項。

6 美國發音

(A) Some desk drawers are open.
(B) A computer station is situated in a corner.
(C) Some binders have been placed on the ground.
(D) A lamp has been turned off.

---

drawer 抽屜　situate 使位於　binder 活頁夾（紙張等綁在一起）
turn off 關閉

翻譯 (A) 有一些書桌的抽屜都開著。
　　(B) 電腦在角落。
　　(C) 地上放有幾個活頁夾。
　　(D) 檯燈關著。

解析 事物與風景的照片
　　(A) [×] 書桌的抽屜是關閉的狀態，開啟的描述是錯的。
　　(B) [○] 電腦在角落的描述是正確的，因此是答案。
　　(C) [×] 活頁夾放在櫃子上，放在地上是錯誤的描述。
　　(D) [×] 檯燈是開啟的狀態，關閉的描述是錯的。

PART 2

7 加拿大發音→美國發音

Where did you purchase this coat?
(A) I can hang your jacket up.
(B) At a department store.
(C) There they are.

---

purchase 購買　hang up 掛上（圖畫、衣服等）
department store 百貨公司

翻譯 你的外套是從哪裡買的？
　　(A) 我會幫你掛外套。
　　(B) 從百貨公司。
　　(C) 那些東西在那邊。

解析 Where 疑問句
　　(A) [×] 因使用了與問題中的 coat（外套）有關的 jacket（夾克），會造成混淆，是錯誤選項。
　　(B) [○] 因回答百貨公司，談到購買外套的地方，這是正確的答案。

(C) [×] 問題詢問外套從哪購買，回答內容卻完全不相關，因此是錯誤選項。

8 🔊 澳洲發音→英國發音

When was the last time that you ate at this restaurant?
(A) **Three weeks ago, I think.**
(B) They loved the salad.
(C) Great, I'll meet you there.

翻譯 你上一次在這間餐廳用餐是什麼時候？
(A) **好像是三個星期前。**
(B) 他們很喜歡那個沙拉。
(C) 好，就在那邊碰面吧。

解析 When 疑問句
(A) [○] 因為是詢問上一次在該餐廳用餐是何時，回答好像是三個星期前，所以是正確答案。
(B) [×] 使用了 restaurant（餐廳）相關的 salad（沙拉），是會造成混淆的選項。
(C) [×] 使用了代表 restaurant（餐廳）的 there，這是會造成混淆的錯誤選項。

9 🔊 加拿大發音→英國發音

Who made these blueprints for the sports stadium?
(A) We joined a basketball club.
(B) **Charles and I.**
(C) Yes, thanks for the blueprints.

blueprint 設計圖，計劃　sports stadium 運動場

翻譯 是誰幫運動場畫了設計圖？
(A) 我們加入籃球同好會了。
(B) **Charles 和我。**
(C) 好，謝謝你的設計圖。

解析 Who 疑問句
(A) [×] 使用了與 sports stadium（運動場）相關的 basketball，這是會造成混淆的錯誤選項。
(B) [○] 回答是 Charles 和自己，因談到畫設計圖的人，所以這是正確答案。
(C) [×] 疑問句回答 Yes，重複使用 blueprints 造成混淆，此為錯誤選項。

10 🔊 美國發音→加拿大發音

How frequently is the recycling picked up?
(A) Let me show you how.
(B) Only paper-based materials.
(C) **Every other week.**

frequently 經常　recycling 資源回收　pick up 拾取、清除
material 材料、物質　every other week 隔週

翻譯 資源回收多久會來收一次？
(A) 我來示範一下怎麼做。
(B) 只有紙張製成的材料。
(C) 隔週。

解析 How 疑問句
(A) [×] 題目詢問多久會進行回收一次，回答卻完全不相關，因此是錯誤選項。
(B) [×] 使用與 recycling（資源回收）相關的 paper-based materials（紙材料），這是會造成混淆的錯誤選項。
(C) [○] 回答隔週，因為與回收頻率相關，因此是正確答案。

11 🔊 澳洲發音→英國發音

Who is scheduled to work the night shift this week?
(A) Because I changed my schedule.
(B) Shift it to the left.
(C) **Ron Walters, I believe.**

be scheduled to 排定要～　night shift 夜班

翻譯 這個星期是誰被排夜班？
(A) 因為我變更行程了。
(B) 請把那個移到左邊。
(C) **好像是 Ron Walters。**

解析 Who 疑問句
(A) [×] 把問題中的 scheduled 改成 schedule 來重覆使用，是會造成混淆的錯誤選項。
(B) [×] 把問題中的 shift（輪班）當作動詞「搬移」使用，是會造成混淆的錯誤選項。
(C) [○] 回答好像是 Ron Walters，內容與這星期上夜班的人有關係，因此是正確答案。

12 🔊 加拿大發音→澳洲發音

Do you know how to use the Skysoft program?
(A) We've never met.
(B) I'll use this one, then.
(C) **Try asking Carlos.**

翻譯 你知道怎麼使用 Skysoft 程式嗎？
(A) 我們不曾見過面。
(B) 那我要使用這個。
(C) **請去問 Carlos。**

解析 助動詞疑問句
(A) [×] 題目詢問 Skysoft 程式的使用方法，但回答卻說我們不曾見面，內容完全不相關，因此是錯誤選項。
(B) [×] 因重複使用問題中的 use，是會造成混淆的錯誤選項。
(C) [○] 這句話的意思是去詢問 Carlos，間接轉達自己不懂 Skysoft 程式的使用方法，因此是正確答案。

May I take my afternoon break a few minutes early?
(A) Sure, go ahead.
(B) There are a few missing parts.
(C) You should have tried the soup.

---

break 休息（時間）　missing 消失的　part 零件

翻譯 我可以提早幾分鐘午休嗎？
(A) 當然可以，你請便吧。
(B) 有幾個零件不見了。
(C) 你應該喝喝看那個湯的。

解析 要求疑問句
(A) [○] 使用 Sure 同意想要提前幾分鐘午休的要求，是正確答案。
(B) [×] 重複使用問題的 a few，是會造成混淆的錯誤選項。
(C) [×] 題目詢問是否能提早幾分鐘午休，卻突然說應該嚐嚐看湯，因此是錯誤選項。

When does the clinic usually close?
(A) It's across from Regions Park.
(B) We have four nurses on staff.
(C) It shuts down at 7 o'clock.

---

clinic 診所　across from ～的對面　on (the) staff 在職的
shut down 關門

翻譯 診所通常幾點關門？
(A) 那個地方在 Regions 公園的對面。
(B) 我們有四名在職的護理師。
(C) 那個地方 7 點關門。

解析 When 疑問句
(A) [×] 明明是詢問診所關門的時間，卻回答位置，這是錯誤選項。
(B) [×] 因使用與問題 clinic（診所）相關的 nurses，是會造成混淆的錯誤選項。
(C) [○] 回答 7 點關門，與診所關門時間有關係，因此是正確答案。

Which briefcase belongs to our client, Mr. Powell?
(A) The meeting was very brief.
(B) This black one is his.
(C) I keep my files in it.

---

briefcase 公事包　belong to 屬於～　brief（時間）短的

翻譯 哪一個是顧客 Powell 先生的公事包？
(A) 會議非常短。
(B) 這個黑色的就是他的。
(C) 我把文件夾保管在那裡面。

解析 Which 疑問句
(A) [×] 使用與問題中 briefcase 發音相似的 brief，是會造成混淆的錯誤選項。
(B) [○] 內容等於回答黑色公事包是 Powell 先生的物品，所以是正確答案。
(C) [×] 使用與問題的 briefcase（公事包）相關的 files（文件夾），搭配可能代表 briefcase（公事包）的 it，是會造成混淆的錯誤選項。

Why did you show up to work late?
(A) Just on Tuesdays and Thursdays.
(B) It should be starting in a few minutes.
(C) I was stuck in traffic.

---

show up 到場、露面　stuck in traffic 塞車

翻譯 為何你會晚到公司？
(A) 只有星期二和星期四。
(B) 幾分鐘內就會開始。
(C) 路上塞車了。

解析 Why 疑問句
(A) [×] 題目詢問為何會晚到公司，回答只有星期二與星期四根本毫不相關，是錯誤選項。
(B) [×] 使用與問題中的 late（晚到）相關的 in a few minutes（幾分鐘內），因此會造成混淆。
(C) [○] 塞車是晚到公司的理由，因此是正確答案。

Who is leading the weekend fitness class, Carl or Jane?
(A) Nobody has been assigned yet.
(B) Only gym members can apply.
(C) Sometime next weekend.

---

lead 帶領　fitness class 運動課程　assign 分配　apply 申請

翻譯 週末是誰帶運動課，Carl 還是 Jane ？
(A) 目前還沒分配任何人。
(B) 只有體育館的會員能申請。
(C) 下週的某個時候。

解析 選擇疑問句
(A) [○] 還沒分配任何人，就代表沒有選擇 Carl 或 Jane，是正確答案。
(B) [×] 使用與問題的 fitness class（運動課程）相關的 gym（體育館），是會造成混淆的錯誤選項。
(C) [×] 重複使用問題中的 weekend，因此會造成混淆。

My plane leaves this evening.
(A) Yes. One ticket, please.
(B) Tomorrow morning as well.
(C) Enjoy your trip.

翻譯 我的飛機今晚出發。
    (A) 是，請給我一張票。
    (B) 明天早上也是。
    (C) 祝你旅途愉快。

解析 直述句
    (A) [×] 使用與問題中的 plane（飛機）有關的 ticket，因此會造成混淆。
    (B) [×] 使用與問題中的 evening（晚上）有關的 morning（早上），因此會造成混淆。
    (C) [○] 回答旅途愉快來祝福對方今晚出發，因此是正確答案。

19 🎧 英國發音→澳洲發音

How is the parking garage renovation progressing?
(A) It's free to park on the street.
(B) I got busy with another project.
(C) Please take out the garbage.

parking garage 停車場　renovation 修理、更新
progress 進行　take out 帶出去　garbage 垃圾

翻譯 停車場的翻修進度如何？
    (A) 停在街上是免費的。
    (B) 我因為其他專案很忙。
    (C) 請把垃圾帶出去。

解析 How 疑問句
    (A) [×] 使用與題目中 parking 發音相似的 park，因此會造成混淆。
    (B) [○] 回答因為其他專案而忙碌，間接傳達停車場翻修尚未進行，所以是正確答案。
    (C) [×] 使用與題目中 garage 發音相似的 garbage，因此會造成混淆。

20 🎧 澳洲發音→英國發音

Isn't it time for the movie to begin?
(A) Not quite yet.
(B) What a great opening scene.
(C) It doesn't end until Sunday.

scene 場面

翻譯 不是已經到電影開始的時間了嗎？
    (A) 還沒有。
    (B) 好精彩的開場。
    (C) 要等到星期天才結束。

解析 否定疑問句
    (A) [○] 回答還沒有，傳達了電影還沒開始的意思，因此是正確答案。
    (B) [×] 使用與 movie（電影）相關的 scene（場景），是會造成混淆的選項。
    (C) [×] 使用與 begin（開始）意思相反的 end（結束），是會造成混淆的選項。

21 🎧 加拿大發音→美國發音

The hole in the conference room wall must be fixed.
(A) I've already contacted a repairperson.
(B) The room is painted a nice color.
(C) Only half of the attendees are here.

hole 洞　conference room 會議室　repairperson 維修人員
attendee 參加者

翻譯 會議室牆上的洞必須要修補。
    (A) 我已經聯絡維修人員了。
    (B) 那個房間漆成很漂亮的顏色。
    (C) 這裡只有一半的參加者。

解析 直述句
    (A) [○] 回答已經聯絡維修人員了，等於提出了解決方案，因此是正確答案。
    (B) [×] 因重複使用 room，所以會造成混淆。
    (C) [×] 因使用與 conference（會議）相關的 attendees（參加者），是會造成混淆的錯誤選項。

22 🎧 加拿大發音→英國發音

What kind of food should we order for the employee appreciation luncheon tomorrow?
(A) Rachel cannot eat seafood.
(B) We are expecting 50 attendees.
(C) I appreciate the service.

appreciation 感謝、賞識　luncheon 午餐
expect 預期、期待　attendee 參加者

翻譯 明天的員工感謝午餐要訂哪一類的餐點？
    (A) Rachel 沒辦法吃海鮮。
    (B) 我們預計有 50 名參加者。
    (C) 我很感謝這項服務。

解析 What 疑問句
    (A) [○] 回答 Rachel 沒辦法吃海鮮，等於間接轉達不能訂海鮮，所以是正確答案。
    (B) [×] 使用與 luncheon（午餐）相關的 attendees（參加者），因此會造成混淆。
    (C) [×] 使用與題目的 appreciation 發音相似的 appreciate，因此會造成混淆。

23 🎧 英國發音→加拿大發音

Where is the security training session being held?
(A) Safety is an important consideration.
(B) On Monday at 3 P.M.
(C) Didn't you check the e-mail?

security 保全、安全　training session 教育訓練課程
consideration 考量事項

翻譯 安全訓練課程在哪裡舉行？
    (A) 安全是重要的考量事項。
    (B) 是星期一下午 3 點。

(C) 你沒有確認電子郵件嗎？

解析 Where 疑問句
- (A) [✗] 使用與題目中 security 發音相似的 Safety，因此會造成混淆。
- (B) [✗] 問題詢問安全訓練課程在哪裡舉行，回答時間是錯的。把 Where 混淆為 When，會讓人以誤以為是 When is the security training session being held?（安全訓練課程何時舉行？），因此不是正確答案。
- (C) [○] 反問是否有確認電子郵件，間接轉達可從中確認舉辦的場所，因此是正確答案。

---

24 🎧 美國發音→英國發音

Should we go swimming on Saturday, or is it going to be too cold?
(A) I've never been to that beach.
(B) The weather will be nice all weekend.
(C) Let me grab you a jacket.

翻譯 我們星期六要去游泳嗎？還是會太冷？
- (A) 我不曾去那個海灘。
- **(B) 整個週末天氣都會很好。**
- (C) 我幫你拿一件夾克。

解析 選擇疑問句
- (A) [✗] 因使用與 swimming（游泳）相關的 beach（海灘），會造成混淆。
- (B) [○] 回答整個週末天氣都會很好，等於間接選擇星期六要去游泳，所以是正確答案。
- (C) [✗] 使用與 too cold（太冷）相關的 jacket（夾克），會造成混淆。

---

25 🎧 美國發音→澳洲發音

This jewelry shop is quite expensive.
(A) The prices seem reasonable to me.
(B) The gold earrings.
(C) Yes, we can stop by the store.

jewelry 寶石　reasonable （價格）恰當的、合理的
stop by 順道拜訪～

翻譯 這間珠寶店的價格相當昂貴。
- **(A) 我覺得價格很合理呀。**
- (B) 是金耳環。
- (C) 是，我們能順道過去那間店。

解析 直述句
- (A) [○] 回答覺得價格很合理，提出了對珠寶店的意見，所以是正確答案。
- (B) [✗] 因使用 jewelry（珠寶）相關的 gold earrings（金耳環），會造成混淆。
- (C) [✗] 因使用和 shop（商店）相同意思的 store（商店），會造成混淆。

---

26 🎧 加拿大發音→美國發音

Are any of these wood sculptures handmade?
(A) No, we don't have a fireplace.
(B) Yes, they all are.
(C) Well, let's make some more.

sculpture 雕刻品　handmade 手工、手製的　fireplace 壁爐

翻譯 這些木雕品當中是否有手工製成的？
- (A) 不，我們沒有壁爐。
- **(B) 是，全都是。**
- (C) 嗯，再多製作幾個吧。

解析 Be 動詞疑問句
- (A) [✗] 使用與 wood（樹木）相關的 fireplace（壁爐），因此會造成混淆。
- (B) [○] 回答 Yes 轉達有手工製成的雕刻品，附加說明全都是，因此是正確答案。
- (C) [✗] 重複把 made 當作 make 使用，因此會造成混淆。

---

27 🎧 美國發音→加拿大發音

Has a director been selected to oversee our regional branch?
(A) The search is ongoing.
(B) No, she originally managed the team.
(C) Please write down the directions.

director 負責人　oversee 監督　regional 地區的　branch 分店
ongoing 持續的　manage 管理　direction 說明事項

翻譯 監督我們這一區分行的負責人已經選出來了嗎？
- **(A) 目前持續在找。**
- (B) 不，她本來在管理那個團隊。
- (C) 請填寫說明事項。

解析 助動詞疑問句
- (A) [○] 回答持續在找當中，等於間接轉達尚未選出負責人，因此是正確答案。
- (B) [✗] 使用和 oversee（監督）意思相同的 manage（管理），因此會造成混淆。
- (C) [✗] 使用與題目中 director 發音相似的 directions，因此會造成混淆。

---

28 🎧 澳洲發音→美國發音

Shouldn't the maintenance worker be here by now?
(A) Now is not a good time for me.
(B) He's waiting in the lobby.
(C) To maintain our current workforce.

maintenance 保養、維護　by now 目前為止　current 目前的
workforce （所有的）職員

翻譯 維修人員不是差不多該到了嗎？
- (A) 對我來說現在不是很好的時機。

(B) 他已經在大廳等了。

(C) 為了維持我們目前的工作團隊。

解析 否定疑問句

(A) [✗] 重複使用 now，因此會造成混淆，是錯誤選項。

(B) [○] 回答他已經在大廳等了，等於轉達維修人員來了，因此是正確答案。

(C) [✗] 使用與題目中 maintenance 發音相似的 maintain，因此會造成混淆。

29 🔊 澳洲發音→美國發音

> Did someone from the accounting department call in sick?
> (A) Apparently, Kyle Alton has the flu.
> (B) I didn't account for those costs.
> (C) The hospital staff is extremely helpful.
>
> accounting department 會計部　call in sick 打電話請假
> apparently 似乎　flu 流感　account for 計入～（的支出）
> extremely 極端地

翻譯 會計部門有人打電話請病假嗎？

(A) Kyle Alton 似乎得流感了。

(B) 我沒有計入那些成本。

(C) 那間醫院的職員非常有幫助。

解析 助動詞疑問句

(A) [○] 回答 Kyle Alton 得流感，等於是間接轉達他請病假，因此是正確答案。

(B) [✗] 使用與題目中 accounting 發音相似的 account，因此會造成混淆。

(C) [✗] 使用與 call in sick（打電話請病假）相關的 hospital（醫院），因此會造成混淆。

30 🔊 英國發音→加拿大發音

> There will be room for everyone on the shuttle bus, right?
> (A) I expect the drive to take an hour.
> (B) The subway was quite busy.
> **(C) I don't think there's enough space.**
>
> room 空位　expect 預期　busy 擁擠的　space 場地、空間

翻譯 每個人在接駁巴士上應該都有座位，對吧？

(A) 我預計開車要一個小時。

(B) 地鐵相當擁擠。

(C) 我不認為有足夠的位子。

解析 附加疑問句

(A) [✗] 使用與 shuttle bus（接駁巴士）相關的 drive（開車），因此會造成混淆。

(B) [✗] 使用與 shuttle bus（接駁巴士）相關的 subway（地鐵），因此會造成混淆。

(C) [○] 回答不認為有足夠的位子，等於轉達接駁巴士沒有足夠的座位，因此是正確答案。

31 🔊 澳洲發音→美國發音

> Can you show me how to install this ceiling fan?
> **(A) In just a couple of minutes.**
> (B) Yes, Tom installed the door.
> (C) I'm a big fan of you.
>
> install 安裝　ceiling 天花板　fan 電扇、風扇、狂熱愛好者

翻譯 可以示範一下該如何安裝這個吊扇嗎？

(A) 再過幾分鐘。

(B) 對，那扇門是 Tom 安裝的。

(C) 我很喜歡你。

解析 要求疑問句

(A) [○] 回答再過幾分鐘，等於同意示範如何安裝吊扇，因此是正確答案。

(B) [✗] 重複使用 installed，因此會造成混淆。

(C) [✗] 重複使用名詞 fan（風扇），因此會造成混淆。

PART 3

32-34 🔊 加拿大發音→美國發音

Questions 32-34 refer to the following conversation.

> M: Hello. This is Nathan Green. ³²I'm calling in regard to the interview I had with your firm for a financial adviser position. I was told I'd be contacted within two weeks of the interview date. ³³But I haven't heard from anyone yet.
> W: Oh, I'm so sorry, Mr. Green. ³³Our accounting director is still reviewing résumés at the moment. He plans to select someone later this afternoon.
> M: I understand. When can I expect to hear back about the decision, then?
> W: ³⁴One of our human resources staff will be letting candidates know tomorrow morning. You'll find out at that time.
>
> in regard to 關於～　interview 面試　financial 財務的
> adviser 顧問　accounting 會計　director 主任　review 檢討
> résumé 履歷　at the moment 此刻　select 選拔
> candidate 應徵者　find out 了解

翻譯 問題 32-34，請參考以下對話。

男：你好，我是 Nathan Green，³² 想要請教貴公司財務顧問一職面試的事。聽說面試完 2 個星期內就會聯絡我，³³ 但我目前還沒收到任何消息。

女：真是抱歉，Green 先生，³³ 我們公司的會計部主任還在審視履歷，預計今天下午會選出人。

男：這樣呀，那大概何時會收到通知？

女：³⁴ 人資部的職員明天早上會通知應徵者。到時候就會收到聯絡。

32 目的問題

翻譯 男子為何要打電話？

(A) 詢問關於面試的事

(B) 接受工作邀請
(C) 為了安排見面
(D) 為了商討專案

解析 題目詢問打電話的目的，一定要聆聽通話時的前半部，男子說自己曾去對方公司面試財務顧問職缺「I'm calling in regard to the interview I had with your firm for a financial adviser position.」，因此 (A) 是答案。

字彙 accept 接受　job offer 工作邀請　arrange 安排

33 理由問題

翻譯 為何會出現延遲？
(A) 沒有繳交申請書。
(B) 某些組員正在休假。
(C) 聘僱委員會還沒召集。
(D) 一些文件還在檢視中。

解析 注意聆聽與問題關鍵字 delay 相關的內容，男子說自己還沒收到任何聯絡「But I haven't heard from anyone yet.」，女子回答「Our accounting director is still reviewing résumés at the moment.」，表示目前會計部主任還在審視履歷，因此答案是 (D)。

換句話說
reviewing résumés 正在審視履歷 → Some documents are being reviewed 一些文件正在審視中

字彙 application form 申請表　submit 繳交
be on vacation 休假中　committee 委員會

34 之後將發生的事

翻譯 人資部的職員明天要做什麼？
(A) 讓應徵者進行參觀。
(B) 聯絡申請者。
(C) 審視履歷。
(D) 為職缺打廣告。

解析 仔細聆聽問題的關鍵詞 tomorrow morning 談到的部分，女子說「One of our human resources staff will be letting candidates know tomorrow morning.」，表示明天早上人資部的職員會負責通知面試者結果。因此答案是 (B)。

換句話說
letting candidates know 通知應徵者 → Contact applicants 聯絡申請者

字彙 applicant 申請者　give a tour 參觀　look over 審視～
advertise 廣告

35-37 [音] 英國發音→澳洲發音

Questions 35-37 refer to the following conversation.

W: Greg, ³⁵the publisher will release my book in two months, so I need a professional profile photo for the cover. It needs to be done as soon as possible. Can you do it?
M: I'm free today and tomorrow. ³⁶If you can come by, we can get it done in about an hour.
W: That sounds great. ³⁷I have a video call with representatives of a public relations firm

scheduled for this afternoon, but I can stop by your studio tomorrow. I'll see you around 10 A.M.

publisher 出版社、出版人　release 發行　professional 專業的
cover 封面　as soon as possible 盡早　free 不受限制的
come by 順道　representative 代表（人）　public relations 宣傳

翻譯 問題 35-37，請參考以下對話。
女：Greg，³⁵ 出版社說我的書兩個月後會發行，封面需要專業的頭像照，必須盡快完成才行，你能辦到嗎？
男：我今天和明天都有空，³⁶ 如果你能順便過來一趟，我們會在一個小時內完成。
女：聽起來很好，³⁷ 我今天下午和公關公司的代表們約好要視訊，但是明天我可以去一趟你的工作室，我們上午 10 點左右見面吧。

35 說話者問題

翻譯 女子最可能從事什麼行業？
(A) 作家
(B) 出版業者
(C) 攝影師
(D) 演員

解析 一定要掌握對話中與身分和職業相關的表達方式，女子說「the publisher will release my book in two months.」，表示出版社兩個月後會發行自己的書，由此可知她是作家。因此答案是 (A)。

字彙 profession 職業（種）

36 意圖掌握問題

翻譯 男子回答「我今天和明天都有空」時，其用意是什麼？
(A) 他將會執行某事務。
(B) 他將會延長截止期限。
(C) 他將會更新行程。
(D) 他要休息一天。

解析 與問題引用句（I'm free today and tomorrow）相關的部分要仔細聆聽，男子說「If you can come by, we can get it[profile photo] done in about an hour.」，表示如果女子能順道去一趟，只要一個小時左右就能完成頭像照，從這句話可知道他準備要執行某事務。

字彙 perform 執行　extend 延長　deadline 截止期限
take a day off 休息一天

37 之後將發生的事

翻譯 女子下午要做什麼？
(A) 參加研討會。
(B) 進行簡報。
(C) 造訪辦公室。
(D) 參加線上會議。

解析 仔細聆聽與問題關鍵字 afternoon 相關的部分，女子預計下午要進行視訊通話（I have a video call ~ scheduled for this afternoon），因此 (D) 是正確答案。

換句話說
have a video call ~ scheduled 預定要視訊通話 → Join an

online meeting 參加線上會議

字彙 attend 參加

38-40 [3w] 澳洲發音→美國發音→英國發音

Questions 38-40 refer to the following conversation with three speakers.

M: ³⁸We've had fewer customers since that new deli opened across the street.
W1: Yeah, some of our regular customers have started eating there instead.
W2: We should do something to get them back. Do you have any ideas, Jason?
M: ³⁹How about reducing what we charge for appetizers and entrées?
W2: That won't do much. I mean, ⁴⁰we're already cheaper than the deli.
W1: ⁴⁰True. We've always been one of the neighborhood's most affordable restaurants.
M: Then, let's have a staff meeting with everyone tonight to discuss other ideas.

deli 熟食店　regular customer 常客
appetizer 開胃菜（提升食慾的料理）　entrée 主菜
neighborhood 鄰近地區、附近　affordable 平價的

翻譯 問題 38-40，請參考以下三方對話。
男：³⁸ 自從馬路對面新開一間熟食店，客人就變少了。
女 1：對呀，我們有好幾個常客都開始去那邊用餐了。
女 2：如果想讓客人回流，我們得想想辦法才行，Jason，你有什麼意見嗎？
男：³⁹ 要不要調降開胃菜和主菜的價格？
女 2：這樣應該沒有太大的幫助，我的意思是，⁴⁰ 我們本來就比那間熟食店更便宜了。
女 1：⁴⁰ 對，我們一直是這附近最平價的餐廳之一。
男：那今晚大家就一起開會，討論一下其他點子吧。

38 問題點問題

翻譯 問題是什麼？
(A) 客人減少了。
(B) 業者關門了。
(C) 客人提出抗議了。
(D) 餐點的品質降低了。

解析 仔細聆聽對話中的負面敘述。男子說「We've had fewer customers since that new deli opened across the street.」，表示自從街對面那家新熟食店開業以來，顧客就減少了，因此 (A) 是正確答案。
換句話說
had fewer customers 客人變少了 → Customers have decreased 客人減少了

字彙 decrease（大小、數量等）減少　complain 抗議

39 提議問題

翻譯 男子提出何種意見？
(A) 推出新的主菜

(B) 調降價格
(C) 僱用更多員工
(D) 提供免費開胃菜

解析 仔細聆聽男子談到與提議相關的部分，他說「How about reducing what we charge for appetizers and entrées?」，提議降低開胃菜與主菜的價格，因此 (B) 是正確答案。

字彙 introduce 引進、介紹

40 提及何事的問題

翻譯 女子談到餐廳的哪些事？
(A) 剛搬到鄰近的地區。
(B) 最近變更了料理方法。
(C) 提供不算貴的餐點。
(D) 準備開 2 號店。

解析 仔細聆聽女子交談時與 restaurant 相關的內容，女子 2 說他們的餐廳原本就比該熟食店更便宜了（we[restaurant] are already cheaper than the deli），女子 1 表示同意，並且說他們一直是這附近最平價的餐廳之一（True. We've always been one of the neighborhood's most affordable restaurants.）。從這番話可知道該餐廳能提供不貴的餐點，因此答案是 (C)。
換句話說
have ~ been one of the ~ most affordable restaurants 最便宜的餐廳之一 → offers inexpensive dishes 提供不貴的食物

字彙 recipe 料理方法　inexpensive 不貴的　dish 食物

41-43 [2w] 加拿大發音→美國發音

Questions 41-43 refer to the following conversation.

M: ⁴¹I've booked my flight to Spain for the trade exhibit next week, but I'm not sure where to stay. ⁴²This is my first time going to Barcelona, so I'm not familiar with the hotels there.
W: It's being held at the new convention center in the harbor district, right? I know of two hotels in the area . . . um, Hotel Costal is closer to the center, but ⁴³I'm concerned since it has higher rates. It's almost $200 for a room.
M: The company will reimburse me up to $250 per night, so ⁴³that's fine. Plus, I'd like to be near the event venue.

book 預約　trade exhibit 貿易展　be familiar with 熟悉的
harbor 港灣　district 地區、區域　rate 費用　reimburse 補償
up to 直到～　venue 場地

翻譯 問題 41-43，請參考以下對話。
男：⁴¹ 我預約了飛往西班牙的班機，為了參加下星期的貿易展示會，但我不知道要住哪裡，⁴² 因為這是我第一次去巴塞隆納，我對那邊的飯店不太熟。
女：貿易展在港灣地區的會議中心舉辦，對吧？我知道那個地區的兩間飯店⋯⋯嗯，雖然 Costal 飯店和會議中心更近，⁴³ 但費用更高，所以我會有顧慮。一個房間將近要 200 美金。

男：公司可支付每晚 250 美金的上限，43 所以這倒是沒關係，而且我想住在距離活動地點較近的地方。

41 之後將發生的事

翻譯 下星期會發生什麼事？
(A) 旅遊博覽會
(B) 商店開幕
(C) 飯店會議
(D) 貿易博覽會

解析 仔細聆聽與問題關鍵詞 next week 相關的部分，男子說「I've booked my flight to Spain for the trade exhibit next week.」，表示為了參加下星期的貿易展，已經預約飛往西班牙的機票，因此 (D) 是正確答案。
換句話說
trade exhibit 貿易展 → trade show 貿易博覽會

42 主題問題

翻譯 對話者主要在談些什麼？
(A) 航班行程
(B) 住宿選擇
(C) 活動場所
(D) 展示會日期

解析 因為是詢問對話的主題，一定要聆聽對話一開始的內容。男子說「This is my first time going to Barcelona, so I'm not familiar with the hotels there.」，表示自己是第一次去巴塞隆納，對當地的飯店不太熟，將對話內容延伸至住宿地點的選擇，因此正確答案是 (B)。

字彙 accommodation 住宿處

43 意圖掌握問題

翻譯 為何男子說「公司可支付每晚 250 美金的上限」？
(A) 為了拒絕提議
(B) 為了解決對方的顧慮
(C) 為了提議
(D) 為了應對不滿

解析 仔細聆聽與問題引用句（The company will reimburse me up to $250 per night）相關的部分，女子說「I'm concerned since it[Hotel Costal] has higher rates. It's almost $200 for a room.」，表達 Costal 飯店的費用更高，一個房間將近 200 美金，所以讓她有所顧慮，男子則回答沒關係（that's fine），由此可知這句話是要解決女子的擔憂，因此答案是 (B)。

字彙 reject 拒絕　address 解決、處理　respond 回應
complaint 抱怨

44-46 🔊 澳洲發音→英國發音

Questions 44-46 refer to the following conversation.

M: Janna, this is Martin Rodriguez. I'm calling to let you know that 44my truck broke down on Freeway 76 near Exit 23 when I was plowing snow from the road. 44/45I need to be picked up.

➡

W: 45I'll dispatch another one of our employees to get you right away. However, I won't be able to send a tow truck until tomorrow afternoon. 46Is the vehicle blocking traffic where it's currently parked?
M: No, I managed to stop on the side of the road, so it should be fine here.

---

break down 故障　freeway 高速公路　plow 除雪
pick up（車子）接送　dispatch（為了特殊目的）派遣
tow 牽引、（汽車、汽船）拖吊　block 抵擋、封鎖　manage 調度

翻譯 問題 44-46，請參考以下對話。
男：Janna，我是 Martin Rodriguez。44 我在道路除雪時，卡車在 76 號高速公路接近 23 號出口處拋錨了，所以我才會打電話給你。44/45 我需要有人來載我。
女：45 我會派另一名職員去接你，但我要等明天下午才能派拖吊車，46 停車的位置會阻礙交通嗎？
男：不會，我成功停在路旁，應該不會造成問題。

44 問題點問題

翻譯 男子的問題是什麼？
(A) 職員沒有時間。
(B) 無法去到高速公路。
(C) 車輛無法運作。
(D) 車庫關閉。

解析 仔細聆聽男子在交談時使用的負面表達，他說「my truck broke down ~. I need to be picked up.」，表示卡車拋錨，對方必須來接自己。因此答案是 (C)。
換句話說
truck broke down 卡車故障了 → vehicle is not functioning 車輛無法啟動

字彙 available 有空的、可利用的　highway 高速公路
accessible 可使用（接近）的　function 運作

45 特定細節問題

翻譯 女子同意要做什麼？
(A) 傳達訊息。
(B) 清除積雪。
(C) 派遣職員。
(D) 聯絡急救人員。

解析 仔細聆聽女子說的話，男子說對方必須來接送自己（I need to be picked up.），女子回答「I'll dispatch another one of our employees to get you right away.」，表示會立刻派一名職員去接人，因此答案是 (C)。

字彙 forward 傳達　emergency personnel 急救人員

46 特定細節問題

翻譯 女子在詢問什麼事？
(A) 是否能拖吊卡車
(B) 是否有阻礙交通
(C) 是什麼原因導致延誤了
(D) 應該何時去接男子

解析 仔細聆聽女子說的話「Is the vehicle blocking traffic where it's currently parked?」，她問停車的位置會阻礙交通嗎，因此答案是 (B)。

字彙 cause 促使

Questions 47-49 refer to the following conversation.

M: Cindy, ⁴⁷could you drive some people to the employee retreat this weekend?
W: I thought we had hired a bus.
M: We reserved two, but the bus company just informed me that ⁴⁸one of the buses had an accident this morning, and their mechanic is out of town this week.
W: Oh, I see. I don't mind driving, and I have room for six others in my SUV.
M: You've made my job a lot easier. I really appreciate this.
W: If you need another vehicle, you should ask Bob Granger in marketing.
M: Do you think he'd be willing to drive?
W: Yes, and ⁴⁹he has a 15-passenger van.

retreat 郊遊 hire（短時間）出租 inform 通知 mechanic 技師
be out of town 出城、在外地 mind 相關、介意 room 空間
be willing to 樂意

翻譯 問題 47-49，請參考以下對話。
男：Cindy，⁴⁷你這個週末可以載幾名員工去郊遊嗎？
女：我還以為我們會請遊覽車。
男：我們請了兩輛遊覽車，但遊覽車公司突然通知 ⁴⁸其中一輛今天早上出車禍，而且技師這個星期出遠門。
女：啊，原來如此，我開車是沒關係，我的休旅車可以載六個人。
男：多虧有你才能讓事情變簡單多了，真的很謝謝你。
女：如果還需要車，那就去問行銷部的 Bob Granger 吧。
男：你覺得他會樂意開車嗎？
女：對，而且 ⁴⁹他有 15 人座的廂型車。

47 請求問題

翻譯 男子請女子做什麼？
(A) 提供交通工具。
(B) 選擇目的地。
(C) 進行購買。
(D) 確認資訊。

解析 仔細聆聽男子提出要求的部分「could you drive some people to the employee retreat this weekend?」，他詢問女子這個週末能否載幾名員工去參加郊遊，從這句話可知道男子要求女子提供交通工具，因此答案是 (A)。
換句話說
drive 接送 → Provide transportation 提供交通工具

字彙 destination 目的地、終點 verify 確認，驗證

48 特定細節問題

翻譯 今天早上發生了什麼事？
(A) 遊覽車受損了。
(B) 活動日期變更了。
(C) 僱用了技師。
(D) 確定預約了。

解析 仔細聆聽與問題關鍵詞 this morning 相關的部分，男子說「one of the buses had an accident this morning, and their mechanic is out of town this week.」，表示其中一輛遊覽車早上發生車禍，而且技師這個星期去出差，由此可知遊覽車毀損的事實，因此答案是 (A)。

字彙 reschedule 變更行程 confirm 確認

49 提及何事的問題

翻譯 關於 Bob Granger，有談到什麼？
(A) 他是一名專業駕駛。
(B) 他有一臺大型車。
(C) 他是活動主辦者。
(D) 他很清楚郊遊場所的位置。

解析 仔細聆聽與問題核心（Bob Granger）相關的內容，女子說「he[Bob Granger] has a 15-passenger van.」，表示 Bob Granger 有 15 人座的廂型車，因此答案是 (B)。

字彙 automobile 車（輛） organizer 主辦人、組織者

Questions 50-52 refer to the following conversation.

M: I was just in the conference room to set up for the board meeting this afternoon, and ⁵⁰I discovered that the projector won't turn on. I think it might be broken.
W: Oh, the projector isn't broken. ⁵¹I unplugged the power cord earlier today in order to use the outlet. I must have forgotten to plug it back in after recharging my cell phone.
M: I see. Well, I've never noticed an outlet in that room. ⁵²Can you tell me where it's located?
W: Sure. It's on the wall opposite the door. There's a table in front of it, which you'll have to move to plug in the cord.

set up 安排、搭建 board meeting 董事會 discover 查出、發現
turn on 開啟 broken 故障的 unplug 拔插頭 power cord 電線
outlet 插座 recharge（再）充電

翻譯 問題 50-52，請參考以下對話。
男：我剛剛在會議室準備今天下午的董事會，⁵⁰發現投影機沒辦法開啟，我覺得應該是故障了。
女：啊，那個投影機不是故障了，⁵¹今天稍早我要使用插座，所以把投影機的插頭拔掉了。我的手機充好電後，一定忘了把投影機的插頭插回去。
男：原來如此，嗯，我完全沒看到那個房間有插座，⁵²可以告訴我在哪裡嗎？
女：沒問題，插座就在門對面的牆壁上，插座前面有一張桌子，想插電就得移動桌子。

50 問題點問題

翻譯 男子談到什麼問題？
(A) 任務尚未完成。
(B) 文件遺失了。
(C) 機器無法啟動。
(D) 辦公室目前正在使用中。

解析 仔細聆聽男子在交談時使用的否定表達方式，他說「I discovered that the projector won't turn on」，表示發現投影機無法啟動，因此答案是 (C)。

換句話說
projector won't turn on 投影機無法啟動 → device is not working 機器無法運作

字彙 assignment（分派的）任務　complete 完成
lost（物品）遺失的　device 機器、裝置　be in use 正在使用

51 特定細節問題

翻譯 女子今天稍早做了什麼事？
(A) 她測試了投影機。
(B) 她把電池充電了。
(C) 她弄丟電話了。
(D) 她參加會議了。

解析 仔細聆聽與關鍵詞 earlier today 相關的部分，女子說「I unplugged the power cord earlier today ~. I must have forgotten to plug it back in after recharging my cell phone.」，表示自己稍早為了讓手機充電，所以拔掉投影機的插頭，後來忘了插回去，由此可知她今天稍早把電池充電了，因此答案是 (B)。

字彙 test 測試　charge 充電、收費

52 特定細節問題

翻譯 男子詢問女子什麼事？
(A) 插座的位置
(B) 電線的長度
(C) 房間的大小
(D) 桌子的高度

解析 仔細聆聽男子說的話「Can you tell me where it[outlet]'s located?」，他詢問是否可以告知插座的位置，因此答案是 (A)。

字彙 length 長度　height 高度

53-55 美國發音→加拿大發音→澳洲發音

Questions 53-55 refer to the following conversation with three speakers.

W: Chris, have you met Nick Walters here? [53]He's just joined our company and will help us prepare the annual financial reports.
M1: Oh, that's great. It's nice to meet you, Nick. Have you worked for an investment bank like ours before?
M2: Yes, actually. I was a financial manager at Opus Investments for about five years.

M1: [54]That's quite a renowned corporation! Well, I'm glad to have you on the team. Is your desk on the ninth floor?
W: It is. He'll be sitting right next to me. [55]Let me lead you there now, Nick.
M2: All right, then. It was a pleasure meeting you, Chris.

---

join 進入公司、參加　financial 會計的、財務的
investment bank 投資銀行　renowned 知名的　lead 帶領

翻譯 問題 53-55，請參考以下三方對話。
女：Chris，你曾見過 Nick Walters 嗎？[53] 他剛來我們的公司，他會幫忙我們準備年度財務報告。
男 1：啊，太好了，Nick，很高興認識你，你先前曾在像我們這樣的投資銀行工作嗎？
男 2：是，我有相關的工作經驗，我曾經在 Opus Investments 公司大約當了 5 年的財務長。
男 1：[54] 那間公司滿有名的！總之我很開心你能加入我們的團隊，你的座位在 9 樓嗎？
女：對，他將會坐在我隔壁，[55] Nick，我帶你去那邊吧。
男 2：好，Chris，認識你很開心。

53 特定細節問題

翻譯 從女子的話來看，每年都要準備什麼？
(A) 財務文件
(B) 產業大會
(C) 教育課程
(D) 投資計劃

解析 仔細聆聽與關鍵句 prepared every year 相關的部分，女子說「He[Nick Walters]~ will help us prepare the annual financial reports.」，表示他會協助準備財務報告，由此可知每年都要準備財務文件，因此答案是 (A)。

54 提及何事的問題

翻譯 關於 Opus Investments 公司有談到哪些事？
(A) 是一間知名的公司。
(B) 位於 9 樓。
(C) 是新成立的公司。
(D) 目前正在重新配置員工。

解析 仔細聆聽與關鍵詞 Opus Investments 相關的內容，男子 1 說「That[Opus Investments]'s quite a renowned corporation!」，表示 Opus Investments 公司是一間知名的公司，因此答案是 (A)。

字彙 well-known 知名的、聞名的　relocate 配置、遷移

55 提議問題

翻譯 女子提議要做什麼？
(A) 準備和管理階層之間的會議。
(B) 帶同事去辦公室。
(C) 安排公司聚會的位子。
(D) 參觀導覽生產工廠。

解析 仔細聆聽與女子提議相關的內容「Let me lead you there[Nick's desk] now, Nick.」，她說要帶 Nick 前往辦公座位，因此答案是 (B)。

字彙 supervisor 主管、監督者　arrange 配置　gathering 聚會
give a tour 讓～參觀　production facility 生產工廠

56-58 [澳] 澳洲發音→美國發音

Questions 56-58 refer to the following conversation.

> M: Beth, I heard that you're giving a presentation at the Dumont Conference Center next week.
> W: That's right. It's for a group of investors interested in one of our company's upcoming projects. [56]I'm a little worried, though. I've never been to the center. And I'm not sure what kind of audiovisual equipment is set up in the rooms.
> M: Can't you just ask someone who works there?
> W: [57]It's closed this week. I guess the lobby is being remodeled.
> M: Hmm . . . Maybe you should speak to Molly Martin in the research department. She attended a workshop at the center last month. So [58]she'll be able to give you the information you need. Her extension is 459.

investor 投資者　upcoming 即將到來　audiovisual 視聽的
set up 設置　remodel 改造　extension 電話分機

翻譯 問題 56-58，請參考以下對話。
　　男：Beth，聽說你下星期要在 Dumont 會議中心進行簡報。
　　女：對，對方是一群對我們公司即將推出的專案感興趣的投資人，[56] 但我有點擔心，因為我不曾去過那個會議中心，我不太清楚裡面裝設了哪些類型的視聽設備。
　　男：不能問在那邊工作的人嗎？
　　女：[57] 那個會議中心這個星期休息，大廳好像在維修。
　　男：嗯……最好能和研究部的 Molly Martin 說一下，她上個月有去參加在那個會議中心舉辦的研討會，所以 [58] 她應該能提供你想要的資訊，她的分機號碼是 459。

56 問題點問題

翻譯 女子的問題是什麼？
　　(A) 無法觀看簡報。
　　(B) 無法參加活動。
　　(C) 無法租借設備。
　　(D) 對某場地不了解。

解析 仔細聆聽女子話中使用負面表達的部分「I'm a little worried, though. I've never been to the center.」，她說自己有點擔心，因為她不曾去過會議中心，由此可知女子對場地不熟悉，因此答案是 (D)。
換句話說
have never been to the center 不曾去過會議中心 → is unfamiliar with a venue 對場地不太熟悉

字彙 unfamiliar 不熟悉

57 理由問題

翻譯 Dumont 會議中心為什麼這星期沒有開放？
　　(A) 正在維修中。
　　(B) 大廳在打掃。
　　(C) 為了準備活動。
　　(D) 在更新音響系統。

解析 仔細聆聽與關鍵詞 closed this week 相關的部分，女子說「It[Dumont Conference Center]'s closed this week. I guess the lobby is being remodeled.」，表示 Dumont 會議中心這個星期沒有開放，而且大廳好像在維修，因此答案是 (A)。

字彙 renovate 翻新

58 方法問題

翻譯 女子該怎麼做才能取得想要的資訊？
　　(A) 和投資者見面
　　(B) 參加研討會
　　(C) 打電話給同事
　　(D) 上網站

解析 仔細聆聽與關鍵句 information ~ requires 相關的內容，男子說「she[Molly Martin]'ll be able to give you the information you need. Her extension is 459.」，表示可以去向 Molly Martin 取得需要的資訊，並告知對方的分機號碼，由此可知透過電話就能取得需要的資訊，因此答案是 (C)。

字彙 coworker 同事

59-61 [加] 加拿大發音→美國發音

Questions 59-61 refer to the following conversation.

> M: [59]I'm trying to decide which of these boats would best suit my needs, but I can't. Would you mind giving me a recommendation?
> W: Of course. [60]We offer over 20 different fishing boats, so I can understand why you're struggling to make up your mind. Are you interested in any specific features?
> M: I'd like one that has fishing rod holders and a built-in cooler for food and drinks. It should also seat at least four people.
> W: We have three models that meet those criteria. [61]Follow me, and I'll show them to you.

suit 合適　needs 需要、要求　recommendation 推薦
offer 待售、提供　struggle 奮鬥　make up one's mind 決定
specific 具體的、特定的　fishing rod 釣竿　built-in 內建的
seat 容納、就座　meet 滿足（需要、需求等）
criterion 基準（criteria 的單數形）

翻譯 問題 59-61，請參考以下對話。
　　男：[59] 我要從這些船當中挑出一艘最適合我的，卻做不到，你能推薦一下嗎？
　　女：沒問題，[60] 我們有超過 20 款不同的釣漁船，所以我能理解您為何遲遲無法做出決定。您有感興趣的具體特點嗎？

男：我想要有釣竿支架，以及可保存食物與飲料的內建冰箱，而且至少要能容納四個人。

女：我們有三種型號都符合這些標準，⁶¹ 請跟我來，我帶您去看型號。

59 特定細節問題

翻譯 男子需要何種幫忙？
(A) 尋找座位
(B) 退貨
(C) 預約旅行
(D) 選擇產品

解析 仔細聆聽與關鍵字 assistance 相關的內容，男子說「I'm trying to decide which of these boats would best suit my needs, but I can't. Would you mind giving me a recommendation?」，表示想要找最合適自己的船，卻遲遲無法決定，於是詢問女子是否能推薦，因此答案是 (D)。

換句話說
decide which of ~ boats would best suit ~ needs 決定哪一艘船最合乎需求 → Selecting a product 選擇產品

字彙 assistance 協助

60 說話者問題

翻譯 女子最可能是誰？
(A) 導遊
(B) 船長
(C) 顧客
(D) 銷售員

解析 仔細聆聽與身分、職業相關的表達方式，女子說「We offer over 20 different fishing boats, so I can understand why you're struggling to make up your mind.」，表達店裡有超過 20 種釣漁船，能夠理解男子難以抉擇的理由，由此可知女子是銷售員，因此答案是 (D)。

字彙 tour guide 導遊　captain 船長　salesperson 銷售員

61 之後將發生的事

翻譯 男子接下來最可能做什麼事？
(A) 觀看一些船隻。
(B) 去其他賣場。
(C) 觀看彩排。
(D) 訂購食物。

解析 仔細聆聽交談內容的最後部分，女子說「Follow me, and I'll show them[models] to you.」，請男子跟著自己一起走，並表示要讓他觀看船隻的模型，由此可知男子接下來要去看船，因此答案是 (A)。

字彙 examine 仔細查看　demonstration 示範

62-64 英國發音→澳洲發音

Questions 62-64 refer to the following conversation and floor plans.

W: Hi. My name is Carla Farrow. ⁶²I have an appointment with Bruce Zimmerman, the accounting manager, at 3 P.M. We're meeting to discuss the annual tax report.

M: Oh, yes. He is expecting you. You can go right in to meet with him now. ⁶³He is already waiting in the meeting room. It's right next to the elevator.

W: Great. Is there a bathroom that I can use first?

M: Yes. There is one in the break room. ⁶⁴I'm going to bring some drinks in a few minutes. Would you like a coffee or water? We also have some sodas.

W: ⁶⁴Some water would be nice.

appointment 約定　accounting 會計
annual 年度的、每年的　break room 休息室

翻譯 問題 62-64，請參考以下對話。

女：你好，我是 Carla Farrow，⁶² 我和會計部經理 Bruce Zimmerman 約好下午 3 點見面，我們要一起商討年度稅務報告。

男：啊，是，他正期待您到來呢，只要進去就能見到他。⁶³ 他已經在會議室等了，會議室就在電梯旁邊而已。

女：真不錯，這裡有化妝室讓我先使用嗎？

男：是，休息室裡有一間化妝室，⁶⁴ 幾分鐘後我會帶飲料過去，您要喝咖啡還是喝水呢？我們也有碳酸飲料。

女：⁶⁴ 給我水就好了。

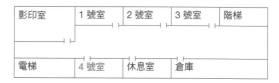

影印室	1 號室	2 號室	3 號室	階梯
電梯	4 號室	休息室	倉庫	

62 特定細節問題

翻譯 Zimmerman 先生最可能是什麼人？
(A) 部門經理
(B) 實習生
(C) 接待員
(D) 營業部長

解析 仔細聆聽與身分、職業相關的表達方式，女子說「I have an appointment with Bruce Zimmerman, the accounting manager, at 3 P.M.」，表示自己下午三點和會計部經理 Bruce Zimmerman 有約，由此可知 Zimmerman 先生是部門經理，因此答案是 (A)。

字彙 receptionist 接待員、受理人員

63 圖片題

翻譯 請看圖片，會議將在哪裡進行？
　　(A) 1 號室
　　(B) 2 號室
　　(C) 3 號室
　　(D) 4 號室

解析 確認平面圖的資訊後，仔細聆聽與關鍵詞 meeting be held 相關的內容，男子說「He[Bruce Zimmerman]is already waiting in the meeting room. It's right next to the elevator.」，表示 Bruce Zimmerman 已經在會議室裡等，而會議室就在電梯旁邊，從平面圖中可知道是在 4 號室進行會議，因此答案是 (D)。

64 特定細節問題

翻譯 女子將很快會收到什麼？
　　(A) 飲料
　　(B) 文件
　　(C) 房間鑰匙
　　(D) 密碼

解析 仔細聆聽與關鍵句 woman receive shortly 相關的內容，男子說「I'm going to bring some drinks in a few minutes. Would you like a coffee or water?」，表示幾分鐘後會帶飲料過去，詢問需要咖啡或水，女子回答給自己水就好了（Some water would be nice.），因此答案是 (A)。

換句話說
shortly 很快地 → in a few minutes 幾分鐘後

字彙 shortly 即將、很快地　pass code 密碼、暗號

65-67 🎧 加拿大發音→英國發音

Questions 65-67 refer to the following conversation and table.

M: Good afternoon. My name is Ben Jenkins, and I'm checking out of Room 405. ⁶⁵Could I get my bill?
W: Certainly, Mr. Jenkins. I'll just pull up your information on the computer. Let's see . . . you canceled the last night of your booking, which means you were only here for one night, right?
M: That's correct.
W: And you didn't order any room service . . . So the total amount owed is $250 plus tax.
M: Oh, ⁶⁶that's unexpected. ⁶⁶/⁶⁷I thought the rate for my room was higher.
W: ⁶⁷It usually is. The regular price is $270 a night. But we're only charging you $250 as part of a special summer promotion.

---

bill 帳單　certainly 毫無疑問、當然　pull up 帶來、停下
booking 預約　owe 有支付的義務　unexpected 出乎預料之外
promotion 促銷活動

翻譯 問題 65-67，請參考以下對話。
　　男：午安，我是 Ben Jenkins，405 號要退房，⁶⁵ 可以給我帳單嗎？

女：沒問題，Jenkins 先生，我先用電腦取得您的顧客資料，我看看……預約的最後一個晚上取消，所以只有在這裡待一個晚上，對嗎？
男：對。
女：而且您沒有使用客房服務……那要支付的金額，含稅後總共是 250 美金。
男：啊，⁶⁶ 真是出乎預料，我還以為我的房間費用會更高一點。
女：⁶⁷ 通常是這樣，定價是一晚 270 美金，但因為有夏季特殊促銷活動，所以只需要 250 美金。

客房類型	定價
標準	250 美金
⁶⁷ 高級	270 美金
豪華	300 美金
奢華	350 美金

65 請求問題

翻譯 男子向女子提出何種要求？
　　(A) 退錢
　　(B) 對帳單
　　(C) 新的客房
　　(D) 優惠

解析 仔細聆聽男子提出要求的相關表達方式，男子問「Could I get my bill?」，詢問能否看一下帳單，由此可知男子請女子提供對帳單，因此答案是 (B)。

換句話說
bill 帳單 → statement 對帳單

字彙 statement 對帳單

66 理由相關問題

翻譯 男子為何覺得驚訝？
　　(A) 價格和他想的不一樣。
　　(B) 客房狀況不太好。
　　(C) 信用卡被拒絕了。
　　(D) 因太晚退房，所以要支付費用。

解析 仔細聆聽與關鍵字 surprised 相關的內容，男子說「that[$250]'s unexpected. I thought the rate for my room was higher.」，表示 250 美金是出乎意料之外的價錢，本以為自己的客房價格會更高，因此答案是 (A)。

換句話說
thought the rate ~ was higher 本以為費用更高 → was expecting a different price 本來認為是其他價錢

字彙 expect 期待　decline 拒絕

67 圖表題

翻譯 請看圖表，男子住的是哪一種房型？
　　(A) 標準
　　(B) 高級
　　(C) 豪華
　　(D) 奢華

解析 確認表格上的資料後，仔細聆聽和關鍵句 room ~ man

stay in 相關的內容，男子說「I thought the rate for my room was higher.」，表示原本以為自己的房間價格會更高，女子則回答「It usually is. The regular price is $270 a night.」，說明正常一晚的價格是 270 美金。因定價每晚是 270 美金，由此可知男子住在 270 美金的高級房型，因此答案是 (B)。

68-70 🎧 英國發音→加拿大發音

Questions 68-70 refer to the following conversation and transit map.

> W: Hello. ⁶⁸I moved to this city recently, and I am wondering . . . How do I get to city hall? Can you help me?
> M: Well, taking the 405 bus is the best way. However, ⁶⁹there's construction being done on the route between Kensington Avenue and Canterbury Avenue, so it is temporarily blocked. The bus will have to make a detour, which will take a lot of time.
> W: Hmm . . . Is there a faster way? I actually don't have much time. City hall closes in an hour.
> M: In that case, ⁷⁰taking a taxi might be a better idea.
> W: How long will that take?
> M: No more than about 30 minutes.
> W: ⁷⁰I think I'll do that then. Thank you.
>
> ---
>
> wonder 想知道　construction 建設、工程　route 路線
> temporarily 暫時　make a detour 繞道

翻譯 問題 68-70，請參考以下對話及交通系統地圖。

女：你好，⁶⁸ 我最近剛搬來這個城市，我想知道要怎麼去市政府？你可以幫忙我嗎？

男：嗯，搭乘 405 號公車會是最好的方法，只不過 ⁶⁹ Kensington 街和 Canterbury 街之間的路線正在施工，所以目前暫時封閉。公車必須繞路，會花費很多時間。

女：嗯……有更快的方法嗎？其實我的時間不多，市政府一個小時後就會關門。

男：既然如此，⁷⁰ 搭計程車應該是更好的選擇。

女：需要多久的時間？

男：大概不超過 30 分鐘。

女：⁷⁰ 那我應該會搭計程車，謝謝你。

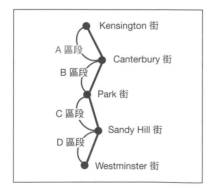

---

68 特定細節問題

翻譯 女子最近做了什麼？

(A) 搬到新的城市。
(B) 獲得工作機會。
(C) 去了公共行政機關。
(D) 購買通行券。

解析 問題是在詢問女子最近做的事情，仔細聆聽與關鍵字 recently 相關的部分，女子說「I moved to this city recently」，表示自己最近搬來這座城市，因此答案是 (A)。

換句話說
moved 搬家了 → Relocated 搬遷了

字彙 government office 公共行政機關　transit pass 通行券

---

69 圖片題

翻譯 請看圖片，哪一個區段暫時封閉了？

(A) A 區段
(B) B 區段
(C) C 區段
(D) D 區段

解析 確認題目的交通系統地圖後，仔細聆聽與關鍵詞 temporarily closed 相關的內容，男子說「there's construction being done on the route between Kensington Avenue and Canterbury Avenue, so it is temporarily blocked」，表示 Kensington 街和 Canterbury 街之間的路線施工中，因此暫時封閉，從圖片中可知道 A 區段暫時封閉，因此答案是 (A)。

換句話說
is ~ blocked 封閉 → is ~ closed 封閉

字彙 segment 部分、區段

---

70 之後將發生的事

翻譯 女子之後要做什麼？

(A) 去公車站。
(B) 檢查建設工地。
(C) 搭計程車。
(D) 重新安排會面。

解析 注意聆聽對話的最後部分，男子說「taking a taxi might be a better idea」，表示搭計程車是更好的選擇，女子回答「I think I'll do that then.」，回覆自己應該會搭計程車，因此答案是 (C)。

字彙 inspect 查看、核查

PART 4

71-73 加拿大發音

Questions 71-73 refer to the following advertisement.

Are you anxious about the stuff that has accumulated in your home this winter? Don't worry about it! Let Stressless Cleaners take care of it for you. [71]Our specialists can handle everything from tidying up your house to disposing of unwanted clothing and electronics devices. We can even help sort out stored items in garages and sheds. [72]Until May 12, you can take advantage of our special spring cleaning offer. All customers who book a four-hour session will get 25 percent off. So, don't delay for another minute! [73]Visit our website to arrange a date and time today.

anxious 憂慮的、擔心的　accumulate 堆積　take care of 看管
specialist 專家　handle 處理（事情）　tidy up 整理乾淨
dispose of 清除　electronic device 電子設備　sort out 處理
store 保管　shed 倉庫　take advantage of 利用
spring cleaning 春季大掃除　offer 優惠　arrange 決定

翻譯 問題 71-73，請參考以下廣告。
　　您是否擔心今天冬天家裡堆積的物品呢？請別擔心！請讓 Stressless Cleaners 為您處理吧！[71] 我們的專家會幫您把家裡打掃乾淨，並處理所有不需要的衣物、電子用品，我們還能協助整理車庫與倉庫保管的物品。[72] 5 月 12 日為止可享有春季大掃除特別優惠，預約 4 小時作業時間的所有顧客都能獲得打 75 折的優惠。因此，連片刻都別猶豫了！[73] 若是想決定日期與時間，今天就請到我們的官網吧。

71 主題問題

翻譯 是哪一類的業者在打廣告？
(A) 裝潢設計公司
(B) 清潔公司
(C) 不動產仲介業者
(D) 家電產品零售店

解析 題目詢問廣告主題，一定要聽清楚短文剛開始的內容。
　　「Our specialists can handle everything from tidying up your house to disposing of unwanted clothing and electronics devices.」，意思是專家會幫忙把家裡清理乾淨，甚至也會清除不需要的衣物與電子用品，由此可知這是打掃公司的廣告，因此答案是 (B)。

字彙 real estate 不動產　retailer 零售店

72 特定細節問題

翻譯 聽眾在 5 月 12 日前可獲得什麼？
(A) 產品樣本
(B) 免費諮詢
(C) 禮品券
(D) 優惠服務

解析 仔細聆聽與關鍵詞 until May 12 相關的部分，廣告說「Until May 12, you can take advantage of our special spring cleaning offer. All customers who book a four-hour session will get 25 percent off.」，表示到 5 月 12 日為止可享有春季大掃除特別優惠，所有預約 4 小時的顧客都能獲得 75 折，因此答案是 (D)。

字彙 consultation 諮詢　gift certificate 商品券

73 理由問題

翻譯 聽眾為何必須進入網站？
(A) 為了付錢
(B) 為了預約
(C) 為了下載優惠券
(D) 為了填寫問卷

解析 仔細聆聽與關鍵詞 visit the website 相關的內容，廣告說「Visit our website to arrange a date and time today.」，表示想要決定日期與時間就在今天登入網站，因此答案是 (B)。
　　換句話說
　　arrange a date and time 決定日期與時間 → schedule an appointment 預約

字彙 make payment 支付　complete 填寫　questionnaire 問卷

74-76 澳洲發音

Questions 74-76 refer to the following telephone message.

Hello, I'm calling for Janine Freeman. This is Jaehyun Kim from JetPeak Airlines. [74]You filed a missing luggage claim for your flight on March 14. Well, your bag was found by one of our baggage handlers. It will be delivered to your home tomorrow afternoon. However, it appears that your suitcase has sustained some light damage. [75]To receive compensation for the damage, you need to send completed application forms to our corporate office. After this call, [76]I will e-mail the forms with instructions on how to fill them out. Please call me at 555-6793 if you have any questions.

file 正式繳交（文件等）　missing luggage 遺失的行李
claim 通知書、索取　baggage 旅行袋、行李
handler 負責人、處理者　sustain 造成（損失）
compensation 索賠、賠償　application form 申請書
instruction 說明

翻譯 問題 74-76，請參考以下電話訊息。
　　您好，我要找 Janine Freeman，我是 JetPeak 航空公司的 Jaehyun Kim，[74] 您針對 3 月 14 日航班的遺失行李提交了相關申請書。嗯，我們的行李裝卸人員發現了您的背包，明天下午就會送到您府上。但您的旅行背包有輕微的毀損，[75] 如果想取得賠償的話，必須將填妥的申請書寄到我們公司的辦公室。通話結束後，[76] 我會把表格與填寫方式的相關說明寄到您的電子信箱。如果有任何疑問，請來電至 555-6793。

74 主題問題

翻譯 說話者主要在說什麼？
(A) 最新政策
(B) 退票
(C) 遺失的物品
(D) 停飛的航班

解析 題目詢問訊息的主題，一定要聽清楚短文剛開始的內容。訊息中談到「You filed a missing luggage claim for your flight on March 14.」，指出乘客針對 3 月 14 日航班遺失的物品繳交申請書，之後就開始談失物的相關內容，因此答案是 (C)。

字彙 misplaced 遺失的

75 特定細節問題

翻譯 Freeman 女士該怎麼做才能獲得賠償？
(A) 繳交文件。
(B) 出示票券。
(C) 與行李裝卸人員交談。
(D) 退還毀損的產品。

解析 仔細聆聽關鍵句 receive compensation 相關的部分「To receive compensation for the damage, you[Ms. Freeman] need to send completed application forms to our corporate office.」，其中說明如果想獲得賠償，Freeman 女士必須將填妥的申請書寄至公司辦公室，因此答案是 (A)。

換句話說
send completed application forms to ~ office 填妥的申請書寄至辦公室 → Submit some paperwork 繳交文件

字彙 submit 繳交　paperwork 文件

76 之後將發生的事

翻譯 說話者之後要做什麼？
(A) 查看旅行背包。
(B) 前往辦公室。
(C) 確認付款。
(D) 寄送電子郵件。

解析 仔細聆聽短文的最後部分，說話者說「I will e-mail the forms with instructions on how to fill them out.」，表示會把表格與填寫方式的相關說明寄到電子信箱，因此答案是 (D)。

字彙 inspect 審視　confirm 確認

77-79 🎧 加拿大發音

Questions 77-79 refer to the following introduction.

[77]I appreciate all of you attending the third annual seminar for writers on Gibbons Island. We have plenty of activities planned for the weekend that will help you develop your skills and get to know your fellow authors. But first, I'd like to introduce the keynote speaker for this year's retreat, Jill Holloway. You've probably heard her name. [78]Ms. Holloway started out as a working mother who wrote in her free time ⏵

and eventually became a best-selling novelist. [79]Today, she is going to talk for a few minutes about her career. Please join me in welcoming her to the stage.

---

plenty of 大量　get to know 了解　fellow 同伴的、朋友的
keynote speaker 主講人　free time 空閒時間　novelist 小說家
career 職涯經歷

翻譯 問題 77-79，請參考以下介紹。
[77]感謝各位蒞臨 Gibbons 島舉辦的第三屆年度作家研討會，這個週末我們準備了很多能提升各位技巧和認識其他作家的活動。不過首先，我要介紹今年活動的主講人 Jill Holloway，各位大概都聽過她的名字，[78]Holloway 女士是一名在職媽媽，剛開始都是利用空閒時間寫作，後來成為了暢銷小說家。[79]今天她將會和我們談一下自己的職涯經歷，請和我一起歡迎她上臺吧。

77 地點問題

翻譯 聽眾最可能在哪裡？
(A) 退休紀念派對
(B) 寫作研討會
(C) 美術展
(D) 頒獎典禮

解析 仔細聆聽短文中與場所相關的部分「I appreciate all of you attending the third annual seminar for writers ~. We have plenty of activities planned ~ that will help you develop your skills and get to know your fellow authors.」，說話者感謝各位參加 Gibbons 島舉辦的第三屆年度作家研討會後，接著說這個週末準備了很多能提升各位技巧和認識其他作家的活動，由此可知聽眾們在參加研討會，因此答案是 (B)。

字彙 retirement 退休、退職　exhibit 展覽
award ceremony 頒獎典禮

78 意圖掌握問題

翻譯 說話者說「各位大概都聽過她的名字」，他的意思是什麼？
(A) 先前已經談過 Jill Holloway。
(B) Jill Holloway 參加過先前的活動。
(C) Jill Holloway 最近獲獎了。
(D) Jill Holloway 很有名。

解析 仔細聆聽與引用句（You've probably heard her name）相關的部分，「Ms. Holloway started out as a working mother who wrote in her free time and eventually became a best-selling novelist.」，說明 Holloway 女士是一名在職媽媽，剛開始是利用空閒時間寫作，後來成為了暢銷作家，由此可知 Holloway 女士很有名，因此答案是 (D)。

79 之後將發生的事

翻譯 聽眾接下來最可能要做什麼？
(A) 討論書。
(B) 登記研討會。
(C) 短暫休息。

(D) 聽演講。

解析 仔細聆聽短文最後的部分「Today, she[Ms. Holloway] is going to talk for a few minutes about her career. Please join me in welcoming her to the stage」，主持人在說完今天對方會和聽眾談主講人的職涯經歷後，就請大家一起歡迎她上臺，由此可知聽眾接下來要聽演講，因此答案是 (D)。

字彙 brief 簡短的　speech 演講

80-82 🎧 澳洲發音

Questions 80-82 refer to the following excerpt from a meeting.

In order to stay competitive with other companies, [80]we're going to change our marketing approach. Right now, most of our advertising budget is spent on television commercials. Moving forward, however, we are going to invest more in online marketing. [81]We've hired a new staff member, Mindy Lineman, to manage our accounts on social media. If you have any questions or suggestions regarding our approach, please direct them to her. Okay . . . our time is almost up, so [82]I'll conclude now. It looks like another team needs to use the conference room.

competitive 具競爭力的　approach 方法、接近
budget 預算　commercial 廣告　invest 投資　manage 管理
account 帳號　regarding 關於～　direct 將～轉給
conclude 結束

翻譯 問題 80-82，請參考以下會議摘錄。
為了維持與其他公司的競爭力，80 我們將改變行銷方法，目前我們的廣告預算大部分都在電視廣告上，但往後我們會投資網路行銷更多一點。為了管理社群媒體的帳號，81 我們聘請了新職員 Mindy Lineman。如果對我們的方法有疑問或有任何提議，希望各位能告訴她。好……時間差不多快到了，82 我就說到這裡為止，其他團隊似乎也要使用會議室了。

80 主題問題

翻譯 說話者主要在談論什麼？
(A) 產品評估
(B) 行銷策略
(C) 職位開缺
(D) 工作時間表

解析 題目詢問會議主題，一定要聽清楚短文的開頭「we're going to change our marketing approach」，在說完將要改變行銷方法後，接著就開始談論新的行銷策略，因此答案是 (B)。

字彙 review 評估、檢討　strategy 策略　job opening 職缺

81 特定細節問題

翻譯 Mindy Lineman 最可能是什麼人？
(A) 公司高層
(B) 企業顧問

(C) 求職者
(D) 新進職員

解析 仔細聆聽與 Mindy Lineman 的身分、職業相關的內容「We've hired a new staff member, Mindy Lineman」，說明公司僱用了新職員 Mindy Lineman，因此答案是 (D)。

字彙 executive 高層、經營團隊　consultant 顧問、諮詢師
job applicant 求職者　hire 新進職員

82 意圖掌握問題

翻譯 說話者為何說「時間差不多快到了」？
(A) 會議行程必須變更。
(B) 截止期限快到了。
(C) 會議差不多該結束了。
(D) 業務還沒完成。

解析 仔細聆聽與引用句（our time is almost up）有關的部分「I'll conclude now. It looks like another team needs to use the conference room.」，內容談到我說到這裡為止，其他團隊似乎也要使用會議室，由此可知會議要結束了，因此答案是 (C)。

字彙 reschedule 變更行程　approach 接近　complete 完成

83-85 🎧 英國發音

Questions 83-85 refer to the following instruction.

For the last part of today's training session, I'd like to explain how to process a product return. When a customer brings an item back to our store, [83]you should first check the receipt to find out when the purchase was made. Keep in mind that refunds cannot be issued after 10 days. Next, inspect the product carefully. [84]If you see any damage, notify your supervisor immediately and let him or her decide whether a refund can be given. [85]The final step is to have the customer fill out and sign a request form. It must include the reason for returning the item. That's it . . . Any questions?

training session 培訓課程　process 處理　find out 查明
keep in mind 記住　issue 頒發　notify 通知　immediately 立即
request form 申請書　include 包含

翻譯 問題 83-85，請參考以下說明。
今天培訓的最後一個階段，我想介紹處理退貨的方法，當客人把商品帶回賣場時，83 各位要先確認收據，了解一下購買時間。請記住如果超過 10 天就無法退款，之後請詳細觀察商品，84 如果發現任何毀損，要立即向主管報告，決定是否予以退款。85 最後客人要填寫申請書和簽名，一定要填寫退貨的理由，我的說明到此結束……有任何問題嗎？

83 特定細節問題

翻譯 根據說話者的介紹，處理退貨時必須先做什麼？
(A) 進行寄送。
(B) 檢查商品。

(C) 確認日期。

(D) 退款。

解析 仔細聆聽問題的核心（done first），「you should first check the receipt to find out when the purchase was made」，內容談到必須先確認收據，了解購買時間，因此答案是 (C)。

換句話說
find out when the purchase was made 了解購買時間 → Confirm a date 確認日期

字彙 examine 檢查

84 理由問題

翻譯 為何聽者必須聯絡上司？

(A) 為了告知商品受損

(B) 為了確認某項要求是否已處理

(C) 為了取得某些書面文件

(D) 為了提供退貨理由

解析 仔細聆聽問題中的關鍵詞 contact a supervisor，「If you see any damage, notify your supervisor immediately」，表示如果發現任何損壞，請立即通知主管，因此答案是 (A)。

字彙 report 呈報、報告　paperwork 文件、文書工作

85 特定細節問題

翻譯 聽者必須請顧客做什麼？

(A) 填寫表格。

(B) 購物。

(C) 取消付款。

(D) 簽約。

解析 仔細聆聽與關鍵句 ask customers to do 相關的內容，「The final step is to have the customer fill out and sign a request form.」，內容談到最後顧客要填寫申請書和簽名，因此答案是 (A)。

字彙 complete 填寫　sign a contract 簽約

86-88 🎧美國發音

Questions 86-88 refer to the following broadcast.

You are listening to WZRL 95, and this is Kennedy Walker. [86]And now for your local news. For those interested, the annual Summer Festival is being held this weekend at Marigold Park. The festival, sponsored by local business Marty's Cupcakes, will feature a variety of exciting events, including face painting, a relay race, and much more! [87]Please keep in mind that there is limited parking on the streets near the park, so you should take a bus if possible. Now, [88]we'll speak with Marty Peters, the owner of Marty's Cupcakes, and he'll tell us exactly how his bakery is getting involved in this year's festivities.

---

be sponsored by 被～贊助　feature 包括　a variety of 各種的
keep in mind 銘記在心　limited 限定的　festivity 慶典（活動）

翻譯 問題 86-88，請參考以下廣播內容。
各位正在收聽 WZRL 95，我是 Kennedy Walker，現在要播報地區新聞，[86] 先告訴感興趣的聽眾一個消息，一年一度的夏季慶典這個週末將於 Marigold 公園舉行。此一慶典由當地業者 Marty's Cupcakes 贊助，包含臉部彩繪、接力賽等各種有趣的活動！[87] 一定要記得公園附近街道上的停車位有限，最好盡可能搭乘公車。現在，[88] 我們來和 Marty's Cupcakes 的老闆 Marty Peters 聊一下吧！他將告訴我們今年他的麵包店會如何參與這次的慶典活動。

86 主題問題

翻譯 廣播主要在談些什麼？

(A) 交通堵塞

(B) 地區活動

(C) 新餐廳

(D) 校園競賽

解析 題目詢問廣播的主題，一定要聽清楚短文的開頭。廣播者說「And now for your local news. ~ the annual Summer Festival is being held this weekend at Marigold Park.」，表示現在要播報地區新聞後，接著說要告訴感興趣的聽眾一個消息，一年一度的夏季慶典這個週末將於 Marigold 公園舉行，因此答案是 (B)。

字彙 traffic jam 交通堵塞　competition 競賽

87 請求問題

翻譯 廣播建議聽眾做什麼？

(A) 利用大眾運輸工具。

(B) 避開主要高速公路。

(C) 提早報名活動。

(D) 進行慈善捐贈。

解析 仔細聆聽短文後半部與要求相關的句子，內容談到「Please keep in mind that there is limited parking on the streets near the park, so you should take a bus if possible.」，表示務必記得公園附近街道的停車位有限，最好能搭乘公車，因此答案是 (A)。

換句話說
take a bus 搭公車 → Use public transportation 利用大眾運輸工具

字彙 public transportation 大眾運輸工具　major 主要
charitable 慈善的

88 特定細節問題

翻譯 之後會由誰來和聽眾說話？

(A) 氣象主播

(B) 廠商老闆

(C) 地區政治人物

(D) 知名廚師

解析 仔細聆聽關鍵詞 hear from next，內容談到「we'll speak with Marty Peters, the owner of Marty's Cupcakes」，表示將和 Marty's Cupcakes 的老闆 Marty Peters 交談，因此答案是 (B)。

字彙 weather forecaster 氣象主播　politician 政治人物

89-91 🎧 英國發音

Questions 89-91 refer to the following telephone message.

Good afternoon. This is Leslie Schwartz calling for Mr. Harvey Lynch. [89]I just wanted to follow up on the discussion we had last Tuesday about our company's product distribution to local grocery retailers. [90]I've gotten in touch with two major grocery sellers, and they have both expressed interest in our line of dairy products. I'm hoping you might be able to spare some time next week to join me when I meet with the owners of these businesses. [91]They are interested in learning more about our product offerings and prices, so we should consider preparing a short presentation for them. Please call me back as soon as you receive this message at 555-2459.

follow up on 跟進　distribution 配送　get in touch with 與～聯絡
dairy product 乳製品　spare 挪出（時間）　as soon as 一…就…

翻譯 問題 89-91，請參考以下電話訊息。
　　午安，我是 Harvey Lynch 先生，我想要找 Leslie Schwartz。[89] 我想追蹤上星期二我們談到我們公司配送產品至當地雜貨零售商的相關討論，[90] 我已經聯絡過兩個主要雜貨供應商，他們都表示對我們的乳製品很有興趣。我希望您能抽出時間，下星期和我一起見那些業者，[91] 因為他們想更進一步了解我們的產品與價格，我們應該考慮為他們準備一個簡短的報告。收到這個訊息時請來電 555-2459。

89 目的問題

翻譯 說話者為何要打電話？
(A) 為了訂購產品
(B) 為了繼續談話
(C) 為了延長期限
(D) 為了取得建議

解析 題目詢問打電話的目的，一定要聽清楚短文一開始的部分。「I just wanted to follow up on the discussion we had last Tuesday」，內容談到要繼續追蹤上星期二討論的事，由此可知說話者是為了延續談話而打電話的，因此答案是 (B)。
換句話說
follow up on the discussion 追蹤討論 → continue a conversation 延續談話

字彙 extend a deadline 延長期限

90 特定細節問題

翻譯 說話者做了什麼事？
(A) 配送樣品。
(B) 拒絕商業提案。
(C) 聯絡零售商。
(D) 確認價目表。

解析 仔細聆聽與關鍵詞 already done 相關的內容，說話者談到「I've gotten in touch with two major grocery

sellers」，表示已和兩個主要雜貨供應商聯絡了，因此答案是 (C)。
換句話說
have gotten in touch with two ~ grocery sellers 已經和兩處的食品供應商聯絡了 → Contacted some retailers 聯絡了零售商

字彙 turn down 駁回　price list 價目表

91 理由問題

翻譯 為何要準備報告？
(A) 為了分享產品的資訊
(B) 為了介紹新進人員
(C) 為了解說新的服務內容
(D) 為了解說運送過程

解析 仔細聆聽與關鍵詞 presentation be prepared 相關的內容，「They[owners] are interested in learning more about our product offerings and prices, so we should consider preparing a short presentation for them.」，其中談到業者想更進一步了解產品與價格，可以考慮幫他們準備簡報說明，由此可知必須準備產品資訊分享相關的報告，因此答案是 (A)。

字彙 recent hire 新進人員　describe 說明、描寫　shipping 運送

92-94 🎧 加拿大發音

Questions 92-94 refer to the following broadcast.

You're listening to *The Literary Hour* on 103 FM. This afternoon, I'll be interviewing [92]Judith Frost, who recently published the novel *Bright Lights*. [93]This is the final book in Frost's popular series about the American film industry. Before I start the interview, I should mention that [94]there have been some changes to Ms. Frost's book-signing schedule. Many people will likely be disappointed. [94]She will appear at Feldman's Books on Saturday, but all of her later appearances have been postponed. The schedule on her official website will be updated shortly. Now, I'd like to welcome Ms. Frost to the program.

publish 出刊　appearance 出席、登場

翻譯 問題 92-94，請參考以下廣播內容。
　　各位正在收聽 103 FM 的 The Literary Hour，今天下午我將採訪 [92] 近期推出小說《Bright Lights》的 Judith Frost，[93] 這是 Frost 關於美國電影產業的人氣系列小說的最後一本。在採訪前，我要告訴各位 [94] Frost 女士的新書簽名會行程有部分變更事項，大概很多人會覺得很失望吧。[94] 雖然星期六她會出現在 Feldman's Books，但之後的行程都延期了。她的官方網站很快就會更新行程。好了，現在就請 Frost 女士加入我們的節目吧。

92 特定細節問題

翻譯 Judith Frost 最可能是誰？
(A) 文學評論家
(B) 小說家

(C) 節目主持人
(D) 電影導演

解析 仔細聆聽對象（Judith Frost）的身分、職業相關的表達方式，從 Judith Frost 於近期推出新書《Bright Lights》（Judith Frost, who recently published the novel *Bright Lights*）這部分來看，可知道她是小說家，因此答案是(B)。

字彙 literary 文學的　critic 評論家、批評者　host 主持人；主持 film director 電影導演

93 提及何事的問題

翻譯 關於《Bright Lights》，提到了什麼？
(A) 它是一套小說的一部分。
(B) 將會拍成電影。
(C) 新聞有進行專題報導。
(D) 尚未出版。

解析 仔細聆聽與（*Bright Lights*）相關的內容，「This[*Bright Lights*] is the final book in Frost's popular series」，指出《Bright Lights》是 Frost 人氣系列作品的最後一部，由此可知《Bright Lights》只是整個系列的一部分，因此答案是(A)。

換句話說
final book in ~ series 一系列的最後一部 →
part of a collection 全套的一部分

字彙 collection 全套　feature（新聞等）專題報導

94 意圖掌握問題

翻譯 說話者說「大概很多人會覺得很失望吧」，他的意思是什麼？
(A) 來賓取消訪談了。
(B) 可獲得新書簽名會入場券的機會有限。
(C) 最近電影收到負面的評價。
(D) 部分活動會晚一點舉辦。

解析 仔細聆聽問題引用句（Many people will likely be disappointed）的前後文，內容談到「there have been some changes to Ms. Frost's book-signing schedule」，表示 Frost 女士的新書簽名會行程有變更，星期六雖然會現身 Feldman's Books，但之後的活動都要延期（She will appear at Feldman's Books on Saturday, but all of her later appearances have been postponed.），由此可知部分活動會晚一點進行，所以答案是(D)。

字彙 availability 可得性、有用性　limited 受限的、限定的

95-97 [美]美國發音

Questions 95-97 refer to the following announcement and schedule.

I am sorry to announce that we have had to cancel Jacklyn Parkerson's lecture next week. We barely sold any tickets, and it would just not be good for her reputation or ours. [95]I have already informed Ms.

Parkerson and offered her a position on the panel. She will be able to speak for about 10 minutes at the beginning of the panel. She is going to introduce corporate responsibility in the tech industry. [96]She will receive the same fee as she is protected from any loss of compensation under her contract. [97]Could you put up a notice to let everyone know?

barely 幾乎沒有　reputation 名聲、聲望
panel 討論會、委員團　introduce 發表、遞交
corporate responsibility 企業的責任
compensation 賠償金、津貼、報酬　contract 契約　put up 告示

翻譯 問題 95-97，請參考以下公告及時間表。
下星期的 Jacklyn Parkerson 講座已經取消了，我們真的感到很遺憾，我們的票幾乎沒賣出去，這對於她或我們的聲譽都會有不好的影響，[95]我已經將這件事告知 Parkerson 女士，並提議她加入座談小組，她在小組討論的前面階段可發言 10 分鐘左右。她會介紹科技產業裡的企業責任。[96]她將收到同樣的費用，因為合約保護她免受任何的報酬損失，[97]各位可以公告通知所有人嗎？

Horgen 文化中心
系列講座

時間	主題
上午 9 點	工資協商
上午 11 點	建立企業品牌
下午 4 點	金融犯罪
[95] 下午 6 點	小組討論

95 圖片題

翻譯 請看圖片，Parkerson 女士何時要進行演講？
(A)上午 9 點
(B)上午 11 點
(C)下午 4 點
(D)下午 6 點

解析 確認時間表的資訊後，仔細聆聽關鍵詞 Ms. Parkerson 的前後文，內容談到「I have already informed Ms. Parkerson and offered her a position on the panel. She will be able to speak for about 10 minutes at the beginning of the panel.」，表示已經將這件事告知 Parkerson 女士，並提議她加入座談小組，可在小組討論的開頭發言 10 分鐘左右。從表格中可知道 Parkerson 女士在下午 6 點會發言，因此答案是(D)。

96 提及何事的問題

翻譯 說話者談到 Parkerson 女士的什麼事情？
(A) 沒有簽約。
(B) 她的講座會錄影。
(C) 她的酬勞不變。
(D) 她是活動的主講人。

解析 仔細聆聽與 Ms. Parkerson 相關的部分，內容談到「She[Ms. Parkerson] will receive the same fee as she is protected from any loss of compensation under her contract.」，她獲得合約的保護，所有的損失都能獲得賠償，因此答案是 (C)。

換句話說
compensation 報酬 → payment 酬勞

97 請求問題

翻譯 聽者被要求做什麼？
(A) 複習講座。
(B) 貼出公告。
(C) 印出印刷品。
(D) 開啟售票處。

解析 仔細聆聽短文中後半段包含要求相關的句子「Could you put up a notice to let everyone know?」，內容詢問聽者是否能貼出公告，因此答案是 (B)。

換句話說
put up 告示 → Post 張貼

字彙 review 複習　handout 印刷物

98-100

Questions 98-100 refer to the following excerpt from a meeting and graph.

Let's take a few minutes to review the performance of the online service our company launched in May. As you know, ⁹⁸customers can use our website to book hotels and flights. Unfortunately, it hasn't attracted as many visitors as expected. Here, look at this graph. As you can see, ⁹⁹we achieved our goal of 5,000 visitors only once. That was in the month immediately after our television advertisement was released. However, this type of marketing campaign is too expensive to do every month. So, ¹⁰⁰I'd like you to come up with some other ideas on how to promote this service.

---

performance 實績　launch 上市　attract 引進　achieve 達成
release 公開、發表　come up with 提出、想出　promote 宣傳

翻譯 問題 98-100，請參考以下會議摘錄及表格。
讓我們來研究一下公司 5 月推出的線上服務的實際績效，就如同各位知道的一樣，⁹⁸ 顧客能使用我們的網站預約飯店與航班，但遺憾的是，吸引的訪客並沒有預期的多。請看這邊，⁹⁹ 我們只達成一次 5,000 名訪客的目標值，當時是我們推出電視廣告後的月份。但每個月都做這類行銷活動的支出太高了，因此，¹⁰⁰ 我希望各位能針對此一服務提出不同的宣傳點子。

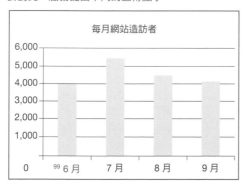

98 說話者問題

翻譯 說話者最可能從事哪一行？
(A) 研究公司
(B) 旅行社
(C) 線上零售業
(D) 運輸公司

解析 仔細聆聽短文中與身分、職業相關的表達方式，「customers can use our website to book hotels and flights」，內容談到旅客可透過公司網站預約飯店與航班，由此可知說話者在旅行社服務，因此答案是 (B)。

字彙 research 研究、調查　travel agency 旅行社

99 圖片題

翻譯 請看圖片，公司在何時推出電視廣告？
(A) 6 月
(B) 7 月
(C) 8 月
(D) 9 月

解析 確認圖片的資訊後，仔細聆聽和關鍵句 run a television advertisement 相關的內容「we achieved our goal of 5,000 visitors only once. That was in the month immediately after our television advertisement was released.」，說明只達成一次 5,000 名訪客的目標值，而當時是推出電視廣告後的月份，由此可知訪客超過 5,000 名是在推出電視廣告的 6 月之後，也就是 7 月，因此答案是 (A)。

字彙 run 進行、運作

100 請求問題

翻譯 說話者請聽者做什麼？
(A) 降低費用。
(B) 提議。
(C) 檢討意見。
(D) 聯絡顧客。

解析 仔細聆聽短文後半段與要求相關的敘述，「I'd like you to come up with some other ideas on how to promote this service」，內容談到希望大家能針對此一服務提出不同的宣傳點子，因此答案是 (B)。

換句話說
come up with ~ ideas 提出點子 → Provide suggestions 提議

字彙 feedback 意見

PART 5

101 填入形容詞

解析 空格位於 be 動詞（is）後面的主詞補語的位置，因此名詞 (A)、動名詞 (C)、形容詞 (D) 都可能是正確答案，空格前的 more 和空格後的 than 一起使用後必須要有「比線上宣傳更有效果」的意思，修飾主詞（promoting ~ online）的形容詞 (D) effective（有效的）是答案。

翻譯 想要吸引年輕消費者，線上宣傳新產品會比電視廣告更有效果。

字彙 attract v. 吸引、魅惑　effect n. 效果、結果；v. 帶來（某種結果）

102 選出動詞

解析 因為是「使用五個不同語言介紹觀光的導遊」，(A) conduct（嚮導、執行）是正確答案。(B) receive 是「接收」；(C) inspect 是「檢查」；(D) distribute 是「分配」。

翻譯 Twins Excursions 公司僱用會使用五種不同語言介紹觀光且具備執照的導遊。

字彙 excursion n.（短暫的）遊覽
licensed adj. 持有執照的、持有的、允許的　tour n. 觀光、旅行

103 填入符合的人稱代詞

解析 名詞片語（medical benefits）前可當作形容詞使用的人稱代詞是所有格，因此 (B) their（他們的）是正確答案。考慮到是介係詞（of）之後的目的語的位置，注意不要選擇受格 (C) them（他們）。

翻譯 員工手冊有提供職員該如何使用醫療保險的相關資訊。

字彙 employee handbook 員工手冊　personnel n. 職員，人員
take advantage of 利用　medical benefit 醫療保險

104 填入名詞

解析 可放在介係詞（for）的受詞位置的是名詞，contribution（捐款）的複數型 (A) contributions 是正確答案。動詞或分詞 (B)、動詞 (C) 與 (D) 無法放在名詞的位置。

翻譯 只要提出要求，捐給 Global Awareness Foundation 的所有捐款皆能收到正式的收據。

字彙 request n. 要求；v. 請求　official adj. 正式的
receipt n. 收據　issue v. 頒發、發表

105 選出名詞

解析 因為從內容來看是「Silent Moon 被提名為最優秀電影獎候選者」，(A) nomination（獲獎候補、提名）是正確答案。(B) subscription 是「申請、訂閱」；(C) destination 是「目的地、目的」；(D) creation 是「創造」。

翻譯 導演 Phillip Anderson 的電影《Silent Moon》被提名為今年最優秀電影獎。

106 對等連接詞

解析 因必須是「上千名的廚師與許多業餘廚師」的意思，(B) and（以及）是正確答案。

翻譯 西雅圖餐飲大會吸引上千名的廚師與許多業餘廚師，獲得了莫大的成果。

字彙 success n.（大）成功、成果　attract v. 招引、吸引
a large number of 大量

107 分辨現在分詞與過去分詞

解析 修飾的名詞（workforce）與分詞是被動關係，意思是「熟練的員工」，過去分詞 (A) experienced 是正確答案。現在分詞 (B) experiencing（有經驗的）如果放在空格，就會變成「正在經歷的員工」，整句話會變很不自然，因此無法當作答案。

翻譯 購物旺季期間，Johnson's 運動服飾店為確保職員能熟練一點，提供額外的員工教育訓練。

字彙 peak season 旺季　ensure v. 確保、保障
workforce n.（所有的）職員

108 完成動詞相關詞語

解析 從整句話來看，意思應該是「只有工作 15 年以上的員工才有資格獲得優秀員工獎」，空格前的 are 和空格後的 to 一起使用後要構成「獲得～的資格」的意思，因此動詞 entitle 的過去分詞 (C) entitled 是正確答案。（be entitled to：有獲得～的資格）(A) accountable 是「具責任」的意思，和介係詞 for 一起使用。（be accountable for：對～有責任）(B) modified 是「修改的」；(D) important 是「重要的」。

翻譯 只有工作 15 年以上的員工才有資格獲得優秀員工獎。

字彙 excellent adj. 優秀的

109 填入和主詞一致的動詞

解析 因為句子中沒有動詞，動詞 (B) 和 (C) 皆可能是答案，因為主詞（The new recruitment process）是單數，單數動詞 (B) requires 是答案。

翻譯 新的招聘程序要求未來所有應徵者都透過電子郵件繳交履歷。

字彙 recruitment n. 招募、招聘　job candidate 應徵者
via prep. 透過

110 選出副詞

解析 整體來看，意思是「近期經濟衰退並不代表失業率一定會上升」，(A) necessarily（一定、必然）是正確答案，組成 not necessarily，意思是「不一定」。(B) expectedly 是「依照預期」；(C) hesitantly 是「猶豫不決」；(D) consciously 是「有意地」。

翻譯 近期經濟衰退並不代表失業率一定會上升。

字彙 economic downturn 經濟衰退　unemployment rate 失業率

111 填入名詞

解析 可放在介係詞（of）的受詞位置的是名詞，因此名詞 (D) encouragement（促進、鼓勵）是正確答案。副詞 (A)、動詞 (B)、過去分詞 (C) 無法放在名詞的位置。

翻譯 在具備環保意識的居民的支持下，地方政府正在城市各個地方建設自行車專用道。

字彙 as a result of 由於　environmentally conscious 具備環保意識的
bicycle lane 自行車專用道

112 選出正確的介係詞

解析 因為正確的意思是「至少要比預定日期提早兩天再次確認預約」，(A) prior to（～之前）是正確答案。(B) provided that 是「倘若」；(C) among 是「在～之間」；(D) since 是「自從～」。

翻譯 Foley 牙科要求患者至少要比預定日期提早兩天再次確認預約。

字彙 dental clinic 牙科　reconfirm v. 再次確認

113 選出正確的「be 動詞 + 過去分詞」

解析 想要構成「收到簽約提議」的意思，就必須是被動型的句子。因此，和 be 動詞（was）一起組成被動型動詞的過去分詞 (A) offered 是正確答案。(B) 和 (C) 當作動詞使用時無法放在 be 動詞後面，就算當作名詞使用，因為和主詞（Susan James）未能達成同位語的關係，因此無法當作答案；(D) 放在 be 動詞（was）後面可變成（主動）進行式，但這個句子會變成「正在提供契約」的意思，語意不順。

翻譯 把原稿寄給多家出版社後，Susan James 終於收到 Spring Books 公司的簽約提議。

字彙 manuscript n. 原稿　dozens of 很多的　contract n. 契約
offer v. 提議；n. 提案

114 選出形容詞

解析 整句話看起來是「因為費用高的關係，猶豫著是否要升級電腦系統」，因此 (A) reluctant（猶豫不決）是正確答案。(B) unanticipated 是「意料之外的」；(C) acceptable 是「可容許的」；(D) vulnerable 是「脆弱的」。

翻譯 Peramo 公司的管理層因為費用高的關係，猶豫著是否要升級電腦系統。

字彙 management n. 管理層

115 選出時態正確的動詞

解析 為了表現出是確保資金後發生的事（聘請研發者的事）而使用未來的時態，因此 (C) will recruit 是正確答案。在表示時間的副詞子句中，使用現在時態的動詞 secures 來呈現未來的情形。

翻譯 Telestar Computing 公司確保資金後，將大規模聘請研發者來落實公司的擴張計劃。

字彙 secure v. 確保　funding n. 資金　carry out 執行

116 選出名詞

解析 根據全文來看，意思應該是「停飛航班的乘客獲得全額退款與優惠券，藉此彌補對他們造成的不便」，因此 (A) compensation（賠償）是正確答案。(B) presentation 是「呈遞、發表」；(C) motivation 是「賦予動機、刺激」；(D) admiration 是「尊敬、感嘆」。

翻譯 停飛航班的乘客獲得全額退款與 500 美元優惠券，藉此彌補對他們造成的不便。

字彙 full refund 全額退費　voucher n. 優惠券、商品券
inconvenience n. 不便

117 選出形容詞

解析 根據全文來看，意思應該是「游泳池的狀況不太好是造成負面評價的主因」，(A) principal（主要的、重要的）是正確答案。(B) considerate 是「考慮周到、體貼的」；(C) secure 是「安全的」；(D) beneficial 是「有益的、有利的」。

翻譯 游泳池的狀況不太好是造成 Central Highland 體育館獲得負面評價的主因。

字彙 negative adj. 負面的　condition n. 狀態、條件

118 選出形容詞慣用語

解析 因為必須是「支持計劃」的意思，有 be supportive of（支持）意思的 (B) supportive 是正確答案。

翻譯 近期的民調顯示，居民支持市議會為了建設新公園而增稅的計劃。

字彙 poll n. 輿論調查　indicate v. 顯示、表明　support v. 支持
supportive adj. 支持的

119 填入副詞

解析 因為需要有副詞修飾動詞（apologized），副詞 (B) quickly（迅速地）是正確答案。名詞 (A)、動詞 (C)、過去分詞 (D) 無法修飾動詞。

翻譯 Cruise 先生因為自己在向股東們演說時說錯話而迅速道歉。

字彙 misspeak v. 說錯話　shareholder n. 股東

120 選出名詞

解析 從內容來看，意思應該是「將會舉辦一系列的講座」，因此 (C) series（一連串、連續）是正確答案。(A) gathering 是「聚會、收集」；(B) means 是「手段、方法」；(D) conclusion 是「結論」。

翻譯 Killiam 公立圖書館在夏天時將會舉辦一連串當地作家的講座。

字彙 host v. 舉辦、開啟

121 副詞子句連接詞

解析 因為這句話是具備主詞（representatives）、動詞（will sign）、受詞（the contract）的完整子句，_____ an agreement is reached 應該視為懸垂修飾語。由於此一懸垂修飾語具備動詞（is reached），可引導的副詞子句連接詞 (A) 和 (D) 都可能是答案。整句的意思應該是「達成協議後就會立刻簽約」，因此 (D) As soon as（一～就立刻）是正確答案。(A) Not only 是與 but also 搭配的對等連接詞，以 not only A but（also）B 的形態使用，意思是「不只 A，還有 B」。

翻譯 達成協議後，雙方公司的代表就會立刻簽約。

字彙 agreement n. 協議、協定　reach v. 達成（目的）、到達
representative n. 代表　corporation n. 公司

122 填入副詞的位置

解析 想修飾動詞（reports）就必須要有副詞，副詞 (A) directly（直接、立刻）是正確答案。過去分詞 (B)、動詞 (C)、動名詞 (D) 無法修飾動詞。

翻譯 身為區域經理，Nissim 女士直接向公司董事會彙報。

字彙 regional manager 區域經理　board of directors 董事會

翻譯 因為必須是「決定租賃辦公空間，而不是購買建築物」的意思，(D) instead of（作為替代）是正確答案。(A) about 是「關於」；(B) on behalf of 是「代表～」；(C) regarding 是「對於～」。

翻譯 Bolton 公司決定幫新的分公司租賃辦公空間，而不是購買建築物。

字彙 rent v. 租賃

124 填入反身代名詞

解析 可修飾空格後的名詞（time）的所有格人稱代名詞 (A)，可放在及物動詞（give）之受詞位置的所有格代名詞 (B)，反身代名詞 (C) 和 (D) 都可能是答案。使用 give 開始的子句（give ~ workouts）是祈使句，因此是省略主詞 you 的句子。因為必須是「運動時要給自己恢復的時間」的意思，主詞（you）和受詞相同時，可放在受詞位置的反身代名詞 (C) yourself 是正確答案。使用所有格人稱代名詞 (A) your 和所有格代名詞 (B) yours 時，就會變成「給你恢復的時間／給你時間」，意思變得相當不順，因此無法當作答案。反身代名詞 (D) itself 在稱呼主詞等事物時使用。

翻譯 為了達到最佳的效果，運動間隔中要給自己恢復的時間。

字彙 recover v. 恢復　workout n. 運動

125 填入 to 不定詞的動詞原形

解析 因為必須符合「為了超越」的意思，所以要使用表示達成目的的 to 不定詞。To 之後必須是動詞原形，(B) surpass 是正確答案。

翻譯 Northpoint Cellular 公司為了超越早已奠定一席之地的其他公司，目前正大量投資新的無線技術。

字彙 heavily adv. 大量、沉重地
well-established adj. 不動搖的、穩定的　surpass v. 超越

126 填入連接副詞

解析 連接詞 and 連接子句（Renewable energy ~ in recent years）與子句（more consumers ~ it），整句的意思應該是「近幾年再生能源變更便宜了，因此更多消費者選擇想要使用再生能源。」，(B) therefore（因此）是正確答案。(A) otherwise 是「否則」；(C) once 是「一旦～就」；(D) instead 是「替代」。

翻譯 近幾年再生能源變更便宜了，因此更多消費者選擇使用再生能源。

字彙 renewable energy 再生能源　affordable adj. 便宜的

127 選出形容詞

解析 「現實的對話與維妙維肖的登場人物獲得評論家的好評」，(D) favorable（善意的）是答案。(A) defective 是「有缺陷的」；(B) renewable 是「可再生的」；(C) artificial 是「人造的」。

翻譯 Joel Hardwick 的第二部小說因為逼真的對話與維妙維肖

的登場人物獲得評論家的好評。

字彙 praise v. 高度評價、稱讚　realistic adj. 現實的　dialog n. 對話
believable adj. 維妙維肖　character n. 登場人物、性格、特徵

128 分辨現在分詞與過去分詞

解析 這是完整的子句，同時具備主詞（The number ~ Edible Magazine）、動詞（has increased），____ that ~ publications 應該要視為是懸垂修飾語。選項中可能成為懸垂修飾語的是分詞 (C) 與 (D)。主句的主詞（The number of subscribers）和分詞構句是主動關係，意思是「超越訂閱者的數量」，現在分詞 (D) exceeding 是正確答案。動詞 (A) 與副詞 (B) 無法成為懸垂修飾語，因此不是答案。

翻譯 Edible 雜誌的訂閱者人數持續增加，已超越其他料理出版品。

字彙 subscriber n. 訂閱者　steadily adv. 逐漸地、穩步地
culinary adj. 料理的、飲食的

129 填入介係詞

解析 意思應該是「促銷活動的第三與第四週的銷售量」，(C) during（～期間）是答案。

翻譯 是否要延長促銷活動，在觀察第三週與第四週的銷售量後會決定。

字彙 monitor v.（追蹤）觀察、監視　extend v. 延長、伸展

130 填入 to 不定詞

解析 這個句子是具備主詞（CanAir's frequent flyer program）和動詞（is designed）的完整子句，_____ passengers ~ airline 應該視為扮演副詞的懸垂修飾語，因此，可成為懸垂修飾語的 to 不定詞 (C) to reward 是正確答案。此時 to reward 是代表目的（為了獎勵）的 to 不定詞，be designed to 是「被設計用於」的慣用表現。名詞或動詞的 (A) 與 (D)、形容詞的 (B) 都無法成為懸垂修飾語。

翻譯 CanAir 公司的飛行常客專案是為了獎勵定期搭乘該航空公司飛機的乘客而設計的。

字彙 frequent flyer 飛行常客　regularly adv. 定期
fly v. 搭乘飛機、飛行　rewarding adj. 有意義的、有報酬的

PART 6

問題 131-134，請參考以下信件。

Victoria Collins 女士
98007 華盛頓州，貝爾維尤
Keystone 街 645 號
致 Collins 女士，

131 上週您來本店諮詢時，您說需要一件特殊的服裝去參加貝爾維尤美術協會的慈善晚宴。

132 我們剛收到設計師 Eleanor Harris 的各種夏季系列服飾，特別是有一件藍色晚禮服您可能會有興趣，這件商品

只有在本店才能買到，但它的尺寸是 S 號，¹³³ 稍微修改一下就能讓禮服合身。

¹³⁴ 您說晚宴是在 5 月舉行，到時候的天氣應該很溫暖，穿上這種輕盈的禮服參加活動應該會很完美，請告訴我您何時可以來一趟。

Miranda Hudson 敬上
Dot 精品店

consultation n. 諮詢、商議　unique adj. 特殊的　outfit n. 服裝
charity n. 慈善（團體）
exclusive adj. 在其他地方無法購買的、獨占的

---

131 填入符合時間的時態動詞

解析 因為有過去時間的表現（last week），過去式 (C) mentioned 是答案。

132 選出名詞

解析 從內容來看，應該是「收到設計師的各種夏季系列服飾」，(A) assortment（各種物品、齊全）是正確答案。(B) estimate 是「估計、估價單」；(C) invitation 是「邀請」；(D) announcement 是「發表、消息」。

133 選出正確的句子

翻譯 (A) 我們擔心那件禮服會太正式。
(B) 有時候衣服放進烘乾機會造成縮水。
(C) 稍微修改一下就能讓禮服合身。
(D) 在全國知名的零售店都有販售。

解析 問題要選擇填入空格的句子，因此要掌握前後文與整體內容的脈絡。前面的部分談到有 Collins 女士可能會感興趣的藍色晚禮服，「This item is exclusive to our shop, but it is a size small.」中談到此一商品雖然在其他地方無法買到，但卻是 S 號，由此可知空格應填入「稍微修改一下就能讓禮服合身」，因此 (C) 是正確答案。

字彙 formal adj. 拘謹的、隆重的　shrink v. 縮水
minor adj. 輕微的、小的　alteration n. 修繕、變化
fit n. 合身的衣服、適合　retail store 零售店

134 選出動詞　掌握前後文的脈絡

解析 文中談到「晚宴是在 5 月___」，(B) discussed（商討）、(C) canceled（取消）、(D) held（舉辦）都可能是答案，但光憑空格的句子並無法判斷，需要掌握前後文與整體文章的脈絡。因為文中談到「到時候的天氣應該很溫暖，穿上這種輕盈的禮服參加活動應該會很完美」（The weather will be warm by then, so a light dress such as this one will be perfect for the event.），可知道晚餐會是在 5 月舉辦，因此 (D) held 是答案。

問題 135-138，請參考以下備忘錄。

日期：12 月 10 日
收件人：全體員工
寄件人：Jonathan Carter，營運長
主旨：政策變更事項　　　　　　　　　　◯

---

¹³⁵ 為了推動更高的效率，經營團隊決定變更明年員工的考績評分方法。¹³⁶ 從 1 月起，全體員工每年都必須參加完善的評估。在此過程會檢討每個人各方面的績效，¹³⁷ 員工將可根據結果得獎金。新制度的相關額外資訊包含在員工手冊的最新版本上，¹³⁸ 文件將於下星期發下。

若是有任何疑問，請聯絡人資部部長 Dave Stewart。

COO n. 營運長　encourage v. 推動
carry out 實施、執行　assessment n. 評估
involve v. 伴隨、包含　aspect n. 側面、觀點
performance n. 成果、實績　updated adj. 最新的
employee manual 員工手冊　personnel n. 人資部、職員們

---

135 選出名詞　掌握整體脈絡

解析 「為了推動更高的效率，經營團隊決定變更明年員工的___方法」，所有選項都可能是答案，單憑空格的句子無法找出正確答案，因此要掌握前後文或整體的脈絡。後面談到「員工每年都必須參加評估」，加上談到「在此過程會檢討每個人各方面的績效」（This process will involve examining all aspects of their performance），由此可知會實施職員評估，因此 (D) evaluations（評估）是答案。

字彙 assignment n. 課題、任務　registration n. 登記

136 選出形容詞，掌握前後文脈絡

解析 從內容來看是「全體員工每年都必須參加___的評估」，所有選項都可能是答案，單憑空格的句子無法找出正確答案，因此要掌握前後文或整體的脈絡。後面談到「在此一過程會檢討每個人各方面的績效」（This process will involve examining all aspects of their performance.），由此可知評估是縝密的，因此 (A) thorough（縝密的、完善的）是答案。

字彙 temporary adj. 暫時的、臨時的
voluntary adj. 自發性　selective adj. 可選擇的

137 填入正確時態的動詞　掌握前後文脈絡

解析 從內容來看，意思是「員工將可根據結果得獎金」，這種情況下單憑空格的句子無法選出正確時態的動詞，必須掌握前後文或整體脈絡。前面談到「在此過程會檢討所有人各方面的績效」（This process will involve examining all aspects of their performance.），由此可知，根據結果得獎金的時間點是未來，因此未來式 (C) will receive 是答案。

138 選出正確的句子

翻譯 (A) 此一過程已經提升表現了。
(B) 文件將於下星期發下。
(C) 一些成員尚未接受評估。
(D) 不過，這些結果並不會讓人訝異。

解析 問題要挑選填入空格中的正確句子，需要掌握前後文或整體的脈絡。「Additional information about the new system has been included in the updated version of the employee manual.」中談到新制度的相關額外資訊包含

在員工手冊的最新版本上，因此空格應該填入「文件將於下星期發下」，所以答案是 (B)。

字彙 distribute v. 分配

問題 139-142，請參考以下廣告。

Quinn Grill 的廚師職務

我們是一間享譽盛名的高級餐廳，目前經營超過 5 年了。

139 因為客人口耳相傳與評論家的正面評價，這段期間客群迅速增加。140 由於我們正在擴張主要用餐空間，所以需要有經驗的廚師。所有應徵者都必須在餐廳工作過 2 年以上，包含製作過種類不同的多元化料理。141 我們還有其他幾項具體的要求條件。142 我們理想中的應徵者必須能承受高壓的環境，並和其他組員合作，包含週末與假日在內都能彈性上班。

請各位把求職信、履歷、推薦函寄到 squinn@quinngrill.com，收件人是 Sophia Quinn。

---

vacancy n. 職位、空缺　fine adj. 高級的
reputation n. 聲望、口碑　be in business 做生意
customer base 客戶群　rapidly adv. 快速地、迅速地
critic n. 評論家、批評家　be in need of 需要
experienced adj. 有經驗的、熟練的　ideal adj. 理想的、完美的
handle v. 承擔、處理　high-pressure adj. 高壓的、充滿壓力的
collaborate v. 合作　reference letter 推薦函

---

139 選出正確的句子

解析 從「這段期間顧客群迅速增加」此一內容來看，單憑空格的句子無法找出正確時態的動詞，必須掌握前後文或整體的脈絡。前面談到「經營超過 5 年了」（we have been in business for over five years），由此可知是從 5 年前開始營業，目前顧客群也持續增加當中，因此現在完成式 (C) has grown 是答案。

字彙 grow v. 增加、成長

140 選出正確的句子

解析 這個句子是具備必要元素（we ~ cooks）的完整子句，___we ~ room 必須視為是懸垂修飾語，此一懸垂修飾語是具備動詞（are expanding）的修飾語，可引導修飾語的副詞子句連接詞 (A)、(C)、(D) 都可能是答案。因為要符合「由於我們正在擴張主要用餐空間，所以需要有經驗的廚師」的意思，因此 (A) Because（因為）是答案。

141 選出正確的句子

翻譯 (A) 所有人都通過規定參加的食品安全課程。
(B) 我們還有其他幾項具體的要求條件。
(C) 面試結果很快就會公布。
(D) 必須立刻帶客人到他們的座位上。

解析 題目要選出填入空格的正確句子，必須掌握前後文或整體的脈絡。前面談到所有應徵者都必須在餐廳工作 2 年以上，後面的「Our ideal candidate will be able to handle a high-pressure environment, collaborate with

---

other members of a team」說，我們理想中的應徵者必須能承受高壓的環境，並和其他組員合作，由此可知該填入空格的是「還有其他幾項具體的要求條件」，所以 (B) 是答案。

字彙 mandatory adj. 義務的　show v. 解說

142 填入形容詞

解析 想要修飾名詞（hours）就必須有形容詞，因此 (C) flexible（具彈性的、可變通的）是答案。

字彙 flexibility n. 變通性、伸縮性　flexibleness n. 伸縮性、柔軟

問題 143-146，請參考以下信件。

Sandra Ericta
租賃業者，Bristol 大樓
95125 加州，舊金山
Main 街 355 號

致 Ericta 女士，

這封信是要通知我將於 9 月 30 日搬離 Bristo 大樓 307 號，143 我依照租約於 30 天前通知您。

144 我很清楚自己有義務讓房子維護在良好的狀態，否則就會拿不回保證金。145 您何時能來檢查房子，確認自己是否滿意，請告訴我一聲。搬完家並把鑰匙交給您後，希望您能在 9 月 30 日把保證金還給我。146 我會在當天把銀行帳號的資料交給您。

謝謝。

John Schroeder 敬上

---

landlord n. 房東、主人　serve as 擔任
vacate v. 空出、離開　rental contract 租賃契約
condition n. 狀態、環境，條件　otherwise adv. 否則
security deposit 保證金　move out 搬走

---

143 分辨現在分詞與過去分詞

解析 修飾的名詞（30 days' notice）與分詞是被動關係，意思是「要求的 30 天前通知」，因此過去分詞 (D) requested 是答案。

144 選出名詞　掌握前後文的脈絡

解析 內容是「我很清楚自己有___讓房子維護在良好的狀態」，(B) obligation（義務）和 (D) option（選擇權）都有可能是答案，單憑有空格的句子無法判斷，必須掌握前後文或整體脈絡。後面的句子談到「否則我就會拿不回保證金」（Otherwise, I will lose my security deposit.），寄件人 Schroeder 先生很清楚自己有義務讓房子維持在良好的狀態，因此 (B) obligation 是答案。

字彙 occupation n. 職業、業務　inquiry n. 詢問

145 選出形容詞

解析 整句的意思應該是「檢查房子，確認自己是否滿意」，(C) satisfactory（滿意的）是答案。

字彙 capable adj. 有能力的　challenging adj. 具挑戰性的
appreciative adj. 感激的

146 選出正確的句子

翻譯 (A) 房客被禁止打鑰匙。
(B) 好像匯錯金額了。
(C) 我會在當天把銀行帳號的資料交給您。
(D) 我今天大概無法搬家具。

解析 問題要在空格中填入合適的句子，必須掌握前後文或整體的脈絡。在前面的句子「I would like my deposit returned to me on September 30 after I move out and hand you the key.」中表示搬完家後就會交還鑰匙，希望對方能在 9 月 30 日退還保證金，由此可知空格應該填入「我會在當天把銀行帳號的資料交給您」，所以 (C) 是答案。

字彙 tenant n. 承租者、房客　prohibit v. 禁止　transfer v. 匯款、傳達

PART 7

問題 147-148，請參考以下廣告。

你剛搬進新大樓或新房子嗎？修補房子需要任何幫助嗎？
那你非常好運，只要打一通電話到：

¹⁴⁷ Harold and Sons 公司
森特維爾地區包含郊外都會提供服務 555-2398

¹⁴⁷ 我們提供包含下列事項在內的廣泛服務。

房屋基礎修繕
安裝家電產品、照明、固定裝置
壁紙與牆壁塗漆
配置家具
鋪設磁磚

Harold Clark 在 25 年前創業，現在他的兒子 Robert、William 和他一起工作，為當地的居民提供到府服務，這個家族的經歷與專業性無與倫比。

¹⁴⁸ 若 6 月來電，無論是訂購 Harold and Sons 公司的哪一項服務，都會免費幫忙設置吊扇或照明設備。

fix up 修理　be in luck 運氣真好　greater adj. 包含郊外的
lighting n. 照明
fixture n. 固定裝置（浴缸、馬桶等無法移動的裝置）
installation n. 設置　wallpaper n. 壁紙　arrangement n. 配置
lay v. 安裝，放置　beyond comparison 無法比較的

---

147 推論題

翻譯 Harold and Sons 公司最可能從事哪一行？
(A) 設計裝潢房子的壁紙圖案。
(B) 把家具搬到另一間房子。
(C) 住宅的維護補修作業。
(D) 專門幫辦公室安裝照明。

解析 這是針對關鍵詞 Harold and Sons 推論的問題，從「Harold and Sons」和「We provide a wide range of services, including: Basic home repairs, ~, Tile laying」等內容來看，其中提到 Harold and Sons 公司提供範圍

相當廣泛的服務，包含基本房屋修繕、鋪設磁磚等，由此可推論出與住宅的維護補修作業有關係，因此答案是 (C)。

字彙 conduct v. 執行　residential adj. 住宅的、居住的
maintenance n. 維護、補修　specialize in 專門從事

148 5W1H 問題

翻譯 顧客在 6 月時能獲得什麼？
(A) 禮品券
(B) 免費服務
(C) 產品樣本
(D) 新的公司目錄

解析 這是詢問顧客在 6 月可獲得什麼（What）的 5W1H 問題，與問題的核心 customers receive in June 有關係，「If you call in the month of June, Harold and Sons will install a ceiling fan or light fixture for free with the purchase of any service.」，文中談到只要在 6 月來電，無論向 Harold and Sons 公司購買何種服務都會免費幫忙安裝吊扇或照明設備，因此答案是 (B)。

換句話說
install a ceiling fan or light fixture for free 免費安裝吊扇或照明設備 → A complimentary service 免費服務

字彙 complimentary adj. 免費的

問題 149-150，請參考以下訊息。

Kelly Orville　　　　　　　　　　　[下午 4 點 30 分]
好，^{149-A/C} 我們決定下星期五不去 Chez Mimi's，而是去 Lococo's Grill 進行員工聚餐。^{149-C} 那邊距離我們辦公室更近。

Nigel Wendt　　　　　　　　　　　[下午 4 點 31 分]
這個決定真是太棒了，^{149-B} 我平常都在那邊吃飯，¹⁵⁰ 已經打電話預約了嗎？剛剛 IT 部門有幾個人說他們能來參加聚餐。

Kelly Orville　　　　　　　　　　　[下午 4 點 33 分]
我本來要打去預約，¹⁵⁰ 但今天真的太忙了。IT 部門有幾個人要參加呢？那間餐廳的位子很多，就算來更多人，應該也會有位子吧。

Nigel Wendt　　　　　　　　　　　[下午 4 點 33 分]
據我所知是 7 個人，但你大概得再確認一下。

after all 終究　mean to 打算要　plenty of 大量的
seat v. 安排座位，讓～坐下　double-check v. 再次確認

---

149 Not/True 題型

翻譯 關於 Lococo's Grill 哪一個不是真的？
(A) 可進行公司聚餐。
(B) Wendt 先生經常去用餐。
(C) 比 Chez Mimi's 更接近公司。
(D) 週末需要預約。

解析 問題是要在短文中找出與關鍵詞 Lococo's Grill 相關的內容，然後和選項進行對照。(A) 在「we'll be having the staff dinner ~ at Lococo's Grill (4:30 P.M.)」中談到要

去 Lococo's Grill 進行員工聚餐，與短文的內容一致。
(B)「I eat there[Lococo's Grill] all the time. (4:31 P.M.)」
中 Wendt 先生說自己常去 Lococo's Grill 用餐，與短
文內容一致。(C)「we'll be having the staff dinner ~ at
Lococo's Grill instead of Chez Mimi's. It's much closer
to our office. (4:30 P.M.)」中談到不去 Chez Mimi's，而
是去 Lococo's Grill 去聚餐，那邊距離辦公室更近，與短
文中的內容一致。(D) 是短文中沒有談到的內容，因此是
答案。

換句話說
eat there all the time 常在那邊用餐 →
It is frequently visited 經常去拜訪
much closer to ~ office 距離辦公室更近 →
nearer to a workplace 距離工作場所更近

字彙 workplace n. 工作場所

150 意圖掌握問題

翻譯 下午 4 點 33 分，Orville 女士談到「I've been meaning
to」時，最有可能是什麼意思？
(A) 打算邀請其他部門的員工。
(B) 不知道有多少員工會參加。
(C) 打算告訴員工變更事項。
(D) 沒有聯絡餐廳。

解析 這是在詢問 Orville 女士意圖的問題，確認引用句「I've
been meaning to」相關的內容，在「Have you called to
make the reservation yet? (4:31 P.M.)」中 Wendt 先生詢
問是否有預約，Orville 女士回答「I've been meaning to
（我正打算預約）」，另在「but I've been really busy
today (4:33 P.M.)」中則表示自己今天真的很忙。由此可
知 Orville 女士因為太忙了，所以未能聯絡餐廳，因此答
案是 (D)。

問題 151-153，請參考以下報導。

Medallion 公司幫助新進員工適應環境

[151] 今年年初，Medallion 為了發展員工的能力而製作了員
工師徒制計劃。— [1] — Medallion Mentoring 計劃會把
新進人員與高層管理人員每兩人分成一組，高層管理人員
不僅會提供資歷發展計劃，還會提供日常工作上的建議。
— [2] —人資部負責人會分配督導給新進人員，每個星期
會安排兩次，每次一小時。— [3] — 另外，[152] 計劃中的所
有督導都必須遵守此一時間條件。

雖然花了好一段時間才開始這項計劃，但參加者慢慢增加
當中，[153] 人資部的負責人把今年的目標設定在全公司有
200 名的導師。— [4] — Medallion 公司董事長 Sally Kay
表示「現在越來越多人關注這項計劃，所以尋找自願成為
督導的主管不會有問題」。

---

pair v. 兩人分成一組、配對　senior-level adj. 高階的
day-to-day adj. 日常的　career n. 資歷　strategy n. 計劃、戰略
coordinator n. 負責人、進行者　assign v. 分配
fulfill v. 遵守、滿足　get ~ off the ground 以~為開始、順利出發
gradually adv. 慢慢地　aim to 以~為目標
companywide adv. 全公司

151 推論題

翻譯 關於 Medallion Mentoring 計劃，暗示了下列哪個內容？
(A) 已經在公司網站上大力宣傳過。
(B) 每一季都需要徵人活動。
(C) 不受到高階經營團隊的支持。
(D) 建立還不到 12 個月。

解析 這是針對關鍵詞 Medallion Mentoring program 的推
論題，在「Earlier this year, Medallion Corporation
created a staff mentoring program to develop the skills
of its employees.」中談到今年年初，Medallion 為了
發展員工的能力而制定了員工師徒制計劃，因此答案是
(D)。

字彙 feature v.（報紙等）專題報導、包含　quarterly adv. 每一季
upper management 高階管理人員　establish v. 成立

152 5W1H 問題

翻譯 督導被要求做什麼？
(A) 滿足最低程度的必要時間。
(B) 每天下班後當義工 2 小時。
(C) 和接受指導的員工的家人見面。
(D) 和負責人定期進行諮詢。

解析 這是詢問督導們被要求做什麼（What）的 5W1H 問
題，與問題的關鍵句 mentors required to do 相關，
「all mentors in the program must fulfill this time
requirement[two one-hour sessions per week]」中談到
計劃中的所有督導都得遵守每個星期進行兩次，每次一
小時的條件，因此答案是 (A)。

換句話說
fulfill ~ time requirement 遵守時間條件 → Meet a minimum
number of necessary hours 滿足最低程度的必要時間

字彙 meet v. 滿足　minimum adj. 最低限度的　necessary adj. 必要的
get together 會面　counseling n. 諮詢

153 將句子放入合適的位置

翻譯 以下句子最適合放入 [1]、[2]、[3] 或 [4] 的哪個位置？
「此一目標預計在 10 月時會達成。」
(A) [1]
(B) [2]
(C) [3]
(D) [4]

解析 問題要找出最適合填入空格的句子，在「This goal is
expected to be achieved by October」中談到此一目
標預計在 10 月會達成，可預測句子前會有和目標相關
的內容。[4] 前面的句子「This year, human resources
coordinators aim to have 200 mentors companywide.」
談到人資部的負責人把今年的目標設定在全公司有 200
名的督導，加入選項 [4] 的句子後，很自然就形成「預計
全公司在 10 月會達成 200 名導師的目標」，因此答案
是 (D)。

字彙 goal n. 目標　achieve v. 達成

154-155 號是下列電子信件的相關問題。

收件人：Leah Young <leahyoung@journeyon.com>
寄件人：Even Harris <evenharris@smartmail.com>
日期：5 月 9 日
主旨：旅行保險
附件：收據、警察報告書
Young 女士，

154 我之所以會寫這封信，是為了針對意外的開銷要求給予理賠。

我最近去墨西哥度假，透過 Journey on Travel Insurance 公司申請旅遊保險，我的保單號碼是 4533906。

我預約科蘇梅爾島的 Fiesta 飯店五個晚上，155 入住第二天，有人跑來我房間偷走了筆電。雖然飯店經理退還我剩下三天的住宿費，但這筆錢根本就無法購買電腦。

據我所知，這種情況下我可以從貴公司獲得 5,000 美元的保險理賠，我的筆電總共是 2,300 美元，附檔是電腦收據和警察報告書的影本。

Evan Harris 敬上

---

reimbursement n. 償還、報銷　unexpected adj. 意外的
insure v. 投保　gain access to 接近
remaining adj. 剩餘的　come close to 差一點就
cover v. 足夠支付～的錢　replacement n. 替換
be entitled to 有資格獲得～　coverage n. 保障

---

154 目的問題

　　Harris 先生為何會寄這封電子郵件？

　　(A) 為了要求理賠

　　(B) 為了預約

　　(C) 為了批評飯店

　　(D) 為了取消付款

解析　題目詢問 Harris 先生寫這封電子郵件的目的，仔細確認短文前面的部分。「I am writing to request reimbursement for an unexpected expense.」中談到之所以會寫信，是為了針對意外的開銷要求給予理賠，因此答案是 (A)。

字彙　compensation n. 賠償　criticize v. 批評

155 5W1H 問題

　　根據信件內容來看，在 Fiesta 飯店發生了什麼事？

　　(A) 客人的客房費被多收了。

　　(B) 電子用品被偷走了。

　　(C) 個人電腦受損了。

　　(D) 要求退錢被拒絕了。

解析　這是詢問 Fiesta 飯店發生什麼（What）事的 5W1H 問題，與關鍵詞 happened at Hotel Fiesta 有關係。「On the second day of my visit, someone gained access to my room and took my laptop computer.」中談到住宿第二天有人跑進房內偷走了筆電，因此答案是 (B)。

換句話說

someone ~ took ~ laptop computer 有人拿走了筆電→
An electronic device was stolen 電子設備被偷走了

字彙　overcharge v. 多收錢　electronic adj. 電子的　device n. 設備
　　　deny v. 拒絕

問題 156-157，請參考以下網頁。

Delta 的驚人優惠折扣
156 當地業者的特殊優惠，您的情報來源

為了 Delta 地區的消費者，我們計劃和商店、餐廳、旅行社、美容室、SPA、居家服務業者打造能在同一個地方完成所有購物的商店。相信您在其他地方絕對無法享有這麼多的優惠。156 今天就去尋找滿滿的優惠折扣吧！

搜尋商品或服務

搜尋業者

此一網站由 Delta Times 報紙提供。

首頁	購物	居家服務	個人服務

優惠折扣 1 號：
Hammerhead 的窗戶清潔
第一次使用住宅窗戶清潔服務時折扣 40 美元
優惠折扣 2 號：
Scrub Masters 的瓷磚與通風口清潔
兩種服務都訂購時，折扣定價的 20%
優惠折扣 3 號：
Bloom 的庭院服務
157 預付 6 個月的每週草地管理服務時，折扣 25%
優惠折扣 4 號：
Swift Swipe 地毯清潔
最多五個房間的地毯清潔服務 1 次，折扣 10%

下一頁繼續，請點擊這邊！〉〉〉

---

source n. 來源、出處　spa n. 水療、溫泉、修養設施
one-stop adj. 在一個地方都能進行的
residential adj. 住宅（用）的　air vent 通風口　lawn n. 草皮
one-time adj. 僅限 1 次的、一度　rug n. 小地毯

---

156 目的問題

　　網頁的目的是什麼？

　　(A) 為了和類似的服務互相比較價格

　　(B) 為了提供當地業者的評價

　　(C) 為了介紹新公司

　　(D) 為了宣傳業者提供的優惠

解析　題目是詢問網頁的目的，仔細確認短文前面的部分，「Your source for special deals at area businesses」中談到「當地業者的特殊優惠，您的情報來源」，接著在「Find a great deal today!」中談到「今天就去尋找滿滿的優惠折扣吧」，因此答案是 (D)。

字彙　compare v. 比較　enterprise n. 公司、企業

157 5W1H 問題

　　景觀美化服務給予多少折扣？

　　(A) 10%

　　(B) 20%

　　(C) 25%

　　(D) 40%

解析 題目詢問景觀美化服務有多少（How much）折扣的 5W1H 問題，與問題的關鍵句 discount ~ offered on landscaping services 有關，「Six months of weekly lawn care services, prepaid, at 25 percent off」中談到預付 6 個月的每週草地管理服務時，可享有 25% 的折扣，因此答案是 (C)。

字彙 landscaping n. 景觀美化

問題 158-160，請參考以下信件。

---

4 月 12 日
Chad Steiner
53705 威斯康辛州，麥迪遜
Elm 街 1420 號，# 32
Steiner 先生，

這封信已經寄送給 Singing Vines 大樓的所有住戶了，相信大家也都知道，這棟建築物的停車場有另外為房客準備位子，158-D 已經有住戶多次抗議無視此項規定的訪客，159 下星期開始我們將會查看停車場內的所有車輛。如果玻璃窗上看不見住戶停車證，那我們就會移除車輛。

請告訴各位的客人，大樓對面的 Elm 街整天任何時段都可免費停車，Boulder 街和 Park 路雖然也能停車，但按小時計費。160 市府規定建築物西側的 160 Devon 大路禁止停車，請記住這一點。

如果有任何疑問或需求，請立刻聯絡我。

Rachel Solomon 敬上
建築物管理員，Singing Vines 大樓

resident n. 居民、住戶　parking lot 停車場
reserve v. 另外保留（位子等）　tenant n. 房客
complaint n. 抗議、不滿　regulation n. 規定
parking pass 停車證　hourly adv. 每小時　prohibit v. 禁止
run v. 延續

---

158 Not/True 題型
Solomon 女士有談到什麼問題？
(A) 大樓沒有清掃。
(B) 費用提高了。
(C) 車輛有刮痕。
(D) 某規定未被遵守。

解析 這是從短文中找出與 Solomon 女士談論的問題相關的內容，與選項對照的 Not/True 問題。(A)、(B)、(C) 在短文中沒有提到，(D) 在「we have received several complaints about visitors ignoring this regulation」中，Solomon 女士說已經有住戶多次抗議無視此項規定的訪客，因此與短文中的內容一致，所以答案是 (D)。

字彙 scratch v. 刮痕

159 5W1H 問題
下星期會發生什麼事？
(A) 會發停車證。
(B) 會檢查車輛。
(C) 房客會被人聯繫。
(D) 大樓要翻修。

解析 這是詢問下星期會發生什麼（What）事的 5W1H 問題，與關鍵詞 next week 有關，「Starting next week, we will be checking all automobiles parked in our lot.」中談到「下星期開始我們將會查看停車場內的所有車輛」，因此答案是 (B)。

字彙 issue v. 頒發、發表　examine v. 檢查

160 5W1H 問題
不允許訪客停車的地方在哪裡？
(A) Elm 街
(B) Boulder 街
(C) Park 路
(D) Devon 大路

解析 這是詢問訪客無法停車的地方在哪裡（Where）的 5W1H 問題，與問題的關鍵句 visitors not allowed to park 有關，在「a city rule prohibits parking on Devon Boulevard」中談到市府規定建築物西側的 Devon 大路禁止停車，所以答案是 (D)。

問題 161-163，請參考以下電子郵件。

收件人：Marcy Sizemore
　　　　　<marcysizemore@fullerchemical.com>
寄件人：Shane Ellis
　　　　　<shaneellis@quantumlaboratories.com>
日期：1 月 14 日
主旨：恭喜
附加：履歷

你好，Marcy，

161 雖然我們最後一次共事已經快 10 年了，但我最近在《Science News》月刊看見你晉升為 Fuller Chemical 公司研發部副總的報導時，162 想起我們早期在 LabSure 公司當研究助理時的日子。我早猜到你終將會因為自己的才能與工作倫理而成功，恭喜你升遷了。

如你所知，我是 Quantum 研究所的品保負責人，我們有一個相當優秀的研究員要離開公司去找其他工作，雖然失去她讓我們很難過，161 但如果你們公司有合適的職位，我想向你推薦她。你會發現她擁有相當棒的學歷，以及在生物學研究領域的豐富經歷，我附上她的履歷，供你審視。

就算沒有空缺，163 你是否能和她見一面，給予她職涯建議呢？如果你有意願幫忙她，希望能告訴我一聲。

希望你在新的職位一切都順利，謝謝。

Shane Ellis 敬上

promotion n. 晉升　vice president 副總　assistant n. 助理
talent n. 才能　work ethic 工作倫理　quality assurance 品質保證
talented adj. 有能力的、有實力的　seek out 尋找
employment opportunity 就業機會　suitable sadj. 合適的
opening n. 空位、空缺　impressive adj. 偉大的
educational background 學歷　a great deal of 許多的
biological adj. 生物學的　career advice 職業建議

---

161 目的問題

Ellis 先生為何會寫電子郵件？
(A) 為了尋求研究計劃的協助
(B) 為了告知他的晉升
(C) 為了提議投資機會
(D) 為了推薦有潛力的職員

解析 這是詢問 Ellis 先生寫信理由的問題，特別要注意的是，短文中間的部分有談到目的相關的內容。「I would like to recommend her[researcher] to you in case you have a suitable opening at your company」文中談到如果收件人的公司有合適的職位，他想推薦該名研究員，因此答案是 (D)。

字彙 investment n. 投資　potential adj. 潛在的

162 5W1H 問題

Sizemore 女士和 Ellis 先生是如何認識的？
(A) 參加同一場會議。
(B) 曾是職場同事。
(C) 透過認識的人見面。
(D) 曾就讀同一所學校。

解析 題目詢問 Sizemore 女士和 Ellis 先生是如何（How）認識彼此的，與問題的關鍵詞 know each other 有關，「It has been nearly 10 years since we last worked together」中談到兩人最後一次共事已經快 10 年了，「I remembered our early days working together as research assistants for LabSure Corporation」中則談到想起一起在 LabSure 公司當研究助理時的日子，因此答案是 (B)。

字彙 coworker n. 同事　acquaintance n. 熟人

163 5W1H 問題

Ellis 先生向 Sizemore 女士建議要做什麼？
(A) 應徵職位
(B) 推薦人才。
(C) 見面。
(D) 聯絡客戶。

解析 題目詢問 Ellis 先生提議 Sizemore 女士做什麼（What），與問題的關鍵句 Mr. Ellis suggest that Ms. Sizemore do 有關。「would you mind meeting her[researcher] to offer career advice?」中 Ellis 先生詢問 Sizemore 女士是否能和研究員見一面，給予她職涯建議，因此答案是 (C)。

字彙 candidate n. 候選人、應徵者

問題 164-167，請參考以下線上對話內容。

Joy Saunders	[下午 2 點 15 分]

各位是否曾在報帳出差費時遇到問題呢？因為最近有不少人在抱怨。

Maurice Watts	[下午 2 點 17 分]

我曾遇到問題，164 我上個月去舊金山參加貿易博覽會時的開銷只有收到部分的金額，但我不清楚原因。我沒有超過 1,000 美元的上限，165 在當月第一週的星期五前就繳交收據，那一天剛好是截止日，對吧？ ➡

Joy Saunders	[下午 2 點 18 分]

沒錯，你有問過會計部哪裡出錯了嗎？

Maurice Watts	[下午 2 點 19 分]

有，但目前還沒收到回覆。

Jennifer Cole	[下午 2 點 20 分]

166 我 1 月時在飯店付的 600 美元幾乎等了快 3 個月，詢問理由後才知道，超過 400 美元的經費必須先取得會計部的許可，否則處理過程可能會多花上幾週的時間。

Charlie Pearson	[下午 2 點 22 分]

我搭乘交通工具就花了超過 500 美元，根本就沒有時間慢慢等報銷。

Joy Saunders	[下午 2 點 25 分]

167 我會打電話詢問會計部經理，我該怎麼做才能加快處理速度。

reimburse v. 報銷　travel expense 出差費
complaint n. 抱怨、不滿事項　run into 遭遇、遇到
portion n. 部分、一部分　trade exhibition 貿易博覽會
exceed v. 超過　limit n. 限度　explanation n. 理由、說明
approve v. 核准　in advance 事先、事前　process v. 處理
afford to 承擔得起

164 Not/True 題型

關於 Watts 先生的敘述有說到什麼？
(A) 他是會計部的職員。
(B) 他就要調到其他分公司了。
(C) 他幫忙準備貿易博覽會。
(D) 他最近去出差了。

解析 這是從短文中找出與問題關鍵詞 Mr. Watts 相關的內容，與選項對照後找出 Not/True 的題目。(A)、(B)、(C) 是短文中沒有談到的內容，(D)「I went to San Francisco for the trade exhibition last month (2:17 P.M.)」中談到 Watts 先生上個月去舊金山參加貿易博覽會，與短文內容一致，因此答案是 (D)。

字彙 transfer v. 調動、移動　organize v. 準備、組織
trade show 貿易博覽會

165 意圖掌握問題

解析 下午 2 點 18 分，Saunders 女士回答「That's correct」，她的意思是什麼？
(A) 會計部門通常都會列印收據。
(B) 截止日是每個月第一週的星期五。
(C) 無論理由是什麼都不能超過 1,000 美元的上限。
(D) 一名組員妥善說明了她的費用。

解析 題目詢問 Saunders 女士的意圖，確認問題引用句「That's correct」前後文的脈絡。在「I submitted my receipts before the first Friday of the month. That's the deadline, right? (2:17 P.M.)」中，Watts 先生談到自己在當月第一週星期五就繳交收據了，並詢問那一天是否就是截止日，Saunders 女士回答「That's correct」（對），由此可知截止日是每個月第一週的星期五，因此答案是 (B)。

字彙 fall on （某個日子）在～、屬於～

166 5W1H 問題

Cole 女士 1 月時在住宿費用方面花了多少錢？
(A) 400 美元
(B) 500 美元
(C) 600 美元
(D) 1,000 美元

解析 題目詢問 Cole 女士於 1 月時在住宿方面花了多少（How much）金額，與問題的關鍵句 spend on accommodations in January 有關，「I had to wait almost three months to get the $600 I paid for a hotel in January. (2:20 P.M.)」中談到 Cole 女士於 1 月在飯店支出的 600 美元幾乎等了快三個月，因此答案是 (C)。

字彙 accommodations n. 住宿設施

167 推論題

關於 Saunders 女士可推論的是什麼？
(A) 她要購買幾張機票。
(B) 她批准了退款請求。
(C) 她將聯絡某部門的經理。
(D) 她向管理階層提出投訴。

解析 這是針對問題關鍵詞 Ms. Saunders 推論的題目，「Let me call the accounting manager and see what I can do to speed things up. (2:25 P.M.)」中 Saunders 女士談到會打電話詢問會計部經理，該怎麼做才能加快處理速度，因此答案是 (C)。

問題 168-171，請參考以下信件。

---

1 月 28 日

Eugene Lee
19801 德拉瓦州，威明頓
Westing 路 66 號

Lee 先生，

Hoyle 地區劇院會盡可能提供最棒的表演藝術體驗，作為一個非營利組織，我們一直以來都依賴地區社群的援助。因此 168 我們要請贊助者定期捐款。— [1] —.

168 附上閣下能放捐款的信封。— [2] —.無論金額多寡都非常歡迎，171 捐贈 100 美元以上的人士可獲得相當棒的優惠。— [3] —.

另外，為了感謝我們忠實的贊助者，我們今天打算把目前為止最野心勃勃的幾個表演搬上舞臺。— [4] —.3 月，我們將推出 169-D 由著名肯亞劇作家 David Kobo 編著的戲劇《Searching for the Homeland》。另外，6 月將會舉辦為期 3 週當地劇作家 Steve Weller 的三部戲劇表演。之後今年秋天，我們將會推出古希臘悲劇系列的表演。

170 我們是威明頓唯一提供免費表演的劇院，我們是因為像您這樣的人士才能維持至今，因此非常感謝閣下一直以來的奉獻。

Kathryn Little 敬上
導演，170 Hoyle 地區劇院

---

strive v. 努力   performing art 表演藝術
nonprofit adj. 非營利性   depend on 依賴   patron n. 贊助人

---

periodically adv. 定期性、週期性   make donations 捐贈
enclosed adj. 封入   appreciate v. 歡迎、鑑賞
substantial adj. 相當的   contribute v. 捐贈
stage v. 登上舞臺；n. 舞臺   ambitious adj. 志向遠大的
put on a play 演出戲劇   famed adj. 著名的
playwright n. 劇作家   classical adj. 古代的
tragedy n. 悲劇   dedication n. 奉獻

---

168 目的問題

解析 這封信的用意是什麼？
(A) 為了請求贊助者捐款
(B) 為了宣傳新的劇院
(C) 為了通知行程變更
(D) 為了徵求表演的演員

解析 這是在詢問信件用意的題目，「we ask that our patrons periodically make donations」中談到請求贊助者定期捐款，「Enclosed is an envelope into which you can place your donation.」中則談到附有能放捐款的信封，因此答案是 (A)。

換句話說
ask that ~ make donations 請求捐款 → solicit money 徵求資金

字彙 solicit v. 徵求   seek v. 尋找

169 Not/True 題型

解析 關於《Searching for the Homeland》，文中提到了什麼？
(A) 將會舉辦三週。
(B) 以希臘悲劇為基礎。
(C) 由 Steve Weller 監製。
(D) 由知名藝術家編著。

解析 這是從短文中找出與問題關鍵詞 Searching for the Homeland 相關的內容，再和選項對照的 Not/True 題型。(A)、(B)、(C) 在短文中沒有談到，(D)「a play by the famed Kenyan playwright David Kobo called Searching for the Homeland」中談到《Searching for the Homeland》是著名肯亞劇作家 David Kobo 的戲劇，因此答案是 (D)。

字彙 run v. 開啟、持續（一段時間）   direct v. 監督

170 推論題

關於 Hoyle 地區戲院有何暗示？
(A) 位於威明頓郊區。
(B) 表演時會使用學生演員。
(C) 入場不需要支付費用。
(D) 週末與國定假日不營業。

解析 這是針對問題的關鍵詞 Hoyle Community Theater 推論的問題，「As the only theater in Wilmington that offers free performances」和「Hoyle Community Theater」中談到寄件人 Hoyle 地區劇院是威明頓唯一提供免費表演的劇院，由此可推論出入 Hoyle 地區劇院不需要入場費，因此答案是 (C)。

換句話說
offers free performances 提供免費表演 →
does not charge money for admission 入場不需要支付費用

字彙 admission n. 入場   national holiday 國定假日

171 將句子放入合適的位置

翻譯 以下句子最適合放入 [1]、[2]、[3] 或 [4] 的哪個位置？
「這些包含當地餐廳的禮券與當地演唱會的門票。」
(A) [1]
(B) [2]
(C) [3]
(D) [4]

解析 題目要找出最適合填入空格的句子，「These include gift cards to restaurants in the area and tickets to local concerts」中談到這些包含當地餐廳的禮券與當地演唱會的門票，由此可猜到句子前面有提供優惠的相關內容。[3] 前面的句子「Substantial benefits are available to those who contribute $100 or more.」中談到無論金額多寡都非常歡迎，捐贈 100 美元以上的人士可獲得相當棒的優惠，加入 [3] 的句子後，自然就能解釋提供給捐贈者優惠的內容，句子也顯得相當通順，因此答案是 (C)。

問題 172-175，請參考以下介紹。

封路

注意，King 街、Queen 街與 Dundas 街的特定區間於 3 月和 4 月將會封閉。¹⁷² 為了進行冬季時受損道路的修補工程，此一封路是必要的。¹⁷³ 由於這些道路都是通往市區的主要路線，不應維持現在的狀態。

請記住以下的行程。

・3 月 6 日至 3 月 20 日－Bathurst 街和 University 街之間的 King 街將會封閉。
・3 月 21 日至 4 月 3 日－Ossington 街和 Kensington 街之間的 Queen 街將會封閉。
・4 月 4 日至 4 月 18 日－University 街和 Young 街之間的 Dundas 街將會封閉。

建議繞到 Royce 街和 Church 街代替上述的街道，如果要使用住宅區的小道路，請記得要隨時遵守降低的速限。

謝謝各位的耐心與諒解。

多倫多公共工程公司委員會敬上

road closure 封路　section n. 區間、部分　major adj. 主要的　route n. 途徑　detour n. 改道、迂迴　residential adj. 住宅區的　observe v. 遵守、觀察　speed limit 速限　at all times 一直　committee n. 委員會

---

172 5W1H 題型

為何有些道路都封閉了？
(A) 為了舉辦慶典
(B) 為了在冬天結束後為些道路
(C) 為了建造新的步道
(D) 為了透過增加車道來拓寬道路

解析 這是詢問道路為何（Why）要封閉的問題，與問題的關鍵詞 some roads being closed 有關，「These closures are necessary to perform required work on parts of these roads that were damaged during the long winter.」中談到，為了進行冬季時受損道路的修補工

程，封路是必要的，因此答案是 (B)。

字彙 take place 舉行、發生　sidewalk n. 步道

173 尋找同義詞

第 1 段第 5 行的「condition」，意思最接近下列何者？
(A) 要求條件
(B) 地區
(C) 狀態
(D) 作業

解析 包含 condition 在內的句子，「The roads are all major routes through the city, and they should not be left in their current condition.」中的 condition 當作「狀態」使用，因此答案是 (C)。

174 Not/True 題型

哪一條道路沒有被封閉？
(A) Queen 街
(B) King 街
(C) Dundas 街
(D) Royce 街

解析 這是從短文中找出與問題關鍵詞 road ~ be closed 相關的句子，再和選項對照的 Not/True 題型。(A)「Queen Street will be closed」中談到 Queen 街會封閉，因此和內容一致。(B)「King Street will be closed」中談到 King 街會封閉，因此和內容一致。(C)「Dundas Avenue will be closed」中談到 Dundas 街會封閉，因此和內容一致。(D)「We suggest using Royce Avenue ~ as detours」中建議繞道使用 Royce 街，和短文中的內容不一樣，因此答案是 (D)。

175 5W1H 問題

文中要求部分駕駛做什麼？
(A) 遵守速限。
(B) 只行駛主要道路。
(C) 聯絡委員會取得資訊。
(D) 利用道路收費站進入道路。

解析 這是在詢問部分駕駛被要求做什麼（What）的問題，與問題的關鍵詞 some drivers asked to do 有關。「If you decide to use smaller residential streets, please remember to observe the reduced speed limit at all times.」中談到如果要使用住宅區的小道路，記得要隨時遵守降低的速限，因此答案是 (A)。

字彙 follow v. 遵守、跟從　toll booth 道路收費站

問題 176-180，請參考以下備忘錄及表格。

---

¹⁷⁶ 收件人：全體員工
寄件人：Chase Milton
日期：12 月 3 日
主旨：職員節日禮物
附件：禮品選擇卡

致全體員工，

相信各位都知道，節日很快就要到來了，[176] 為了感謝大家今年的辛勞，Carrigan Foods 公司將提供火雞、火腿或蔬食籃給全體員工。[179] 肉類製品 12 月 12 日可拿取，但蔬食籃將會在 12 月 16 日才準備好。

[177] 每位員工只能選擇一個禮物，請多加留意。為了知道各位的選擇，請填寫附件的卡片，並於 12 月 6 日前繳交給各位的主管。若是不想收到任何物品，我們會視作是要把物品送給為街友供餐的地區食物銀行。

希望各位能好好享受禮物與即將到來的節日。

Chase Milton 敬上
董事長，Carrigan Foods 公司

---

indicate v. 顯示　turn in 呈交、交還
food bank 食物銀行（貧困者可免費獲得食物的地方）
homeless n. 街友　coming adj. 即將來臨、下次的

Carrigan Foods 公司
職員禮物選擇卡

請檢查收到食品的標籤上的保管方法，所有產品都必須冷藏或冷凍保管。[178] 建議工作時間結束後從行政室把禮物帶走，避免長時間放置在辦公室或車內。

如果預定分發禮物的日期沒有出勤上班，希望您請同事幫忙領取帶走。超過既定領取日期的食品我們無法幫忙保管，希望各位多加注意，沒有帶走的食物將會捐給食物銀行。

---

[179] 名稱：Selena Kim
員工 ID 編號：1002532
[180-D] 部門：行銷
[180-B] 分機號碼：7457
[180-A] 請從下列選項中選擇一個。
[179] ■ 冷凍火雞
□ 冷凍火腿
□ 蔬食籃

我想把禮物捐給食物銀行：是□　否■

---

storage n. 保管、儲存　instruction n. 方法、指示
refrigerated adj. 冷藏的　frozen adj. 冷凍的
administration office 行政室　shift n. 輪班時間、調動
distribute v. 分配、發布　arrange v. 準備、配置
hold v. 持有、抓住　designated adj. 既定的、指定的
give v. 捐贈、給予

176 5W1H 問題

Carrigan Foods 計劃要做什麼？
(A) 準備節日晚餐。
(B) 向員工表達感謝。
(C) 提供烹飪技術的相關課程。
(D) 送禮品券給部分顧客。

解析 這是在詢問 Carrigan Foods 公司計劃做什麼（What）的問題，確認與問題關鍵詞 Carrigan Foods planning to do 相關的內容。第一篇短文（備忘錄）的「To: All employees」和「To thank everyone for their hard work

this year, Carrigan Foods will provide each employee with a turkey, ham, or basket of vegetarian food.」中談到為了感謝全體員工今年的辛勞，Carrigan Foods 公司將提供火雞、火腿或蔬食籃，因此答案是 (B)。

字彙 organize v. 準備、組織　technique n. 技術、技巧
gift card 禮品券

177 尋找同義詞

在備忘錄第 2 段第 1 行的「select」，意思最接近下列何者？
(A) 投票
(B) 選擇
(C) 分配
(D) 喜好

解析 在包含短文之 select 的句子「Please keep in mind that each employee is allowed to select only one gift.」中，select 作為「選擇」的意思使用，因此 (B) 是正確答案。

178 5W1H 問題

根據內容來看，建議職員做什麼？
(A) 聯絡當地的食物銀行。
(B) 立刻前往保管處。
(C) 業務結束後去取得物品。
(D) 事先決定領取時間。

解析 這是詢問建議職員做什麼事（What）的問題，確認問題關鍵詞 employees advised to do 相關的內容。第二個短文的「It is recommended that you pick up your gift from the administration office when your shift ends」中談到，建議工作時間結束後從行政室把禮物帶走，因此答案是 (C)。
換句話說
pick up your gift ~ when your shift ends 工作時間結束時帶走禮物 → Claim an item after finishing work 完成工作時去拿物品

字彙 claim v. 獲得、主張

179 推論題

Kim 女士最可能會在何時收到她的禮物？
(A) 12 月 3 日
(B) 12 月 6 日
(C) 12 月 12 日
(D) 12 月 16 日

解析 先確認問題的關鍵詞 Ms. Kim 填寫的表格。
線索1 從第二篇短文的「Name: Selena Kim」與「■ Frozen turkey」中可知道 Kim 女士選擇冷凍火雞，但因為沒有提示何時能收到火雞，所以要確認相關內容。
線索2 從第一篇短文的「The meat products will be available on December 12」中可確認肉類產品 12 月 12 日可使用。
綜合兩篇的內容來看，可知道 Kim 女士選擇的冷凍火雞 12 月 12 日可領取，因此答案是 (C)。

180 Not/True 題型

表格中並沒有要求什麼資訊？

(A) 品項偏好
(B) 電話號碼
(C) 領取時間
(D) 部門名稱

解析 這是從短文中找出談論過的內容，與選項對照的 Not/True 問題，因此確認第二篇短文。(A)「Please pick one of the following options[items]」談到可從下列物品中擇一，與短文的內容一致。(B)「Phone Extension: 7457」中可確認分機號碼，與短文的內容一致。(C) 是短文中沒有談到的內容，因此此答案。(D)「Division: Marketing」中可確認部門名稱，與短文的內容一致。

字彙 preference n. 選擇、喜愛

問題 181-185，請參考以下廣告及電子郵件。

第 15 屆年度圖書販售

位於 [183] Ferris 街的 Carlton 圖書館將於 8 月 2 日星期五舉行第 15 屆年度圖書銷售，請各位把已經不看的書籍都交給服務臺的工作人員。[181-A/B/C] 我們的人員會檢查書本是否有撕破、水造成的毀損，以及空白處是否有字跡。如果書本的狀況佳，我們會以適當的價格購買。

另外，我們的圖書館 2 樓販售各種不同的中古書籍，包含古詩的翻譯本以及最新暢銷書等。[183] 所有的平裝書是 5 美元，精裝書是 12 美元。此外，我們還販售 8 美元的大型手提包、20 美元的背包、11 美元的筆記本等各種類型的圖書館物品。

[182] 所有銷售獲得的收益將會捐給提供孩童教學的慈善機構 Appleton 教育協會，想要取得更多關於圖書販售活動的資訊，請至 www.carltonsale.org。

lie around 亂放　margin n. 空白、邊緣
be in good condition 狀態佳　reasonable adj. 適當的、合理的
on sale 販售中、優惠中的　translation n. 翻譯（本）
ancient adj. 古詩　poetry n. 詩
contemporary adj. 最新的、現代的　paperback n. 平裝書
proceeds n. 收益　institute n.（教育、學術）協會
charitable adj. 慈善的、仁慈的　tutoring n. 教學

收件人：<questions@appleton.org>
寄件人：Sally Fisher<sallyfisher44@fastmail.com>
主旨：義工機會
日期：8 月 4 日
附件：履歷

敬啟者，

兩天前，[183] 我在 Carlton 圖書館的銷售活動中購買了 5 美元的物品，收到了 Appleton 教育協會的傳單，[184-A] 雖然先前不曾聽過貴機構的事，但仔細閱讀過傳單後，讓我對您們的貢獻變得相當感興趣。

[184-C] 我是最近退休的前任高中英文教師，但我還在尋找某種程度上能繼續教育工作的途徑，我對於教導閱讀與寫作面臨困難的人有豐富的經驗，我相當喜歡這類工作。因此，我想知道貴機構是否有擔任義工或兼職的機會。

[185] 雖然我星期四會在地區文化會館當志工，大部分的時間都有空。附件有我的履歷，期待很快就能收到閣下的回信。　→

Sally Fisher 敬上

volunteer n. 志工　read over 仔細閱讀　former adj. 先前的
retire v. 退休　be looking to do 計劃去做
extensive adj. 大量的、廣闊的　struggle v. 掙扎、努力
available adj. 有空的、可利用的

181 Not/True 題型

根據廣告內容來看，下列哪一項是圖書館員工不會確認的？
(A) 水造成的毀損
(B) 撕破的頁面
(C) 文字旁的筆跡
(D) 不見的封面

解析 這是詢問問題關鍵句 library staff ~ check used books for 的 Not/True 題目，在談到圖書館員工的第一篇短文中確認相關內容。(A)、(B)、(C)「Our staff will check these books[used books] to make sure that they don't have any torn pages, water damage, or writing in the margins.」中談到，人員會檢查書本是否有撕破、水造成的毀損、以及空白處是否有字跡，和短文中的內容一致。短文中沒有談到 (D) 的內容，因此此答案。

字彙 moisture n. 水分、濕氣　rip v. 撕破　cover n. 封面、蓋子

182 5W1H 問題

販售圖書獲得的收入會如何使用？
(A) 協助非營利組織
(B) 改造閱覽室
(C) 提供資金給公立學校
(D) 宣傳新的雜誌

解析 題目詢問販售圖書獲得之收入的用途（What），在談到關鍵詞 the money raised by the book sale 的廣告中確認相關內容。第一篇短文的「The proceeds from all sales will be donated to the Appleton Institute, a charitable organization that provides tutoring to children.」中談到，所有銷售獲得的收益將捐給提供孩童教學的慈善機構 Appleton 教育協會，因此答案是 (A)。

字彙 raise v. 募集、抬高　nonprofit adj. 非營利的
reading room 閱覽室　public school 公立學校
market v. 廣告、推出（商品）

183 5W1H 問題

Fisher 女士在 Carlton 圖書館裡買了什麼？
(A) 背包
(B) 平裝書
(C) 精裝書
(D) 筆記本

解析 因為是詢問 Fisher 女士在 Carlton 圖書館購買了什麼（What）物品，先確認 Fisher 女士寄出的電子郵件。
線索1 在第二篇短文（電子郵件）的「I bought a $5 item at the Carlton Library's book sale event」中，Fisher 女士說自己在 Carlton 圖書館的活動中購買了 5 美元的物品，但 Carlton 圖書館的圖書銷售活動中沒有說明 5 美元的物品是什麼，必須從公告確認相關內容。

線索2 在第一篇短文（公告）的「The Carlton Library ~ is holding its 15th Annual Book Sale」和「All paperbacks are $5」中，可確認 Carlton 圖書館的販售活動中的平裝書都是 5 美元。

綜合以上來看時，可知道 Fisher 女士在 Carlton 圖書館的活動中買了 5 美元的平裝書。因此答案是 (B)。

184 Not/True 題型

下列哪一項與 Fisher 女士的職業經歷相符？
(A) 她先前曾在 Appleton 教育協會工作。
(B) 她出書幫助有困難的讀者。
(C) 她曾是教職人員。
(D) 她在圖書館提供英文教學。

解析 這是詢問關鍵詞 her professional experience 的 Not/True 題型，在談論 Fisher 女士資歷的第二篇短文（電子郵件）中確認相關內容。(A)「I had never heard of your organization[Appleton Institute] before」中表示先前沒聽過 Appleton 教育協會，因此和短文內容不符。(B) 是短文中沒有提過的內容。(C)「I am a former high school English teacher who has recently retired.」中談到自己是最近退休的高中英文教師，與短文內容一致，因此答案是 (C)。(D) 是短文中沒有談到的內容。

換句話說
a former ~ teacher who has recently retired 最近退休的老師 → was employed as an educator 被僱用為教職人員

字彙 experience n. 資歷、經驗 educator n. 教職人員

185 5W1H 問題

為什麼 Fisher 女士星期四沒空？
(A) 因為語言課程的日程變了。
(B) 因為在書店工作
(C) 因為讀書會每週都有聚會
(D) 因為當志工

解析 題目詢問 Fisher 女士為何（Why）星期四沒空，確認與問題關鍵句 Ms. Fisher not available on Thursdays 相關的電子郵件內容。在第二篇短文（電子郵件）的「I am available on most days of the week, although on Thursdays I perform charity work at a community center.」中談到 Fisher 女士幾乎大部分的時間都有空，但星期四要去地區文化會館進行慈善活動，因此答案是 (D)。

換句話說
perform charity work 從事慈善工作 → has a volunteer position 擁有志工工作

字彙 book club 讀書會 position n. 業務、工作

問題 186-190，請參考以下廣告、電子郵件及表格。

RB 銀行

186 請在 RB 銀行開設帳戶，利用我們的特殊服務。
存款超過 2,500 美元以上時，可享有 60 天的免費交易與現金優惠。*

・存 2,500 美元至 49,999 美元時，100 美元優惠 + 免費交易 ➡

・187 存 50,000 美元至 99,999 美元時，250 美元優惠 + 免費交易
・存 100,000 美元至 249,999 美元時，500 美元優惠 + 免費交易
・存 250,000 美元以上時，750 美元優惠 + 免費交易

186 為何要選擇 RB 銀行呢？
・收費合理，沒有手續費
・186-D 為了所有投資者準備的教育訓練資料
・186-B 可選擇的多元化投資類型
・186-C 財務顧問 24 小時的支援
・桌電與行動裝置容易使用的交易軟體

*服務有效時間到 4 月 30 日，基本交易手續費是 9.99 美元，諮詢請來電 555-2975，或寄電子郵件至 info@rbbank.com，或者也能到我們全國 60 個分行中的其中一個。

---

take advantage of 利用　trading n. 交易、買賣
incentive n. 優惠，獎勵金　deposit v. 存錢；n. 儲蓄、保證金
fair adj. 合理的、公平的　pricing n. 定價
hidden adj. 隱藏的、神祕的　fee n. 手續費、費用
round-the-clock adj. 全天候　financial adviser 財務顧問
valid adj. 有效的　nationwide adj. 全國性的

收件人：Beth Viola <b.viola@ambercrafts.com>
寄件人：Ron Campbell <r.campbell@rbbank.com>
主旨：閣下的帳戶
日期：4 月 21 日

Viola 女士，

187 感謝您在 RB 銀行開設投資帳戶，昨天已經收到您的 50,000 美元存款，您的現金獎勵大約要 60 天後才會送出，希望您能多加留意。

關於您提出的其他問題，通常想貸款的業者有兩種選擇，188/189 第一種是 SBA 貸款，189 這是為了員工未滿 50 名的公司準備的方案，188 利率是 4.9%，最多可貸到 100,000 美元。188 另一個選擇是 CTA 貸款，這是員工人數 50 名以上的企業才能申請的方案，利率是 3.9%，最多可貸到 500,000 美元。如果想知道貸款方案的其他資訊或申請方法，請到我們的官網看。

Ron Campbell 敬上
財務顧問

---

borrow v. 借貸、借　loan n. 貸款　interest rate 利率
borrower n. 借款人　instruction n. 說明

RB 銀行
貸款申請書

公司資訊
189 公司名稱：Amber Crafts 公司
190 所有人：Beth Viola
地址：24016 維吉尼亞州，羅阿諾克，Fairfax 街 527 號
電話：555-2308
電子信箱：b.viola@ambercrafts.com

189 貸款類型：SBA 貸款
☑ 閱讀過 RB 銀行隱私權保護政策後請點擊此處。 ➡

190 繳交的資料必須包括申請書與營業執照影本，請多加注意。

privacy agreement 隱私權保護政策　business license 營業執照

186 Not/True 題型

下列關於 RB 銀行的描述，哪一個在文中並未出現？
(A) 收取業界最低的手續費。
(B) 有各種不同的投資選擇。
(C) 提供 24 小時的金融服務。
(D) 為了投資者提供教育訓練資料。

解析 題目詢問關於 RB 銀行的內容，哪一個在文中並未談到，因此要在談到 RB 銀行的第一篇短文（廣告）中找出相關內容。(A) 是短文中並未談到的內容，因此是答案。(B) 在「Why choose RB Bank?」與「Various investment types to choose from」中表示之所以會選擇 RB 銀行，是因為有多元化的投資類型，因此和短文中的內容一致。(C) 「Round-the-clock support from financial advisers」中說財務顧問會 24 小時給予支援，和短文中的內容一致。(D) 「Educational resources for every investor」中提到為了所有投資者準備的教育訓練資料，和短文中的內容一致。

換句話說
Various investment types to choose from 可選擇的多元化投資類型 → a range of investment options 多元化投資選擇
Round-the-clock support from financial advisers 財務顧問全天候的支援 → 24-hour financial support 全天候的金融支援
Educational resources for every investor 為了所有投資者準備的教育訓練資料 → learning materials for investors 為了投資者準備的教育訓練資料

字彙 a range of 多樣的

187 5W1H 問題

Viola 女士開設投資帳戶會收到多少現金？
(A) 100 美元
(B) 250 美元
(C) 500 美元
(D) 750 美元

解析 問題的關鍵句 cash will Ms. Viola receive for opening an investment account 中詢問 Viola 女士開設投資帳戶會收到多少（How much）現金，因此先確認寄給 Viola 女士的電子郵件。
線索1 在第二篇短文（電子郵件）的「Thank you for opening an investment account with RB Bank. Your deposit of $50,000 was received yesterday. ~ your cash bonus to be released.」中談到 Viola 女士在 RB 銀行開設投資帳戶存入 50,000 美元，而且會給予現金獎勵，但因為沒有提到會給予多少現金獎勵，因此要從廣告中確認相關內容。
線索2 在第一篇短文（廣告）的「Open an investment account with RB Bank ~. Get ~ a cash incentive when you deposit $2,500 or more.」中，談到從 RB 銀行開設投資帳戶後若是存 2,500 美元以上就能獲得現金優惠，從「$250 incentive ~ with deposit of $50,000 to $99,999」中可確認存 50,000 至 99,999 美元時可獲得 250 美元的獎勵。

綜合兩個部分來看，因為 Viola 女士開設投資帳戶時存了 50,000 美元，應該可獲得現金 250 美元，所以答案是 (B)。

188 5W1H 問題

從電子郵件的內容來看，CTA 貸款比 SBA 貸款更有利的是哪一個部分？
(A) 加入獎勵更多
(B) 利率更低
(C) 貸款期間更長
(D) 申請程序比較沒那麼複雜

解析 題目詢問 CTA 貸款的哪一點（What）比 SBA 貸款更為有利，從談論到問題關鍵詞 CTA 貸款與 SBA 貸款的電子郵件中查看相關的內容。在第二篇短文（電子郵件）的「The first is the SBA Loan.」與「Up to $100,000 may be borrowed at a 4.9-percent interest rate.」中有談到 SBA 貸款的利率是 4.9%，「The other option is the CTA Loan.」與「For this loan, up to $500,000 is available to the borrower at a 3.9-percent interest rate.」中談到 CTA 貸款的利率是 3.9%，由此可知 CTA 貸款的利率比 SBA 貸款更低，所以答案是 (B)。

字彙 advantage n. 有利因素、優勢　generous adj. 大量的、豐富的　signup n. 加入　borrowing n. 貸款　complex adj. 複雜的

189 推論題

關於 Amber Crafts，有何暗示？
(A) 持有者正在尋找投資者。
(B) 近期開了其他分店。
(C) 產品在多個國家販售。
(D) 僱用的職員未滿 50 名。

解析 先確認談到問題關鍵詞 Amber Crafts 的表格。
線索1 在第三篇短文（表格）的「Company Name: Amber Crafts」與「Loan Type: SBA Loan」中談到 Amber Crafts 公司申請了 SBA 貸款，卻沒有提出 SBA 貸款的相關資訊，因此確認電子郵件的相關內容。
線索2 在第二篇短文（電子郵件）的「The first is the SBA Loan. This is for companies with fewer than 50 employees.」中談到 SBA 貸款是員工未滿 50 名的公司可申辦的方案。
綜合兩個部分來看，因為 Amber Crafts 公司申請了 SBA 貸款，可知道該公司的員工未滿 50 名，所以答案是 (D)。

字彙 look for 尋找、尋求　multiple adj. 多個、多樣的

190 5W1H 問題

Viola 女士被要求提供什麼？
(A) 人事紀錄
(B) 財務報表
(C) 營業執照
(D) 合法契約

解析 題目詢問 Viola 女士被要求提供什麼（What），因此要確認 Viola 女士填寫的表格內容。在第三篇短文（表格）的「Please note that you must include a copy of your company's business license with your application.」中談到繳交的資料必須包括申請書與營業執照影本，因此答案是 (C)。

字彙 personnel records 人事紀錄　financial statement 財務報表
operating adj. 經營上的　permit n. 許可證；v. 允許
legal adj. 合法的

問題 191-195，請參考以下說明、廣告和信件。

關於 Empire 集團

短短 25 年，Empire 集團就成為具備建設與融資能力的房地產開發龍頭。

目前 [191-C]Empire 集團在包含紐約、舊金山、洛杉磯等 45 個城市進行商辦與住宅建案。過去 2 年，Empire 集團在馬來西亞、加拿大、德國建設辦公建築與住宅，藉此鞏固在國際上的地位。不僅如此，集團在美國還建造了由 Blackwood 公司與 Le Clare 公司等大型企業營運的 32 間飯店。

近期 Empire 集團的事業擴展到澳洲，[192] 在澳洲的初期目標是在高收入人口多的城市提升員工的人數，就和在其他地區一樣。

---

leader n. 先驅、領導者　property n. 房地產、財產
experience n. 能力、經驗　financing n. 融資
carry out 執行　commercial adj. 商業的　residential adj. 居住的
establish v. 堅定、設立　presence n. 存在、影響力
operator n. 公司、經營者　initial adj. 初期的、一開始的
aim n. 目標、目的　workforce n. 職員、勞動力
population n. 人口

---

[192]Empire 集團澳洲分公司正在徵求幾個正職適任人員。想要應徵就請把履歷寄到 jobs@empiregroup.au。

秘書
- [192] 兩個職位（布里斯本與墨爾本）
- 職務包含行政支援
- 一定要能配合出差
- 具備在企業工作 2 年以上之資歷的大學畢業者尤佳

[195] **人資部職員**
- 兩個職位（墨爾本和伯斯）
- 職務包含處理職員相關業務，以及支援招募活動
- 必須具備 3 年以上相關資歷，以及人力資源管理學的學位
- [195] 優先僱用具備專業資格證的應徵者

簽約專家
- 四個職位（雪梨與伯斯）
- 職務包含管理供應商關係以及談判商務合約
- 必須具備 5 年以上的房地產資歷，以及企業管理學的學位

[193] **行銷職員**
- [192] 兩個職位（布里斯本和伯斯）
- 職務包含調查與開發廣告活動
- [193-D] 必須擅長使用辦公軟體與表達演說
- [193-B] 必須具備 3 年以上的房地產資歷，以及大學學歷

➡

---

qualified adj. 合格的、勝任的　executive assistant 秘書
duty n. 職務、任務　willing adj. 樂意的、心甘情願的
priority n. 優先權　negotiate v. 談成、協商
real estate 房仲業　proficient adj. 精通的　adept at 熟練的

Empire 集團澳洲分公司
www.empiregroup.au

7 月 14 日

Chen 女士，

感謝您的應徵與面試，[194] 但很遺憾的是，我們決定錄取其他應徵者。

[195] 您的資歷與教育程度都滿足我們的基本要求，但我們選擇的應徵者具備尚未取得的幾項資格證照。

希望您之後求職順利，建議您之後可以應徵 Empire 集團的其他職位，公司目前在澳洲還處於初期階段，就業務發展有進一步規劃，特別是在您所在的墨爾本。

Leonora Mitchell 敬上
僱用專家

---

in terms of 就～而言　continued adj. 延續、持續的
early stage 初期階段　further adj. 另外的、更進一步的

---

191 Not/True 題型

關於 Empire 集團的敘述，哪一個是正確的？
(A) 剛開始是一間金融服務公司。
(B) 大部分的辦公室都在歐洲。
(C) 建造商業與居住用建築物。
(D) 建造的部分飯店下個月要開幕了。

解析 題目詢問關鍵詞 Empire Group 的相關敘述，確認與 Empire 集團相關的第一篇短文（說明）。(A) 和 (B) 是短文中沒有談到的內容，(C) 「Empire Group carries out commercial and residential construction projects」中談到 Empire 集團在執行商辦與住宅建案，與短文的內容一致，所以答案是 (C)。(D) 是短文中沒有談到的內容。

192 推論題

關於布里斯本，可推論出什麼？
(A) 可應徵的工作最多。
(B) Empire 集團澳洲總公司的所在地。
(C) 有很多高收入的居民。
(D) 是準備舉辦房地產博覽會的地方。

解析 先確認有談到關鍵詞 the city of Brisbane 的廣告。
線索1 在第二篇短文（廣告）的「Empire Group Australia is seeking qualified candidates to fill several full-time positions.」和「Two positions（Brisbane and Melbourne）」、「Two positions（Brisbane and Perth）」當中談到 Empire 集團澳洲分公司正在召募幾個正職人員，包括布里斯本，但沒提到 Empire 集團澳洲分公司的僱用資訊，因此要確認說明文。
線索2 在第一篇短文（說明）的「its[Empire Group] initial aim in Australia is to increase its workforce in cities that have a large population of upper-income residents」當中談到澳洲的 Empire 集團的初期目標是，

提升高收入人口多的城市的職員數量。

綜合來看時，Empire 集團澳洲分公司徵求職員的布里斯本有很多的高收入居民，因此答案是 (C)。

字彙 job opening 工作機會、職缺　exposition n. 博覽會、展示會

193 Not/True 題型

關於廣告的行銷職務，哪一個是真的？
(A) 包含超過銷售目標的獎勵。
(B) 只開放給具備行銷系學位的應徵者。
(C) 偶爾需要去國外出差。
(D) 需具備優秀的電腦實力。

解析 這是在詢問關鍵詞 marketing positions 的問題，從談過 marketing positions 的第二篇短文（廣告）中確認相關內容。(A) 是短文中不曾談過的內容。(B)「Marketing associate」和「Must be college graduates with 3+ years of real estate work experience」中只有談過行銷職員的職務，沒有提到資歷的內容，因此與短文內容不符。(C) 是短文中沒有出現的內容。(D)「Must be proficient in office software」中談到必須擅長使用辦公軟體，與短文內容一致，所以答案是 (D)。

換句話說
be proficient in office software 擅長使用辦公軟體 →
good computer skills 優秀的電腦實力

字彙 exceed v. 超過　be open to 對～開放
occasional adj. 非經常的、偶爾的

194 尋找目的

Mitchell 女士為何會寫信？
(A) 為了恭賀成功被錄取者
(B) 為了請應徵者來面試
(C) 為了回絕求職者
(D) 為了要求提供詳細的履歷

解析 題目是要找出 Mitchell 女士寫信的用意，確認 Mitchell 女士的信件內容。第三篇短文（信件）的「Unfortunately, we have decided to give the job to another applicant.」中該公司表示很遺憾，因為他們決定錄取其他應徵者，並解釋對方被淘汰的理由，因此答案是 (C)。

字彙 successful applicant 成功錄取者　invite v. 要求、邀請
reject v. 不合格、拒絕　detail n. 詳細情報、細節問題
work history 履歷

195 推論題

Chen 女士應徵了哪一種職務？
(A) 秘書
(B) 人資部的職員
(C) 簽約專家
(D) 行銷職員

解析 在關鍵句 position ~ Ms. Chen ~apply for 中有詢問 Chen 女士應徵何種職務，因此要先確認寄給 Chen 女士的信件。
線索1 在第三篇短文（信件）的「Although you met our basic requirements in terms of experience and education, the applicant we selected has several certificates that you have not yet received.」中談到，

雖然 Chen 女士的資歷與教育程度符合基本要求，但錄取者擁有 Chen 女士未具備的多項資格證照。由於沒有談到證照持有者應徵的職務，所以要在廣告中確認內容。
線索2 在第二篇短文（廣告）的「Human resources worker」和「Priority given to candidates with professional certification」當中可知道人資部的職務會優先錄取具備專業證照的應徵者。

綜合兩者來看，可知因為 Chen 女士是應徵人資部的職務，所以會優先錄取有證照的人，正確答案是 (B)。

問題 196-200，請參考以下網頁、電子郵件和手冊。

---

www.pps.org

費城保護協會（PPS）

196 拜費城保護協會舉辦的活動所賜，費城得以舉辦國內最大公共美術展覽之一，每個人都能享有免費觀賞作品的機會。

這裡有幾個方法能讓各位支持我們執行保護公共美術的任務。

• 198 加入 PPS 個人會員，接受 PPS 特別活動的事前邀約。
• 成為 PPS 企業的合作夥伴，每年都能免費參加我們準備的半年一次的晚宴。
• 點擊此處捐款，無論金額多寡。197 捐贈時可獲得免費的 PPS 咖啡馬克杯。

preservation n. 保護　thanks to 由於
boast v. 擁有（值得驕傲的東西）、誇耀　ongoing adj. 進行中的
collection n. 展示（會）、收集（品）　background n. 背景、出身
access n. 機會、途徑　mission n. 任務、使命
advance adj. 事前的；v. 前進　semiannual adj. 半年一次的
banquet n. 晚餐、宴會　at no cost 不需支付費用、免費

收件人：Marilyn Johnson <m.johnson@pps.org>
寄件人：Dixie Piper <p.piper@solomon.edu>
主旨：課程活動
日期：5 月 2 日

Johnson 女士，

198 我最近加入了費城保護協會的個人會員，我想帶我的 6 年級美術班去參加您的宣傳手冊上的自助旅遊。199 如果可以的話，我想帶學生們去可以素描的湖泊或河流附近，活動時間是星期五上午 9 點到 12 點，午餐時間則以野餐的方式結束。199 另外，您的自助旅遊中似乎也有租借自行車的選項，為了這次的活動，我想要租自行車。為了能制定具體的計劃，希望您能提供一下意見。

謝謝。

Dixie Piper 敬上

ideally adv. 可能的話、理想地　lead v. 帶領、引導
end with 結束於　concrete adj. 具體的

費城保護協會的自助旅遊

自助旅遊是享受費城公共美術非常好的一個方法！請進行下列費城保護協會準備的其中一項旅遊方式吧。

200-D 自然中心
200-A 2 小時的旅程

費城美術館
1 小時的旅程

在 28,000 平方公尺空間中充滿整齊且綠意盎然的樹木，來參觀充滿現代美術魅力的公共藝術作品。（200-D 庭院只有平日上午 9 點至下午 3 點開放。）

美術館周圍地區是許多雕刻作品的誕生地，為了能欣賞更多的美術品，請立刻前往此一美術館。

（美術館外部區域星期一禁止民眾進出。）

199/200-C Kelly 路
200-A 2.5 小時的旅程

里滕豪斯廣場
1 小時的旅程

199 沿著 Schuylkill 河經過途中的無數戶外雕刻品，同時享受悠閒的旅遊。（199/200-C 自行車可在 Floyd 大廳租借。）

里滕豪斯廣場是費城成立以來就一直存在的美麗公園，請好好欣賞廣場上的各種歷史雕刻品。

詳情請至 www.pps.org。

---

fascinating adj. 吸引人的　amid prep. 在～之中、當中
well-tended adj. 整齊的　greenery n. 綠樹
ground n. 庭園、地面　leisurely adj. 悠閒的、從容的
a number of 大量的　sculpture n. 雕刻品
on the way 在途中　home n. 誕生地、故鄉
date back to 起源於、追溯至　founding n. 設立、樹立

196 推論題
費城保護協會最可能是在做什麼的？
(A) 提供當地學生美術教學。
(B) 管理城市的觀光產業。
(C) 提供資金保存近代建築物。
(D) 保存美術品供民眾觀賞。

解析 這是針對關鍵詞 Philadelphia Preservation Society 推論的問題，確認有談論到費城保護協會的網站。在第一篇短文（網頁）的「Thanks to the work of the Philadelphia Preservation Society, Philadelphia boasts one of the largest ongoing collections of public art in the country.」中談到因為費城保護協會舉辦活動的關係，費城才能進行全國數一數二的公共美術展，「People from all backgrounds can enjoy access to these works at any time for free.」中則提到每個人都能享有免費觀賞作品的機會，由此可推論費城保護協會是為了讓大眾觀賞而保存美術品，所以答案是 (D)。

字彙 tourist industry 觀光產業　modern adj. 近代的、現代的　maintain v. 保存、維護　artwork n. 美術品

197 5W1H 問題
捐款者能獲得什麼？
(A) 會員折扣
(B) 免費商品
(C) 寫有資訊的小冊子
(D) 免費體驗課程

解析 題目詢問要提供什麼（What）給捐款者，確認談到關鍵

句 offered to those who give a donation 的網頁。在第一篇短文（網頁）的「Get a free PPS coffee mug when you donate.」中談到捐款時可獲得免費的 PPS 咖啡馬克杯，因此答案是 (B)。

換句話說
a free ~ coffee mug 免費咖啡馬克杯 →
A complimentary item 免費商品

198 推論題
關於 Piper 女士的暗示為何？
(A) 可收到 PPS 活動的邀請。
(B) 近期參加了戶外教學。
(C) 為了她的團體取得資金。
(D) 將會對 PPS 進行一次捐款。

解析 先確認問題的關鍵詞 Ms. Piper 寫的電子郵件。
線索 1 在第二篇短文（電子郵件）的「I recently signed up as an individual member of the Philadelphia Preservation Society」中談到 Piper 女士最近加入費城保護協會的個人會員，但沒有談到費城保護協會個人會員的相關資訊，因此要從網頁中確認相關內容。
線索 2 在第一篇短文（網頁）的「Join as a PPS individual member and receive advance invitations to PPS special events.」中可確認加入 PPS 個人會員，就會收到 PPS 特殊活動的邀請。綜合兩者來看，因為 Piper 女士已經加入 PPS 個人會員，之後能收到 PPS 特殊活動的邀請，所以答案是 (A)。

字彙 field trip 戶外教學　secure v. 確保、獲得

199 5W1H 問題
Piper 女士對哪一種旅遊感興趣？
(A) 自然中心
(B) Kelly 路
(C) 費城美術館
(D) 里滕豪斯廣場

解析 先確認問題的關鍵詞 Ms. Piper 寫的電子郵件。
線索 1 在第二篇短文（電子郵件）的「I'd like to lead the students on a tour near a lake or river」中，Piper 女士說想帶學生們去湖泊或河川附近旅遊，在「Also, I'd prefer to rent bikes for this activity since one of your self-guided tours seemed to have that option.」中則談到「自助旅遊中似乎也有租借自行車的選項，為了這次的活動，還想要租自行車。」不過，文中並未提到可去湖泊或河川，以及租借自行車的旅遊是哪一個，因此必須從小冊子中確認相關內容。
線索 2 在第三篇短文（小冊子）的「Kelly Drive」和「Take a leisurely trip along the Schuylkill River」、「Bike rentals available」當中談到選擇 Kelly 路旅遊時，可沿著 Schuylkill 河參觀，並且租借自行車。
綜合這兩者來看時，由此可知 Piper 女士對可沿著河川旅遊並租借自行車的 Kelly 路遊覽比較有興趣，所以答案是 (B)。

200 Not/True 題型
關於自助旅遊的描述，提到了什麼？
(A) 各自都需要一個小時才會結束。

(B) 讓學生和團體打折。

(C) 適合所有騎自行車的人。

(D) 部分在特定日子無法使用。

解析 此為詢問關鍵詞 self-guided tours 的題目，在談到自助旅遊時的第三篇短文（小冊子）中確認相關內容。(A)在「2-hour trip」和「2.5-hour trip」當中談到有 2 小時與 2.5 小時的旅遊，和短文內容不一致。(B) 是短文中沒有提過的內容。(C) 在「Kelly Drive」和「Bike rentals available」中談到只有 Kelly 路可租借自行車，與短文的內容不一致。(D)「Nature Center」和「Grounds are open on weekdays only」中談到自然中心的庭園只有平日開放，和短文的內容一致，所以答案是 (D)。

換句話說
open on weekdays only 只有平日開放 → unavailable on certain days of the week 每週特定日子無法使用

字彙 complete v. 結束、完成　suitable adj. 適合的

LISTENING TEST

p.112

1 (D)	2 (D)	3 (A)	4 (D)	5 (A)
6 (B)	7 (A)	8 (A)	9 (C)	10 (B)
11 (A)	12 (C)	13 (B)	14 (C)	15 (B)
16 (B)	17 (C)	18 (A)	19 (A)	20 (C)
21 (B)	22 (C)	23 (B)	24 (C)	25 (C)
26 (B)	27 (A)	28 (C)	29 (C)	30 (A)
31 (A)	32 (C)	33 (C)	34 (B)	35 (D)
36 (A)	37 (A)	38 (A)	39 (C)	40 (B)
41 (A)	42 (C)	43 (C)	44 (A)	45 (D)
46 (C)	47 (A)	48 (C)	49 (A)	50 (C)
51 (B)	52 (D)	53 (B)	54 (B)	55 (D)
56 (C)	57 (C)	58 (A)	59 (B)	60 (D)
61 (B)	62 (B)	63 (A)	64 (B)	65 (B)
66 (B)	67 (D)	68 (C)	69 (B)	70 (A)
71 (C)	72 (B)	73 (B)	74 (A)	75 (A)
76 (B)	77 (B)	78 (A)	79 (B)	80 (A)
81 (A)	82 (A)	83 (B)	84 (D)	85 (A)
86 (D)	87 (D)	88 (B)	89 (D)	90 (D)
91 (C)	92 (D)	93 (B)	94 (A)	95 (B)
96 (B)	97 (B)	98 (A)	99 (C)	100 (B)

READING TEST

p.124

101 (D)	102 (B)	103 (A)	104 (D)	105 (A)
106 (B)	107 (A)	108 (B)	109 (A)	110 (A)
111 (B)	112 (A)	113 (B)	114 (C)	115 (C)
116 (C)	117 (B)	118 (A)	119 (C)	120 (C)
121 (D)	122 (D)	123 (C)	124 (D)	125 (C)
126 (C)	127 (C)	128 (B)	129 (A)	130 (A)
131 (C)	132 (A)	133 (A)	134 (D)	135 (A)
136 (D)	137 (C)	138 (B)	139 (B)	140 (C)
141 (D)	142 (A)	143 (A)	144 (C)	145 (C)
146 (C)	147 (B)	148 (C)	149 (D)	150 (A)
151 (C)	152 (D)	153 (C)	154 (C)	155 (C)
156 (C)	157 (D)	158 (C)	159 (C)	160 (D)
161 (B)	162 (C)	163 (A)	164 (C)	165 (C)
166 (D)	167 (B)	168 (A)	169 (B)	170 (D)
171 (C)	172 (B)	173 (D)	174 (B)	175 (A)
176 (A)	177 (C)	178 (A)	179 (D)	180 (B)
181 (D)	182 (B)	183 (C)	184 (A)	185 (A)
186 (A)	187 (B)	188 (D)	189 (C)	190 (D)
191 (B)	192 (D)	193 (A)	194 (B)	195 (D)
196 (C)	197 (B)	198 (D)	199 (B)	200 (D)

PART 1

1 🔊 澳洲發音

(A) He is walking up some steps.
(B) He is relaxing in a lobby.
(C) He is drinking from a cup.
(D) He is reading a newspaper.

relax 休息

翻譯 (A) 他在爬樓梯。
　　(B) 他在大廳休息。
　　(C) 他在用茶杯喝東西。
　　(D) 他在看報紙。

解析 1 人照片
　　(A) [✕] 男子坐在階梯上，正在爬樓梯（walking up）的描述是錯誤的。
　　(B) [✕] 照片中的場所並非大廳（lobby），因此這是錯誤的選項。
　　(C) [✕] drinking（正在喝東西）此一描述和男子的動作無關，因此是錯誤的選項。
　　(D) [○] 男子在看報紙的描述是最正確的答案。

2 🔊 美國發音

(A) They are looking at a computer.
(B) They are putting on safety gear.
(C) They are moving some equipment.
(D) They are reviewing some documents.

safety gear 安全裝備

翻譯 (A) 他們正在看電腦。
　　(B) 他們戴著安全裝備。
　　(C) 他們正在搬運一些裝備。
　　(D) 他們正在檢視一些文件。

解析 2 人以上的照片
　　(A) [✕] 人物都在看文件，看電腦的描述是錯誤的。
　　(B) [✕] putting on（穿戴）與人物的動作沒有關係，因此是錯誤的選項。注意不要把代表已經是穿戴衣服、帽子、鞋子等狀態的 wearing 和正在穿戴的動作 putting on 搞混。
　　(C) [✕] moving（正在搬運）和人物的動作沒關係，因此是錯誤選項。
　　(D) [○] 描述人物在檢視文件的選項是正確答案。

3 🔊 加拿大發音

(A) Some cars are parked along a street.
(B) A lamppost has fallen over.
(C) There are many vehicles driving by the building.
(D) A truck is being towed.

---

lamppost 路燈柱（燈柱）　fall over 倒下、跌倒
vehicle 車輛、交通工具　tow 拖吊、拖

翻譯 **(A)** 有一些車輛沿街停放。
　　(B) 路燈柱倒下了。
　　(C) 經過建築物的車輛有很多。
　　(D) 卡車正在被拖吊。

解析 事物與風景照
　　(A) [○] 車輛沿街停放的描述是最正確的選項。
　　(B) [×] 路燈柱是豎立的狀態，倒下是錯誤的描述。
　　(C) [×] 車輛都是停放的狀態，經過建築物的描述是錯誤的。
　　(D) [×] 照片中無法確認卡車正在被拖吊（is being towed），因此是錯誤選項。

4 🔊 澳洲發音

(A) A man is leaning against the bookcase.
(B) A picture is being displayed on the wall.
(C) A medical device is being plugged in.
(D) A man is resting his elbow on a desk.

---

lean against 靠著　bookcase 書櫃　display 展示
medical device 醫療設備　plug in 插上～的插座　rest 躺、倚靠
elbow 手肘

翻譯 (A) 一名男子倚靠著書櫃。
　　(B) 圖畫展示在牆壁上。
　　(C) 醫療設備目前插著插頭。
　　(D) 一名男子把手肘放在桌上。

解析 1 人照片
　　(A) [×] 男子不是靠著書櫃，而是倚靠書桌，因此這是錯誤的選項。
　　(B) [×] 因為從照片中無法確認牆上是否展示了圖畫（picture），因此是錯誤選項。
　　(C) [×] 照片中雖然能看見醫療設備，但插頭沒有插上（is being plugged in），因此是錯誤選項。
　　(D) [○] 男子的手肘放在書桌上是最正確的描述，此一選項是答案。

5 🔊 美國發音

(A) A bicycle is positioned next to a building.
(B) Some lines are being painted on a road.
(C) A door is propped open.
(D) Some flowers are being planted in pots.

---

position 放在～、擱　prop 支撐　plant 種植

翻譯 **(A)** 自行車放在建築物旁。
　　(B) 路上正在畫幾條線。
　　(C) 門是開著的狀態。
　　(D) 花盆正在種一些花朵。

解析 事物與風景照
　　(A) [○] 自行車停放在建築物旁的描述是最正確的，因此是正確答案。
　　(B) [×] 路上早已畫有好幾條線，因此「正在畫」（are being painted）的動作是錯誤的描述。
　　(C) [×] 門是關閉的狀態，開啟的描述是錯誤的。
　　(D) [×] 花盆中已經種了好多花，因此正在種植（are being planted）是錯誤的描述。

6 🔊 英國發音

(A) A man is removing his apron.
(B) Produce is in boxes at an outdoor market.
(C) A woman is hanging up a sign.
(D) Customers are lined up to buy groceries.

---

apron 圍裙　produce 農產品、收種物　outdoor 戶外的、屋外的
hang up 掛上　line up 排隊

翻譯 (A) 男子正在脫圍裙。
　　(B) 農產品在露天市場上的箱子內。
　　(C) 女子正在掛標示牌。
　　(D) 顧客們在排隊購買雜貨。

解析 2 人以上的照片
　　(A) [×] 男子穿著圍裙，正在脫圍裙是錯誤的描述。
　　(B) [○] 農產品在露天市場的箱子內是最正確的描述，因此是答案。
　　(C) [×] hanging up（正掛著）與女子的動作沒有關係，因此是錯誤選項。由於使用了照片中的標示牌（sign）一字，所以會造成混淆。
　　(D) [×] 從照片中無法看見排隊購買雜貨的客人，因此是錯誤選項。由於使用了照片中雜貨（groceries）一字，所以會造成混淆。

PART 2

7 美國發音→澳洲發音

Where is the locker room located?
(A) Across from the entrance.
(B) To change my clothes.
(C) It was donated.

locker room 更衣室　locate 位於～　across from ～的對面
entrance 入口　donate 捐贈

翻譯　更衣室在哪裡？
　　　(A) 在入口的對面。
　　　(B) 為了換衣服。
　　　(C) 那個已經捐贈了。

解析　Where 疑問句
　　　(A) [○] 回答在入口的對面，因談到更衣室的位置，所以是正確答案。
　　　(B) [×] 使用和 locker room（更衣室）相關的 clothes（衣服），所以會造成混淆，是錯誤選項。
　　　(C) [×] 使用與 located 發音相似的 donated，是會造成混淆的錯誤選項。

8 加拿大發音→美國發音

Why are you going to visit the shopping mall?
(A) I need a new shirt.
(B) In my shopping bag.
(C) Because a customer took it.

customer 客人、顧客

翻譯　為什麼你要去購物中心？
　　　(A) 我需要新襯衫。
　　　(B) 在我的購物包裡。
　　　(C) 因為有客人拿走了。

解析　Why 疑問句
　　　(A) [○] 內容中談到需要新襯衫，因有談到去購物中心的理由，所以是正確答案。
　　　(B) [×] 因重複使用問題中的 shopping，是會造成混淆的錯誤選項。
　　　(C) [×] 因使用了和問題的 shopping mall（購物中心）相關的 customer（客人），是會造成混淆的錯誤選項。

9 美國發音→加拿大發音

How often does the bus stop here?
(A) On top of the car.
(B) Do you have my bus pass?
(C) About every 30 minutes.

on top of 在～之上　bus pass 車票

翻譯　公車多久會來一班？

（A) 在汽車的上面。
（B) 你有拿我的車票嗎？
(C) 大概每 30 分鐘一班吧。

解析　How 疑問句
　　　(A) [×] 因使用了和問題的 bus（公車）相關的 car（汽車），是會造成混淆的錯誤選項。
　　　(B) [×] 因使用了和問題的 bus（公車）相關的 bus pass（車票），是會造成混淆的錯誤選項。
　　　(C) [○] 回答每隔 30 分鐘會來一班，因談到公車來的頻率，所以是答案。

10 美國發音→澳洲發音

When are you holding interviews for the receptionist position?
(A) For the main reception desk.
(B) Within the next week.
(C) I'm excited to begin the job!

hold an interview 面試、與～面會　receptionist 接待員
position 職務、工作

翻譯　你何時要去面試接待員的職務？
　　　(A) 為了主要接待處。
　　　(B) 下星期內。
　　　(C) 我很高興能開始這份工作！

解析　When 疑問句
　　　(A) [×] 因使用與 receptionist 發音相似的 reception desk，是會造成混淆的錯誤選項。
　　　(B) [○] 內容談到下星期內，因有談到面試的時間，所以是正確答案。
　　　(C) [×] 因使用和問題的 position（職務）相關的 job（工作），是會造成混淆的錯誤選項。

11 澳洲發音→美國發音

Can I use your phone to make a brief call?
(A) Yes, no problem.
(B) No, in the telephone book.
(C) A pretty short walk.

brief（時間）短的　telephone book 電話簿

翻譯　我可以用你的電話進行簡短的通話嗎？
　　　(A) 是，沒問題。
　　　(B) 不，在電話簿裡面。
　　　(C) 就走一小段路吧。

解析　請求疑問句
　　　(A) [○] 回答 Yes 同意想借電話使用的要求，是正確答案。
　　　(B) [×] 因使用和問題中的 phone（電話）相關的 telephone book（電話簿），是會造成混淆的錯誤選項。
　　　(C) [×] 因使用和問題中的 brief（〔時間〕短）相同意思的 short（〔時間〕短），是會造成混淆的錯誤選項。

12 英國發音→加拿大發音

Which banquet guests will be seated at the front table?
(A) Well, these chairs should be moved.
(B) This is a nice place for an event.
(C) Our company's board members.

banquet 宴會　seat 坐、請～坐下　board member 董事會成員

翻譯 哪些宴會嘉賓會坐在前面的桌子？
(A) 嗯，這些椅子必須要搬走。
(B) 這裡是舉辦活動的好地方。
(C) 我們公司的董事會成員。

解析 Which 疑問句
(A) [×] 因使用了和問題中的 seated（坐著的）相關的 chairs（椅子），是會造成混淆的錯誤選項。
(B) [×] 因使用了和問題中的 banquet（宴會）相關的 event（活動），是會造成混淆的錯誤選項。
(C) [○] 回答董事會成員，因談到坐在前面桌子的嘉賓，所以是正確答案。

13 英國發音→美國發音

What is the matter with your motorcycle?
(A) That's the problem.
(B) The back tire has a hole.
(C) My brother is a mechanic, too.

motorcycle 摩托車　mechanic 技師

翻譯 你的摩托車有什麼問題嗎？
(A) 那就是問題。
(B) 後輪破洞了。
(C) 我弟弟也是技師。

解析 What 疑問句
(A) [×] 使用和問題的 matter（問題）相同意思的 problem（問題），是會造成混淆的錯誤選項。
(B) [○] 回答後輪破洞了，因談到摩托車發生問題，所以是正確答案。
(C) [×] 因使用了和 motorcycle（摩托車）相關的 mechanic（技師），是會造成混淆的錯誤選項。

14 澳洲→英國發音

Who is responsible for updating the employee manual?
(A) Ms. Dunlap wrote the reports.
(B) Employees found it quite helpful.
(C) It has yet to be decided.

responsible for 對～負責的　manual 小冊子　quite 相當
helpful 有用的、有幫助的

翻譯 是誰負責更新員工手冊的？
(A) Dunlap 女士寫了那些報告書。
(B) 職員們發現那相當有幫助。

(C) 目前還沒決定。

解析 Who 疑問句
(A) [×] 因使用了和問題中的 employee manual（員工手冊）相關的 report（報告），是會造成混淆的錯誤選項。
(B) [×] 因問題中的 employee 以 employees 重複使用，因此造成了混淆，另也使用和 employee manual（員工手冊）相關的 helpful（有用的），是會造成混淆的錯誤選項。
(C) [○] 回答目前還沒決定，間接表達不清楚是誰負責更新，所以是正確答案。

15 澳洲發音→美國發音

How large is the new couch in the waiting area?
(A) There's a furniture store nearby.
(B) Big enough for four people.
(C) I'll wait for you after the show.

couch 沙發　waiting area 等候室　furniture 傢俱

翻譯 等候室裡的新沙發有多大？
(A) 附近有傢俱店。
(B) 足夠讓四個人坐。
(C) 表演結束後我會等你。

解析 How 疑問句
(A) [×] 因使用和問題的 couch（沙發）相關的 furniture（傢俱），是會造成混淆的錯誤選項。
(B) [○] 回答足夠讓四個人一起坐，因談到沙發的尺寸，所以是正確答案。
(C) [×] 使用和 waiting 發音相似的 wait，是會造成混淆的錯誤選項。

16 澳洲發音→英國發音

Where is Peter right now?
(A) He is the supervisor.
(B) Weren't you just with him?
(C) That's the wrong number.

supervisor 主管、監督者

翻譯 Peter 現在在哪裡？
(A) 他是主管。
(B) 你剛剛不是和他在一起嗎？
(C) 那是錯誤的號碼。

解析 Where 疑問句
(A) [×] 因使用了可代表 Peter 的 He，是會造成混淆的錯誤選項。
(B) [○] 反問對方剛剛不是和他在一起，間接回答不清楚 Peter 在哪裡，因此是正確答案。
(C) [×] 使用 wrong（錯誤）引起混淆，問題中的 right 是「立即」的意思，它同時也有「正確」的意思，和 wrong（錯誤）相反。

17 加拿大發音→美國發音

This television came with a scratch on it.
(A) Our electronics are on sale.
(B) The colors match well.
(C) We can exchange it for you.

scratch 刮、刮痕　electronics 電器　on sale 優惠中的
match 合適、一致　exchange 交換

翻譯　這個電視送來時就有刮痕了。
　　　(A) 我們的電器目前有優惠。
　　　(B) 顏色很搭。
　　　(C) 我們可以幫您換過。

解析　直述句
　　　(A) [×] 因使用和 television（電視）相關的 electronics
　　　　　（電器），是會造成混淆的錯誤選項。
　　　(B) [×] 使用了和 scratch 發音相似的 match，是會造成
　　　　　混淆的錯誤選項。
　　　(C) [○] 回答可以幫忙換過，等於是提出電視有刮痕之問
　　　　　題的解決方案，因此是答案。

18 英國發音→加拿大發音

Would you empty the trash can?
(A) Sure, just a second.
(B) Buy a black garbage can.
(C) Yes, I can fill it.

empty 空的　trash can 垃圾桶　garbage can 垃圾桶　fill 填補

翻譯　你可以把垃圾桶清空嗎？
　　　(A) 當然，請等一下。
　　　(B) 請購買黑色垃圾桶。
　　　(C) 好，我來填補。

解析　請求疑問句
　　　(A) [○] 回答 Sure，同意清除垃圾桶的要求，因此這是
　　　　　正確答案。
　　　(B) [×] 因使用和問題的 trash can（垃圾桶）相同意思
　　　　　的 garbage can（垃圾桶），是會造成混淆的錯誤選
　　　　　項。
　　　(C) [×] 因使用和問題的 empty（空的）意思相反的 fill
　　　　　（填補），是會造成混淆的錯誤選項。

19 美國發音→加拿大發音

Isn't it time to leave for the sales seminar?
(A) We're heading out right now.
(B) The instructor left them out.
(C) Next to the convention center.

sales 銷售　head out 出發　instructor 講師　leave out 除去
convention center 會議中心（會議場所、住宿設施等集中的綜合大
樓）

翻譯　是不是該出發去參加銷售研討會了？
　　　(A) 我們現在出發。

(B) 講師把他們排除在外。
(C) 在會議中心旁邊。

解析　否定疑問句
　　　(A) [○] 回答現在出發，等於間接回答參加銷售研討會的
　　　　　時間到了，因此是正確答案。
　　　(B) [×] 因使用和 seminar（研討會）相關的 instructor
　　　　　（講師），是會造成混淆的錯誤選項。
　　　(C) [×] 因使用和 seminar（研討會）相關的 convention
　　　　　center（會議中心），是會造成混淆的錯誤選項。

20 英國發音→澳洲發音

One of the firm's lawyers left a voice message for you.
(A) I work for a big law firm.
(B) All of the legal documentation.
(C) I'll listen to it now.

firm 公司　lawyer 律師　voice message 語音訊息　legal 法律的
documentation 文件、紀錄

翻譯　公司的一名律師留了語音訊息給你。
　　　(A) 我在大型法律事務所工作。
　　　(B) 所有的法律文件。
　　　(C) 我現在聽。

解析　直述句
　　　(A) [×] 因使用和 lawyers 發音相似的 law，是會造成混
　　　　　淆的錯誤選項。
　　　(B) [×] 因使用和 lawyers（律師們）相關的 legal
　　　　　documentation（法律文件），是會造成混淆的錯誤
　　　　　選項。
　　　(C) [○] 回答現在聽，因已經傳達會確認訊息，所以是正
　　　　　確答案。

21 澳洲發音→英國發音

Do you know where the information desk is?
(A) That desk comes with drawers.
(B) I can show you if you'd like.
(C) Yes, the shopper was informed.

information desk 服務臺　come with 伴隨　drawer 抽屜
informed 知情的

翻譯　你知道服務臺在哪裡嗎？
　　　(A) 那張書桌有抽屜。
　　　(B) 如果你願意的話，我可以帶你去。
　　　(C) 是，購物者已經知道了。

解析　包含疑問詞 Where 的一般疑問句
　　　(A) [×] 因重覆使用問題出現的 desk，是會造成混淆的
　　　　　錯誤選項。
　　　(B) [○] 回答只要對方願意，就可以帶對方去，等於間接
　　　　　回答知道服務臺在哪裡，所以是正確答案。
　　　(C) [×] 使用和 information 發音相似的 informed，是會
　　　　　造成混淆的錯誤選項。

22 加拿大發音→美國發音

Is Dr. Campbell available this afternoon?
(A) Most of our clinic's doctors.
(B) No, but you can keep them.
(C) I'm afraid his schedule is booked.

available 有時間的　clinic 診所　book 預約

翻譯 Campbell 醫生今天下午有空嗎？
(A) 我們診所的大部分醫生。
(B) 不，但你可以保留那些東西。
(C) 對不起，他的行程已經滿了。

解析 Be 動詞疑問句
(A) [×] 因使用和問題的 Campbell 醫生相關的 clinic（診所），是會造成混淆的錯誤選項。
(B) [×] 詢問 Campbell 醫生下午是否有時間，因回答「你可以保留那些東西」，和問題完全不相關，所以是錯誤的選項。
(C) [○] 回答對不起，他的行程已經滿了，等於是間接回答 Campbell 醫生下午沒空，因此是正確的選項。

23 加拿人發音→英國發音

I would like to order a large pepperoni pizza.
(A) Actually, the smaller piece is mine.
(B) Where would you like it delivered?
(C) No, with extra cheese.

order 訂購　actually 其實、實際上　piece 塊

翻譯 我想訂大份的美國臘腸披薩。
(A) 其實比較小塊的是我的。
(B) 請問要送去哪裡？
(C) 不，要另外加起司。

解析 直述句
(∧) [×] 因使用和問題的 pizza（披薩）相關的 piece（塊），所以是錯誤的選項。
(B) [○] 反問要送去哪裡，要求追加訂購披薩需要的資訊，這是正確答案。
(C) [×] 因使用和問題的 pizza（披薩）相關的 cheese（起司），所以是錯誤的選項。

24 加拿大發音→英國發音

Jane is moving out tomorrow, isn't she?
(A) Yes, yesterday afternoon.
(B) I can't move it alone.
(C) So far as I know.

move out 搬出去　so far as 就～來說

翻譯 Jane 明天搬出去，不是嗎？
(A) 是，昨天下午。
(B) 我一個人沒辦法搬。
(C) 據我所知是這樣。

解析 附加疑問句
(A) [×] 使用和問題的 tomorrow（明天）相關的 yesterday（昨天），是會造成混淆的錯誤選項。
(B) [×] 重覆使用 move（搬家），當作「搬運」的意思，是會造成混淆的錯誤選項。
(C) [○] 回答據自己所知是這樣，因轉達 Jane 明天要搬出去，所以是正確答案。

25 加拿大發音→澳洲發音

Did you find the correct part to fix the copier?
(A) Ten copies, please.
(B) Some factory machines.
(C) The component will arrive today.

part 零件　copier 影印機　component 零件、要素

翻譯 找到修理影印機需要的正確零件了嗎？
(A) 麻煩十份。
(B) 有一些工廠的機器。
(C) 零件今天會送來。

解析 助動詞疑問句
(A) [×] 使用和 copier 發音相似的 copies，是會造成混淆的錯誤選項。
(B) [×] 因使用和 copier（影印機）相關的 machines（機器），是會造成混淆的錯誤選項。
(C) [○] 那個零件今天會送到，因間接回答已經找到修理影印機需要的零件，所以是正確答案。

26 英國發音→澳洲發音

The Internet doesn't seem to be working.
(A) That doesn't feel warm enough.
(B) Did you try restarting your laptop?
(C) Yes, I work out every day.

restart 重新開始　laptop 筆電　work out 運動

翻譯 網路似乎無法正常運作。
(A) 感覺好像還不夠溫暖。
(B) 你有重新啟動筆電嗎？
(C) 對，我每天運動。

解析 直述句
(A) [×] 問題是在說網路沒有啟動，但選項卻回答還不夠溫暖，答非所問，因此是錯誤選項。
(B) [○] 反問是否有重新啟動筆電，因提出解決網路沒有正常運作的方法，所以是正確答案。
(C) [×] 因使用和 working 發音相似的 work out，是會造成混淆的錯誤選項。

27 英國發音→加拿大發音

Has the grocery store across the street closed down?
(A) It will in about a week.
(B) For the grand opening.
(C) You can store them here.

---

grocery store 雜貨店　close down 關門、倒閉
grand opening 開店、開張　store 店；保管

翻譯　馬路對面的雜貨店結束營業了嗎？
(A) 大概一個星期後吧。
(B) 為了開幕。
(C) 那些東西可以保管在這裡。

解析　助動詞疑問句
(A) [○] 回答大概是一個星期後，因傳達雜貨店還沒關門，等於是提供結束營業的日期資訊，所以是正確答案。
(B) [×] 因使用和問題的 closed down（關門）相反意思的 grand opening（開幕），是會造成混淆的錯誤選項。
(C) [×] 重覆使用 store（商店），當作動詞「保管」的意思，是會造成混淆的錯誤選項。

28 美國發音→澳洲發音

Is Mr. Irving coming to the dinner, or will he join us another time?
(A) He joined the organization a year ago.
(B) The clock in the restaurant is broken.
(C) He should be here momentarily.

---

join 一起進行、加入　organization 組織　broken 故障的
momentarily 立刻

翻譯　Irving 先生會來參加晚餐嗎？還是下次才會參加？
(A) 他一年前加入了那個組織。
(B) 餐廳的時鐘故障了。
(C) 他很快就會來這裡。

解析　選擇疑問句
(A) [×] 重覆使用 join（一起進行），當作「加入」的意思，是會造成混淆的錯誤選項。
(B) [×] 因使用和 dinner（晚餐）相關的 restaurant（餐廳），是會造成混淆的錯誤選項。
(C) [○] 回答他很快就會來這裡，因為 Irving 先生選擇參加晚餐，所以是正確答案。

29 加拿大發音→英國發音

The hotel we reserved has an outdoor pool, right?
(A) Thank you for making a reservation with us.
(B) No, the gathering took place indoors.
(C) Yes, I just checked that information online.

---

outdoor 戶外的　gathering 聚會　take place 舉辦、發生
indoors 在室內

翻譯　我們預約的飯店有戶外泳池，對吧？
(A) 謝謝您的預約。
(B) 不，那個聚會在室內舉辦。
(C) 對，我剛剛在網路上確認過那項資訊了。

解析　附加疑問句
(A) [×] 因重覆使用了問題中 reserved（已經預約）的名詞 reservation，是會造成混淆的錯誤選項。
(B) [×] 因使用和 outdoor（戶外的）相關的 indoors（在室內），是會造成混淆的錯誤選項。
(C) [○] 回答 Yes，傳達預約的飯店裡有戶外泳池後，補充說明已經在網路上確認過那項資訊，因此是答案。

30 澳洲發音→英國發音

The number of people visiting our website increased in July.
(A) Our online marketing must be working.
(B) Let's count all of the letters.
(C) Between April and May.

---

increase 增加　working 有效果的　count 計算

翻譯　造訪我們網站的人數在 7 月時增加了。
(A) 我們的線上行銷一定有發揮效果。
(B) 試著計算所有的字母。
(C) 在 4 月和 5 月之間。

解析　直述句
(A) [○] 回答線上行銷一定有發揮效果，因談到造訪網站的人數增加了，所以是正確答案。
(B) [×] 使用和 number（數字）相關的 count（計算），是會造成混淆的錯誤選項。
(C) [×] 使用和問題的 July（7 月）相關的 April and May（4 月和 5 月），是會造成混淆的錯誤選項。

31 美國發音→加拿大發音

Did any of the diners ask for some more food?
(A) No one said anything to me.
(B) The diner on Jefferson Street.
(C) I think it tastes very good.

---

diner 用餐者、餐廳　ask for 要求～

翻譯　有沒有用餐者要求多一點食物？
(A) 沒有人告訴我任何事。
(B) 是 Jefferson 街的餐廳。
(C) 我覺得味道很棒。

解析　助動詞疑問句
(A) [○] 回答沒有人告訴自己任何事，間接傳達沒有人要求多一點食物，因此是正確答案。
(B) [×] 把問題中的 diners（用餐者）當作 diner「餐廳」的意思使用，是會造成混淆的錯誤選項。
(C) [×] 因使用和 food（食物）相關的 tastes（有～的味道），是會造成混淆的錯誤選項。

PART 3

32-34 [3刂] 澳洲發音→英國發音

Questions 32-34 refer to the following conversation.

M: ³²Can you move the image of the car a little to the right? The text is blocking the vehicle's logo, which needs to be displayed on the cover of this magazine.

W: Sure. I'll also have to increase the size of the picture, so the full car is in view. ³³Are there any other adjustments you think should be made? This is our last chance before we present the design in our meeting today.

M: Everything else looks good to me. However, ³⁴I think we should stop by Ms. Anderson's office briefly and see if she has any additional comments.

W: ³⁴All right. Let's go there now.

---

block 賭塞、擋住　display 顯示　cover 封面　adjustment 調整
present 發表、交出　stop by 順便拜訪~　briefly 短暫地
additional 額外的

問題 32-34，請參考以下對話。

男：³² 你可以把車子的圖片稍微移到右邊嗎？文字遮住了車輛的標誌，雜誌封面要能看見標誌。

女：沒問題，我還必須增加圖片的尺寸，為了方便看到完整的汽車。³³ 你認為還有其他需要調整的地方嗎？這是我們在今天會議上發表設計前的最後機會。

男：其他看起來都不錯，但 ³⁴ 我認為應該先去一趟 Anderson 女士的辦公室，看看她是否有其他意見。

女：³⁴ 好，我們現在就過去吧。

32 特定細節問題

翻譯 說話者在進行何種作業？
(A) 車輛設計
(B) 櫥窗商品陳列
(C) 出版品封面
(D) 公司網站

解析 仔細聆聽與關鍵詞 working on 相關的內容，男子對女子說：「Can you move the image of the car~? The text is blocking the vehicle's logo, which needs to bedisplayed on the cover of this magazine.」，詢問能否把車子的圖片稍微右移，因為文字遮住了車輛的標誌，而雜誌封面要能看見標誌。透過這對話可知，說話者在進行出版品封面的相關作業，因此 (C) 是正確答案。

字彙 window display 櫥窗的商品陳列　publication 出版物

33 特定細節問題

翻譯 女子詢問男子什麼事？
(A) 何時會列印文件
(B) 為什麼要刪除照片
(C) 草案是否還需要變更
(D) 誰會參加會議

解析 仔細聆聽女子說的話，女子對男子說：「Are there any other adjustments you think should be made?」，詢問對方是否還有需要修正的地方。因此答案是 (C)。

換句話說
any other adjustments ~ should be made 其他該修正的部分
→ requires more changes 需要更多的變更

字彙 remove 刪除　draft 草案

34 之後將發生的事

翻譯 說話者接下來最可能做什麼？
(A) 選擇設計。
(B) 前往辦公室。
(C) 購買車子。
(D) 檢查車輛。

解析 仔細聆聽對話最後的部分，男子說他認為應該去一趟 Anderson 女士的辦公室（I think we should stop by Ms. Anderson's office briefly），女子表示同意，回答「好，現在就去吧」（All right. Let's go there now.）。從對話可知兩人準備前往辦公室，因此答案是 (B)。

字彙 examine 查看

35-37 [3刂] 加拿大發音→英國發音

Questions 35-37 refer to the following conversation.

M: ³⁵I need help making some bouquets for a wedding. ³⁶Andria was supposed to assist me with the flower arrangements, but she is sick today. So I'm behind schedule, and I'm not sure whether I will be able to prepare the order on time.

W: No problem. ³⁷I can start bringing flowers and ribbons into the workroom. Or would you like me to do something else instead?

M: I already have plenty of materials in there. It would be great if you could start bunching and tying red and white roses together. The bouquets should have roughly an even number of each color. I really appreciate the assistance!

---

assist 幫助　flower arrangement 插花
behind schedule 進度落後的　on time 準時　workroom 工作室
material 材料　bunch 聚集　tie 綁住　roughly 幾乎　even 同樣的

翻譯 問題 35-37，請參考以下對話。

男：³⁵ 我需要有人幫忙我準備結婚典禮的花束。³⁶ Andria 本來會幫忙插花，但她今天身體不舒服，所以我的進度落後了，不知道是否能準時完成訂單。

女：沒問題，³⁷ 我先把花和緞帶拿進工作室。還是你希望我先做其他事呢？

男：那裡面已經有很多材料了，你可以先把紅玫瑰和白玫瑰綁在一起，花束中每種顏色花朵的數量都必須差不多，真的很謝謝你的幫忙！

35 說話者問題

翻譯 說話者最可能在什麼地方工作？
(A) 辦公用品店

(B) 宴客場地
(C) 雜貨店
(D) 花店

解析 仔細聆聽對話中和身分、職業相關的部分，男子說需要有人幫忙準備結婚典禮的花束（I need help making some bouquets for a wedding.），兩人繼續談論製作花束的相關內容，由此可知說話者在花店工作，因此答案是 (D)。

字彙 office supplies 辦公用品　grocery store 雜貨店

36 理由問題

翻譯 為何男子的進度會落後？
(A) 同事不在。
(B) 訂單變更了。
(C) 活動提前了。
(D) 送貨延遲了。

解析 仔細聆聽問題關鍵詞 behind schedule 的前後文，男子表示：「Andria 本來要幫忙插花，但她今天生病了，所以進度落後」（Andria was supposed to assist me with the flower arrangements, but she is sick today. So I'm behind schedule.），從這句話可知道 Andria 不在，因此答案是 (A)。

字彙 unavailable 不存在的、無法使用的　ahead 在前面

37 提議問題

翻譯 女子提議說要幫忙做什麼？
(A) 拿東西過來。
(B) 和客人交談。
(C) 約定碰面。
(D) 拆除包裝紙。

解析 仔細聆聽女子說要幫忙男子做什麼，女子說：「會先把花和緞帶搬到工作室」（I can start bringing flowers and ribbons into the workroom.），因此答案是 (A)。

換句話說
bringing flowers and ribbons 把花和緞帶拿過來 →
Get some supplies 把物品帶過來

字彙 set up 安排、建立　remove 拆卸、清除　package 包裝紙、箱子

38-40 🎧 英國發音→加拿大發音→澳洲發音

Questions 38-40 refer to the following conversation with three speakers.

W: ³⁸Did you two get the e-mail from the administrative team? I read through it this morning, and apparently our building's parking lot will be reserved for clients starting next week.

M1: I never saw that. Where are employees supposed to leave their cars?

M2: At the garage on Elm Street . . . ³⁹The company will cover the cost of parking passes. We just need to submit a receipt each month.

W: Personally, I'm really unhappy about the policy. ⁴⁰That garage is three blocks away. Getting to the office is going to be really inconvenient. ⏺

M1: Yeah, you're right. We should ask our manager whether there is another option for parking.

administrative 管理的　read through 細心瀏覽
apparently 看來、顯然　parking lot 停車券　reserve 指定為
cover 負擔（警備損失）　parking pass 停車權　submit 提交
receipt 收據　personally 個人地　inconvenient 不方便的

翻譯 問題 38-40，請參考以下三人對話。
女：³⁸ 兩位是否有收到行政團隊的電子郵件呢？我今天早上仔細讀過了，看來我們大樓的停車場從下星期開始被指定為客戶專用的停車場。
男 1：我完全沒看見那個部分。員工的車要停在哪裡呢？
男 2：Elm 街的停車場……³⁹ 公司會負擔停車券的費用，我們只要每個月交出收據就行了。
女：我個人對這項政策真的很不滿，⁴⁰ 那個停車場距離辦公室有三個街區，走到辦公室真的很不方便。
男 1：對，沒錯，我們應該去詢問經理是否有其他的停車方案。

38 特定細節問題

翻譯 女子今天早上做了什麼？
(A) 閱讀訊息。
(B) 造訪其他部門。
(C) 檢視了收據。
(D) 寄送了電子郵件。

解析 仔細聆聽有談到關鍵詞 this morning 的部分，女子詢問男子是否有收到行政團隊的電子郵件，並表示自己早上已經看過信件了（Did you two get the e-mail from the administrative team? I read through it this morning.），因此答案是 (A)。

字彙 review 檢視

39 提及何事的問題

翻譯 內容中談到公司的哪個部分？
(A) 要搬遷到其他大樓。
(B) 要擴大停車場。
(C) 幫員工核銷費用。
(D) 為了客戶舉辦特別活動。

解析 仔細聆聽談論到關鍵字 company 的部分，男 2 說公司會幫忙負擔停車券的費用（The company will cover the cost of parking passes.），因此答案是 (C)。

換句話說
cover the cost 負擔費用 → reimburse ~ for a fee 核銷費用

字彙 expand 擴充　reimburse 核銷

40 問題點問題

翻譯 女子在擔心什麼事？
(A) 使用券的費用
(B) 設施的位置
(C) 罰金的金額
(D) 停車場的大小

解析 仔細聆聽女子話中的負面內容，她說：「那個停車場

距離辦公室有三個街區，走到辦公室真的很不方便」（That garage is three blocks away. Getting to the office is going to be really inconvenient.），從這番話可知道女子很在意設施的位置，因此答案是 (B)。

字彙 fine 罰金

41-43 🎧 美國發音→澳洲發音

Questions 41-43 refer to the following conversation.

W: [41]This is Jennifer Burke calling from Cool Fit, the nation's leading athletic wear store. May I please speak with Catherine Brady?

M: I'm Ms. Brady's personal assistant. [42]May I ask what the purpose of this call is? She's not interested in speaking with any telemarketers.

W: Oh no, sir. I'm simply calling to let her know that [43]her membership with our company will expire at the end of next month. She can easily renew it, however, by providing me with some basic information. If you could please connect me to her, I'll help her do that.

---

leading 頂級的、領先的　athletic wear 運動服
personal assistant 個人秘書　expire 結束　renew 延長

問題 41-43，請參考以下對話。
女：[41] 我是全國最頂尖的運動服飾店 Cool Fit 公司的 Jennifer Burke。我是否能和 Catherine Brady 談一下呢？
男：我是 Brady 女士的個人秘書。[42] 可以請教您有什麼事嗎？她沒有意願和電話推銷員通話。
女：不是那樣的，我只是想告知 [43] 她在本公司的會員資格到下個月底為止，只要她願意提供幾項基本資料，就能輕鬆延長會員的資格。只要幫我轉接給她，我就能幫忙延長會員的資格。

41 說話者問題

翻譯 女子在哪裡工作？
(A) 服飾店
(B) 運動設施
(C) 傢俱店
(D) 雜誌公司

解析 仔細聆聽對話中與身分、職業相關的部分，女子說自己是全國最頂尖的運動服飾店 Cool Fit 公司的 Jennifer Burke（This is Jennifer Burke calling from Cool Fit, the nation's leading athletic wear store.），從這句話可知道她在服飾公司上班，因此答案是 (A)。

字彙 fitness 運動、健康

42 特定細節問題

翻譯 男子想知道什麼事？
(A) 產品的價格
(B) 賣場的位置
(C) 來電的理由
(D) 專案的主旨

解析 仔細聆聽男子說的話，男子詢問來電的用意（May I ask what the purpose of this call is?），因此答案是 (C)。

43 特定細節問題

翻譯 女子說什麼就要到期了？
(A) 優惠券
(B) 出版品訂閱
(C) 會員資格
(D) 租賃契約

解析 仔細聆聽與關鍵詞 expire soon 相關的內容，女子說 Brady 女士的會員資格到下個月底（her[Ms. Brady] membership with our company will expire at the end of next month），因此答案是 (C)。

字彙 publication 出版品　subscription 訂閱

44-46 🎧 澳洲發音→美國發音

Questions 44-46 refer to the following conversation.

M: Hello. This is Gerald Short calling from Actercorp. [44]I attended your organization's recent seminar on sales planning at the Fairfield Hotel. [45]I just want to ask if you can provide me with the video recording of the presentation Raymond Eston gave on profit forecasting. I'd like to have it for reference.

W: Yes, Mr. Short, I can do that. [46]Shall I send it to the same e-mail address you used to register for last month's event?

M: Actually, [46]I think it would be better to send it to my personal account at gerryshort@usermail.net.

---

attend 參加　forecasting 預測　for reference 作為參考、參考
register 登錄　account 帳號

翻譯 問題 44-46，請參考以下列對話。
男：您好，我是 Actercorp 公司的 Gerald Short。[44] 我參加了貴公司近期在 Fairfield 飯店舉辦的銷售策略研討會。[45] 我只是想請教您能否提供 Raymond Eston 針對利潤預測簡報的影片，我想用來當作參考。
女：是，Short 先生，我會提供影片給您。[46] 只要寄到您報名上個月活動時使用的電子信箱就行了嗎？
男：其實，[46] 如果能寄到我個人信箱 gerryshort@ usermail.net 會更好。

44 提及何事的問題

翻譯 男子談到研討會的什麼事？
(A) 在飯店舉辦。
(B) 少數人參加。
(C) 由 Actercorp 贊助。
(D) 著重在數位出版業。

解析 仔細聆聽男子話中和關鍵字 seminar 有關係的部分，男子說參加了女子公司近期在 Fairfield 飯店舉辦的研討會（I attended your organization's recent seminar ~ at the Fairfield Hotel.），因此答案是 (A)。

45 特定細節問題

翻譯 男子希望女子提供什麼東西？
(A) 一些聯絡資訊
(B) 申請書
(C) 一些指示事項
(D) 影片檔案

解析 仔細聆聽男子說的話，男子詢問女子是否能提供影片檔案給自己（I just want to ask if you can provide me with the video recording of the presentation.），因此答案是 (D)。

字彙 registration form 申請書　direction 指示、方向

46 請求問題

翻譯 男子提出何種要求？
(A) 開設新帳號
(B) 前往系列講座
(C) 使用其他電子信箱
(D) 親自送交物品

解析 注意聆聽對話後半部與要求相關的句子，女子問男子：「只要寄到您報名上個月活動時使用的電子信箱就行了嗎？」（Shall I send it to the same e-mail address you used to register for last month's event?），男子則表示寄到自己的個人信箱會更好（I think it would be better to send it to my personal account.），因此答案是 (C)。

字彙 lecture series 系列講座　in person 親自

47-49 🎧加拿大發音→美國發音

Questions 47-49 refer to the following conversation.

> M: Hello. I want some information about trips to Asia. I'm interested in the cultural tours of Thailand and Vietnam I saw in your advertisements.
> W: Sure. [47]Our most popular tour provides guests with an opportunity to learn how to make traditional crafts in Vietnam.
> M: [47]Maybe that's not the best choice. I've always been interested in exotic cuisine.
> W: OK. We also have a tour that includes cooking classes in Thailand. [48]Here are the pamphlets about it.
> M: That's perfect. Can I book that for next month?
> W: Yes. [49]Please give me a moment to open our booking system.

opportunity 機會　traditional 傳統的　craft 工藝
exotic 異國的　cuisine 料理、食物　pamphlet 小冊子、宣傳冊

翻譯 問題 47-49，請參考以下對話。
　　男：你好，我需要亞洲旅遊的相關資訊，我對在你廣告上看見的泰國與越南文化旅遊很感興趣。
　　女：沒問題，[47] 我們最受歡迎的觀光旅遊會提供機會讓

顧客能學習越南的傳統工藝。
男：[47] 這可能不是最好的選擇。因為我一直都對異國料理很感興趣。
女：了解，我們也有包含在泰國上料理課程的旅遊，[48] 這裡有相關的小冊子。
男：太棒了，我可以預約下個月嗎？
女：好，[49] 我們會開啟預約系統，請等一下。

47 意圖掌握問題

翻譯 男子說：「因為我一直都對異國料理很感興趣」，他的意思是什麼？
(A) 想要其他的選項。
(B) 不擔心費用。
(C) 不曾吃過泰國料理。
(D) 想要廣告的優惠

解析 仔細聆聽和引用句子（I've always been interested in exotic cuisine）相關的內容。女子說：「我們最受歡迎的觀光旅遊會提供機會讓顧客能學習越南的傳統工藝」（Our most popular tour provides guests with an opportunity to learn how to make traditional crafts in Vietnam.），男子表示這可能不是最好的選擇（Maybe that's not the best choice.），從這句話可知道他希望有其他的選項，因此答案是 (A)。

字彙 taste 吃、品嚐　deal 優惠商品、物品

48 特定細節問題

翻譯 女子給男子什麼東西？
(A) 優惠券
(B) 行程表
(C) 小冊子
(D) 票券

解析 仔細聆聽和關鍵句 woman give to the man 相關的內容，女子表示也有包含在泰國上料理課程的小冊子（Here are the pamphlets about it[a tour that includes cooking classes in Thailand].），從這句話可知道女子拿小冊子給男子，因此答案是 (C)。
換句話說
pamphlets 宣傳冊子 → Brochures 小冊子

字彙 brochure （指南、廣告用）小冊子

49 之後將發生的事

翻譯 女子接下來最可能做什麼？
(A) 確認預約系統。
(B) 更新旅遊行程表。
(C) 重啟電腦。
(D) 寄書。

解析 仔細聆聽對話最後的部分，女子說：「會開啟預約系統，請對方等一下」（Please give me a moment to open our booking system.），由此可知女子要確認預約系統，所以答案是 (A)。
換句話說
booking 預約 → reservation 預約

字彙 timetable 行程表　reboot 重啟

Questions 50-52 refer to the following conversation.

> W: Excuse me. I'm staying in Room 232 with my husband, but we'd like to be moved.
>
> M: May I ask the reason?
>
> W: Well, ⁵⁰our room is right by the elevator, and we heard people coming and going all last night.
>
> M: I'm so sorry for the inconvenience.
>
> W: ⁵⁰It was very annoying. We couldn't even sleep.
>
> M: I see. Well, ⁵¹it looks like I can move you to Room 240 later today. But I'm afraid the other rooms are all booked. How does that sound?
>
> W: Good—as long as it's the same price as our current room.
>
> M: ⁵²Usually, it's $20 more. That's because it's a premium room, not a standard. But I'll waive the extra costs in this case.

---

inconvenience 不便　annoying 討厭的
waive 不強求執行（規則等）

翻譯 問題 50-52，請參考以下對話。
　　女：不好意思，我和我先生住在 232 號房，但我們希望能換房間。
　　男：可以詢問一下理由嗎？
　　女：嗯，⁵⁰ 我們房間就在電梯旁邊，昨天整晚都聽到別人進進出出的聲音。
　　男：造成兩位不便，真的很抱歉。
　　女：⁵⁰ 這樣真的很煩人，我們根本沒辦法睡覺。
　　男：我知道了。嗯，⁵¹ 我今天稍晚應該能幫兩位換到 240 號房，很遺憾，其他房間都有人預約了。您覺得怎麼樣呢？
　　女：好，希望價格和我們現在的房間一樣。
　　男：⁵² 通常要多加 20 美金，因為這是尊爵房型，不是標準房型，但這次免收這筆額外費用。

50 問題點問題

翻譯 女子談到了什麼問題？
(A) 設施備品不足。
(B) 飯店的預約不見了。
(C) 房間位於很吵鬧的位置。
(D) 帳單不正確。

解析 仔細聆聽女子話中含有負面情緒的內容，女子說自己住的房間就在電梯旁邊，昨天整晚都聽到別人進進出出的聲音（our room is right by the elevator, and we heard people coming and going all last night），並表示這樣很煩人，根本就無法睡覺（It was very annoying. We couldn't even sleep.），因此答案是 (C)。

字彙 be short on 缺乏　supplies 備品、儲存品　bill 帳單
inaccurate 不正確的

51 推論題

翻譯 關於 240 號房，暗指了什麼？
(A) 今晚已經有預約了。

(B) 是唯一可使用的房間。
(C) 最近已經整修了。
(D) 位於走廊盡頭。

解析 仔細聆聽和關鍵詞 Room 240 相關的部分，男人表示待會應該能幫顧客換到 240 號房，但很遺憾的是其他房間都有人預約了（it looks like I can move you to Room 240 later today. But I'm afraid the other rooms are all booked.），由此可知 240 號房是唯一能使用的房間，因此答案是 (B)。

字彙 available 可使用的　be located at 位於～

52 提議問題

翻譯 男子表示願意做什麼？
(A) 正式提出投訴。
(B) 要求修繕。
(C) 尋找主管。
(D) 提供免費升級。

解析 仔細聆聽男子要採取的處理方式，男子說：「因為這是尊爵房型，不是標準房型，通常要多加 20 美金，但這次免收這筆額外費用」（Usually, it[Room 240]'s $20 more. That's because it's a premium room, not a standard. But I'll waive the extra costs in this case.），由此可知男子是免費幫忙升級，因此答案是 (D)。

字彙 file 正式提出（訴訟、申請等）　formal 正式的
complaint 投訴、抗議　supervisor 管理者

Questions 53-55 refer to the following conversation.

> W: Hello. ⁵³I bought boots here yesterday, but I think I was overcharged. A sales clerk told me to speak to someone at the customer service desk. Here's my receipt.
>
> M: Just a minute . . . Um, I don't see the problem. The amount you paid matches the price of that product.
>
> W: But I belong to the Elite Loyalty Club, so shouldn't I receive a 10 percent discount?
>
> M: Oh, ⁵⁴I'm sorry. That program was just launched last week, and our employees sometimes forget to ask whether customers are members.
>
> W: You'll refund the amount that I was overcharged to my credit card, then?
>
> M: Of course. ⁵⁵I just need you to fill out this form.

---

overcharge 索取（金額）太高　match 一致
belong to 隸屬（俱樂部、組織）　launch 開始　fill out 填寫

翻譯 問題 53-55，請參考以下對話。
　　女：你好，⁵³ 我昨天在這裡買了靴子，但好像被多收錢，銷售員請我來跟客服櫃檯的人說明。我的收據在這裡。
　　男：等一下……嗯，我看起來沒有問題，您支付的金額和商品價格是一致的。
　　女：但我是 Elite Loyalty Club 會員，不是應該有 10%

的折扣嗎？

男：啊，⁵⁴ 對不起，那個方案上星期才開始，我們的職員偶爾會忘記詢問顧客是不是會員。

女：那我的信用卡多刷的部分會退還嗎？

男：沒問題，⁵⁵ 請填一下這個表格。

53 地點問題

翻譯 對話最可能是在哪裡進行的？
(A) 在生產工廠
(B) 在門市
(C) 在金融機構
(D) 在旅行社

解析 仔細聆聽對話中與場所相關的部分，女子說自己昨天在這裡買了靴子，但好像被多收錢，銷售人員請她去告訴客服櫃檯的人員（I bought boots here yesterday ~. A sales clerk told me to speak to someone at the customer service desk.），由此可知對話是在門市進行的，因此答案是 (B)。

字彙 production facility 生產設施　financial institution 金融機構　travel agency 旅行社

54 意圖掌握問題

翻譯 為什麼男子會說「那個方案上星期才開始」？
(A) 為了表達對要求的關切
(B) 為了解釋出錯原因
(C) 為了宣傳新的服務
(D) 為了對耽誤表示歉意

解析 仔細聆聽問題的引用句子「That program was just launched last week.」，男子說職員偶爾會忘記詢問顧客是不是會員，並表達歉意（I'm sorry. ~ and our employees sometimes forget to ask whether customers are members.），由此可知是在解釋出錯原因，所以答案是 (B)。

字彙 concern 憂慮　promote 宣傳　delay 延遲

55 請求問題

翻譯 男子要求女子做什麼？
(A) 出示信用卡。
(B) 之後再來。
(C) 試穿其他商品。
(D) 填寫文件。

解析 仔細聆聽男子話中和要求相關的內容，男子請女子填寫表格（I just need you to fill out this form.），因此答案是 (D)。

換句話說
fill out ~ form 填寫表格 → Complete a document 填寫文件

字彙 merchandise 商品　complete 填寫

Questions 56-58 refer to the following conversation with three speakers.

W1: ⁵⁶We are looking for someone to lend us a hand at the booth for our energy drink here at the Extreme Sports Expo. Have you done any promotional work like that?

M: Yes. I have worked at trade shows and have done food demonstrations.

W1: Great. I think you can start immediately as you already have experience. ⁵⁶Ms. Jones, could you show Sam where our booth is?

W2: Certainly. Follow me. ⁵⁷You will set up and restock the drinks.

M: It's a little chilly in here, Ms. Jones. Can I wear my coat?

W2: Actually, ⁵⁸I'll get the uniform you need to wear now. It includes a jacket. That should be sufficient.

---

lend a hand 給予幫助　promotional 宣傳的　demonstration 演示
set up 交出、設置　restock 再裝滿　chilly 寒冷的、冰冷的
sufficient 充分的

翻譯 問題 56-58，請參考以下三人對話。

女 1：⁵⁶ 我們在找人協助極限運動博覽會的能量飲攤位，你曾做過這種宣傳工作嗎？

男：是，我曾在貿易博覽會上工作，也曾參加美食展。

女 1：好，因為你已經有經驗，應該可以直接開始，⁵⁶ Jones 女士，可以帶 Sam 看看我們的攤位在哪裡嗎？

女 2：沒問題，請跟我來。⁵⁷ 你負責擺放和補齊飲料。

男：這裡有點冷耶，Jones 女士，我可以穿外套嗎？

女 2：其實 ⁵⁸ 我會帶你要穿的制服來，也有外套，這樣應該就夠了。

56 場所問題

翻譯 對話最可能是在哪裡進行的？
(A) 在製造設施
(B) 在咖啡廳
(C) 在博覽會場
(D) 在健身中心

解析 仔細聆聽對話中與場所相關的部分，女 1 說在找人協助極限運動博覽會能量飲攤位（We are looking for someone to lend us a hand at the booth for our energy drink here at the Extreme Sports Expo.），後來請女 2 Jones 女士帶 Sam 去攤位的所在位置（Ms. Jones, could you show Sam where our booth is?），由此可知對話場所是在博覽會場，因此答案是 (C)。

換句話說
Expo 博覽會 → exposition 博覽會

字彙 exposition center 博覽會場

---

57 特定細節問題

翻譯 男子的新工作內容是什麼？
　　(A) 示範新的工具
　　(B) 搭建攤位
　　(C) 準備飲料
　　(D) 確認溫度

解析 仔細聆聽和關鍵詞 new assignment 相關的內容，女
　　2 對男子說要擺放和補充飲料（You will set up and
　　restock the drinks.），從這句話可知道男子的工作內容
　　是準備飲料，因此答案是 (C)。

字彙 consist of 由～組成　erect 建立、設立　organize 準備、組織

58 之後將發生的事

翻譯 Jones 女士接下來要做什麼？
　　(A) 提供工作服。
　　(B) 列印操作手冊。
　　(C) 準備付款。
　　(D) 品嚐新的飲料。

解析 仔細聆聽對話最後的部分，女 2（Jones 女士）說會
　　帶男子要穿的制服來（I'll get the uniform you need to
　　wear now），因此答案是 (A)。

換句話說
uniform 制服 → work clothes 工作服

59-61 [美] 美國發音→加拿大發音

Questions 59-61 refer to the following conversation.

W: Doug, can you give me some help with this
report? I'm trying to create a spreadsheet, but I'm
not that familiar with this document format. ⁵⁹My
deadline is this weekend, so I'm kind of pressed
for time.

M: Sure, Sarah. I can take a look at it. What are you
having trouble with?

W: Well, ⁶⁰I want to list these sales amounts from
smallest to largest. But the data gets mixed up
when I try to do it.

M: You just need to click on this green button. There
. . . everything should be ordered how you want it
now. Also, ⁶¹if you have similar issues with using
this program, the website for the spreadsheet
software offers lots of helpful tips.

format 格式　familiar with 熟悉的　be pressed for time 時間緊迫
take a look 看一下　list（依照特定順序）列舉　mix up 混合

翻譯 問題 59-61，請參考以下對話。
　　女：Doug，你能幫忙我完成這個報告嗎？我想製作電子
　　　　試算表，但我不熟悉這個文件的格式，⁵⁹ 因為截止
　　　　日是這個週末，時間有點趕。
　　男：沒問題，Sarah，我看一下，你遇到什麼困難呢？
　　女：嗯，⁶⁰ 我想把這些銷售額依照順序從小到大列出，
　　　　但如果我這樣做，資料就會混在一起。
　　男：只要點擊綠色按鍵就行，像這樣……就會依照你的
　　　　意思排列，⁶¹ 此外，使用這個程式如果發生類似的

問題，電子試算表軟體的網站上有提供很多有用的
資訊。

59 提及何事的問題

翻譯 女子談到什麼關於報告的事？
　　(A) 是她的主管製作的。
　　(B) 這星期必須交出去。
　　(C) 包含不正確的資訊。
　　(D) 為了開會，必須列印出來。

解析 注意聆聽女子話中和關鍵字 report 相關的內容，女子說
　　截止日是這個週末（My deadline is this weekend.），
　　因此答案是 (B)。

字彙 include 包含　inaccurate 不確的　gathering 會議、聚會

60 特定細節問題

翻譯 女子想做什麼？
　　(A) 影印。
　　(B) 計算。
　　(C) 把檔案上傳到網站。
　　(D) 重新排列數值。

解析 仔細聆聽對話中女子說的話，女子說：「想把這些銷售
　　額依照順序從小到大列出」（I want to list these sales
　　amounts from smallest to largest.），因此答案是 (D)。

換句話說
list ~ sales amounts from smallest to largest 依照銷售額的最
小數值列舉至最大數值 → Rearrange some figures 重新排列數值

字彙 post（資訊、照片）上傳至（網頁）　rearrange 重新排列
figure 數值、數字

61 特定細節問題

翻譯 男子說女子可以從網路上找到什麼？
　　(A) 申請書
　　(B) 對程式的支援
　　(C) 訂單相關資訊
　　(D) 軟體樣品

解析 仔細聆聽男子話中和關鍵字 online 相關的內容，男子對
　　女子說：「使用程式如果發生類似的問題時，電子試算
　　表軟體的網站上有提供很多有用的資訊」（if you have
　　similar issues with using this program, the website for
　　the spreadsheet software offers lots of helpful tips），
　　因此答案是 (B)。

字彙 registration form 申請書　assistance 幫助

62-64 [英] 英國發音→加拿大發音

Questions 62-64 refer to the following conversation
and schedule.

W: Carl, ⁶²have you confirmed the agenda for our
automotive engineering conference? Several
industry executives will be there next month, so I
want to make sure everything's well organized.

M: ⁶²Not yet. There's just one issue with the order of
presentations. I was just informed that ⁶³the first

speaker won't arrive until 12 P.M. I guess there was a problem with his train reservation, so he has to take a later one from Boston than originally planned.

W: Well, we'll need to switch his time with another speaker's, then. ⁶⁴Could you get in touch with one of the afternoon speakers? How about Fred Jones or Peter Wright?

M: OK. I'll give them both a call. Once I confirm the change, I'll update the schedule and e-mail it to you.

---

confirm 確定　agenda 議事日程（決定會議案件的順序）
automotive 汽車的　conference 會議、學會
executive 代表、領導階層　organized 有計劃的
issue 問題　inform 通知　originally 當初　switch 轉換
get in touch with 與～聯絡

翻譯 問題 62-64，請參考以下對話和行程表。

女：Carl，⁶² 關於汽車工程會議的議事日程，你確認了嗎？下個月幾位業界高層人士都會去那邊，我想先確認一切是否都安排好了。

男：⁶² 還沒好，演講的順序出了問題，我剛接獲通知 ⁶³ 第一個講者要等到中午 12 點才會抵達，他的火車預約發生了問題，好像得從波士頓搭乘比預定計劃更晚的列車。

女：嗯，那就得把他的時間和其他講者更換才行，⁶⁴ 你可以聯絡下午的講者嗎？Fred Jones 或 Peter Wright 怎麼樣呢？

男：我知道了，我會試著打給他們兩個，確定變更事項後我會更新日程，並且寄電子郵件給您。

簡報日程表	
講者	時間
⁶³ John Foreman	上午 9：00～上午 10：30
Harry Garcia	上午 10：30～中午 12：00
Fred Jones	下午 1：30～下午 3：00
Peter Wright	下午 3：00～下午 4：30

62 主題問題

翻譯 說話者主要在談論什麼？
(A) 活動場所
(B) 演講日程
(C) 申請的截止期限
(D) 會議主題

解析 這是詢問對話主題的問題，仔細聆聽對話剛開始的部分，掌握整個語境。女子詢問男子汽車工程會議的日程確定了嗎（have you confirmed the agenda for our automotive engineering conference?），男子回答還沒，因演講順序發生了問題（Not yet. There's just one issue with the order of presentations.），因此答案是 (B)。

63 圖片題

翻譯 請看圖片，誰會從波士頓來？
(A) John Foreman
(B) Harry Garcia
(C) Fred Jones
(D) Peter Wright

解析 確認日程表的資訊後，仔細聆聽與問題關鍵字 Boston 相關的部分，男子說第一個講者要等到中午 12 點才會抵達，他的火車預約發生了問題，好像得從波士頓搭乘比預定計劃更晚的列車（the first speaker won't arrive until 12 P.M. ~ he has to take a later one[train] from Boston），因此答案是 (A)。

64 請求問題

翻譯 女子向男子提出何種要求？
(A) 另外寄送邀請函。
(B) 聯絡講者。
(C) 和場地管理者見面。
(D) 延長截止日。

解析 仔細聆聽女子話中和要求相關的內容，女子問男子是否可連絡下午的講者（Could you get in touch with one of the afternoon speakers?），因此答案是 (B)。

字彙 send out 傳送、發送　extend 延長

65-67 美國發音→澳洲發音

Questions 65-67 refer to the following conversation and map.

W: Good morning, Alan. ⁶⁵I saw that the city maintenance department put a sign on my front door about a plan to spray for weeds in Wrigley Park. Did you get the same one?

M: I did, and ⁶⁶I'm worried about it. The spray can be harmful to people's health.

W: I agree. Also, it's not necessary, since there aren't very many weeds growing in the park.

M: Well, there are some in ⁶⁷the area where the children usually play . . . you know, right between the stream and the picnic area.

W: True, but I'd still prefer not to have chemicals used there.

---

maintenance 維持（管理）　sign 告示、看板
spray 噴灑；（殺蟲劑、香水等的）噴霧　weed 雜草
harmful 有害的　stream 溪流　chemical 化學物質

翻譯 問題 65-67，請參考以下對話和地圖。

女：你好，Alan，⁶⁵ 我看見城市維護管理部在我前門貼了要在 Wrigley 公園噴除草劑的公告，你也有收到嗎？

男：我也收到了，⁶⁶ 但我很擔心，噴灑除草劑可能危害大家的健康。

女：我也同意，而且那個公園的雜草並不多，我認為沒有那種必要。

男：嗯，⁶⁷ 小朋友主要玩耍的地方有一些……就在溪流和野餐區之間。

女：對，但我希望那邊不要使用化學物質。

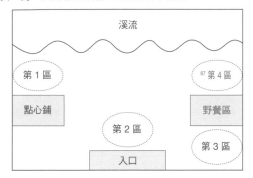

65 特定細節問題

翻譯 女子最近做了什麼？
(A) 安裝新的門。
(B) 閱讀公告。
(C) 申請草皮照護服務。
(D) 聯絡技師。

解析 仔細聆聽與問題關鍵詞 recently do 相關的內容，女子說：「看見城市維護管理部在大門貼了要在 Wrigley 公園噴除草劑的公告」（I saw that the city maintenance department put a sign on my front door about a plan to spray for weeds in Wrigley Park.），從內容中可知道女子最近閱讀了公告，因此答案是 (B)。

字彙 notification 通知書、告知　lawn care 草皮管理

66 問題點問題

翻譯 男子為何會擔心？
(A) 官員拒絕了要求。
(B) 城市的計劃可能會造成負面影響。
(C) 遊樂區已經封閉了。
(D) 維護管理作業還沒完成。

解析 仔細聆聽男子話中與負面表達相關的內容。男子對計劃表示很擔心，並說噴灑殺蟲劑會危害大家的健康（I'm worried about it[plan]. The spray can be harmful to people's health.），因此答案是 (B)。

換句話說
harmful to people's health 危害健康的 → have a negative impact 造成負面影響

字彙 official 官員　reject 拒絕　impact 影響　close down 封閉

67 圖片題

翻譯 請看圖片，孩童們主要在哪裡玩耍？
(A) 第 1 區
(B) 第 2 區
(C) 第 3 區
(D) 第 4 區

解析 確認圖片資訊後，仔細聽與問題關鍵詞 children usually play 相關的內容。男子說：「小朋友主要玩耍的地方有一些……就在溪流和野餐區之間」（the area where the

children usually play ~, right between the stream and the picnic area），圖片顯示孩子主要在 4 號區域玩耍，因此 (D) 是正確答案。

68-70 ⏳ 澳洲發音→英國發音

Questions 68-70 refer to the following conversation and graph.

M: Michelle, can you look over the results of the customer questionnaires we released . . . the ones about our new speaker system, BeatBox 2?

W: I already did. ⁶⁸I was surprised to learn that it isn't as popular as the previous model, though. Look for yourself.

M: I see. I guess we need to figure out which aspect of the BeatBox 2 to improve upon first.

W: ⁶⁹The aspect with the worst customer satisfaction level can be easily adjusted, so let's discuss the second lowest first.

M: Yeah, that makes sense. ⁷⁰Can you give me a hard copy of this graph? I want to show it to our director this afternoon.

W: Sure thing.

look over 檢討　questionnaire 問卷調查表　figure out 弄明白
aspect 側面　improve 改善　customer satisfaction 顧客滿意度
adjust 調整、調節　hard copy 紙本

翻譯 問題 68-70，請參考以下對話和圖表。
男：Michelle，可以檢討一下我們發放的顧客問卷調查結果嗎？是關於新音響系統 BeatBox 2 的內容。
女：我已經做了，不過 ⁶⁸ 得知它沒有比先前的型號更受歡迎，讓我相當訝異，你親自看一下吧。
男：這樣呀，看來得先了解該改善 BeatBox 2 的哪一個部分。
女：⁶⁹ 顧客滿意度最低的部分可輕易調整，就先討論第二低的部分吧。
男：對，沒錯，⁷⁰ 可以給我一份紙本的圖表嗎？我下午會拿去讓董事看。
女：沒問題。

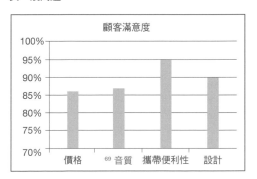

68 理由問題

翻譯 女子為何感到訝異？
(A) 公司停止機器的生產。
(B) 音響系統太貴了。

(C) 產品的受歡迎度相對較低。

(D) 公司宣布要回收。

解析 仔細聆聽與問題關鍵字 surprised 相關的部分，女子說自己得知 BeatBox 2 沒有先前的型號那樣受歡迎時相當訝異（I was surprised to learn that it[BeatBox 2] isn't as popular as the previous model.），因此答案是 (C)。

字彙 production 生產　device 設備　relatively 相對地
recall 召回、想起

69 圖表題

翻譯 請看圖表，哪一個部分會立即檢討？
(A) 價格
(B) 音質
(C) 攜帶便利性
(D) 設計

解析 確認圖表的資訊後，仔細聆聽與問題關鍵句 aspect ~ be addressed immediately 相關的內容。女子說：「顧客滿意度最低的部分可輕易調整，就先討論第二低的部分吧」（The aspect with the worst customer satisfaction level can be easily adjusted, so let's discuss the second lowest first.），從圖表中可知道音質會立即進行檢討，因此答案是 (B)。

字彙 portability 攜帶便利性

70 之後將發生的事

翻譯 男子今天下午大概會做什麼？
(A) 和董事見面。
(B) 和顧客交談。
(C) 影印圖表。
(D) 測試新產品。

解析 仔細聆聽與問題關鍵詞 this afternoon 有關的部分。男子詢問是否可提供圖表的紙本，並表示下午要拿給董事看（Can you give me a hard copy of this graph? I want to show it to our director this afternoon.），由此可知男子下午會和董事見面，因此答案是 (A)。

PART 4

71-73 🔊 英國發音

Questions 71-73 refer to the following introduction.

Good morning, everyone. I'm delighted to introduce Mr. Juan Hernandez. 71Mr. Hernandez is taking over as the general manager of this branch of Homerson Bank. He has been employed by a number of financial firms during his 20 years in the industry. Most recently, 72he led a training session for administrative workers at a major bank in New York. To allow Mr. Hernandez to get to know staff better, 73a dinner is being held at Norman's Restaurant over on Rexford Drive this evening. You're all invited, so please try to make it.

➡

delighted 欣喜　take over as 接管　branch 分行　employ 僱用
a number of 很多的　training session 培訓課程
administrative 行政的　get to know 去熟悉　make it 參加

翻譯 問題 71-73，請參考以下介紹。
大家好，很高興能向各位介紹 Juan Hernandez 先生，71 Hernandez 先生將要接任 Homerson 銀行分行的總經理職務。他在這個業界的 20 年間曾受僱於多間金融公司，最近 72 他在紐約的一間主要銀行進行了行政職員培訓課程。為了讓 Hernandez 先生能更了解職員，73 今天晚上在 Rexford 路的 Norman's 餐廳舉辦了晚宴。各位全都受邀參加，請盡可能到場吧。

71 場所問題

翻譯 聽者最可能在什麼地方？
(A) 地區文化中心
(B) 職業介紹所
(C) 金融機構
(D) 公共行政機關

解析 仔細聆聽短文中與場所相關的用法，文中提到 Juan Hernandez 先生將要接任 Homerson 銀行分行的總經理職務（Mr. Hernandez is taking over as the general manager of this branch of Homerson Bank.），由此可知聽者是在金融機構，因此答案是 (C)。

字彙 community center 地區文化中心
employment agency 職業介紹所
financial institution 金融機構　government office 公共行政機關

72 特定細節問題

翻譯 Hernandez 先生在紐約做了什麼事？
(A) 面試職員。
(B) 舉辦研習會。
(C) 獲獎。
(D) 成立公司。

解析 仔細聆聽與問題關鍵句 Mr. Hernandez do in New York 相關的內容，文中談到 Hernandez 先生在紐約開設了研修課程（he[Mr. Hernandez] led a training session ~ in New York），因此答案是 (B)。

換句話說
led a training session 開設研修課程 →
conducted a workshop 舉辦研習會

字彙 interview 面試　conduct 帶領、實施　found 設立

73 之後將發生的事

翻譯 聽者今天晚上大概會做什麼？
(A) 參加職員的新訓。
(B) 去餐廳聚餐。
(C) 開車去會議中心。
(D) 參加教育課程。

解析 仔細聆聽與問題關鍵詞 this evening 相關的部分。文中談到今天晚上在 Norman's 餐廳舉辦了晚宴，大家全都受邀參加，請盡可能到場（a dinner is being held at Norman's Restaurant ~ this evening. You're all invited, so please try to make it.），因此答案是 (B)。

字彙 dining establishment 餐廳 training course 教育課程

74-76 [3w] 美國發音

Questions 74-76 refer to the following announcement.

This is an announcement for all passengers of Brava Airways Flight 788 to Madrid. [74]Due to an unexpected technical malfunction with your aircraft, Flight 788 has been canceled. As Brava Airways does not have any other flights to Madrid this evening, [75]the airline will be giving passengers hotel vouchers. We will also book everyone a replacement flight for tomorrow morning. [76]Further information about the situation is available at our service desk near Gate 35. On behalf of Brava Airlines, we apologize for this inconvenience and thank you for choosing to travel with us.

passenger 乘客 unexpected 出乎意料的 technical 技術性的
malfunction 缺陷 aircraft 飛機 voucher 使用券
replacement 替代 on behalf of 代表～ inconvenience 不便

翻譯 問題 74-76，請參考以下公告。
搭乘飛往馬德里的 Brava 航空公司 788 號班機的旅客請注意，[74] 788 航班因為出乎預料的技術性故障而取消，由於 Brava 航空公司今晚沒有其他飛往馬德里的航班，[75] 航空公司會提供飯店使用券給各位旅客，我們還會幫各位旅客預約明早出發的替代航班。[76] 關於目前狀況的更多資訊可以詢問 35 號登機門附近的服務櫃檯。造成各位旅客不便，在此代表 Brava 航空公司表示歉意，感謝各位搭乘本公司的航班。

74 理由問題

翻譯 為何會取消航班？
(A) 因為飛機發生技術性的故障。
(B) 氣象條件相當惡劣。
(C) 發生安全問題。
(D) 機場停電了。

解析 仔細聆聽與問題關鍵詞 flight cancellation 相關的內容。文中提到 788 航班因為出乎預料的技術性故障而取消（Due to an unexpected technical malfunction with your aircraft, Flight 788 has been canceled.），因此答案是 (A)。
換句話說
technical malfunction 技術故障 →
mechanical issue 技術性問題

字彙 mechanical 技術性、機械性 weather condition 氣象條件
severe （氣候寒冷、炎熱等情形）嚴重的

75 特定細節問題

翻譯 特定乘客將能獲得什麼？
(A) 住宿券
(B) 費用優惠
(C) 座位升級
(D) 全額退款

解析 仔細聆聽與關鍵句 provided to certain passengers

相關的內容。文中提到航空公司會提供飯店使用券給旅客（the airline will be giving passengers hotel vouchers），因此答案是 (A)。

字彙 accommodation 住宿、住處 fare 費用

76 特定細節問題

翻譯 根據說話者，服務櫃檯在哪裡？
(A) 登機手續櫃檯旁邊
(B) 登機門附近
(C) 餐廳對面
(D) 售票處旁

解析 仔細聆聽與問題關鍵詞 service desk 相關的內容。文中提到如果想知道關於更多的資訊，可以去詢問 35 號登機門附近的服務櫃檯（Further information about the situation is available at our service desk near Gate 35.），由此可知是在登機門附近的服務櫃檯，所以答案是 (B)。

字彙 check-in 搭乘手續

77-79 [3w] 加拿大發音

Questions 77-79 refer to the following advertisement.

[77]Are you looking for a musical instrument that's just right for you? Then stop by Spark to browse our newly stocked selection of products. [78]Spark's sales representatives are experts in various musical styles, and we promise excellent service. We're confident that our staff can assist you with any instrument-related questions or concerns you might have. And from now until the end of the month, we are offering a discount of up to 60 percent off select goods. [79]Simply come down to 10 Westchester Street to take advantage of this spectacular limited-time deal.

look for 尋找 stop by 順便拜訪 browse 瀏覽
stock （商店等的物品）進貨 expert 專家
select 選定的、篩選 take advantage of 利用～
spectacular 巨大的、壯觀的

翻譯 問題 77-79，請參考以下廣告。
[77] 您在尋找適合自己的樂器嗎？那就來 Spark 看一下我們嚴選的新產品。[78] Spark 的銷售員是各種音樂風格的專家，保證提供優質服務。有關於樂器的任何問題，我們工作人員也保證會幫忙。另外，從現在開始到本月底，我們篩選的商品最高可享 60% 的折扣。[79] 請來 Westchester 街 10 號享受期間限定的優惠。

77 特定細節問題

翻譯 Spark 是哪一類型的業者？
(A) 不動產仲介辦公室
(B) 樂器店
(C) 音樂學院
(D) 顧問公司

解析 仔細聆聽與問題關鍵字 Spark 相關的內容。開頭詢問是否在尋找適合自己的樂器後，便提議去 Spark 參觀嚴

選的新產品（Are you looking for a musical instrument that's just right for you? Then stop by Spark to browse our newly stocked selection of products.），由此可知 Spark 是樂器店，因此答案是 (B)。

字彙 real estate 房仲業　academy 學院

78 提及何事的問題

翻譯 說話者談到 Spark 工作人員的哪些事？
(A) 知道很多種類的音樂。
(B) 具備 10 年的資歷。
(C) 一個星期內都在現場。
(D) 提供個人的培訓。

解析 注意聆聽和問題關鍵詞 Spark's staff 相關的內容。文中提到 Spark 的銷售員是各種音樂風格的專家（Spark's sales representatives are experts in various musical styles），因此答案是 (A)。

換句話說
experts in various musical styles 有各種音樂風格的專家 → familiar with different kinds of music 熟悉各種不同的音樂

字彙 be familiar with 很熟悉　on site 現場的

79 方法問題

翻譯 聽者該怎麼樣才能獲得折扣？
(A) 利用諮詢電話
(B) 參觀設施
(C) 進入網頁
(D) 寄電子信件給銷售員

解析 仔細聆聽與問題關鍵詞 receive a discount 相關的內容，文中談到前往 Westchester 街 10 號可享受期間限定的優惠（Simply come down to 10 Westchester Street to take advantage of this ~ deal.），因此答案是 (B)。

字彙 hotline 諮詢電話

80-82 ♪ 澳洲發音

Questions 80-82 refer to the following talk.

Hi, everyone. My name is Kevin Baker, and I'm the director of the Mariposa Community Center. In just a moment, I'll be introducing tonight's special guest, [80]Gregory Smyth, who is the CEO of the Body First chain of fitness centers. He will be lecturing on the health benefits of exercise. Before that, however, I'd like to discuss an important issue with you. The city cut our funding by 30 percent. [81]Our budget is no longer sufficient to operate the center, so it'd be nice if you could help us out. Any amount, great or small, will be appreciated, so please speak to me after the lecture if you are able to contribute. [82]OK, Mr. Smyth. You can now come up to the podium.

lecture 講課　cut 減少　funding 財務支援、資金
budget 預算（案）　sufficient 充足的　operate 操作、經營
help out 幫忙　contribute 捐贈、贈與　podium 講臺、指揮臺

翻譯 問題 80-82，請參考以下談話。
大家好，我的名字是 Kevin Baker，我是馬里波薩地區文化中心的負責人。待會我將介紹今晚的貴賓[80] 連鎖健身中心 Body First 的執行長 Gregory Smyth，他會講關於運動對健康有益的課程。但在那之前，我想和大家討論一件重要的事。市政府的資金支援減少了 30%，[81] 我們的預算無法維持中心的運作，因此希望各位能幫助我們，無論金額多寡我們都會很感激。如果各位能捐款的話，請在演說結束時告訴我一聲。[82] 好，Smyth 先生，請上來講臺吧。

80 特定細節問題

翻譯 Gregory Smyth 最可能是誰？
(A) 公司管理階層人員
(B) 公務員
(C) 醫藥專家
(D) 大學教授

解析 仔細聆聽與對方（Gregory Smyth）的身分、職業相關的用法。內容提到 Gregory Smyth 是連鎖健身中心 Body First 的執行長（Gregory Smyth, who is the CEO of the Body First chain of fitness centers），因此答案是 (A)。

字彙 executive 管理階層、經營團隊
government official 公務員、政府關係者

81 意圖掌握問題

翻譯 為何說話者會談到「市政府的資金支援減少了 30%」？
(A) 為了請求一些捐款
(B) 為了公告行程變更
(C) 為了提供關閉的理由　　　．
(D) 為了提供幾個存錢方法

解析 仔細聆聽與問題引用句 The city cut our funding by 30 percent 相關的部分。文中談到因預算無法維持中心的運作，希望大家能給予幫助，無論金額多寡都會很感激（Our budget is no longer sufficient to operate the center, so it'd be nice if you could help us out. Any amount, great or small, will be appreciated），從這句話可知道希望大家能給予一些捐款，因此答案是 (A)。

字彙 donation 捐贈（金）　closure 封閉、停業

82 之後將發生的事

翻譯 接下來會發生什麼事？
(A) 講者將登上舞臺。
(B) 健身課將要開始了。
(C) 預算案將要公開。
(D) 將會討論慈善募款活動。

解析 仔細聆聽短文最後的部分，文中談到 Smyth 先生可以上去講臺了（OK, Mr. Smyth. You can now come up to the podium.），因此答案是 (A)。
換句話說
come up to the podium 上去講臺 → take the stage 上去舞臺

字彙 take the stage 上舞臺　release 公開、發表
charity drive 慈善募款活動

83-85 🎧加拿大發音

Questions 83-85 refer to the following excerpt from a meeting.

> [83]I want to end our meeting by talking about how our line of tablet devices has been selling. The TabTech L2—our newest addition to the line—is doing very well. This is in large part thanks to [84]the successful promotional campaign that our partner On Point Solutions created for us. However, the TouchBolt's sales performance has decreased over the last three months. This decline is concerning as our analyses suggest that it should still be selling well. I would like each of you to spend the rest of the morning going over the customer reviews of the product posted on our website. [85]At 12:30 P.M., we'll meet again to talk about these comments. Maybe this will help us figure out the problem.

addition 新增的　thanks to 幸虧　promotional 宣傳的
decrease 減少　decline 減少　analysis 分析　go over 檢討～
review 評價　post 上傳（資訊等至網頁）　figure out 弄清楚

翻譯　問題 83-85，請參考以下會議摘錄。
[83] 會議的最後，我想要談一下我們的平板系列的銷售狀況。這個系列近期新增的 TabTech L2 賣得相當好，有很大的部分 [84] 都要歸功於我們的合作公司 On Point Solutions 宣傳活動成功的關係。不過，過去三個月 TouchBolt 的銷售成績下滑，根據我們的分析，它應該還要賣得不錯才對，這種銷售減少的狀況讓人感到擔憂。我希望各位在今天早上剩下的時間內，好好檢視一下顧客上傳至網站的產品評價。[85] 中午 12 點 30 分我們再來談談顧客的意見，說不定這會有助於我們解決問題。

83 主題問題

翻譯　說話者主要在談些什麼？
(A) 設計缺陷
(B) 銷售成績
(C) 廣告策略
(D) 部門擴大

解析　題目詢問會議的主題，一定要聽清楚短文剛開始的內容。文中談到會議的最後想要談一下平板系列的銷售狀況（I want to end our meeting by talking about how our line of tablet devices has been selling.），後來繼續談論銷售成績，因此答案是 (B)。
換句話說
how ~ devices has been selling 設備銷售狀況 → Sales performance 銷售成績

字彙　flaw 缺陷　performance 成績　strategy 策略　expansion 擴張

84 特定細節問題

翻譯　根據說話者，On Point Solutions 公司做了什麼事？
(A) 生產零件。
(B) 管理資金。
(C) 配送商品。
(D) 舉行活動。

解析　仔細聆聽與問題關鍵詞 On Point Solutions 相關的部分。文中談到 On Point Solutions 的宣傳活動很成功（the successful promotional campaign ~ On Point Solutions created for us），由此可知 On Point Solutions 公司舉辦了活動，因此答案是 (D)。

字彙　manufacture 生產　distribute 流通

85 理由問題

翻譯　為何今天下午要開會？
(A) 為了討論顧客的意見
(B) 為了測試機器的功能
(C) 為了規劃新的產品系列
(D) 為了檢視財務分析

解析　仔細聆聽與問題關鍵詞 this afternoon 相關的內容，文中談到中午 12 點 30 分要再來談談顧客的意見（At 12:30 P.M., we'll meet again to talk about these comments[customer reviews].），因此答案是 (A)。
換句話說
talk about these comments 談論這些意見 →
discuss customer feedback 討論顧客的意見

字彙　feature 機能

86-88 🎧澳洲發音

Questions 86-88 refer to the following instruction.

> First of all, [86]I appreciate everyone coming in to help with the store's inventory. Now, [87]the store's storage area was reorganized yesterday. So, our first goal this evening is to transfer the necessary stock from the back room to the sales floor. After that, we'll need to count those products and then compare the actual numbers against what our records say. You've all done this before. [88]So you know that if there are any inconsistencies between the two, you should report it to me or one of the other managers immediately. OK, let's get started.

appreciate 感謝　inventory 庫存　storage 儲存、保管
reorganize 改組　transfer 轉移　sales floor 賣場
compare 比較　inconsistency 不一致　immediately 立即

翻譯　問題 86-88，請參考以下說明。
首先，[86] 很感謝來幫忙整理賣場庫存的各位。好，[87] 昨天賣場的倉庫已經重新整頓好了，所以今晚我們的第一個目標是從後面的房間把需要的庫存搬到賣場。接下來，我們要清點產品，再比較實際數量與我們的記錄。各位先前都做過這件事，[88] 如果發現數量有誤差時，就必須立即告知我或是其他任何一位經理。好，開始吧。

86 目的問題

翻譯　談話的主要目的是什麼？
(A) 為了要求員工加班到很晚
(B) 為了說明賣場的規定
(C) 為了跟員工們談郊遊的事
(D) 為了說明工作內容

解析 這是詢問談話目的的題型，仔細聆聽短文剛開始的部分。文中在感謝所有來幫忙整理庫存的員工後，就開始說明整理賣場庫存的順序（I appreciate everyone coming in to help with the store's inventory），因此答案是 (D)。

字彙 inform 通知　outing 郊遊　describe 說明、描述

87 特定細節問題

翻譯 昨天發生什麼事了？
(A) 促銷活動結束了。
(B) 找到遺失的物品。
(C) 僱用員工了。
(D) 整理倉庫了。

解析 仔細聆聽與關鍵字 yesterday 相關的部分，文中談到昨天已經整理過賣場的倉庫了（the store's storage area was reorganized yesterday），因此答案是 (D)。

字彙 promotion 促銷活動　misplaced 遺失的

88 意圖掌握問題

翻譯 說話者說「各位先前都做過這件事」，他的意思是什麼？
(A) 曾犯下失誤。
(B) 流程應該令人熟悉。
(C) 專案很快就會結束。
(D) 變更事項即將宣布。

解析 仔細聆聽問題的引用句 You've all done this before。文中談到如果員工發現數量有誤差時，就必須告知自己或是其他任何一位經理（So you know that if there are any inconsistencies between the two, you should report it to me or one of the other managers immediately.），因此答案是 (B)。

字彙 procedure 步驟　announce 通知

89-91 🌐英國發音

Questions 89-91 refer to the following announcement.

I've been asked by [89]the head of human resources, Philip Calandra, to notify everyone about some changes that have been made to our employee attendance system. [90]First, you should go to the main page of our intranet. Here, you can set up an account for the new system. Simply follow the steps on the screen to create an account. After that has been completed, [91]I suggest that you watch the training video in the upper left-hand corner of the page to learn more about how to log your work hours each day. Please feel free to contact me with any questions.

notify 告知　attendance 出席　set up 設立、安裝
account 帳號　complete 完成、填寫　log 記錄

翻譯 問題 89-91，請參考以下公告。

[89]人資部主管 Philip Calandra 要我通知各位關於職員出缺勤系統的變更事項。[90]首先，各位必須先登入我們內部網路的主頁，接著就能在那邊建立新系統所需的帳號，只要依照畫面上的順序建立帳號就行了。完成後，為了更進一步了解每天記錄各位工作時間的方法，[91]建議各位能觀看一下畫面左上角的教育訓練影片。如果有任何疑問，歡迎隨時聯絡我。

89 特定細節問題

翻譯 Philip Calandra 是誰？
(A) 公司董事
(B) 主管
(C) 培訓講師
(D) 電腦技師

解析 仔細聆聽 Philip Calandra 的身分與職業稱呼。文中談到 Philip Calandra 是人資部主管（the head of human resources, Philip Calandra.），因此答案是 (B)。

字彙 board member 董事　departmental 部門的　instructor 講師
technician 技師

90 請求問題

翻譯 說話者要求聽者先做什麼？
(A) 分發小冊子。
(B) 在出缺勤記錄簿上簽名。
(C) 下載員工守則。
(D) 進入網站。

解析 仔細聆聽短文中後部分與要求相關的用法和句子。文中談到必須先登入公司內部網路的主頁（First, you should go to the main page of our intranet.），因此答案是 (D)。

字彙 pass out 分發　brochure 小冊子　employee manual 員工手冊

91 提議問題

翻譯 說話者提出何種建議？
(A) 刪除帳號
(B) 報名研討會
(C) 觀看影片
(D) 填寫問卷調查

解析 仔細聆聽短文中後半部與提議相關的用法和句子。文中提到建議觀看網頁左上角的教育訓練影片（I suggest that you watch the training video in the upper left-hand corner of the page），因此答案是 (C)。

字彙 delete 刪除　register 登記　survey（問卷）調查

92-94 🌐加拿大發音

Questions 92-94 refer to the following telephone message.

Good morning, Ms. James. [92]My name is Carter Swain, and I am the owner of Swain Salon. I want to apologize for your unsatisfactory experience last week. My associate informed me about your complaint. The person who provided you the service is no longer working here, and [93]I can assure you all of my current employees are well-trained and knowledgeable about chemical-sensitivity issues. Therefore, [94]on top of providing you a full refund, I'd like to send you a coupon for $40 off your next visit. I will actually perform your treatment myself. So call me back at 555-4983, and I'll schedule an appointment for you.

---

unsatisfactory 不滿意　complaint 不滿、抱怨　assure 保障
well-trained 熟練的　knowledgeable 有見識的、淵博的
on top of 不僅、除～之外　treatment 管理、待遇

翻譯　問題 92-94，請參考以下電話訊息。
　　　早安，James 女士，[92] 我的名字是 Carter Swain，我是 Swain 沙龍的老闆。我想針對上星期讓客人不愉快的事表達歉意，同事告訴我客人您的不滿，當時提供服務的人已經離職了，[93] 我可以保證現在的所有工作人員都受過培訓並很清楚化學產品敏感性的問題。因此，我們不僅會全額退費，[94] 下次您來光顧本店時還會提供 40 元的優惠券。我會親自為您服務，只要來電 555-4983，我就會為您預約。

92 說話者問題

翻譯　說話者很可能在哪裡工作？
　　　(A) 客服中心
　　　(B) 職業仲介所
　　　(C) 化學工廠
　　　(D) 美容院

解析　仔細聆聽對話中與身分、職業相關的用法。說話者表示自己的名字叫做 Carter Swain，是 Swain 沙龍的老闆（My name is Carter Swain, and I am the owner of Swain Salon.），由此可知他在沙龍工作，因此答案是 (D)。
　　　換句話說
　　　Salon 沙龍 → beauty shop 美容院

字彙　employment agency 職業介紹所

93 意圖掌握問題

翻譯　為何說話者會說「當時提供服務的人已經離職了」？
　　　(A) 為了暗示會僱用更多的職員
　　　(B) 為了保證不會再發生問題
　　　(C) 為了告知部分服務已經無法使用
　　　(D) 為了建議重新調整預約日程

解析　仔細聆聽與問題引用句 The person who provided you the service is no longer working here 相關的部分。說話者表示現在的所有工作人員都受過培訓並很清楚化學產品敏感性的問題（I can assure you all of my current employees are well-trained and knowledgeable about chemical-sensitivity issues），由此可知是為了保證不再發生問題，因此答案是 (B)。

字彙　hire 僱用　guarantee 保障

94 特定細節問題

翻譯　聽者最可能會獲得什麼？
　　　(A) 金錢上的補償
　　　(B) 額外的教育訓練
　　　(C) 免費物品
　　　(D) 到府服務

解析　仔細聆聽與問題關鍵句 listener ~ receive 相關的內容。文中談到不僅會全額退費，下次光顧時還會提供 40 元的優惠券（on top of providing you a full refund, I'd like to send you a coupon for $40 off your next visit），由此可知能獲得金錢上的補償，所以答案是 (A)。

字彙　financial 財務的　compensation 補償　complimentary 免費的

95-97 美國發音

Questions 95-97 refer to the following telephone message and schedule.

Good morning, Jim. This is Beth from CV Productions. I just got your e-mail about [95]the Mountain Music Festival we're holding this year to raise money for school art programs. [96]To answer your question, your band will be staying at Days Hotel, which is near the site of the performance. Oh . . . also, another thing. I just found out that the event schedule has been changed. Three bands will play on Saturday instead of Sunday. So you and the other members of The Black Hats will play first on Sunday night. [97]The band that was supposed to play before you will be the opening act on Saturday.

---

festival 慶典　raise 募集（錢、捐款）　site 場所
find out 得知、查出　opening act 開幕表演

翻譯　問題 95-97，請參考以下電話訊息和日程表。
　　　你好，Jim，我是 CV Productions 公司的 Beth。我剛收到你的來信，內容是關於籌備 [95] 今年學校藝術課程資金而舉辦的山地音樂慶典。[96] 我現在就來回答你的問題，你的樂團會住在 Days 飯店，飯店就在表演場地的附近。啊……還有一件事，我剛剛得知活動日程變更了，有三個樂團將在星期六演出，而不是在星期日。因此你和 The Black Hats 的其他成員會在星期日晚上第一個表演，[97] 原本在你們之前的樂團則在星期六開幕時表演。

山地音樂慶典-日程表	
星期六	下午 9:00 – The Early Birds 下午 11:00 – Open Source
星期日	下午 7:00 –[97] Green Wave 下午 9:00 – The Black Hats 下午 11:00 – Cherry Blossom

95 提及何事的問題

翻譯　說話者談到慶典的什麼事？
　　　(A) 由音樂家主持。
　　　(B) 那是慈善活動。
　　　(C) 每年舉辦。

(D) 移動到新的場所。

解析 仔細聆聽與問題關鍵字 festival 相關的部分，文中談到為了籌備學校藝術課程資金要舉辦山地音樂慶典（the Mountain Music Festival we're holding this year to raise money for school art programs），從山地音樂慶典這個部分可知道是慈善活動，因此答案是 (B)。

字彙 musician 音樂家　charity event 慈善活動

96 特定細節問題

翻譯 聽者最可能詢問哪方面的問題？
(A) 裝備
(B) 住宿
(C) 費用
(D) 交通

解析 仔細聆聽與問題關鍵句 listener ~ ask about 相關的內容。說話者表示自己現在就來回答問題，並表示該樂團會住在 Days 飯店（To answer your question, your band will be staying at Days Hotel），由此可知聽者曾問過住宿的相關問題，所以答案是 (B)。

字彙 accommodation 住宿

97 圖表題

翻譯 請看圖表，哪一個樂團在星期六晚上第一個表演？
(A) Open Source
(B) Green Wave
(C) The Black Hats
(D) Cherry Blossom

解析 確認日程表資訊後，仔細聆聽和核心句子 perform first on Saturday night 相關的內容。文中談到原本在 The Black Hats 之前的樂團在星期六開幕時表演（The band that was supposed to play before you[The Black Hats] will be the opening act on Saturday.），從日程表中可知道 Green Wave 是星期六晚上第一個表演的團體，所以答案是 (B)。

換句話說
perform first 第一個表演 → be the opening act 負責開幕表演

字彙 perform 表演

98-100 ③ 加拿大發音

Questions 98-100 refer to the following talk and list of rooms.

[98]The upcoming Chicago Restaurant Convention is the best opportunity we'll get for showcasing our new product. This will be the largest exposition of its kind in the country, and [99]it's coming just two weeks before we officially release the oven. Six of our staff members will be traveling with us to the exposition. [99]We'll be giving our presentation about the oven on the exposition's second day, July 23, so we'll travel there via bus on July 22. We've booked rooms at the Chicago Continental, one of the best hotels in the

➡

city. [100]Each staff member will be staying in a room with a king-sized bed.

---

upcoming 即將到來的、即將來臨的
showcase 介紹、展示、公開活動　exposition 博覽會、展示會
officially 官方的　via 透過、藉由

翻譯 問題 98-100，請參考以下談話和客房目錄。
[98] 即將到來的芝加哥餐廳大會是我們介紹新產品的絕佳機會。這將是此類會展在國內最大的一個，[99] 那是在烤箱正式上市前的兩個星期。我們有六名員工會一起去，博覽會的第二天 7 月 23 日我們會展示推廣烤箱。我們 7 月 22 日會搭公車前往那邊，而且我們預約了那個城市最棒的飯店之一的芝加哥洲際飯店，[100] 每位員工都能自己住一間配有加大尺寸床鋪的房間。

芝加哥洲際套房	
客房	床的種類
Master room	1 個單人一般尺寸的床
[100] Deluxe room	1 個加大尺寸的床
Premium Room	2 個一般尺寸的床
Gold room	2 個加大尺寸的床

98 提及何事的問題

翻譯 說話者談到哪個部分和芝加哥餐廳大會有關？
(A) 提供宣傳商品的好機會。
(B) 要求參加者支付高額的入場費。
(C) 每年變得更受歡迎。
(D) 吸引全世界的參加者。

解析 仔細聆聽與問題關鍵詞 Chicago Restaurant Convention 相關的部分，文中提到「即將到來的芝加哥餐廳大會是我們介紹新產品的絕佳機會」（The upcoming Chicago Restaurant Convention is the best opportunity we'll get for showcasing our new product.），因此答案是 (A)。

換句話說
the best opportunity ~ for showcasing ~ product 介紹商品的最佳機會 → a good chance to market a product 宣傳商品的好機會

字彙 market 廣告、販售　admission 入場、入學

99 說話者問題

翻譯 說話者最可能從事哪一個行業？
(A) 餐旅服務
(B) 商業用不動產
(C) 家電製造
(D) 餐廳管理

解析 仔細聆聽短文中和身分、職業相關的用法，文中談到應該是在烤箱正式上市前的兩個星期（it[Chicago Restaurant Convention]'s coming just two weeks before we officially release the oven），接著又說會展示推廣烤箱（We'll be giving our presentation about the oven），由此可知他是從事家電製造領域，所以答案是 (C)。

字彙 hospitality 接待客人、接待、招待　appliance 家電產品

100 圖表題

翻譯 請看圖表，職員將入住哪一種類型的套房？
(A) Master room
(B) Deluxe room
(C) Premium Room
(D) Gold room

解析 確認提示的客房資訊後，注意聆聽與問題關鍵詞 employees staying in 相關的內容，內容提到每位員工都能自己住一間配有加大尺寸床的房間（Each staff member will be staying in a room with a king-sized bed.），由表中可知道職員是住在 Deluxe room，所以答案是 (B)。

PART 5

101 填入副詞

解析 想要修飾動詞（opposed），就必須要有副詞，因此副詞 (D) strongly（強烈地）是正確答案。形容詞 (A) 和 (B)、以及名詞 (C) 皆無法修飾動詞。

翻譯 MYK 公司強烈反對政府限制餐廳與咖啡廳的營業時間。

字彙 oppose v. 反對　regulate v. 規制、控制　opening hour 營業時間

102 填入介係詞

解析 因為整句話必須是「除了管理者之外」的意思，所以 (B) except（除了～之外）是正確答案。(A) within 是「～以內」；(C) across 是「穿過～」；(D) since 是「自～以來」。

翻譯 除了管理者之外，沒有人能關掉商店的緊急警報裝置。

字彙 deactivate v. 使～停止、停用　alarm system 警報裝置

103 填入不定代名詞／形容詞

解析 空格是主詞的位置，所以必須放名詞，因為必須是「大部分都能完成專案」的意思，所以代表「大部分」的 (A) most 是正確答案。(B) no 是形容詞，沒有名詞無法放在主詞的位置；(C) each 和單數動詞一起使用，因後面是複數動詞（were），所以無法當作答案；(D) another 是指另一個的意思，因此不符合語境。

翻譯 新方案讓研究人員遇到了一點小困難，但大部分人都能完成專案。

字彙 researcher n. 研究員　minor adj. 輕微的、較小的

104 選出名詞

解析 因為語境上是「訂購辦公用品前必須先取得同意」的意思，所以 (D) permission（同意）是正確答案。(A) distribution 是「分配、流通」；(B) confession 是「自白、告白」；(C) situation 是「情況、環境」。

翻譯 職員們額外訂購辦公用品前必須先取得同意。

字彙 obtain v. 獲得　office supply 辦公用品

105 填入正確的人稱代名詞

解析 因需要能放在主詞位置的人稱代名詞，所以 (A) they（他們）是正確答案。

翻譯 投資者抗議他們無法獲得公司財務狀況相關的資訊。

字彙 complain v. 抗議、抱怨　access v. 存取、使用　financial status 財務狀況

106 填入關係代名詞

解析 關係子句（attor neys ~ cases）中需要所有格關係代名詞來修飾名詞（attorneys），並形成主詞「公司律師們」之意思，因此答案是 (B) whose。

翻譯 Parker and Dean 公司是唯一同時有律師能處理民、刑事訴訟的在地法律事務所。

字彙 attorney n. 律師、代理人　deal with 對付、處理　civil adj. 民事上的、市民的　criminal adj. 刑事上的、犯罪的　legal adj. 法律的　case n. 訴訟（事件）

107 填入名詞

解析 可放在介係詞（for）之受詞位置的是名詞，(A) referral（介紹）是正確答案。動詞 (B)、動詞 (C) 和分詞 (D) 無法放在名詞的位置。

翻譯 患者請 Marple 醫師介紹眼科醫生。

字彙 eye specialist 眼科醫生　refer v. 參考、談及

108 選出形容詞

解析 從語境上來看，意思應該是「壯觀的景色和溫和的氣候讓聖塔羅莎成為前景看好的度假勝地」，因此 (B) promising（有前途的）是正確答案。

翻譯 壯觀的景色和溫和的氣候讓聖塔羅莎成為前景看好的度假勝地。

字彙 spectacular adj. 壯觀的、驚人的　scenery n. 景色　mild adj. 溫和的、溫暖的　climate n. 氣候、氛圍　resort n. 度假勝地　contribute v. 捐獻　propose v. 提議　collect v.收集

109 填入符合語態的動詞

解析 因句子中沒有動詞，動詞 (A)、(B)、(D) 都可能是答案。因為是「授予學位」的意思，後面有受詞（degrees），主動語態的動詞 (A) grants 是正確答案。

翻譯 Southwest 大學授予工程學、哲學等相當多元化領域的學位。

字彙 a wide variety of 相當多樣化　field n. 領域　engineering n. 工程學　philosophy n. 哲學　grant v. 授予、承認

110 填入介係詞

解析 整句話的意思必須是「在開會前要把經費報告交給會計部」，(A) before（在～之前）是正確答案。(B) around 是「在～周圍」；(C) in front of 是「在～前面」；(D) along 是「沿著～」。

翻譯 在和 Thompson 女士開會前，請將經費報告交給會計部。

字彙 expense report 經費報告　accounting department 會計部

111 填入非比較級

解析 因空格後面是 than，所以比較級的 (B) lower 是正確答案。

翻譯 長時間的乾旱造成水庫的水位比任何時候都更低。

字彙 prolonged adj. 長時間持續的、長期的　drought n. 乾旱
water level 水位　reservoir n. 水庫
lowly adj.（地位）低的；adv. 寒酸地

112 填入副詞

解析 必須要有副詞修飾動名詞片語（searching for new ways），因此 (A) continually（不斷地）是正確答案。形容詞 (B)、動詞 (C)、形容詞 (D) 無法修飾動名詞片語。

翻譯 Peter Lee 去年不斷尋找新方法向年輕消費者推銷他的軟體。

字彙 market v. 行銷、販售；n. 市場　continuous adj. 繼續的、持續的
continual adj. 再三的、不斷的

113 選出動詞

解析 因為整個語境是「部門管理人的主要作用是讓員工朝向公司訂立的目標邁進」的意思，(B) guide（指引）是正確答案。(A) adopt 是「採納、採用」；(C) initiate 是「開始」；(D) establish 是「設立」。

翻譯 部門管理人的主要作用是讓員工朝向公司訂立的目標邁進。

字彙 supervisor n. 管理者　stated adj. 既定的、定期的

114 分辨 in/at/on 後填入

解析 介係詞 in（在～之後）適合用在期間（two weeks）之前，因此 (C) in 是正確答案。

翻譯 應徵者大概 2 週後會接到公司的通知，請多加留意。

字彙 applicant n. 應徵人員　notify v. 通知
approximately adv. 大約、幾乎

115 選出動詞

解析 整句話的語境是「變更為包含更亮的顏色與更大的圖片」，alter 的過去分詞 (C) altered（變更）是正確答案。(A) 的 partner 是「合夥、合作」；(B) 的 practice 是「練習、執行」；(D) 的 relieve 是「緩和、減少」。

翻譯 我們會依照您的要求，讓網站的設計變更為包含更亮的顏色與更大的圖片。

字彙 request v. 要求；n. 要求　include v. 包含

116 填入 to 不定詞

解析 可以在後面修飾名詞 a contract 的過去分詞 (B) 和 to 不定詞 (C) 其中一個是正確答案。從「供給石油與天然氣的契約」此一部分來看，可連接受詞（oil and natural gas）並從後面修飾名詞（a contract）的是 to 不定詞 (C) to supply，因此它是答案。過去分詞 (B) supplied 無法接受詞，因此不是答案。

翻譯 Perot Petrochemicals 公司簽訂了供給石油和天然氣給公用事業公司的契約。

字彙 sign a contract 簽約　natural gas 天然氣
utility company 公用事業公司

117 填入時態一致的動詞

解析 因為內容談到未來的時間（by the end of next week），未來式 (B) will be ready 是正確答案。

翻譯 我們最新型電視產品的說明書會在下週末前準備好送印。

字彙 latest adj. 最新的　manual n. 說明書；adj. 手動的

118 選出副詞

解析 從語境來看應該是「會定期派遣行銷人員去賣場協助行銷活動」的意思，(A) periodically（定期）是正確答案；(B) absently 是「心不在焉」；(C) mistakenly 是「失誤」；(D) formerly 是「以前」。

翻譯 我們會定期派遣行銷人員去賣場協助行銷活動。

119 填入並置句子結構

解析 從內容上來看是「忙著見當地的民眾，並說明自己的政策」的意思，對等連接詞 and 要連接的 be busy（in）的受詞有兩個，and 前面有動名詞片語 meeting local citizens，and 後面的空格也必須是動名詞，因此答案是 (C) explaining。be busy (in) –ing「忙著進行～」是慣用語。

翻譯 在選舉活動中，政治人物忙著見當地的民眾，並說明自己的政策。

字彙 campaign n. 選舉活動　citizen n. 居民、民眾　policy n. 政策

120 填入副詞子句連接詞

解析 這是具備主詞（All fees）、動詞（must be received）的完整句子，a bill ~ course 必須視為是懸垂修飾語。因為是具備動詞（has been issued）的懸垂修飾語，可連接的副詞子句連接詞 (A) 和 (C) 其中一個是答案。因為整句話的意思必須是「所有學費必須在課程帳單發送後一個月內收到」，所以 (C) after（在～之後）是正確答案。

翻譯 所有學費必須在課程帳單發送後一個月內收到。

字彙 fee n. 學費、報酬　bill n. 帳單　issue v. 發給　course n. 課程

121 選出形容詞

解析 整句話的意思看起來是「為了讓居民們能更方便使用公車站，目前正在該地區重新配置公車站」，因此 (D) accessible（可進入的、容易使用的）是正確答案。(A) increased 是「增加的」；(B) adverse 是「不利的、負面的」；(C) constructive 是「建設性的」。

翻譯 市議會為了讓居民們能更方便使用公車站，目前正在該地區重新配置公車站。

字彙 city council 市議會　relocate v. 重新配置、移動
bus stop 公車站　resident n. 居民

122 填入名詞子句連接詞

解析 動詞（discussed）的受詞位置的子句（the new tax regulations ~ industry）前必須是名詞子句連接詞，(A)、(B)、(D) 皆有可能是答案。因為此一名詞子句是具備主詞（the new tax regulations）、動詞（would affect）、受詞（the automobile industry）的完整句子，引導完整句子的 (D) how 是正確答案。放在不完整句子前面的名詞子句連接詞 (A) 與複合關係代名詞 (B) 無法成為答案。

翻譯 底特律會計大會的主講者探討了新稅制將會如何影響汽車產業。

字彙 keynote speaker 主講者　regulation n. 規定、限制
affect v. 對～造成影響　automobile n. 汽車

123 填入與動詞數量一致的主詞

解析 因為動詞（is prohibited）是單數，後面可接受詞（animals），單數的動名詞 (C) Feeding 是正確答案。分詞或形容詞 (B) 後面必須修飾名詞 animals，並加上複數動詞，所以不是答案。

翻譯 全國的國立公園和保護區都禁止餵食動物。

字彙 prohibit v. 禁止、讓~ 無法進行　national park 國立公園
conservation area 保護區　feed v. 餵食、供給；n. 飼料

124 填入介係詞

解析 和動詞 comply 一起使用的介係詞 (D) with 是正確答案。

翻譯 建設在住宅區附近的工廠必須遵守嚴格的環境保護規定。

字彙 residential area 住宅區　comply v. 依照（法令、命令等）
strict adj. 嚴格的　environmental adj. 環境保護的、環境的

125 分辨現在分詞與過去分詞

解析 這是具備主詞（The company）、動詞（is known for）、受詞（its high-quality work）的完整句子，the new Italian restaurant 必須視為懸垂修飾語。選項中可成為懸垂修飾語的是分詞 (A) 和 (C)，受分詞修飾的名詞（The company）與分詞是主動關係，意思是「公司建造」，現在分詞 (C) building 是答案。

翻譯 建設新義大利餐廳的那間公司以高水準的作業聞名。

字彙 be known for 以～聞名

126 選出動詞

解析 從句子來看，意思應該是「財務評估完成後就會送出去」，finalize 的過去式 (C) finalized（最後完成）是正確答案。(A) nominate 是「提名（候選人）、任命」；(B) consume 是「消費」；(D) misplace 是「放錯地方」。

翻譯 完成財務評估後，就會送去 Newfield Electronics 公司的

法務部門。

字彙 financial adj. 財務的　assessment n. 評估
legal department 法務部

127 分辨動名詞與名詞

解析 句子中，位於 be 動詞（is 前面 Overland Resources 是主詞的位置。可在主詞最前面，同時連接受詞（the merger~ Overland Resources）的是動名詞，因此答案是 (C) Approving。名詞 (D) 後面不能放受詞。

翻譯 批准 Corus 公司和 Overland Resources 公司間的合併預計需要花上政府官員幾個星期的時間。

字彙 merger n. 合併　government official 政府官員
approve v. 同意

128 選出動詞

解析 整句話的語境是「將會在週末進行維修，為了把對辦公室運作造成的影響降至最低程度」，(B) minimize（最小化）是正確答案。(A) subtract 是「減掉、去除」；(C) disturb 是「妨礙」；(D) consider 是「考慮」。

翻譯 Portman 大樓將會在週末進行維修，以把對辦公室運作造成的影響降至最低程度。

字彙 carry out 執行、實施　effect n. 影響、效果
operation n. 營運、作業

129 填入介係詞

解析 由於意思應該是「橫跨全國」，因此 (A) across 是正確答案。

翻譯 據報導，在嚴酷的冬季風暴期間，全國各地出現了創紀錄的低溫。

字彙 record low 歷史新低　report v. 報導、報告
severe adj. 冷酷的、苛刻的

130 選出形容詞

解析 Although 後面的副詞子句與句子的連接必須自然一點，從語境上來看是「雖然出版了各種主題的書籍，但主要著重於歐洲的歷史」，(A) main（主要的、最重要的）是正確答案。(B) cooperative 是「協助的」；(C) convenient 是「方便的」；(D) previous 是「之前、前」。

翻譯 Steven Harris 雖然出版了各種主題的書籍，但他主要著重於歐洲的歷史。

字彙 publish v. 出版　a variety of 多元的　focus n. 焦點、著重點

PART 6

問題 131-134，請參考以下列電子郵件。

收件人：Linda Shute <lshute@plustech.com>
寄件人：Stanley Robinson
　　　　<srobinson@midwayexhibitions.com>
主旨：辦公用品貿易博覽會
日期：4 月 23 日

你好，Shute 女士，

¹³¹ 我之所以會寫這封信，是因為最近有人取消預約，我們辦公用品貿易博覽會上還有一個展位。我記得你對上個月錯過申請截止日感到相當失望，現在又有機會可以報名了。不過，你必須盡快表明自己的意願。¹³² 想要參加必須支付 250 美元，¹³³ 可以透過轉帳或前來我們的辦公室。

我強烈建議你參加。¹³⁴ 這項活動多年來不斷吸引粉絲，今年同樣也會再次聚集創下記錄的訪客人數。

Stanley Robinson 敬啟
顧客管理部

cancellation n. 取消預約、被取消之物　recall v. 記憶、使～想起
disappointed adj. 失望的　second chance 第二次機會
indicate v. 明示　following n. 粉絲、追隨者

---

131 填入介係詞

解析 原因是最近有人取消預約，所以多了一個展位，表示理由的介係詞 (C) due to（因為～）是正確答案。(A) in spite of 是「儘管～」；(B) opposite 是「～的對面」；(D) as long as 是引導子句的連接詞，因此無法成為答案。

132 填上時態正確的動詞　掌握整體的語境

解析 因為句子中沒有動詞，動詞 (A) 和 (C) 都可能是答案。從語境來看，意思是「想要參加必須支付 250 美元」，此時光憑空格的句子無法選出時態正確的動詞，必須掌握前後文或整體語境再選出答案。前面曾提到「可再次報名貿易博覽會的機會（you now have a second chance to register）」，並表示要盡快表示意願，由此可知參加博覽會支付費用的時態是未來式。因此答案是未來式的 (A) will need。

133 選出正確的句子

翻譯 **(A) 可以透過轉帳或前來我們的辦公室。**
　　(B) 博覽會期間有很多人造訪了該展位。
　　(C) 有幾個參展公司能使用的空位。
　　(D) 報名截止日已經過大幅調整。

解析 此一題型是要選出填入空格的正確句子，因此要掌握語境。前面提到想要參加就必須支付 250 美元（You (will need) to pay a fee of $250 to participate.），由此可知空格應該填入銀行轉帳或前往辦公室，所以答案是 (A)。

字彙 bank transfer 銀行轉帳　widely adv. 範圍廣的、廣泛
opening n. 空位　significantly adv. 相當地、大幅度

134 填入關係詞

解析 這個句子是具備主詞（This）、動詞（is）、補語（an event）的完整子句，a growing following over the years 必須視為是懸垂修飾語，因為此一懸垂修飾語在修飾前面的名詞「an event」，(C) 包含可修飾名詞的現在分詞，(D) 包含主格關係代名詞與關係子句的動詞，因此兩者都可能是答案。因為必須是「這項活動多年來不斷吸引粉絲」的意思，(D) which has attracted 不僅引導把 an event 當作先行詞的關係子句，在關係子句中有可扮演主詞的主格關係代名詞（which）和關係子句的動

詞（has attracted），因此這是正確答案。包含現在分詞在內的 (C) 是被動狀態，後面無法放受詞（a growing following），動詞 (A) 和 (B) 無法從後面修飾名詞。

字彙 attract v. 吸引、招引

問題 135-138，請參考以下新聞。

Edge Technologies 的彈性工時制度
Sarah Peterson 撰寫

6 月 11 日——Edge Technologies 公司執行長 Gerald McCarthy 宣布他的公司將採用彈性工時制度。¹³⁵ 如果真的完全施行此一制度，所有員工都有權選擇調整每天的工作時間。舉例來說，原本早上 9 點上班的員工，如果變成早上 7 點上班就能提早 2 個小時下班，¹³⁶ 每天要工作的總時間維持一樣，所有人都必須持續每天在辦公室工作 8 小時。

新制度明訂的目標是讓所有職員都能發展更好的工作、生活平衡，¹³⁷ McCarthy 先生希望這樣能提振公司的士氣。¹³⁸ 此一政策的制定，是為了應對科技公司在員工工作福利方面日益提升的競爭力。

flextime n. 彈性工時　adopt v. 採用
put ~ into practice 執行　adjust v. 調整
eight-hour day 一天工作 8 小時　stated adj. 官方的、規定的
work-life balance 工作生活平衡　morale n. 士氣、鬥志
competitiveness n. 競爭力　in terms of 在～方面、關於
benefit n. 福利政策、優勢、利益

---

135 填入名詞與數量／人稱一致的代名詞　掌握語境

解析 因為有單數動詞（puts），單數主詞 (A) 和 (C) 皆有可能是答案，單憑空格所在的句子無法判斷，必須掌握前後文或整個語境。前面的句子談到他的公司（his company）採用彈性選擇上班時間的制度，要填入空格的代名詞所指的對象是 company。因此，代表單數事物名詞（company）的代名詞 (A) it 是正確答案。

136 選出正確的句子

翻譯 (A) 職員可自由在家補足缺失的時間。
　　(B) 賣場週末也會繼續營業。
　　(C) 日程不會再以週為單位來變動。
　　(D) 每天要工作的總時間維持一樣。

解析 這是要選出填入空格之句子的題型，必須掌握前後文或整體的語境。前面有舉例說原本早上 9 點上班的員工，如果變成早上 7 點上班就能提早兩個小時下班（For example, a staff member who comes in at 7:00 A.M. instead of 9:00 A.M. will be able to leave two hours earlier.），後面則談到所有人每天都必須在辦公室工作 8 小時（Everyone must continue to work an eight-hour day at the office.），因此要填入空格的是「每天要工作的總時間維持一樣」，所以答案是 (D)。

字彙 make up 補充、組成　missing adj. 丟失的、遺漏的、消失的
on a weekly basis 以一週為單位

137 填入連接副詞　掌握整體語境

解析 空格是在句首的連接副詞的位置，需要掌握前面句子與

116

空格所在之句子的關係後選出答案。前面談到新制度的明訂目標是讓所有員工都能發展更好的工作生活平衡，空格所在的句子中談到 McCarthy 希望這樣能提振公司的士氣。由此可知，句子中使用的 (C) In this way（以這種方式）是正確答案。

字彙 nevertheless adv. 儘管如此　despite that 儘管

138 填入符合時態的動詞

解析 主詞（The policy）和動詞（create）有「政策考量」的意思，被動態動詞 (B) was created 是正確答案。

字彙 create v. 研發、創造

問題 139-142，請參考以下廣告。

Tree Doctor 公司

樹木只要細心照顧就能活很久，139 為了延長你樹木的壽命，必須妥善管理才行。140 Tree Doctor 公司的職員都擁有管理樹木的豐富知識，因為他們全都是經驗豐富、獲得認證的專家。為了評估樹木的狀態，我們的專家可以前往你的地產。141 具體來說，他們會查找生病的樹枝與根部。142 如果你考慮種植新的樹木，他們會針對該種植哪一種樹木才會在土中長得好，給予建議。如果想更進一步了解我們的服務和預約，請進入我們的網站 www.treedoctor.com。

take care of 照顧　proper adj. 恰當的、適當的
care n. 管理、照顧、關注　certified adj. 公認的、認證的
professional n. 專家；adj. 專業的　a great deal of 很多的
property n. 持有地、建築、不動產　evaluate v. 評價、鑑定

---

139 填入 to 不定詞

解析 因為必須是「為了延長樹木的壽命」的意思，代表目的的 to 不定詞 (B) To prolong 是正確答案。

字彙 prolong v. 讓~延長、延長

140 選出形容詞　掌握整體語境

解析 從語境上來看，意思是職員都擁有管理樹木的___知識，(A) prior（事前的）；(C) extensive（範圍廣的、廣闊的）；(D) partial（部分的、不完整的）皆有可能是答案，單憑空格的句子無法判斷，必須掌握前後文或整體語境。後面的句子談到他們全都是經驗豐富、獲得認證的專家（This is because they are all certified professionals with a great deal of experience.），由此可知是職員擁有豐富的知識，因此答案是 (C) extensive。

141 選出正確的句子

翻譯 (A) 因此，他們熟知各種不同的治療方法。
(B) 特定的樹木已經從庭院中移除了。
(C) 某些肥料對很多樹種有害。
(D) 具體來說，他們會查找生病的樹枝與根部。

解析 題目要選出填入空格的正確句子，必須掌握前後文或整體的語境。前面的句子談到為了評估樹木的狀態，

專家可以前往對方的地產（Our experts can visit your property to evaluate the condition of your trees.），具體來說，空格必須填入評估樹木狀態的內容，因此是「具體來說，他們會查找生病的樹枝與根部」，所以答案是 (D)。

字彙 be familiar with 對~熟悉的　a variety of 各式各樣的
treatment n. 治療（方法）　yard n. 庭院　fertilizer n. 肥料
species n. 物種　diseased adj. 生病的　branch n. 樹枝
root n. 根

142 填入時態正確的動詞

解析 因內容談到「如果有考慮種植新的樹木，他們會針對該種植哪一種樹木才會在土中長得好，給予建議」，從情境來看是未來的狀況，因此未來式 (A) will grow 是正確答案。

問題 143-146，請參考以下電子郵件。

收件人：Belle Rogers <brogers@smail.com>
寄件人：Aaron Cooper <aaroncooper@moneyphase.com>
主旨：歡迎！
日期：1 月 31 日

Rogers 女士，

143 我代表公司全體同仁歡迎成為新顧客的您，很開心您能選擇我們幫忙管理投資組合。

144 我們很清楚規劃您的財務需要時間、耐心和努力，可供選擇的投資選項相當多樣化，要選出適合自己的標的需要指引，我們保證能提供專業的建議。

希望您能告訴我何時方便進行第一次會面，145 屆時我們要討論您的短期與長期財務目標。146 請來電 555-1221 或寄電子郵件回答我。再次歡迎您，期望我們能建立成功的關係！

Aaron Cooper 敬上
投資分析師

on behalf of 代表~　manage v. 管理、營運
finance n. 財務、資金　patience n. 忍耐、耐心
a wide variety of 各式各樣的　guidance n. 引導、指導
assure v. 保證、使~確信　expert adj. 專業的；n. 專家

---

143 選出名詞　掌握整體語境

解析 從語境上來看是「歡迎成為新____的您」，因此所有選項都可能是答案，單憑空格的句子無法判斷，必須掌握前後文或整體的語境。後面談到很開心對方能選擇自己公司幫忙管理投資組合（We are thrilled that you have chosen our company for assistance with managing your investment portfolio.），由此可知收件人是公司的新顧客，所以答案是 (A) customer（顧客）。

字彙 owner n. 所有人　vendor n. 販售者

144 選出動詞　掌握整體的語境

解析 從語境上來看是「____財務需要時間、耐心和努力」，

所有選項都可能是答案，光憑空格所在的句子無法判斷，必須掌握前後文或整體的語境。後面談到可供選擇的投資選項相當多樣化，要選出適合自己的標的需要指引（There are a wide variety of investment options to choose from, and selecting the right ones requires guidance.），之後則說能提供專業的建議（we will provide you with expert advice），因此可以知道是要規劃財務，所以答案是 (C) planning（計劃）。

字彙 transfer v. 轉讓、移動　decrease v. 減少、減　cancel v. 取消

145 選出正確的句子

翻譯 (A) 我們相信這些建議可以提升您的收益。
(B) 很感謝您透過電子郵件給予財務上的相關建議。
(C) 屆時我們要討論您的短期與長期財務目標。
(D) 我們認為必須變更約定的日期。

解析 題目要選出適合填入空格的句子，必須掌握前後文或整體的語境。前面的句子請對方告知何時方便進行第一次會面（Please let me know when it would be convenient to hold our first meeting.），空格適合填入「屆時我們要討論您的短期與長期財務目標」，因此答案是 (C)。

字彙 reschedule v. 變更日程

146 填入相關連接詞

解析 和相關連接詞 either 符合的 (C) or 是正確答案。either A or B 和片語動詞（contact me）、片語動詞（reply to this e-mail）連接在一起。

PART 7

問題 147-148，請參考以下公告。

> 布蘭登堡的第三屆年度冬季慶典活動將於 12 月 2 日舉辦，147-B Muller 路沿路都會擺放裝飾品，Hasting 街上則會有冰雕，147-C Rossellini 路和 Peters 街交叉口的溜冰場於早上 8 點到下午 6 點會開放給民眾使用。
>
> 147-D 當晚的主要活動是晚上 10 點在 Sterner 路上的大松樹點燈，之後 147-A 布蘭登堡樂隊將會演奏各種節日歌曲。148 燈光會一直亮到新年的第一天為止，隔天都市公園管理員會負責拆除。
>
> decoration n. 裝飾（物）　sculpture n. 雕刻品
> ice rink 溜冰場　intersection n. 交叉路　lighting n. 點燃、照明
> brass band 管樂隊　afterward adv. 之後

147 Not/True 題型
下列哪一個不是冬季慶典活動的特點？
(A) 音樂演奏
(B) Peters 街的裝飾品
(C) 溜冰場的營運
(D) 樹木的點燈

解析 這是從短文中找出與關鍵句 a feature of the Winter Festival Ceremony 相關的內容，再和選項對照的 Not/True 題型。(A) 布蘭登堡樂隊將會演奏各種假日歌曲（the Brandenburg Brass Band will play a variety of

holiday songs）和短文內容一致。(B) Muller 路沿路都會擺放裝飾品（Decorations will be placed along Muller Way），但 Peters 街並不是擺放裝飾品，和短文內容不符，因此答案是 (B)。(C) 溜冰場會開放給民眾使用（the ice rink ~ will be open to skaters），和短文內容一致。(D) 當晚的主要活動是在大松樹上點燈（The main event of the night will be the lighting of the large pine tree），和短文內容一致。

換句話說
play a variety of holiday songs 演奏各種假日歌曲 →
performance of some music 音樂演奏
the ice rink ~ will be open 溜冰場將會開放 →
operation of a skating rink 溜冰場的營運

字彙 feature n.（活動等的）有趣事物、特色　operation n. 營運

148 5W1H 問題
新年第一天後會發生什麼事？
(A) 冰雕會被清除。
(B) 城市公園會重新開放。
(C) 照明會被拆除。
(D) 將會舉辦紀念儀式。

解析 題目詢問新年第一天後會發生什麼（What）事情，屬於 5W1H 問題。注意問題的關鍵詞 after New Year's Day，燈光會一直亮到新年的第一天為止，隔天就會拆下（The lights will stay up until New Year's Day, and they will be removed the next day），因此答案是 (C)。

字彙 take down 取下

問題 149-150，請參考以下信件。

> 5 月 12 日
> John Simon
> 85701 亞利桑那州，圖森
> North 街 772 號
>
> Simon 先生，
>
> 很感謝您同意由世界文化基金會在 Flagstaff 主辦的晚宴發表演說。149 大家都很高興能聽到您發表安地斯山脈地區古代文化的相關研究。因為您是活動的主講人，150 將會在我們的會長 Ernesto Paramo 之後進行演說。接著，大學生 Will Meyer 會播放他近期去哥倫比亞旅行的影片，結束後則會供應晚餐。
>
> 閉幕詞將由 Robert Shelling 負責，他目前經營 Flagstaff 文化院。
>
> 您的姓名已經加入我們的邀請名單，只要到場就行了，期待您的范臨。
>
> Roberto Marquez 敬啟
>
> organize v. 主辦、準備　conduct v. 進行
> ancient adj. 古代的　keynote speaker 主講人
> guest list 嘉賓名單　show up 到達、出現

149 推論題
Simon 先生最可能是誰？
(A) 基金會首長

(B) 研習會主辦人

(C) 電影製作者

(D) 研究員

解析 這是針對問題關鍵詞 Mr. Simon 推論的題目，文中談到大家都很高興能聽到 Simon 先生發表安地斯山脈地區古代文化的相關研究（Everyone is excited to hear about the studies you've conducted about the ancient cultures of the Andes Mountains region.），因此可推測 Simon 先生是研究員，所以答案是 (D)。

字彙 head n. 首長、負責人　filmmaker n. 電影製片人　researcher n. 研究員

150 5W1H 問題

誰會比 Simon 先生更早上臺？

(A) Ernesto Paramo

(B) Will Meyer

(C) Robert Shelling

(D) Roberto Marquez

解析 這是詢問誰（Who）會比 Simon 先生更早上臺的 5W1H 問題，因為和問題的關鍵詞 precede Mr. Simon 有關係。文中談到「您將會在我們的會長 Ernesto Paramo 之後進行演說」（you [Mr. Simon]'ll be giving your speech right after our organization's president, Ernesto Paramo），所以答案是 (A)。

字彙 precede v. 處於～之前

問題 151-152，請參考以下訊息。

Tony Webb	[下午 1 點 15 分]
你有聽說 Dave Jonson 下星期就要離開了嗎？	
Laura Hughes	[下午 1 點 17 分]
有，151-A/152 他剛才和我一起去吃午餐時說自己接受新工作的邀約了。	
Tony Webb	[下午 1 點 19 分]
他不是唯一的一個。152 公司會很快再僱用更多員工嗎？	
Laura Hughes	[下午 1 點 21 分]
對，人資部下星期會面試更多應徵我們部門的人。我已經同意要去 151-B 協助新人的教育訓練。	
Tony Webb	[下午 1 點 21 分]
好，這是當然的呀！151-D 光憑這麼少數的人要趕上所有的行銷期限真的太困難了。	
Laura Hughes	[下午 1 點 22 分]
151-D 我也很清楚，我的團隊成員都很擔心這件事，總之我再收到消息就會告訴你。	

offer n. 邀約、提案；v. 提議　meet v. 趕上（期限等）

151 Not/True 題型

關於 Hughes 女士的敘述哪一個是錯的？

(A) 最近和同事一起去吃飯。

(B) 為了工作，將會幫新員工進行教育訓練。

(C) 收到其他公司的工作邀約。

(D) 她是行銷部門的成員。

解析 這是從短文中找到和問題關鍵詞 Ms. Hughes 相關的內容，再和選項對照的 Not/True 題型。(A) Hughes 女士說自己和 Dave Jonson 剛剛一起去吃午餐（When he[Dave Jonson] and I were out for lunch earlier today(1:17 P.M.)），因此和短文內容一致。(B) Hughes 女士說會協助新人教育訓練（I've agreed to help with the training for newly hired employees.(1:21 P.M.)），和短文內容一致。(C) 是短文中沒有談到的內容，因此答案是 (C)。(D) Webb 先生說光憑這麼少數的人要趕上所有的行銷期限真的太困難了（It's been really hard to meet all of our marketing deadlines with so few people(1:21 P.M.)），Hughes 女士回答自己很清楚，並表示自己的團隊成員也都很擔心這件事（I know. Everyone on my staff has been worried about that.(1:22 P.M.)），因此和短文的內容一致。

換句話說

help with the training for newly hired employees 協助新職員的教育訓練 → prepare new employees 為新職員作準備

字彙 colleague n. 同事　prepare v. 讓～準備好　position n. 職務

152 意圖掌握問題

下午 1 點 19 分，Webb 先生說「He's not the only one」，他的意思最可能是什麼？

(A) 業務將會分配給其他人。

(B) 培訓文件必須更新。

(C) 已經有好幾名應徵者選上了。

(D) 其他組員離職了。

解析 題目詢問 Webb 先生的意圖，確認問題的引用句（He's not the only one）整體語境。文中 Hughes 女士和 Dave Jonson 一起去吃午餐時談到他接受新的工作邀約（When he[Dave Jonson] and I were out for lunch earlier today, he mentioned that he had accepted an offer of a new job.(1:17 P.M.)），接著 Webb 先生說不是只有他而已（He's not the only one），且詢問公司是否很快就會僱用更多的新員工（Will the company hire more staff soon?(1:19 P.M.)），由此可知其他組員已經離職了，因此答案是 (D)。

字彙 resign v. 離職、放棄

問題 153-154，請參考以下電子郵件。

收件人：Mitchell O'Connor〈moconnor@fastmail.com〉
寄件人：Playback Streaming 公司〈support@playback.com〉
主旨：Secrets of Paris
日期：9 月 19 日
O'Connor 先生，
感謝您使用媒體內容串流服務第 1 名的 Playback Streaming，我們的紀錄顯示您曾觀看由 153-CSam Marshall 監製且首次在 HistoryNow 頻道播放的紀錄片《Secrets of Paris》，我們一直都鼓勵顧客要寫觀賞評論，若您想要寫，只需要點擊想發表意見的影片底下按鍵即可。154 作為特別優惠，評論 100 部以上影片的人會晉升為

「優質用戶」，可獲得相當於 50 美金的免費電影和電視秀。

再次感謝您使用我們的服務。

Playback Streaming 公司顧客支援部門

media n. 媒體　direct v. 監督　air v. 播放
encourage v. 建議　review n. 評論；v. 評價
beneath prep. 底下　incentive n. 優惠、獎勵
award v. 給予、授予　status n. 等級、地位
eligible adj.（配合特定條件）有資格的
complimentary adj. 免費的

153 Not/True 題型
哪一部分和《Secrets of Paris》有關？
(A) 是根據一本知名的書籍。
(B) 獲得最優秀導演獎。
(C) 首次在歷史頻道中播放。
(D) 可額外購買。

解析 這是從短文中找出和問題關鍵詞 Secrets of Paris 相關的內容，進而和選項對照的 Not/True 題型。(A) 和 (B) 是短文中沒有提到的內容，(C) 談到由 Sam Marshall 監製且首次在 HistoryNow 頻道播放的紀錄片《Secrets of Paris》（the documentary Secrets of Paris, ~ first aired on the HistoryNow Channel），和短文中的內容一致，因此 (C) 是正確答案。(D) 是短文中不曾出現過的內容。

字彙 be based on 以～為基礎

154 5W1H 問題
用戶若寫 100 則評論，能獲得什麼？
(A) 電影的 DVD
(B) 額外的會員點數
(C) 1 年的訂閱
(D) 免費的媒體內容

解析 這是在詢問用戶寫 100 則以上評論時可獲得什麼（What）的 5W1H 問題，與問題的關鍵句 customers receive if they write 100 reviews 有關係。文中談到評論 100 部以上影片的人會晉升為「優質用戶」，可獲得相當於 50 美金的免費電影和電視秀（those who review 100 items or more are ~ eligible to receive $50 worth of complimentary movies and TV shows），因此答案是 (D)。

換句話說
complimentary movies and TV shows 免費電影和電視秀 → Free media content 免費的媒體內容

字彙 copy n. 影本　yearlong adj. 1 年間的　subscription n. 訂閱

問題 155-157，請參考以下網頁。

前往布林克里科學中心探險吧

參觀布林克里科學中心這棟共 3 層樓的博物館不需要任何理由。在這裡可以和大眾一起共享科學的驚奇。在我們的設施中可以 155-C 參觀聲波、龍捲風、距離地球很遙遠的行星等所有的展覽，所以請帶各位的朋友和家人一起來吧！

博物館營運時間

週二－週五：上午 9 點到下午 5 點
週六－週日：上午 9 點到下午 6 點
155-D 每週一公休

票價
一般入場 10 美元
學生 8 美元
65 歲以上 6 美元
156-C 布林克里大學學生免費入場
未滿 6 歲孩童免費入場

156-D 每個月第一個星期二，所有布林克里科居民都能免費入場，需要居住證明。

路線
汽車：行駛 20 號州際公路，從 60 號出口往 Grant 路方向移動，接著 157 左轉往 Lessing 路移動，科學中心就在左側。
地鐵：
在 Havel 街站的 2 號出口往右迴轉至 Wallace 街，前進 100 公尺後 157 請往右轉向 Lessing 路，科學中心就在右側。
公車：80 號和 125 號公車都會停靠科學中心前。

explore v. 探險　excuse n. 理由、藉口　story n.（建築的）樓層
dedicated to 致力於　wonder n. 驚異　exhibit n. 展示（品）
sound wave 聲波　distant adj. 遙遠的　general adj. 一般的
admission n. 入場、入場費　admit v. 允許入場、批准
proof of residence 居住證明書

155 Not/True 題型
關於布林克里科學中心，有何敘述？
(A) 有專門為了孩童準備的特別空間。
(B) 吸引很多國外的參觀者。
(C) 有關於氣候的展覽。
(D) 假日時沒有營業。

解析 這是從短文中找到和關鍵詞 Brinkley Science Center 相關的內容，再和選項對照的 Not/True 題型。(A) 和 (B) 是短文中沒有談到的內容。(C) 中談到你可以看到和龍捲風相關的展覽（you can view exhibits on ~ tornadoes），和短文中的內容一致，因此答案是 (C)。(D) 說星期一沒有營業（Closed on Mondays），和短文內容不符。

換句話說
exhibits on ~ tornadoes 有關於龍捲風的展覽 → weather-related exhibit 和氣象相關的展覽

字彙 attract v. 吸引

156 5W1H 問題
誰絕對不會被收取入場費？
(A) 年長者
(B) 未滿 6 歲孩童的父母親
(C) 布林克里大學的學生
(D) 布林克里的居民

解析 題目詢問誰（Who）絕對不會被收取入場費，和問題的關鍵詞 never charged for admission 有關。因文中談到布林克里大學學生免費入場（Free admission for students attending Brinkley College），所以正確答案是 (C)。(D) 說每個月第一個星期二所有布林克里居民都

能免費入場（On the first Tuesday of every month, all residents of Brinkley are admitted for free.），這是錯誤選項。

換句話說
never charged for admission 絕對不會收入場費的 →
Free admission 免費入場

157 推論題
布林克里科學中心最可能在什麼地方？
(A) Grant 路
(B) Have 街
(C) Wallace 街
(D) Lessing 路

解析 這是針對關鍵詞 Brinkley Science Center ~ located 進行推論的題目。文中談到左轉往 Lessing 路移動，科學中心就在左側（turn left onto Lessing Way. The center will be on your left.），往右轉向 Lessing 路，科學中心就在右側（turn right onto Lessing Way. The center will be on your right），由此可推測科學中心位於 Lessing 路，因此答案是 (D)。

問題 158-160，請參考以下徵人廣告。

Heimart 徵求全職銷售職員

Heimart 是專門提供平價的家庭用品與家電產品的領頭歐洲零售業者，— [1] —。158-A 在紐約、芝加哥、洛杉磯的第一間美國賣場成功後，158-D 我們預期針對美國其他主要城市新分店的職缺填補人手。

159 門市的員工要負責日常的作業，像是卸下新庫存、填補架上的貨物、以及保持門市的整潔。— [2] —依照表現也可能提供不同的職務機會，各位可學習使用收銀機、服務顧客的方法等。— [3] —

應徵者必須是 21 歲以上，同時具備類似職務的經驗。160 員工必須要有彈性安排工作日程的意願。— [4] —合格者可獲得具有競爭力的時薪、醫療保險、定期獎金、以及持續性的職業訓練。

想要應徵請來信 jobs@heimart.com。

---

full-time adj. 全職的　store associate 銷售員
leading adj. 領頭的　specialize in 專門從事
appliance n. 家電產品　look to 期待、等待
be responsible for 對～負責任　carry out 執行
routine adj. 常規的　unload v. 裝卸、卸貨
orderly adj. 井然有序的　register n.（金錢）收銀機
be willing to 有意願、樂意　flexible adj. 可變動的
successful candidate 合格者　competitive adj. 具備競爭力的
wage n. 薪資、薪水

---

158 Not/True 題型
關於 Heimart 的敘述提到什麼？
(A) 美國的第一個賣場將要開幕了。
(B) 販售各種辦公用傢俱。
(C) 提供家庭送貨服務。
(D) 有好幾個城市都有工作機會。

解析 這是從短文中找出和問題關鍵字 Heimart 相關的內容，

再和選項對照的 Not/True 題型。(A) 說因為紐約、芝加哥、洛杉磯的第一間門市都成功了（the success of our first American stores in New York, Chicago, and Los Angeles），和短文中的內容不符。(B) 和 (C) 是短文中沒有談到的內容。(D) 預計為美國其他主要城市新分店的職缺填補人手（we are looking to fill positions at new locations in other major US cities），和短文的內容一致，因此答案是 (D)。

字彙 carry v. 辦理

159 5W1H 問題
門市員工的工作是什麼？
(A) 調整日程
(B) 尋找產品供應商
(C) 維持清潔
(D) 運送訂購物品

解析 這是詢問門市員工工作內容是什麼（What）的 5W1H 問題，與問題的關鍵詞 responsibility of a store associate 有關。文中談到平常的工作是要保持門市的整潔等（As a store associate, you will be responsible for carrying out routine tasks, such as ~ keeping the store clean and orderly at all times.），因此答案是 (C)。

換句話說
keeping ~ clean 維持整潔 → Maintaining cleanliness 維持清潔

字彙 arrange v. 調整　maintain v. 維持

160 將句子放入合適的位置
翻譯 以下句子最適合放入 [1]、[2]、[3] 或 [4] 的哪個位置？
「包含不定期的早班與晚班的輪班。」
(A) [1]
(B) [2]
(C) [3]
(D) [4]

解析 題目是要選出最適合填入空格的選項，文中談到包含不定時的早班和晚班的輪班（This includes early morning and night shifts on occasion），因此可猜到句子前面應該是和工作時間有關的內容。[4] 因談到員工必須要有彈性安排工作日程的意願（Employees should be willing to work on a flexible schedule.），如果加入 [4] 的句子，整句話就是「員工必須要有彈性安排工作日程的意願，包含不定期的早班與晚班的輪班。」，因此答案是 (D)。

字彙 shift n. 輪班　on occasion 不時

問題 161-163，請參考以下備忘錄。

收件人：Brumfield 的全體職員
寄件人：Fred Sears，人資部主管
日期：5 月 10 日
主旨：改造作業

相信大家也都知道，161 Brumfield 公司從下星期開始將展開為期一個月的四樓改造作業，161-C 這會讓目前在那個地方工作的行銷部門職員座位出現問題。162 原本我們考慮

➔

TEST
3
NEW TOEIC 950 聽力+閱讀 5 回達標

要讓他們坐在大樓不同樓層的辦公空間。但經過一番苦思後，我們最後認為這不是一個好方案，因為行銷的職員常要講電話，¹⁶² 如果這樣安排，他們可能會讓工作需要安靜的其他部門職員很傷腦筋。

因此，¹⁶¹⁻C/3 我們決定要把大樓二樓的大會議室當作該組人員的臨時作業空間，IT 部門明天會去那邊安裝需要的電腦和印表機。¹⁶³ 三樓職員休息室旁邊比較小的會議室，在下個月左右是其他部門職員唯一能使用的會議室。

謝謝各位。

---

aware adj. 意識到的　undergo v. 進行　create v. 引起、製造
space n. 處所、空間　look into 檢討　seat v. 請～坐下、容納
consideration n. 費心、考慮　conclude v. 結論
arrange v. 配置　bothersome adj. 令人傷腦筋的、麻煩的
silence n. 安靜　temporary adj. 暫時的　break room 休息室

161 Not/True 題型

關於 Brumfield 公司，有提到什麼事？
(A) 目前正在擴張行銷部。
(B) 要改造辦公室。
(C) 要搬遷 IT 部門。
(D) 正在更新電腦。

解析　這是從短文中找到問題關鍵詞 Brumfield Co.，再和選項對照的 Not/True 題型。(A) 是短文中沒有談到的內容。(B) 內容談到 Brumfield 公司從下星期開始將展開為期一個月的四樓改造作業（Brumfield Co. will be undergoing a month-long renovation of its fourth floor starting next week），和短文的內容一致，因此 (B) 是正確答案。(C) 談到目前在四樓工作的行銷部門職員會出現座位問題（This creates a space problem for the marketing department employees currently working there[fourth floor].），後來說請加上下引號（we have decided to create a temporary work area for the team ~ on the second floor of the building），由此可知搬遷的不是 IT 部門，而是行銷部門，所以和短文中的內容不符，(D) 是短文中沒有談到的內容。

字彙　expand v. 擴張　relocate v. 讓～移動

162 5W1H 問題

為什麼行銷部職員沒有分散配置在各個樓層？
(A) 必須一起進行大部分的業務。
(B) 準備重要的簡報。
(C) 可能會造成其他職員的困擾。
(D) 必須互相討論專案。

解析　這是在詢問行銷部為什麼（Why）沒有分散在各個樓層的 5W1H 問題，因為和問題的核心句子 marketing staff not be spread out over several floors 有關。文中談到「原本我們考慮要讓他們坐在大樓不同樓層的辦公空間」（We initially looked into seating them[marketing staff] in various available workstations on the other floors of the building.）、「如果這樣安排，可能會讓工作需要安靜的其他部門職員很傷腦筋」（arranging them in this way would be bothersome to other department members whose jobs require silence），因此答案是 (C)。

換句話說
bothersome to other department members 讓其他部門的職員很傷腦筋的 → disruptive to other workers 對其他職員造成困擾的

字彙　spread out 散開　assignment n.（分配的）業務
disruptive adj. 引起混亂的

163 推論題

針對大會議室可推論出什麼？
(A) 部分職員將會無法使用。
(B) 位於影印室旁邊。
(C) 上個月重新粉刷過。
(D) 先前被當作職員休息室使用。

解析　這是針對問題關鍵詞 main conference room 推論的題目，文中談到請加上下引號（we have decided to create a temporary work area for the team[marketing team] in the main conference room on the second floor of the building）、比較小的會議室是其他部門職員唯一能使用的會議室」（The smaller meeting room ~ will be the only one available for members of other departments to use），因此可推測部分職員無法使用大會議室，所以答案是 (A)

字彙　unavailable adj. 無法使用的　refurbish v. 翻新
lounge n. 休息室

問題 164-167，請參考以下訊息。

Carol Medina [上午 11 點 41 分]
¹⁶⁴ 我正在規劃公司的尾牙，我希望有人能幫忙我。

Annie Sanders [上午 11 點 42 分]
我很樂意幫忙，你希望我做什麼？

Carol Medina [上午 11 點 43 分]
我還沒找到舉辦尾牙的地點，¹⁶⁵ 你可以幫忙我找合適的宴會場地嗎？我們必須預約 12 月 22 日。

Annie Sanders [上午 11 點 43 分]
¹⁶⁵ 沒問題。今年有多少人參加？

Carol Medina [上午 11 點 44 分]
目前還不確定，因為每個員工都能邀請一名客人來，所以我們得聯絡每個人，詢問他們是否會帶人來。

Vincent Bryce [上午 11 點 45 分]
這件事我現在能處理，我會寫信給公司的所有員工，明天午餐前我會把預估的人數告訴兩位。

Annie Sanders [上午 11 點 46 分]
太完美了，餐點呢？¹⁶⁶ 需要我去找外燴業者嗎？

Carol Medina [上午 11 點 47 分]
不需要。¹⁶⁶ Bellwood Fine Foods 公司的菜單很棒，而且價格也很合理。¹⁶⁷ 過去 6 年來我們用過他們的服務很多次。

---

year-end party 尾牙　could use 希望能獲得
lend a hand 給予幫助　look for 尋找、取得
suitable adj. 合適的　banquet hall 宴會場　intend to 預定要～
catering n. 供給食物　reasonable adj.（價格）適當的

164 尋找目的

Medina 女士為何會聯絡同事？

(A) 為了告知即將到來的活動
(B) 為了要求關於餐點的建議
(C) 為了要求關於業務的協助
(D) 為了表達對專案的關注

解析 題目是要找出 Medina 女士聯絡同事的用意，因此要仔細確認短文前面的部分。內容談到她正在規劃公司的尾牙，希望有人能幫忙（I'm planning the company's annual year-end party. I could really use some help. (11:41 A.M.)），因此 (C) 是正確答案。

換句話說
help 幫助 → assistance 幫助

字彙 assistance n. 幫助

165 5W1H 問題

Sanders 女士同意要做什麼？

(A) 確認參加者人數。
(B) 聯絡外燴業者。
(C) 尋找場地。
(D) 寄送邀請函。

解析 這是詢問 Sanders 女士同意什麼（What）事的 5W1H 問題，與問題的關鍵句 Ms. Sanders agree to do 有關係。Medina 女士詢問 Sanders 女士是否可以幫忙找合適的宴會場地（Could you look for a suitable banquet hall?(11:43 A.M.)），Sanders 女士回答當然沒問題（Sure.(11:43 A.M.)），因此 Sanders 女士要幫忙找場地，所以答案是 (C)。

換句話說
look for a suitable banquet hall 尋找合適的宴會場 → Find a venue 尋找場地

字彙 attendance n. 參加者（人數）、參加　caterer n. 外燴業者
venue n. 場所

166 意圖掌握問題

上午 11 點 47 分，Medina 女士回答「No need」，她最可能有何用意？

(A) 要詢問變更菜單的事。
(B) 知道參加者的人數。
(C) 已經確認過大廳是否可使用。
(D) 要和特定外燴業者合作。

解析 題目是詢問 Medina 女士的意圖，確認問題的引用詞語（No need）整體語境，Sanders 女士問：「需要幫忙找外燴業者嗎？」（Would you like me to look for catering companies as well?(11:46 A.M.)），Medina 女士回答不需要（No need），並表示「Bellwood Fine Foods 公司的菜單很棒，而且價格也很合理，過去 6 年來我們用過他們的服務很多次」（Bellwood Fine Foods has excellent menu options and reasonable prices. (11:47 A.M.)），由此可知 Medina 女士和特定外燴業者合作，所以答案是 (D)。

字彙 availability n. 使用可能性、可使用

167 推論題

關於 Bellwood Fine Foods 公司，文中暗示了什麼？

(A) 專門為小規模團體舉辦派對。
(B) 已經營業好幾年了。
(C) 提供數量有限的菜單選項。
(D) 最近調降價格了。

解析 這是針對關鍵詞 Bellwood Fine Foods 進行推論的題目，文中談到過去 6 年多次和外燴業者合作（We've used them[Bellwood Fine Foods] often over the past six years.(11:47 A.M.)），由此可推論出 Bellwood Fine Foods 公司已經營業很多年了，所以答案是 (B)。

字彙 specialize in 專攻　be in business 營業中　limited adj. 限定的

問題 168-171，請參考以下新聞。

工程公告

East Parsons，6 月 3 日—交通部長 Claudia Rittora 今天在記者會中表示新的地鐵路線－綠線從 9 月起將要施工，這條鐵路線會服務 Peterson 和 Forest Falls 郊區，168 包含在 Pew 街、Jackson 街、Crispin 大路設站，之後會和通往市區的紅線相會。— [1] —

Rittora 女士 169 表示之所以會決定規劃通往郊區的地鐵路線，是因為必須去市區的通勤族表示強烈不滿。— [2] — 一通往郊區的公車只有幾班而已，而且每班間隔的時間太長了，曾經有電車路線銜接郊區，沿著 Jackson 街和 Wollford 街停靠，170-C/171 但經營那條路線需要耗費相當多的費用，170-D/171 而且使用的乘客也不多。— [3] —

因為郊區人口大幅增加，新的地鐵路線應該會更為成功，— [4] —綠線每天會營運 24 小時，每天都會行駛，每隔 10 分鐘就會有一班車，想知道更多資訊的人只要前往 www.eastparsonscity.gov 就行了。

---

press conference 記者會　commissioner n. 長官
undergo v. 進行、經歷　service to 運行至～
suburban adj. 郊外的　neighborhood n. 地區、鄰居
merge v. 合併　downtown adv. 朝市中心；n. 市區
suburb n. 郊外　in response to 響應　commute v. 通勤
outlying adj. 偏僻的　infrequent adj. 罕見的　interval n. 間隔
tram n. 電車　extend to 延伸至～　outer adj. 外圍的
costly adj. 昂貴的

168 尋找同義詞

第 1 段第 5 行的「merge」，意思最接近下列何者？

(A) 相會
(B) 堆積
(C) 返回
(D) 交易

解析 這裡的 merge 是「會合」的意思，因此 (A)「相會」是正確答案。

169 5W1H 問題

為何會建設新的地鐵路線？

(A) 為了縮短住在市區的居民的通勤時間
(B) 為了處理郊區居民的不滿
(C) 為了容納新建地區的居民

(D) 為了彌補取消的公車服務

解析 這是在詢問為什麼（Why）要建蓋新地鐵路線的 5W1H 問題，和問題的核心句子 the new subway line be constructed 有關。文中談到之所以會決定規劃通往郊區的地鐵路線，是因為必須去市區的通勤族表示強烈的不滿（the decision to build a subway line in the suburbs was made in response to the many complaints that have been made by people who must commute to the city），因此答案是 (B)。

換句話說
was made in response to the many complaints 為了回應許多的不滿 → address ~ dissatisfaction 處理不滿

字彙 commuting time 通勤時間　address v. 處理、辦理
dissatisfaction n. 不滿　accommodate v. 容納
compensate v. 加強、補償　cancellation n. 取消、中止
bus service 公車運行

---

170 Not/True 題型

關於電車路線的敘述，提到什麼？
(A) 每天可運行 24 小時。
(B) 由私人企業擁有。
(C) 造價昂貴。
(D) 只有少數人使用。

解析 這是從短文中找出和問題關鍵詞 tram line 相關的內容，再和選項對照的 Not/True 題型。短文中沒有談到 (A) 和 (B)，(C) 營運那條路線需要耗費相當多的費用（it[tram line] was very costly to operate），但不清楚建設時投入了多少金額，所以和短文內容不符。(D) 使用的乘客也不多（not many people used it[tram line]）和短文內容一致，所以答案是 (D)。

字彙 operational adj. 可運行的

---

171 將句子放入合適的位置

翻譯 以下句子最適合放入 [1]、[2]、[3] 或 [4] 的哪個位置？
「結果市政府在 20 年前決定要停止行駛。」
(A) [1]
(B) [2]
(C) [3]
(D) [4]

解析 題目是要掌握語境，從中選出最適合填入句子的位置。內容談到「結果市政府在 20 年前決定要停止行駛」（As a result, the city decided to end this service 20 years ago），可猜測在句子前面有談到先前的交通設施停駛的理由。[3] 前面的句子談到經營那條路線需要耗費相當多的費用，而且使用的乘客也不多（it[tram line] was very costly to operate, and not many people used it），可以知道只要加入 [3] 的句子就能自然解釋電車停駛的理由，所以正確答案是 (C)。

問題 172-175，請參考以下表格。

《THE NORTHWEST LEDGER》

172 姓名：Mohammed Abbar
訂閱：■每日　　　□每週　　　□每週 2 次
地址：155 號 Winateka 路，華盛頓州塔科馬 98401

172 我想要的：
□變更訂閱　　　■取消訂閱

如果要變更訂閱，請選擇服務：
□每日　　　□每週　　　□每週 2 次

如果要取消的話，請勾選理由：
□搬家。
□無法負擔訂閱費用。
□對內容的品質不滿意。
■其他

如果是其他理由，請詳細填寫：

原本我是為了知道每天地區發生的事情才會訂閱《The Northwest Ledger》報刊，但 173 最近幾年我都使用 TacomaToday.com 和其他網站取得資訊來源，加上我比先前更忙，坐著看大份報紙的機率就變更低了。

174 改善《THE NORTHWEST LEDGER》的相關建議：

貴公司的報紙主要都在提供國內運動聯盟的報導，174 我認為應該多報導我們地區的棒球聯賽和曲棍球的新聞，餐廳食評也要更多一點。

只要交出此一表格，175 您的服務就會變更或停止，為了確認完成申請內容，信件將會寄送到您於上方填寫的地址。若是沒有收到信件，請來信 subscriptions@northwestledger.com 聯絡我們。

subscription n. 訂閱　daily adj. 每天的；n. 日刊
weekly adj. 每週的；n. 週刊　semiweekly adj. 每週 2 次的
rely on 依賴~　be less likely to 不太可能~　coverage n. 報導
story n. 記事、故事　devoted to 將用於~、奉獻於~
discontinue v. 中斷　confirm v. 證實、確認

---

172 目的問題

Abbar 先生為什麼要填寫表格？
(A) 為了申請週刊郵件
(B) 為了停止收到報刊
(C) 為了變更郵件寄送地址
(D) 為了抱怨新聞

解析 因為題目是要找出 Abbar 先生填寫表格的理由，因此要詳細確認短文前面的部分，「NAME: Mohammed Abbar」和「I WOULD LIKE TO: ■ Cancel my subscription」，表示 Abbar 先生不想再收到報紙，因此答案是 (B)。

換句話說
Cancel ~ subscription 取消訂閱 → stop getting a newspaper 停止接收報紙

字彙 sign up for 申請　mailing n. 郵件
mailing address 郵件寄送地址

173 推論題

關於 Abbar 先生，可以做出什麼推論？
(A) 最近搬到塔科馬了。
(B) 喜歡閱讀小說出版物。
(C) 想要延長訂閱。
(D) 偏好線上新聞來源。

解析 這是針對關鍵詞 Mr. Abbar 進行推論的題目，文中談到最近幾年都使用 TacomaToday.com 和其他網站取得資訊（in recent years, I have been getting news from TacomaToday.com and other websites instead），因此答案是 (D)。

字彙 fiction n. 小說 publication n. 出版物 renew v. 延長、更新 news source 新聞來源、新聞出處

174 推論題

關於《The Northwest Ledger》，文中暗示了什麼？
(A) 沒有評論欄。
(B) 具備有限的地區體育欄。
(C) 不是每天發行。
(D) 有線上的版本。

解析 這是針對問題關鍵詞 The Northwest Ledger 推論的題型，「SUGGESTIONS FOR IMPROVING THE NORTHWEST LEDGER:」和「I think there should be more stories devoted to our local baseball league and hockey teams.」中談到「改善《THE NORTHWEST LEDGER》的相關建議：貴公司的報紙主要都在提供國內運動聯盟的報導，我認為應該多報導我們地區的棒球聯賽和曲棍球的新聞」，由此可推論《The Northwest Ledger》報刊的地區體育版很有限，所以答案是 (B)。

字彙 section n.（新聞等的）欄位、部分 limited adj. 受限的 on a daily basis 以每天為單位、每天

175 推論題

Abbar 先生會收到什麼？
(A) 確認信件
(B) 禮券
(C) 全額退款
(D) 免費圖書

解析 這是針對問題關鍵句 Mr. Abbar ~ receive 推論的題型。文中談到服務將會變更或停止，為了確認完成申請內容，信件將會寄送到填寫的地址（your service will be changed or discontinued. To confirm that this has been done, you will receive a letter），因此可推測 Abbar 先生將會收到確認信件，所以答案是 (A)。

字彙 confirmation n. 確認 complimentary adj. 免費的

問題 176-180，請參考以下電子郵件和產品說明。

收件人：Angelica Lucci<angelica@craincameras.com>
寄件人：Brad Farley <brad@ craincameras.com >
主旨：產品說明書
日期：1 月 28 日

Angelica，

我負責製作我們新的 Selector 數位相機宣傳文，具體來說是我們線上購物網站照片旁的文字，不過，我在進行此一工作時的特定方面遇到了些許的困難。176/178 因為我想把重點放在先前型號 ProViewer 沒有的相機功能，176 你是這兩款型號相機的負責人，不知道你是否能幫忙我？舉例來說，我想知道 ProViewer 有沒有臉部偵測功能。另外，它的容量有沒有 4 GB？如果沒有的話，我想在 Selector 的產品說明書中強調這一類的功能，我對 Selector 新的錄影功能感到有些混亂，你可以告訴我詳細的資訊嗎？希望你能抽空回答我的問題，謝謝！

Brad Farley 敬上

assign v. 負責、配定 publicity material 宣傳物
aspect n. 層面、狀態、觀點 assignment n. 負責業務、分配
feature n. 功能、特徵 product manager 產品負責人
face-detection n. 臉部辨識 storage n. 儲存
capacity n. 容量、能力 highlight v. 強調

CRAIN CAMERAS 公司的新 SELECTOR 數位相機

177 新的 Selector 相機在各方面都很優秀，無論是專家或業餘攝影師都非常適合。178 Selector 和先前的型號一樣可儲存 4GB 的照片，在各種不同的照明下都能使用。不過，為了讓它有更多發揮空間、使用更便利、以及更加精巧，我們增加了很多新功能。

■SELECTOR 擁有自動調整焦點的臉部辨識功能，可鮮明呈現人物的臉部。
■我們還延長了電池的壽命，在沒有充電的情況下，SELECTOR 最久可持續 20 個小時。
■179-D Selector 最久可拍攝 30 分鐘的影片，因為影片都具備高解析度，所以相當清晰。179-B 也可使用幾乎所有影片編輯軟體來轉換為各種不同的格式。

此外，180 所有商品附加可擺放相機的三腳架，三腳架可調整高度，讓您在高角度或低角度都能拍攝照片。

professional adj. 專家的、熟練的 alike adv. 兩者都、差不多
lighting n. 照明 versatile adj. 多用途的、多才多藝的
accessible adj. 使用簡單、可存取得
sophisticated adj. 精巧的、高性能的、洗鍊的
adjust v. 調整、適應 last v. 持續 recharge v.（再）充電
shoot v. 拍攝、拍照 detailed adj. 詳細的
be converted into 轉換為～ come with 伴隨～
foldout adj. 摺疊的 tripod n. 三腳架 mount v. 上升、增加

176 目的問題

Farley 先生為何寫這封信？
(A) 為了要求產品相關的資訊
(B) 為了針對顧客諮詢採取後續措施
(C) 為了要求校正文件
(D) 為了提出行銷戰略

解析 題目是要找出 Farley 先生寫信的用意，因此要確認 Farley 先生的信件內容。第一篇短文（電子郵件）中談到想把重點放在先前型號 ProViewer 沒有的相機功能（I'd like to focus on the features of this camera that were not included in our previous model ~.），並詢問對方是這兩款型號相機的負責人，不知道是否能幫忙

（Since you're the product manager for both camera models, could you help me with this?），因此答案是 (A)。

字彙 follow up 採取後續措施　proofread v. 校正

---

177 尋找同義詞

產品說明書中第 1 段第 1 行的詞彙「outstanding」，意思最接近何者？

(A) 明顯的
(B) 過期的
(C) 優秀的
(D) 具備意義

解析 產品說明書中包含 outstanding 的句子是「Perfect for professional and amateur photographers alike, the new Selector camera is outstanding in every way.」，該句子中的 outstanding 是「優秀的」的意思，因此 (C) 是正確答案。

---

178 推論題

關於 ProViewer 有提到什麼？

(A) 最多可儲存 4GB 的資料。
(B) 在專業人士之間相當受歡迎。
(C) 大約在一年前推出。
(D) 自動對焦物品。

解析 先確認與問題關鍵字相關的電子郵件。
線索 1 在第一篇短文（電子郵件）談到 ProViewer 是先前的型號（our previous model, the ProViewer），不過，因為沒提出先前型號的相關資訊，所以要確認產品說明書中的相關內容。
線索 2 在第二篇短文（產品說明書）可確認先前的型號可儲存 4GB 的照片（As with our earlier models, the Selector can store up to four gigabytes of photographs）。
綜合兩個部分來看時，可知道先前的型號 ProViewer 最多可儲存 4GB 的照片，所以答案是 (A)。

字彙 release v. 發行

---

179 Not/True 題型

產品說明書如何描述 Selector 的影片功能？

(A) 額外付費就能加裝。
(B) 需要特定的程式軟體。
(C) 把畫面傳送到線上帳號。
(D) 可拍攝 30 分鐘的影片。

解析 這是詢問關鍵詞 Selector's video feature 的 Not/True 題型。在談到 Selector 影片功能的第二篇短文（產品說明書）中可確認相關的內容。(A) 是短文中沒談到的內容。(B) 和短文的內容不符，短文中說可採用幾乎所有影片編輯軟體來轉換為各種不同的格式（They[videos] can also be converted into various formats using almost any video-editing software.）。(C) 是短文中未提到的內容。(D) 因為短文中談到最久可拍攝 30 分鐘的影片（The Selector can shoot videos of up to 30 minutes in length.），和內容一致，所以答案是 (D)。

換句話說
shoot videos of up to 30 minutes in length 最多能拍攝 30 分鐘的影片 → allows for filming of half-hour videos 可拍攝半小時的影片

字彙 footage n. 場面

---

180 5W1H 問題

根據產品說明書來看，Selector 有搭配什麼？

(A) 額外的電池
(B) 可調整的三腳架
(C) 攜帶收納袋
(D) 多種鏡頭

解析 這是詢問 Selector 配備有什麼（what）的 5W1H 問題，在談論到問題關鍵詞 Selector come with 的產品說明書中確認相關的內容。第二篇短文（產品說明書）中談到所有產品都配有可折疊的三腳架，而且能調整高度（all units come with a foldout tripod ~. The tripod is adjustable），所以答案是 (B)。

字彙 a selection of 多樣的

問題 181-185，請參考以下廣告和電子郵件。

致 West Carver 的居民

這星期因為要舉辦為期三天的波多黎各文化慶典，所以有幾條道路會封街：

■[183] Madeline 街的 100 到 800 街區會有舞者和樂隊進行波多黎各遊行，7 月 2 日星期五上午 8 點到下午 12 點將會封街。

■MacDunn 街的 200 到 500 街區要進行 [181-A] 傳統音樂表演，7 月 3 日星期六上午 11 點到下午 5 點將會封街。

■Harrison 街的 300 到 600 街區會舉辦玩 [181-B] 滑水道和各種慶典遊樂設施的娛樂之日，7 月 4 日星期天下午 2 點到 10 點將會封街。

Carver 公園會舉辦包含唱歌、舞蹈、[181-C] 抽獎的更多活動，7 月 3 日和 4 日上午 9 點和下午 11 點之間會舉辦。

[182] 如果因為身心障礙難以外出行動，請來信 services@sanmiguel.gov 聯絡我們的政府職員，我們會做出安排，接送各位去感興趣的活動。

marching band 樂儀隊　fun and games 娛樂和遊戲
feature v. 特別包含　ride n. 遊樂設施　raffle for ～的抽獎
disability n. 障礙　arrangement n. 準備

收件人：Lucy Garcia <lgarcia@puertoricanfestival.com>
寄件人：Michael Gomez <mgomez@fastmail.com>
主旨：幾個問題
日期：7 月 3 日

Garcia 女士，

我的名字是 Michael Gomez，是 West Carver 的居民，[183] 昨天我聽見沿著我家裡前面的街道移動的大型遊行聲，於是便上網搜尋了解一下，[184] 我先前曾住過波多黎各，對協助地區居民慶祝我的文化傳統很有興趣，請問是否還需要義

工呢？我可以在社區周圍貼海報、引導參加者進行特定活動、設置活動需要的帳篷。¹⁸⁵另外，因為我有貨車，可以幫忙運載備品。如果有辦法能協助這項活動，請記得告訴我，期待您的回信。

Michael Gomez 敬上

---

celebrate v. 紀念　heritage n. 文化遺產、傳統
put up 張貼、告示　attendee n. 參加者
set up 設置、建立　pick up 裝載、載送
drop off 放下、下降　assist v. 幫助、有助益

---

181 Not/True 題型
下列哪一個不是公告中出現的選項？
(A) 音樂表演
(B) 水上遊樂器具
(C) 抽獎
(D) 試吃活動

解析 這是詢問與關鍵詞 an attraction 相關內容的 Not/True 題型，確認第一篇短文（公告）中與 an attraction 相關的內容。(A) a performance of traditional music 中談到有傳統音樂表演，因此符合短文內容。(B) a waterslide 有談到滑水道，所以和短文內容一致。(C) 短文中有談到抽獎（raffle for gifts）。(D) 是短文中沒有談到的內容，因此答案是 (D)。

字彙 attraction n. 喜聞樂見的事物、吸引、景點　prize drawing 抽獎

---

182 5W1H 問題
居民應該何時聯絡政府職員？
(A) 無法購買票的時候
(B) 無法走到場所時
(C) 想要更進一步了解慶典時
(D) 想觀看活動的影片時

解析 這是詢問居民何時（When）該聯絡政府職員的 5W1H 問題，在公告中確認與關鍵句 residents contact a government official 相關的內容，第一個短文（公告）談到如果因身心障礙而難以外出行動時可聯絡政府代表（If you have any disabilities that make it difficult to walk around town, we encourage you to contact a government representative），因此答案是 (B)。
換句話說
difficult to walk around town 在城鎮中很難移動 → cannot get to a location on foot 難以步行到某個地點

字彙 get to 前往、達到（階段）　on foot 走路、徒步

---

183 推論題
關於 Gomez 先生，提到了什麼？
(A) 先前曾表演過。
(B) 家人目前來 West Carver 玩。
(C) 家位於 Madeline 街。
(D) 要搬到新的社區。

解析 先確認問題關鍵詞 Mr. Gomez 寫的電子郵件。
線索1 第二篇短文（電子郵件）談到「昨天我聽見沿著家裡前面的街道移動的大型遊行聲」（I heard a large parade passing down the street my house is situated

on），但因為沒有談到遊行是在哪個街道進行，所以要確認公告中的內容。
線索2 從第一篇短文（公告）中可確認 Madeline 街要進行波多黎各遊行，所以將會封街（Madeline Street will be closed ~ for a Puerto Rican parade）。
綜合兩個部分來看時，可知道遊行是在 Madeline 街進行，Gomez 先生的家位於 Madeline 街，所以答案是 (C)。

---

184 5W1H 問題
Gomez 先生為什麼會想當慶典的義工？
(A) 先前曾在波多黎各住過。
(B) 倉庫有多的裝飾品。
(C) 喜歡煮傳統料理。
(D) 想在非營利組織工作。

解析 這是詢問 Gomez 先生為什麼（Why）會想要當義工的 5W1H 問題，必須從電子郵件中確認和關鍵句 Mr. Gomez want to volunteer at the festival 相關的內容。在第二篇短文（電子郵件）中談到他先前曾住過波多黎各，對協助地區居民慶祝他的文化傳統很有興趣，並且詢問是否還需要義工（As I am a former resident of Puerto Rico, I'm interested in helping local residents celebrate my heritage. Are you still accepting volunteers?），因此答案是 (A)。

字彙 decoration n. 裝飾品、裝飾　storage n. 倉庫、儲存
cuisine n. 料理、食物　nonprofit adj. 非營利的

---

185 5W1H 問題
Gomez 先生提出願意提供什麼協助？
(A) 利用他的車搬運物品。
(B) 在網路上發布廣告。
(C) 封鎖特定的街道。
(D) 清理公園的垃圾。

解析 這是 Gomez 先生提議做什麼事（What）的 5W1H 問題，從電子郵件中確認和關鍵句 Mr. Gomez offer to do 相關的內容。第二篇短文（電子郵件）談到 Gomez 先生有貨車，可以幫忙運載備品（I also have a truck, so I can pick up and drop off supplies.），因此答案是 (A)。
換句話說
pick up and drop off supplies 運送備品 →
Transport items 運輸物品

字彙 transport v. 搬運、運送　block off 封鎖、擋住

問題 186-190，請參考以下說明文、邀請函和信件。

Opal 美術館
訪客通知

¹⁸⁶ Opal 美術館的訪客有 Fairfield、Morrison、Gosling 三個停車場可以選擇。Gosling 停車場距離活動場地最近，Morrison 停車場則和美術館的正門最近。

請一定要從自動機那邊領取停車券，離開時可利用其中一臺機器使用信用卡或現金付款，如果想獲得美術館會員的折扣，¹⁸⁷請使用 Gosling 停車場的機器掃描您的 Opal 美術館會員卡。

---

189 時間	非會員費用	189 會員費用
未滿 1 小時	10 美元	8 美元
1-2 小時	12 美元	10 美元
2-3 小時	14 美元	12 美元
3-4 小時	16 美元	14 美元
189 4 小時以上	20 美元	189 18 美元

若是有任何疑問，請來電美術館管理室 555-6698。

garage n. 停車場、車庫　access n. 出入、存取
front entrance 正門　automated adj. 自動的、自動化的
payable adj. 可支付的　administrative office 管理室

---

189 Kerry Fulton 女士
Opal 美術館的長期會員
6 月 5 日星期五，189 下午 5-10 點
Crystal 廳舉辦的季度活動-
正式邀請您參加與藝術家的晚餐。

這次春季我們美術館要 188-D 舉辦 5 小時的晚餐活動，介紹在國際上獲得好評的雕刻家 Alexandra Galanos 和她的最新展覽 Crossing the Road，190 展覽的揭幕式於 6 月 12 日在 Alabaster 別館舉行。188-D 晚宴在晚上 8 點進行，之後是 Galanos 女士的演說，以及博物館館長 Darrell Finn 的發表。

Gosling 停車場 6 月第一週將會進行上漆作業，貴賓必須停在其他的停車場之一。

longtime adj. 長期的、很久　formally adv. 正式、官方
quarterly adj. 各季的　acclaimed adj. 獲得好評的
sculptor n. 雕刻家　exhibit n. 展示（品）
unveil v. 舉行揭幕式、公開　wing n. 別館、附屬建築
promptly adv. 正確地、及時　announcement n. 發表

---

190 6 月 12 日
Darrell Finn
Opal 美術館，館長室
08618 紐澤西州，特倫頓
Morrison 街 400 號

Finn 先生，

我對您上週活動的成功表示讚賞，您的演說令人很感動，身為美術館的一員，我覺得很榮幸。

另外，我想說 190 今天我參加了 Galanos 女士的展示開幕儀式，不只是雕刻作品而已，活動場地的改造也讓我印象深刻。

謝謝您。期待美術館未來的活動。

Kerry Fulton 敬上

commend v. 稱讚、推薦　inspiring adj. 令人感動的、鼓勵的
impressed adj. 使~欽佩

186 目的問題

說明文的主旨是什麼？

(A) 為了告知停車的選項
(B) 為了告知新的費用
(C) 為了提供幾個安全提醒
(D) 為了宣傳美術館會員券

解析 題目是要找出說明文的主旨，因此要確認說明文的內容。第一篇短文（說明文）談到 Opal 美術館的訪客有 Fairfield、Morrison、Gosling 三個停車場可以選擇（Visitors to the Opal Museum of Art have three parking options: the Fairfield Lot, the Morrison Lot, and the Gosling Garage.），因此答案是 (A)。

字彙 reminder n. 注意、提醒　membership n. 會員券、會員資格

187 推論題

關於 Gosling 停車場有何描述？
(A) 它是最貴的停車場。
(B) 有可以掃描卡片的機器。
(C) 距離美術館的入口最近。
(D) 因為市府活動的關係，最近封閉了。

解析 這是針對問題關鍵詞 Gosling Garage 推論的題型，因此要確認和 Gosling 停車場有關係的說明文。第一篇短文（說明文）中談到請使用 Gosling 停車場的機器掃描 Opal 美術館會員卡（scan your Opal Museum of Art membership card at a machine in the Gosling Garage），因此可推論有可掃描的機器，所以答案是 (B)。

188 Not/True 題型

翻譯 關於 Galanos 女士的描述，提到了什麼？
(A) 先前曾造訪過 Opal 美術館。
(B) 將會針對雕刻進行講課。
(C) 和 Finn 先生簽約了。
(D) 將在活動上進行演說。

解析 這是詢問關鍵詞 Ms. Galanos 的 Not/True 題型，在第二篇短文（邀請函）中確認與 Galanos 女士相關的內容。(A)、(B)、(C) 是短文中沒談到的內容，(D) 因內容有談到將會舉辦 5 小時的晚宴活動（our museum will hold a five-hour dinner event），晚宴結束後 Galanos 女士會進行演說（Dinner will be ~ followed by a speech from Ms. Galanos），因和短文內容相符，所以答案是 (D)。
換句話說
a speech 演說 → make some remarks 進行演說

字彙 sign a contract 簽約　make remarks 演說
gathering n. 活動、聚會

189 5W1H 問題

如果 Fulton 女士參加全程活動，應該要支付多少停車費用？
(A) 10 美元
(B) 14 美元
(C) 18 美元
(D) 20 美元

解析 問題的關鍵句在詢問 Fulton 女士參加全程活動需要支付多少（How much）停車費用（Ms. Fulton pay for parking if she stays for the entire event），所以先確認寄給 Fulton 女士的邀請函。

線索1 第二個短文（邀請函）的「Ms. Kerry Fulton, As a longtime member of the Opal Museum of Art, You are formally invited to Dinner with the Artist」和「5-10 P.M.」中談到身為 Opal 美術館會員的 Fulton 女士受邀參加活動，活動時間是下午 5-10 點。不過，因為沒有談到 Opal 美術館停車費的資訊，要在停車費用說明文中確認相關內容。

線索2 第一篇短文（說明文）談到 Opal 美術館停車場 4 小時以上的會員費用是 18 美元（Period, 4 or more hours；Member Fee, $18）。

綜合兩個部分來看，Opal 美術館的會員 Fulton 女士在活動期間 5 小時都停車時，需要支付的費用是 18 美元，因此答案是 (C)。

字彙 entire adj. 整個、全部的

190 5W1H 問題

根據信件來看，6 月 12 日時讓 Fulton 女士印象深刻的是什麼？
(A) Galanos 女士有益的講課
(B) 重新塗漆的 Crystal 廳
(C) Finn 先生的設施參觀
(D) 改善的 Alabaster 別館

解析 在問題的關鍵句 Ms. Fulton impressed with on June 12 中詢問 6 月 12 日時讓 Fulton 女士感動的是什麼（What），所以先確認 Fulton 女士寄出的信。

線索1 第三篇短文（信件）中談到 6 月 12 日（June 12）和參加 Galanos 女士的展示揭幕儀式時因為場地的改造而深受感動（I attended the opening of Ms. Galanos's exhibit today. I was impressed with ~ the renovations that were made in the area where the exhibition was held），不過，因為沒有談到 Galanos 女士舉辦展示的場地在哪裡，所以要確認邀請函的內容。

線索2 第二篇短文（邀請函）中談到 Galanos 女士的最終展示揭幕儀式 6 月 12 日在 Alabaster 別館舉行（her[Ms. Galanos] latest exhibit ~ which will be unveiled in the Alabaster Wing on June 12）。

綜合兩個部分來看時，Galanos 女士的揭幕儀式在 Alabaster 別館舉行，Fulton 女士在 6 月 12 日時因改造的 Alabaster 別館而深受感動，所以答案是 (D)。

字彙 informative adj. 有益的　tour n. 參觀、觀光

問題 191-195，請參考以下網頁、電子郵件和後記。

www.sbntc.com		
節目日程	聯絡處	即將上映

我們需要創業家！

你是擁有新產品或創意的創業家或發明家嗎？

如果是的話，我們藍寶石廣播網（SBN）正在找你！

191-B 我們廣播網正在收購美國最受歡迎的電視節目《Lion's

Den》的版權，SBN 工作室計劃製作以新加坡為主的版本。191-A/D 參加者將在節目拍攝期間向由當地四位知名企業家組成的小組發表他們的產品或創意。每次發表結束時，小組成員就會提問，並且決定是否要投資他們的產品或創意，他們會投資自己的資金，194 SBN 這一季總共會製作 12 集。

2 月 8 日至 2 月 10 日在新加坡 SBN 工作室會進行選角，點擊這裡填寫線上申請書，191-C 只有獲得選秀資格的人才會收到聯絡。

call for 需要　entrepreneur n.（涉及風險的）創業家、企業家
businessperson n. 企業家　inventor n. 發明家
network n. 網路、廣播網　right n. 版權、權利
prominent adj. 著名的、重要的　casting n. 選秀、選角
qualify for 獲得～的資格

收件人：Susan Tsang<susantsang@rubydevelopments.com>
寄件人：Dennis Ping<dping@sbntc.com>
主旨：Lion's Den Asia
日期：1 月 29 日

Tsang 女士，

很高興您能以投資者的身分對我們的節目表示感興趣，我們已經聘請 Chanchai Akkarat 董事長和 Deepa Sidhu 董事長參加節目的演出，193 Trinity Manufacturing 公司的執行長 Mi-young Choi 目前還在考慮是否要擔任第四個位子，還要確認是否能調整她的工作行程以參加節目。

雖然是 4 月初開始製作，192 但在那之前我想先和您以及其他小組成員見面詳細討論各位負責的部分，因此，我將請您 3 月 28 日來我們新加坡市中心的辦事處參加會議。

再次感謝您同意參加我們的節目！

Dennis Ping 敬上

製作人，Lion's Den Asia

appear v. 出演、出現　investor n. 投資者
responsibility n. 負責的工作、職務　in detail 詳細地
downtown adj. 市區的；adv. 在市中心　part n. 一員、部分

http://www.couchtvreviewer.com/realitytv/lionsdenasia/

193/194 電視節目：Lion's Den Asia　194 廣播網：SBN
播出時間：每週三下午 8 點　194 評論人：Abdul Hassan

我是原版《Lion's Den》節目的忠實粉絲，得知要製作亞洲版本時我相當興奮。194 我看過節目的前面六集，內容沒有讓我失望，主持人 Rajiv Sunder 魅力十足，所有的小組成員都很有趣，193 特別是 Mi-young Choi 相當有才氣，經常會對發表者提出出乎預料之外的問題。此外，Chanchai Akkarat 還讓嚴肅的節目添加了些幽默，我也很欣賞 Susan Tsang 頻繁對創業家提出投資邀約。

相反地，195 小組委員 Deepa Sidhu 目前只有提議要投資三名創業家，這個部分讓我覺得有些擔心。我認為她應該對投入資金這件事更敞開心胸，但整體來說，就像美國版本，我對這版本也同樣滿意。

original adj. 原著的、最初的　host n. 進行者、主持人
charming adj. 愉快的、具魅力的　clever adj. 具才氣的、賢明的
unexpected adj. 出乎預料之外、突發的
appreciate v. 高度評價、感謝　frequent adj. 頻繁的、屢次
in contrast 相比之下　so far 目前為止　open to 開放的

191 Not/True 題型

關於《Lion's Den》的描述，哪一個不是真的？
(A) 讓地區創業家參加。
(B) 在新加坡首度播出。
(C) 為了節目參加者進行試鏡。
(D) 包含參賽者的發表。

解析 這是在詢問關鍵詞 Lion's Den 的 Not/True 題型，因此要在談到《Lion's Den》的第一篇短文（網頁）中確認相關內容。(A) 和 (D) 談到參賽者將在節目期間向由當地四位知名企業家組成的小組發表他們的產品或創意（Participants will present their product or idea to a panel of four prominent businesspeople from the region during the show.），因此和短文的內容一致。(B) 收購美國電視節目《Lion's Den》的版權，SBN 工作室計劃製作以新加坡為主的版本（Our network has purchased the rights to the popular American television program Lion's Den, and we plan to produce a version based in Singapore at the SBN studios.），因此和內容不符，所以 (B) 是正確答案。(C) 只有聯絡取得試鏡資格的人（Only those who qualify for auditions will be contacted.），因此和短文內容相符。

換句話說
businesspeople from the region 地區的企業家 → regional entrepreneurs 在地創業家
Participants will present their product or idea 參加者會發表他們的產品或創意 → presentations by contestants 參賽者的發表

字彙 feature v. 出演、當作特徵　contestant n. 參賽者

192 5W1H 問題

Ping 先生為什麼會在 3 月 28 日準備會議？
(A) 為了取得部分創意的許可
(B) 為了協商發表者的報酬
(C) 為了把投資人介紹給製作團隊
(D) 為了討論小組成員的義務

解析 這是詢問 Ping 先生為什麼（Why）要在 3 月 28 日開會的 5W1H 問題，因此要確認 Ping 先生寫的電子郵件內容。第二篇短文中談到請對方 3 月 28 日參加會議，更進一步討論小組委員負責的工作（I would like to meet with you and the other members of our panel before then to discuss your responsibilities in more detail. Therefore, I will require you to attend a meeting ~ on March 28.），所以答案是 (D)。

換句話說
discuss ~ responsibilities 討論負責的工作 → discuss the obligations 討論義務

字彙 arrange v. 安排、籌備　secure v. 獲得　approval n. 同意
negotiate v. 協商、談判　compensation n. 報酬、賠償
obligation n. 義務、職責

193 推論題

Choi 女士可能做了什麼？
(A) 為了參加節目而變更行程。
(B) 為了小組成員而面試了幾名企業家。
(C) 協商在地電視廣播網的收購案。
(D) 和製造公司的共同經營者合作。

解析 先確認有談到問題關鍵詞 Ms. Choi 的電子郵件。
線索1 第二篇短文（電子郵件）中談到 Choi 女士還要看看能否調整工作行程來上節目《Lion's Den Asia》（Mi-young Choi ~ still has to see if her work schedule can be adjusted to join the show[Lion's Den Asia].），但沒有說 Choi 女士確定要參加《Lion's Den Asia》，因此要確認評論的內容。
線索2 第三篇短文（評論）中談到 Choi 女士確定會參加《Lion's Den Asia》（TELEVISION PROGRAM: Lion's Den Asia；Mi-young Choi is especially clever, often asking presenters unexpected questions.）。
綜合兩個部分來看時，因為 Choi 女士參加了《Lion's Den Asia》，所以變更了工作行程，所以答案是 (A)。

字彙 partner with 和~合作　associate n. 共同經營者、合作者、夥伴

194 推論題

關於 Hassan 先生的提示，有何提示？
(A) 收到試鏡的相關信件聯絡
(B) 《Lion's Den Asia》的節目中有一半的集數都沒有看。
(C) 認為《Lion's Den Asia》不如原版有趣。
(D) 先前與其中一名參加的投資者見面。

解析 先確認問題關鍵詞 Mr. Hassan 寫的後記。
線索1 第三篇短文（評論）中 Hassan 先生看過 SBN 廣播網的《Lion's Den Asia》節目的前面六集「TELEVISION PROGRAM: Lion's Den Asia」和「NETWORK: SBN」、「REVIEWER: Abdul Hassan」和「I have watched the first six episodes of the show」，但沒談到 SBN 廣播網的《Lion's Den Asia》總共有幾集，所以要確認網頁的內容。
線索2 第一篇短文（網頁）中談到《Lion's Den Asia》總共要製作 12 集「SBN will produce a total of 12 episodes for this season[Lion's Den Asia].」。
綜合兩個部分來看時，《Lion's Den Asia》總共有 12 集，Hassan 先生有一半都沒看過，因此答案是 (B)。

字彙 personally adv. 直接

195 5W1H 問題

Hassan 先生對哪位小組委員表示擔憂？
(A) Chanchai Akkarat
(B) Susan Tsang
(C) Mi-young Choi
(D) Deepa Sidhu

解析 這是在詢問 Hassan 先生對哪位（Which）小組委員表示擔憂，屬於 5W1H 問題，因此要確認和關鍵句 Mr. Hassan express concern about 相關的評論。第三篇短文（評論）中談到 Hassan 先生對小組委員 Deepa Sidhu 目前只有提議要投資三名創業家，這個部分讓他

覺得有些擔心（I'm a bit worried that panel member Deepa Sidhu has only offered to be an investor for three of the entrepreneurs so far），因此答案是 (D)。

字彙 express concern 表示擔憂

問題 196-200，請參考以下報導、廣告和電子郵件。

Richmond Sun 報刊

健康的速食來了

菲德里克堡，7 月 9 日—196-B 國內第一間有機快餐店 Fresh Goods 將於下個月在第 95 號高速公路上開幕，業者 Libby Hawkins 希望它成為數百家裡第一間為旅人提供快速、健康、平價餐點的地方。

20 年前開始經營自己的農場以來，Hawkins 女士一直都是有機產品的支持者，目前 196-C 她的農場是維吉尼亞州最大的牛奶和乳酪生產業者之一。她本人經常去旅行，197 當她在意識到休息站販售的健康食物不足時，19/200 她便決定開「Fresh Goods」。

200 目前她正在努力建立農場供應網，提供有機食材給 Fresh Goods，參加活動的農場主人有機會獲得有機農認證和合理的價格，不過，為了保證材料的新鮮度，200 成為此一供應網成員的農場不能距離餐廳超過 50 英里以上。

on the way 順便、在途中　organic adj. 有機的
proprietor n. 業主、所有者　affordable adj. 平價的、可負擔的
supporter n. 支持者、擁護者　lack n. 缺乏、不足
rest stop 休息站　work on 付出努力　certification n. 認證、保證
fair price 合理的價格　ingredient n. 材料、成分
part n. 一員、部分

第 4 屆 198-A 年度 Culpeper 秋收感謝祭
198-B 9 月 8 日星期五到 9 月 10 日星期日為止

9 月 8 日：研討會
下午 5 點・Spotswood 飯店咖啡廳，Davis 街 215 號
與維吉尼亞食品合作社（VFC）理事 Emmett Ashby 共議
更多的細節詳閱 www.vfc.org

9 月 9 日：參觀農場
上午 11 點-下午 1 點・Westover 農場，Mill 路 15384 號
下午 1 點-3 點・Whisper Hill 飼育場，Yowell 路 899 號
下午 3 點-5 點・Salt Cedar 孵化場，Maple 路 11452 號

9 月 10 日：農夫市集
198-D 使用當地栽培的材料準備的社區用餐時間
Great Meal
可攜帶一起分享的料理（非必須）
下午 2 點−4 點 30 分・農夫市集
下午 5 點・Great Meal
199 農夫市集和 Great Meal 將會在 Chandler 街 308 號的
Kingsbrook 公園舉辦

harvest festival 秋收感謝祭　cooperative n. 合作組合；adj. 合作的
field n. 飼育場　hatchery n. 孵化場　farmer's market 農夫市集
dish n. 料理、碟子　optional adj. 選擇性的

➡

收件人：Marvin Cooper <m.cooper@harrisonburg.net>
寄件人：Libby Hawkins <l.hawkins@freshgoods.com>
主旨：見面
日期：8 月 29 日

Cooper 先生，

200 感謝您近期成為我的農場供應網的一員，並決定提供雞肉給我們的餐廳。另外，關於您來信提出的問題，我希望在即將到來的 Culpeper 秋收感謝祭和您見面，雖然我無法去參觀您的 Salt Cedar 孵化場，199 但隔天我可以抽空在 Great Meal 順道去您在農夫市集上的攤位，如果有任何問題，只要來電 555-2498 就行，謝謝，我們很快就會見面了！

Libby Hawkins 敬上

spare time 空閒時間

---

196 Not/True 題型
關於 Hawkins 女士的農場，有何描述？
(A) 預計明年要擴張。
(B) 位於 95 號高速公路附近。
(C) 生產乳製品。
(D) 供應給全國的餐廳。

解析 這是詢問與關鍵詞 Ms. Hawkins's farm 相關內容的 Not/True 題型，因此要確認有談論到 Hawkins 女士的第一篇短文（報導）內容。(A) 這是短文沒有談到的內容。(B) 內容談到 Fresh Goods 會開在 95 號高速公路（The country's first organic fast food restaurant, Fresh Goods, opens next month on Interstate 95.），Hawkins 女士的農場不是在 95 號高速公路，因此和短文內容不符。(C) 文中談到 Hawkins 女士的農場是維吉尼亞州最大的牛奶與乳酪產業者之一（her[Ms. Hawkins] farm is one of Virginia's biggest producers of milk and cheese），和短文內容相符，所以答案是 (C)。(D) 是短文中沒有談到的內容。

換句話說
one of ~ biggest producers of milk and cheese 最大的牛奶與乳酪生產業者之一 → produces dairy products 生產乳製品

字彙 dairy product 乳製品　nationwide adv. 全國性的；adj. 全國的

197 5W1H 問題
是什麼促成 Hawkins 女士開設餐廳？
(A) 刊載在食品業雜誌上的某篇報導
(B) 部分場所無法選擇對健康有益的食物
(C) 經由先前的同事推薦
(D) 為自家產品尋找市場的需要

解析 題目詢問 Hawkins 女士開餐廳的動機是什麼（What），屬於 5W1H 問題，因此要確認與關鍵句 caused Ms. Hawkins to open her restaurant 相關的內容。第一篇短文（報導）中談到 Hawkins 女士明白休息站販售的健康食品不足（she decided to open Fresh Goods when she noticed the lack of healthy dishes sold at rest stops），於是便決定開餐廳 Fresh Goods，所以答案是 (B)。

換句話說
the lack of healthy dishes sold at rest stops 休息站販售的健康食品太少→ The unavailability of healthy food options at some locations 部分場所無法取得健康食品

字彙 publish v. 刊載、出版
unavailability n. 無法使用　former adj. 先前的

198 Not/True 題型
關於 Culpeper 秋收感謝祭的描述哪一個是正確的？
(A) 通常一年舉辦兩次。
(B) 會持續一個星期。
(C) 由政府贊助。
(D) 呈現當地的食品。

解析 這是與問題關鍵詞 the Culpeper Harvest Festiva 相關的 Not/True 題型，因此必須確認談論到 Culpeper 秋收感謝祭的第二篇短文（廣告）。(A) 文中談到年度 Culpeper 秋收感謝祭（Annual Culpeper Harvest Festival），和短文內容不符。(B) 內容談到 9 月 8 號星期五至 9 月 10 號星期日為止（Friday, September 8, to Sunday, September 10），和短文內容不符。(C) 短文中並沒有談到相關內容。(D) 使用當地栽培食材準備的 Great Meal（Followed by the Great Meal ~ prepared with locally grown ingredients），和短文內容一致，所以答案是 (D)。

字彙 be sponsored by 由～贊助

199 5W1H 問題
Hawkins 女士想要在哪裡和 Cooper 先生見面？
(A) Spotswood 飯店
(B) Kingsbrook 公園
(C) Salt Cedar 孵化場
(D) Westover 農場

解析 問題的核心句子是 Ms. Hawkins want to meet Mr. Cooper，問題是在詢問 Hawkins 女士想要從哪裡（Where）和 Cooper 先生見面，所以要先確認 Hawkins 女士寄的電子郵件。
線索1 在第三篇短文（電子郵件）中談到 Hawkins 女士說在農夫市集可以順便去一趟 Cooper 先生的攤位（I can spare some time ~ to stop by your[Mr. Cooper] booth at the Farmer's Market），但因為沒有談到農夫市集在哪裡，所以要確認廣告內容。
線索2 第二篇短文（廣告）談到農夫市集將在 Kingsbrook 公園舉行（Both the Farmer's Market and the Great Meal will be held at Kingsbrook Park）。
綜合兩個部分來看時，可知道 Hawkins 女士說要在農夫市集和 Cooper 先生見面，因此答案是 (B)。

200 推論題
關於 Cooper 先生可推論出什麼？
(A) 會在 Great Meal 上提供一些料理。
(B) 他的設施已經營運超過 10 年。
(C) 第一次參加慶典。
(D) 他的農場距離 Fresh Goods 在 50 英里內。

解析 先確認寄給問題關鍵詞 Mr. Cooper 的電子郵件。
線索1 第三篇短文（電子郵件）中 Hawkins 女士對

Cooper 先生近期成為農場供應網一員這件事表示感謝（Thank you for recently becoming a member of my network of farms），但因為沒有提到關於 Hawkins 女士的農場供應網成員的資訊，所以要確認相關報導內容。
線索2 第一篇短文（報導）談到 Hawkins 女士正在努力建立農場供應網，提供有機食材給 Fresh Goods（she[Ms. Hawkins] decided to open Fresh Goods)和（Currently, she is working on establishing a network of farms that will supply organic ingredients for Fresh Goods.），並且談到供應網成員的農場不能距離餐廳超過 50 英里以上（farms that will be part of this network can be no farther than 50 miles from the restaurant[Fresh Goods]）。
綜合兩個部分來看時，Cooper 先生已經成為 Hawkins 女士的農場供應網的一份子，因此可以知道他的農場距離 Fresh Goods 沒有超過 50 英里，所以答案是 (D)。

字彙 operate v. 營運、啟動

TEST 4

PART 1

1 🔊 加拿大發音

(A) He is rolling up his sleeves.
(B) He is removing items from a container.
(C) He is sitting on a bed.
(D) He is facing away from some boxes.

roll up one's sleeves 捲起某人的袖子　remove 清除
container 容器　face away 轉頭

翻譯 (A) 他正在捲袖子。
(B) 他在清除容器中的物品。
(C) 他坐在床上。
(D) 他背對著一些箱子。

解析 1 人照片
(A) [×] 男子已經是捲起袖子的狀態，正在捲袖子（is rolling up）是錯誤的描述。
(B) [×] removing（正在清除）和圖中男子的動作沒有關係，因此是錯誤選項。照片中使用了容器（container），所以會造成混淆。
(C) [×] 男子是站立的狀態，坐著是錯誤的描述。
(D) [○] 男子背對著幾個箱子是最恰當的描述，因此是正確答案。

2 🔊 澳洲發音

(A) The man is lifting a load with a work truck.
(B) The man is labeling some packages.
(C) The man is climbing up the scaffolding.
(D) The man is getting out of the vehicle.

lift 抬起來　load 貨物、行李　label 貼標籤　package 箱子
climb up 爬上　scaffolding 支架　get out of（從車輛等）下來

翻譯 **(A) 男子正在駕駛作業車搬起貨物。**
(B) 男子正在箱子上貼標籤。
(C) 男子正在爬支架。
(D) 男子正在下車。

解析 1 人照片
(A) [○] 男子正在駕駛作業車搬起貨物，這是最恰當的描述，因此是正確答案。
(B) [×] labeling（正在貼標籤）和男子的動作沒關係，因為照片中有箱子（packages），所以會造成混淆。
(C) [×] climbing up（正在攀爬）和男子的動作沒關係，因此是錯誤選項。
(D) [×] 男子坐在作業車上，因此和下車的動作沒關係，所以是錯誤選項。

3 美國發音

(A) The man is riding in an elevator.
(B) A bucket is being emptied.
(C) The man is cleaning some tiles.
(D) A sign is being carried away.

ride in 搭乘　empty 清空　carry away 搬走

翻譯 (A) 男子正在搭乘升降梯。
(B) 桶子正在被清空。
(C) 男子正在清理磁磚。
(D) 告示牌正在被搬走。

解析 1 人照片
(A) [×] 男子在升降梯外面，搭乘升降梯是不對的描述，這是錯誤選項。
(B) [×] 照片中雖然有桶子，但並非正在清空（is being emptied）的狀態，是錯誤選項。
(C) [○] 男子正在清理磁磚是最恰當的描述，是正確答案。
(D) [×] 告示牌是立著的狀態，搬走告示牌是錯誤的描述。

4 英國發音

(A) Some books have been left on a shelf.
(B) A woman is inspecting some items in a box.
(C) A woman is purchasing some reading material.
(D) Some products have been wrapped.

inspect 檢查、調查　reading material 讀物
wrap 包裝、把～包起來

翻譯 **(A) 架子上擺了好幾本書。**
(B) 有一名女子正在檢查箱子裡的物品。
(C) 有一名女子正在購買讀物。
(D) 有些產品已經包裝好了。

解析 2 人以上的照片
(A) [○] 架子上擺了好幾本書是最恰當的描述，這是正確答案。
(B) [×] 因照片中沒有箱子（box），所以是錯誤選項。
(C) [×] 照片中沒有正在購買讀物（purchasing some reading material）的女子，所以是錯誤選項。
(D) [×] 照片中雖然有產品，但無法確認是否已經包裝（have been wrapped），因此是錯誤選項。

5 澳洲發音

(A) A computer monitor has been turned on.
(B) There are windows on one side of the wall.

(C) Books have been spread out on the desks.
(D) One of the keyboards is being used.

turn on 開啟　spread out 散開

翻譯 (A) 電腦螢幕被開啟了。
(B) 一邊的牆面有窗戶。
(C) 書已經在書桌上散開了。
(D) 其中一個鍵盤已經在使用了。

解析 事物與風景照
(A) [×] 電腦螢幕是關閉的狀態，電腦螢幕開啟是錯誤的描述。
(B) [○] 一個牆面上有窗戶是最恰當的描述，因此是正確答案。
(C) [×] 因為照片中沒有書本（Books），所以是錯誤選項。
(D) [×] 照片中雖然有鍵盤，但並非使用中（is being used）的狀態，所以是錯誤選項。

6 美國發音

(A) Some trees are being trimmed.
(B) Some lamps are hanging from a fence.
(C) A garden gate has been shut.
(D) A lawn is being watered.

trim 修剪、修整　shut 關閉　lawn 草地

翻譯 (A) 有幾棵樹正在修剪中。
(B) 有幾盞燈掛在柵欄上。
(C) 庭園出入口關閉了。
(D) 草皮正在灑水。

解析 事物與風景照
(A) [×] 照片中雖然有樹木，但並非修剪中的狀態（are being trimmed），因此是錯誤選項。
(B) [×] 因為無法確認照片中的柵欄是否掛有燈具，所以是錯誤選項。
(C) [○] 庭園出入口關閉是最恰當的描述，這是正確答案。
(D) [×] 照片中雖然有草皮，但沒有在灑水（is being watered），所以是錯誤選項。

PART 2

7 加拿大發音

What time does this restaurant close?
(A) We have no more tables available.
(B) Mostly Italian food.
(C) Usually around 10 P.M.

available 可使用的

翻譯 這間餐廳幾點關門？
(A) 我們沒有可就坐的桌子了。
(B) 大部分都是義式料理。

(C) 通常都是晚上 10 點左右。

解析 What 疑問句
    (A) [×] 使用和問題 restaurant（餐廳）相關的 tables（桌子），是會造成混淆的選項。
    (B) [×] 使用和問題 restaurant（餐廳）相關的 food（食物），是會造成混淆的選項。
    (C) [○] 回答通常是晚上 10 點，因談到餐廳關門的時間，所以是正確答案。

8 🔊 英國發音

> Where do you think you lost your wallet?
> (A) I don't think it's the right size.
> (B) You didn't pay for the ticket.
> **(C) At the movie theater, I believe.**

wallet 皮夾　pay for 支付～的費用

翻譯 你認為你在哪裡弄丟皮夾的？
    (A) 我不認為那是正確的尺寸。
    (B) 你沒有付門票錢。
    (C) 我想是在電影院。

解析 Where 疑問句
    (A) [×] 題目詢問在哪裡弄丟皮夾，回答卻說「尺寸不符」，與內容無關，因此是錯誤選項。
    (B) [×] 使用與 wallet（皮夾）相關的 pay for（支付～的費用），是會造成混淆的選項。
    (C) [○] 回答「我想是在電影院」，因談到弄丟皮夾的場所，所以是正確答案。

9 🔊 美國發音

> Who forgot to put away the paint brushes?
> **(A) I think it was Fidel.**
> (B) Thanks, I meant to paint it.
> (C) Beside those bushes.

put away 收起來　paint brush 油漆刷　bush 草叢、灌木叢

翻譯 誰忘記收好油漆刷？
    (A) 我想是 Fidel。
    (B) 謝謝，我本來想粉刷的。
    (C) 在草叢旁邊。

解析 Who 疑問句
    (A) [○] 回答「我想是 Fidel」，因有談到忘記收好油漆刷的人，所以是正確答案。
    (B) [×] 把問題中的 paint（油漆）當作動詞（漆油漆）使用，是會造成混淆的選項。
    (C) [×] 使用和 brushes 發音相似的 bushes，是會造成混淆的選項。

10 🔊 加拿大發音→英國發音

> Why did you order a different computer chair?
> (A) You'll get another reminder.
> (B) Use these order forms.

(C) My current one gives me back pain.

order 訂購、訂貨　reminder 提醒　current 現在的　back 背後
pain 傷痛、疼痛

翻譯 為什麼你訂了不一樣的電腦椅？
    (A) 你會再收到提醒。
    (B) 請使用這些訂購單。
    (C) 現在那張椅子讓我的背好痛。

解析 Why 疑問句
    (A) [×] 使用和 different（不一樣）相同意思的 another（另一個），是會造成混淆的錯誤選項。
    (B) [×] 反覆使用名詞 order（訂購），是會造成混淆的錯誤選項。
    (C) [○] 回答現在的椅子會讓背很痛，因談到訂購其他電腦椅的理由，所以是正確答案。

11 🔊 澳洲發音→英國發音

> When do you leave work today?
> **(A) In a couple of hours.**
> (B) I was working on a proposal.
> (C) Leave the check here.

leave work 下班　a couple of 一對、幾個的　proposal 企劃書
check 支票

翻譯 你今天幾點下班？
    (A) 再過幾個小時。
    (B) 我正在寫企劃書。
    (C) 支票請放這邊。

解析 When 疑問句
    (A) [○] 回答再過幾個小時，因談到下班的時間，所以是正確答案。
    (B) [×] 因把 work（職場）當作動詞 was working（作業）使用，是會造成混淆的錯誤選項。
    (C) [×] 因把 leave（離開）當作「放置」的意思使用，是會造成混淆的錯誤選項。

12 🔊 美國發音→澳洲發音

> What impressed you the most about the novel?
> (A) Yes, it was written by Jason Crawford.
> **(B) The main character.**
> (C) Oh, I found it at a local bookstore.

impress 使～留下深刻印象　novel 小說
main character 主角　local 地區的、當地的

翻譯 那本小說讓你印象最深的是什麼？
    (A) 是，那是 Jason Crawford 寫的。
    (B) 是主角。
    (C) 啊，我是在當地的書店找到它的。

解析 What 疑問句
    (A) [×] 使用 Yes 回答疑問詞疑問句，因此是錯誤選項。
    (B) [○] 回答主角，因談到對那本小說印象最深刻的對象，所以是正確答案。

(C) [×] 使用和 novel（小說）相關的 bookstore（書店），因此是錯誤選項。

13 🔊 加拿大發音→美國發音

Can we practice for Friday's presentation now?
(A) After lunch would be better for me.
(B) My soccer team practices daily.
(C) Last Saturday night.

---
practice 練習　daily 每天

翻譯 我們現在可以練習星期五的簡報嗎？
(A) 午餐過後對我來說會比較好。
(B) 我們的足球隊每天都在練習。
(C) 上星期六晚上。

解析 提議疑問句
(A) [○] 回答午餐後會更好，因間接拒絕現在練習的提議，所以是正確答案。
(B) [×] 因把問題中的 practice 重複以 practices 的方式使用，是會造成混淆的錯誤選項。
(C) [×] 因使用與 Friday（星期五）相關的 Saturday（星期六），是會造成混淆的錯誤選項。

14 🔊 美國發音→加拿大發音

Which company should we hire to print our flyers?
(A) Print enough for everyone.
(B) To post them around the neighborhood.
(C) The same one we used last time.

---
hire 僱用　flyer 廣告單、宣傳單　post 張貼
neighborhood 鄰近地區

翻譯 我們應該請哪間公司印刷廣告單？
(A) 請列印足夠的量給大家。
(B) 為了將它們張貼在附近。
(C) 和上次一樣的那間。

解析 Which 疑問句
(A) [×] 因重複使用 print，是會造成混淆的錯誤選項。
(B) [×] 因使用可代表 flyers（廣告單）的 them，是會造成混淆的錯誤選項。
(C) [○] 回答和上次一樣的那間，因談到印刷廣告紙的業者，所以是正確答案。

15 🔊 美國發音→加拿大發音

When can I expect my merchandise to arrive?
(A) You can save the rest for later.
(B) Yes, according to experts.
(C) No later than March 12.

---
merchandise 購買的物品　save 留存　rest 其餘的
according to 根據　expert 專家　no later than 最晚不超過

翻譯 我的商品預計何時會送到？
(A) 你可以保留其他的之後使用。
(B) 對，根據專家的說法。

(C) 最慢 3 月 12 日會送到。

解析 When 疑問句
(A) [×] 題目詢問購買物品何時會送達，回答內容卻無關，因此是錯誤選項。
(B) [×] 用 Yes 回答疑問詞疑問句，是錯誤選項。
(C) [○] 回答最晚 3 月 12 日，因談到物品的抵達日期，所以是正確答案。

16 🔊 美國發音→加拿大發音

Who told you about the board of directors' election results?
(A) I received my test results.
(B) Tell Sam about these suggestions.
(C) My manager made an announcement.

---
board of directors 董事會、理事會　election 選舉
suggestion 意見、提議　make an announcement 宣布

翻譯 是誰告訴你董事會選舉結果的？
(A) 我收到測試結果了。
(B) 請把這些意見告訴 Sam。
(C) 我的經理宣布的。

解析 Who 疑問句
(A) [×] 因重複使用 results，是會造成混淆的錯誤選項。
(B) [×] 把問題中的 told 以 tell 的型態重複使用，是會造成混淆的錯誤選項。
(C) [○] 回答自己的經理宣布的，因談到告知選舉結果的人物，所以是正確答案。

17 🔊 美國發音→加拿大發音

Have you decided on the location of the fashion show?
(A) The clothing line is amazing.
(B) Will you be relocating?
(C) Ashley is handling that.

---
decide on 決定　relocate 調動、遷移　handle 處理、應付

翻譯 時裝秀的表演地點已經決定好了嗎？
(A) 那個服裝系列真的很棒。
(B) 你會被調動嗎？
(C) Ashley 正在處理。

解析 助動詞疑問句
(A) [×] 因使用和 fashion show（時裝秀）相關的 clothing line（服裝系列），是會造成混淆的錯誤選項。
(B) [×] 因使用和 location 發音相似的 relocating，是會造成混淆的錯誤選項。
(C) [○] 因談到 Ashley 正在處理，間接回答自己並非負責人，所以是正確答案。

18 美國發音→加拿大發音

I'd like to book a flight from Baltimore to San Francisco.
(A) Sorry, I haven't been there.
(B) I can help with that.
(C) Pick it up at the gate.

book 預約　flight 班機　pick up 領取　gate 登機門

翻譯 我想預約從巴爾的摩出發前往舊金山的班機。
(A) 很抱歉,我沒去過那個地方。
(B) 我可以幫忙這件事。
(C) 請去登機門領取。

解析 直述句
(A) [×] 文中談到想要預約班機,回答不曾去過那邊是答非所問,因此是錯誤選項。
(B) [○] 回答將給予協助,等於同意預約班機的要求,因此是正確答案。
(C) [×] 因使用和問題中的 flight(班機)相關的 gate(登機門),是會造成混淆的錯誤選項。

19 澳洲發音→英國發音

Are the training participants in the conference room?
(A) The train leaves at 10 A.M.
(B) We can make room for the equipment.
(C) It has been canceled.

participant 參加者　conference room 會議室　room 空間、位子
equipment 裝備

翻譯 參加培訓者是否在會議室?
(A) 那班火車上午 10 點離開。
(B) 我們可以為了設備挪出空間。
(C) 已經取消了。

解析 Be 動詞疑問句
(A) [×] 因使用和 training 發音相似的 train,是會造成混淆的錯誤選項。
(B) [×] 因把 room(室、房)重複當作「空間、位子」的意思使用,是會造成混淆的錯誤選項。
(C) [○] 回答已經取消了,間接告知參加培訓者沒有在會議室,因此是正確答案。

20 澳洲發音→美國發音

How much will it cost to repair the delivery van?
(A) They offer free delivery.
(B) Shouldn't we just replace it?
(C) The rental costs $30 a day.

van 貨車、廂型車　replace 交替、替換　rental 使用費、租金

翻譯 修理貨車需要多少錢?
(A) 他們提供免費配送。
(B) 我們是不是該直接替換它?
(C) 租金一天 30 美元。

解析 How 疑問句
(A) [×] 因重複使用 delivery,是會造成混淆的錯誤選項。
(B) [○] 反問是不是該替換了,間接回答修理費相當高,因此是正確答案。
(C) [×] 把問題中的 cost 重複以 costs 的型態使用,是會造成混淆的錯誤選項。

21 澳洲發音→英國發音

Hasn't our latest speaker model been selling well?
(A) Yes, but only in certain states.
(B) I'll speak to her now.
(C) Profits from a manufacturing firm.

latest 最新的　state 國家、州　profit 利潤
manufacturing firm 製造公司

翻譯 我們最新型號的揚聲器不是賣得很好嗎?
(A) 對,但僅限部分的州。
(B) 我現在跟她說。
(C) 那是製造公司的利潤。

解析 否定疑問句
(A) [○] 使用 Yes 回答最新型號的揚聲器銷售不錯,附加解釋只有在部分的州,因此是正確的答案。
(B) [×] 因使用和 speaker 發音相似的 speak,是會造成混淆的錯誤選項。
(C) [×] 因使用和 selling(販售中的)相關的 Profits(收益),是會造成混淆的錯誤選項。

22 加拿大發音→美國發音

I don't think we were sent the correct books.
(A) Oh, these are the novels I ordered.
(B) A textbook publisher.
(C) Send a sample by today.

novel 小說　textbook 教科書　publisher 出版社、出版者

翻譯 我不認為我們收到了正確的書。
(A) 啊,這些是我訂購的小說。
(B) 是教科書出版社。
(C) 今天之內送出樣品。

解析 直述句
(A) [○] 回答那是自己訂購的小說,間接告知收到的書是對的,因此是正確答案。
(B) [×] 因使用與問題中的 books(書籍)相關的 textbook(教科書),是會造成混淆的錯誤選項。
(C) [×] 把問題中的 sent 重複以 send 的型態使用,是會造成混淆的錯誤選項。

23 英國發音→加拿大發音

How will I finish our report while you're on vacation?
(A) Mandy can help.
(B) At a popular resort.
(C) I wish I could go.

be on vacation 正值休假

翻譯 你休假的期間我要怎麼完成我們的報告書？
  (A) Mandy 可以幫忙。
  (B) 在一個熱門度假村。
  (C) 真希望我能去。

解析 How 疑問句
  (A) [○] 回答 Mandy 可以幫忙，間接告知自己休假時可向 Mandy 尋求協助完成報告，因此是正確答案。
  (B) [×] 因使用和 vacation（放假）相關的 resort（度假村），是會造成混淆的錯誤選項。
  (C) [×] 題目詢問對方放假時自己該如何完成報告，此回答無關，因此是錯誤選項。

24 美國發音→加拿大發音

Is our food going to be delivered soon, or will it take a while longer?
(A) It was surprisingly spicy.
(B) I can call and find out.
(C) As soon as you cook it.

take 花費（時間）　surprisingly 令人訝異地
spicy 辣的　find out 查明　as soon as 一～就～

翻譯 我們的食物很快就會送到，還是需要多一點時間？
  (A) 這個辣到讓人很訝異。
  (B) 我打電話問問看。
  (C) 你開始烹飪時。

解析 選擇疑問句
  (A) [×] 因使用和 food（食物）相關的 spicy（辣的），是會造成混淆的錯誤選項。
  (B) [○] 回答會打電話詢問，等於間接告知不清楚食物何時會送到，所以是正確答案。
  (C) [×] 使用和 food（食物）相關的 cook（料理），而且重複使用 soon，是會造成混淆的錯誤選項。

25 英國發音→澳洲發音

Our ferry has arrived at the dock.
(A) Lock the doors when you're done.
(B) OK, I'll grab my luggage.
(C) After the boat tour.

ferry 渡輪、渡船　dock 碼頭　lock 上鎖　grab （匆忙）帶過來
luggage 行李

翻譯 我們的渡輪已經抵達碼頭。
  (A) 結束後請鎖門。
  (B) 我知道了，我會把行李帶過來。
  (C) 在乘船遊覽後。

解析 直述句
  (A) [×] 因使用和 dock 發音相似的 lock，是會造成混淆的錯誤選項。
  (B) [○] 回答 OK 表示知道渡輪抵達碼頭，附加說明要去拿行李，因此是正確答案。
  (C) [×] 因使用與 ferry（渡輪）相關的 boat（小船），是會造成混淆的錯誤選項。

26 澳洲發音→英國發音

Would you bring this document to the head of the finance team?
(A) Some official documents.
(B) I think he already has a copy of it.
(C) Yes, we met with the CEO.

document 文件　finance team 財務組　official 官方的

翻譯 可以幫我把這份文件拿去給財務組的主管嗎？
  (A) 一些官方的文件。
  (B) 我認為他已經有影本了。
  (C) 好，我們見過執行長了。

解析 要求疑問句
  (A) [×] 因重複把問題中的 document 以 documents 的型態使用，是會造成混淆的錯誤選項。
  (B) [○] 回答他應該已經有影本了，等於間接拒絕把文件轉交給財務組的主管，因此是正確答案。
  (C) [×] 因使用和 head（組織的首長）相關的 CEO（執行長），是會造成混淆的錯誤選項。

27 加拿大發音→美國發音

The event's date has changed again, hasn't it?
(A) Yes, it was a success.
(B) I'm afraid so.
(C) You never sign up for the event.

sign up for 報名參加

翻譯 那個活動的日期又變了，不是嗎？
  (A) 對，那是一大成功。
  (B) 恐怕是這樣。
  (C) 你不曾報名過那個活動。

解析 附加疑問句
  (A) [×] 因使用代表 event（活動）的 it，是會造成混淆的錯誤選項。
  (B) [○] 回答恐怕是這樣，等於轉達活動日期又變更了，因此是正確答案。
  (C) [×] 因重複使用 event，是會造成混淆的錯誤選項。

28 加拿大發音→英國發音

Isn't our new factory going to be built in Jacksonville?
(A) On the plant floor.
(B) According to our manager.
(C) Yes, my house is being built.

plant 工廠　floor 工地、地面　according to 根據

翻譯 我們的新工廠不是預定蓋在 Jacksonville 嗎？
  (A) 在工廠工地。
  (B) 我們的經理是這樣說。
  (C) 是，我的房子正在建造中。

解析 否定疑問句
  (A) [×] 因使用和 factory（工廠）相同意思的 plant（工廠），是會造成混淆的錯誤選項。

(B) [○] 回答我們的經理是這樣說，間接回答新工廠預定蓋在 Jacksonville，因此是正確答案。

(C) [×] 因重複使用 built，是會造成混淆的錯誤選項。

29 [加拿大發音→英國發音]

We missed the shipping deadline for a customer last week.
(A) Mr. Clemens already informed me.
(B) No, he arrived last week.
(C) Be sure not to miss the talk.

---

shipping 船運、海運　deadline 截止日　inform 通知
be sure to 務必～　miss 錯過　talk 演講

翻譯 我們上星期錯過客戶的出貨期限。
(A) Clemens 先生已經告訴我了。
(B) 不，他上星期就抵達了。
(C) 請別錯過那個演講。

解析 直述句
(A) [○] 回答 Clemens 先生已經告訴我了，等於轉達知道錯過出貨期限，因此是正確答案。
(B) [×] 重複使用 last week，是會造成混淆的錯誤選項。
(C) [×] 把 missed 以 miss 的型態重複使用，是會造成混淆的錯誤選項。

30 [澳洲發音→美國發音]

Did you change your e-mail address?
(A) Sorry, I'm out of change.
(B) It's the same as before.
(C) Thanks for sending me the message.

---

change 變更；零錢　be out of 用完

翻譯 你換電子信箱了嗎？
(A) 抱歉，我沒有零錢了。
(B) 那和先前一樣。
(C) 謝謝你傳訊息給我。

解析 助動詞疑問句
(A) [×] 因反覆把 change（改變）當名詞「零錢」的意思使用，是會造成混淆的錯誤選項。
(B) [○] 回答和先前一樣，等於告知電子信箱沒有變更，所以是正確答案。
(C) [×] 因使用和 e-mail（電子郵件）相關的 message（訊息），是會造成混淆的錯誤選項。

31 [加拿大發音→澳洲發音]

The lights were turned off in the garage, right?
(A) We turned it into a kitchen.
(B) I made sure to double-check.
(C) Yes, this color is much lighter.

---

light 電燈；明亮的　turn off 關閉　garage 車庫
turn ~ into 使～變成　make sure to 確定會
double-check 再次確認

翻譯 車庫的燈都關了，對吧？
(A) 我們把它變成廚房了。
(B) 我有再確認。
(C) 好，這個顏色亮多了。

解析 附加疑問句
(A) [×] 因重複使用 turned，是會造成混淆的錯誤選項。
(B) [○] 回答自己會再次確認，間接表示車庫的燈已經關了，所以是正確答案。
(C) [×] 因使用和 lights 發音相似的 lighter，是會造成混淆的錯誤選項。

PART 3

32-34 [加拿大發音→美國發音]

Questions 32-34 refer to the following conversation.

M: Good afternoon. ³²This is Woodbridge Medical Facility. How may I assist you?
W: Hello. May I please speak with Dr. Anderson? This is one of his patients, Jennifer Ford.
M: I'm so sorry, Ms. Ford, but Dr. Anderson is in the staff cafeteria having lunch right now. ³³I can take down a message for him, if you'd like.
W: Yes, please. I'd just like to let him know that ³⁴my back pain has improved. So, I won't need a refill of the medication he prescribed me last month.

---

medical facility 醫療設施　assist 幫助　take down 作筆記
pain 痛症　improve 變更好、改善　refill 補充；補充品
medication 藥、藥物　prescribe 為～開處方

翻譯 問題 32-34，請參考以下對話。
男：午安，³² 這裡是 Woodbridge 醫療中心，需要什麼幫忙嗎？
女：您好，我可以和 Anderson 醫生談一下嗎？我是 Jennifer Ford，他的病人之一。
男：真的很抱歉，Ford 女士，Anderson 醫生目前在員工餐廳吃午餐。³³ 如果你願意，我可以幫你留言給他。
女：好，麻煩您了，我只是想告訴他 ³⁴ 我的腰痛改善了，所以上個月他開給我的處方藥不需要補充了。

32 說話者問題

翻譯 男子最可能是什麼人？
(A) 店員
(B) 櫃檯人員
(C) 藥師
(D) 醫生

解析 仔細聆聽對話中和身分、職業相關的用法，男子說這裡是 Woodbridge 醫療中心（This is Woodbridge Medical Facility. How may I assist you?），藉由詢問女子需要什麼協助，可知道男子是櫃檯人員，因此答案是 (B)。

字彙 cashier 店員　receptionist 櫃檯人員　pharmacist 藥師

33 提議問題

翻譯 男子表示願意做什麼？
(A) 留言。
(B) 傳送簡訊。
(C) 開藥。
(D) 延後預約。

解析 仔細聆聽男子會幫女子做什麼，男子表示「如果需要的話，可以幫你留言給他」（I can take down a message for him, if you'd like.），因此答案是 (A)。

換句話說
take down a message 寫下訊息 → Write a note 留言

字彙 postpone 延後

34 提及何事的問題

翻譯 關於女子，提到了什麼？
(A) 她預計會晚一點到。
(B) 她上個月背部受傷了。
(C) 她的狀況好轉了。
(D) 她付的款項沒有讓對方收到。

解析 仔細聆聽對話中和女子相關的內容，女子說自己的腰痛改善了（my back pain has improved），因此答案是 (C)。

字彙 expect to 預期要　condition 狀態

35-37 🔊 澳洲發音→英國發音

Questions 35-37 refer to the following conversation.

M: Hello. ³⁵You've reached Delta Card. How can I help you today?
W: Hi. This is Lauren O'Day. ³⁵/³⁶I'm calling about my recent credit card bill. ³⁶There's a $125 fee that I didn't expect.
M: OK . . . ³⁶That's the annual fee for your account. It covers services such as credit protection, our rewards program, and our hotel discount program.
W: ³⁷I'm sure this is a mistake. I've had this card for over a year, and ³⁷I've never had to pay this before.
M: The fee is waived for the first 12 months as part of our promotion for new account holders. It's all explained in your cardholder's agreement.
W: Oh . . . I wasn't aware of that. I should have looked at it closer.

credit card 信用卡　annual fee 年費　account 信用交易、帳號
cover 包含、負擔（損失）　reward 酬金
waive 不會套用（規則等）　promotion 促銷活動
account holder 帳號持有者　agreement 契約書、協議書

翻譯 問題 35-37，請參考以下對話。
男：您好，³⁵ 您聯絡了 Delta 卡公司，今天需要什麼幫忙？
女：您好，我叫做 Lauren O'Day，³⁵/³⁶ 我想要詢問近期的信用卡帳單，³⁶ 因為沒想到會多了 125 美元的費用。
男：原來如此……³⁶ 那是顧客您的信用卡年費，包含信

用保護、我們的獎勵計劃、飯店優惠計劃等的服務費用。
女：³⁷ 我確定一定哪裡有出錯，我用這張卡片已經超過 1 年了，³⁷ 先前從來不曾需要支付年費。
男：該費用是我們為了新帳戶持有者進行之促銷活動的一環，第一年不會收取費用，在您的卡片持有契約書中都有說明。
女：啊……我不知道耶，看來當初得詳細閱讀內容。

35 說話者問題

翻譯 男子最可能在哪裡工作？
(A) 法律事務所
(B) 金融機構
(C) 零售店
(D) 保全公司

解析 仔細聆聽對話中與身分、職業相關的用法，男子說對方聯絡了 Delta 卡公司，並詢問今天需要什麼幫忙（You've reached Delta Card. How can I help you today?），女子表示想要詢問近期的信用卡帳單（I'm calling about my recent credit card bill.），由此可知男子是在金融機構工作，因此答案是 (B)。

字彙 law office 法律事務所　financial institution 金融機關
retail outlet 零售店　security 保全的；保安

36 提及何事的問題

翻譯 關於女子信用卡的描述為何？
(A) 有定期的會費。
(B) 提供現金回饋獎勵。
(C) 有一筆飯店住宿的費用
(D) 1 年內有效。

解析 仔細聆聽與問題關鍵詞 woman's credit card 相關的內容，女子說是因為近期信用卡帳單才打電話的，並表示有自己意料之外的 125 美元（I'm calling about my recent credit card bill. There's a $125 fee that I didn't expect.），男子則回覆那是女子的信用卡交易的年費（That's the annual fee for your account.），因此答案是 (A)。

換句話說
annual fee 年費 → regular fee 定期會費

字彙 valid 有效的、妥當的

37 意圖掌握問題

翻譯 女子為何會說「我用這張卡片已經超過 1 年了」？
(A) 為了要求更換
(B) 為了表達對服務的滿意
(C) 為了詢問某一筆費用
(D) 為了要求免費的贈禮

解析 仔細聆聽與問題引用句 I've had this card for over a year 相關的部分，女子說自己確定年費一定是搞錯了（I'm sure this[annual fee] is a mistake.）之後，又說自己先前不曾付過（I've never had to pay this before），由此可知是為了詢問費用的事情，因此答案是 (C)。

字彙 replacement 交替、替換

Questions 38-40 refer to the following conversation with three speakers.

M1: ³⁸I think we should upgrade our office lights.

W: I agree. ³⁹Our current ones are way too bright. I find them distracting.

M2: So, Mark, what kind of lighting do you have in mind?

M1: Well, I read about ones that automatically adjust their brightness when it gets darker outside.

M2: That sounds good, but are they within our budget?

M1: Our office is fairly large, so installing them certainly wouldn't be cheap.

W: We should keep in mind that if the new lights help increase worker productivity, they would be worth the cost.

M2: Let's see what the other managers think about the idea. ⁴⁰I'll bring this up at the weekly meeting on Thursday.

---

upgrade 改善　distracting 分散注意力的、干擾的
lighting 照明　have in mind 考慮到　automatically 自動地
adjust 調整　brightness 亮度　budget 預算　fairly 頗為、相當
keep in mind 牢記　productivity 生產力　worth 值得
bring up 談論

翻譯 問題 38-40，請參考以下三人對話。
男 1：³⁸ 我認為應該改善一下我們辦公室的照明。
女：我同意，³⁹ 目前的照明太亮，會讓人無法集中注意力。
男 2：所以 Mark 你認為要換哪一種照明？
男 1：嗯，我知道有一種當外面變暗時可自動調整亮度的照明。
男 2：這也不錯，但那在預算範圍內嗎？
男 1：我們的辦公室很大，安裝那種照明應該不便宜吧。
女：我們必須記得，如果新照明有助於提升員工的生產力，那就值得花這筆費用。
男 2：去了解一下其他經理對這項意見有何看法吧，⁴⁰ 星期四的週會我會提出這件事。

38 主題問題

翻譯 說話者主要在談些什麼？
(A) 改善軟體
(B) 生產力降低
(C) 推出產品
(D) 改善辦公室

解析 因為題目在詢問對話主題，一定要仔細聆聽對話剛開始的部分，男子 1 認為照明必須改善（I think we should upgrade our office lights.），之後的對話都在討論改善辦公室，因此答案是 (D)。

字彙 decline 減少　launch 發行、開始

39 提及何事的問題

翻譯 女子談到辦公室照明的哪些事？
(A) 太亮了。
(B) 使用太多電力。
(C) 安裝得不牢固。
(D) 太老舊。

解析 注意聆聽女子話中和關鍵詞 office lights 相關的內容，女子說現在的照明太亮了（Our current ones[office lights] are way too bright. I find them distracting.），導致無法集中注意力，因此答案是 (A)。

字彙 electricity 電力　poorly 不牢固、不好　out of date 老舊的

40 之後將發生的事

翻譯 下星期四會發生什麼事？
(A) 會修理照明。
(B) 會開放新的空間。
(C) 會舉辦定期會議。
(D) 會宣布預算刪減。

解析 仔細聆聽和關鍵詞 next Thursday 相關的部分，男子 2 說星期四進行定期開會時會試著提這件事（I'll bring this up at the weekly meeting on Thursday.），由此可知下星期四會舉辦定期會議，因此答案是 (C)。

字彙 regular 定期的　budget cut 刪減預算　announce 宣布

Questions 41-43 refer to the following conversation.

W: Hello, Greg. This is Carol from Westfield International. I want to tell you that ⁴¹I received the catalog you sent me on behalf of your firm yesterday. I have some questions about the CrystalSet.

M: Yes, that's our latest tablet. What are you curious about in particular?

W: Well, ⁴²I'm wondering if it comes in multiple sizes. The catalog says it's 10 inches wide, but we'd like something bigger for our staff.

M: Right now, that's the only version available. However, a larger model will be launched in early summer. ⁴³If you want, I can call again when I have more details about the exact release date.

---

catalog 目錄　on behalf of 代表　latest 最新的　curious 好奇的
in particular 特別、尤其　wonder 想知道　multiple 多樣的
available 可使用的　launch 上市　release 上市、公開

翻譯 問題 41-43，請參考以下對話。
女：您好，Greg，我是 Westfield International 公司的 Carol。我想告訴您 ⁴¹ 我昨天收到您代表公司寄給我的目錄了，我對 CrystalSet 有幾個疑問。
男：對，那是我們的最新型平板，您對哪些地方有疑問？
女：嗯，⁴² 我想知道它是否有多種尺寸，目錄上寫著它是 10 吋，但我們想要給員工使用更大的尺寸。

男：目前這是唯一可取得的款式，但初夏時會推出更大的尺寸，43 如果需要的話，等掌握上市日期的相關資訊時，我會再次打電話給您。

41 特定細節問題

翻譯 昨天寄送了什麼？
(A) 替代零件
(B) 電子設備
(C) 個人信件
(D) 產品目錄

解析 注意聆聽和問題關鍵詞 delivered yesterday 相關的內容，女子說昨天收到男子代表公司寄出的目錄了（I received the catalog you sent me on behalf of your firm yesterday），由此可知昨天送來的東西是目錄，所以答案是 (D)。

字彙 replacement 替代、交換　part 零件　electronic device 電子設備

42 特定細節問題

翻譯 女子詢問男子什麼事？
(A) 產品上市日
(B) 出版物的價格
(C) 物品的尺寸
(D) 平板的重量

解析 仔細聆聽女子說的話，女子說想知道平板是否有其他尺寸（I'm wondering if it[tablet] comes in multiple sizes），因此正確答案是 (C)。

字彙 publication 出版物　weight 重量

43 提議問題

翻譯 男子提議幫忙做什麼？
(A) 分享財務細節。
(B) 晚點會再次致電。
(C) 向上司確認。
(D) 提議其他型號。

解析 仔細聆聽男子說要幫女子做的事情，男子對女子說：「如果需要的話，等掌握上市日期的相關資訊時，我會再次打電話給您」（If you want, I can call again when I have more details about the exact release date.），因此答案是 (B)。

字彙 share 分享　financial 財務的　call back 再次致電
supervisor 上司、管理者

44-46 🎧 澳洲發音→英國發音

Questions 44-46 refer to the following conversation.

M: 44Here are copies of the reports that we'll need for our presentation on the firm's accounting procedures.
W: Thanks. I don't know about you, but 45I'm a bit nervous about tomorrow. I've never spoken in front of such a large group. And many of the managers I report to will be there.

M: If you want, 46we can stay a bit later than usual tonight to practice our parts. Doing that should make tomorrow a lot easier.
W: All right. 46That's a really good idea. I'll meet you in the main conference room at 7 P.M.

accounting 會計　procedure 程序　report 練習

翻譯 問題 44-46，請參考以下對話。
男：44 這是公司會計程序簡報需要的報告影本。
女：謝謝，雖然我不清楚你怎麼樣，45 但我對明天的事感到有些緊張。我不曾在那麼多人面前說話，而且我上頭的很多經理應該都會到場。
男：如果你想要的話，46 今天晚上可以待到比平常更晚一點，練習我們的部分，這樣明天就會簡單一點。
女：好，46 這個主意真是太棒了，我們晚上 7 點會議室見吧。

44 特定細節問題

翻譯 根據男子的話，可知道他們必須做什麼？
(A) 撰寫報告。
(B) 簡報。
(C) 檢討財務帳目。
(D) 設置投影機。

解析 仔細聆聽男子說的話，男子談到公司會計程序簡報需要的報告影本（Here are copies of the reports that we'll need for our presentation on the firm's accounting procedures.），從對話中可知道談話者準備要簡報，因此答案是 (B)。

字彙 account （會計）帳簿、帳號　set up 設置

45 問題點問題

翻譯 女子為何會擔心？
(A) 她對某事務沒有信心。
(B) 她無法參加會議。
(C) 她把文件放錯位置。
(D) 她計算發生錯誤。

解析 仔細聆聽女子話中與負面表達相關的部分，她談到對明天的事覺得有些緊張，自己從來不曾在那麼多人面前說話（I'm a bit nervous about tomorrow. I've never spoken in front of such a large group.），由此可知女子對工作缺乏自信，所以答案是 (A)。

字彙 confident 自信的　misplace 隨意擱置　calculation 計算

46 之後將發生的事

翻譯 說話者今晚會做什麼？
(A) 審視一些數據
(B) 與主管會面
(C) 工作到更晚
(D) 預約研討會座位

解析 仔細聆聽與關鍵詞 this evening 相關的內容，男子說如果想要練習，今天晚上可以待到比平常更晚一點（we can stay a bit later than usual tonight to practice our parts），女子回答這個主意真是太棒了，下午 7 點會議室見吧（That's a really good idea. I'll meet you in the main conference room at 7 P.M.），由此可知說話者今晚會比較慢離開公司，所以正確答案是 (C)。

字彙 look over 檢討　figure 數值、數字

47-49 ③加拿大發音→英國發音→美國發音

Questions 47-49 refer to the following conversation with three speakers.

> M: ⁴⁷I'd like to invite the two of you to a birthday party I'm having this Saturday evening at my home.
> W1: I'm definitely interested in joining.
> W2: Me too. I'm supposed to meet a friend for dinner that night, but I can do it another time.
> M: Great. Do you know where I live?
> W2: It's the blue house on Briar Lane, isn't it?
> M: Actually, I moved a few months back. ⁴⁸My new house is at 321 Folgers Drive. It's across the street from Janes Park.
> W1: Sounds good. When should we arrive? And I'll bring snacks to share.
> M: The party starts at 7 P.M., Laura. And . . . ⁴⁹Kelly, will you bring over some drinks to the party, then?

definitely 當然、肯定　join 參加　actually 事實上、實際上
share 分享

翻譯 問題 47-49，請參考以下三人對話。
男：⁴⁷ 我想邀請兩位參加這星期六晚上我們家舉辦的生日派對。
女 1：我當然想參加。
女 2：我也是，我那天晚上原本和朋友約好要一起吃飯，但我可以改天。
男：好，你們知道我家在哪裡嗎？
女 2：是 Briar 路的藍色房子，不是嗎？
男：其實我幾個月前搬走了，⁴⁸ 我的新家在 Folgers 路 321 號，在 Janes 公園的另一邊。
女 1：聽起來不賴，我們何時要到場呢？我會帶點心去一起吃。
男：Laura，生日派對在晚上 7 點才開始。還有……⁴⁹ Kelly，你可以帶幾瓶飲料來派對嗎？

47 主題問題

翻譯 對話主要在談些什麼？
(A) 公司晚餐
(B) 介紹住宅
(C) 志工活動
(D) 私人聚會

解析 題目詢問對話的主題，男子說想邀請其他人去參加在自己家舉辦的生日派對（I'd like to invite the two of you to a birthday party I'm having ~ at my home.），內容是在談論私人聚會，因此答案是 (D)。

字彙 house showing （為了販售或租賃）住宅介紹
volunteer 自願的；志工　gathering 聚會

48 特定細節問題

翻譯 男子說 Folgers 路上有什麼？
(A) 百貨公司
(B) 公司
(C) 住宅
(D) 超市

解析 仔細聆聽和關鍵詞 Folgers Drive 相關的內容，男子表示自己的新家在 Folgers 路 321 號（My new house is at 321 Folgers Drive.），因此答案是 (C)。

換句話說
house 家 → residence 住宅

字彙 department store 百貨公司　workplace 職場　residence 住宅

49 特定細節問題

翻譯 男子請 Kelly 帶什麼過去？
(A) 書
(B) 禮物
(C) 點心
(D) 飲料

解析 仔細聆聽男子話中和關鍵詞 Kelly ~ bring 相關的部分，男子請 Kelly 帶幾瓶飲料去生日派對（Kelly, will you bring over some drinks to the party, then?），因此答案是 (D)。

換句話說
drinks 飲料 → Beverages 飲料

50-52 ③澳洲發音→英國發音

Questions 50-52 refer to the following conversation.

> M: Good afternoon, and welcome to Clothing Works. What can I help you with today?
> W: Hello. ⁵⁰I just purchased this dress for a business conference I'm going to in Frankfurt tomorrow. Unfortunately, it looks like the salesperson who assisted me forgot to remove the security tag at the checkout counter.
> M: I'm sorry about that. I can go ahead and remove it for you. ⁵¹I'll just need to see your receipt for the item.
> W: Oh, yes. Here it is. Just so you know, I'm in a bit of a hurry. ⁵²I've got to catch the shuttle bus to the airport hotel in 30 minutes.

conference 會議　salesperson 銷售員　assist 幫助
remove 移除　security 保安　checkout counter 結帳處
be in a hurry 迅速地　catch （依照公車、火車等的時間）搭乘

翻譯 問題 50-52，請參考以下對話。
男：午安，歡迎來到 Clothing Works，我能幫您什麼忙呢？
女：您好，⁵⁰ 為了明天在法蘭克福的商務會議，我剛購買了一件禮服，但很不巧的是，協助我的銷售人員在櫃檯忘記拆下安全標籤了。
男：對不起，我立刻幫您拆下。⁵¹ 我只需要先確認一下商品的收據。

女：啊，好，它在這裡。只是讓你知道，我趕時間。⁵²因為我 30 分鐘後要搭前往機場飯店的接駁車。

50 理由問題

翻譯 女子為何要去法蘭克福？
　　(A) 為了去找親戚
　　(B) 為了檢查設施
　　(C) 為了去見設計師
　　(D) 為了參加會議

解析 仔細聆聽與關鍵字 Frankfurt 相關的內容，女子表示自己為了明天在法蘭克福的會議購買了一件禮服（I just purchased this dress for a business conference I'm going to in Frankfurt tomorrow.），由此可知女子為了參加會議要前往法蘭克福，所以答案是 (D)。

字彙 relative 親戚　inspect 檢視

51 請求問題

翻譯 男子請女子做什麼？
　　(A) 和經理談話。
　　(B) 前往其他分店。
　　(C) 移除安全標籤。
　　(D) 提出購買證明。

解析 仔細聆聽男子話中和要求相關的內容，男子表示要確認物品的收據（I'll just need to see your receipt for the item.），從這句話可知道男子請女子出示購買證明，因此答案是 (D)。

換句話說
receipt for the item 物品的收據 → proof of purchase 購買證明

字彙 branch 分店　protective 保護用的　proof of purchase 購買證明

52 之後將發生的事

翻譯 女子 30 分鐘後最可能要做什麼？
　　(A) 與某人相約。
　　(B) 搭乘接駁車。
　　(C) 回到零售店。
　　(D) 搭乘飛機。

解析 仔細聆聽與關鍵詞 half an hour 相關的內容，女子表示 30 分鐘後要搭乘接駁車前往機場飯店（I've got to catch the shuttle bus to the airport hotel in 30 minutes.），因此答案是 (B)。

字彙 schedule 安排行程　get on 搭乘　retail outlet 零售店
board 搭乘

53-55 🔊 美國發音→加拿大發音

Questions 53-55 refer to the following conversation.

W: ⁵³I'm interested in traveling abroad to Lima for my upcoming vacation period. I've looked at several tour packages on your website, but I'm not sure which one would be best for me. I want some guided tours, but I'd also like a bit of freedom to explore on my own. ➲

M: ⁵⁴Then I recommend going with the Peru Adventure package. That one has the most flexible itinerary.
W: How much does that one cost?
M: Here are the price details for all of our packages. Also, ⁵⁵if you sign up for a membership today, you'll be able to get a discounted rate on your trip.

abroad 海外　upcoming 即將發生　guided tour 有導遊的旅遊
freedom 自由　explore 勘查　flexible 靈活的
itinerary 旅行計劃（表）　rate 價格、費用

翻譯 問題 53-55，請參考以下對話。
　　女：⁵³ 在即將到來的假期，我想出國去利馬旅行。我在您的網站上看見好幾個旅遊方案，但我不知道哪一個比較適合我。雖然我也希望有導遊，但也希望能有自己探索的自由。
　　男：⁵⁴ 那我建議祕魯冒險之旅，那個行程最有彈性。
　　女：那個方案多少錢？
　　男：這裡有所有方案的價格資訊。另外，⁵⁵ 如果今天加入會員，就能獲得優惠價格。

53 特定細節問題

翻譯 女子在考慮什麼？
　　(A) 接受一份夏季工作
　　(B) 擔任導遊
　　(C) 前往國外旅行
　　(D) 變更旅行計劃

解析 仔細聆聽與關鍵詞 woman considering 相關的內容，女子說在即將到來的假期想出國去利馬旅行（I'm interested in traveling abroad to Lima for my upcoming vacation period.），因此答案是 (C)。

字彙 summer job 暑假打工　accept 同意、接受　tour guide 旅行導遊
overseas 到國外的

54 理由問題

翻譯 男子為何會推薦祕魯冒險之旅？
　　(A) 包含高級飯店房間。
　　(B) 能幫忙節省旅費。
　　(C) 可提供更多的彈性。
　　(D) 因含有免費贈品。

解析 仔細聆聽和關鍵詞 Peru Adventure package 相關的內容，男子推薦祕魯冒險之旅，因為該行程較能彈性利用時間（Then I recommend going with the Peru Adventure package. That one has the most flexible itinerary.），因此答案是 (C)。

換句話說
has the most flexible itinerary 有最具彈性的旅程 → offers more flexibility 提供更大的彈性

字彙 save 節省（費用、時間、努力等）　flexibility 彈性
come with 伴隨　complimentary 免費的

55 特定細節問題

翻譯 男子說加入會員有什麼好處？
　　(A) 旅遊保險
　　(B) 優惠價格

(C) 免費旅遊指南

(D) 追加的觀光景點

解析 仔細聆聽與關鍵詞 benefit ~ membership provide 相關的內容，男子說今天加入會員就能獲得優惠價格（If you sign up for a membership today, you'll be able to get a discounted rate on your trip），因此答案是(B)。

字彙 insurance 保險　reduced 折扣的、減少的　guidebook 旅遊指南　additional 附加的　destination 觀光地、目的地

56-58 🔊 澳洲發音→美國發音

Questions 56-58 refer to the following conversation.

M: [56]I've got a shipment of computer hardware devices for Alicia Carson. They're from TechnicStore. [56]Where would you like me to put the package?

W: Oh, thanks. [57]Please just place it on top of the desk right near the window there. I appreciate it.

M: Certainly. Could you please sign this form indicating your acceptance of the delivery? It's required by the sender in order to confirm that you've successfully received the items.

W: OK . . . Yes . . . it looks like everything listed here is in the package. [58]I'll go ahead and do that, then.

---

shipment 運送品、運輸　package 包裹　place 放置
indicate 顯示　acceptance 接納、同意　confirm 確認

翻譯 問題 56-58，請參考以下對話。

男：[56] 我這邊有 Alicia Carson 的電腦硬體設備包裹，包裹是來自 TechnicStore，[56] 我應該放在哪裡呢？

女：啊，謝謝，[57] 請幫我放在那邊窗戶附近的桌上。感謝你。

男：沒問題，可以在單子上簽名，表示已經收到貨品了嗎？因為寄件人需要確認您有順利收到東西。

女：我知道了……好……列在上面的東西似乎都在包裹裡，[58] 那我就快點簽名吧。

56 說話者問題

翻譯 男子最可能是什麼人？

(A) 送貨員

(B) 個人助理

(C) 電腦工程師

(D) 部門主管

解析 注意對話中與身分、職業相關的用法，男子說有 Alicia Carson 的電腦硬體設備包裹（I've got a shipment of computer hardware devices for Alicia Carson.），接著詢問包裹應該放在哪裡（Where would you like me to put the package?），可見男子是送貨員，答案是 (A)。

字彙 assistant 助理

57 請求問題

翻譯 女子要求男子做什麼？

(A) 寄送包裹至新地址。

(B) 確認箱子的內容物。

(C) 去一趟服務臺。

(D) 把包裹放在桌上。

解析 仔細聆聽女子話中與要求相關的內容，女子請男子把包裹放在桌上（Please just place it[package] on top of the desk），因此答案是 (D)。

字彙 contents 內容物　stop by 順便拜訪

58 之後將發生的事

翻譯 女子接下來最可能做什麼？

(A) 在文件上簽名。

(B) 審視已購買商品的清單。

(C) 聯絡最初的寄件人。

(D) 訂購其他硬體。

解析 仔細聆聽對話最後的部分，女子說會快點簽名（I'll go ahead and do that[sign]），因此答案是 (A)。

字彙 signature 簽名　look over 查看　original 最初的、原來的　place an order 訂購

59-61 🔊 英國發音→加拿大發音

Questions 59-61 refer to the following conversation.

W: Hi, Walter. [59]I thought you were visiting our branch in Toronto this week.

M: [59]That's right. I flew out there on Monday and got back yesterday. [60]I had to interview some candidates for the manager position. The current head of the branch . . . um, Peter Greer . . . he has decided to resign.

W: How did it go?

M: Well, a couple of candidates look promising, but none of them are ideal. I'm going to recommend that we promote someone else.

W: Interesting. Do you have anyone in mind?

M: Well, [61]the assistant manager is the most obvious choice, but she has requested a transfer to our Vancouver office. So, [61]I'm thinking of recommending the head of the sales team instead.

---

fly out 搭飛機前往　candidate 應徵者　current 目前的
resign 辭職　promising 有潛力的　ideal 理想的
promote 晉升、促使　have in mind 考慮到、想好
obvious 明顯、顯然的　transfer 轉移、移動

翻譯 問題 59-61，請參考以下對話。

女：您好，Walter，[59] 我以為您這星期會去參訪我們在多倫多的分店。

男：[59] 對，我星期一搭飛機去，昨天回來了。[60] 我因為分店長的職缺必須面試好幾個應徵者，目前的分店長……嗯，Peter Greer……他決定要離職了。

女：面試進行得如何？

男：嗯，目前有幾名應徵者看起來有潛力，但他們都不算理想，我應該會提議讓其他人升遷吧。

女：真是有意思，你腦中有人選嗎？

男：這個嘛，[61] 副店長是最顯而易見的選擇，但她已經申請調到溫哥華辦公室，所以 [61] 我在考慮推薦行銷團隊的負責人。

59 特定細節問題

翻譯 男子這星期初做了什麼？
(A) 和某團隊負責人交談。
(B) 去出差。
(C) 參加研習會。
(D) 要求升遷。

解析 仔細聆聽與關鍵詞 earlier in the week 有關的內容，女子表示以為男子這星期會去多倫多的分店（I thought you were visiting our branch in Toronto this week.），男子回答沒錯，並說自己星期一搭飛機去，昨天回來（That's right. I flew out there on Monday and got back yesterday.），由此可知男子這星期去出差，所以答案是 (B)。

字彙 participate 參加　promotion 升遷

60 理由問題

翻譯 為何會進行面試？
(A) 分店長就要離職了。
(B) 將要擴店了。
(C) 部門的人手不足。
(D) 工作邀約被拒絕了。

解析 仔細聆聽與關鍵詞 interviews conducted 相關的內容，男子說自己因為分店長的職缺必須面試好幾個申請者，目前的店長決定要辭職了（I had to interview some candidates for the manager position. The current head of the branch ~ has decided to resign.），因此答案是 (A)。

字彙 expand 擴張　understaffed 人手不足的　job offer 工作邀約
turn down 拒絕

61 意圖掌握問題

翻譯 男子為何提到「她已經申請調到溫哥華辦公室」？
(A) 為了說明無法採用某選項的原因
(B) 為了強調職位的重要性
(C) 為了推薦其他分店
(D) 為了鼓勵女子做出決定

解析 仔細聆聽與引用句 she has requested a transfer to our Vancouver office 相關的部分，男子說副店長是最顯而易見的選擇（the assistant manager is the most obvious choice），但她已經申請調到溫哥華辦公室，所以目前在考慮推薦行銷團隊的負責人（I'm thinking of recommending the head of the sales team instead），由此可知他是在解釋無法採用某選項的原因，所以答案是 (A)。

字彙 unavailable 無法採用的　stress 強調　importance 重要性
encourage 鼓勵　make a decision 決定

62-64 英國發音→澳洲發音

Questions 62-64 refer to the following conversation and product list.

W: I was really surprised by the sales figures for our latest watch line. They've sold better than we expected.
M: So was I. [62]The watch with the round face is doing especially well. Although it was released most recently, it has sold the most this year.
W: Yes, that is quite surprising. [63]Unfortunately, we're running out of that model now.
M: Can't we make more of them?
W: I've contacted our factory supervisor, and she is planning to increase production.
M: That's good. [64]With the holiday season coming up, demand will probably increase even more.
W: Exactly. Watches are always popular gifts.

---

sales figures 銷售額　face（鐘的）正面　run out of 用完、耗盡
demand 需要；要求

翻譯 問題 62-64，請參考以下對話和商品目錄。
女：最新的手錶產品銷售額讓我相當驚訝，銷售狀況比我們預期的還要更好。
男：我也一樣。[62] 圓錶的銷售狀況特別好，雖然它近期才上市，卻是今年銷售最好的。
女：對，真的很驚人，[63] 不過很遺憾的是，那個型號已經快沒了。
男：不能再多生產一點嗎？
女：我聯絡工廠主管了，她已經在規劃增產了。
男：太好了，[64] 隨著假期到來，需求可能會大幅增加。
女：對，手錶一直都是受歡迎的禮物。

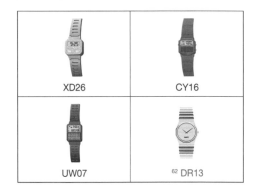

XD26　　CY16
UW07　　[62] DR13

62 圖片題

翻譯 請看圖片，哪一個型號是近期推出的？
(A) XD26
(B) CY16
(C) UW07
(D) DR13

解析 確認產品目錄的資訊後，仔細聆聽與關鍵詞 most recently released 相關的內容。文中談到圓錶的銷售狀況特別好，雖然它是近期才上市的，卻是今年銷售最好的（The watch with the round face is doing especially well. Although it was released most recently, it has sold the most this year.），從目錄中可知道 DR13 型號是最近推出的，因此答案是 (D)。

63 問題點問題

翻譯 女子談到什麼問題？
(A) 新手錶的評價是負面的。
(B) 某個品項的庫存快用光了。
(C) 工廠停產了。
(D) 某主管在徵才方面遇到了困難。

解析 仔細聆聽女子話中反面的表達，女子談到：「不過很遺憾的是，那個型號已經快沒了。」（Unfortunately, we're running out of that model[The watch with the round face] now.）因此答案是 (B)。

字彙 negative 反面的　run low 快用完、不足
shut down 使～停止　have trouble -ing 在～方面有困難

64 理由問題

翻譯 男子為何認為銷售會提升？
(A) 部分品項已被放上促銷了。
(B) 手錶越來越受歡迎。
(C) 僱用外部的行銷公司。
(D) 假期就要到了。

解析 仔細聆聽和關鍵詞 sales to increase 相關的內容，男子說隨著假期的到來，需求可能會大幅增加（With the holiday season coming up, demand will probably increase even more.），因此答案是 (D)。

65-67 英國發音→加拿大發音

Questions 65-67 refer to the following conversation and graph.

> W: Alton, have you finished editing the latest job advertisement for the engineer position?
> M: Yes. But [65]I still need to post it online. I'm planning to take care of that right after lunch.
> W: [66]We need to hire another employee as soon as possible as we can't continue with the mall construction project until we find someone.
> M: Yes, filling this role is a priority right now.
> W: Have you thought about posting the advertisement on industry job boards?
> M: I have. In the past, [67]we got the highest number of applications in the month that we uploaded job listings to a site that targets engineers. So, I'm going to publish it there.
>
> edit 編輯　latest 最新的　job advertisement 徵人廣告
> post 刊登　take care of 處理　fill 填補（某個職務）
> priority 優先順位　job board 徵人欄　application 申請書
> job listing 徵人目錄　target 以～為對象　publish 刊載

翻譯 問題 65-67，請參考以下對話及圖表。
女：Alton，最新的工程師徵人廣告已經編輯好了嗎？
男：好了，不過 [65] 我還必須刊登在網路上。我打算午餐後進行。
女：[66] 因為我們必須等徵到人才能繼續執行購物中心建設專案，所以必須要盡快找到人。
男：對，現在當務之急就是填補這個職缺。
女：你有考慮在行業徵人欄中刊登廣告嗎？

男：我已經想到了。以前 [67] 我們曾把徵人清單上傳至工程師網站，而那個月收到的履歷數量最多，所以我要在那邊刊登廣告。

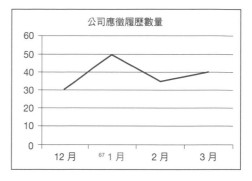

公司應徵履歷數量

65 特定細節問題

翻譯 男子還必須做什麼？
(A) 刊登廣告。
(B) 準備面試。
(C) 聯絡最近的應徵者。
(D) 幫新人進行教育訓練。

解析 仔細聆聽與關鍵詞 still need to do 相關的內容，男子說還必須刊登在網路上（I still need to post it[job advertisement] online），因此答案是 (A)。

字彙 applicant 應徵者　train 教育訓練

66 理由問題

翻譯 根據女子說的話來看，為何急著徵人？
(A) 就要舉行會議了。
(B) 專案暫停中。
(C) 主要職員離職了。
(D) 團隊進行重組了。

解析 仔細聆聽與關鍵詞 hiring decision urgent 相關的內容，女子說：「因為我們必須等徵到人才能繼續執行購物中心建設專案，所以必須要盡快找到人」（We need to hire another employee as soon as possible as we can't continue with the mall construction project until we find someone.），因此答案是 (B)。

字彙 approach 即將到來　on hold 暫停中、保留中　key 重要的
quit 放棄　reorganize 重新編列

67 圖片題

翻譯 請看圖片，徵人廣告是何時刊登上網站？
(A) 12 月
(B) 1 月
(C) 2 月
(D) 3 月

解析 確認圖片的資訊後，仔細聆聽和核心句子 job openings advertised on the website 相關的內容。男子說把徵人清單上傳至工程師網站的那個月收到的履歷數量最多（we got the highest number of applications in the month that we uploaded job listings to a site that targets engineers），由此可知徵人廣告是在 1 月時刊登網站的，所以答案是 (B)。

Questions 68-70 refer to the following conversation and seating chart.

M: Good morning. [68]I'm checking in for my flight to Oakland. [69]Here's my passport.

W: Thank you. Do you have any luggage besides that carry-on bag?

M: No, that's it. I'm going on a short trip.

W: OK. I'll finish confirming your reservation, then. Hmm . . . It appears that the seat you originally booked has been reassigned. [70]Two passengers traveling with a baby need the cot area that is located in front of the seat. I apologize for the inconvenience.

M: In that case, [70]can I move to a window seat?

W: [70]Yes, I'll put you in the same row as you were, just on the other side of the aisle.

---

check in 進行登機報到手續　passport 護照　luggage 行李
carry-on bag 攜帶用背包　reassign 重新分派　cot 嬰兒床
in that case 既然那樣、假如是那樣　row 行、列　aisle 通道、走廊

翻譯 問題 68-70，請參考以下對話及座位配置圖。
　　男：[68] 您好，我要辦理飛往奧克蘭班機的登機報到手續。[69] 這是我的護照。
　　女：謝謝，除了隨身背包之外，是否還有其他行李？
　　男：沒了，這是全部的行李，這是一趟短程旅行。
　　女：好，那我現在就確認您的預約，嗯……您原本預約的座位被重新分配了，[70] 帶著小孩的兩名乘客需要前面能放嬰兒床的座位。造成您的不便，真的很抱歉。
　　男：那 [70] 可以換到窗戶旁的座位嗎？
　　女：[70] 好，我會把您換到同一排走廊的另一邊。

嬰兒床					
窗戶	A-1	A-2	走廊	A-3	[70] A-4	窗戶

68 場所問題

翻譯 說話者最可能在哪裡？
　　(A) 渡輪港口
　　(B) 機場
　　(C) 火車站
　　(D) 公車站

解析 仔細聆聽和場所相關的用法，男子說要辦理搭乘飛往奧克蘭班機的登機手續（I'm checking in for my flight to Oakland.），從這句話可知道說話者在機場，所以答案是 (B)。

字彙 ferry 渡輪　port 港口

69 特定細節問題

翻譯 男子把什麼交給女子？
　　(A) 信用卡
　　(B) 遺失物申報書

(C) 行李
(D) 身分識別證

解析 仔細聆聽和關鍵詞 give to the woman 相關的內容，男子對女子說這是我的護照（Here's my passport.），因此答案是 (D)。
換句話說
passport 護照 → identification 身分識別證

字彙 missing-item 遺失物　identification 身分證

70 圖片題

翻譯 請看圖片，男子會被安排哪個座位？
　　(A) A-1
　　(B) A-2
　　(C) A-3
　　(D) A-4

解析 確認座位配置圖後，仔細聆聽和關鍵詞 seat ~ given 相關的內容。女子說帶著小孩的兩名乘客需要前面能放嬰兒床的座位（Two passengers ~ need the cot area that is located in front of the seat.），接著表示會把男子換到同一排走廊的另一邊（Yes, I'll put you in the same row as you were, just on the other side of the aisle.），由此可知和嬰兒床前面的座位是同一排，走道對面最旁邊的 A-4 是男子的座位，所以答案是 (D)。

PART 4

Questions 71-73 refer to the following recorded message.

Thank you for calling the Gramsfield City Library. [71]Our facility is currently closed for renovations. We will reopen on Tuesday, February 23, at 9 A.M. [72]During our temporary closure, checked-out library materials may be returned through the book drop slot on the right side of the building. All late fee payments made on our website will be processed normally. As for books that were placed on reserve before February 23, they may be picked up at the circulation desk when the library reopens. [73]Should you have any urgent issues, please call 555-6632. Have a nice day.

---

renovation 整修、翻新　temporary 臨時的　closure 封閉
check out （圖書館等）借書　book drop 還書箱
process 處理　normally 正常地　pick up 尋找、取物
circulation desk 還書櫃檯　urgent 緊迫的

翻譯 問題 71-73，請參考以下語音訊息。
　　感謝您來電 Gramsfield 市立圖書館，[71] 我們的圖書館正在整修中，因此目前休館中，於 2 月 23 日星期二上午 9 點再次開館。[72] 暫時休館的期間，借出的圖書館讀物可透過建築物右邊的圖書館還書箱交還。網站上支付的所有延滯費都會正常處理，2 月 23 日前預約的書籍可在重新開館時從租借處領取。[73] 如果有緊急狀況，請來電 555-6632，那麼祝您有愉快的一天。

71 理由問題

翻譯 該設施為何要休館？
(A) 紀念假日。
(B) 建築物整修。
(C) 設備必須檢驗。
(D) 系統必須升級。

解析 仔細聆聽關鍵詞 facility closed 相關的部分，文中談到圖書館正在整修而休館中（Our facility is currently closed for renovations.），因此正確答案是 (B)。

字彙 celebrate 紀念　repair 修理　inspect 檢驗

72 特定細節問題

翻譯 講者談到休館期間聽者能做什麼？
(A) 還書。
(B) 領取讀物。
(C) 更新借書證。
(D) 前往其他分館。

解析 仔細聆聽與關鍵詞 during a closure 相關的內容，文中談到暫時休館的期間，租借的圖書館資料可透過建築物右邊的圖書館還書箱交還（During our temporary closure, checked-out library materials may be returned through the book drop slot on the right side of the building.），因此答案是 (A)。

字彙 renew 更新　library card 借書證

73 方法問題

翻譯 聽者該如何處理緊急情況？
(A) 去找職員
(B) 打電話
(C) 填寫線上表單
(D) 寄送電子郵件

解析 仔細聆聽與關鍵詞 urgent issues 相關的內容，文中談到如果有緊急狀況請來電 555-6632（Should you have any urgent issues, please call 555-6632.），因此答案是 (B)。

字彙 address 處理（困難的問題等）　dial a number 打電話

74-76 ③⑪美國發音

Questions 74-76 refer to the following instruction.

My name is Cameron Bell. [74]For today's training session, I'll be showing you all how to use our company's accounting software, NextBook. You'll see that the software is already loaded on the computers in front of you, and [75]an ID number is required to log into the program. I'll give each of you those numbers in just a moment. But before we start using NextBook, [76]my assistant is going to pass out these instruction manuals for your reference. Keep these with you throughout the morning, as I'll be referring to them multiple times.

training session 教育訓練（課程）　pass out 分發（物品）
instruction manual 使用說明書　for reference 供作參考的
refer to 引用、提及

翻譯 問題 74-76，請參考以下說明。
我的名字是 Cameron Bell，[74] 今天的培訓課程我要告訴各位公司會計軟體 NextBook 的使用方法。各位面前的電腦已經安裝該軟體了，[75] 登入程式需要 ID 號碼，我會把號碼告訴各位。但在我們開始使用 NextBook 前，[76] 我的秘書會把參考用的使用說明書發給各位，因為整個上午會多次引用，所以請各位都要帶在身上。

74 說話者問題

翻譯 說話者最可能是誰？
(A) 電腦維修人員
(B) 研究分析師
(C) 公司培訓人員
(D) 銷售人員

解析 仔細聆聽短文中與身分、職業相關的用法，文中談到今天的培訓課程會告訴各位公司會計軟體 NextBook 的使用方法（For today's training session, I'll be showing you all how to use our company's new accounting software, NextBook.），由此可知說話者是公司的培訓人員，所以答案是 (C)。

字彙 analyst 分析師　trainer 教育者、培訓人員
sales representative 銷售人員

75 提及何事的問題

翻譯 說話者談到關於 NextBook 的什麼事？
(A) 數個月前改版了。
(B) 電腦讀取時需要一點時間。
(C) 獲得董事長同意了。
(D) 使用時需要特殊的號碼。

解析 仔細聆聽和關鍵字 NextBook 相關的內容，文中談到登入程式需要 ID 號碼（an ID number is required to log in to the program[NextBook]），因此答案是 (D)。

換句話說
ID number is required to log into 登入時需要 ID 號碼 →
requires a special code to access 使用時需要特殊的號碼

字彙 approve 同意　code 號碼、暗號　access 使用、存取

76 特定細節問題

翻譯 秘書會發下什麼？
(A) 申請書
(B) 教育訓練資料
(C) 事務裝備
(D) 電子儀器

解析 仔細聆聽和關鍵詞 assistant pass out 相關的內容，文中談到秘書會把參考用的使用說明書發給各位（my assistant is going to pass out these instruction manuals for your reference），因此 (B) 是正確答案。

字彙 application form 申請書　electronic device 電子設備

Questions 77-79 refer to the following broadcast.

Good afternoon. This is Arlene Vickers, and I've got your traffic report. The unexpectedly heavy snow that began falling at 6 A.M. is still being cleared by city snow plows. [77]A representative of the transportation department, John Harris, said that the work will likely take a couple of hours to complete. [78]Motorists are urged to drive carefully, especially when crossing the Harborview Bridge as ice has reportedly formed on it. And if you were planning on taking the Park Expressway into the downtown area, you may want to reconsider. [79]The snowy conditions have resulted in several accidents, bringing traffic to a standstill. Use Kensington Street or Fourth Avenue instead.

traffic report 交通資訊　unexpectedly 出乎預料
heavy snow 暴雪　snow plow 鏟雪車　urge 強烈勸告
reportedly 據說　form 形成　expressway 高速公路
downtown 市區　reconsider 重新考慮
result in 導致、造成　standstill 停滯、停止

翻譯　問題 77-79，請參考以下廣播。
午安，我是 Arlene Vickers，為各位播報交通資訊。因為上午 6 點突然降下出乎預料的暴雪，所以目前都市鏟雪車還在進行清理。[77] 交通部的職員 John Harris 說鏟雪作業需要 2 個小時左右才會完成，[78] 強烈建議各位駕駛開車時要小心一點，根據了解，由於 Harborview 橋上結冰了，所以過橋時要特別小心。另外，如果要利用 Park 高速公路前往市區，你可能需要重新考慮。[79] 因為降下大雪的關係，造成多處發生意外，所以交通壅塞。請各位駕駛改為利用 Kensington 街或 4 號街。

77 特定細節問題

翻譯　John Harris 最可能是誰？
(A) 記者
(B) 氣象播報員
(C) 鏟雪車駕駛
(D) 公務員

解析　仔細聆聽短文中關於對象 John Harris 的身分、職業的相關用法，文中談到交通部的職員 John Harris （A representative of the transportation department, John Harris），因此可知道 John Harris 是公務員，所以答案是 (D)。

字彙　journalist 記者　weather forecaster 氣象播報員
　　　operator （機械等的）駕駛　public official 公務員

78 提及何事的問題

翻譯　關於 Harborview 橋的描述，說到了什麼？
(A) 那邊是事故現場。
(B) 橋上結冰了。
(C) 是前往市區唯一的路。
(D) 雪已經全部清除了。

解析　仔細聆聽和關鍵詞 Harborview Bridge 相關的內容，文中談到「強烈建議各位駕駛開車時要小心一點，根據了

解，由於 Harborview 橋上結冰了，所以過橋時要特別小心」（Motorists are urged to drive carefully, especially when crossing the Harborview Bridge as ice has reportedly formed on it.），由此可知 Harborview 橋上結冰了，因此答案是 (B)。
換句話說
ice has ~ formed 結冰 → frozen over 結凍
字彙　site 現場　freeze over 冰封　completely 完全地

79 意圖掌握問題

翻譯　說話者談到「你可能需要重新考慮」，她的意思是什麼？
(A) 活動可能會延期。
(B) 交通號誌異常。
(C) 必須使用其他道路。
(D) 最近的某個報導尚未經過證實。

解析　仔細聆聽和引用句 you may want to reconsider 相關的部分。因為降下大雪的關係，造成多處都發生意外，所以交通壅塞，請各位駕駛改為利用 Kensington 街或 4 號街（The snowy conditions have resulted in several accidents, bringing traffic to a standstill. Use Kensington Street or Fourth Avenue instead.），由此可知必須使用其他道路，因此答案是 (C)。

字彙　postpone 延期　traffic light 紅綠燈　properly 適當地
　　　alternative 其他的、可替代的　route 路、途徑

Questions 80-82 refer to the following excerpt from a meeting.

Starting from next week, we will begin planning a TV advertising campaign for a major Taiwanese beverage manufacturer, Refresh. [80]A representative from the firm will be visiting our headquarters next Friday to discuss how the company wants its brand portrayed in the advertisements. [81]I've asked the research team to put together a short presentation on work that we've done for similar organizations in the past. As usual, Peter Zimmer will lead the design team, and he'll be present at the meeting as well. [82]If anyone has a question about their role for the upcoming campaign, please contact me at extension 567 at any time.

beverage 飲料　manufacturer 製造業者
representative 代表（人）　headquarters 總公司
portray 描寫、描繪　put together 準備、蒐集、裝配
as usual 像往常一樣　lead 帶領　extension 分機號碼

翻譯　問題 80-82，請參考以下會議摘錄。
下星期開始，我們將為臺灣的主要飲料製造業者 Refresh 公司企劃電視廣告活動。[80] 該公司的代表下星期五將會來我們的總公司，為了商討在廣告中呈現自家公司的方式，[81] 我已經請研究團隊準備過去類似組織進行過之作業的相關簡短報告。就和平常一樣，Peter Zimmer 將同樣率領設計團隊，也會參加會議。[82] 如果對自己在即將進行的活動中的角色有任何疑問，隨時都能撥打分機號碼 567 聯繫我。

80 之後將發生的事

翻譯 說話者講到會發生什麼事？
(A) 製造工廠將會開門。
(B) 飲料產品將要上市。
(C) 電視廣告即將完成。
(D) 顧客將要造訪公司。

解析 仔細聆聽和關鍵詞 next week 相關的內容，文中談到該公司的代表下星期五將會造訪總公司（A representative from the firm will be visiting our headquarters next Friday），因此答案是 (D)。

換句話說
A representative from the firm will be visiting ~ headquarters 該公司的代表將會造訪總公司 →
A client will come to an office 客戶將會來公司

字彙 manufacturing plant 製造工廠　release 上市
commercial 廣告

81 請求問題

翻譯 說話者請研究團隊做什麼？
(A) 開始調查顧客。
(B) 修訂報告書。
(C) 從線上分享結果。
(D) 準備簡單的報告。

解析 仔細聆聽短文中後部分與要求相關的部分，文中談到「我已經請研究團隊準備過去替類似組織進行過之作業的相關簡短報告」（I've asked the research team to put together a short presentation on work），因此答案是 (D)。

換句話說
put together a short presentation 準備簡短的報告 → Prepare a brief presentation 準備簡單的報告

字彙 survey（問卷）調查　make a correction 修訂、校正

82 理由問題

翻譯 聽者為什麼應該聯絡說話者？
(A) 為了提出疑問
(B) 為了協調行程
(C) 為了確認參加
(D) 為了自願接下工作

解析 仔細聆聽和關鍵詞 contact the speaker 相關的內容，文中談到「如果對自己在即將進行的活動中的角色有任何疑問，隨時都能聯絡我」（If anyone has a question about their role for the upcoming campaign, please contact me），因此答案是 (A)。

字彙 coordinate 調整　confirm 確認　attendance 參加、出席
volunteer for 自願~

83-85 [澳] 澳洲發音

Questions 83-85 refer to the following introduction.

I'd like to ask you all to please welcome Gerald Kramer, the new senior director of Hampton Insurance. [83]Mr. Kramer has significant experience overseeing ➡

workers at major insurance providers. [84]He has also lived and worked abroad, achieving near-native proficiency in Spanish. That's a major reason why Mr. Kramer was brought on—to aid us in assisting our many Spanish-speaking clients. One of his main tasks will be to provide further professional development in language skills for all staff going forward. To celebrate the fact that Mr. Kramer is now joining our office, [85]we will be holding a casual staff get-together next Friday evening at 7 P.M.

senior director 常務理事　significant 相當的、重要的
oversee 監督　achieve 達到　proficiency 流暢、熟練　aid 幫助
going forward 向前走　celebrate 紀念　casual 非正式的
get-together 聚會

翻譯 問題 83-85，請參考以下介紹。
請各位一起歡迎 Hampton 保險公司的新常務理事 Gerald Kramer，[83] Kramer 先生先前在一流保險公司督導員工，這方面有相當的資歷。[84] 他還曾在海外工作，西班牙文幾乎和母語一樣流暢，這就是我們聘請 Kramer 先生的主要原因——就是為了協助使用西班牙文的許多顧客。他的主要工作之一是協助全體職員的語言實力獲得大幅度的專業性成長。為了慶祝 Kramer 先生加入我們公司，[85] 我們下星期五晚上 7 點要舉辦非正式的員工聚餐。

83 特定細節問題

翻譯 Kramer 先生在哪方面有豐富的經驗？
(A) 販售保險商品
(B) 管理職員
(C) 處理客訴事項
(D) 處理公司的合併

解析 仔細聆聽和核心句子 have a lot of experience 相關的內容，文中談到 Kramer 先生先前在一流保險公司督導員工，在那方面有相當的資歷（Mr. Kramer has significant experience overseeing workers at major insurance providers.），因此答案是 (B)。

字彙 handle 處理、操作　merger（組織事業體的）合併

84 提及何事的問題

翻譯 說話者提到 Kramer 先生的什麼事？
(A) 他想要演講。
(B) 他曾住在其他國家。
(C) 他拒絕其他工作邀約。
(D) 他將要僱用秘書。

解析 仔細聆聽和關鍵詞 Mr. Kramer 相關的內容，文中談到 Kramer 先生曾居住在國外（He[Mr. Kramer] has also lived ~ abroad），因此答案是 (B)。

字彙 give a talk 演講　refuse 拒絕

85 之後將發生的事

翻譯 下星期五什麼事很可能會登場？
(A) 語言課程
(B) 貿易博覽會

(C) 營業會議

(D) 非正式聚餐

解析 仔細聆聽和關鍵詞 next Friday 相關的內容，文中談到下星期五晚上 7 點要舉辦非正式的員工聚餐（we will be holding a casual staff get-together next Friday evening at 7 P.M.），因此答案是 (D)。

換句話說
casual staff get-together 非正式員工聚餐 → An informal gathering 非正式聚會

字彙 trade fair 貿易博覽會　informal 非正式的、非正規的　gathering 聚會

86-88 🔊 加拿大發音

Questions 86-88 refer to the following speech.

86Thank you all for attending the annual shareholders' meeting for Freemont Industries. I am pleased to be here, representing Freemont as its CEO for the last 15 years. For those who don't know, 87the magazine *BizSurprise* just named us one of Canada's most successful businesses in its most recent monthly edition. That's a huge honor, and it has motivated us to work even harder to maintain our standing in the coming years. But before I discuss future plans, CFO for Freemont Jennifer Harvey will be presented with a special award in recognition of her hard work. 88Ms. Harvey, please join me on the stage and say a few words.

annual 年度的　shareholders' meeting 股東大會
represent 代表、代替　name 命名　edition（刊物的）號、版
honor 榮耀　motivate 賦予動機　maintain 維持
standing 地位、聲望　present 授予、贈送　award 獎
recognition 表彰、認識　say a few words 說幾句話

翻譯 問題 86-88，請參考以下演說。
86 感謝各位參加 Freemont Industries 公司的年度股東大會，很高興能以 Freemont 公司 15 年的執行長代表本公司參加此一大會。有些人還不知道，87 BizSurprise 雜誌最新一期把我們列為加拿大最成功公司之一，這是非常大的榮幸，同時也帶給我們動力，往後幾年要更加努力維持現在的地位。但在我談論往後的計劃之前，Freemont 公司要先頒特殊獎給財務長 Jennifer Harvey 表揚她的辛勞。88 Harvey 女士，請上臺和我一起講幾句話吧。

86 聽者問題

翻譯 聽者最可能是誰？
(A) 企業總裁
(B) 銀行行員
(C) 公司股東
(D) 雜誌編輯

解析 仔細聆聽短文中和身分、職業相關的部分，文中談到感謝大家參加 Freemont Industries 年度股東大會（Thank you all for attending the annual shareholders' meeting for Freemont Industries），由此可知聽眾是股東，所以答案是 (C)。

字彙 bank teller 銀行行員　stakeholder 股東　editor 編輯

87 推論題

翻譯 關於 BizSurprise 雜誌，可推論出什麼？
(A) 出版月刊。
(B) 想採訪執行長。
(C) 贊助企業博覽會。
(D) 必須僱用更多的作家。

解析 仔細聆聽和關鍵字 BizSurprise 相關的部分，文中談到 BizSurprise 雜誌最新一期把 Freemont 列為加拿大最成功公司之一（the magazine BizSurprise just named us one of Canada's most successful businesses in its most recent monthly edition），由此可知 BizSurprise 雜誌出版刊物，所以答案是 (A)。

字彙 publish 出刊、發行　sponsor 贊助　fair 博覽會

88 請求問題

翻譯 說話者請 Harvey 女士做什麼？
(A) 頒獎。
(B) 演說。
(C) 幫獲獎者拍手。
(D) 坐在位子上。

解析 仔細聆聽短文後面和要求相關的句子，文中談到請 Harvey 女士過來講句話（Ms. Harvey, please ~ say a few words.），因此答案是 (B)。

換句話說
say a few words 說幾句話 → Make a speech 演說

字彙 applaud 拍手

89-91 🔊 加拿大發音

Questions 89-91 refer to the following excerpt from a meeting.

Over the past several months, 89/90we in the City Recreation Department have noticed that many of our public parks have had an unusually large amount of litter. 90In one way, this is to be expected. It is tourist season, after all. Still, having empty bags and bottles on the ground makes our parks unattractive to visitors. We need to come up with solutions. 91One idea I have is to conduct an advertising campaign that informs people about the importance of keeping our parks clean. We could put up posters to remind people to properly dispose of waste. 91I was also thinking about running radio ads highlighting the importance of cleaning up litter. If anyone has other ideas, please feel free to suggest them now.

recreation 休養、娛樂　unusually 不尋常地　litter 垃圾
be to be expected 當然　after all 總之、終究
come up with 想出　conduct 進行　properly 適當地
dispose of 清除、處理　highlight 強調

翻譯 問題 89-91，請參考以下會議摘錄。
過去幾個月，89/90 我們都市遊憩部門發現許多公立公園

都有異常的大量垃圾。⁹⁰ 從某個層面來看這是理所當然的。畢竟，目前是旅遊旺季，但地上的空袋子和瓶子會導致公園根本無法吸引遊客，因此我們需要思考解決對策。⁹¹ 我的想法是舉辦宣傳活動，讓大家都知道維護公園整潔的重要性，我們也能貼海報提醒大家要適當處理垃圾。⁹¹ 我也有考慮透過廣播廣告強調清理垃圾的重要性，如果各位有其他想法，儘管告訴我一聲。

89 說話者問題

翻譯 說話者最可能是什麼人？
(A) 電臺主持人
(B) 市府職員
(C) 觀光導覽員
(D) 廣告負責人

解析 仔細聆聽短文中和身分、職業相關的用法「we in the City Recreation Department have noticed that many of our public parks have had an unusually large amount of litter」，說話者所在的都市遊憩部門發現許多公立公園都有異常的大量垃圾，從這句話可知道說話者是市政府的職員，所以答案是 (B)。

字彙 host 主持人　executive 負責人、經營者

90 意圖掌握問題

翻譯 說話者為何會說「畢竟，目前是旅遊旺季」？
(A) 為了表達公園附近有很多觀光巴士的原因
(B) 為了表達必須在特定日期前完成
(C) 為了說明公園很多垃圾的原因
(D) 為了建議舉辦促銷活動

解析 仔細聆聽和引用句 It is tourist season, after all 相關的部分，文中談到發現許多公立公園都有異常的大量垃圾，從某個層面來看這是理所當然的（we ~ have noticed that many of our public parks have had an unusually large amount of litter. In one way, this is to be expected.），因此答案是 (C)。

字彙 note 顯現、標示　certain 特定的

91 提議問題

翻譯 說話者提出何種意見？
(A) 分發垃圾袋
(B) 利用廣告
(C) 召募臨時職員
(D) 與清潔公司談談

解析 仔細聆聽短文中和提議相關的句子，說話者表示自己有一個想法，就是舉辦宣傳活動讓大家都知道維護公園整潔的重要性（One idea I have is to conduct an advertising campaign that informs people about the importance of keeping our parks clean.），接著又說也有考慮透過廣播廣告強調清理垃圾的重要性（I was also thinking about running radio ads highlighting the importance of cleaning up litter.），因此答案是 (B)。

字彙 hand out 分發　temporary 臨時的　speak to 與～談談

92-94 〔澳洲發音〕

Questions 92-94 refer to the following announcement.

As a reminder, a new overtime policy will be implemented on Friday. ⁹²All overtime will have to be approved in advance by a supervisor. If you have any questions, ⁹³speak with Rhonda Levy in human resources. She's covering for her supervisor, Brittany Jacobs, who's on leave. OK, let's turn to project schedules. The company wants to release the SDX Digital Camera in mid-July now, so ⁹⁴I need the marketing plan by June 10 instead of June 23. I know . . . we have only five people. ⁹⁴So, Sandra and Debbie, I'm going to assign some of your team members to this project, but I'll extend your team's deadlines in return.

reminder 提醒　overtime 超時的、加班　implement 施行
approve 核准　in advance 提前
cover for 頂替（工作崗位）　be on leave 休假中
assign 配定　extend 延長　in return 作為交換

翻譯 問題 92-94，請參考以下公告。
在此提醒一下，新的加班政策將於星期五實施，⁹² 所有加班都必須事前獲得主管同意。如果有任何疑問，⁹³ 請去和人資部的 Rhonda Levy 談，她目前暫時代理休假中的主管 Brittany Jacobs 的職務。好，接下來就來談專案日程吧，因為現在公司在 7 月中旬要推出 SDX 數位相機，⁹⁴ 6 月 10 日之前我就要行銷企劃，而不是 6 月 23 日。我知道……我們只有 5 個人而已，Sandra 和 Debbie，⁹⁴ 我會安排你們的幾名組員參與這項專案，但會以延長團隊的截止日來交換。

92 特定細節問題

翻譯 根據說話者，哪一件事須獲得批准？
(A) 放假
(B) 額外工作時間
(C) 產品設計
(D) 經營團隊的變更

解析 仔細聆聽和關鍵字 approved 有關的部分，文中談到所有加班都必須事前獲得主管的同意（All overtime will have to be approved in advance by a supervisor.），因此答案是 (B)。

換句話說
overtime 加班 → Additional work 額外工作

字彙 time off 休假、休息　work hours 工作時間

93 特定細節問題

翻譯 Brittany Jacobs 最可能是誰？
(A) 人事科職員
(B) 銷售員
(C) 攝影專家
(D) 教育訓練講師

解析 仔細聆聽短文中和 Brittany Jacobs 的身分、職業相關的用法，文中談到和人資部的 Rhonda Levy 談，她

目前暫時代理休假中的主管 Brittany Jacobs 的職務
（speak with Rhonda Levy in human resources. She's
covering for her supervisor, Brittany Jacobs），由此可
知 Brittany Jacobs 是人資部的職員，所以答案是 (A)。

換句話說
human resources 人資部 → personnel 人事科

字彙 photography 拍照、攝影術　expert 專家

94 意圖掌握問題

翻譯 說話者說「我們只有五個人而已」，他的意思是什麼？
(A) 重要的決定無法達成協議。
(B) 公司很快就會僱用更多職員。
(C) 想完成業務需要一些協助。
(D) 有幾名職員必須加班。

解析 仔細聆聽和引用句 we have only five people 相關的內
容，文中談到 6 月 10 日之前就要行銷企劃，而不是 6
月 23 日（I need the marketing plan by June 10 instead
of June 23），並說會安排幾名組員參與這項專案（So,
Sandra and Debbie, I'm going to assign some of your
team members to this project），由此可知是「想完成
業務需要一些協助」，所以答案是 (C)。

95-97 ᴬ 美國發音

**Questions 95-97 refer to the following telephone
message and price list.**

Mr. Harrison, 95this is Beth Williams calling from Viva
Rentals at the Dallas International Airport regarding
your inquiry. To respond to your first question, we're
open from 6 A.M. until 11 P.M. daily, so your 9 P.M.
arrival time won't be a problem. 96You also mentioned
that you would like to reserve a minivan because you
are traveling with four coworkers. Unfortunately, we
don't have any available for the date you arrive, but
we do have another type of vehicle that can seat five
people comfortably. I'll e-mail you some information
now. Once you've made your choice, 97please visit our
website to reserve your vehicle.

---
inquiry 詢問　respond 回答　arrival time 抵達時間
coworker 同事　seat （建築物、車輛等）收容、有～人的座位
comfortably 方便、舒適地

翻譯 95-97 號是與下列電話訊息和價目表有關的題目。
Harrison 先生，95 我是達拉斯國際機場 Viva Rentals 的
Beth Williams，就您的問題致電。針對您的第一個問
題，我們的營業時間是每天上午 6 點到下午 11 點，下
午 9 點抵達不會造成問題。96 您也提到自己是和另外 4
名同事一起行動，所以想要預約迷你廂型車。但很遺憾
的是，您抵達的日期已經沒有迷你廂型車了，不過有其
他可容納 5 個人的車種。我現在就把資料寄到您的電子
信箱，等您選好後就 97 請到我們的官網預約車輛。

Viva Rentals		
種類	容納人數	每日費用
跑車	**2** 名	**32 00** 美元
四門轎車	4 名	22 00 美元
96 SUV	6 名	28 00 美元
迷你廂型車	**8** 名	34 00 美元

95 目的問題

翻譯 說話者為何打電話？
(A) 為了確認預約
(B) 為了提供特價商品
(C) 為了回答幾個問題
(D) 為了提供商店的位置

解析 題目詢問打電話的用意，一定要仔細聽清楚對話剛開始
的部分。文中談到說話者是達拉斯國際機場 Viva Rentals
的 Beth Williams，是為了回答顧客的問題才打電話
的（this is Beth Williams calling from Viva Rentals ~
regarding your inquiry），由此可知是為了回答問題才打
電話的，因此答案是 (C)。

96 圖表題

翻譯 請看圖表，顧客最可能會選擇哪一種車型？
(A) 跑車
(B) 四門轎車
(C) SUV
(D) 迷你廂型車

解析 確認價格表後，仔細聆聽和關鍵詞 vehicle ~ choose
相關的內容，文中談到因為是和另外 4 名同事一起行
動，所以想要預約迷你廂型車，不過很遺憾的是，在
抵達的日期已經沒有迷你廂型車了，不過有其他可容
納 5 個人的車種（You also mentioned that you would
like to reserve a minivan ~. Unfortunately, we don't
have any available for the date you arrive, but we do
have another type of vehicle that can seat five people
comfortably.），由此可知顧客應該會選擇可容納 5 名以
上乘客的 SUV，所以答案是 (C)。

97 特定細節問題

翻譯 文中請顧客做什麼？
(A) 準時還車。
(B) 線上預約。
(C) 確認旅行日期。
(D) 親自交出表格。

解析 仔細聆聽和關鍵詞 instructed to do 相關的內容，文中談
到請到我們的官網預約車輛（please visit our website to
reserve your vehicle），因此答案是 (B)。

換句話說
visit ~ website to reserve 登入網站預約 →
Make an online booking 線上預約

字彙 return 交還　on time 準時　verify 確認　in person 親自

Questions 98-100 refer to the following broadcast and map.

> In local business news, ⁹⁸Western Development announced that it took over its former rival, Bedford Properties. Jill Myers, president of Western Development, said that the acquisition will provide her company with the resources needed to launch several new developments. ⁹⁹The most significant of these will be the building of a large shopping mall. Construction will begin on June 3. Moreover, Ms. Myers stated that Western Development is relocating to a larger office. ¹⁰⁰The company has rented a building on Oak Street next to City Hall to serve as its new headquarters. The transition is expected to be complete by May 25.

take over 接手　former 先前的　acquisition 收購
resource 資源、資產　launch 開始　significant 重要的
state 正式說明　rent 租借　serve 可作為（特別、特定的用途）使用
transition 轉移、移動、執行

翻譯 問題 98-100，請參考以下廣播和地圖。

這裡是地區經濟新聞，⁹⁸ Western Development 公司表示已收購先前的競爭對手 Bedford Properties 公司，Western Development 公司的董事長 Jill Myers 說此一收購能提供多項展開新開發案所需要的資源，⁹⁹ 當中最重要的是建設大型商場，工程將在 6 月 3 日開工。另外，Myers 女士說 Western Development 公司將會搬遷到更大的辦公室，¹⁰⁰ 公司租下市政府旁 Oak 街的建築物當作新的總公司使用，預計會在 5 月 25 日前完成搬遷。

	建築物 A		市立圖書館
¹⁰⁰ 建築物 B	市政府	Ocean 街	建築物 C
Oak 街			
百貨公司	建築物 D		地鐵站

98 主題問題

翻譯 廣播主要在談什麼事？
(A) 收購公司
(B) 購買建築物
(C) 活動場所
(D) 土地開發

解析 題目詢問廣播的主題，仔細聆聽短文前面的部分。內容談到 Western Development 公司表示已收購先前的競爭對手 Bedford Properties 公司（Western Development announced that it took over its former rival, Bedford Properties），因此是在談論收購公司的事，所以答案是 (A)。

換句話說
took over ~ former rival 收購先前的競爭業者 →
A corporate acquisition 收購公司

字彙 property 建築物、財產

99 之後將發生的事

翻譯 6 月 3 日會發生什麼事？
(A) 搬遷公司。
(B) 開始專案。
(C) 經營者將要退休。
(D) 辦公室會再次開門。

解析 仔細聆聽和關鍵詞 June 3 相關的內容，文中談到當中最重要的是建設大型商場，工程將在 6 月 3 日開工（The most significant of these[developments] will be the building of a large shopping mall. Construction will begin on June 3.），由此可知 6 月 3 日專案就會開始，所以答案是 (B)。

字彙 executive 經營者、決策者　retire 退休

100 圖表題

翻譯 請看圖表，Western Development 公司租下哪一個建築物？
(A) 建築物 A
(B) 建築物 B
(C) 建築物 C
(D) 建築物 D

解析 確認地圖資訊後，仔細聆聽有談到關鍵字 rent 的部分。內容談到公司租下市政府旁 Oak 街的建築物當作新的總公司使用（The company has rented a building on Oak Street next to City Hall to serve as its new headquarters.），由此可知 Western Development 公司租下了建築物 B，所以答案是 (B)。

PART 5

101 填入時態正確的動詞

解析 因為有代表過去時間的用語（recently），所以過去時態 (C) purchased 是正確答案。

翻譯 Sanders Industries 公司最近購入能讓生產量倍增的最尖端機器。

字彙 high-tech adj. 最尖端的　double v. 倍增　output n. 生產量

102 填入和動詞型態一致的主詞

解析 空格是主詞的位置，因此可成為主詞的代名詞 (A) 和 (B) 皆可能是答案，因為動詞（is pleased）是單數，所以代表單數的 (A) Each 是正確答案。(B) All 必須讓動詞和後面的名詞數量一致，所以必須和複數動詞一起使用。(C) Other 和 (D) Their own 是形容詞，不能放在名詞當主詞的位置。

翻譯 接受調查的每位職員對擴大退休的計劃感到很滿意。

字彙 survey v.（問卷）調查、檢驗　be pleased with 滿足於　expansion n. 擴大　retirement n. 退休

103 填入名詞

解析 可放在所有格（the train's）後面的是名詞，名詞 (D) departure 是正確答案。動詞 (A) 和 (C)、以及是動詞或

分詞的 (B) 無法放在名詞的位置。

翻譯 暴雪讓火車的出發時間延後 4 個小時以上。

字彙 heavy snowfall 暴雪　delay v. 延後、往後　depart v. 出發
departure n. 出發、離開

104 填入頻率副詞

解析 因為整句話必須是「因為該地區一整年都充滿觀光客，所以總是有滿滿的客人」的意思，(B) always（總是）是正確答案。(D) soon（即將）是待會將發生某件事或過了一會發生了某件事的情況下使用的時間副詞，因此不能當作答案。

翻譯 因為該地區一整年都充滿觀光客，所以 Shoreline 餐廳總是有滿滿的客人。

字彙 busy adj. 熙熙攘攘的、忙碌的　be filled with 充滿～
year-round adv. 全年地　exactly adv. 準確地

105 填入否定代名詞／形容詞

解析 空格是主詞的位置，因此必須放名詞，指示代名詞 (A)、(B)、(C) 都有可能是答案。整句話的意思必須是「大多數的新事業在 5 年內都會失敗，但有些則相當成功」，因此 (C) some（有些）是正確答案。使用 (A) any（任何）與 (B) these（這些）則會讓意思變不順，所以無法當作答案。

翻譯 大多數的新事業在 5 年內都會失敗，但有些則相當成功。

字彙 fail v. 失敗

106 選出動詞

解析 語境看來是「讓房仲評估房子」的意思，assess 的過去式 (C) assessed（評估）是正確答案。(A) perform 是「執行」、「實施」；(B) appear 是「出現」；(D) outline 是「描繪輪廓」。

翻譯 王小姐在出售她的房子前，先讓房仲評估房子。

字彙 real estate agent 房屋仲介　offer for sale 出售

107 分辨現在分詞與過去分詞

解析 被修飾的名詞（seats）和分詞是被動關係，意思是「預約座位」，因此過去分詞 (B) reserved 是正確答案。

翻譯 頒獎儀式上有為獲獎者的家人和同事預留 30 個座位。

字彙 recipient n. 接受者　coworker n. 同事
awards ceremony 頒獎儀式

108 填入祈使句的動詞

解析 這是介系詞片語（In order to ~ security）後面的句子沒有主詞的祈使句，因此當作祈使句必須使用的動詞原形 (A) include 是正確答案。

翻譯 為了維護帳號的安全，密碼至少要一個數字和字母。

字彙 maintain v. 維持、持續　account n. 帳號、帳戶
security n. 安全、警備

109 選出形容詞

解析 從語境來看意思是「Findera 建設公司為提高國際知名度，將越南住宅市場的快速成長視為機會」，(B) rapid（急速的、快速的）是正確答案。(A) best 是「最棒的」；(C) original 是「原來的」；(D) adverse 是「負面的、不利的」。

翻譯 Findera 建設公司為提高國際知名度，將越南住宅市場的快速成長視為機會。

字彙 take advantage of 把～當作機會　profile n. 認知度

110 分辨現在分詞與過去分詞

解析 被修飾的名詞（ending）和分詞是主動關係，意思是「非常開心的結局」，因此現在分詞 (C) thrilling 是正確答案。分辨 thrill 等情緒動詞的現在分詞和過去分詞時，主詞如果感受到情緒時就是過去分詞，主詞如果是情緒的原因就使用現在分詞。此時主詞（ending）是讓人開心的原因，所以必須使用現在分詞（thrilling）。

翻譯 很多評論家都稱讚導演 John Parker 讓其最新動作片有令人開心的結局。

字彙 critic n. 評論家　praise v. 稱讚　ending n. 結尾、結局
thriller n. 驚悚小說　thrill n. 顫動、刺激；v.（使）激動

111 填入時態和時間表現一致的動詞

解析 因為有表示未來的用語（The upcoming sale），所以 (D) will save 是正確答案。(A) 是複數動詞，所以無法成為答案。

翻譯 Westside Electronics 公司即將到來的折扣銷售將讓購物者節省大量購買電視的錢。

字彙 upcoming adj. 即將發生、這次的　a great deal of 許多的
save v. 節約、拯救

112 選出形容詞

解析 語境來看意思是「發現新電腦型號中有缺陷的零件後就將其召回了」，因此 (D) defective（有瑕疵的）是正確答案。(A) functional 是「實用性的、功能性的」；(B) adjustable 是「可調整的」；(C) portable 是「攜帶用的、容易移動的」。

翻譯 RubioTech 公司發現新電腦型號中有瑕疵的零件後就將其召回了。

字彙 recall v. 召回、記起　discover v. 查出　contain v. 包含、抑制
component n. 零件、要素

113 填入動名詞

解析 介系詞（Before）的受詞位置可放名詞 (A) 和 (B) 以及動名詞 (D)，把名詞（Carla Evans）當作受詞，可放在介系詞受詞位置的動名詞 (D) contacting 是正確答案。名詞前無法連接其他名詞，或是沒有介系詞，因此名詞 (A) 和 (B) 無法成為正確答案。

翻譯 在連絡 Carla Evans 安排面試日期之前，Harris 先生早已看過她履歷上的資料了。

字彙 schedule v. 安排行程　verify v. 確認、認證　résumé n. 履歷
contact n. 聯絡；v. 聯絡

114 填入 to 不定詞

解析 動詞 need 後面必須放 to 不定詞，(B) to register 是正確答案。動詞原形 (A)、動名詞 (C)、動詞或分詞 (D) 無法放在動詞 need 的後面。

翻譯 想參加會議的人至少要在 7 天前事先報名。

字彙 attend v. 參加　in advance 事先、提前　register v. 登錄

115 選出副詞

解析 從語境上來看是「訂單寄送到錯誤的地址」的意思，(D) accidentally（不小心、意外地）是正確答案。(A) generously 是「寬容地」；(B) mutually 是「互相、共通」；(C) productively 是「有生產力的」。

翻譯 TriGem Chemicals 公司承認誤將客戶的訂單寄送到錯誤的地址。

字彙 admit v. 承認、認同、自白

116 選出名詞

解析 語境上來看必須是「產品的運送必須依照契約條件在 3 天內完成」的意思，因此 (B) contract（契約）是正確答案。(A) figure 是「數值、人物」；(C) research 是「調查、研究」；(D) concept 是「概念、觀念」。

翻譯 產品的運送必須依照契約條件在 3 天內完成。

字彙 terms n. 條件、用語

117 填入介係詞

解析 因必須是「增加了 15%」的意思，所以 (D) by（表示程度或數量）是正確答案。

翻譯 XL550 平板電腦的銷售從推出新版本的運作系統後就增加了 15%。

字彙 Increase v. 增加　operating system 運作系統　release v. 上市

118 填入強調副詞

解析 比較級（higher）前面的空格必須放強調比較級的副詞，(B) much 是正確答案。(A) very 或 (D) so 修飾形容詞或副詞，無法強調比較級。(C) more 以「more + 原形」的形態呈現比較級，very 強調最高級時以「the + very +最高級」的形態使用。

翻譯 Ice River 國家公園 10 月的造訪人數遠遠高於前一個月。

字彙 previous adj. 先前的

119 完成動詞相關句子

解析 語境上來看必須是「公司管理階層的餐廳將變成職員休息室」的意思，和空格後面的介係詞 into 一起使用後變成「轉換為」的 (A) converted 是正確答案（convert A into B：A 轉換為 B）。(B) convince 是「使確信、說服」；(C) consent 是「同意」；(D) conceal 是「隱藏、隱匿」。

翻譯 公司管理階層的餐廳在改造期間將變成職員休息室。

字彙 executive adj. 管理職用的；n. 高層　cafeteria n. 自助餐廳
lounge n. 休息室　renovation n. 改造、補修

120 填入形容詞

解析 空格是 be 動詞（is）後面的主詞補語的位置，名詞 (A) 和 (B)、現在分詞 (C)、形容詞 (D) 四個選項都可能是答案。因為必須是「國家限制使用化石燃料的同時，能否繼續擴大經濟規模是有爭議的」的意思，因此正確答案是形容詞 (D) debatable（有爭議的）。單數名詞 (A) 必須和冠詞一起使用，複數名詞 (B) 無法和單數動詞 is 一起使用。就算使用動詞 debate 的現在分詞 (C) debating（有爭議的），主詞 It 就代表空格後面的「國家限制使用化石燃料的同時，能否繼續擴大經濟規模」（whether countries ~ fossil fuel use），因此 It 無法成為爭議的主體，所以無法成為正確答案。

翻譯 國家限制使用化石燃料的同時，能否繼續擴大經濟規模是有爭議的。

字彙 fossil fuel 化石燃料

121 選出副詞

解析 從語境上來看必須是「剛開始打算向海外擴張，但後來決定專注於提升國內的銷售量」的意思，因此 (C) initially（起初）是正確答案。(A) negatively 是「消極地」；(B) currently 是「現在」；(D) rarely 是「稀少」。

翻譯 Poole Automotive 公司剛開始打算向海外擴張，但後來決定專注於提升國內的銷售量。

字彙 expand v. 擴張　overseas adv. 國外　increase v. 增加
domestic adj. 國內的

122 填入介係詞

解析 因必須是「飯店之間」的意思，(D) among（在～之間）是正確答案。(A) before 是「在～之前」；(B) toward 是「朝向～」；(C) onto 是「向～之上」。

翻譯 每晚只需要 50 美元的 Warren 飯店在當地許多飯店間被視為特價旅館。

字彙 consider v. 把～當作、認為
bargain n. 特價品、便宜物品；v. 討價還價

123 選出形容詞

解析 從語境上來看應該是「有興趣更進一步瞭解公司福利制度的應徵者」的意思，(C) interested（有興趣的）是正確答案。

翻譯 有興趣更進一步瞭解公司福利制度的應徵者可以登入我們的網站。

字彙 find out 查出、發現　benefits package 福利制度
obsess v. 使～強迫　display v. 展示　stimulate v. 刺激

124 完成動詞相關句子

解析 整句話的意思應該是「為了區分公司最新型微波爐和

先前的型號」，和空格後的介系詞 from 一起使用，搭配後完成「區分」意思的 (D) differentiate 是正確答案（differentiate A from B：區分 A 和 B）。(A) concentrate 是「集中、專心」，和介系詞 on 一起使用（concentrate on：專注於）；(B) handle 是「處理」；(C) designate 是「指定」。

翻譯 為了區分公司最新型微波爐和先前的型號，Langford Appliances 公司展開了重大的行銷活動。

字彙 microwave n. 微波爐　launch v. 開始、上市
major adj. 重大的、重要的

125 選出名詞

解析 整句話的意思是「根據會員對中心區位置的偏好，挑選 Debran 中心做為開會的地點」，(B) preference（偏好、偏好度）是正確答案。(A) performance 是「成果、表演」；(C) collection 是「收集、一群」；(D) exception 是「例外、反對」。

翻譯 零售商協會根據會員對中心區位置的偏好，挑選 Debran 中心做為開會的地點。

字彙 association n. 協會、聯盟　based on 根據～
central adj. 中央（區）的

126 填入副詞子句連接詞

解析 這句話是完整的子句，具備了必要的元素（Mr. Cooper made appointments），____he ~ job 必須視為是懸垂修飾語。這是有動詞（had decided）的子句，可引導它的副詞子句連接詞 (A) Once（一～就～）是正確答案。介系詞 (B)、副詞 (C) 和 (D) 無法引導懸垂修飾語。

翻譯 一決定要找新工作，Cooper 先生就和幾間招聘事務所約好要見面。

字彙 make an appointment with 和～約定
recruitment agency 招聘顧問

127 填入關係詞

解析 這句話是完整的句子，具備了主詞（Pacer Industries）、動詞（purchased）、受詞（a factory），____ produces ~ components 必須視為是懸垂修飾語，因此選項中可引導懸垂修飾語的關係詞 (B) that 是正確答案。此一懸垂修飾語是關係子句，從後面修飾前面的名詞（a factory）。代名詞 (A) it 無法引導懸垂修飾語，名詞子句連接詞 (C) what 和 (D) whether 是引導主詞、受詞、補語之名詞子句的連接詞，因此無法放在關係詞的位置。

翻譯 Pacer Industries 公司收購了在中國境內生產各種電子零件的工廠。

字彙 a wide range of 各式各樣的　electronic component 電子零件

128 填入比較級

解析 因為必須是「只要能縮短工時」的意思，比較級 (B) shorter 是正確答案。(A) 和動詞 (C) 無法修飾名詞（hours），「最高級 + 名詞」前面主要必須是 the 或是所有格，因此 (D) 無法成為答案。

翻譯 最近的民意調查顯示，大部分的上班族只要能縮短工

時，就會願意接受減薪。

字彙 poll n. 民意調查、投票　suggest v. 啟示、暗示
take a pay cut 接受減薪　shortly adv. 不久　shorten v. 縮短

129 填入關係代名詞

解析 先行詞（anyone）是人物，要填入空格的關係代名詞必須在關係子句（____stays there ~ month）中扮演主詞的作用。因此主格人物關係代名詞 (A) who 是正確答案。

翻譯 只要每個月能住 4 晚以上，Paxton 飯店就會給予 20% 的折扣。

130 選出動詞

解析 因為語境上必須是「捐款提供國立古代美術館財務上的支援」，所以答案是 (C) provide（提供）。(A) notify 是「通知」；(B) interpret 是「解析、說明」；(D) confront 是「對抗」。

翻譯 Lumour 公司的捐款提供國立古代美術館財務上的支援。

字彙 donation n. 捐款、捐贈　funding n. 財務支援、資金
ancient adj. 古代的

PART 6

問題 131-134，請參考以下新聞。

是連鎖店呢？還是選擇自營業呢？

4 月 11 日——創業者面臨一個困難的決定，該開加盟店呢？還是當自營業者呢？[131] 兩種都各有優點和缺點，加盟店的老闆不需要花費幾年的時間去提升知名度，而是由總公司給予支援；[132] 另一方面，自營業者有更多自由能選擇產品，也能決定產品的價格。必須考慮的另一個要素是初期的投資，[133] 雖然經營加盟店只需要初期的小額投資金，但部分收益也必須要交給總公司。[134] 反之，自營業老闆雖然創業費用較高，但卻能擁有所有的收入。

---

franchise n. 加盟店　entrepreneur n. 創業者
face v. 面臨、正視　brand recognition 品牌認知度
headquarters n. 總公司　set v. 決定　initial adj. 初期的
in contrast 相反地

---

131 選出正確的句子

翻譯 (A) 大部分的人都偏好去國際連鎖店購物。
(B) 許多業者在營業的第一年都虧損。
(C) 市面上的幾個品牌價格都相當昂貴。
(D) 兩個選擇都有優點和缺點。

解析 題目是要選出填入空格的正確句子，必須掌握前後文的語境或整體的語境。前面的句子談到創業者面臨一個困難的決定，該開加盟店呢？還是當自營業者呢？（A difficult decision that an entrepreneur faces is whether to open a franchise or an independent business.），空格後面則在說明加盟店和自營業者的優點和缺點，由此可知空格應該填入兩個選項都有優點和缺點，所以答案是 (D)。

字彙 lose money 虧損　operation n. 營業、運用
on the market 市面上的　significantly adv. 相當地、顯著地
overpriced adj. 過於昂貴的

132 填入人稱代名詞

解析 名詞（prices）前面是可像形容詞一樣使用的人稱代名詞是所有格，因此 (D) their（它們的）是正確答案。

133 填入副詞子句連接詞

解析 這個句子是具備必備要素（some profits ~ headquarters）的完整子句，____ running a franchise ~ investment 必須視為是懸垂修飾語。此一懸垂修飾語是具備動詞（requires）的句子，可引導它的副詞子句連接詞 (B) 和 (C) 皆有可能是答案。因為必須是「雖然經營加盟店只需要初期的小額投資金，但部分收益也必須要交給總公司」的意思，所以正確答案是 (C) Although（儘管~但是）。

字彙 except prep. 不包含

134 選出動詞　掌握語境

解析 從語境來看意思是「反之，自營業老闆能_____所有的收入」，所有的選項都可能是答案。光憑空格的句子無法選出正確答案，必須掌握前後文或整體的語境，前面的句子談到經營加盟店只需要初期的小額投資金，但部分收益也必須要交給總公司（some profits must be paid to the corporate headquarters），由此可知這句話是自營業老闆能擁有所有的收入，所以 (D) keep（自己保有）是正確答案。

字彙 estimate v. 推算、評價　waste v. 浪費　eliminate v. 消除、移除

問題 135-138，請參考以下公告。

> 致全體顧客：
>
> 能告知我們 Hamby-Russ 公司和 Carmona 公司合併的消息，本人覺得很開心。135 本月初，我們位於西雅圖的總公司已經以 Hamby-Russ & Carmona 的名義開始運作。
>
> 136 此一合併規劃了近 10 個月。這段期間兩家公司為了制定可提供購物者最佳娛樂產品的戰略而進行了大規模的協商，關於公司的組織結構，目前正在調整當中，137 但我們會維持目前所有的職員。如此一來各位就能和先前的銷售員一起處理工作，我們的電話也不會變更，138 如果有任何問題，不要猶豫，立刻來電 555-3438 聯絡我們行政組。
>
> ---
> merge v. 合併　operate v. 營運　under the name 以~的名義
> negotiate v. 協商　extensively adv. 廣泛地
> recreational adj. 娛樂的、心情轉換的
> as for 就~而言　organizational structure 組織結構
> adjust v. 調整　original adj. 既有的、原來的
> salesperson n. 銷售員　administrative adj. 行政的

135 填入介系詞

解析 想要完成「這個月初」的意思，就必須是 At the start of the month，因此 (B) At（在~）是正確答案，(A) While 是副詞子句連接詞，引導主詞和動詞所在的句子。

136 選出正確的句子

翻譯 (A) 我們決定完全停止營運是最好的方法。
(B) 春季購物季是我們一年當中最忙碌的時期。
(C) 此一合併規劃了 10 個月。
(D) 協議完成就會發表。

解析 題目詢問填入空格的正確句子，必須掌握前後文或整體的語境。前面談到 Hamby-Russ 公司和 Carmona 公司合併，後面談到這段期間兩家公司為了制定可提供購物者最佳娛樂產品的戰略而進行了大規模的協商（During this time, both companies negotiated extensively to develop a strategy for providing shoppers with the best recreational products available.），由此可知空格處應該填入此一合併規劃了近 10 個月，所以答案是 (C)。

字彙 cease v. 中斷　entirely adv. 完全　agreement n. 協議
finalize v. 結束

137 選出動詞　掌握前後文的語境

解析 從語境上來看，意思是「現有的全體職員將會____」，所有選項都可能是正確答案，單從語境上來看，憑空格中的句子無法選出正確答案，必須掌握前後文或整體的語境。文中談到因此可以和先前的銷售員一起處理工作（As a result, you will be able to work with the same salespeople that you had before.），由此可知是現有的全體職員都還會留著，所以答案是 (A) maintain（維持）。

字彙 transfer v. 移動、轉移　replace v. 更換、代替
dismiss v. 解僱、解散

138 助動詞後面填入動詞原形

解析 助動詞（Do）之後必須是動詞原形 (A) 或是 (B)，因為必須是具備主動意思的「不要猶豫，要立刻聯絡」，所以主動語態 (A) hesitate 是正確答案。

字彙 hesitate v. 猶豫、遲疑

問題 139-142，請參考以下顧客後記。

> 139 為了近期去邁阿密的旅行，我計劃透過 EZ Auto 公司租車，因為這間公司的每天租車的費用比其他競爭公司更低，所以我才會選擇這間公司。不過，當我抵達機場附近的 EZ Auto 公司時，我卻無法使用原本預約的 SUV，140 很明顯對方弄錯日期了，因為那邊還有貨車，於是我便拜託對方讓我租貨車。141 不過，對方通知我更大的車輛必須支付全額的費用，那個價格比 SUV 的全額更高。EZ Auto 的職員為了彌補自己的失誤，應該要提供免費升級服務才對，142 所以我決定以後不會再使用這間公司的服務。
>
> ---
> recent adj. 最近的　arrange v. 計劃、整理
> competitor n. 競爭公司　unavailable adj. 無法使用的
> lot n. 腹地　compensate v. 補償

139 選出名詞　掌握整體語境

解析 因為語境上是「計劃＿＿＿車輛」，所有選項都有可能是答案，只憑空格的句子無法選出正確答案，必須掌握前後文或整體的語境。文中談到該公司每天的租車費用更低（lower daily rates for travelers），後面的部分則說無法使用預約的 SUV（the SUV I had reserved was unavailable），由此可知已經計劃租車了，所以答案是 (B) rental（租借）。

字彙 repair n. 修理、補修　inspection n. 檢查　delivery n. 運送

140 選出正確的句子

翻譯 (A) 他們沒有我的導航系統申請紀錄。
(B) 很遺憾的是，沒有其他車輛。
(C) 看來日期發生錯誤了。
(D) 我已經要求退款了。

解析 題目選出填入空格的正確句子，必須掌握前後文或整體的語境。前面談到自己無法預約的 SUV（the SUV I had reserved was unavailable），由此可知空格應該填入無法使用預約車輛的原因，也就是日期發生錯誤，所以 (C) 是正確答案。後面的句子談到因為那邊還有貨車，於是我便拜託對方讓我租貨車（As there was a truck on the lot, I asked to rent it instead.），所以 (B) 無法成為答案。

字彙 apparently adv. 看來、據～所知

141 填入符合時態的動詞

解析 因為獨立子句沒有動詞，(A)、(B)、(D) 都有可能是答案，主詞（I）和動詞（inform）具備「我收到通知」的被動意思，所以被動式的動詞 (A) was informed 是正確答案。Inform 是有兩個受詞的動詞，此一句子是在主動態變成被動態，間接受詞（I）變成主詞，直接受詞（that ~ vehicle）留在動詞的後面。

字彙 inform v. 通知、告知

142 填入 to 不定詞

解析 動詞 decide（have decided）後面必須放 to 不定詞，所以 (A) to use 是正確答案。

問題 143-146，請參考以下備忘錄。

寄件人：Diane Langston，營業部長
收件人：全體員工
日期：9 月 23 日
主旨：秋季馬拉松街道封閉

年度 Renfield 秋季馬拉松將於本星期五舉行。[143] 活動期間附近部分的街道會封閉，請多加留意。[144] Sandy Brook 路和我們建築物旁的停車場上午 9 點至下午 2 點無法進入。因此，如果各位平常都是開車上班，就必須想想其他方案。[145] 舉例來說，29 號街有各位可使用的停車場。從辦公室步行 5 分鐘的距離，各位也能搭乘行駛 Davis 路的公車，那邊距離這裡兩個街區，公車路線可在網路上查詢。[146] 如果需要任何幫助，只要告訴我就行了。

take place 舉行、發生　garage n. 停車場、車庫
normally adv. 平常　assistance n. 幫助

143 填入可修飾其他名詞的名詞

解析 因為是複合名詞「鄰近街道」的意思，所以變成複合名詞的 (C) neighborhood 是正確答案。

字彙 neighborly adj. 具備社交性的、親切的
neighbor n. 鄰居、周圍的人
neighborliness n. 像鄰居的、睦鄰友好

144 選出形容詞　掌握前後文的語境

解析 整句話是「Sandy Brook 路和我們建築物旁的停車場上午 9 點至下午 2 點＿＿＿」，(A) safe（安全的）和 (C) inaccessible（無法進入的）都有可能是答案。光憑空格的句子無法找出正確答案，必須掌握前後文或整體的語境。前面的句子談到活動期間附近部分的街道會封閉，請多加留意（Be aware that some ~ streets may be closed during the event.），後面則談到如果各位平常都是開車上班，就必須想想其他方案（So if you normally drive to work, you should make other plans.），由此可知 Sandy Brook 路和建築物旁的停車場上午 9 點至下午 2 點無法進入，所以答案是形容詞 (C) inaccessible。

字彙 vulnerable adj. 脆弱的、軟弱的　acceptable adj. 可容許的

145 選出正確的句子

翻譯 (A) 如果各位能遠距工作，我推薦那樣做。
(B) 所幸我們只是短暫遇到不便而已，
(C) 辦公室在馬拉松結束後就會開門。
(D) 舉例來說，29 號街有各位能使用的停車場。

解析 題目選出填入空格的正確句子，必須掌握前後文或是整體的語境。前面句子談到如果各位平常都是開車上班，就必須想想其他方案（So if you normally drive to work, you should make other plans.），後面的句子說這個地方從辦公室步行 5 分鐘就能到（It is only a five-minute walk from the office.），由此可知空格必須填入「舉例來說，29 號街有各位能使用的停車場」，所以答案是 (D)。

字彙 telecommute v. 遠距辦公

146 沒有 if 的假設語氣

解析 因為必須是「如果需要任何幫助，只要告訴我就行了」，(B) Should you need 是正確答案。Should + 主詞 + 動詞原形意思是「如果是～的話」，這是從假設未來 If + 主詞 + should + 動詞原形中省略 If，由主詞和助動詞（should）形成的倒裝。假設語氣未來句子中省略 If 時，形成 Should + 主詞 + 動詞原形，主詞 + will（can, may, should）+ 動詞原形的形態。

PART 7

問題 147-148，請參考以下線上後記。

---

https://www.oakridge.com/customerreviews

顧客名稱：Ruth Bell

評分：★

日期：4 月 3 日

產品：Lucas 咖啡桌

2 月 10 日我在 Oakridge Furniture 公司訂購了咖啡桌，整體來說我對這個傢俱很滿意，設計相當棒，具備現代風，147-C 桌子非常適合我的新大樓的客廳，147-A 組裝也相當簡單。148 我之所以會從可能的五顆星中只給這間公司一顆星，是因為我訂購的物品抵達的時間比預期的還要更久。原本被告知 3 月 8 日會運送，但一直等到 3 月 26 日才送到我家，好像是公司的運送系統出現技術性錯誤，導致桌子送錯地址。照理說該公司應該要向我道歉或給予折扣，但我卻沒有收到任何回應，所以我不會再購買 Oakridge Furniture 公司的物品了。

---

order v. 訂購；n. 訂購品　overall adv. 全面地
assemble v. 組合　originally adv. 原來
drop off 運送（物品）　distribution n. 運送、流通
result in 變成（某種結果）

147 Not/True 題型

關於 Bell 女士的描述提到什麼？

(A) 沒辦法組裝桌子。

(B) 將會退還一件傢俱。

(C) 搬到新的居住地了。

(D) 正在尋找新的大樓。

解析 這是要從短文中找出和關鍵詞 Ms. Bell 相關的內容，並且和選項對照的 Not/True 題型。(A) 文中談到組裝也相當簡單（It was also very easy to assemble.），因此和短文內容不符。(B) 短文中沒有談到此一內容。(C) 文中談到桌子的尺寸和新大樓的客廳相當搭（the table is just the right size for the living room of my new apartment），由此可知 Bell 女士搬家了，與短文內容相符，所以答案是 (C)。(D) 是短文中沒談到的內容。

字彙 residence n. 居住地、住宅

148 5W1H 問題

Bell 女士為何給該公司較差的評論？

(A) 物品已經沒有庫存。

(B) 道歉信太晚寄出了。

(C) 商品在運送過程中毀損了。

(D) 沒有依照預定日期送到。

解析 這是在詢問 Bell 女士為什麼（Why）給該公司負評的 5W1H 問題，與問題的關鍵詞 a poor review 有關，文中談到 Bell 女士之所以只有給一顆星，（The reason that I am giving this company only one star out of a possible five is that my order took much longer than expected to arrive.），是因為訂購的物品比預期還要更久才送到，所以答案是 (D)。

換句話說
a poor review 負評 → only one star out of a possible five 五顆星中只有一顆星
took much longer than expected to arrive 送達的時間比預期的還要更晚 → did not arrive on schedule 沒有在預定時間內抵達

字彙 be in stock 有庫存　package n. 商品、包裹
in transit 運送途中　on schedule 依照預定

問題 149-150，請參考以下對話。

Mia Heilig　　　　　　　　　　　　　[下午 2 點 37 分]
您好，Chantal，我的班機因為氣候不佳而誤點了，149-A 所以我不清楚自己何時能抵達蒙特婁。

Chantal Lacroix　　　　　　　　　　　[下午 2 點 39 分]
誤點多久呢？150 不過您仍是今晚就會到，對吧？

Mia Heilig　　　　　　　　　　　　　[下午 2 點 45 分]
看起來不太妙，因為我的出發時間延後 3 個小時，149-C/150 大概無法趕上從丹佛轉搭的班機吧，大概得搭乘下一班機，150 但我還不清楚時間。

Chantal Lacroix　　　　　　　　　　　[下午 2 點 47 分]
真是遺憾，149-D 總之抵達丹佛時請告訴我更新的抵達時間，屆時我會立刻與駕駛安排必要的準備。

---

delay v. 延誤；n. 誤點　departure time 出發時間
push back（時間等）延後　mean v. 結果是、意味著
connecting flight 轉機航班　available adj. 可使用的
arrival time 抵達時間　arrangement n. 準備

149 Not/True 題型

關於 Heilig 女士的描述哪一個是正確的？

(A) 已經從蒙特婁出發了。

(B) 她會去載 Lacroix 女士。

(C) 她將搭乘多個航班。

(D) 她在丹佛聯絡 Lacroix 女士了。

解析 這是要從短文中找出與關鍵詞 Ms. Heilig 相關的內容，並且和選項對照的 Not/True 題型。(A) 文中談到不清楚何時會抵達蒙特婁（I'm not sure when I'll be arriving in Montreal (2:37 P.M.)），因此和短文內容不符。(B) 這是短文中沒有談到的內容。(C) 因文中談到必須要轉機（I'll miss my connecting flight in Denver. I'll have to get on the next available one (2:45 P.M.)），和短文的內容相符，所以答案是 (C)。(D) Lacroix 女士請 Heilig 女士抵達丹佛時聯絡自己（call me when you get to Denver (2:47 P.M.)），因此和短文內容不符。

字彙 pick up 用車接送　multiple adj. 多個、多數的

150 意圖掌握問題

下午 2 點 45 分，Heilig 女士說「It's not looking good」，她的意思最可能是什麼？

(A) 無法換票。

(B) 可能無法退款。

(C) 無法聯絡司機。

(D) 今天晚上可能無法抵達。

解析 這是在詢問 Heilig 女士意圖的題目，確認和引用句（It's not looking good）相關的前後文語境。

Lacroix 女士詢問 Heilig 女士今天晚上是否仍然能抵達（You'll still be getting here tonight, right?(2:39 P.M.)），Heilig 女士回答看起來看起來不太妙（It's not looking good），後來又說：「大概無法趕上從丹佛轉搭的班機吧，大概得搭乘下一班機，但我還不清楚時間」（I'll miss my connecting flight in Denver. I'll have to get on the next available one, but I don't know when that will be.(2:45 P.M.)），由此可知 Heilig 女士今晚無法抵達，所以答案是 (D)。

字彙 exchange v. 交換　refund n. 退款

問題 151-152，請參考以下廣告。

Video Marketing 公司
36575 阿拉巴馬州，莫比爾
Highland 街 372 號
555-8230

151-C Video Marketing 公司為您的業務提供各種影片製作服務，包含提供創意、劇本製作、選角、導演、拍攝、編輯等。

我們會幫所有類型和規模的團體製作影片，如果需要行銷活動、產品說明會或教育研討會的影片，請與我們聯絡。我們會聘請熟悉影片製作過程各個階段的專家。當然我們的拍攝設備和舞臺道具都是最佳的品質。

152 11 月 1 日到 12 月 31 日為止，我們將會為小型業主提供冬季特別優惠，為企業製作 30 秒的影片，只需要 2,000 美元，之後我們的線上行銷團隊會提供如何在社交媒體網站上宣傳影片的訣竅。如此一來您的廣告將會被廣大觀眾看到，不需要支付龐大的費用購買電視臺的播出時間。想要獲得此一優惠或取得更多關於我們公司的資訊，請到我們的官網 www.videomarketingenterprise.com。

---

generation n. 產出、發生　script n. 腳本　directing n. 演出
filming n. 攝影　editing n. 編輯
product demonstration 產品說明會　professional n. 專家
knowledgeable adj. 有見識的　not to mention 更不用說
props n. 道具　promote v. 宣傳　audience n. 觀眾
costly adv. 費用大的　airtime n. 播出時間
television network 廣播公司　in general 整體來說

---

151 Not/True 題型
關於 Video Marketing 公司，暗指了什麼事？
(A) 只有少數幾名職員。
(B) 舉辦電影製作者的研討會。
(C) 提供各種服務。
(D) 販售影片製作裝備。

解析 這是從短文中找出和關鍵詞 Video Marketing Enterprise 相關的內容，然後和選項對照的 Not/True 題型。(A) 和 (B) 是短文中沒談到的內容。(C) 文中談到「Video Marketing 公司為您的業務提供各種影片製作服務，包含提供創意、劇本製作、選角、導演、拍攝、編輯等」（At Video Marketing Enterprise, we offer various video production services for your business, including idea generation, script writing, casting, directing, filming, and editing.），和短文內容相符，所以答案是 (C)。(D)

短文中沒有談到相關的內容。

字彙 filmmaker n. 電影製作者　a wide range of 各式各樣的

152 5W1H 問題
11 月 1 日到 12 月 31 日會發生什麼事？
(A) 網頁將會更新。
(B) 公司將要擴大。
(C) 將要舉辦行銷活動。
(D) 社群媒體平臺將要上市。

解析 這是在詢問 11 月 1 日到 12 月 31 日會發生什麼（What）事的 5W1H 問題，與問題的關鍵句 from November 1 to December 31 有關，文中談到 11 月 1 日到 12 月 31 日為止，我們將會為小型業主提供冬季特別優惠（From November 1 to December 31, we are offering a special winter deal for small business owners.），因此答案是 (C)。
換句話說
offering a special ~ deal 提供特別的折扣 →
A promotion will be held 舉辦促銷活動

字彙 expand v. 擴張　promotion n. 促銷活動、宣傳　launch v. 上市

問題 153-154，請參考以下電子郵件。

收件人：全體講師
寄件人：Adam Fitzpatrick
　　　　<afitzpatrick@hardingbusinessinstitute.com>
主旨：最新資訊
153 日期：6 月 17 日

大家好，

如各位所知，153 昨天的颱風導致 Farley 大樓的地下室淹水，因此我們在地下室進行的課程全都暫時搬到隔壁大樓 Sherman 中心，下面有臨時教室的分配表。

課程	講師	教室
吸引投資者加入您的新公司	Mark Helling	200
品牌商品化 101	Jesse Weiner	205
高級財務會計	Helen Boucher	207
社群媒體行銷	Megan Davis	210

各位的上課時間一樣，學生們今天下午將會收到電子郵件通知相關的情況，Farley 大樓的管理者 154 Alfred King 說會在接下來 3 天內把淹水的房間全都清掃乾淨和補修，並表示下星期一就能再次啟用。

若是任何疑問請聯絡我。

Adam Fitzpatrick 敬上
校長，Harding 商務學院

---

basement n. 地下室　flood v. 淹水　typhoon n. 颱風
temporarily adv. 臨時　meet v. 開啟（課程等）、聚集
assignment n. 配定　advanced adj. 高級的、先進的
financial accounting 財務會計　notify v. 通知
clean out 清除乾淨　available adj. 可使用的

153 5W1H 問題

根據備忘錄來看，6 月 16 日發生了什麼事？

(A) 發生颱風了。

(B) 有幾堂課被取消了。

(C) 一些考試評分了。

(D) 有一名講師放假了。

解析 這是詢問 6 月 16 日會發生什麼（what）事情的 5W1H 問題，與問題的關鍵字 June 16 有關，從 Date: June 17 可知道製作備忘錄的日期是 6 月 17 日，文中談到昨天的颱風（yesterday's typhoon），由此可知 6 月 16 日發生了颱風，所以答案是 (A)。

字彙 storm n. 暴風　correct v. 評分、訂正

154 5W1H 問題

King 先生對 Fitzpatrick 先生說了什麼？

(A) Sherman 中心的 2 樓開放中。

(B) 行銷相關課程可依照計劃舉行。

(C) 修復淹水造成的損害太過昂貴無法進行。

(D) Farley 大樓的地下室下星期就能使用。

解析 這是詢問 King 先生對 Fitzpatrick 先生說了什麼（What）的 5W1H 問題，與問題的關鍵句 Mr. King tell Mr. Fitzpatrick 有關，King 先生告訴備忘錄製作者 Fitzpatrick 先生淹水的房間下星期一可再次使用（Alfred King ~ informed me that the flooded rooms ~ will be available for use again next Monday.），因此答案是 (D)。

字彙 as scheduled 按照計劃　water damage 水損害

問題 155-157，請參考以下公告。

公告

[155] 支持 Thomas Anderson 市長再生回收計劃的 Bristo 市議會同意今年底前會和 Sanders Waste Management 公司結束合約，屆時所有的廢棄物都由 Perry Waste and Recycling 公司負責處理。

[156-A] 此一再生回收的結果是，Bristo 的居民從 1 月 1 日開始將要做垃圾分類。金屬、玻璃、紙張將被放入綠色垃圾桶，一般垃圾要放在黑色垃圾桶。新垃圾桶這星期將和詳細的小手冊一起送出，[157] 建議居民仔細檢查印刷好的指南書。

---

mayor n. 市長　initiative n. 計劃　conclude v. 結束、完成
contract n. 契約　separate v. 使～分離　bin n. 垃圾桶
along with 和～在一起　pamphlet n. 小冊子

155 目的問題

公告的目的是什麼？

(A) 為了要求議會開會

(B) 為了表明對專案的支持

(C) 為了告知變更服務

(D) 為了報告方案的成功

解析 題目詢問公告目的，文中談到 Bristo 市議會同意今年底前會和 Sanders Waste Management 公司結束合約，屆時所有的廢棄物都由 Perry Waste and Recycling 公司負責處理（The Bristol City Council ~ has agreed to conclude its contract with Sanders Waste Management by the end of the year. From that point on, all waste will be handled by Perry Waste and Recycling.），因此答案是 (C)。

字彙 call for 要求　report v. 報告

156 Not/True 題型

關於回收計劃有談到什麼？

(A) 將在明年施行。

(B) 由前市長提議。

(C) 將由議會議員管理。

(D) 更大型計劃的一部分。

解析 這是在短文中找出和關鍵詞 recycling initiative 有關的內容，然後和選項對照的 Not/True 題型。(A) 文中談到此一再生回收的結果是，Bristo 的居民從 1 月 1 日開始將要做垃圾分類（As a result of this recycling initiative, Bristol residents will be asked to separate their trash beginning January 1.），和短文中的內容相符，因此正確答案是 (A)。(B)、(C)、(D) 是短文中沒有談到的內容。

字彙 take effect 施行

157 5W1H 問題

Bristol 的居民被鼓勵做什麼？

(A) 更常丟垃圾。

(B) 只用一種垃圾桶。

(C) 參加市議會的會議。

(D) 閱讀文件。

解析 這是在詢問 Bristol 居民被鼓勵做什麼（What）的 5W1H 問題，和關鍵句 Bristol residents encouraged to do 有關，文中談到建議居民仔細檢查印刷好的指南書（Residents are advised to review the printed guidelines carefully），因此答案是 (D)。

換句話說
are ~ encouraged 被鼓勵 → are advised 被建議
review the printed guidelines 檢討印刷的指南書 →
Read a document 閱讀文件

字彙 dispose of 丟棄、處分

問題 158-161，請參考以下新聞。

《On the Loose Again》預計將在 Goldwin 戲院上映

[158-A/C/160-A] 人氣喜劇《On the Loose》的續集《On the Loose Again》將於 5 月 16 日在 Goldwin 劇院上映，[158-C] 兩部電影的主角 Max Walter 和 Elena Marconi 都會參加，在電影上映前會先簡單拍照。[159] 戲院開放時就會進行紅毯活動，電影在 1 個小時後上映，時間是 6 點到 8 點。電影結束後，會有全體演員和製作團隊的問題時間，最後在 8 點 30 分時舉辦簽名會。

《On the Loose Again》的劇情銜接前一部電影的結尾，描述一名逃犯與妻子嘗試避開警察，並在美國南部展開逃亡行動。[160-A/B] 製作包括《Above Ground》和《Special

➡

Investigation》在內等許多人氣電視影集的導演 Jamie Moya [160-A] 接替原著電影導演 Richard Weber，因為第一部電影票房不錯，預計《On the Loose Again》也會吸引相當多的觀眾。[161] 想要試映會門票的人應至 www.goldwintheater.com/tickets 或是來電 555-3716 早早事先購買。

---

premiere v. 開封；n. 首映　sequel to ～的續集　star n. 主演
be in attendance 參加　photo shoot 拍攝照片
question-and-answer session 問答時間　cast n. 全體演員
feature v. 描繪（特徵）、特別包含　escaped adj. 逃出的
criminal n. 犯罪者　numerous adj. 很多的　replace v. 接替、代替
draw v. 拖拉　obtain v. 得到、獲得　well adv. 相當地、頗為
in advance 事前、事先

---

158 Not/True 題型

關於《On the Loose Again》的描述，哪一個正確？
(A) 是該系列的第三部電影。
(B) 特別受青少年歡迎。
(C) 由和第一部電影相同的演員主演。
(D) 獲得肯定的評價。

解析　這是從短文中找出和關鍵詞 On the Loose Again 相關的內容，並且和選項對照的 Not/True 題型。(A) 文中談到《On the Loose Again》是《On the Loose》的續集（On the Loose Again, the sequel to the popular comedy On the Loose），和短文內容不符。(B) 短文中沒有談到此一內容。(C) 文中談到《On the Loose》和續集《On the Loose Again》兩部電影的主角是 Max Walter 和 Elena Marconi（On the Loose Again, the sequel to the popular comedy On the Loose）、（The stars of both films—Max Walter and Elena Marconi—），由此可知和第一部是相同的演員，和短文內容相符，所以 (C) 是正確答案。(D) 短文中沒有談到此一內容。

字彙　review n. 評價

159 找出同義詞

第 1 段第 6 行的單字「shown」在意思上和＿＿最相近。
(A) 露出的
(B) 報告的
(C) 執行的
(D) 上映的

解析　在包含 shown 的句子「The red carpet event will begin as soon as the theater opens, and the film will be shown one hour later, from 6 P.M. to 8 P.M.」中，shown 的意思是「上映的」，所以答案是 (D)。

160 Not/True 題型

關於 Moya 先生有何描述？
(A) 他是《On the Loose》的導演。
(B) 以電視作品聞名。
(C) 他是 Marconi 女士的朋友。
(D) 他寫了《On the Loose Again》的劇本。

解析　這是從短文中找出和關鍵詞 Mr. Moya 相關的內容，然後

和選項對照的 Not/True 題型。(A)「On the Loose Again, the sequel to ~ On the Loose」和「Director Jamie Moya ~ replaced Richard Weber, the director of the original movie.」中談到 Jamie Moya 接替原著電影《On the Loose》之導演 Richard Weber，因此和短文內容不符。(B)「Director Jamie Moya, who has also produced numerous popular television series」中談到導演 Jamie Moya 製作了許多受歡迎的電視影集，和短文中的內容一致，所以正確答案是 (B)。(C) 和 (D) 是短文中沒有談到的內容。

換句話說
has ~ produced numerous popular television series 製作了許多受歡迎的電視影集 → is known for ~ work in television 以電視作品聞名

字彙　be known for 因～而聞名　script n. 腳本

161 5W1H 問題

報導建議大家做什麼？
(A) 下午 8 點前進戲院。
(B) 早點購票。
(C) 參加攝影。
(D) 參加線上抽籤。

解析　這是詢問新聞建議大家去做什麼（What）的 5W1H 問題，與關鍵句 advise people to do 有關，在文中談到想要試映會門票的人必須提早購買（Those wishing to obtain tickets to the premiere should buy them well in advance），因此答案是 (B)。

字彙　raffle n. 抽籤、彩券

問題 162-165，請參考以下線上對話內容。

Robin Underwood　　　　　　　　[下午 8 點 30 分]
大家好，我好像找到能吸引體育館新會員的方法了。

Franklin Bates　　　　　　　　　[下午 8 點 31 分]
真是開心，[162-B] 我們因為大街那邊新開的健身房失去了很多客人，你的計劃是什麼？

Robin Underwood　　　　　　　　[下午 8 點 33 分]
[163] 申請 6 個月會員的新會員可免費 1 個月，申請 1 年則可免費 2 個月。

Norma Flores　　　　　　　　　　[下午 8 點 34 分]
很多體育館也有類似的促銷活動，[164] 我們大概得做更多。

Robin Underwood　　　　　　　　[下午 8 點 35 分]
這就是我計劃請既有會員向朋友推薦我們的理由，介紹別人來報名的會員可獲得免費的體育館背包當作禮物。

Franklin Bates　　　　　　　　　[下午 8 點 37 分]
這樣應該會很有效果，[165] 你希望我把這項資訊新增到網站嗎？我教的第一堂運動課程是明天下午 1 點，午餐前應該有時間能進行。

Robin Underwood　　　　　　　　[下午 8 點 38 分]
好像還不錯，Norma，可以請你把新政策的相關說明貼在體育館嗎？

Norma Flores　　　　　　　　　　[下午 8 點 38 分]
沒問題，我會去告訴其他職員，讓他們告訴其他客人。　→

come up with 找到（解答、錢等）　attract v. 吸引
waive v. 沒有套用（規則等）、放棄（權利等）
sign up 登記　existing adj. 既有的　put up 頒布
notice n. 告示　notify v. 通知

162 Not/True 題型
關於 Underwood 女士工作的體育館，提到了什麼？
(A) 開第二個分店。
(B) 有新的競爭者。
(C) 將要搬遷到其他位置。
(D) 提供 2 個月的會員券。

解析 這是從短文中找到和關鍵詞 gym where Ms. Underwood works 相關的內容，並且和選項對照的 Not/True 題型。
(A) 短文中沒有談到的內容。(B) 短文中談到「我們因為下面新開的健身房失去了很多客人」（We've lost a lot of customers to the fitness center that recently opened down the street.(8:31 P.M.)），和短文內容相符，所以答案是 (B)。(C) 和 (D) 是短文中沒有談到的內容。
換句話說
the fitness center that recently opened 最近開業的健身房 →
a new competitor 新的競爭者

字彙 competitor n. 競爭者

163 意圖掌握問題
下午 8 點 34 分，Flores 女士寫「Lots of other gyms have similar promotions」，她的意思最可能是什麼？
(A) 想要模仿其他優惠。
(B) 同意提議。
(C) 對計劃沒把握。
(D) 需要確認幾個細節問題。

解析 題目詢問 Flores 女士的意圖，因此要確認引用句（Lots of other gyms have similar promotions）相關的語境。內容中 Underwood 女士說明計劃是申請 6 個月會員的新會員可免費 1 個月，申請 1 年則可免費 2 個月（We can waive one month's fee for new members who sign up for a six-month membership and two months' fees if it's an annual membership. (8:33 P.M.)），後來 Flores 女士表示很多體育館也有類似的促銷活動（Lots of other gyms have similar promotions），並說「我們大概得做更多才行」（Maybe we need to do more. (8:34 P.M.)），由此可知到 Flores 女士對計劃沒有把握，因此答案是 (C)。

字彙 imitate v. 模仿、效仿　doubtful adj. 不能確定的

164 5W1H 問題
部分既有會員有資格獲得什麼？
(A) 商品券
(B) 減少費用
(C) 提升會員資格
(D) 免費商品

解析 這是在詢問部分既有會員有資格獲得什麼（What）的 5W1H 問題，和關鍵句 some existing members be eligible to receive 有關，「Members[existing members]

who get someone else to sign up here will receive a free gym bag as a gift. (8:35 P.M.)」中談到介紹別人來報名的會員可獲得免費的體育館背包當作禮物，因此答案是 (D)。

字彙 be eligible to 有～的資格　gift certificate 禮品券
reduction n. 減少　complimentary adj. 免費的

165 推論題
Bates 先生明天早上最可能做什麼？
(A) 列印通知書。
(B) 指導運動課程。
(C) 更新網站。
(D) 和職員開會。

解析 這是針對關鍵詞 Mr. Bates ~ do tomorrow morning 進行推論的題型，在「Would you like me to add this information to our website? The first exercise class I teach isn't until 1:00 P.M. tomorrow, so I'll have time to do it before lunch. (8:37 P.M.)」中 Bates 先生詢問是否需要把資訊更新到網站上，自己教的第一堂運動課程要明天下午 1 點，午餐前應該有時間能進行，換句話說就是有時間把資訊更新至網站上，所以答案是 (C)。
換句話說
add ~ information 增加資訊 → Update 更新

問題 166-168，請參考以下通知。

職場健康研究協會
www.whra.org

[166] 職場健康研究協會（WHRA）10 月 10 日與 11 日於 WHRA 機關舉辦第 5 屆年度職場健康學會。身為多個研究團體的聯盟，WHRA 把職員的福利視為主要目標。

今年學會會針對睡眠、營養、運動對職場生產力造成的影響，提供最新資訊給全體參加者。[167-B] 課程主題和講者的額外細節問題將於 8 月 7 日確定，並公布於 www.whra.org/events。

[167-D] 如果想報名就請填寫線上申請書。[167-A] 如果是 WHRA 的會員，兩天都參加的總費用可獲得 30% 的優惠，報名時請提供會員編號，若是想申請會員，請前往網站的會員頁面。

[168] 登記日期是 8 月 1 日至 9 月 15 日，若是想取消登記，請在 9 月 21 日前來信 rebecca.smith@whra.org。過了此一日期就不會給予退款，若是有任何疑問或諮詢事項，只要來信 fifthconference@whra.org 就行了。

workplace n. 工作場所　association n. 協會
alliance n. 聯盟、同盟　well-being n. 福利　primary adj. 主要的
latest adj. 最新的　nutrition n. 營養　productivity n. 生產力
finalize v. 敲定、最後確定　grant v.（認證後正式）給予、同意

---

166 推論題
關於 WHRA，有提到什麼？
(A) 即將要開始新的研究專案。
(B) 是在最近成立的。
(C) 有成立海外辦公室。
(D) 先前舉辦過學會。

解析 這是針對 WHRA 推論的題目，「The Workplace Health Research Association (WHRA) is holding its Fifth Annual Workplace Health Conference」中談到職場健康研究協會（WHRA）要舉辦第 5 屆年度職場健康學會，由此可知 WHRA 先前舉辦過學會，因此答案是 (D)。

字彙 establish v. 設立　operate v. 營運　overseas adv. 海外
host v. 主持

167 Not/True 題型
　　下列關於活動的描述哪一個沒有提到？
　　(A) 參加者有資格獲得折扣。
　　(B) 活動計劃會刊登在網站上。
　　(C) 想參加必須成為會員。
　　(D) 參加者可在網站上報名。

解析 這是從短文中找到和關鍵字 event 相關的內容，並且和選項對照的 Not/True 題型。(A)「If you are a member of WHRA, you will receive 30 percent off」中談到 WHRA 會員可獲得 30% 的折扣，和短文內容相符。(B)「Additional details about lecture topics and presenters will be ~ posted on www.whra.org/events」中談到課程主題和講者的額外細節問題會刊登在網站上，和短文內容一致。(C) 短文中沒有談到此一內容，所以答案是 (C)。(D)「To register, please fill out the online registration form.」中談到想要報名就去填寫線上申請書，和短文內容一致。

換句話說
receive 30 percent off 獲得 30% 的折扣 → qualify for a discount 有獲得折扣的資格
Additional details about lecture topics and presenters 課程主題和講者的額外細節問題 → A program 活動計劃

字彙 qualify for 獲得～的資格　program n. 活動計劃

168 5W1H 問題
　　參加者必須在哪個日期之前報名？
　　(A) 8 月 1 日
　　(B) 8 月 7 日
　　(C) 9 月 15 日
　　(D) 9 月 21 日

解析 這是在詢問參加者必須在什麼（What）日期前報名的 5W1H 問題，和關鍵詞 date ~ participants register 有關，文中談到報名在 9 月 15 日結束（Registration ~ ends on September 15.），因此答案是 (C)。

問題 169-171，請參考以下報導。

> **Stanton 的租賃房地產需求持續上升**
>
> 由於過去 10 年間 Stanton 的就業市場都很好，169 租賃住宅的需求持續上升中。— [1] 一在市中心商業區工作的人想住在市區，市場調查顯示，他們寧願租房子，也不想要購買昂貴的市區地產，負擔高額的貸款。— [2] 一開發業者利用此一趨勢在該地區與周圍建設高樓層大型建築物。— [3] 一雖然目前已經建設大量的大樓社區，171 但 Stanton 內物件的高度需求讓每月的租金持續上升當中。— [4] —170 房地產專家預計此一動向在滿足需求之前還會再持續好幾年。　➡

property n. 不動產　demand n. 需求　need n. 需求、需要
rental housing 租賃住宅　climb v. 上升　steadily adv. 穩定地
upward adv. 向上　business district 商業區
market survey 市場調查　take out a loan 貸款
real estate 房子、房地產　take advantage of 利用
trend n. 趨勢　high-rise adj. 高層的　expert n. 專家
predict v. 預計　pattern n. 動向　satisfy v. 使～滿足

169 主題問題
　　報導主要在談論什麼？
　　(A) 高層建築物的人氣
　　(B) 地區內對租賃住宅的高度需求
　　(C) 市區房地產下跌的價格
　　(D) 預測的郊區成長動向

解析 這是在詢問報導主要談論內容尋找主題的類型，文中談到租賃住宅的需求持續上升中（the need for rental housing has climbed steadily upward），而這也說明了 Stanton 內的高度租賃需求，所以答案是 (B)。

換句話說
the need for rental housing has climbed steadily upward 租賃住宅的需求持續上升中 → High rental housing demand 高漲的租賃住宅需求

字彙 popularity n. 聲望　multi-story adj. 高樓層的、多層的
urban adj. 市中心的　forecast v. 預報　suburb n. 郊區、城郊

170 推論題
　　關於 Stanton 租賃住宅市場，提示了什麼？
　　(A) 已經達到高峰了。
　　(B) 預計將會有相當程度慢下來。
　　(C) 短時間內將會維持目前上升的趨勢。
　　(D) 正受到高失業率影響。

解析 這是針對關鍵詞 Stanton's rental housing market 推論的題型，「Real estate experts predict that the pattern will continue for a few more years before demand is satisfied.」中談到房地產專家預計此一動向在滿足需求之前還會再持續好幾年，因此答案是 (C)。

字彙 peak n. 頂端　considerably adv. 相當地
unemployment n. 失業

171 將句子放入合適的位置
翻譯 以下句子最適合放入 [1]、[2]、[3] 或 [4] 的哪個位置？
　　「但變昂貴的費用未能阻止人們租房子。」
　　(A) [1]
　　(B) [2]
　　(C) [3]
　　(D) [4]

解析 這是根據短文語境選出合適位置的題型，在「However, the rising costs have not prevented people from renting」中談到變昂貴的費用未能阻止人們租房子，因此可猜到前面的部分有談論到租金變昂貴的內容。[4] 前面的句子「monthly rental fees continue to rise due to high demand for units in Stanton」談到 Stanton 內物件的高度需求讓每月的租金持續上升當中，如果把句子放進 [4]，就會是「儘管每月租金持續上漲，人們還是想要租房子」的意思，因此答案是 (D)。

換句話說
monthly rental fees continue to rise 每月租金持續上漲中 →
rising costs 上漲的費用

字彙 prevent v. 阻止、預防

問題 172-175，請參考以下備忘錄。

日期：5 月 5 日
收件人：全體員工
寄件人：Joel Smith，人資部主管
主旨：員工福利

大家好，

管理者之間曾針對企業的福利制度進行多次討論。

172-B Smartech 公司剛開始時，我們只能提供員工基本的
健保而已。— [1] —不過，172-D 3 年前公司成立以來，172-
A 我們的銷售有相當的成長。— [2] —因此我們決定要改
善員工福利制度。175 7 月 1 日起將會提供基本的牙醫健
保，— [3] —173 員工們也能選擇是否要額外支付費用獲得
更多牙醫健保項目，若是想利用此一福利，請填寫申請書
交到人資部。174 關於此一福利變更的最新員工手冊將會
在下星期送出，— [4] —若是有任何疑問請來信 j.smith@
smartech.com，或是來辦公室一趟。謝謝。

Joel Smith 敬上

employee benefits 員工福利　benefits package 福利制度
health insurance 健保　found v. 設立　significant adj. 相當的
revenue n. 銷售　dental adj. 牙齒的、牙科的
coverage n.（保險等的）保障
take advantage of 利用（機會等）　updated adj. 最新的

172 Not/True 題型
關於 Smartech 公司的描述哪一個沒有提及？
(A) 銷售增加了。
(B) 成立以來都有提供健康保險。
(C) 職員可獲得年度獎金。
(D) 於 3 年前成立。

解析 這是從短文中找出和關鍵字 Smartech 相關的內容，
並且和選項對照的 Not/True 題型。(A)「we have
experienced significant revenue growth」中談到銷
售有相當程度的成長，因此和內容相符。(B)「When
Smartech first opened, we could only provide basic
health insurance to employees.」中談到 Smartech 公
司剛成立時就有提供基本健康保險給員工，因此和內
容一致。(C) 是短文中沒有談論到的內容，因此答案是
(C)。(D)「Since the company was founded three years
ago」中指出公司在 3 年前成立，因此和內容相符。
換句話說
have experienced significant revenue growth 銷售有顯著的成
長 → revenues have increased 銷售增加了

字彙 founding n. 設立

173 5W1H 問題
職員們要如何獲得額外的保險保障？
(A) 聯絡管理者
(B) 可從線上選擇

(C) 繳交醫療診斷書
(D) 額外支付費用

解析 這是在詢問職員該如何（How）獲得額外保險保障的
5W1H 問題，與關鍵句 acquire additional insurance
coverage 有關，「Employees will also have the option
of paying extra for more dental insurance coverage.」
中談到員工們也能選擇是否要額外支付費用擴大牙醫健
保範圍，因此答案是 (D)。

字彙 acquire v. 獲得　option n. 選擇權
medical report 醫療診斷書、診療報告

174 5W1H 問題
下星期會發生什麼事？
(A) 將要施行某政策。
(B) 將要分發某文件。
(C) 將要協議契約。
(D) 將要安排職員會議的日程。

解析 這是在詢問下星期會發生什麼（What）事的 5W1H 問
題，和問題的關鍵詞 next week 有關，「An updated
employee manual ~ will be sent to all staff members
next week.」中談到最新的員工手冊將會在下星期送
出，因此答案是 (B)。
換句話說
An updated employee manual ~ will be sent 將要發送最新的
員工手冊 → A document will be distributed 將要分發文件

字彙 implement v. 執行　distribute v. 分發　negotiate v. 協議

175 將句子放入合適的位置

翻譯 以下句子最適合放入 [1]、[2]、[3] 或 [4] 的哪個位置？
「它會負擔定期檢查和清洗的費用，而不是重大的牙科
診療。」
(A) [1]
(B) [2]
(C) [3]
(D) [4]

解析 這是根據短文語境選出合適位置的題型，「This will
cover the costs of regular checkups and cleaning but
not major dental work」中談到「它會負擔定期檢查與
清洗的費用，而不是重大的牙科診療」，因此該句子是
和牙科定期檢查與洗牙費用有關的部分，[3] 前面的句子
「Starting July 1, basic dental care will be provided.」
談到 7 月 1 日開始會提供基本的牙醫健保，如果把句子
放在 [3]，整句話的意思就是 7 月 1 日開始雖然會提供基
本的牙醫健保，但不是重大的診療，而是負擔定期檢查
與洗牙的費用，所以答案是 (C)。

字彙 cover v. 負擔（經費）、覆蓋　regular checkup 定期檢驗

問題 176-180，請參考以下報導和表格。

Launch Technologies 公司回收筆電

5 月 13 日的記者會，Launch Technologies 的執行長
Jasmine Hong 宣布 176 公司要回收 Edge X 和 Glide **780**
兩款筆電。177 去年販售超過 **75 萬**臺，所以本次的回收規
模超過該公司先前的回收。　●

Hong 女士說 ¹⁸⁰ Edge XL 的電源線有瑕疵，這些零件在電腦運作時容易過熱，在某些情況下會導致筆電著火。「雖然收到報告的事例只有少數，但我們非常認真替顧客的安全著想，這就是我們請購買筆電者立刻退還的原因。」公司同時也決定要回收 Glide 780，因為有瑕疵的硬碟會讓筆電突然停止運作。

¹⁷⁸ 持有其中一種型號的顧客都能全額退款，並且獲得 Launch Technologies 公司所有產品皆適用的 200 美元商品券。

recall v. 回收；n. 回收　press conference 記者會
issue v. 發表；n. 案件　defective adj. 有缺陷的、不完整的
component n. 零件、組成要素　be prone to 易於
overheat v. 過熱；n. 過熱　catch on fire 著火　instance n. 事例
take ~ seriously 認真看待　at the same time 同時
faulty adj. 有缺陷的、不完整的　shut down 停止、靜止
unexpectedly adv. 突然、出乎預料　be eligible to 具備~的資格

---

¹⁸⁰ 產品退換表格
Launch Technologies 公司
26003 西維吉尼亞州，Wheeling
Cumberland 路 2839 號

■顧客資訊　　　　　　　　　日期：5 月 14 日

^{179/180} 名稱：Garret Brewer
電子郵件：gbrewer@breweraccounting.com
電話號碼：555-4119
地址：43203 俄亥俄州，哥倫布，Park 路 990 號 314 室

¹⁸⁰ 產品名稱	數量	¹⁸⁰ 事由
Edge XL	7	製造公司回收的產品

■意見

¹⁷⁹ 我購買此一電腦是要讓我公司的員工使用，退還這些電腦顯然一定會造成相當不便，為了讓我能立即訂購替代的電腦，希望在 5 月 16 日前能處理退款的部分。退款必須退到我先前購買時使用的企業信用卡，若是需要額外的資訊，只要透過上面的號碼聯絡我就行了，謝謝。

obviously adv. 明顯地　significant adj. 相當地　process v. 處理
replacement n. 替代品、替補人員　owe v. 有該支付的義務
reach v. （用電話）聯絡

176 尋找同義詞
第 1 段第 3 行的「issued」和____的意思最相近。
(A) 決定
(B) 分配
(C) 認同
(D) 宣布

解析 內容「the company has issued a recall for two of its laptops」中包含的 issued 是「宣布」的意思，因此答案是 (D)。

177 推論題
關於 Launch Technologies 公司可推論出什麼？
(A) 上個月推出了筆電。
(B) 先前曾回收產品。

(C) 成立時間超過 10 年以上了。
(D) 最近僱用了新的執行長。

解析 這是針對問題關鍵詞 Launch Technologies 推論的題型，確認報導中關於 Launch Technologies 公司的內容，第一篇短文中談到本次的回收規模比先前的都還要更龐大（these models ~ making this recall larger than any others the company has ever had before），由此可推論 Launch Technologies 公司先前也曾回收產品，所以答案是 (B)。

字彙 establish v. 設立　decade n. 10 年

178 5W1H 問題
Edge XL 和 Glide 780 的購買者將能收到什麼？
(A) 免費軟體程式
(B) 電腦週邊用品的折扣
(C) 免費維修服務
(D) 可用於未來購買的點數

解析 這是在詢問 Edge XL 和 Glide 780 的購買者能獲得什麼（What）的 5W1H 問題，在短文中確認和關鍵句 buyers of the Edge XL and the Glide 780 receive 相關的內容。在第一篇短文中談到持有其中一種型號的顧客都能全額退款，並獲得 Launch Technologies 公司所有產品皆適用的 200 美元商品券（Customers who own either model[Edge XL or Glide 780] are eligible to receive ~ a $200 voucher that can be used for any Launch Technologies product.），因此答案是 (D)。
換句話說
a $200 voucher that can be used for any ~ product 所有產品皆能使用的 200 美元商品券 → Credit for a future purchase 可用於未來購買的點數

字彙 accessory n. 週邊產品、飾品　complimentary adj. 免費的

179 推論題
Brewer 先生最可能是什麼人？
(A) 產品檢驗師
(B) 企業主
(C) 電腦技術師
(D) 工廠員工

解析 這是針對問題關鍵詞 Mr. Brewer 推論的題型，在 Brewer 先生製作的表格中確認相關的內容。在第二篇短文中談到 Brewer 先生購買電腦是要讓我公司的員工使用（Name: Garret Brewer；I purchased these computers to be used by the staff working at the company I own.），由此可推論 Brewer 先生是企業主，所以答案是 (B)。

字彙 inspector n. 檢驗員

180 推論題
下列哪一個和 Brewer 先生購買的電腦有關係？
(A) 附有更換零件。
(B) 會突然關機。
(C) 啟動時會變熱。
(D) 硬碟槽需要更新。

解析 先確認和問題關鍵句 the devices purchased by Mr. Brewer 相關的表格。

線索1 第二篇短文中談到 Brewer 先生說 Edge XL 是製造公司回收的產品，因此填寫了退貨單「Product Return Form」、「Name: Garret Brewer」、「Product Name, Edge XL」、「Reason, Product recalled by manufacturer」，不過因為沒有談到 Edge XL 被公司回收的理由，所以要在報導中確認相關的內容。

線索2 第一篇短文中談到 Edge XL 的電源線有瑕疵，這些零件在電腦運作時容易過熱（the Edge XL has a defective power cable. This component is prone to overheating when the computer is running）。

綜合兩個部分來看時，可知道 Brewer 先生購買後想要退貨的電腦 Edge XL 在啟動時會發生過熱的情況，所以答案是 (C)。

換句話說
overheating when the computer is running 電腦啟動時會過熱 → become hot while being operated 啟動期間會變熱

字彙 come with 伴隨　replacement component 更換零件　without warning 沒有事先告知

問題 181-185，請參考以下網站和線上後記。

Captain Jack's Seafood			
介紹	選單	位置	後記

位於布里奇波特海灘的 Captain Jack's Seafood 是在 10 年以前由 Jack Hoult 創立的，他是一個當地的漁夫，夢想是開一間屬於自己的海鮮料理餐廳。這間餐廳剛開始面臨附近海鮮餐廳的激烈競爭，但 Hoult 先生利用新鮮並完美烹調的料理讓 Captain Jack's Seafood 成為深受歡迎的餐廳，事實上，181-B Food & Drink 雜誌在許多報導中都稱 Captain Jack's Seafood 是布里奇波特最棒的海鮮料理專門餐廳。

Captain Jack's Seafood 是以龍蝦和蟹肉蛋糕等特色海鮮聞名，182 這裡的美味飲料也是居民們特別喜歡的，183 試著品嘗幾項價格合理的當日特別料理。

183 星期四—蟹肉蛋糕　　星期五—炸魚薯條
星期六—炸魷魚　　　　星期日—龍蝦

184 下午 6 點前抵達就能獲得下次可使用的優惠券。建議事先預約，想要預約請來電 555-2243。

found v. 創立、建立　face v. 面臨、朝向
competition n. 競爭　early years 初期
dedication n. 奉獻、貢獻　eatery n. 餐廳、餐飲店
name v. 說話、命名　favorite n. 特別喜歡之物；adj. 非常喜歡的
special n. 特別菜單；adj. 特別的　reasonable price 合理價格

Captain Jack's Seafood			
介紹	選單	位置	後記

姓名：Carmen Vasquez
評分：★★★☆☆

我上星期滿心期待去了 Captain Jack's Seafood，朋友說那邊是市區最棒的海鮮餐廳，菜單的選擇相當多。➡

183/184 星期四下午 5 點我就抵達餐廳了，但還是等了 30 分鐘，我在餐廳外面站了一段時間終於才輪到我，但等服務生把菜單交給我又等了 10 分鐘，我訂了調酒和今日特殊菜單，183 後來在服務生把食物端上來之前，我有 40 分鐘的時間都沒看見服務生。

整體來說我想給 Captain Jack's Seafood 三顆星，食物和飲料都很棒，氣氛也非常舒適。185 但員工需要熟悉一下能以更迅速、有效的方式處理顧客需求的方法。

amazed adj. 嚇一跳　selection n. 可供挑選之物、選擇
disappear v. 不見了　beverage n. 飲料
atmosphere n. 氛圍　welcoming adj. 感到愜意的、歡迎的
efficiently adv. 有效率地

181 Not/True 題型
關於 Captain Jack's Seafood，提到了什麼？
(A) 最近變更菜單了。
(B) 獲得某出版物的肯定。
(C) 廚師大部分都是漁夫。
(D) 有多間分店。

解析 這是詢問關鍵詞 Captain Jack's Seafood 的 Not/True 題型，在第一篇短文中確認與 Captain Jack's Seafood 相關的內容。(A) 短文中沒有談論到的內容。(B) 短文中談到 Food & Drink 雜誌有很多文章都稱 Captain Jack's Seafood 為布里奇波特最棒的海鮮料理專門餐廳（Food & Drink Magazine has named Captain Jack's Seafood in many of its articles as the best seafood restaurant in Bridgeport），因此和短文內容相符，所以 (B) 是正確答案。(C) 和 (D) 是短文中沒談到的內容。

字彙 publication n. 出版品、發表　mostly adv. 大部分、幾乎

182 5W1H 問題
根據網頁內容來看，居民特別喜歡 Captain Jack's Seafood 的什麼？
(A) 周圍漂亮的景色
(B) 美味的飲料
(C) 有禮貌的服務員
(D) 可選擇對健康有益的食物

解析 這是詢問居民去 Captain Jack's Seafood 特別喜歡什麼（What）的 5W1H 問題，因此從網頁中確認和關鍵句 locals especially enjoy at Captain Jack's Seafood 相關的內容。第一篇短文中談到 Captain Jack's Seafood 的美味飲料特別深受當地人的喜愛（its delicious drinks are favorites among locals），因此答案是 (B)。

換句話說
locals especially enjoy 居民特別喜歡 → favorites among locals 居民特別喜愛的東西

字彙 surrounding adj. 周圍的、環繞的　view n. 展望、觀點　tasty adj. 美味的　polite adj. 有禮貌的

183 推論題
Vasquez 女士最可能點了什麼料理？
(A) 蟹肉蛋糕
(B) 炸魚薯條
(C) 炸魷魚
(D) 龍蝦

解析 問題是在詢問關鍵人物 Vasquez 女士點了什麼料理，因此要先確認 Vasquez 女士填寫的線上後記。

線索1 在第二篇短文中談到 Vasquez 女士是星期四去 Captain Jack's Seafood（When I got there[Captain Jack's Seafood] ~ on Thursday.），當天她點了今日特餐，不過沒有談到 Vasquez 女士點了餐點是什麼，因此要在網頁中確認相關內容。

線索2 第一篇短文中談到 Captain Jack's Seafood 的星期四特餐是蟹肉蛋糕（Try one of several daily specials~Thursdays – Crab Cakes）。

綜合兩個部分來看時，可知道 Vasquez 女士的星期四今日特餐是蟹肉蛋糕，所以答案是 (A)。

184 推論題

關於 Vasquez 女士可推論出什麼？
(A) 訂閱了食品雜誌。
(B) 坐在戶外的座位。
(C) 最近搬到布里奇波特了。
(D) 獲得日後可使用的優惠券。

解析 先確認關鍵人物 Vasquez 女士寫的線上後記。

線索1 第二篇短文中談到星期四下午 5 點就抵達餐廳了，但還是等了 30 分鐘（When I got there, however, there was a 30-minute wait, despite it being only 5 P.M. on Thursday.），因為沒有談到 5 點抵達時的狀況，所以要在網頁中確認相關內容。

線索2 第一篇短文中談到下午 6 點前抵達就能獲得下次可使用的優惠券（Arrive before 6 P.M., and you will also receive a coupon for your next visit.）。

綜合兩個部分來看，因為 Vasquez 女士是下午 6 點前抵達餐廳，所以可知道她獲得了之後可使用的優惠券，所以答案是 (D)。

字彙 subscribe v. 訂閱

185 尋找同義詞

線上後記第 2 段第 3 行的「address」，意思最接近下列何者？
(A) 根據（法律、命令等）
(B) 記錄
(C) 對～說話
(D) 處理～

解析「But the staff members need to learn how to address their customers' needs more quickly and efficiently.」中包含 address，在該句子中的意思是「處理」，因此答案是 (D)。

問題 186-190，請參考以下兩封電子信件和日程表。

收件人：Tom Gonzales <t.gonzales@gmail.com>
寄件人：Cecilia Wiggins <c.wiggins@topsmile.net>
主旨：臨時變更事項
日期：5 月 25 日

Gonzales 先生，

186 您想要檢查口腔健康的日期，剛好 Makata 醫師沒有時

間，真的很遺憾。據我所知您是預約 4 月 12 日，187/188-C 但 Makata 醫師受同事所託要幫忙，187 您預約的那一天，Makata 醫師會去參加艾爾帕索的學會。188-A 她要等到 6 月 16 日才會回來診療室。是否可以把您的預約改到下星期呢？186 我可以幫您預約您比較方便的上午 10 點，煩請抽空回覆一下。

Cecilia Wiggins 敬上

regret v. 遺憾　available adj. 有時間的　oral adj. 口腔相關的
checkup n. 健康診斷　fill in for 代替做事
not ~ until 直到～才　due adj. 預計的

187/189 第 15 屆南部地區牙科學會

6 月 12 日到 14 日，Bamba 飯店，187 艾爾帕索，德克薩斯州

187/189 6 月 14 日星期六日程

時間	活動	場所	188-D 演說者
189 上午 8 點- 11 點 30 分	189 研討會：牙齒攝影與數位處理	189 Javelina 廳	Stephen Gentry 醫師
上午 9 點- 11 點 30 分	授課：挑選牙齒手術的工具	Oryx 室	Warren Francis 醫師
上午 11 點 30 分- 下午 1 點 30 分	午餐時間		
下午 1 點 30- 2 點 30 分	研討會：患者客服的優秀性	Javelina 廳	Janine Kirst 醫師
下午 1 點 30 分- 3 點	會議：新牙科醫生的財務戰略	Oryx 室	Heather Wallace 醫師
188-B 下午 2 點- 4 點 30 分	188-B 授課：患者保險相關議題	Finch 室	187/188-B/D Noemi Makata 醫師

通知：會員可免費參加任何一堂課程或會議，不過，參加 189 研討會需要支付費用，被取消時則會退款。

regional adj. 地區的　dental adj. 牙科的、牙齒的
processing n. 處理　material n. 工具、材料
excellence n. 優秀、卓越　strategy n. 戰略、策略
issue n. 案件、問題　surrounding adj. 相關的、環繞的
free of charge 免費　in the event of 在～的情況下

收件人：Kyle Green <k.green@srdc.org>
寄件人：Larry Ayala <l.ayala@bamba.com>
主旨：您的擔憂事項
189 日期：6 月 13 日

Green 先生，

我們已經拜託技師檢查 Javelina 廳的空調，不過很遺憾的是，空調應該要修理才行，最快也要等到明天早上才能完成，造成不便真的很抱歉，189 這也表示明天中午在 Javelina 廳進行的南部地區牙科學會必須取消。190 另外，我已經將你對自助餐溫度的擔憂轉達 Lopez 女士了，她會讓放在外頭的食物保溫到午餐結束為止。若是還需要其他協助，請來電我的手機 555-4106 聯絡我。

Larry Ayala 敬上
Bamba 飯店

concern n. 憂慮、擔心　inconvenience n. 不方便
temperature n. 溫度　make sure 確保　keep warm 保暖
further adj. 另外的　assistance n. 協助

186 推論題

Wiggins 女士最可能是什麼人？
(A) 設施持有者
(B) 活動協調者
(C) 學會演講者
(D) 醫院櫃檯人員

解析 這是針對關鍵人物 Ms. Wiggins 推論的題型，因此要從 Wiggins 女士寄送的電子郵件中確認內容。在第一篇短文中 Wiggins 女士告知收件人他想預約的口腔健康檢查當天醫生不在，並且表示遺憾（I regret to inform you that Dr. Makata will not be available on the date you requested for your oral health checkup.），後來又說可幫忙預約對方方便的時間點（I could schedule an appointment for your preferred time），由此可推論 Wiggins 女士是醫院的櫃檯人員，所以答案是 (D)。

字彙 coordinator n. 協調者　clinic n. 診所
receptionist n. 櫃檯人員

187 5W1H 問題

Gonzales 先生和 Makata 醫生約好何時見面？
(A) 4 月 12 日
(B) 5 月 25 日
(C) 6 月 14 日
(D) 6 月 16 日

解析 在 Mr. Gonzales supposed to meet with Dr. Makata 當中，詢問 Gonzales 先生何時（When）和 Makata 醫生見面，因此必須先確認寄給 Gonzales 先生的電子郵件。
線索1 第一篇短文中談到 Gonzales 先生預約的那一天，Makata 醫師必須去艾爾帕索參加學會（Dr. Makata ~ will be at a conference in El Paso on the day scheduled for you [Mr. Gonzales]），卻沒有提到 Makata 醫師去參加學會的日期，因此要確認一下日程表。
線索2 在第二篇短文中談到 Makata 醫師前往艾爾帕索參加第 15 屆南部地區牙科學會 6 月 14 日的日程（15th Southern Regional Dental Conference, El Paso, Schedule for Saturday, June 14', Dr. Noemi Makata）。綜合兩個部分來看時，因為 Makata 醫師是參加艾爾帕索 6 月 14 日舉辦的學會活動，因此 Gonzales 先生原本是和 Makata 醫師約 6 月 14 日，所以答案是 (C)。

188 Not/True 題型

關於 Makata 醫師的描述，沒有提到什麼？
(A) 6 月 16 日將回到崗位。
(B) 上午將要參加研討會。
(C) 她將代替同事工作。
(D) 她將在活動中演講。

解析 這是詢問關於 Makata 醫師沒有談到的內容，屬於 Not/True 的題型，因此要先從電子郵件和行程表中確認與 Makata 醫師相關的內容。(A) 第一篇短文中談到 Makata

醫師要 6 月 16 日才會回到診療室（She [Dr. Makata] is not due back in the office until June 16.），因此和短文內容相符。(B) 從第二篇短文「2:00-4:30 P.M., Lecture, Dr. Noemi Makata」中可知道 Makata 醫師參加下午的授課，所以和內容不符，因此答案是 (B)。(C) 第一篇短文談到同事請 Makata 醫師幫忙（Dr. Makata was asked to fill in for a colleague），所以和短文內容相符。(D) 第二篇短文談到 Makata 醫師是演講者（Speaker, Dr. Noemi Makata），因此和短文內容一致。

字彙 be present 參加　associate n. 同伴

189 推論題

關於南部地區牙科學會可推論出什麼？
(A) Francis 醫師的授課將會被取消。
(B) 午餐會有額外的其他選項。
(C) Kirst 醫師的活動可能會延期。
(D) 部分研討會參加者將能獲得退款。

解析 先確認談論到關鍵詞 the Southern Regional Dental Conference 的第二封電子郵件。
線索1 第三篇短文的「Date: June 13」和「we will have to cancel the event for the Southern Regional Dental Conference being held in that hall[Javelina Hall] before lunchtime tomorrow」中的寄信日期是 6 月 13 日，明天午餐時間之前在 Javelina 廳舉行的南部地區牙科學會活動必須取消，不過沒談到 6 月 14 日午餐時間前 Javelina 廳舉行的學會活動相關資訊，所以要在行程表中確認相關內容。
線索2 第二篇短文的「15th Southern Regional Dental Conference」、「Schedule for ~ June 14」和「8:00-11:30 A.M., Workshop, Javelina Hall」中談到 6 月 14 日上午 8 點至 11 點 30 分 Javelina 廳舉辦的學會活動是研習會，「a fee may be charged for attending a workshop. All fees may be refunded in the event of cancellation.」中談到參加研習會要支付費用，取消時將會進行退款。
綜合兩個部分來看時，因為 Javelina 廳上午舉辦的研討會將要取消，部分研討會參加者將能獲得退款，因此答案是 (D)。

190 5W1H 問題

Green 先生擔憂什麼事？
(A) 空間可能太擁擠。
(B) 食物會變冷。
(C) 無法和管理者交談。
(D) 資料可能會比較晚發放。

解析 這是在詢問 Green 先生在擔憂什麼（What）事的 5W1H 問題，在第二個電子郵件中確認和關鍵詞 Mr. Green's concern 相關的內容。在「I spoke to Ms. Lopez regarding your[Mr. Green] concern about the temperature of the buffet food. She will make sure that any dishes left out are kept warm」中，寄件人表示 Green 先生很擔心自助餐的溫度，因此會確保所有剩餘的食物不會變涼，由此可看出 Green 先生擔心的是食物可能變涼，所以答案是 (B)。

字彙 crowded adj. 擁擠的、複雜的　distribute v. 分配、分發

191-195 號是與下列廣告單、電子郵件和後記相關的內容。

193 Billings 飯店的 Thumping Thursdays

下班後請到 Gordon's Grill 和我們一起享受美妙的音樂、美食和紅酒！

在欣賞現場音樂表演的同時，坐在陽臺上的椅子或坐在草地上，下午 5 點到晚上 10 點是我們的晚餐時間，現場音樂演出的日期和音樂家名單如下。191 如果天氣狀況佳，所有公演會從下午 6 點進行到 8 點。依照市政府規定，酒類無法在草地上飲用，更多的細節問題請到 www.billingshotel.com 查看。

7 月 10 日：Mister Misty	193 **8 月 14 日**：Roxy Blues
7 月 17 日：Elder Lake	**8 月 21 日**：Terry Crank
193 7 月 24 日：Roxy Blues	8 月 28 日：Mister Misty
7 月 31 日：Mister Misty	193 **9 月 4 日**：Roxy Blues
8 月 7 日：Elder Lake	193 9 月 11 日：Mister Misty

take a seat 坐下、就坐　lawn n. 草皮　per prep. 經由、每一　regulation n. 規定、規制　alcoholic beverage 酒類

收件人：Walt Galvin <galvinw@stompmail.com>
寄件人：Pauline Eagan <eaganp@bluemail.com>
主旨：可進行的表演
日期：7 月 4 日

Walt，

還記得我曾留名片給 Billings 飯店的活動管理者 Dena Harris 嗎？嗯，192/193 她今天聯絡了我，詢問你和 Deacon Delta 的同事們是否願意去 一個叫 Thumping Thursdays 的飯店活動參加表演。聽說 193 她本來和 Roxy Blues 簽約了，但後來因為他們受邀去愛丁堡的藍調慶典表演就退出了。

她希望你們能頂替 Roxy Blue 原本分配到的所有時段。192 目前你的樂團只有每個星期五晚上會在 Cowhead Lounge 表演，193 所以相信有充分的時間能準備表演。我已經告知 Harris 女士說 Deacon Delta 目前有時間可參加活動，希望你能確認可以接下。

Pauline 敬上

business card 名片　apparently adv. 聽說、看來　book v. 和～簽訂演出契約、預約　back out 退出、取消　cover v. 頂替（工作崗位）　time slot n. （分配的）時段　plenty of 充分的、很多的

TRIP TALES

www.triptales.com

官網 > 宿泊設施後記 > Billings 飯店後記

密西西比州的夢 ★★★★☆

194 Isabel Calhoun 於 9 月 20 日刊登

194 我這個月初參加了在該飯店舉行的朋友婚禮，在該飯店住了 4 天 3 夜，房間雖然很簡單，但很舒適，還有免費的

WiFi。雖然我更喜歡飯店的另一間餐館 Gordon's Grill 的料理，但 Polk Room 的早餐自助餐也不錯。194 這個飯店一個很棒的地方，就是我第一天晚上吃飯時表演的藍調樂隊 Mister Misty，附近有很多可以做和可以看的東西，195 這次旅行唯一讓我感到不滿的是，早上 8 點就因為外面的施工噪音被吵醒了，後來我才知道原來是因為這間飯店要蓋新的大樓，整體來說，飯店的 CP 值不錯，也讓我覺得很好玩，所以我相當推薦其他旅行的人，特別是喜歡藍調音樂的人。

decent adj. 不錯的、合宜的　entire adj. 整體的
discover v. 知道、發現　wing n. 建物
overall adv. 整體來說；adj. 整體的
value n. 價值　particularly adv. 特別地

---

191 5W1H 問題

根據廣告單來看，有什麼因素能讓主辦者取消音樂活動？
(A) 市府法規
(B) 氣候不佳
(C) 進行中的維修
(D) 其他預約活動

解析 這是詢問什麼（What）因素可讓主辦者取消音樂活動的 5W1H 問題，因此要確認與關鍵句 cause organizers to cancel a musical event 相關的內容。在第一篇短文中談到如果氣候狀況佳，所有活動都會進行（All performances[music performances] will run ~ if the weather permits.），由此可知只要氣候狀況不佳就會取消活動，所以答案是 (B)。

字彙 inclement adj. （氣候）不佳的　ongoing adj. 進行中的

192 推論題

Eagan 女士最可能是誰？
(A) 活動管理者
(B) 餐廳老闆
(C) 樂團經紀人
(D) 業餘音樂家

解析 因為這是針對關鍵詞 Ms. Eagan 進行推論的題型，因此要確認 Eagan 女士寫的電子郵件。在第二篇短文中談到「she contacted me today to ask if you and your fellow members of Deacon Delta would be willing to play at a hotel event」，Eagan 女士詢問收件人和 Deacon Delta 的同事是否有意願在飯店的活動中表演，Eagan 女士還說目前 Deacon Delta 樂團只有每個星期五晚上有表演（I only have your band[Deacon Delta] scheduled to perform on Friday nights），因此可推論 Eagan 女士是樂團經紀人，所以答案是 (C)。

193 推論題

關於 Deacon Delta 的描述是什麼？
(A) 在愛丁堡的演唱會行程可能要變更。
(B) 過去曾和 Roxy Blues 一起表演。
(C) 為了音樂慶典的表演而參加徵選。
(D) 可能會在 Billings 飯店進行三次表演。

解析 新確認寄給關鍵詞 Deacon Delta 成員的電子郵件。

線索1 在第二篇短文中談到 Deacon Delta 收到飯店活動 Thumping Thursdays 詢問是否有意願參加表演（she contacted me today to ask if you and your fellow members of Deacon Delta would be willing to play at a hotel event called Thumping Thursdays），後來談到希望 Deacon Delta 能代替原本要表演的 Roxy Blues 所分配到的所有時段「she had originally booked Roxy Blues, but they backed out ~. She'd like you[Deacon Delta] to cover all of their time slots.」、「you'll have plenty of time for these performances」，不過沒有談到 Roxy Blues 在活動中的表演日期，因此要確認廣告單的內容。

線索2 在第一篇短文中的「Thumping Thursdays at the Billings Hotel」和「July 24: Roxy Blues」、「August 14: Roxy Blues」、「September 4: Roxy Blues」可確認 Roxy Blues 在 Billings 飯店的活動總共有三次。

綜合兩個部分來看時，因為 Roxy Blues 在 Billings 飯店的表演有三次，所以可推論 Deacon Delta 在該飯店的表演是三次，所以答案是 (D)。

字彙 spot n. 演出、地點

194 推論題

Calhoun 女士大概是在何時看 Mister Misty 的表演？
(A) 7 月 10 日
(B) 8 月 28 日
(C) 9 月 4 日
(D) 9 月 11 日

解析 因為是在詢問 Calhoun 女士何時觀看 Mister Misty 的表演，所以要先確認 Calhoun 女士寫的後記。

線索1 第三篇短文中談到「Posted on September 20 by Isabel Calhoun」和「I stayed at this hotel[Billings Hotel] earlier this month」，Calhoun 女士是在 9 月初入住 Billings 飯店，「The hotel also had a great blues band called Mister Misty on the first night I ate there.」則提到自己入住期間曾有一個叫做 Mister Misty 的藍調樂團，但因為沒有談到 Mister Misty 在 9 月初的表演時間，所以要確認廣告單中的內容。

線索2 第一篇短文談到 September 11: Mister Misty，可確定 Mister Misty 在 9 月 11 日時有表演。

綜合兩個線索來看時，Calhoun 女士於 9 月初時曾待過 Billings 飯店，由此可知 Calhoun 女士是在 9 月 11 日時看過表演，所以答案是 (D)。

195 5W1H 問題

Calhoun 女士對 Billings 飯店有何不滿？
(A) 房間的裝飾方式
(B) 可選擇的食物太少
(C) 部分工程造成的干擾
(D) 和觀光景點之間的距離

解析 這是在詢問 Calhoun 女士對 Billings 飯店有何不滿（What）的 5W1H 問題，因此要確認和關鍵句 Ms. Calhoun dislike about the Billings Hotel 有關的後記。

第三篇短文中談到 Calhoun 女士對整體來說唯一的不滿就是早上 8 點就被窗外的施工噪音吵醒（My only complaint about this entire trip was getting woken up at 8 A.M. by construction noise outside my window.），由此可知 Calhoun 女士對飯店的工程造成的干擾覺得很不滿，所以答案是 (C)。

換句話說
construction noise 工程噪音 → The disturbances caused by some work 部分工程造成的干擾

字彙 decorate v. 裝飾 food items 食品 disturbance n. 騷亂、騷動

問題 196-200，請參考以下廣告、網頁和公告。

使用 Glider 達到自我管理改善

Glider 是所有身體部位都適用的多功能按摩工具，高頻率波震動可舒緩壓力和痛症，並協助身體達到恢復效果。196-C Glider 同時也是一種智慧型儀器，記錄使用的統計數據，並提供即時資訊和程序建議。Glider 與 Glider 線上應用程式同步，功能就像日常健康追蹤器一樣。

Glider 已經被專業運動選手和運動專業診所所使用，現在就訂購你的機器，成為數千名滿意的顧客之一。如果成為我們的新客戶，就能在 Glider 上享受 10% 的優惠折扣，請上 www.gliderdevice.net 看看，我們同時也歡迎批發客戶。

198 9 月成為批發合作業者，下訂單就能獲得 20% 的優惠。

---

multifunctional adj. 多功能的　high-frequency n. 高頻率
vibration n. 震動　statistics n. 統計（資料）　sync v. 同步化
function v. 健康　wellness n. 健康　clinic n. 診所
wholesale adj. 批發的、大規模的；n. 批發
account n. 顧客、交易處

Glider
www.gliderdevice.net

首頁	購物	資訊	合作	支援

批發資訊

197 Glider 可以批發訂購，在健康專業諮詢中心、健身工作室或運動組織使用設備且進行推廣，除了在現場宣傳設備外，197 我們推薦大家在社交媒體頁面上露出，只要上傳設備的宣傳內容就有資格獲得免費的周邊商品。

199 關於諮詢事項請直接來信 b.perez@glider device.net 聯絡 Brianna Perez，她會親自指導正確的使用方法，這是提供每位新批發客戶的免費服務。

---

partnership n. 合夥、合作　available adj. 可使用的
workout n. 運動　apart from 除外、除了~
on-site adv. 在現場的　feature v. 刊登；n. 特徵
entitle to 賦予~資格　instruct v. 教、指示

Pursuit Pilates 員工公告
198 9 月 14 日（當週）

198/199Pursuit Pilates 於上星期成為 Glider 按摩機器的正式批發合作夥伴，根據我個人的經驗看來，我認為這個設備相當有效果，只要顧客能定期使用，相信一定能獲得效果。

199 關於這方面的進展，每位講師都要參加 9 月 30 日下午 7 點的研討會，Glider 代表會親自教導我們設備的正確使用方法，200 請在研討會前就先下載 Glider 軟體應用程式。最後，我希望大家能夠鼓勵我們的客戶在工作室直接購買 Glider 機器，我們將在購買前把他們可試用的展示型號放在接待處。

---

official adj. 官方的　in connection with 關於
development n. 進展、成長、發展　workshop n. 研討會
accompany v. 伴隨、和～一起　reception n. 接待處

---

196 Not/True 題型

關於 Glider 的描述哪一個是正確的？
(A) 是一系列產品中最新的型號。
(B) 由健身專家設計。
(C) 提供即時意見給使用者。
(D) 附有 30 天內退款的保證。

解析 這是在詢問關鍵詞 Glider 的 Not/True 題型，從第一篇短文中確認和 Glider 相關的內容。(A) 和 (B) 是短文中沒有談論到的內容。(C)「The Glider is ~ a smart device, recording statistics on its use and providing live information and program suggestions.」中談到 Glider 會記錄使用統計，同時也會提供即時資訊和程序建議，是一種智慧型機器。由於和短文內容相符，所以答案是 (C)。(D) 短文中沒有談到此一內容。

換句話說
live information 即時資訊 → live feedback 即時意見

字彙 series n. 系列、系列物　come with 配有　warranty n. 保證

197 5W1H 問題

文中鼓勵批發客戶做什麼？
(A) 在社群媒體中宣傳設備。
(B) 定期訂購。
(C) 取得官方認證。
(D) 簽 2 年的契約。

解析 這是在詢問建議批發客戶做什麼（What）的 5W1H 問題，在網頁上確認和 wholesale customers encouraged to do 相關的內容。在第二篇短文中談到「The Glider is available for wholesale orders.」和「we recommend that you feature it on your social media page」，由此可知 Glider 可批發訂購，且建議在社群媒體露出，所以答案是 (A)。

換句話說
feature ~ on ~ social media page 在社群媒體網頁露出 → Promote ~ on social media 在社群媒體宣傳

字彙 on a regular basis 定期地　certificate n. 認證、證明書
commitment n. 承諾、契約

198 推論題

關於 Pursuit Pilates 可推論出什麼？
(A) 開辦線上課程。
(B) 先前曾購買其他按摩工具。
(C) 獲得了 20% 的優惠。
(D) 會員人數增加了。

解析 先確認和關鍵詞 Pursuit Pilates 相關的公告。
線索1 在第三篇短文中「Week of September 14」和「Pursuit Pilates became an official wholesale partner of the Glider massage device last week」談到 9 月 14 日的公告說 Pursuit Pilates 已經在上星期成為 Glider 按摩機器的正式批發合作夥伴，但因為沒有談到 9 月 14 日上一週成為批發合作夥伴的優惠是什麼，所以要確認廣告內容。
線索2 第一篇短文中談到九月成為合作夥伴，下單就能獲得 20% 的優惠（This September, become a wholesale partner and receive 20 percent off your order.）。
綜合兩個部分來看時，由於 Pursuit Pilates 是在 9 月 14 日成為 Glider 按摩機器的正式批發合作夥伴，所以可獲得 20% 的優惠，因此答案是 (C)。

199 推論題

關於 Brianna Perez 的暗示為何？
(A) 具備軟體工程學位。
(B) Glider 的共同創辦人之一。
(C) 同意 9 月 30 日的聚會。
(D) 定期在 Pursuit Pilates 運動。

解析 先確認與問題關鍵詞 Brianna Perez 相關的網頁。
線索1 在第二篇短文中談到如果有任何疑問可聯絡 Brianna Perez，且可以直接向她學習設備的正確使用方法，這是提供給每一位新批發合作夥伴的免費服務（For inquiries, please contact Brianna Perez directly ~. You will be instructed by her personally on how to use the device correctly. This is a free service offered to any new wholesale account.），因為沒有談到 Brianna Perez 何時指導設備使用方法的詳細資訊，所以要在公告中確認相關內容。
線索2 第三篇短文中「Pursuit Pilates became an official wholesale partner of the Glider massage device ~」和「In connection with this development, each instructor is being asked to attend a workshop on September 30 at 7 P.M. A Glider representative will instruct us directly on the correct use of the device.」中談到 Pursuit Pilates 成為 Glider 按摩設備正式的批發合作夥伴，每位講師都必須參加 9 月 30 日下午 7 點的研習會，Glider 代表會親自教導設備的正確使用方法。
綜合兩個線索來看時，可知道 Glider 代表 Brianna Perez 同意 9 月 30 日的聚會，並且會指導 Pursuit Pilates 設備的使用方法，所以答案是 (C)。

字彙 degree n. 學位　cofounder n. 共同創辦人

200 5W1H 問題

Pursuit Pilates 的職員被要求做什麼？
(A) 下載程式。
(B) 安裝設備。
(C) 參加營業會議。
(D) 訓練新的組員。

解析 這是在詢問 Pursuit Pilates 的職員被要求做什麼（What）的 5W1H 問題，在談到 employees at Pursuit

Pilates asked to do 的公告中確認相關的內容。在第三篇短文的「Please download the accompanying Glider software application before the workshop.」中談到在參加研習會前最好先下載 Glider 軟體的應用程式，因此答案是 (A)。

TEST 5

PART 1

1 🔊 澳洲發音

(A) She is holding up a car hood.
(B) She is writing on a clipboard.
(C) She is repairing a motorcycle.
(D) She is speaking on the phone.

---

hold up 支撐　repair 修理

翻譯 (A) 她在撐著汽車的引擎蓋。
　　(B) 她在筆記板上寫字。
　　(C) 她在修理摩托車。
　　(D) 她在講電話。

解析 1 人照片
　　(A) [✕] holding up（支撐著～）和女子的動作無關，因此是錯誤選項。因使用照片中的汽車引擎蓋（car hood），所以會造成混淆。
　　(B) [✕] writing（寫字）和女子的動作無關，因此是錯誤選項。
　　(C) [✕] 照片中沒有摩托車（motorcycle），因此是錯誤選項。
　　(D) [○] 女子正在講電話是最正確的描述，所以是正確答案。

2 🔊 英國發音

(A) Some people are sitting on a log.
(B) Some people are hiking up a hill.
(C) A man is pouring liquid into a cup.
(D) A woman is tying her shoelace.

---

log 原木　pour 使～流動、倒　liquid 液體　tie 綁、捆
shoelace 鞋帶

翻譯 **(A)** 有些人坐在一根圓木上。
　　(B) 有些人在健行走上山丘。
　　(C) 男子正在將液體倒入杯中。
　　(D) 女子正在綁鞋帶。

解析 2 人以上的照片
　　(A) [○]「有些人坐在一根圓木上」的描述最為正確，因此是答案。
　　(B) [✕] hiking（健行）與圖中人物的動作無關，因此是錯誤選項。
　　(C) [✕] pouring（使～流動、倒）與男子的動作無關，因此是錯誤選項。因使用了杯子（cup），所以可能造成混淆。
　　(D) [✕] tying（綁、捆）與女子的動作無關，因此是錯誤選項。因使用了鞋帶（shoelace），所以可能造成混淆。

3 ᴴᵉ 加拿大發音

(A) The man is resting his arm on a table.
(B) Some flowers are arranged in a vase.
(C) Pillows are stacked on the floor.
(D) A television is mounted on the wall.

rest 擱、倚靠　pillow 枕頭　mount 使~固定、放上

翻譯 (A) 男子把手臂靠在餐桌上。
　　 (B) 有幾朵花插在花瓶中。
　　 (C) 枕頭堆疊在地上。
　　 (D) 電視固定在牆上。

解析 1 人照片
　　 (A) [✗] 男子是伸出手臂的狀態，靠在餐桌上是不對的描述，這是錯誤選項。
　　 (B) [✗] 照片中沒有花（flowers），這是錯誤選項。因使用照片中花瓶（vase），所以會造成混淆。
　　 (C) [✗] 枕頭放在沙發上，說堆疊在地上是不對的描述，這是錯誤選項。
　　 (D) [○] 電視固定在牆上是最正確的描述，所以是正確答案。

4 ᴴᵉ 澳洲發音

(A) A worker is climbing onto a platform.
(B) A worker is spraying water with a hose.
(C) A railing is being painted.
(D) A ladder is attached to a wall.

climb onto 爬上　platform 平臺、講臺　spray 噴灑　railing 欄杆
attach to 貼上

翻譯 (A) 一名工人正在爬到平臺上。
　　 (B) 一名工人正在使用管子噴水。
　　 (C) 欄杆正在塗漆。
　　 (D) 梯子貼著牆壁。

解析 1 人照片
　　 (A) [✗] climbing onto（爬上）和工人的動作無關，所以是錯誤選項。
　　 (B) [○] 工人使用管子噴水是最正確的描述，因此是正確答案。
　　 (C) [✗] 因照片中沒有（railing），這是錯誤選項。
　　 (D) [✗] 因照片中沒有梯子（ladder），這是錯誤選項。

5 ᴴᵉ 英國發音

(A) A vehicle is passing by a storefront.
(B) A passenger is stepping off a bus.
(C) A train track leads into a tunnel.
(D) A roof is being installed on a shop.

vehicle 車輛、交通工具　storefront 商店前、商店正面
passenger 乘客　step off 走下~　lead into 導向~　install 安裝

翻譯 **(A) 一部車輛正經過商店前面。**
　　 (B) 一名乘客從公車下來。
　　 (C) 列車路線通往隧道。
　　 (D) 一間商店正在裝設屋頂。

解析 事物與風景的照片
　　 (A) [○] 一部車輛正經過商店前是最恰當的描述，所以是正確答案。
　　 (B) [✗] 因照片中無法確認有乘客下車，這是錯誤選項。
　　 (C) [✗] 因照片中無法確認列車路線通往隧道，這是錯誤選項。
　　 (D) [✗] 雖然照片中有看見屋頂，但並非正在裝設（is being installed）的狀態，所以是錯誤選項。

6 ᴴᵉ 美國發音

(A) A square is covered with fallen leaves.
(B) There is a statue in a plaza.
(C) A building is being constructed.
(D) A fountain is surrounded by a fence.

square 廣場　statue 銅像　plaza 廣場　construct 建設
fountain 噴泉　surround 環繞、包圍

翻譯 (A) 落葉覆蓋住廣場。
　　 (B) 廣場上有銅像。
　　 (C) 一棟建築正在建造中。
　　 (D) 噴泉被柵欄圍住了。

解析 事物與風景的照片
　　 (A) [✗] 因照片中沒有落葉（fallen leaves），這是錯誤選項。使用照片中的廣場（square），所以會造成混淆。
　　 (B) [○] 廣場上有銅像是最恰當的描述，所以是正確答案。
　　 (C) [✗] 照片中雖然有建築物，但並非正在建造（is being constructed）的狀態，所以是錯誤選項。
　　 (D) [✗] 照片中沒有噴泉（fountain），因使用照片中的柵欄（fence），所以會造成混淆。

PART 2

7 ᴴᵉ 加拿大發音→美國發音

Who is your supervisor?
(A) Yes, I respect our supervisor.
(B) For a new project.
(C) The man standing over there.

supervisor 主管、監督者　respect 尊敬

翻譯 誰是你的主管？
　　 (A) 是，我很尊敬我們的主管。

(B) 為了新的專案。
(C) 站在那邊的男子。

解析 Who 疑問句
(A) [×] 因重複使用問題的 supervisor，是會造成混淆的錯誤選項。
(B) [×] 因使用和問題中的 supervisor（主管、監督者）相關的 project（專案），是會造成混淆的錯誤選項。
(C) [○] 回答在那邊的男子，因談論到自己的主管是誰，所以是正確答案。

8 ⓘ 澳洲發音→英國發音

When is this tree going to be removed?
(A) John planted a pine tree.
(B) Before the end of the week.
(C) We moved the furniture.

remove 清除、消除　pine tree 松樹　furniture 傢俱

翻譯 這棵樹何時會移除？
(A) John 種了一棵松樹。
(B) 這個週末之前。
(C) 我們搬運了傢俱。

解析 When 疑問句
(A) [×] 因重複使用問題中的 tree，是會造成混淆的錯誤選項。
(B) [○] 回答這個週末之前，因回答移除樹木的時間，所以是正確答案。
(C) [×] 因使用和 removed 發音相似的 moved，是會造成混淆的錯誤選項。

9 ⓘ 加拿大發音→英國發音

What job did you apply for?
(A) We appreciate your application.
(B) Computer technician.
(C) Come after the interview.

apply for 申請　appreciate 感激　application 申請
technician 技術員

翻譯 你申請哪個職務？
(A) 謝謝你的申請。
(B) 電腦技師。
(C) 請在面試後來吧。

解析 疑問句
(A) [×] 因使用和 apply for（申請）相關的 application（申請），是會造成混淆的錯誤選項。
(B) [○] 回答電腦技師，因為已經回答職務，所以是正確答案。
(C) [×] 因使用和 job（職務）相關的 interview（面試），是會造成混淆的錯誤選項。

10 ⓘ 美國發音→加拿大發音

Why is Ms. Albright leaving our department?
(A) Oh, not until next month.
(B) To work at headquarters.
(C) Yes, we're ready to go.

department 部門　headquarters 總公司

翻譯 Albright 女士為何離開我們部門？
(A) 啊，要等下個月。
(B) 為了在總公司上班。
(C) 是，我們做好離開的準備了。

解析 Why 疑問句
(A) 題目詢問 Albright 女士離開部門的原因，回答時間是答非所問，因此是錯誤選項。
(B) [○] 回答為了在總公司工作，因說出 Albright 女士離開部門的原因，所以是正確答案。
(C) [×] 疑問詞疑問句回答 Yes，因此這是錯誤選項。因使用和問題的 leaving（離開）相同意思的 go（離開），所以會造成混淆。

11 ⓘ 澳洲發音→英國發音

Who is able to train the new cashier?
(A) The train is behind schedule.
(B) From one of the clerks.
(C) Clarence, the day manager.

train 培訓；火車　cashier 出納員
behind schedule 比預期更晚　clerk 店員、職員

翻譯 誰能幫新來的出納員進行教育訓練？
(A) 火車比預期的更晚。
(B) 來自其中一名店員。
(C) 日班經理 Clarence。

解析 Who 疑問句
(A) [×] 因把問題的 train（教育訓練）以名詞「火車」的意思重複使用，是會造成混淆的錯誤選項。
(B) [×] 因使用和問題的 cashier（出納員）相關的 clerks（店員），是會造成混淆的錯誤選項。
(C) [○] 回答日班經理 Clarence，因談到可幫新人教育訓練的人物，所以是正確答案。

12 ⓘ 加拿大發音→澳洲發音

Where did you buy this briefcase?
(A) To carry my work files.
(B) Some amazing accessories.
(C) Through an online retailer.

briefcase 公事包　carry 攜帶　retailer 零售商

翻譯 這個公事包在哪裡買的？
(A) 為了攜帶我的工作文件。
(B) 一些很棒的飾品。

(C) 透過線上零售商。

解析 Where 疑問句
　　(A) [×] 題目詢問購買公事包的場所，因回答購買公事包的理由，所以是錯誤選項。
　　(B) [×] 因使用和問題 briefcase（公事包）相關的 accessories（飾品），是會造成混淆的錯誤選項。
　　(C) [○] 回答透過線上零售商，因談到購買公事包的場所，所以是正確答案。

13 🎧 澳洲發音→英國發音

How much do the brown shoes cost?
(A) They're on sale for $50.
(B) Whichever color you want.
(C) The shop specializes in footwear.

cost 花費　on sale 特價中　specialize 專攻　footwear 鞋子

翻譯 那雙褐色鞋子多少錢？
　　(A) 它們特價 50 美元。
　　(B) 你想要的顏色都有。
　　(C) 那間店專門販售鞋子。

解析 How 疑問句
　　(A) [○] 回答價格是 50 美元，因回答鞋子的價錢，這是正確答案。
　　(B) [×] 因使用和問題的 brown（褐色）相關的 color（顏色），是會造成混淆的錯誤選項。
　　(C) [×] 因使用和問題 shoes（鞋子）相同意思的 footwear（鞋子），是會造成混淆的錯誤選項。

14 🎧 澳洲發音→美國發音

This bakery sells fresh bread daily, right?
(A) No, a sales representative.
(B) Yes, that's correct.
(C) The bread has been sliced.

fresh 新鮮的、現做的　daily 每天
sales representative 銷售員　slice 切薄

翻譯 這間麵包店每天都會販售剛出爐的麵包，對吧？
　　(A) 不，是銷售員。
　　(B) 對，沒錯。
　　(C) 麵包已被切成薄片。

解析 附加疑問句
　　(A) [×] 使用和問題的 sells（販售）相關的 sales representative（銷售員），是會造成混淆的錯誤選項。
　　(B) [○] 使用 Yes 回應這間麵包店會販售剛出爐的麵包，因此是正確答案。
　　(C) [×] 因重複使用問題中的 bread，是會造成混淆的錯誤選項。

15 🎧 澳洲發音→英國發音

Why do you want images of the venue?
(A) Here is the camera.
(B) For a business pamphlet.
(C) I imagine it was hard.

image 照片、圖　venue 場地　pamphlet 小冊子　imagine 想像

翻譯 為什麼你想要那個場地的照片？
　　(A) 這裡有相機。
　　(B) 為了公司的小冊子。
　　(C) 我覺得那很困難。

解析 疑問句
　　(A) [×] 因使用和問題的 images（照片）相關的 camera（照相機），是會造成混淆的錯誤選項。
　　(B) [○] 回答為了公司的小冊子，因為有談到想要照片的理由，所以是正確答案。
　　(C) [×] 因使用和 images 發音相似的 imagine，是會造成混淆的錯誤選項。

16 🎧 加拿大發音→美國發音

Who is organizing the park cleanup?
(A) I've never heard about that.
(B) Across from a dry cleaner.
(C) Should I park nearby?

organize 準備、計劃　cleanup 大掃除　across from 在～的對面

翻譯 誰在準備公園的大掃除？
　　(A) 我沒有聽說。
　　(B) 在乾洗店對面。
　　(C) 我必須在附近停車嗎？

解析 Who 疑問句
　　(A) [○] 回答沒有聽說，等於間接說自己不清楚是誰在準備公園的大掃除，所以是正確答案。
　　(B) [×] 因使用和 cleanup 發音相似的 cleaner，是會造成混淆的錯誤選項。
　　(C) [×] 因重複使用與問題的 park（公園）有關係的「停車」，這是會造成混淆的錯誤選項。

17 🎧 英國發音→加拿大發音

I'd like to order an appetizer before dinner.
(A) That's a good idea.
(B) The order is for Table 3.
(C) Because my meal is cold.

order 點餐；訂單　appetizer 開胃菜　meal 餐點

翻譯 我想在晚餐前點一份開胃菜。
　　(A) 好主意。
　　(B) 那個訂單是 3 號桌的。
　　(C) 因為我的餐點是冷的。

解析 直述句
  (A) [○] 回答好主意，等於同意想在晚餐前點開胃菜的意見，所以是正確答案。
  (B) [×] 因重複把問題的 order（點餐）當作名詞「訂單」使用，這是會造成混淆的錯誤選項。
  (C) [×] 因使用和問題的 dinner（晚餐）相關的 meal（食物），這是會造成混淆的錯誤選項。

---

18 美國發音→加拿大發音

Would you tell Mark about tomorrow's presentation?
(A) They didn't say anything.
(B) An informative speech.
(C) No problem.

---

presentation 報告　informative 有益的　speech 演講

翻譯 你能跟 Mark 說一下明天報告的事嗎？
  (A) 他們什麼都沒有說。
  (B) 這是一場很有幫助的演講。
  (C) 沒問題。

解析 要求疑問句
  (A) [×] 因使用和問題的 tell（說）相同意思的 say（說），是會造成混淆的錯誤選項。
  (B) [×] 因使用和問題的 presentation（報告）相關的 speech（演講），是會造成混淆的錯誤選項。
  (C) [○] 回答沒問題，因同意告知 Mark 關於演講的事，所以是正確答案。

---

19 英國發音→澳洲發音

Do you need any help, or can you finish filing these records yourself?
(A) I guess so.
(B) Oh, you don't need to call her.
(C) I'll be fine. Thanks.

---

file 整理　record 紀錄（文件）

翻譯 需要幫忙嗎？還是你能自己整理好紀錄文件？
  (A) 應該是吧。
  (B) 啊，不需要打電話給她。
  (C) 我應該可以，謝謝你。

解析 選擇疑問句
  (A) [×] 題目詢問是否需要幫忙，或者自己就能整理好紀錄文件，回答「應該是吧」等於答非所問，是錯誤選項。
  (B) [×] 因重複使用問題的 need，是會造成混淆的錯誤選項。
  (C) [○] 回答應該可以，因表達自己可獨自整理好紀錄文件，是正確的答案。

---

20 澳洲發音→英國發音

My notebook is missing again.
(A) We missed you, too.
(B) I saw it beside the photocopier.
(C) The receptionist found some keys.

---

missing 不見的　miss 思念　beside 在～旁邊
photocopier 影印機　receptionist 接待員

翻譯 我的筆記本又不見了。
  (A) 我們也很想念你。
  (B) 我在影印機旁邊看見了。
  (C) 接待員找到了幾把鑰匙。

解析 直述句
  (A) [×] 因使用和 missing 發音相似的 missed，是會造成混淆的錯誤選項。
  (B) [○] 回答我在影印機旁邊看見了，因告知對方筆記本的位置，這是正確的答案。
  (C) [×] 使用和問題 missing（不見的）相關的 found（找到了），是會造成混淆的錯誤選項。

---

21 加拿大發音→美國發音

What is the dress code for the year-end gathering?
(A) The retirement celebration.
(B) He's giving a special address.
(C) Business casual should be fine.

---

gathering 集會　retirement 退休　celebration 紀念活動
give an address 演說

翻譯 尾牙的穿著規定是什麼？
  (A) 是退休紀念活動。
  (B) 他正在進行特別演說。
  (C) 商務休閒風應該就行了。

解析 What 疑問句
  (A) [×] 因使用和問題的 year-end gathering（尾牙）相關的 celebration（紀念活動），是會造成混淆的錯誤選項。
  (B) [×] 使用和 dress 發音相似的 address，是會造成混淆的錯誤選項。
  (C) [○] 回答商務休閒風應該就行了，因談到尾牙的穿著規定，所以是正確的答案。

---

22 美國發音→澳洲發音

Where is the closest bathroom to the conference room?
(A) The conference is about sales tactics.
(B) It starts at 1:30 P.M.
(C) There's a floor plan near the elevator.

---

tactic 戰術、手法　floor plan 樓層說明圖、平面圖

翻譯 距離會議室最近的廁所在哪裡？
  (A) 那是關於銷售手法的會議。

(B) 下午 1 點 30 分開始。
(C) 電梯附近有樓層說明圖。

解析 Where 疑問句
(A) [×] 因重複使用問題中的 conference，這是會造成混淆的錯誤選項。
(B) [×] 問題詢問距離會議室最近的廁所，回答時間是不對的，使用和 conference（會議）相關的 starts at 1:30 P.M.（下午 1 點 30 分開始），因此會造成混淆。
(C) [○] 回答電梯附近有樓層說明圖，等於間接回答不清楚距離會議室最近的廁所在哪裡，所以是正確答案。

Our athletic footwear line will launch next year.
(A) We're standing in line near the entrance.
(B) Only 20 athletes attended.
(C) Yes. It is expected to do well.

athletic 運動的　footwear 鞋子　launch 上市　entrance 出入口
athlete 運動選手　attend 參加　expect 期待

翻譯 我們的運動鞋系列將於明年上市。
(A) 我們在出入口附近排隊。
(B) 只有二十名運動選手參加。
(C) 沒錯，預計會很順利。

解析 直述句
(A) [×] 因把問題的 line（〔商品〕系列）當作「排隊」使用，這是會造成混淆的錯誤選項。
(B) [×] 因使用和 athletic 發音相似的 athletes，這是會造成混淆的錯誤選項。
(C) [○] 使用 Yes 表示知道明年運動鞋系列將要上市，並附加說明預計會進行順利，因此是正確答案。

24 英 英國發音→加拿大發音

Can I purchase tickets for the concert at the venue?
(A) It's a really good band.
(B) They must be ordered online.
(C) No, I saw them live in concert.

purchase 購買　venue 現場、場地

翻譯 在現場可以購買演唱會門票嗎？
(A) 那個樂團真的很棒。
(B) 那必須在線上訂購。
(C) 不，我是在演唱會看他們的現場演出。

解析 助動詞疑問句
(A) [×] 使用和問題的 concert（演唱會）相關的 band（樂團），這是會造成混淆的錯誤選項。
(B) [○] 回答必須在線上訂購，因間接告知現場無法購買演唱會門票，因此是正確的答案。
(C) [×] 因重複使用問題的 concert，這是會造成混淆的錯誤選項。

Is the front door locked, or do I need to take care of that?
(A) Take as many as you want.
(B) I'll go find out.
(C) No, that's my bike lock.

lock 上鎖；鎖　take care of 處理　find out 查明
bike 自行車

翻譯 玄關的門上鎖了嗎，還是需要我處理？
(A) 你想要多少就帶去吧。
(B) 我去了解一下。
(C) 不，那是我的自行車的鎖。

解析 選擇疑問句
(A) [×] 題目詢問「玄關的門上鎖了嗎，還是需要我處理」，回答「你想要多少就帶去吧」是答非所問，因此是錯誤選項。
(B) [○] 回答會去了解狀況，間接回答不清楚玄關的門是否鎖上了，所以是正確答案。
(C) [×] 因重複把問題的 locked（上鎖的）當作名詞 lock（鎖）使用，這是會造成混淆的錯誤選項。

26 加 加拿大發音→英國發音

The city library is closed for repairs until next month.
(A) I heard about that recently.
(B) Check your library card.
(C) April is actually the best time to travel.

library 圖書館　repair 修理　library card 借書證

翻譯 因為市立圖書館要整修，所以要關閉到下個月。
(A) 我最近聽說了。
(B) 請確認借書證。
(C) 4 月其實是最適合旅遊的時期。

解析 直述句
(A) [○] 回答最近聽說了，因表示自己早已知道圖書館要封館，所以是正確答案。
(B) [×] 因重複使用問題的 library，這是會造成混淆的錯誤選項。
(C) [×] 因使用和問題的 month（月份）相關的 April（4 月），這是會造成混淆的錯誤選項。

27 澳 澳洲發音→美國發音

Aren't we supposed to bring food to Charlie's party?
(A) There aren't enough gloves.
(B) Everything will be provided.
(C) I suppose he will show up.

be supposed to 應該　provide 提供　suppose 認為
show up （在預定的地方）出現

翻譯 我們應該帶食物去 Charlie 的派對不是嗎？
(A) 沒有足夠的手套。

TEST 5　PART 2　**181**

TEST 5　NEW TOEIC 950！聽力+閱讀 5 回達標

(B) 全部都有提供。

(C) 我認為他會出現。

解析 否定疑問句

(A) [×] 題目詢問是否要帶食物去參加派對，回答「手套不夠」是答非所問，因此是錯誤選項。

(B) [○] 回答全都會提供，因間接表示不需要帶食物去，所以是正確的答案。

(C) [×] 因使用和 supposed to 發音相似的 suppose，是會造成混淆的錯誤選項。

Can I get a ride with you to the theater?
(A) The performance got great reviews.
(B) Did you enjoy the movie, too?
(C) I've got room in my car.

get a ride 搭乘（交通工具）　theater 戲院　performance 公演
room 位子、空間

翻譯 我能和你一起搭車去戲院嗎？
(A) 那個表演獲得相當棒的評價。
(B) 你也很喜歡那部電影嗎？
(C) 我的車有位子。

解析 要求疑問句

(A) [×] 由於使用了和問題的 theater（戲院）相關的 performance（表演），這是會造成混淆的錯誤選項。

(B) [×] 使用和問題的 theater（戲院）相關的 movie（電影），這是會造成混淆的錯誤選項。

(C) [○] 回答車上有位子，間接同意一起搭車去戲院的提議，所以是正確的答案。

Didn't you say you have to work over the holiday weekend?
(A) Yes, but Rachel is going to cover my shift.
(B) Over by the cabinet.
(C) No, Friday was the delivery date.

cover 代替　shift 值班時間　cabinet 櫃子
delivery 配送、運送

翻譯 你不是說週末連休要工作嗎？
(A) 是，不過 Rachel 會幫我代班。
(B) 在那個櫃子旁邊。
(C) 不，星期五是交貨日。

解析 否定疑問句

(A) [○] 回答 Yes 表示自己曾說過，再附加說明 Rachel 會幫自己代班，所以是正確答案。

(B) [×] 因重複使用問題的 over，這是會造成混淆的錯誤選項。

(C) [×] 因使用與問題的 weekend（週末）相關的 Friday（星期五），這是會造成混淆的錯誤選項。

When can I come over to collect the sales report?
(A) How about Wednesday afternoon?
(B) Sales have been really strong.
(C) It's a large collection.

strong 上漲的、強勁的

翻譯 我什麼時候可以來拿營業報告？
(A) 星期三下午怎麼樣呢？
(B) 銷售真的很強勁。
(C) 這是為數龐大的收藏品。

解析 When 疑問句

(A) [○] 反問星期三下午怎麼樣，詢問對方關於去拿營業報告時間的意見，這是正確答案。

(B) [×] 重複使用問題的 sales，這是會造成混淆的錯誤選項。

(C) [×] 因使用和 collect 發音相似的 collection，是會造成混淆的錯誤選項。

Will we be holding the customer appreciation day event at Albertville Park?
(A) You can park behind the building.
(B) We don't have the budget for it this year.
(C) I really appreciate all your hard work.

翻譯 我們要在 Albertville 公園舉辦顧客感恩日活動嗎？
(A) 你的車停在建築物後面就行了。
(B) 我們今年沒有給這活動的預算。
(C) 我真的很感謝你的辛勞。

解析 助動詞疑問句

(A) [×] 把問題中的 Park（公園）當作動詞「停車」的意思使用，這是會造成混淆的錯誤選項。

(B) [○] 回答今年沒有預算，間接表示今年不會舉辦感謝顧客的活動，因此是正確答案。

(C) [×] 使用和 appreciation 發音相似的 appreciate，是會造成混淆的錯誤選項。

PART 3

Questions 32-34 refer to the following conversation.

M: Welcome to Golden Touch Restaurant. Will you be dining alone tonight?

W: Oh, no . . . I'm not here to eat. [32]I believe I lost my wallet here earlier. I had lunch with some business partners at a long table by the window. I had my wallet when I paid for the bill, but I later realized it was missing from my purse. [33]Would you ask your staff members if they've found it?

M: I'm sorry to hear that. We have a lost-and-found

basket in the manager's office. ³⁴If you could tell me what the wallet looks like, I'll check the basket.

---

dine 用餐　business partner 商業夥伴　realize 明白
missing 不見的　lost-and-found 失誤保管（所）

翻譯　問題 32-34，請參考以下對話。
男：歡迎來到 Golden Touch 餐廳，今晚一人用餐嗎？
女：啊，不是……我不是來用餐的，³² 我的皮夾好像在這裡弄丟了。我和幾名商業夥伴一起坐在窗戶旁的長桌吃午餐，在付錢時皮夾都還在身上，後來我才發現沒有在手提包裡。³³ 可以幫我問一下其他員工是否有找到我的皮夾嗎？
男：真是遺憾，我們經理的辦公室裡有失物保管籃，³⁴ 只要告訴我皮夾的外觀，我會去確認看看。

32 問題點問題

翻譯　女子的問題是什麼？
(A) 忘記預約。
(B) 遺失個人物品。
(C) 把皮夾放在家裡。
(D) 對餐點不滿。

解析　仔細聆聽女子話中負面的敘述，女子說自己剛剛好像在餐廳裡弄丟了皮夾（I believe I lost my wallet here[restaurant] earlier.），因此答案是 (B)。

字彙　make a reservation 預約　personal belonging 個人物品

33 特定細節問題

翻譯　女子希望男子做什麼？
(A) 換到其他座位。
(B) 和一些職員說。
(C) 從帳單中扣除費用。
(D) 把午餐菜單帶過來。

解析　仔細聆聽女子說的話，女子詢問男子是否可以問其他員工有找到自己的皮夾嗎（Would you ask your staff members if they've found it[wallet]?），因此答案是 (B)。

字彙　remove 移除、消除

34 之後將發生的事

翻譯　女子接下來最可能做什麼？
(A) 就座。
(B) 回去上班。
(C) 描述物品。
(D) 點餐。

解析　仔細聆聽對話的最後部分，男子說：「只要告訴我皮夾的外觀，我會去確認看看」（If you could tell me what the wallet looks like, I'll check the basket.），由此可知女子接下來要描述皮夾的外觀，因此答案是 (C)。
換句話說
tell ~ what the wallet looks like 描述皮夾的外觀 → Describe an item 描述物品

字彙　take a seat 坐下　describe 描述　place an order 訂購

35 35-37　[加拿大發音→英國發音→澳洲發音]

Questions 35-37 refer to the following conversation with three speakers.

M1: Did you two see our office lobby? It looks amazing.
W: Yeah, ³⁵the new sofas and chairs are great. Very modern. They're a huge improvement over our previous furniture.
M2: I wonder, though, about the cost. They look expensive. Seeing as how our profits were down last year, can we afford them?
M1: Actually, ³⁶the company's finances improved last quarter. Brandon is planning to announce the news at this afternoon's staff meeting.
M2: Oh, I can't attend that because I have to go see a client. ³⁷Let me know what he says tomorrow.
W: ³⁷Sure, I can do that.

---

amazing 驚人的　modern 現代的　improvement 發展、改善
wonder about 對～好奇　seeing as 鑑於～　profit 收益、利益
afford 負擔　finance 財務、資金　quarter 季
announce 通知、宣布　attend 參加

翻譯　問題 35-37，請參考以下三人對話。
男1：兩位有看過我們辦公室的大廳嗎？看起來非常棒。
女：是，³⁵ 新沙發和椅子真的很不錯，非常有現代風，相較於先前的傢俱，這是非常大的進步。
男2：不過我很好奇那多少錢，看起來很貴，鑑於我們去年的營收比較低，我們負擔得起嗎？
男1：其實 ³⁶ 公司的財務狀況比上一季還好，Brandon 將在今天下午的會議中宣布這件事。
男2：啊，我必須去見客戶，所以沒辦法參加會議，³⁷ 明天再告訴我他說些什麼吧。
女：³⁷ 沒問題，我可以的。

35 特定細節問題

翻譯　什麼東西更換了？
(A) 座位
(B) 接待處
(C) 大廳桌子
(D) 檔案櫃

解析　仔細聆聽與關鍵字 replaced 相關的內容，女子說新沙發和椅子真的很不錯（the new sofas and chairs are great），由此可知座位更換了，所以答案是 (A)。

字彙　replace 更換　seating 座位　reception desk 接待處
filing cabinet 檔案櫃

36 特定細節問題

翻譯　公司最近做了什麼事？
(A) 申請貸款。
(B) 退送物品了。
(C) 提升收益了。
(D) 僱用職員。

解析 仔細聆聽和關鍵詞 recently do 相關的內容，男子說公司上一季的財務狀況獲得改善了（the company's finances improved last quarter），由此可知公司最近的收益提升了，所以答案是 (C)。

字彙 apply for 申請、報名　loan 貸款　merchandise 物品　increase 提升、增加

37 特定細節問題

翻譯 女子同意做什麼？
(A) 概述會議。
(B) 聯絡客戶。
(C) 提出意見。
(D) 查看預算案。

解析 仔細聆聽女子說的話，男子 2 拜託女子隔天告訴自己會議內容（Let me know what he says tomorrow.），女子回答當然沒問題（Sure, I can do that.）。由此可知女子會概述會議內容，所以答案是 (A)。

字彙 summarize 概述　look over 查看　budget 預算案、預算

38-40 加拿大發音→美國發音

Questions 38-40 refer to the following conversation.

M: Jane, I've got a problem. [38]I'm supposed to get together with David Corey from Grandoff Industries at 3 P.M. But our CEO just asked me to meet with her at the same time.
W: Can you reschedule one of your appointments?
M: Um, [39]I'm actually wondering if you'd be willing to meet with Mr. Corey instead. He has some questions about the revised estimate for the warehouse. Your team created it.
W: OK. That'll be fine. [40]I'll look over the cost analysis now to prepare. I want to make sure I'm ready to answer his questions.

get together with 和～見面　reschedule 變更日程
wonder 好奇　revised 修正的、變更的　estimate 估價單
warehouse 倉庫　look over 檢討　analysis 分析結果

翻譯 問題 38-40，請參考以下對話。
男：Jane，我有麻煩，38 我約好下午 3 點和 Grandoff Industries 公司的 David Corey 見面，但剛剛我們的執行長約我在同一個時間見面。
女：你可以變更一下行程嗎？
男：嗯，39 其實我想知道你是否能代替我去見 Corey 先生，他對倉庫修改的估價單有幾項疑問，那是由你們團隊製作的。
女：好，應該沒問題，40 我現在就去看費用分析結果來做準備。我要確保能夠回答他的問題。

38 問題點問題

翻譯 男子的問題是什麼？
(A) 無法聯絡顧客。
(B) 行程上有衝突。
(C) 已經忘記約定了。

(D) 錯失截止期限。

解析 仔細聆聽男子話中的負面敘述，男性說下午 3 點和 David Corey 約好要見面（I'm supposed to get together with David Corey ~ at 3 P.M. But our CEO just asked me to meet with her at the same time.），但執行長卻約在同一個時間見面，因此答案是 (B)。

字彙 conflict 衝突、相衝；（計劃等）重疊　miss 錯失

39 意圖掌握問題

翻譯 男子為何會說「那是由你們團隊製作的」？
(A) 為了提醒她答應要幫忙
(B) 為了表達她對專案很清楚
(C) 為了稱讚她是位受重視的員工
(D) 為了向她表達有問題

解析 仔細聆聽和問題引用句 Your team created it 相關的部分，男子詢問女子是否可代替自己去見 Corey 先生，他對修改後的倉庫估價單有疑問（I'm actually wondering if you'd be willing to meet with Mr. Corey instead. He has some questions about the revised estimate for the warehouse.），這句話表現出女子對專案很清楚，因此答案是 (B)。

字彙 commend 稱讚　valued 高度評價、珍貴的

40 之後將發生的事

翻譯 女子接下來最可能做什麼？
(A) 和執行長見面。
(B) 取消專案。
(C) 拜訪工廠。
(D) 審視文件。

解析 仔細聆聽對話最後的部分，女子說現在要查看費用分析結果做準備（I'll look over the cost analysis now to prepare.），因此答案是 (D)。
換句話說
look over the cost analysis 查看費用分析結果 →
Review a document 審視文件

字彙 cancel 取消　review 檢討、審查

41-43 英國發音→澳洲發音

Questions 41-43 refer to the following conversation.

W: [41]We have quite a few people going to the team retreat at The Learning Camp. I hope there's plenty of parking available.
M: [41]Why not pay for a bus to take us? It's a long enough drive to make it worthwhile.
W: No, I don't think we have enough people for that. There are only 21 people from our company attending the event. [42]I wonder if any of our staff own a large van. Then some people can ride together.
M: We could rent two vans from Hart Street Car Rental. Each holds about a dozen people. That

way, everybody could leave their cars at the office. ⁴³I'll call them to ask about prices.

翻譯 問題 41-43，請參考以下對話。
女：⁴¹ 我們有相當多人要去參加 The Learning Camp 的出遊，希望有足夠的停車空間。
男：⁴¹ 要不要花錢請巴士來接送我們？這段車程很長，我覺得相當值得。
女：不，人好像也沒多到能請巴士接送，我們公司參加活動的人只有 21 個而已，⁴² 不知道我們的員工是否有大型廂型車，那樣就能載好幾個人。
男：我們應該能去 Hart Street 租車店租兩臺廂型車，每臺車可容納 12 個人，這樣大家的車子就能都停在公司，⁴³ 我會打電話詢問價格。

41 主題問題

翻譯 說話者主要在談論什麼？
(A) 出遊的經費
(B) 廂型車的停車空間
(C) 前往營區的路線說明
(D) 前往活動的交通工具

解析 這是詢問對話主題的題型，一定要聆聽對話剛開始的部分，女子說有相當多人要去參加 The Learning Camp 的出遊，希望有足夠的停車空間（We have quite a few people going to the team retreat ~. I hope there's plenty of parking available.），男子回答要不要花錢請巴士來接送（Why not pay for a bus to take us?），後來就在談論前往活動搭乘的交通工具，因此答案是 (D)。

字彙 expense 經費、費用　direction 指引

42 特定細節問題

翻譯 女子想知道什麼事？
(A) 接駁車需要多少錢
(B) 員工是否有廂型車
(C) 誰要駕駛租賃的車輛
(D) 停車場的位置

解析 仔細聆聽女子說的話，女子說想知道是否有員工擁有廂型車（I wonder if any of our staff own a large van.），因此答案是 (B)。

字彙 rental 租賃的　parking garage 停車場

43 之後將發生的事

翻譯 男子接下來最可能做什麼？
(A) 搭乘巴士。
(B) 打電話。
(C) 報名活動。
(D) 比較價格。

解析 仔細聆聽對話最後的部分，男子說會打電話到 Hart Street 租車店詢問價格（I'll call them[Hart Street Car Rental] to ask about prices.），由此可知男子將會打電話，所以答案是 (B)。

44-46 🎙️加拿大發音→英國發音

Questions 44-46 refer to the following conversation.

M: So, ⁴⁴how should we spend our final day in Hawaii? We can go on a guided hike in the mountains from 2 P.M. to 5 P.M. That sounds fun. Or we could take beginner surfing lessons.
W: ⁴⁵I don't want to choose until Rachel gets back from the spa, since she should have a say, too.
M: Fair enough. When is she going to return?
W: At 11 o'clock, so in about an hour.
M: Well, ⁴⁶why don't you look this over in the meantime? It's a pamphlet that I picked up in the reception area. It details the day trips offered by the resort.

翻譯 問題 44-46，請參考以下對話。
男：⁴⁴ 好，在夏威夷的最後一天要怎麼過？下午 2 點到 5 點我們可以在導遊的帶領下去爬山，應該會很有趣，不然我們也能去上新手衝浪的課程。
女：⁴⁵ 我想要等 Rachel 去溫泉回來後再選擇，因為她也應該有發言權。
男：好，她何時會回來？
女：她 11 點回來，所以是一個小時以內。
男：嗯，⁴⁶ 這段期間要不要先看這個？這是我在大廳拿來的小冊子，它詳細說明渡假村提供的一日遊。

44 主題問題

翻譯 對話主要在談些什麼？
(A) 選擇飯店房間
(B) 準備度假
(C) 決定活動
(D) 支付旅費

解析 這是詢問對話主題的題型，一定要仔細聆聽對話剛開始的部分。男子詢問在夏威夷的最後一天該怎麼過（how should we spend our final day in Hawaii?），後來談到有兩個活動可以選擇（We can go on a guided hike in the mountains ~. Or we could take beginner surfing lessons.），因此答案是 (C)。

字彙 select 選擇

45 提及何事的問題

翻譯 關於 Rachel，提到了什麼事？
(A) 她去泡溫泉。
(B) 她對衝浪課程有興趣。
(C) 她住在夏威夷。
(D) 她 11 點要開會。

解析 仔細聆聽和關鍵字 Rachel 相關的部分，女子說想要等

Rachel 泡溫泉回來後在選擇（I don't want to choose until Rachel gets back from the spa），因此答案是 (A)。

46 特定細節問題

翻譯 男子給女子什麼東西？
(A) 旅行背包
(B) 紀念品
(C) 鑰匙
(D) 小冊子

解析 仔細聆聽與關鍵句 give to the woman 相關的內容，女子詢問這段時間要不要先看這個，那是自己從大廳拿來的（why don't you look this over in the meantime? It's a pamphlet that I picked up in the reception area.），因此答案是 (D)。

換句話說
Pamphlet 小冊子 → Brochure 小冊子

字彙 souvenir 紀念品

47-49 🎧 美國發音→加拿大發音

Questions 47-49 refer to the following conversation.

W: Hello, Mr. Smith. This is Elaine Fredericks from Cortez Coffee. I'm wondering if you've received your monthly order as my records don't indicate whether you have.
M: ⁴⁷Our coffee shop got everything on time as usual. And ⁴⁸the free samples of Honduran coffee that you gave us to try out really impressed our customers. I plan to purchase some with my next order.
W: That's good news. I can send a shipment of only those coffee beans today if you don't want to wait a full month until your next scheduled delivery.
M: I suppose that would work. ⁴⁹Please mail four boxes.

indicate（使用文字）標示　on time 及時　as usual 和平常一樣
impress 給予深刻印象　shipment 配送品、運輸品
mail 郵寄

翻譯 問題 47-49，請參考以下對話。
女：您好，Smith 先生，我是 Cortez 咖啡的 Elaine Fredericks。我們的紀錄沒有標示顧客是否有收到每月的訂貨，所以我想知道您是否有收到。
男：⁴⁷ 我們咖啡廳一如往常準時收到所有的東西了，另外，⁴⁸ 您免費提供試用的 Honduran 咖啡樣品讓客戶們留下深刻的印象，我打算下一次的訂單要購買一些。
女：太好了，如果您不想等到下個月的預定配送日，我今天可以只寄出那些咖啡豆。
男：應該可以吧，⁴⁹ 請寄給我四箱。

47 說話者問題

翻譯 男子最可能是誰？
(A) 清潔業者的老闆
(B) 商店會計帳簿負責人

(C) 運送卡車的駕駛
(D) 咖啡廳經營者

解析 仔細聆聽對話中與身分、職業相關的用法，男子說自己的咖啡廳一如往常都準時收到所有的物品（Our coffee shop got everything on time as usual.），由此可知男子是咖啡廳老闆，所以答案是 (D)。

字彙 cleaning 打掃　bookkeeper 會計帳簿負責人

48 特定細節問題

翻譯 配送品和什麼一起寄出？
(A) 樣品商品
(B) 修訂的請款單
(C) 辦公用品
(D) 特別優惠券

解析 仔細聆聽和問題關鍵詞 sent with a shipment 相關的內容，男子說女子免費提供試用的 Honduran 咖啡樣品讓客戶們留下深刻的印象（the free samples of Honduran coffee that you gave us to try out really impressed our customers），由此可知和配送品一起寄出的是樣品商品，所以答案是 (A)。

字彙 revise 修訂　office supply 辦公用品

49 請求問題

翻譯 男子拜託女子做什麼？
(A) 寫電子郵件。
(B) 寄送幾個箱子。
(C) 使用優惠券。
(D) 退換幾個商品。

解析 仔細聆聽男子話中和要求相關的用語，男子請女子寄四箱（Please mail four boxes），因此答案是 (B)。

換句話說
mail ~ boxes 郵寄~箱子 →
Send some packages 寄幾個包裹

字彙 package 箱子、包裹　voucher 優惠券、商品券

50-52 🎧 澳洲發音→美國發音

Questions 50-52 refer to the following conversation.

M: Excuse me, ⁵⁰can you show me where the new novels are shelved?
W: ⁵⁰They're right next to the checkout area. Are you looking for any title in particular?
M: Two, actually. *The Old Bride* by Phyllis McNeal and *Voting for Peanuts* by . . . um . . . I forget the author's name.
W: It's Dale Daniels, if I'm not mistaken. But I'm afraid we're sold out of that one. ⁵¹/⁵²It was recently featured on a famous talk show and after that, it sold quickly.
M: ⁵²Of course. I heard it was popular. Well, when will more copies be available?
W: Just a moment. Let me check now.

novel 小說　shelve 放置架上　checkout 結帳處　look for 尋找
title 書籍、標題　in particular 特別地、特地　actually 事實上
mistaken 弄錯的　sold out 賣光
feature（新聞、雜誌等）以～為專題

翻譯　問題 50-52，請參考以下對話。
男：不好意思，⁵⁰ 可以告訴我新的小說放在哪裡的架上嗎？
女：⁵⁰ 就在結帳處旁邊，您有特別要找的書嗎？
男：其實有兩本，Phyllis McNeal 的 The Old Bride 和 Voting for Peanuts⋯⋯嗯⋯⋯我忘記作家的名字了。
女：如果我沒記錯的話，應該是 Dale Daniels，但很遺憾的是全都賣完了。⁵¹/⁵² 最近知名的脫口秀節目談到這本書後，就在短時間內銷售一空。
男：⁵² 我想也是，聽說那本書很受歡迎。嗯，那何時才能買到新書？
女：等等，我現在確認一下。

50 場所問題

翻譯　對話最可能是在哪裡進行的？
(A) 在書店
(B) 在圖書館
(C) 在出版博覽會
(D) 在廣播公司工作室

解析　仔細聆聽對話中和場所相關的用法，男子詢問新上市的小說擺放的位置（can you show me where the new novels are shelved?），女子回答在結帳區旁邊（They're right next to the checkout area.），由此可知是在書店交談，所以答案是 (A)。

字彙　bookstore 書店　publishing 出版　expo 博覽會、展示會

51 提及何事的問題

翻譯　女子談到關於《Voting for Peanuts》的什麼事？
(A) 是在《The Old Bride》之後出版的。
(B) 放在服務臺後面的架子上。
(C) 是透過媒體提升知名度的。
(D) 由脫口秀主持人著作的。

解析　仔細聆聽和關鍵詞 Voting for Peanuts 相關的內容，女子說最近《Voting for Peanuts》因為被脫口秀報導而變有名（It [Voting for Peanuts] was recently featured on a famous talk show），因此答案是 (C)。
換句話說
featured on a ~ talk show 脫口秀節目報導 →
publicized in the media 透過媒體提升知名度

字彙　publicize 張揚、受矚目　media（新聞、電視等的）媒體
host 主持人

52 意圖掌握問題

翻譯　為何男子會說「聽說那本書很受歡迎」？
(A) 為了表達興奮
(B) 為了表現自己不覺得訝異
(C) 為了解釋決定事項
(D) 為了推薦新刊圖書

解析　仔細聆聽和引用句 I heard it was popular 相關的部分，女子說最近知名的脫口秀節目把書報導出來後，它就在短時間內銷售一空（It[Voting for Peanuts] was recently featured on a famous talk show and after that, it sold quickly.），男子表示認同，並詢問何時可購買新書（Of course. ~ Well, when will more copies be available?），由此可知男子是為了表現自己一點都不訝異，所以答案是 (B)。

字彙　indicate 表現　recommend 推薦

53-55 ③ 加拿大發音→美國發音

Questions 53-55 refer to the following conversation.

M: Have you seen the documentary called *Help Yourself*? ⁵³It focuses on ways to treat and prevent illnesses with healthy food and supplements.
W: No, I haven't, but I've read positive reviews about it.
M: ⁵⁴I found it informative and consistent with our nutritional consultation services. I wonder if we can buy a copy of it and play it in the waiting room.
W: I bet the movie can be downloaded for a fee online.
M: True. But before we show the film, ⁵⁵you should watch it as well to make sure you find it appropriate.
W: I'll do that this weekend, and then we can discuss if we want to show it here.

focus on 專注於　treat 治療　prevent 預防　illness 疾病
supplement 補充物　review 評價　informative 有益的
consistent 和～一致的　nutritional 營養的　consultation 諮詢
bet 肯定　appropriate 適當的

翻譯　問題 53-55，請參考以下對話。
男：你看過紀錄片《Help Yourself》嗎？⁵³ 它著重在使用健康食品與保健食品治療與預防疾病的方法。
女：不，我還沒看，但我看過關於它的正面評價。
男：⁵⁴ 我認為那很有幫助，也符合我們營養諮詢服務主旨，我們很好奇是否能買一片在等待室播放。
女：那部電影應該可以在線上付費下載。
男：對，但在播放那部電影前，⁵⁵ 我認為你應該也要先看一下是否合適。
女：這個週末我會看，之後我們就能討論是否要在這裡播放。

53 提及何事的問題

翻譯　男子談論關於《Help Yourself》的什麼事？
(A) 今年拍攝的。
(B) 在當地戲院上映。
(C) 由知名演員演出。
(D) 以食品的選擇為主題。

解析　仔細聆聽和關鍵詞 Help Yourself 相關的內容，男子說紀錄片著重在使用健康食品與保健食品治療與預防疾病的方法（It[*Help Yourself*] focuses on ways to treat and prevent illnesses with healthy food and supplements.），因此答案是 (D)。

字彙 film 攝影 feature 由（演員）主演 well-known 知名的 deal with 處理

54 特定細節問題

翻譯 說話者提供什麼樣的服務？
(A) 產品廣告
(B) 營養諮詢
(C) 影片販售
(D) 職涯建議

解析 仔細聆聽和關鍵詞 type of service 相關的內容，男子說紀錄片和自己的營養諮詢服務主旨相符（I found it[documentary] ~ consistent with our nutritional consultation services.），由此可知說話者提供營養諮詢服務，所以答案是 (B)。

字彙 advertising 廣告（業） career 發展、經歷

55 提議問題

翻譯 男子提出何種意見？
(A) 觀看紀錄片
(B) 在其他房間等待
(C) 拍攝廣告
(D) 把資料傳到線上

解析 仔細聆聽男子話中與提議相關的用語，男子表示認為女子應該也要先看一下紀錄片內容是否合適（you should watch it[documentary] as well to make sure you find it appropriate），因此答案是 (A)。

字彙 commercial 廣告 material 資料、材料

56-58 🔊英國發音→美國發音→澳洲發音

Questions 56-58 refer to the following conversation with three speakers.

W1: Macy, [56]I think we could cut costs by stopping the water bottle deliveries to our offices and installing a filtration system instead.
W2: Right. That would also reduce plastic waste.
W1: We should ask if it's in the budget. [57]There's Andrew, the accounting department manager . . . Andrew, is there money to purchase a water filtration system in the budget?
M: I think so. Those systems cost a lot, but it would cut costs in the long term.
W1: Thanks. [58]Then, I will do some research and get a few estimates.
W2: [58]I also have some time. Let's have a look now.

---

install 安裝 filtration system 過濾裝置
in the long term 長期上來看 estimate 估價（額）

翻譯 問題 56-58，請參考以下三人對話。
女 1：Macy，[56] 我認為我們可以停止配送水瓶，利用安裝過濾裝置來減少費用。

女 2：對，這樣也能減少塑膠垃圾。
女 1：我們得問一下是否在預算內，[57] 會計部經理 Andrew 在耶……Andrew，我們有預算可以買淨水器嗎？
男：大概吧，那種裝置需要大量的費用，但長期來說可以省錢。
女 1：謝謝，[58]那我去研究一下取得估價。
女 2：[58]我也有一點時間，現在就去看一下吧。

56 主題問題

翻譯 對話主要在談什麼？
(A) 活動開展
(B) 節省水電的費用
(C) 防止環境汙染
(D) 嘗試使用新的供水來源

解析 這是詢問對話主題的題型，仔細聆聽短文前面的部分。對話中女子 1 認為可以停止配送水瓶，利用安裝過濾裝置來減少費用（I think we could cut costs by stopping the water bottle deliveries to our offices and installing a filtration system instead），由此可知對話在談論新的供給水源，因此答案是 (D)。

字彙 launch 開始、啟動

57 說話者問題

翻譯 男子在哪個部門工作？
(A) 會計
(B) 配送
(C) 人力資源
(D) 維修

解析 仔細聆聽短文中和身分、職業相關的用語，女子 1 說會計部經理 Andrew 在場（There's Andrew, the accounting department manager ~.），由此可知男子是會計部門的職員，所以答案是 (A)。

字彙 accounting 會計 human resources 人力資源 maintenance 整備、維護

58 特定細節問題

翻譯 女子決定要做什麼？
(A) 重新調整會議。
(B) 去取得部分的運送品。
(C) 訂購新裝置。
(D) 取得幾個估價。

解析 仔細聆聽和關鍵詞 women decide to do 相關的內容，女子 1 說自己會去研究且取得幾項估價（Then, I will do some research and get a few estimates.），女子 2 回答自己也有一點時間，現在就去看一下（I also have some time. Let's have a look now.），因此答案是 (D)。

換句話說
get a few estimates 取得幾項估價 →
Get some price quotes 取得一些估價

字彙 quote 估價

59-61 英國發音→加拿大發音

Questions 59-61 refer to the following conversation.

W: My family is in town, and ⁵⁹I'm trying to figure out something fun to do with them. I've taken them to the museums, shopping areas, and parks. I can't think of anything else that they might enjoy.

M: ⁶⁰Why don't you see the new musical at the Central Arts Center? It features country songs performed in the style of rock.

W: Maybe I will. That sounds interesting. Do you know if there are shows on weekends?

M: There definitely are some on Saturdays, but I'm not sure about Sundays. ⁶¹I'll text the website address to you now, so you can check.

figure out 想出～　feature 特別包含、當作特徵　definitely 明確地

翻譯 問題 59-61，請參考以下對話。
　　女：我的家人在市區，⁵⁹ 我想要和他們去做些有趣的事，我帶他們去了博物館、購物地區和公園，我想不到其他能讓他們覺得開心的事。
　　男：⁶⁰ 你們要不要看看中央美術中心新推出的音樂劇？那邊還特別包含使用搖滾風格演奏的鄉村歌曲。
　　女：也許我會這樣做，應該很有趣吧，週末是否也有表演？
　　男：我確定星期六有表演，星期天就不清楚了，⁶¹ 我現在把網址傳給你，你就確認一下吧。

59 特定細節問題

翻譯 女子試著做什麼？
　　(A) 計劃娛樂。
　　(B) 說服朋友和她一起去。
　　(C) 宣傳地區活動。
　　(D) 購買博物館門票。

解析 仔細聆聽和關鍵詞 trying to do 相關的內容，女子說自己想找一些有趣的事和家人去做（I'm trying to figure out something fun to do with them[family]），因此答案是 (A)。
換句話說
Figure out something fun 想一些有趣的事 →
Plan some entertainment 計劃娛樂活動

字彙 entertainment 娛樂、消遣、娛樂表演　convince 說服
promote 宣傳

60 提議問題

翻譯 男子提出何種建議？
　　(A) 去公園郊遊
　　(B) 去購物中心
　　(C) 觀賞表演
　　(D) 去郊外旅遊

解析 仔細聆聽男子話中與提議相關的用語，男子建議去中央美術中心觀看音樂劇（Why don't you see the new musical at the Central Arts Center?），所以正確答案是 (C)。

換句話說
see the ~ musical 觀看音樂劇 →
Watching a performance 觀賞表演

字彙 countryside 郊外、田園地區

61 之後將發生的事

翻譯 男子說要做什麼？
　　(A) 詢問建築物的地址。
　　(B) 分享線上連結。
　　(C) 確認表演時間。
　　(D) 列出幾個名勝。

解析 仔細聆聽對話最後的部分，男子說現在要把網址傳給女子，讓女子能自己確認（I'll text the website address to you now, so you can check.），因此答案是 (B)。
換句話說
text the website address 使用訊息傳送網址 →
Share an online link 分享線上連結

字彙 inquire 諮詢　share 分享　attraction 景點、名勝

62-64 美國發音→澳洲發音

Questions 62-64 refer to the following conversation and business card.

W: ⁶²I'm here to pick up the business cards your shop printed for me. My name is Helga Kim.

M: Yes, Ms. Kim. I have your completed order right here. Please look them over and make sure the information is correct.

W: Hmm . . . It looks like there's an error. ⁶³The operational hours and contact information are fine. However, the number "31" was incorrectly printed as "37."

M: Oh, my apologies. ⁶⁴I'll fix that part and print new ones for you right away, which should only take about 10 minutes.

pick up （從某處）取得、領取　order 訂購物　look over 檢查
error 錯誤　contact information 聯絡處

翻譯 問題 62-64，請參考以下對話和名片。
　　女：⁶² 我是來拿我在你們店裡列印的名片，我的名字是 Helga Kim。
　　男：好，Kim 女士，這是你訂購的名片，請仔細看一下，確認資料是否正確。
　　女：嗯……好像有一個地方錯了，⁶³ 營業時間和聯絡方式沒錯，但數字「31」印成「37」了。
　　男：啊，真是抱歉，⁶⁴ 我現在立刻修正後列印新的，大概需要 10 分鐘左右的時間。

> Helga's 乾洗店
> 老闆 Helga Kim
>
> 電話：555-6922
> 每天營業時間：上午 9 點─下午 7 點
> ⁶³ 地址：Pine 路 37 號
> 電子郵件：helga@cleanwiz.net

62 目的問題

翻譯 女子為何要去那間店？
(A) 為了確認金額
(B) 為了客訴
(C) 為了挑選材料
(D) 為了取得物品

解析 這是詢問對話主旨的題型，一定要認真聽清楚對話剛開始的部分，女子說自己是去男子店裡拿名片的（I'm here to pick up the business cards your shop printed for me.），因此答案是 (D)。

換句話說
pick up the business cards 來拿名片 →
collect some items 來拿東西

字彙 verify 確認　make a complaint 抗議、抱怨　collect 領取

63 圖片題

翻譯 請看圖片，哪一項資料錯了？
(A) 電話號碼
(B) 街道地址
(C) 每天營運時間
(D) 電子信箱

解析 這是詢問錯誤資訊的問題，確認名片上的資訊後，仔細聆聽是否有不符的內容。女子說營業時間和聯絡方式沒錯，但數字「31」印成「37」了（The operational hours and contact information are fine. However, the number "31" was incorrectly printed as "37."），從名片上可知道是地址有問題，所以答案是 (B)。

字彙 contain 裝有、包含

64 特定細節問題

翻譯 完成什麼需要 10 分鐘？
(A) 洗衣服
(B) 修理影印機
(C) 填寫表格
(D) 列印新的名片

解析 仔細聆聽和關鍵字 10 minutes 有關的部分，男子說修訂後就會列印新的名片，大概需要 10 分鐘左右的時間（I'll fix that part and print new ones[business cards] for you right away, which should only take about 10 minutes.），因此答案是 (D)。

字彙 garment 服裝　photocopier 影印機　fill out 填寫　card 名片

65-67 🔊 英國發音→加拿大發音

Questions 65-67 refer to the following conversation and list.

W: Hi. ⁶⁵I'm calling about the booking my company made at your facilities for our upcoming conference. I'm wondering if it's possible to make some last-minute changes.
M: Possibly. What specific changes?
W: Well, 200 people ended up registering . . . that's 100 more than we were expecting. I'm not sure if the original room we booked is large enough. ☞

M: Hmm . . . yes, we'll have to move your event to another space, since ⁶⁶the room you originally booked can seat only 100 people. Luckily, all of our other rooms are free, so we can easily relocate you.
W: Great. ⁶⁷We'll also need to double our catering order to provide meals to all the extra attendees.

make a change 變更　last-minute 最後一刻的　specific 具體的
end up （最後）成為　original 原來的　seat 容納　luckily 幸虧
double 加倍　catering 提供食物　attendee 參加者

翻譯 問題 65-67，請參考以下對話和目錄。
女：您好，⁶⁵ 我之所以會打電話，是要談談我們公司要舉辦會議和貴公司租借場地的事，我想知道最後是否還能進行幾項變更。
男：大概吧，具體來說是要變更哪些事項？
女：嗯，報名人數有 200 名……這已經比我們預期的 100 名還要多，我不知道我們原本預定的會議室是否夠大。
男：嗯…是，⁶⁶ 原本預約的會議室只能容納 100 個人，看來活動得移動到其他地方才行，幸好我們的其他會議室是空置的狀態，要移動到其他會議室很簡單。
女：好，⁶⁷ 為了提供餐點給所有後來參加的人，訂單也必須變成兩倍。

會議室	最大容納人數
⁶⁶ Majesty 廳……………100 名	
Throne 廳……………150 名	
Scepter 廳……………200 名	
Royalty 廳……………250 名	

65 目的問題

翻譯 女子為何會打電話？
(A) 為了報名活動
(B) 為了詢問會議講者
(C) 為了詢問設施的位置
(D) 為了更新預約

解析 這是詢問打電話用意的題型，一定要仔細聆聽對話剛開始的部分。內容談到女子之所以會打電話，是要談談其公司要舉辦會議租借場地的事，想知道最後是否還能進行幾項變更（I'm calling about the booking my company made at your facilities for our upcoming conference. I'm wondering if it's possible to make some last-minute changes.），因此答案是 (D)。

換句話說
make some ~ changes 變更一些 →
update a reservation 更新預約

字彙 sign up for 報名

66 圖片題

翻譯 請看圖片，女子本來預約哪一種會議室？

(A) **Majesty 廳**
(B) Throne 廳
(C) Scepter 廳
(D) Royalty 廳

解析 確認目錄的資訊，仔細聆聽和關鍵詞 originally booked 相關的部分，男子說原本預約的會議室可容納 100 個人（the room you originally booked can seat only 100 people），從目錄中可知道女子原本是預約 Majesty 廳，所以答案是 (A)。

67 請求問題

翻譯 女子提出何種要求？
(A) 追加餐點
(B) 報告裝備
(C) 變更的會議室目錄
(D) 追加嘉賓的入場券

解析 仔細聆聽女子話中與要求相關的用法，女子想要提供餐點給新增的參加者，訂餐量就會增加為兩倍（We'll also need to double our catering order to provide meals to all the extra attendees.），因此答案是(A)。

換句話說
double ~ catering order 訂餐增加為兩倍 →
Additional food 追加餐點

68-70 🔊加拿大發音→美國發音

Questions 68-70 refer to the following conversation and service options.

M: Hello. Thank you for calling Velco. This is Marvin. How may I help you?
W: Hi. My name is Sandra Smith. ⁶⁸I'd like to change my phone plan.
M: Will this be a temporary change?
W: No, it will be ongoing. ⁶⁸Starting this month, I need to make regular calls to new clients in other countries.
M: Um . . . You currently have the Gold Plan. ⁶⁹I'd recommend switching to a different plan. There is one that includes free international calling.
W: Great. I'll do that then.
M: OK. ⁷⁰I'll change your plan now. You should be able to make free calls in about an hour.

---

plan 收費制、制度　temporary 暫時的　ongoing 持續的
starting 開始　regular 經常、定期的　switch 改變
international 國際的、跨國的

翻譯 問題 68-70，請參考以下對話和服務選項。
男：您好，謝謝您來電 Velco 公司，我是 Marvin，請問需要什麼服務呢？
女：您好，我的名字是 Sandra Smith，⁶⁸ 我想變更電話的費率。
男：這是暫時的變更嗎？
女：不，以後也會繼續維持，⁶⁸ 我從這個月開始經常要打電話給國外的新客戶。
男：嗯……您目前有黃金方案，⁶⁹ 我建議變更為其他費

率，有一個就包含可免費撥打國際電話。
女：好，那就用那個吧。
男：我知道了，⁷⁰ 我現在就變更顧客的費率，一個小時後您就能免費通話。

	青銅費率	白銀費率	黃金費率	⁶⁹ 白金費率
免費國內電話	✓	✓	✓	✓
免費國際電話				✓
無限訊息		✓	✓	✓
無限網路			✓	✓

68 理由問題

翻譯 女子為何要變更服務費率？
(A) 她建立了新的商業關係。
(B) 需要額外的電話線。
(C) 想要升級為智慧型手機。
(D) 要去國外出差。

解析 仔細聆聽問題中和（change ~ service plan）相關的內容，女子說想要變更電話費率（I'd like to change my phone plan.），並表示從這個月開始經常要打電話給國外的新客戶（Starting this month, I need to make regular calls to new clients in other countries.），因此答案是 (A)。

字彙 establish 建立、確立　relationship 關係　additional 額外的

69 圖片題

翻譯 請看圖片，男子建議哪一種費率？
(A) 青銅費率
(B) 白銀費率
(C) 黃金費率
(D) 白金費率

解析 確認服務選項的資訊後，仔細聆聽和關鍵字 recommend 相關的部分，男子建議女子變更為其他費率，有一個就包含可撥打免費國際電話（I'd recommend switching to a different plan. There is one that includes free international calling.），從圖表中可知道男子推薦的白金費率，所以答案是 (D)。

70 之後將發生的事

翻譯 男子接下來大概會做什麼？
(A) 提供贈品。
(B) 徵收款項。
(C) 更新帳號。
(D) 撥打電話。

解析 仔細聆聽短文中最後的部分，男子回答要幫女子變更費率（I'll change your plan now.），由此可知要更新帳戶，所以答案是 (C)。

字彙 free gift 贈品　payment 款項、欠款

PART 4

71-73 英國發音

Questions 71-73 refer to the following telephone message.

This is Lindsay Kruger calling for Tyler Sharp. Mr. Sharp, I'm sorry to inform you that [71]I won't be able to meet with you tomorrow to listen to your sales proposal. [72]Unfortunately, a personal matter with a relative has come up, and I'll be taking the day off. I would like to reschedule the meeting for later this week—perhaps Thursday. As I'll be out of the office for the rest of today as well, [73]please leave a message with my assistant at 555-7558 to let me know if this will work for you. I apologize again for the cancellation and hope to hear back from you soon.

sales proposal 銷售提案（書）　relative 親戚
come up 出現、發生　take a day off 休息一天
reschedule 變更日程　perhaps 或許、可能　assistant 秘書

翻譯 問題 71-73，請參考以下電話訊息。
我是打電話給 Tyler Sharp 的 Lindsay Kruger。Sharp 先生，很抱歉，[71] 我明天無法和您開會聽銷售提案了。[72] 真是遺憾，因為我明天要休假去處理和親戚相關的私事。我希望會議時間能改到本週稍晚的時候，也許星期四。由於我今天剩下的時間也不會待在辦公室，[73] 希望您能回電告知自己是否方便，請來電至 555-7558 告訴我的秘書。對於取消會議這一點再次表示抱歉，希望您很快就能來電。

71 特定細節問題

翻譯 明天原本要討論什麼事呢？
(A) 工作日程
(B) 取消專案
(C) 就業機會
(D) 銷售提議

解析 仔細聆聽和關鍵字 tomorrow 相關的部分，內容談到明天要和對方開會聽銷售提議（I won't be able to meet with you tomorrow to listen to your sales proposal），因此答案是 (D)。
換句話說
sales proposal 銷售提案 →
sales proposition 銷售提議

字彙 proposition 提案、提議

72 理由問題

翻譯 會議為何一定要延後？
(A) 必須處理和家人相關的事。
(B) 航班超額預約了。
(C) 職員去國外出差中。
(D) 辦公室經理身體狀況不佳。

解析 仔細聆聽與關鍵詞 a meeting be postponed 相關的內容，打電話的人表示真是遺憾，因為明天要休假去

處理和親戚相關的私事，後來又說希望延到本週稍晚（Unfortunately, a personal matter with a relative has come up, and I'll be taking the day off. I would like to reschedule the meeting for later this week ~.），所以答案是 (A)。
換句話說
a personal matter with a relative 和親戚相關的私事 →
A family matter 家庭事務

字彙 postpone 延期、延後　handle 處理　ill 身體狀況不佳、生病

73 請求問題

翻譯 說話者向聽者提出何種要求？
(A) 去辦公室一趟。
(B) 聯絡秘書。
(C) 致電至手機。
(D) 寄送電子郵件。

解析 仔細聆聽短文後面和要求相關的用法，內容談到為了知道對方是否也同意變更的日期，希望對方能打給秘書告知一聲（please leave a message with my assistant ~ to let me know if this will work for you），因此答案是 (B)。

字彙 stop by 順便拜訪

74-76 美國發音

Questions 74-76 refer to the following news report.

Now it's time for Radio ZPS's morning traffic update. Due to an accident that took place 30 minutes ago, [74]Lincoln Bridge has been closed to vehicles and pedestrians. Although nobody was injured, a railing was damaged and is currently being fixed. Also, [75]the vehicles involved in the accident need to be towed from the scene before the bridge will once again be accessible. This should be taken care of within the hour. For the time being, however, [76]I encourage commuters to cross the Hubert River by using West Bridge.

traffic update 交通快訊　pedestrian 行人　be injured 受傷
railing 欄杆　involve（狀況、事件、活動對人物）牽連
tow 拖吊　scene 現場、狀況　accessible 可使用的
take care of 處理、照顧　for the time being 短時間內
commuter 通勤者

翻譯 問題 74-76，請參考以下新聞報導。
現在是廣播 ZPS 的晨間交通快訊，因為 30 分鐘前發生了車禍，[74] 目前 Lincoln 橋禁止車輛和行人使用，雖然沒有人受傷，但因為欄杆受損，目前正在修復當中。另外，[75] 在橋樑再次開通前，會把受意外牽連的車輛拖離現場，應該會在一小時內處理完畢。不過，在這段時間內，[76] 我建議通勤族最好利用 West 橋通過 Hubert 河。

74 特定細節問題

翻譯 目前哪一件事還在進行中？
(A) 賽跑
(B) 設置標誌

(C) 建物施工
(D) 補修橋樑

解析 注意聆聽和關鍵詞 still taking place 相關的內容，內容談到 Lincoln 橋禁止車輛和行人通行，雖然沒有人受傷，但因為欄杆受損，目前正在修復當中（Lincoln Bridge has been closed to vehicles and pedestrians. ~ a railing was damaged and is currently being fixed.），所以答案是 (D)。

字彙 sign 標誌、看板　installation 安裝

75 之後將發生的事

翻譯 一個小時內大概會發生什麼事？
(A) 會另外提供最新的資訊。
(B) 社區活動將要開始了。
(C) 將車輛從某一處搬移。
(D) 醫院會再次開門。

解析 仔細聆聽和關鍵詞 within the hour 相關的部分，內容談到受車禍牽連的車輛將會拖離現場，且在一小時內會處理（the vehicles involved in the accident need to be towed from the scene ~. This should be taken care of within the hour.），因此答案是 (C)。

換句話說
the vehicles ~ need to be towed from the scene 車輛必須拖離現場 → Cars will be moved from an area 將車輛從某一處搬移

字彙 further 額外的　update 最新資訊

76 提議問題

翻譯 說話者提出何種意見？
(A) 使用其他途徑
(B) 提早出門上班
(C) 使用大眾交通工具
(D) 避開十字路口

解析 仔細聆聽短文後面與提議相關的部分，內容談到建議通勤者利用 West 橋穿越 Hubert 河（I encourage commuters to cross the Hubert River by using West Bridge），因此答案是 (A)。

字彙 commute 通勤　public transport 大眾運輸
intersection 十字路口

77-79 🇨🇦加拿大發音

Questions 77-79 refer to the following announcement.

Good morning, everyone. As scientific consultants, [77]you've been asked to come here today to discuss my company's plan to open a factory. [78]We've found a location that could be ideal, but . . . uh . . . Actually, it's near a residential area. [78/79]I'm worried that our plant might have a negative impact on the natural surroundings and local residents as it will produce some chemical waste. [79]Therefore, we have to develop a strategy for disposing of the waste properly so that it cannot get into the local rivers. That's where you all come in. I want your ideas on how such a system might be developed. ⟳

consultant 顧問　ideal 理想的、完美的　plant 工廠　impact 影響
surrounding 環境、周圍　chemical waste 化學廢棄物
dispose 處理　get into 進入
come in 參加（工作、事業等）、干涉

翻譯 問題 77-79，請參考以下公告。
大家早安，今天邀請身為科學界顧問的各位來，[77] 是為了討論我們公司要開設工廠的計劃。[78] 我們已經找到理想的位置了，不過……其實那邊位於住宅區附近。[78/79] 因為工廠會排放一些化學廢棄物，我擔心會對自然環境與當地居民造成不良的影響。[79] 因此，我們必須研發能確實處理廢棄物的戰略，讓廢棄物無法流入當地河川。這就是要仰賴各位的地方了。我希望各位能提供點子研發這類系統。

77 特定細節問題

翻譯 公司在計劃做什麼？
(A) 搬遷總公司。
(B) 訂購一些化學產品。
(C) 開設新工廠。
(D) 讓一些員工轉調。

解析 仔細聆聽和關鍵詞 company planning to do 相關的內容，文中談到聽話者受邀來到此地是為了討論公司開設工廠的計劃（you've been asked to come here today to discuss my company's plan to open a factory），由此可知公司要開設新工廠，所以答案是 (C)。

換句話說
factory 工廠 → plant 工廠

字彙 transfer 轉調、轉移

78 意圖掌握問題

翻譯 說話者為何談到「其實那邊位於住宅區附近」？
(A) 為了打發潛在的擔憂
(B) 為了強調是便利的位置
(C) 為了提議搬遷設施
(D) 為了指出複雜的因素

解析 仔細聆聽與引用句 Actually, it's near a residential area 相關的部分，文中談到已經找到理想的場所（We've found a location that could be ideal），後來表示擔心會對自然環境與當地居民造成不良的影響（I'm worried that our plant might have a negative impact on the natural surroundings and local residents ~.），由此可知是為了指出與設立工廠相關的複雜因素，所以答案是 (D)。

字彙 dismiss 甩掉、斷然拒絕　highlight 強調　point out 指出、注目

79 特定細節問題

翻譯 說話者在擔心什麼？
(A) 財務費用
(B) 環境汙染
(C) 生產日程
(D) 政府政策

解析 仔細聆聽和關鍵字 concerned 相關的內容，文中談到

因為工廠會排放一些化學廢棄物，擔心會對自然環境與當地居民造成不良的影響。因此必須研發能確實處理廢棄物的戰略，讓廢棄物無法流入在地河流（I'm worried that our plant might have a negative impact on the natural surroundings ~ as it will produce some chemical waste. Therefore, we have to develop a strategy for disposing of the waste properly so that it cannot get into the local rivers.），所以答案是 (B)。

換句話說
a negative impact on the natural surroundings 對自然環境的負面影響 → Environmental pollution 環境汙染

字彙 financial 財務的、財政的　environmental pollution 環境汙染
policy 政策

80-82 ⦿ 澳洲發音

Questions 80-82 refer to the following instruction.

> [80]I'm here today to share some tips on job hunting. As a professional recruiter, I've seen thousands of résumés and job applications, so I can tell you what's effective and what's not. [81]I know what you might be thinking . . . how hard can it be to apply for a job? You'd be surprised. [81]Many people make very basic mistakes, such as not proofreading their résumés and cover letters. However, even [82]one incorrectly spelled word can leave a bad impression on a hiring manager. I'll be teaching you how to catch things like these so that you can best position yourself for success.

job hunting 求職　recruiter 招募人員　résumé 履歷
application 申請書　proofread 校對　spell 拼寫
leave a bad impression 留下壞印象　position 擺在～的位置

翻譯 問題 80-82，請參考以下說明。
[80] 我今天之所以會站在這裡，是為了和各位分享求職的幾項訣竅，身為專業的招聘負責人，我看過數千份的履歷和入職申請書，因此我可以告訴各位哪一種有效，哪一種沒有效果。[81] 我知道各位的想法……遞出履歷有多困難？各位大概會嚇一跳吧，[81] 很多人都會犯下沒有校正履歷和自我介紹這一類非常基本的失誤。但是，[82] 連一個拼寫錯誤的單字都可能給招募經理留下不好的印象。我會教導各位找出這類問題的方法，讓各位在往成功的路上把自己放到最好的位置。

80 主題問題

翻譯 說話者主要在談些什麼？
(A) 工作關係的建議
(B) 給求職者的指導
(C) 職涯抉擇
(D) 執行工作培訓

解析 題目詢問主題，內容談到今天是為了分享幾個求職訣竅而來的（I'm here today to share some tips on job hunting.），後來談起指導求職者的內容，所以答案是 (B)。

字彙 guidance 指導、說明　job seeker 求職者
career path 前途、職涯規劃　pursue 執行、追求
job training 工作培訓

81 意圖掌握問題

翻譯 說話者說：「各位大概會很驚訝」，他想暗示什麼？
(A) 文件有幾個地方出錯。
(B) 程序變得更複雜了。
(C) 需要的條件比較新穎。
(D) 問題很容易發生。

解析 仔細聆聽和問題引用句 You'd be surprised 相關的部分，內容談到「我知道各位的想法……遞出履歷有多困難」（I know what you might be thinking . . . how hard can it be to apply for a job?），並表示許多人都會犯下非常基本的錯誤（Many people make very basic mistakes），由此可知是很容易發生問題，所以答案是 (D)。

字彙 process 程序、過程　requirement 需要條件

82 特定細節問題

翻譯 根據說話者，什麼事可能會留下壞印象？
(A) 冗長的自我介紹
(B) 不夠充足的資歷
(C) 拼寫錯誤
(D) 不恰當的服裝

解析 仔細聆聽和關鍵詞 leave a bad impression 有關的部分，文中談到連一個拼寫錯誤的單字都可能給招募經理留下不好的印象（one incorrectly spelled word can leave a bad impression on a hiring manager），因此答案是(C)。

換句話說
incorrectly spelled word 拼寫不正確的單字 → Spelling mistakes 拼寫錯誤

字彙 insufficient 不充分的　spelling 拼寫　inappropriate 不恰當的
attire 服裝

83-85 ⦿ 加拿大發音

Questions 83-85 refer to the following speech.

> [83]As the manager of CRT Center, I'm happy to see that so many people have come to celebrate the grand opening of the complex. [84]This venue will be the new location for all games played by our city's amateur baseball team, the Dallas Snakes. Throughout the afternoon, fans will be able to explore the complex, including the field, general seating area, and luxury suites. But before you head inside, I want to give special thanks to the residents of the Dallas community. [85]I'd also like to express my gratitude to Mayor Kent Berkley for providing such overwhelming support for the construction of the facility. Without his help, it wouldn't have been possible to build this state-of-the-art complex.
>
> ➡

grand opening 開張、開店　complex 綜合球場、綜合大樓
explore 探索　field 競賽場　luxury suite 奢華包廂
give thanks to 對～表示感謝　express gratitude 表達感謝之意
mayor 市長　overwhelming 極大的、壓倒性的
state-of-the-art 最尖端的

翻譯 問題 83-85，請參考以下演說。

> 83 身為 CRT 中心的管理者，很高興見到這麼多人為了慶祝綜合球場的開幕而來。84 這個場地將成為本市業餘棒球隊 Dallas Snakes 所有比賽的新場地，整個下午球迷們可參觀包含球場、一般觀眾席、奢華包廂等整個綜合大樓。但前往內部之前，我想特別感謝達拉斯地區的居民。85 另外，我想感謝對建設此一設施給予強力支持的市長 Kent Berkley，如果沒有市長的支持，大概就無法建蓋此一最尖端綜合球場。

83 說話者問題

翻譯 說話者最可能是誰？
- **(A) 設施管理者**
- (B) 政府官員
- (C) 專業運動選手
- (D) 企業投資人

解析 仔細聆聽短文中和身分、職業相關的用語，說話者表示身為 CRT 中心的管理者，很高興見到這麼多人為了慶祝綜合球場的開幕而來（As the manager of CRT Center, I'm happy to see that so many people have come to celebrate the grand opening of the complex.），由此可知說話者是設施管理者，所以答案是 (A)。

字彙 government official 政府官員　athlete 運動選手　investor 投資者

84 特定細節問題

翻譯 CRT 中心將被用於什麼？
- (A) 慈善拍賣
- **(B) 運動場**
- (C) 產業大會
- (D) 地區聚會

解析 仔細聆聽和關鍵詞 CRT Center be used for 相關的內容，內容談到這裡將成為本市業餘棒球隊 Dallas Snakes 所有比賽的新場地（This venue[CRT Center] will be the new location for all games played by our city's amateur baseball team），所以答案是 (B)。

> 換句話說
> games played by ~ baseball team 棒球隊的比賽
> → Sporting events 運動比賽

字彙 charity 慈善　auction 拍賣　sporting event 運動比賽　gathering 聚會、集會

85 提及何事的問題

翻譯 關於 Kent Berkley，提到了什麼？
- (A) 監督了部分的工程。
- (B) 最近和市長見面了。
- **(C) 支援了專案。**
- (D) 計劃要進行演說。

解析 仔細聆聽和關鍵詞 Kent Berkley 相關的部分，說話者表示自己想感謝對建設此一設施給予強力支持的市長 Kent Berkley（I'd also like to express my gratitude to Mayor Kent Berkley for providing such overwhelming support for the construction of the facility.），因此答案是 (C)。

> 換句話說
> providing ~ support for the construction of the facility 為了建蓋設施而給予支持 → supported a project 支持了專案

字彙 oversee 監督

86-88 🔊澳洲發音

Questions 86-88 refer to the following telephone message.

> Hi, Sheena? It's John Murray. 86I'm a student in your Tuesday guitar class. 87I was wondering if you have any recommendations for an electric guitar. Since you've been playing for years, I figured that you'd be the best person to ask. I'm considering buying one, and I want to make sure I choose something that's right for me. I need a guitar that's affordable and not too heavy as I'll be carrying it around pretty frequently. 88As for a brand, there isn't a specific one that I like more than another . . . so I'm flexible. Please give me a callback when you get a chance. Thanks!
>
> figure 認為、判斷　affordable （價格）適當的、正確的
> frequently 經常　as for 就~而言　flexible 可變通的、靈活的
> callback 回電話

翻譯 問題 86-88，請參考以下訊息。

> 您好，是 Sheena 嗎？我是 John Murray，86 我是您星期二的吉他課程的學生。87 我想知道您有沒有推薦的電子吉他，因為您已經演奏很多年了，我認為請教您是最合適的。我在考慮買電子吉他，我想挑一個最適合自己的，我需要價格適當且不會太重的吉他，因為我會經常攜帶它行動。88 我沒有特別喜歡的品牌……所以我的選擇很彈性，有機會請回電話給我，謝謝！

86 聽者問題

翻譯 聽者最可能是誰？
- (A) 演唱會籌辦者
- **(B) 音樂講師**
- (C) 學校事務官
- (D) 商店老闆

解析 仔細聆聽短文中與身分、職業相關的用語，說話者表示是對方星期二吉他課程的學生（I'm a student in your Tuesday guitar class.），由此可知聽者是音樂講師，所以答案是 (B)。

字彙 instructor 講師　secretary （機關等的）事務官、秘書

87 目的問題

翻譯 訊息的主要用意是什麼？
- (A) 回答問題
- (B) 預約演奏者
- (C) 報名課程
- **(D) 徵求意見**

解析 這是詢問訊息主旨的題型，仔細聆聽短文剛開始的內容，掌握整體的語境。說話者表示希望對方介紹不錯的電子吉他（I was wondering if you have any recommendations for an electric guitar.），由此可知是在徵求意見，所以答案是 (D)。

字彙 performer 演奏者

88 意圖掌握問題

翻譯 說話者為何說「我的選擇很彈性」？
(A) 因為行程從容。
(B) 沒有特別喜歡的品牌。
(C) 有時間上課。
(D) 喜歡的演奏者很多。

解析 仔細聆聽與引用句 I'm flexible 相關的部分，當事者說自己沒有特別喜愛的品牌（As for a brand, there isn't a specific one that I like more than another），由此可知他沒有偏愛的品牌，所以答案是 (B)。

字彙 open 悠閒的、沒有約定的　preference 偏好（度）
available 有時間的

89-91 🔊 英國發音

Questions 89-91 refer to the following speech.

It's been a pleasure to spend 25 years as creative director for Magique Perfume House. [89]Now that I'm retiring, I'd like to briefly reflect on my working life. One of my greatest achievements and memories was working with so many of you to market the Evening Rose line of perfume. [90]That campaign played a key role in expanding our company into international markets. I still think of it as a highlight of my career. However, [91]the experience I value the most was getting the chance to get to know you all better. You're such wonderful people, and I'll miss interacting with you so often.

---

creative director 創意總監　retire 退休　briefly 短暫地、簡單地
reflect on 深思　market 行銷　line 產品系列、種類
play a key role 扮演重要角色　highlight 最重要的部分
career 職涯　value 珍視　interact 交流、互動

翻譯 問題 89-91，請參考以下演說。
我很高興擔任 Magique Perfume House 的創意總監 25 年，[89] 因為我要退休了，所以想短暫回顧一下自己的職場生活。我最棒的成果與回憶之一，就是和各位共同行銷 Evening Rose 香水產品，[90] 那個活動在我們公司擴展到國際市場時扮演相當重要的角色，我至今還是認為那是我的職場生涯中最重要的一部分。但 [91] 我最珍視的經驗就是有機會能更進一步認識各位，各位是相當棒的人，我將會很懷念和各位交流的歲月。

89 場地問題

翻譯 聽者最可能在什麼地方？
(A) 招聘面試
(B) 貿易博覽會
(C) 退休紀念活動
(D) 節日派對

解析 仔細聆聽短文中和場所相關的用語，說話者表示自己要退休了，所以想短暫回顧一下自己的職場生活（Now that I'm retiring, I'd like to briefly reflect on my working life.），由此可知聽者在參加退休紀念活動，所以答案是 (C)。

字彙 recruitment 僱用、新招聘　trade show 貿易博覽會
retirement 退休　celebration 紀念活動

90 特定細節問題

翻譯 說話者為何會說某廣告活動很重要？
(A) 吸引外國媒體的關注。
(B) 獲得獎項。
(C) 使用新的技術。
(D) 對公司的擴大有所貢獻。

解析 仔細聆聽和關鍵詞 a campaign significant 相關的內容，說話者談到：「那個活動在我們公司擴展到國際市場時扮演相當重要的角色」（That campaign played a key role in expanding our company into international markets.），所以答案是 (D)。

換句話說
played a key role in expanding ~ company into international markets 公司擴展至國際市場時扮演重要的角色 →
helped grow a business 對公司的擴大有所貢獻

字彙 attract media attention 吸引輿論的關注

91 提及何事的問題

翻譯 說話者表示自己最珍視什麼？
(A) 職員的貢獻
(B) 專案的目的
(C) 海外的經驗
(D) 和同事們的關係

解析 仔細聆聽和關鍵詞 values the most 相關的部分，說話者表示自己最珍視的經驗就是有機會能更進一步認識同事（the experience I value the most was getting the chance to get to know you all better），所以答案是 (D)。

字彙 purpose 目的

92-94 🔊 美國發音

Questions 92-94 refer to the following report.

Yesterday afternoon, [92]the Harlington County School Board formally announced plans to build a second high school. There is currently only one high school in the district, and that institution alone is no longer able to meet the demands of the local community. The new one will serve students living in the western part of the district. Ultimately, both facilities will accommodate roughly 2,000 students. [93]During the announcement, school board chair Yolanda Moya said that construction of the school will take place over 10 months—from April to January. Given how many classrooms are overcrowded at the moment,

➡

[94]most students and parents approve of this government project.

---

county school 公立學校　formally 正式地　district 地區
institution 機構、團體　meet 滿足　serve 滿足（要求、需求等）
ultimately 終究　accommodate 容納　roughly 約略
given 考慮到　overcrowded 過度擁擠的　approve of 贊成、同意

翻譯　問題 92-94，請參考以下報導。

　　昨天下午，[92] Harlington 公立學校委員會正式宣布要建蓋第二個高中的計劃案，該地區只有一所高中，光靠一間教育機構已無法滿足當地需求。新學校可滿足住在該地區西部之學生的需求，就結果來說，兩所學校應該可以容納 2,000 名的學生。在公布的過程中，[93] 學校委員會會長 Yolanda Moya 說建蓋學校的工程將從 4 月進行到 1 月，耗時 10 個月，考量到目前教室過度擁擠的因素，目前[94] 大部分的學生和家長都很贊成政府的專案。

92 主題問題

翻譯　報導主要在說些什麼？
(A) 要多蓋一所學校
(B) 培訓幾位教師
(C) 任命新校長
(D) 擴大目前的教育課程

解析　這是詢問報導主題的問題，一定要聆聽短文前面的部分。文中談到 Harlington 公立學校委員會宣布要建蓋第二個高中的計劃案（the Harlington County School Board formally announced plans to build a second high school），後來就在談論蓋新學校的事，所以答案是 (A)。

字彙　establish 設立　appoint 任命　principal 校長　expand 擴大　curriculum 教育課程

93 特定細節問題

翻譯　Yolanda Moya 昨天宣布了什麼事情？
(A) 辦公室的位置
(B) 課程的規模
(C) 開發的費用
(D) 專案的期程

解析　仔細聆聽與關鍵句 Yolanda Moya announce yesterday 相關的內容，文中談到 Yolanda Moya 說建蓋學校的工程將從 4 月進行到 1 月，共耗時 10 個月（During the announcement, ~ Yolanda Moya said that construction of the school will take place over 10 months），因此答案是 (D)。
換句話說
construction of the school will take place over 10 months 學校的建設將花費 10 個月 → The length of a project 專案的時長

字彙　size 規模　length 期間

94 提及何事的問題

翻譯　關於家長的描述說到了什麼？
(A) 他們不希望孩子換學校。
(B) 針對上星期的案件進行了投票。
(C) 接受政府的企劃案。

(D) 認為費用應該降低。

解析　仔細聆聽和 parents 相關的問題，文中談到大部分的家長都很贊成政府的專案（most ~ parents approve of this government project），因此答案是 (C)。

字彙　relocate 搬遷　expense 費用　lower 降低

95-97 ③ 英國發音

Questions 95-97 refer to the following talk and form.

---

[95]Thank you for stopping for this brief demonstration of Joytone Industries' newest electric keyboard, the TouchFone 1000. As you can see, [96]the device has a variety of buttons on the front panel. These buttons control different sound effects, of which there are over 100. Moreover, the TouchFone 1000 is our most energy-efficient keyboard. Lastly, since [97]the TouchFone 1000 is our lightest model yet, it is easy to transport. Right now, I'll hand out some flyers that include technical details about this product. Anyone who's interested in trying the device is free to experiment with this one.

---

brief 簡略的、短的　demonstration 彩排、展示　electric 電子的
a variety of 各種的　control 調節　energy-efficient 能源效率佳的
technical 技術性的　transport 搬動、搬運　hand out 發放

翻譯　問題 95-97，請參考以下談話和表格。

　　[95] 謝謝各位為了 Joytone Industries 公司的最新電子琴 TouchFone 1000[96]展示專程來一趟，就如同各位看見的一樣，此一電子琴前面的面板有多個按鍵，這些按鍵可調整音效。另外，TouchFone 1000 具備最優秀的能源效率，最後，因為 [97] 這是我們目前最輕的型號，搬運相當方便。現在我會把寫有產品技術細節的宣傳單發給大家，想玩一玩的人都能試試看。

產品規格	
產品重量	價格
[97] 20 磅	2,000 美元
25 磅	1,750 美元
28 磅	1,000 美元
35 磅	2,200 美元

95 主題問題

翻譯　哪一種產品正被展示？
(A) 掃除用品
(B) 數位列印機
(C) 樂器
(D) 平面螢幕電視

解析　題目詢問對話的主題，所以一定要留意開頭。「Thank you for stopping for this brief demonstration of ~ electric keyboard」中說「謝謝各位過來觀看電子琴的簡短展示」，因此 (C) 是正確答案。

字彙　appliance 用品　musical instrument 樂器　flat screen 平面螢幕（的）

96 特定細節問題

翻譯 說話者指出前面的面板有什麼？
(A) 顯示螢幕
(B) 操作鍵
(C) 電源位置
(D) 警告標示器

解析 仔細聆聽和關鍵詞 on the front panel 相關的部分，此一裝置正面的面板有按鍵，這些按鍵可調整各種音響效果（the device has a variety of buttons on the front panel. These buttons control different sound effects），由此可知正面面板上有操作鍵，所以答案是 (B)。

換句話說
buttons control different sound effects 按鍵可調整各種音響效果 → Control buttons 操作鍵

字彙 display screen 顯示螢幕　warning 警告、注意　indicator 指示器

97 圖片題

翻譯 請看圖片，TouchFone 1000 多少錢？
(A) 2,000 美元
(B) 1,750 美元
(C) 1,000 美元
(D) 2,200 美元

解析 確認表格的資訊後，仔細聆聽和關鍵詞 TouchFone 1000 相關的部分，內容談到 TouchFone 1000 是目前最輕的型號（the TouchFone 1000 is our lightest model yet.），由此可知它是 2,000 美元，所以答案是 (A)。

98-100 🎧 澳洲發音

Questions 98-100 refer to the following tour information and map.

Welcome to Dwyers' Sweets. I'm Raymond Watts, the factory's manager. [98]We've been making candy at this location for 100 years. You may be surprised to learn that most of our candies start off with the same base, cooked sugar, as you can see here. [99]When we get to the flavoring department in the next area, we'll show you how we give each type of candy its individual taste. Using this basic technique, we produce more than 150 varieties of candy that are sold around the world. [100]When we finish our tour, we'll give you some of our best-selling products to try.

---

start off with 開始於　base 主要成分、主材料
flavoring 香料、調味料　individual 各自不同的、各自的
try 試吃、試穿

翻譯 問題 98-100，請參考以下觀光指南和地圖。
歡迎來到 Dwyers' Sweets，我是工廠經理 Raymond Watts，[98]我們在這個地方製造糖果已經有 100 年的歷史了，就如同大家看見的一樣，或許大家會很驚訝發現，我們大多數的糖果原來是以煮過的糖當作基底。[99]到了下一個區域的調味部門後，大家就會知道我們是如何給每種糖果創造出各自的味道。我們就是用這一基本技術，生產出超過 150 種糖果賣到全世界。[100] 等參觀結束

時，我們會讓各位試吃我們最暢銷的幾種產品。

98 特定詳細資料

翻譯 Dwyers' Sweets 的特徵是什麼？
(A) 生產 100 種糖果。
(B) 開第二間分店。
(C) 工廠經營了一世紀。
(D) 一直都是家族企業。

解析 仔細聆聽和 characteristic of Dwyers' Sweets 相關的內容，文中談到這個地方製造糖果已經 100 年了（We've been making candy at this location for 100 years.），所以答案是 (C)。

字彙 remain 餘留、留下　family-owned business 家族企業

99 圖表題

翻譯 請看圖表，參訪待會要往哪走？
(A) 第 1 區
(B) 第 2 區
(C) 第 3 區
(D) 第 4 區

解析 仔細聆聽和關鍵詞 tour group go next 相關的內容，文中談到只要去下一個區域調味部門，就會知道如何賦予各種糖果其各自的味道（When we get to the flavoring department in the next area, we'll show you how we give each type of candy its individual taste.），由此可知觀光團接下來要去調味區，所以答案是 (B)。

100 特定細節問題

翻譯 聽者在完成參觀後能獲得什麼？
(A) 糖果的樣品
(B) 暢銷商品的目錄
(C) 海外分店的位置
(D) 禮品券

解析 仔細聆聽和關鍵詞 receive after the tour 相關的內容，說話者表示參觀結束時，會提供幾種最暢銷的產品試吃（When we finish our tour, we'll give you some of our best-selling products[candies] to try.），因此答案是 (A)。

字彙 gift voucher 禮品券

PART 5

101 分辨意思後填入名詞

解析 因意思是「出示身分證」，(A) identification（身分證）是正確答案。使用 (B) identity（身分）就會變成「出示身分」，意思就會顯得不自然。

翻譯 訪客進入研究所或機密區時必須要出示身分證。

字彙 research facility 研究所　access v. 存取、進入
sensitive adj. 機密的、敏感的　identification n. 身分證、識別
identity n. 身分、本身

102 選出形容詞

解析 語境上是「雖然擴展至餐飲業，但主要還是著重於時尚」的意思，(C) primary（為主、主要的）是正確答案。(A) high 是「高的」；(B) multiple 是「複合的、多數的」；(D) outside 是「外部」。

翻譯 Orex Enterprises 雖然擴展至餐飲業，但主要還是著重於時尚。

字彙 focus n. 重心、焦點　expand v. 擴張、發展
restaurant business 餐飲業

103 選出符合時態的詞彙

解析 因為主詞（Mr. Kurtz）感到滿足，所以要使用被動語態。和 be 動詞（was）一起形成被動語態動詞的過去分詞 (A) pleased 是正確答案。Be 動詞後面是補語，雖然也能放名詞 (D)，但會變成「Kurtz 先生滿足」的意思，整句話就會很不通順，所以 (D) 無法成為答案。

翻譯 Kurtz 先生相當滿意契約協商，那項協商讓工資提升了15%。

字彙 contract n. 契約　negotiation n. 協商、協議
result in 造成～的結果　please v. 使～滿足、取悅

104 填入 those

解析 句子的主詞位置空著，因為空格後是關係子句（who ~ website），受關係子句修飾後，代表「透過公司網站繳交履歷的人」的 (C) those 是正確答案。關係代名詞 (B) 和 (D) 的前面必須要有先行詞，所以無法成為答案。

翻譯 只有透過公司網站繳交履歷的人才會被列為該實習職位的人選。

字彙 submit v. 繳交　résumé n. 履歷　consider v. 考慮

105 填入副詞

解析 想要修飾動名詞（selling），就必須放副詞，(A) exclusively（僅僅、專門）是正確答案。名詞 (B)、動詞 (C)、形容詞 (D) 無法修飾動名詞。

翻譯 Pete's Produce 以只有販售有機水果和蔬菜聞名。

字彙 be well-known for 以～聞名　organic adj. 有機的
exclusion n. 除外、排除　exclude v. 不包括、排除
exclusive adj. 排他的、獨占的、高檔的

106 填入符合時態的動詞

解析 因為有和過去完成式一起使用的「By the time + 過去式動詞（opened）」，所以過去完成式 (D) had established 是正確答案。

翻譯 SolarTech 公司在歐洲開設第一間工廠時，在美國和亞洲都已經設有工廠了。

字彙 facility n. 設施、設備　establish v. 設立、建立

107 填入副詞

解析 想修飾動詞（work）就必須要有副詞，因此副詞 (D) routinely（日常的、常規的）是正確答案。動詞或分詞 (A)、名詞或形容詞 (B)、名詞 (C) 無法修飾動詞。

翻譯 Flemwell 百貨公司的職員在繁忙的假期通常要加班。

字彙 work overtime 加班　route v.（經由～）發送
routine n. 日常；adj. 日常的

108 填入介系詞

解析 因為必須是「使用機場各個地方的自動報到機臺」的意思，所以 (B) throughout（～到處）是正確答案。

翻譯 Air East 公司的乘客們被建議去使用機場各個地方的自動報到機臺。

字彙 be advised to do 被建議去做　automated adj. 自動的
check-in n. 搭機報到手續

109 選出動詞

解析 語境上來看是「無限量訊息發送和流量使用的手機費率，避免衍生額外費用」的意思，所以答案是 (D) avoid（避開）。(A) prepare 是「準備」；(B) shorten 是「縮短」；(C) comply 是「遵從」；(A) prepare 如果當作「防止出乎預料的費用」使用，就必須和介系詞 for 搭配。

翻譯 顧客可藉由申請無限量訊息發送和流量使用的手機費率，避免衍生額外費用。

字彙 unexpected adv. 出乎預料的　fee n. 費用
cellular adj. 手機的　unlimited adj. 無限的　usage n. 使用

110 填入 to 不定詞的 in order to

解析 這是同時具備了主詞（Employees）、動詞（must contact）、受詞（the human resources department）的完整子句，___ request a leave of absence 應該視為懸垂修飾語。因此引導動詞（request）且代表目的「要求請假」的 (B) in order to 是正確答案。To 不定詞代表目的時，可使用 in order to 或 so as to 代替 to。
副詞 (A) 和 (D) 無法成為懸垂修飾語，因介系詞 (C) 引導沒有動詞的句子，所以無法成為答案。

翻譯 職員必須聯絡人資部才能要求請假。

字彙 contact v. 聯絡　leave of absence 請假

111 選出名詞

解析 語境上是「根據租賃契約條件，房客必須在搬家前一個月告知」的意思，(A) terms（條件）是正確答案。(B) 的 right 是「權利」；(C) cause 是「理由」；(D) sign 是「記號、信號」。

翻譯 根據租賃契約條件，房客必須在搬家前一個月告知。

字彙 under prep. 根據（協議、法律等）
lease agreement 租賃契約　tenant n. 房客
give a month's notice 1 個月前告知
move out（原本居住的屋子）搬出去

112 填入疑問詞

解析 這是在 be 動詞（is）補語位置的句子（the name ~ announced）前填上名詞子句連接詞的題型，空格後有具備主詞（the name ~ CEO）、動詞（will be announced）的完美句子，因為意思必須是「公布新任執行長名字的時候」，(A) when（的時候）是正確答案。因為空格後有完整的子句，引導不完整子句的 (B) 和 (D) 無法成為答案。

翻譯 這個星期三會宣布 Zoltek Engineering 公司新任執行長的名字。

字彙 announce v. 宣告

113 分辨現在分詞與過去分詞後填入

解析 這是具備主詞（Athletes）、動詞（participated in）、受詞（the World Tennis Tournament）的完整句子，more than 50 countries 必須視為是懸垂修飾語。選項中可成為懸垂修飾語的分詞是 (A) 和 (B)，受分詞修飾的名詞（Athletes）和分詞是主動關係，意思是「代表的運動選手」，因此現在分詞 (A) representing 是正確答案。held last year in Guangzhou 是修飾受詞（the World Tennis Tournament）的懸垂修飾語。

翻譯 超過 50 個國家的體育代表選手參加了去年在廣州舉行的世界網球競賽。

字彙 athlete n. 運動選手　participate in 參加　tournament n. 比賽
represent v. 代表　representation n. 表現、代表

114 選出名詞

解析 因語境上是「鄉下的居民持續搬遷到城市」，(B) relocation（遷移）是正確答案。(A) arrangement 是「安排、協議」；(C) environment 是「環境」；(D) discovery 是「發現」。

翻譯 鄉下的居民持續搬遷到城市，造成馬尼拉出現住宅短缺的情況。

字彙 continued adj. 持續的　resident n. 居民　rural adj. 鄉下的
urban adj. 城市的　create v. 引起　housing shortage 住宅短缺

115 選出名詞

解析 語境上是「公告事項後，就會開始講即將到來的教育研討會細節」的意思，(D) emerge（為人所知、出現）是正確答案。(A) compile 是「編輯」；(B) include 是「包含」；(C) appoint 是「任命、指定」。由於空格後沒有

受詞，因此只能放不及物動詞 emerge。

翻譯 公告事項後，就會開始講即將到來的教育研討會細節。

字彙 following prep. 在～之後

116 填入介系詞

解析 題目的意思應該是「直到 2 月的第一週」，所以 (C) until（直到～）是正確答案。(A) about 表示「關於～」；(B) towards 表示「朝向～」；(D) except 表示「除了～之外」。

翻譯 所有關於公司可能合併的討論事項全都保留到 2 月的第一週。

字彙 potential adj. 潛在的　merger n. 合併　put on hold 保留

117 填入形容詞

解析 可修飾名詞（candidate）的形容詞 (C) inadequate（不恰當的）是正確答案。副詞 (A)、名詞 (B) 和 (D) 無法修飾名詞。

翻譯 因為缺乏專業經驗，就行銷職務上 Ross 先生被視為不夠格的求職者。

字彙 consider v. 認為　candidate n. 申請人　lack v. ～不足
professional adj. 專業的；n. 專家　inadequately adv. 不足地
inadequacy n. 不恰當、不足　inadequateness n. 不充分

118 選出形容詞

解析 Although 後面的副詞子句與後面句子的連結必須自然一點，語境上來看是「參加是自願制，但職員參與度非常高」，因此答案是 (B) voluntary（自發性的）。(A) precise 是「精準的」；(C) significant 是「重要的」；(D) persistent 是「堅持不懈、執意的」。

翻譯 HPS 公司參加社會責任委員會完全是自願制，但職員參與度非常高。

字彙 social responsibility 社會責任　committee n. 委員會
purely adv. 全然　involvement n. 參加、參與

119 填入 to 不定詞

解析 在動詞 allow 的受格補語必須放 to 不定詞，因此 (D) to return 是正確答案。

翻譯 圖書館正門旁邊設置的新收納箱，讓使用者也能在設施關閉後交還讀物。

字彙 place v. 放置；n. 場所　main entrance 正門
patron n. 使用者　material n. 資料

120 選出副詞

解析 Because 後面的副詞子句與後面句子的連接必須自然一點，因為語境上是「每季都會發行一次，訂閱者每年可獲得最新資訊」，因此答案是 (A) quarterly（每一季）。(B) properly 是「適當地」；(C) constantly「不斷地」；(D) recently 是「最近」。

翻譯 因為 SharpBiz 雜誌每季都會發行一次，訂閱者每年可獲得四次最新的重要經濟新聞。

字彙 an update on ～的最新資訊
essential adj. 主要的、必要的；n. 必備的事物

121 填入名詞

解析 可放在及物動詞（have）受詞位置的是名詞，因此名詞 (A) influence（影響）是正確答案。空格前放形容詞（greater）也是告知那是名詞位置的線索。形容詞 (B)、動詞或分詞 (C)、動詞 (D) 無法放在名詞的位置。

翻譯 根據最近的調查顯示，電視廣告對消費者造成的影響勝過報章雜誌的廣告。

字彙 advertisement n. 廣告

122 填入介系詞

解析 因為必須是「針對海外擴張狀況發表聲明」的意思，(C) regarding（針對～）是正確答案。(A) behind 是「在～後面」；(B) beyond 是「越過」；(D) within 是「之內」。

翻譯 Edgecom 公司今天將針對其海外擴張狀況發表聲明。

字彙 issue a statement 發表聲明　status n. 狀況、地位
overseas adj. 海外的；adv. 前往海外　expansion n. 擴張

123 選出動詞

解析 因語境上是「超過每月行動裝置數據分配量的顧客將會被額外收取費用」，所以答案是 (B) incur（受到、發生〔損失等〕）。(A) replace 是「代替」；(C) switch 是「轉變」；(D) possess 是「擁有」。

翻譯 超過每月行動裝置數據分配量的顧客將會被額外收取費用。

字彙 allocation n. 分配量、分配

124 選出名詞

解析 語境上是「夏季折扣銷售將會是購物者購買各種新鞋的好機會」，(A) opportunity（機會）是正確答案。(B) contribution 是「貢獻」；(C) appearance 是「出場、外貌」；(D) restoration 是「修復」。

翻譯 Mayfield Footwear 公司的夏季折扣銷售將會是購物者購買各種新鞋的好機會。

字彙 purchase v. 購買；n. 購買　a variety of 多樣的

125 副詞子句連接詞

解析 這是具備必要元素（Software products ～ purchase）的完整子句，＿＿＿＿they are ～ receipt 必須視為是懸垂修飾語。此一懸垂修飾語是有動詞（are accompanied）的句子，能引導修飾語的副詞子句連接詞 (B)、(C)、(D) 皆有可能是答案，因為必須是「必須要有發票正本才能退款」的意思，(D) as long as 是「只要～就」，因此是正確答案。(B) although 是「儘管」；(C) so that 是「以至於」的意思，因此不符合語境。

翻譯 Digital Age 公司的軟體產品只要和發票正本一起交還，就能在購買一個月內退款。

字彙 refund v. 退還；n. 退款　accompany v. 和～一起、陪伴

original receipt 收據正本

126 填入和主詞數量一致的動詞

解析 因為句子沒有動詞，動詞 (A) 和 (D) 都可能是答案，由於主詞（The revised environmental regulations）是複數，複數動詞是 (D) are aimed 是正確答案。be aimed at 是「以～為目標」的意思，是一種慣用語。

翻譯 修訂後的環境法規目標是減少當地工廠排放的溫室氣體量。

字彙 revised adj. 改正的、修訂的　environmental adj. 環境的
regulation n. 管制　greenhouse gas 溫室氣體　emit v. 釋放

127 填入相關連接詞

解析 和相關連接詞 but also 搭配的 (B) Not only 是正確答案，這是不定詞（Not）放在句子前面，讓主詞和動詞倒裝的句子。

翻譯 購買者不僅很滿意那棟房子的價格，對那邊的位置也給予高度的評價。

字彙 appreciate v. 高度評價、感謝

128 分辨人物名詞與抽象名詞

解析 可放在介系詞（for）受詞位置的是名詞，名詞 (A) 和 (D) 都有可能是正確答案，因為意思是「如果想獲得獎助金的資格」，抽象名詞 (A) assistance（支援、援助）是正確答案。人物名詞 (D) 想變成「若是想獲得助手的資格」的意思，就必須和「To qualify as a financial assistant」一起使用，因此它無法成為答案。

翻譯 若是想獲得獎助金的資格，學生們每學期都必須繳交獎助金申請書。

字彙 qualify v. 獲得資格　financial adj. 財務的
funding n. 財務支援、資金　request n. 請願（書）；v. 請求
term n. 學期

129 選出動詞

解析 語境上是「預計今年的收益將會減少，所以降低了預期銷售額」，reduce 的過去式 (C) reduced（降低）是正確答案。(A) overtake 是「超過」；(B) connect「連結」；(D) compliment 是「讚美」。

翻譯 Nesbit Software 公司預計今年的收益將會減少，所以降低了預期銷售額。

字彙 sales projections 預測銷售（額）　revenue n. 收益、銷售
decrease v. 減少

130 選出形容詞

解析 由於語境上是「先前的筆電型號比最新筆電型號更受歡迎」，(D) previous（先前的）是正確答案。(A) various 是「各式各樣的」；(B) relative 是「相對的」；(C) customary 是「慣常的」。

翻譯 Core Electronics 公司推出的前型號筆電比其最新筆電型號更受消費者歡迎。

字彙 release v. 發行、發布　latest adj. 最新的

PART 6

問題 131-134，請參考以下電子郵件。

收件人：Allan White <a.white@trytek.com>
寄件人：Joseph Winfield <j.winfield@trytek.com>
日期：3 月 12 日
主旨：入職研討會

Allan，

很高興能告訴各位，我們為新實習生準備的入職研討會計劃進行得很順利，不過還有一件重要事項尚未解決。131 我們還需要安排行銷部的人進行簡短的報告，但目前還沒有人聯絡我說要參加研討會。132 說不定職員們認為這需要花費很多的時間，133 所以請告訴所有人，演說者只會針對實習生的日常業務演說 10 分鐘而已。134 此外，你還得提醒大家研討會的參加者可獲得 200 美元，藉此補償他們的時間和努力。

謝謝。
Joe 敬上

---

planning n. 計劃　orientation n. 新人訓練
proceed v. 進行、前進　smoothly adv. 順利地
detail n.（詳細）事項；v. 詳細告知　unresolved adj. 未解決的
duty n. 業務、任務　remind v. 提醒　contributor n. 參加者、原因
compensation n. 補償

131 助動詞後面填入動詞原形

解析 空格前和 would 一起像助動詞一樣使用的用語「would like to + 動詞原形」的型態，(D) like to participate 「想參加」是正確答案。另外，「would like to + 動詞原形」是「想要做～」的意思。(B) 是「would have + p.p.」的形態，因為會變成「應該很想參加」的意思，顯得相當不自然，所以無法成為答案。

132 選出正確的句子

解析 (A) 講者已經開始排練演講了。
(B) 說不定職員們認為這需要花費很多的時間。
(C) 新成員同樣也為了發表自己的經驗而參加了。
(D) 對被指名的職員來說參加是義務。

解析 題目要選出填入空格的正確句子，因此必須掌握前後文或整體的語境。前面談到還需要安排人員進行簡短的演說，但目前還沒收到任何人的聯絡（We still need to schedule a short presentation ~, but I have not heard from anyone），後面則說請告訴所有人演說者只會針對實習生的日常業務演說 10 分鐘而已（So, please let everyone know that the presenter will talk ~ for only 10 minutes.），由此可知空格應該填入「說不定職員們認為這需要花費很多的時間」，所以答案是 (B)。

字彙 rehearse v. 排練　join v. 參加、結合　mandatory adj. 義務性的　specified adj. 明示的

133 選出形容詞　掌握整體的語境

解析 從語境上來看是「講者會針對實習生的___工作進行演

說」，(B) momentary（瞬間的）、(C) regular（日常的）、(D) ongoing（持續進行中的）都有可能是答案。光憑空格所在的句子無法選出正確答案，因此必須掌握前後文或整體的語境。因為前面談到目前正在進行為新實習生準備的入職研討會計劃，由此可知講者將針對實習生的日常工作進行演說，所以答案是 (C) regular。

字彙 momentary adj. 瞬間、片刻的　ongoing adj. 繼續進行中

134 填入連接副詞　掌握整體語境

解析 空格與逗號是句子最前面的連接副詞的位置，必須掌握前面的句子與空格所在句子的意思才能選出正確答案。前面的句子要求告訴所有人講者只要演說 10 分鐘，空格的句子則是說必須提醒參加研討會的所有人可獲得 200 美元，因此在前面句子談論的內容加上新資訊時使用的 (B) In addition（另外）是正確答案。

字彙 unfortunately adv. 不幸地　namely adv. 即　nevertheless adv. 儘管如此

問題 135-138，請參考以下廣告。

Madison Woodworks 公司
1987 年設立

135 您在計劃改造房子或辦公室嗎？請利用 Madison Woodworks 公司費心製作的精巧產品搭配各位的新裝潢吧，我們公司供給切斯特菲爾德郡的家庭與企業優質工藝品已經超過 30 年的時間了，無論是喜歡傳統風或是現代風，相信一定都能在我們店裡找到讓各位往後多年都很能觀賞的物品。136 如果喜歡客製化的產品，請和我們的內部設計師進行諮詢，打造獨有的餐桌、書桌或椅子。今天請來參觀我們位於曼徹斯特 Stockport 路 627 號的店面吧，137 到 7 月底前享有購買現成家具都有優惠，敬請把握。各位在線上也能觀看目錄，138 若是想瀏覽我們的所有系列產品，請到 www.madisonwoodworks.com。

---

complement v. 加強、補充　finely adv. 精巧地
craft v. 用心製作　handmade adj. 手工藝的
contemporary adj. 現代化的　consult v. 諮詢
take advantage of 利用　ready-made adj. 已經製作的、成品的

135 選出動詞　掌握前後文語境

解析 語境上來看是「您在計劃___房子或辦公室嗎？」，所有選項都可能是答案，光憑空格所在的句子無法選出正確答案，因此要掌握前後文或整體的語境。後面的句子談到「請利用 Madison Woodworks 公司費心製作的精巧產品搭配各位的新裝潢吧（Complement your new interior with finely crafted items from Madison Woodworks.）」，由此可知整句話是「您在計劃改造房子或辦公室嗎」，所以答案是 (B) renovate（改造）。

字彙 leave v. 離開、出發　finance v. 提供資金　promote v. 宣傳、促進

136 分辨現在分詞與過去分詞

解析 被修飾的（items）和分詞是被動關係，意思是「個人化的產品」，過去分詞 (D) personalized 是正確答案。

字彙 personalize v. 個人化

137 選出名詞　掌握整體的語境

解析 語境上是「在 7 月底前購買現成家具有優惠」，所有選
項都可能是答案，光憑空格所在的句子無法選出正確答
案，因此要掌握前後文或整體的語境。前面談到販售產
品用在居家與辦公環境，又提到桌子、餐桌與椅子，可
知這是家具店，因此答案是 (C) furniture（傢俱）。

字彙 fabric n. 纖維　gadget n. 工具　structure n. 建築物

138 選出正確的句子

解析 (A) 技術人員小組將會去各位的家裡檢查產品。
　　(B) 只要各位把保證書交給我們就能更換產品。
　　(C) 使用內附的說明書與幾項簡易工具，即可組裝。
　　**(D) 若是想瀏覽我們的所有系列產品，請到 www.
　　madisonwoodworks.com。**

解析 題目要選出填入空格的正確句子，因此要掌握前後文或
整體的語境。前面的句子談到在線上也能瀏覽目錄（You
can also view our catalog online.），由此可知空格必須
填入如果想觀看所有的系列產品就必須去官網，所以答
案是 (D)。

字彙 inspect v. 檢驗、檢查　assemble v. 組合
　　browse v. 瀏覽　entire adj. 整體的　collection n. 收藏品、收集品

問題 139-142，請參考以下備忘錄。

收件人：全體職員
寄件人：Jason Fraser，人資部
日期：8 月 5 日
主旨：專業性研發講座

[139] 管理層很高興宣布今年秋天開始，Hearthstone
Appliances 公司的職員將有資格獲得與業務領域相關的學
術費用補貼，參加的職員都能收到 50% 的學費補助，[140]
這筆金額將在他們選擇的課程成功結業後支付。

[141] 只有參加獲得公認之教育機關開設的課程才能獲得補
貼，另外，還有幾項限制可能會造成某些人無法參加。[142]
因此，強烈建議在報名課程前要先和人資部的職員預約會
面。

---

management n. 管理層　academic adj. 大學的、學業的
related to 與～相關的　responsibility n. 業務、責任
reimburse v. 補償　tuition fee 學費
deliver v. 給予（演講等）、運送　approved adj. 批准的、認可的
funding n. 財務支援、資金　restriction n. 制約、規定

139 形容詞慣用語

解析 因為必須是「有資格獲得補貼」的意思，可變成 be
eligible to do（有～的資格）的 (A) eligible 是正確答
案。

字彙 prominent adj. 重要的　social adj. 社會的
　　preferable adj. 更合意的

140 選出正確的句子

解析 **(A) 這筆金額將在他們選擇的課程成功結業後支付。**
　　(B) 區域經理被要求至少要指導 20 小時的教育訓練。
　　(C) 學校的職員可獲得教科書與其他教材的折扣。
　　(D) 人資部將會收集求職的履歷。

解析 題目是在挑選填入空格的正確句子，因此要掌握前後文
或整體的語境。前面的句子談到參加的職員都能收
到 50% 的學費補助（Participating employees will be
reimbursed for 50 percent of their total tuition fees.），
因此空格應該填入「這筆金額將在他們選擇的課程成功
結業後支付」，因此答案是 (A)。

字彙 completion n. 結束、完成　district manager 區域經理
　　be required to do 被要求做　lead v. 指導、率領
　　material n. 用具、材料　application n. 申請（書）、適用
　　job opening 職缺

141 分辨現在分詞與過去分詞

解析 這是具備（employees）、動詞（may receive）、受
詞（funding）的完整句子，___ a class ~ institution 應
該要視為是懸垂修飾語。選項中可能產生歧義的現在分
詞 (C) 與過去分詞 (D)，受修飾的名詞（employees）
與分詞是主動關係，意思是「上課的職員」，因此現在
分詞 (C) taking 是正確答案。delivered by an approved
educational institution 是修飾 a class 的懸垂修飾語。

142 填入連接副詞　掌握前後文的語境

解析 空格是句子最前面的連接副詞的位置，掌握前面句子與
空格所在句子在意義上的關係後選出正確答案。前面談
到有幾項限制可能會造成某些人無法參加，空格所在的
句子是強烈建議在報名課程前要先和人資部的職員預約
會面，因此顯示因果的 (C) Consequently（因此）是正
確答案。

字彙 likewise adv. 同樣地　afterward adv. 之後
　　for instance adv. 舉例來說

問題 143-146，請參考以下廣告。

PEN AND PAPER：在此通知我們的開業日期。

11 月 1 日請來和我們一起慶祝開業，[143] Pen and Paper
是供應所有種類的企業設備、文具類、其他辦公用品的零
售商。

[144] 只要是各位在工作空間需要的任何物品，在我們店裡確
定都能找到。只要告訴我們的職員您需要的物品，他們就
能提供多種品項讓各位選擇。我們不僅提供裝訂服務，也
有小冊子和名片等各種印刷作業。

[145] 當天我們會為來光臨本店的每位顧客提供各種贈品，不
僅如此，第 100 名顧客可獲得 100 美元的禮券。[146] 它在
購買本店的任何一項物品時都能使用，所以請來 Emerald
街 550 號和我們共同參加這項特殊活動吧！

---

grand opening 開業、開張　stationery n. 文具類
office supplies 辦公用品　workspace n. 作業空間
a range of 各種的　in addition to 除～之外　business card 名片
giveaway n. 贈品；adj. 廉價的　gift card 禮品券

143 填入修飾其他名詞的名詞

解析 因為「零售店」是複合名詞，形成複合名詞的名詞 (D) establishment 是正確答案，如果空格加入分詞 (C)，就會變成「設立的零售店」，整句話變得不通順。

字彙 establish v. 設立　establishment n. 商店

144 選出動詞　掌握前後文的語境

解析 從語境上來看是「只要是各位在工作空間需要的任何物品，在我們店裡確定都能___」，所有選項都可能是正確答案。光憑空格所在的句子無法選出正確答案，因此要掌握前後文或整體的語境。後面談到只要告訴我們的職員您需要的物品，他們就會提供多種品項讓各位選擇（Just tell ~ what you are looking for, and they'll provide you with a range of options），由此可知是說需要的物品都能在商店中找到，因此答案是 (A) find（尋找）。

字彙 deliver v. 運送　repair v. 修理、導正　exchange v. 交換

145 填入和先行詞數量一致的主格關係子句的動詞

解析 主格關係子句（who ~ on that day）沒有動詞，因此動詞 (A)、(B)、(C) 皆可能是答案。主格關係詞（who）的先行詞（any customer）是單數，因「顧客來」的主動意思是正確的，因此主動語態單數動詞 (B) enters 是答案。

146 選出正確的句子

解析 **(A) 它在購買本店的任何一項物品時都能使用。**
(B) 開幕時我們公司的執行長將會參加。
(C) 我們商店的翻修已經完成了。
(D) 我們明天將會宣布贈品的中獎名單。

解析 題型是要選出填入空格的正確句子，必須掌握前後文或整體的語境。前面的句子談到第 100 名顧客可獲得 100 美元的禮券（the 100th customer will receive a $100 gift card），由此可知後面要填入「它在購買本店的任何一項物品時都能使用。」，所以答案是 (A)。

字彙 complete v. 完成

PART 7

問題 147-148，請參考以下問卷調查。

Petra's Grill

盡可能提供顧客最棒的用餐經驗是我們的使命，我們很歡迎顧客提供意見，請填寫此一簡單的表格，然後投入出口旁邊的箱子，謝謝！

閣下是否有獲得迅速的服務呢？
---是　　　-X-否

閣下認為餐點的品質怎麼樣呢？
---很棒　　　-X-相當好　　　---很滿足　　　---不好

閣下的主餐是什麼？
烤雞和搭配義式調味醬的蔬菜沙拉　　　　　　●

餐點的價值是否符合其價格？
-X-是　　　　　　---否

多久會來光臨一次 Petra's Grill？
---經常　　　---偶爾　　　---幾乎不來　　　147-X-第一次來

意見

147 我認為下次來應該會更棒，因為我之後會確定在沒有這麼忙的時候來，我的服務生很親切有禮，但他同時也在服務其他顧客，148 她過了很久才發現我，並把菜單拿過來。

---

questionnaire n. 問卷　mission n. 使命、任務
dining n. 用餐　prompt adj. 迅速的　rate v. 評價
server n. 服務生　deal with 處理、關於　polite adj. 有禮的

147 推論題

從問卷中可推論出什麼事？
(A) 餐廳主要提供義式料理。
(B) 顧客有意願再到 Petra's Grill 用餐。
(C) 餐廳最近改建了。
(D) 為了反映顧客的意見，已經變更菜單了。

解析 這是根據問卷內容推論的題型，因問題中沒有關鍵字，因此要從問卷中確認與各個選項關鍵字相關的內容。"-X-This was my first visit" 中談到第一次造訪 Petra's Grill 餐廳，從 I think my next visit here will be better 中可推論出顧客有意願再去該餐廳用餐，所以答案是 (B)。

字彙 primarily adv. 主要　serve v. 提供（食物）　cuisine n. 料理
intend to 有～的意願

148 5W1H 問題

顧客在餐廳碰上了什麼問題？
(A) 餐點送來時早已變涼了。
(B) 當下沒有空桌。
(C) 服務生經過一段時間後才發現他。
(D) 菜單中的品項太貴了。

解析 這是詢問顧客在餐廳發生什麼（What）問題的 5W1H 問題，因為與問題的關鍵句 problem ~ the customer have 有關，文中談到服務生過了很久發現他，並把菜單拿過來（it took a very long time for her[server] to notice me and bring over a menu），所以答案是 (C)。

換句話說
took a very long time ~ to notice 花了很長的時間才發現 →
took a while to be acknowledged 花了一段時間才被注意到

字彙 acknowledge v. 告知收悉、認同（事實）
overpriced adj. 太昂貴的

問題 149-151，請參考以下廣告。

---
6 月 4 日是米林頓州立公園首次向大眾開放 50 週年的紀念日，為了慶祝此一重要的時刻，感謝各位對我們努力保護野生動物的支持，149 包含露營車 55 美元、每輛車 35 美元、摩托車 25 美元，149/150 及步行者或自行車騎士 10 美元的一般入場費，在 6 月 4 日到 6 月 10 日將不收取。此一優惠只適用入場費，但不含團體旅行、露營區、小艇或租借釣具等設備，請多加留意。另外，151 如果在這段期間進入公園，待到 6 月 11 日或之後，離開時將會收取費用。　　●

---

mark v. 紀念；n. 標示　in honor of 慶祝
milestone n. 重要時刻　wildlife n. 野生動物　entry fee 入場費
pedestrian n. 步行者　waive v. 不適用、放棄
exemption n. 免除　entrance fee 入場費
organized tour 團體旅行　camping site 露營地
fishing gear 釣魚工具　charge v. 要價

149 主題問題

公告的主題是什麼？
(A) 設施停車規定的變更
(B) 團體對保護環境的努力
(C) 遊憩地區可以暫時免費入場
(D) 州立公園舉辦的紀念日宴會

解析 這是詢問公告主題的題型，特別要注意此一問題談論到
與主題相關的內容。文中談到米林頓州立公園 6 月 4 日
至 6 月 10 日不會收取一般入場費（our[Millington State
Park] regular entry fees ~ will be waived from June 4
until June 10），因此答案是 (C)。

換句話說
entry fees ~ will be waived from June 4 until June 10 入場費
6 月 4 日到 6 月 10 日將免收 → Temporary free admission 暫時
免費入場
Park 公園 → a recreational area 遊憩區域

字彙 regulation n. 規定、管制　environmental adj. 環境保護的、環境的
admission n. 入場　recreational area 休閒區

150 5W1H 問題

騎自行車進公園需要支付多少錢？
(A) 10 美元
(B) 25 美元
(C) 35 美元
(D) 55 美元

解析 這是詢問騎乘自行車前往公園需要支付多少（How
much）入場費的 5W1H 問題，與問題的關鍵詞 cost
to enter the park on a bicycle 相關，騎乘自行車的人
每位的入場費是 10 美元（entry fees of ~ $10 per ~
cyclist），所以答案是 (A)。

151 推論題

關於米林頓州立公園的暗示，哪一個是正確的？
(A) 以車輛內的人數為基準向訪客收費。
(B) 其安排的導覽行程對大型團體給予折扣。
(C) 定期請大眾贊助支持
(D) 訪客可停留幾天。

解析 這是針對關鍵詞 Millington State Park 推論的題型，
文中談到「如果在這段期間進入公園，待到 6 月 11 日
或之後」（if you enter the park during this period but
stay until June 11 or later），由此可知是遊客們可待在
米林頓州立公園好幾天，所以答案是 (D)。

換句話說
stay until June 11 or later 停留到 6 月 11 日或之後 →
stay for multiple days 停留幾天

字彙 based on 以~為基準　regularly adv. 定期地

問題 152-153，請參考以下訊息。

Brad Lee	上午 9 點 34 分

我剛接到我們管理的其中一個建築物的房客的電話，她在
5 號街的 Plaza Tower 的 202 號。

Sara Godfrey	上午 9 點 35 分

[152] 她因為大廳翻修施工的噪音生氣了嗎？這個星期已經收
到那棟大樓住戶的多次抗議。

Brad Lee	上午 9 點 36 分

不，不是那樣的，聽說西雅圖的公司聘用她，工作從下個
星期開始，所以她這個月就要搬走，但她是簽 1 年的約，
[153] 她想知道是否得支付違約金。

Sara Godfrey	上午 9 點 38 分

這要看情況。[153] 她必須在這個月底前找到新的房客，不然
她就得支付違約金。

Brad Lee	上午 9 點 39 分

其實她說自己的弟弟對那間房子有興趣，我會叫他這星期
填寫好申請書，之後就會和屋主談談看。

tenant n. 房客　property n. 建築物、財產
complaint n. 抗議、抱怨　resident n. 住戶、居民
move out 搬出去　apartment n. 房間、大樓
lease agreement 租賃契約　penalty n. 違約金、罰金

152 推論題

關於 Plaza Tower 提到了什麼？
(A) 為西雅圖的公司所有。
(B) 1 年內建蓋完成。
(C) 有幾個空房間。
(D) 目前正在翻修中。

解析 這是針對關鍵詞 Plaza Tower 推論的題型，在詢問房客
是否因為大廳翻修施工造成的噪音而生氣後，回答 Plaza
Tower 的許多住戶都提出抗議（Is she[tenant] upset
about the noise from the renovation work in the lobby?
I've gotten a lot of complaints from the residents of that
building[Plaza Tower] this week. (9:35 A.M.)），由此可
推論 Plaza Tower 目前正在翻修中，所以答案是 (D)。

字彙 be owned by 被~擁有的　vacant adj. 空置的

153 意圖掌握問題

上午 9 點 38 分，Godfrey 女士寫「That depends」，
她的意思最可能是什麼？
(A) 契約還沒簽名。
(B) 很難聯絡上房東。
(C) 找到新房客就不需要支付違約金。
(D) 有一處房產在特定日期後可能就無法使用。

解析 這是詢問 Godfrey 女士意圖的題型，確認與問題引用句
（That depends）相關的前後文的語境。文中談到說想
知道是否支付違約金（She[tenant] wants to know if
she will have to pay a penalty. (9:36 A.M.)），Godfrey
女士回答還不確定（That depends.），如果這個月底沒
能找到新的房客就得支付違約金（She has until the end
of the month to find a new tenant. Otherwise, she will

have to pay. (9:38 A.M.)），由此可知只要找到新的房客就不需要支付違約金，因此答案是 (C)。

字彙 agreement n. 合約　waive v. 不適用（規則等）、省略
unit n. 一件傢俱、單位

問題 154-156，請參考以下電子郵件。

收件人：Diana Mansfield <dmans@timemail.com>
寄件人：Herbal Greens 公司顧客支援部門
　　　　<cs@herbalgreens.com>
日期：8 月 2 日
主旨：會員

Mansfield 女士，

您在過去幾個月間曾多次向我們訂購，但後來我們知道您尚未加入 155-B 我們網站上的會員，— [1] —雖然沒有加入會員也能購買我們的商品，但 154 成為會員的理由有好幾個。

首先，156 您不需要每次購買時都填入物品寄送地址、電話號碼、信用卡詳細資料。— [2] —另外，您可以收到每週促銷活動的最新資訊，看到原本不會知道的優惠好康。— [3] —155-B 再加上只有會員才能累積點數，成為會員後，155-D 您就能獲得每次訂購時花費總金額的 10%，155-A 這可折抵下次購物金額，或任其累積到之後使用。— [4] —

開設帳戶不需要 2 分鐘的時間，也不需要支付任何費用。建議您今天就加入，多加利用 Herbal Greens 公司的會員優惠。

Clay Lewis 敬啟
Herbal Greens 公司客服支援部門

---

place an order 訂購　sign up for 加入、報名
numerous adj. 許多的　shipping address 物品寄送地址
otherwise adv. 否則　build up 堆積
put toward （部分費用）補貼、給予　accumulate v. 累積
take advantage of 利用

---

154 目的問題

電子郵件的主旨是什麼？
(A) 為了說明如何開設線上帳號
(B) 為了說服顧客成為會員
(C) 為了請顧客變更密碼
(D) 為了說明會員升級的優惠

解析 這是找出電子郵件主旨的題型，在文中談到應該成為會員的理由有好幾個（there are numerous reasons to become a member），接著告知成為會員就能獲得的優惠，所以答案是 (B)。

字彙 set up 開設、建立　convince v. 說服　describe v. 說明

155 Not/True 題型

關於顧客點數沒有談到的是哪一個部分？
(A) 購買物品時可使用。
(B) 只有網站上的會員能獲得。
(C) 經過一段時間就會過期。
(D) 每次支付訂單費用時就能獲得。

解析 這是從短文中找出和關鍵詞 loyalty credit 相關的內容，

並對照選項的 Not/True 題型。(A) 文中談到點數可補貼下次購物時的費用（You can put this credit toward the cost of your next purchase），和短文內容相符。(B) 「a membership on our website」和「only members can build up loyalty credit」中談到只有加入網站的會員才能累積點數，因此和短文內容相符。(C) 這是短文中沒有談到的內容，因此 (C) 是正確答案。(D) 文中談到每次訂購時可獲得總金額的 10%（you will earn 10 percent of the total amount you spend whenever you place an order），和短文內容一致。

換句話說
whenever ~ place an order 每次訂購時 →
each time an order is paid for 每次支付訂單費用時

字彙 expire v. 到期　acquire v. 取得、獲得

156 將句子放入合適的位置

翻譯 以下句子最適合放入 [1]、[2]、[3] 或 [4] 的哪個位置？
「這些資訊在顧客準備結帳時會自動填入必填項目。」
(A) [1]
(B) [2]
(C) [3]
(D) [4]

解析 這是選出最適合填入句子之位置的題型，「This information will be automatically inputted into the necessary fields when you are ready to check out」中談到這些資訊在準備結算時會自動填入必填項目，因此可猜出句子前面談到的內容。[2] 前面的句子「you will no longer be required to enter your shipping address, telephone number, and credit card details each time you make a purchase」談到不需要每次購買時都填入物品寄送地址、電話號碼、信用卡詳細資料，由此可知 [2] 要填入的句子是每次購買時不需要輸入寄送地址、電話號碼、信用卡詳細資料，系統會自動輸入，所以答案是 (B)。

字彙 automatically adv. 自動　input v. 輸入　field n. 項目
check out 計算

問題 157-158，請參考以下廣告。

Tam Bakery –市區最棒的蛋糕！

您有生日、結婚或其他重要活動的計劃嗎？如果想要完美的蛋糕紀念特殊活動，請范臨於 Harbor 街和 Elm 街轉角處的 Tam Bakery 吧。我們優秀的蛋糕師傅會為您製作便宜又美味的藝術作品，157-B 為了能創造出您心目中預期的蛋糕，他們會與您緊密合作，再加上 157-A 我們會使用最棒的材料，也提供純素與低脂肪的選項。5 月 15 日至 6 月 15 日，158 我們為了紀念 10 週年，157-C/158 所有客製化蛋糕都會給予 10% 的優惠，所以別猶豫了，快點光臨我們的店面，開始規劃完美的蛋糕。

想要取得更多關於 Tam Bakery 和我們提供之產品的資訊，就請來 www.tambakery.com。

---

occasion n. 活動　talented adj. 優秀的
affordable adj. 平價的　ensure v.（一定）確保、保障
envision v. 構想、想像　vegan adj. 純素的　low-fat adj. 低脂的
anniversary n. 週年（紀念日）　stop by 順便拜訪

---

157 Not/True 題型

下列哪一個和 Tam Bakery 的蛋糕沒關係？
(A) 使用高品質的材料製成。
(B) 可由顧客構思蛋糕。
(C) 可使用優惠的價格購買。
(D) 將會運送到活動場所。

解析 這是從短文中找出和關鍵詞 Tam Bakery's cakes 相關的內容，並和選項對照的 Not/True 題型。(A)「we use only the best ingredients」中談到只使用最頂尖的食材，和短文內容相符。(B)「They will work closely with you to ensure that the cake you receive is the one you envisioned.」中談到為了讓顧客收到符合自己心目中預期的蛋糕，將會和顧客密切合作，和短文內容相符。(C)「we are reducing the prices of all custom cakes by 10 percent」中談到所有訂購的蛋糕將會優惠 10% 的價格，和短文內容一致。(D) 這是短文沒有談到的內容，因此答案是 (D)。

字彙 high-quality adj. 高品質的　at a discount 優惠的價格
venue n. 場所

158 推論題

關於 Tam Bakery 有何暗示？
(A) 產品在線上販售。
(B) 將要開其他分店。
(C) 已經經營多年了。
(D) 網站上有食譜。

解析 這是針對關鍵詞 Tam Bakery 推論的題型，在「we are reducing the prices ~ to celebrate our 10th anniversary」中談到為了紀念 10 週年，所有訂購的蛋糕都會給予 10% 的優惠，因此可推論出 Tam Bakery 經營多年了，所以答案是 (C)。

字彙 branch n. 分店　be in business 營業　recipe n. 食譜

問題 159-162，請參考以下新聞。

9 月 7 日—Brytwells 百貨公司的發言人宣布今天是公司 31 年以來首次 159 變更公司的商標，顧客熟悉的經典紅色與黃色設計將會變為更具現代風，這是 160 執行長 Marcus Cathwell 為了改變公司的形象付出的眾多努力之一，兩個月前 Jackson Stevens 退休後，就由 Marcus Cathwell 接任。

20 多年來，Brytwells 都和提供更多種類平價物品的新百貨公司展開激烈競爭。每年都有幾個賣場結束營業，161 預計未來 12 個月內會有其他 5 處停止營運，Cathwell 先生承認 Brytwells 品牌早就該進行更新，並表示確信新的商標很契合公司的其他變化，162-A 這些包括新的現代店面配置，以及引進 15 個年輕人的服裝品牌。

162-C Brytwells 開設的第一家店位於國內東北部，這區的 Brytwells 分店將於 10 月最先開始使用這個商標，162-D 全國的其他 Brytwells 分店則會在秋季結束前引進新的公司商標。

spokesperson n. 發言人　familiar with 對～熟悉的
replace v. 改變、替代　modern adj. 具現代風的
move up into 晉升為～　retire v. 隱退　decade n. 10 年
face v. 面臨（狀況）　stiff adj. 激烈的
variety n. 很多種類、多樣性　closure n. 倒閉
result v. 發生　be set to 預定進行～　cease v. 中斷
operation n. 營運　acknowledge v. 承認
overdue adj. 早就該發生的　fit in 與～符合、合得來
contemporary adj. 現代的　layout n. 配置　adopt v. 引進、採納

159 主題問題

報導主要在談論什麼？
(A) 關於新店家商標的構想
(B) 全國連鎖店的關閉
(C) 企業象徵的變化
(D) 零售店之間的競爭

解析 題目詢問新聞主要報導的主題，因此要確認短文前面的部分，在「the company will change its logo」中談到公司將變更商標，接著說明變更商標的相關變化，所以答案是 (C)。

字彙 symbol n. 象徵　retailer n. 零售店

160 Not/True 題型

關於 Cathwell 先生，提到了什麼？
(A) 製作平面圖。
(B) 3 月時被僱用的。
(C) 近期晉升了。
(D) 成立了公司。

解析 這是從短文中找出與關鍵詞 Mr. Cathwell 相關的內容，並和選項對照的 Not/True 題型。(A) 和 (B) 是短文沒有談論到的內容。(C)「CEO Marcus Cathwell, who moved up into his position when Jackson Stevens retired two months ago」中談到執行長 Marcus Cathwell 在兩個月前 Jackson Stevens 退休後，就晉升了，和短文內容一致，因此答案是 (C)。(D) 則是短文中沒有談到的內容。

換句話說
moved up into ~ two month ago 兩個月前升遷了 →
was recently promoted 近期晉升了

字彙 floor plan 平面圖　found v. 設立

161 推論題

明年最可能會發生什麼事？
(A) Brytwells 會推出新的網站。
(B) Brytwells 的所有分店將會降低價格。
(C) Brytwells 的多個賣場將會關閉營業。
(D) Brytwells 的執行長即將卸任。

解析 這是針對關鍵詞 next year 推論的題型，在「another five[five stores] are set to cease operations within the next 12 months」中談到預計未來 12 個月內會有其他 5 處停止營運，由此可推論明年 Brytwells 有多間賣場將要結束營業，所以答案是 (C)。

換句話說
cease operations 停止營運 → close down 停業

字彙 launch v. 上市、公開　close down 停業　resign v. 卸任

162 Not/True 題型

關於 Brytwells 的描述，並未說到什麼？
(A) 將要開始販售更多針對年輕人的商品。
(B) 本店將要搬遷。
(C) 在東北地區開了第一間賣場。
(D) 全國都有分店。

解析 這是從短文中找出和關鍵字 Brytwells 相關的內容，並和選項對照的 Not/True 題型。(A)「These[changes] include ~ the introduction of 15 clothing brands for young people.」中談到公司的變化包含引進 15 個年輕人的服裝品牌，和短文的內容相符。(B) 是短文中沒有談到的內容，因此是正確答案。(C)「the northeastern region of the nation, where Brytwells opened its initial store」中談到 Brytwells 開的第一間賣場位於國內的東北部，和短文的內容相符。(D)「Other Brytwells stores across the country」中談到全國有其他 Brytwells 分店，和短文的內容相符。

換句話說
introduction of ~ clothing brands for young people 引進年輕人的服裝品牌 → begin selling more products for young people 將要開始販售更多針對年輕人的商品

字彙 relocate v. 遷移

問題 163-165，請參考以下廣告。

公告

Hopewell 製作公司 7 月 8 日將要拍攝 A New Life 的一個場景，此一長篇電影由 Christina Harvey 和 Mike Mann 主演，由 Herbert Mercer 負責監督。

163 徵求 18 歲以上的人都能來參加臨時演員的試鏡。165-D 臨演選角於 7 月 1 日中午到下午 8 點在 West Newton 高中舉行，164 所有參加者都該攜帶駕照、護照、或是包含照片的其他種類的正式身分證。

163/165-C 臨時演員主要是在購物中心的短暫場景中扮演群眾，165-A 拍攝將需要花費 10 到 12 個小時，而且會久站和等待。會提供食物，165-B 最後還會有小贈品的抽獎，工資是每小時 9 美元。

---

film v. 攝影   scene n. 場面   feature-length adj. 長篇的
star v. 擔任主角、主演   invite v. 徵求、招待
extra n. 臨演   driver's license 駕照   official adj. 官方的
identification n. 身分證   primarily adv. 主要   crowd n. 群眾
sequence n. 場面   shoot n. 拍攝   involve v. 伴隨
wait around 無所事事地等   raffle n. 抽獎

---

163 5W1H 問題

根據公告來看，Hopewell 製作公司建議大家做什麼？
(A) 去外燴工作。
(B) 設置裝備。
(C) 帶領參觀攝影棚。
(D) 參加拍片演出

解析 這是在詢問 Hopewell 製作公司建議民眾做什麼（What）的 5W1H 問題，與問題關鍵句 Hopewell Productions encouraging people to do 相關，「Anyone

over the age of 18 is invited to audition as an extra.」中談到徵求 18 歲以上的人都能來參加臨時演員的試鏡，「Extras will be used primarily as crowd members for a short sequence」則談到臨時演員主要是在購物中心的短暫場景中扮演群眾，所以答案是 (D)。

字彙 catering n. 外燴   set up 設置   conduct v. 指引   set n. 攝影場

164 5W1H 問題

參加者應該攜帶什麼去 West Newton 高中？
(A) 銀行帳戶收支明細
(B) 履歷和自我介紹書
(C) 身分證明書
(D) 表演的影片

解析 這是詢問參加者應攜帶什麼（What）去 West Newton 高中的 5W1H 問題，與問題關鍵句 participants bring to West Newton High School 相關，在「all participants must bring a driver's license, a passport, or some other type of official photo identification」中談到所有參加者都該攜帶駕照、護照、或是包含照片的其他種類的正式身分證，因此答案是 (C)。

換句話說
a driver's license, a passport, or some other type of official photo identification 駕照、護照、或有照片的其他正式身分證 →
A form of identification 身分證明書

字彙 bank statement （銀行帳號的）收支款明細
cover letter 自我介紹書   recording n. 錄影、錄音

165 Not/True 題型

關於拍攝提到了什麼？
(A) 將會持續好幾天。
(B) 包含贈品抽獎。
(C) 大部分都在戶外進行。
(D) 中午開始。

解析 這是在短文中找出與關鍵字 shoot 相關的內容，並和選項對照的 Not/True 題型。(A)「The shoot will take 10 to 12 hours」中談到拍攝大概是 10 到 12 小時，和短文內容不符。(B)「a raffle for small prizes will be held at the end」中談到最後會有贈品的抽獎活動，和短文的內容相符，所以答案是 (B)。(C)「Extras will be used ~ for a short sequence that takes place in a mall.」中談到臨時演員將會安排在購物中心的短暫場景中，和短文內容不符。(D)「The casting call ~ will take place ~ from noon」中談到試鏡從中午開始，並不是中午開始拍攝，所以和內容不符。

換句話說
a raffle for small prizes 小贈品的抽獎 →
a prize drawing 贈品抽獎

字彙 last v. 持續   prize drawing 贈品抽獎

問題 166-169，請參考以下電子郵件。

收件人：Pingvillian 飯店預約部門
　　　　<rsvn@pingvillianhotel.com>
寄件人：Alice Rolstin <alirol@alertmail.com>
日期：9 月 10 日
主旨：住宿

敬啟者，

我之所以會寫這封信是因為我 166-A/D 透過線上旅行社 Frewel.com 預約貴飯店的房間，我有兩項請求，一 [1] 一 首先，我和我的丈夫要求延遲入住，166-C 我們會在 9 月 17 日下午 11 點 30 分抵達清邁。169 如果網頁上的資訊正確的話，我們大概會在午夜時抵達飯店。一 [2] 一

另外，您應該知道我們是 9 月 25 日退房，但回程的班機變更了，166-C 我們將於 24 號下午 8 點離開。一 [3] 一 167 因為我們不會按照原訂計劃在 24 號晚上留宿飯店，我想知道可否取消我們預定的最後一天，在 24 號下午 6 點退房？一 [4] 一168 雖然我知道退房時間是中午，但如果能讓我們待到要搭乘計程車去機場，會幫我們很大的忙。

謝謝您挪出時間，期待入住 Pingvillian 飯店的那一天到來。

Alice Rolstin 敬啟

---

in regard to 關於　travel agency 旅行社
late check-in 延遲入住（午夜後的入住）　land v. 抵達
midnight n. 午夜　accurate adj. 準確的
be supposed to 應該要做　check out（飯店等）退房
depart v. 離開、出發　look forward to 期待

---

166 Not/True 題型

關於 Rolstin 女士，哪一個是真的？
(A) 透過網站預約了。
(B) 將會比預期更早抵達飯店。
(C) 會待在清邁到下個月。
(D) 在 Pingvillian 飯店預約了兩個房間。

解析 這是從短文中找出和關鍵詞 Ms. Rolstin 相關的內容，並和選項對照的 Not/True 題型。(A)「the reservation I made ~ through ~ Frewel.com.」中談到是透過 Frewel.com 預約，和短文內容相符，所以答案是 (A)。(B) 是短文中沒有談到的內容。(C)「We should be landing in Chiang Mai ~ on September 17.」和「we will be departing ~ on the 24th」中談到 9 月 17 日抵達清邁並於 24 日離開，所以和短文內容不符。(D)「the reservation I made for a room at your hotel」中談到在飯店中預約了一個房間，所以和短文內容不符。

167 尋找同義詞

第 2 段第 3 行的單字 originally 在意思上和____最相近。
(A) 獨特地
(B) 完全地
(C) 不同地
(D) 最初地

解析 在包含 originally 的句子「Since we won't be spending the night of the 24th at your hotel as originally planned,

I was wondering if we could cancel our reservation for the final day」中把 originally 當作「起初」的意思使用，因此此答案是 (D)。

168 5W1H 問題

Rolstin 女士提出什麼要求？
(A) 獎勵優惠券
(B) 延後退房時間
(C) 載送到機場
(D) 額外住宿一晚

解析 這是詢問 Rolstin 女士要求什麼（What）的 5W1H 問題，與問題的關鍵詞 Ms. Rolstin ask for 有關，「I know your check-out time is noon, but if we could stay until it is time for us to get a taxi to the airport, it would really be helpful.」談到 Rolstin 女士雖然很清楚退房時間是中午，但表示如果能延後到自己搭車去機場為止應該能幫上很大的忙，所以答案是 (B)。

字彙 compensation n. 補償　voucher n. 優惠券、商品券

169 將句子放入合適的位置

翻譯 以下句子最適合放入 [1]、[2]、[3] 或 [4] 的哪個位置？
「上面寫著從機場搭計程車需要 15 至 20 分鐘左右。」
(A) [1]
(B) [2]
(C) [3]
(D) [4]

解析 這是選出最適合填入句子之位置的題型，「It says getting a taxi from the airport only takes about 15 to 20 minutes」中談到從機場搭計程車需要 15 至 20 分鐘的時間，由此可猜測前面有談到從機場搭乘計程車所需要的時間。[2] 前面的句子「I believe we will arrive at the hotel by midnight if the information on your web page is accurate.」中談到如果網站上的資訊正確的話，我們大概會在午夜時抵達飯店，只要把句子放入 [2]，整句話的意思就是官網上寫從機場搭計程車需要 15 到 20 分鐘，所以大概午夜時會抵達飯店，語意通順自然，所以答案是 (B)。

問題 170-171，請參考以下新聞。

廢水處理場是否建造依舊不明

民眾對當地政府想在 Komlossy 建設一座廢水處理廠的計劃保持半信半疑的態度，如果市政府的水利部門批准這項建設，那麼當地的住宅和商業不動產的持有人勢必都將繳納更多的稅來支付其費用。此一系統的建設需要花費 5 千 2 百萬美元，未來每個月的運作和維護需要 42 萬美元，雖然部分納稅人不想停止使用目前便宜許多的系統，但多數人認為此一新型系統值得額外付費。至少 170 它不會像先前一樣讓任何一種汙染物質流入河流或湖泊。171 這個議題將於 11 月 6 日 Komlossy 的水質管理理事會中深入探討。

➔

---

proposal n. 計劃、提案
wastewater treatment center 廢水處理場
uncertainty n. 半信半疑、不確定性
municipal adj. 市政的、地方政府的　approve v. 批准
residential adj. 居住（用）的　commercial adj. 商業（用）的
subsequent adj. 隨後的　taxpayer n. 納稅人
be reluctant to 不情願　majority n. 多數　at the very least 至少
permit v. 可進行（某件事）　contaminant n. 汙染物質
issue n. 議題、主題　in depth 深入的

170 推論題

關於目前的廢水系統提到了什麼？
(A) 是造成水源汙染的原因之一。
(B) 運作非常昂貴。
(C) 去年安裝的。
(D) 大部分的居民都很支持。

解析 這是針對問題關鍵詞 current wastewater system 推論的題型，「it[new system] will not permit any contaminants to enter nearby rivers and lakes, as the old one does」中談到新系統會防止任何一種汙染物質和先前一樣流入河水與湖泊中，因此可推論目前的廢水系統是造成水質汙染的原因之一，所以答案是 (A)。

換句話說
permit ~ contaminants to enter nearby rivers and lakes 汙染物流入附近的江河與湖泊 → contributes to water pollution 成為水質汙染的原因

字彙 contribute v. 是～的原因之一、貢獻　water pollution 水質汙染

171 5W1H 問題

根據報導來看，11 月份會發生什麼事？
(A) 市政府將要展開新的設施建設工程。
(B) 市民將要表決是否要蓋廢水處理場。
(C) 將開會審視市政計劃。
(D) 整個城市將要執行新的稅制。

解析 這是在詢問 11 月會發生什麼（What）事的 5W1H 問題，與問題的關鍵字 November 相關，「The issue [construction of wastewater treatment center] will be discussed in depth at Komlossy's Water Quality Control Board meeting on November 6.」中談到蓋廢水處理場的議題將在 11 月 6 號 Komlossy 的水質管理理事會的會議中深入討論，所以答案是 (C)。

字彙 vote on 表決　sewage n. 汙水　implement v. 執行

問題 172-175，請參考以下線上對話內容。

Soomin Park [下午 6 點 38 分]
計劃變更了，172 Lawson 女士剛剛傳訊息說 6 月 4 日不需要我們的服務了，她的婚禮改到 9 月 16 日，她希望我們的攝影工作室在那天幫忙拍攝婚禮和婚宴。

Lauren Jean [下午 6 點 41 分]
那應該會造成問題吧，那天我一整天都要負責其他顧客的活動，況且我們目前 6 月 4 號沒有任何預約。

Taylor Morgan [下午 6 點 43 分]
173 她的婚禮在 9 月 16 日時也是在同一個地方和時間舉行

嗎？如果是我就可以，我下午都有空。

Soomin Park [下午 6 點 44 分]
謝謝你，Taylor，173 時間和場所都和先前說的一樣，174 我跟 Lawson 女士說如果 6 月 4 號我們有其他預約，那她的保證金就會挪到 9 月 16 號的訂單，174/175 如果沒有她就會失去保證金。

Lauren Jean [下午 6 點 45 分]
這樣就說得過去，175 我們那天拒絕了本來想請我們的幾個潛在顧客。事到如今仔細想想，說不定他們還會有人需要攝影師。

Soomin Park [下午 6 點 45 分]
真的嗎？如果有空就去聯絡看看吧。

photography n. 攝影　reception n. 招待會　cover v. 負責
transfer v. 搬動　deposit n. 保證金　prospective adj. 潛在的
get in touch with 和～聯絡

172 5W1H 問題

Lawson 女士為什麼聯絡 Park 女士？
(A) 為了安排在攝影工作室的拍攝
(B) 為了協商優惠的價格
(C) 為了通知場所變更
(D) 為了變更預約日程

解析 這是詢問 Lawson 女士為什麼（Why）聯絡 Park 女士的 5W1H 問題，與問題的關鍵句 Ms. Lawson contact Ms. Park 有關，「Ms. Lawson just texted me to say she will no longer be requiring our services on June 4. Her wedding date has been moved to September 16, and she wants our studio to do the photography ~ on that day instead.(6:38 P.M.)」中談到 Lawson 女士傳訊息通知 Park 女士說 6 月 4 號不需要拍照了，因為她的婚禮改成 9 月 16 日，所以她希望改成那天拍照，因此答案是 (D)。

字彙 arrange v. 計劃　photo shoot 拍照　negotiate v. 協商
notify v. 通知　reschedule v. 變更日程

173 推論題

關於 Lawson 女士的婚禮可推論出什麼？
(A) 將在戶外舉辦。
(B) 將會由 **Morgan** 先生進行拍攝。
(C) 已經支付全額了。
(D) 一個月後舉辦。

解析 這是針對問題關鍵詞 Ms. Lawson's wedding 推論的題型，「Is her[Ms. Lawson] wedding still going to be at the same place and time on September 16? If so, I can do it. (6:43 P.M.)」中談到 Morgan 先生詢問 Lawson 女士說 9 月 16 日的婚禮是否在相同場所相同時段進行，如果是的話，他就能去進行拍攝。「The time and venue are the same as previously requested. (6:44 P.M.)」中則說 Park 女士回答時間和場所都在同一樣，由此可推論 Morgan 先生將會去 Lawson 女士的婚禮幫忙拍攝，所以答案是 (B)。

字彙 pay in full 支付全額

174 5W1H 問題

6 月 4 日攝影工作室如果沒有收到任何預約會發生什麼事？

(A) Park 女士將要擬定新合約草稿。

(B) Jean 女士就有時間參加婚禮。

(C) Lawson 女士就會失去部分已支付的費用。

(D) Morgan 先生就無法去某個場所。

解析 這是在詢問 6 月 4 日攝影工作室若是沒能收到預約會發生什麼（What）事的 5W1H 問題，與問題的關鍵句 happen if the studio cannot make a booking for June 4 有關，「I told Ms. Lawson that if we[studio] get another booking for June 4, we will transfer her deposit to her bill for September 16. If not, she will lose the deposit. (6:44 P.M.)」中談到 Park 女士對 Lawson 女士說 6 月 4 日如果有收到其他客人的預約，那她的保證金就會移到 9 月 16 日的訂單，如果沒有收到預約，她就會失去保證金，所以答案是 (C)。

字彙 draft v. 編制草案

175 意圖掌握問題

下午 6 點 45 分，Jean 女士回答「That makes sense」時，她最有可能想說什麼？

(A) 想要抱怨其他客人。

(B) 打算要確認帳號。

(C) 認為那項決定很合理。

(D) 認為保證金應該退還。

解析 這是詢問 Jean 女士 意圖的題型，因此要先確認問題的引用句（That makes sense）。「If not, she[Ms. Lawson] will lose the deposit. (6:44 P.M.)」中談到 Park 女士說如果 6 月 4 號沒有收到預約，Lawson 就會失去保證金，Jean 女士回答「That makes sense.」（這樣很合理），「We turned down several other prospective clients who wanted to hire us for that day. (6:45 P.M.)」中談到曾拒絕想聘請自己去攝影的其他潛在顧客，由此可知 Jean 女士認為那項決定很合理，所以答案是 (C)。

字彙 complain v. 抱怨　account n. 帳號　reasonable adj. 合理的

問題 176-180，請參考以下廣告和報導。

沃特敦音樂祭

[178] 6 月 5 日星期六到 6 月 6 日星期日，沃特敦市舉辦所有音樂愛好者都很享受的活動！[176-C] 沃特敦音樂祭會有 Kayla Swank、Sienna Hanson、Tristan Woodlawn 等鄰近地區的歌手連續兩天蒞臨演出。[176-B/178] 表演會在 Morton 競賽場外圍與內部設置的多個舞臺上進行。[177] 憑門票獲准進入所有表演場地與餐廳。成人入場需要支付 30 美元，10 歲以下的孩童可免費進入。

音樂祭由 New Wave 公司贊助，那是一間營業將近 30 年的音樂與圖書零售業者，[179] 為了能獲得 Darrell Lane 的全國巡迴演唱會的後臺通行證，千萬別錯過綜合園區旁邊的 New Wave 公司的攤位，更多的資訊與門票的購買請至 www.watertownmusicfest.com。

---

surely adv. 肯定地、確定地　vocalist n. 歌手
surrounding adj. 鄰近的　set up 設置　arena n. 競賽場
access n. 利用、存取　dining facility 餐廳　entry n. 入場
be sponsored by 由～贊助　be in business 營業中
complex n. 綜合園區　win v. 獲得、獲勝
backstage pass 後臺通行證　nationwide adj. 全國性的

非常受歡迎的地區慶典

Marcus Cooper 筆

6 月 10 日—本月稍早舉行的沃特敦音樂祭是該城市的主要活動，[178] 今年音樂家們在兩天內吸引兩萬名以上的聽眾，之所以能辦到是因為場地變更了，比起去年的 Westfield 場館，這次 6 月的場地有更大空間給更多舞臺。

當地餐廳的老闆 Nancy Welsh 表示他們全家人都非常喜愛那項慶典，Welsh 女士表示，「那個活動有可以讓我的三個小孩跑跑跳跳的足夠空間，我一邊沉浸在很棒的音樂，同時也享受了愉快的時光，[179] 我甚至還參加 New Wave 公司贊助的贈品活動，結果我獲得了原本就規劃參加的 8 月份演唱會的後臺通行證！」

6 月份沒能參加的人，[180-C] 可以下載音樂祭的智慧型手機 App 了解明年活動的最新資訊。

major adj. 重大的、主要的　draw in 吸引
incredibly adv. 極其　plenty of 充分的、許多的
take part in 參加　giveaway n. 贈品
result in 結果是　make it 參加、成功

176 Not/True 題型

關於沃特敦音樂祭有何描述？

(A) 舉辦超過 10 年了。

(B) 應該會有室內與戶外的表演區域。

(C) 國際知名人士會參加表演。

(D) 因為其他活動而延期了。

解析 這是詢問關鍵詞 the Watertown Music Festival 的 Not/True 題型，因此要從沃特敦音樂祭的第一篇短文中確認相關內容。(A) 是短文中沒有談論到的內容。(B) 「Performances will be given on multiple stages that have been set up both outside and within the Morton Arena.」中談到 Morton 競賽場外面和內部都設有多個舞臺，因此和短文內容相符，所以答案是 (B)。(C) 「The Watertown Music Festival will be a ~ celebration featuring vocalists from the surrounding region」中談到沃特敦音樂祭會有鄰近地區的歌手表演，因此和短文內容不符。(D) 是短文中沒談到的內容。

字彙 international adj. 國際的　celebrity n. 知名人士

177 尋找同義詞

廣告第 1 段第 8 行的單字「grant」的意思和＿＿＿最相近。

(A) 允許

(B) 簽名

(C) 調查

(D) 要求

解析 在包含 grant 的句子中「Tickets will grant access to all performance areas and dining facilities.」，grant 被當作「允許」的意思使用，因此答案是 (A)。

178 推論題
關於 Westfield 競賽場提到了什麼？
(A) 每年都被當作音樂祭場地使用。
(B) 夏天時將會關閉。
(C) 場地沒有比 Morton 競賽場更寬敞。
(D) 將要改造成有用餐的空間。

解析 先確認和問題關鍵詞 the Westfield Arena 相關的報導。
線索1 第二篇短文「This year, musical artists drew in more than 20,000 audience members ~. What helped make this possible was the change of venue. This June's location allowed more space ~ than Westfield Arena did last year.」中談到今年之所以能吸引 2 萬名以上的聽眾，是因為變更場地的關係，這次 6 月的場地有更多的空間可設置比去年在 Westfield 競賽場更多的舞臺。但因為沒談到 6 月的活動場地在哪裡，所以從廣告中確認相關的內容。
線索2 第一篇短文「From ~ June 5 through ~ June 6, the city of Watertown is hosting an event」中談到 6 月 5 日到 6 月 6 日沃特敦將會舉辦活動，「Performances will be given ~ both outside and within the Morton Arena.」則談到表演會在 Morton 競賽場的內部與外側進行，所以可確定 6 月的活動場地是 Morton 競賽場。
綜合兩個部分來看，可知道 Westfield 競賽場沒有比 Morton 競賽場更寬敞，所以答案是 (C)。

字彙 close down 封閉 spacious adj. 寬敞的

179 5W1H 問題
Welsh 女士計劃 8 月份時去看哪一名歌手的演出？
(A) Kayla Swank
(B) Darrell Lane
(C) Sienna Hanson
(D) Tristan Woodlawn

解析 這是詢問 Welsh 女士計劃 8 月去看哪一個（Which）歌手的 5W1H 問題，先確認和關鍵句 performer ~ Ms. Welsh plan to see in August 相關的內容。
線索1 在第二篇短文中「"I[Ms. Welsh] even took part in a prize giveaway sponsored by New Wave, which resulted in me winning backstage passes to a concert I was already planning on attending in August!"」談到 Welsh 女士參加 New Wave 公司贊助的贈品活動，結果獲得了原本就打算參加的 8 月份演唱會的後臺通行證，不過卻沒有談到 New Wave 公司的抽獎活動中提供的後臺通行證是哪位歌手表演，所以要從廣告中確認相關內容。
線索2 在第一篇短文中「Be sure not to miss New Wave's booth ~ for a chance to win backstage passes to a concert on Darrell Lane's nationwide tour.」談到在 New Wave 公司的攤位有機會獲得 Darrell Lane 的全國巡迴演唱會的後臺通行證。
綜合兩個部分來看時，可知道 Welsh 女士參加的活動是

提供 Darrell Lane 的演唱會後臺通行證，Welsh 女士計劃 8 月份去看 Darrell Lane 的演唱會，所以答案是 (B)。

180 Not/True 題型
關於智慧型手機 App 的描述為何？
(A) 6 月將會有幾項設計變化。
(B) Welsh 女士的孩子下載了 App。
(C) 會有關於下次音樂祭的詳細資訊。
(D) 去年當地的雜誌有介紹。

解析 這是詢問關鍵詞 the smartphone application 的 Not/True 題型，因此要從談到智慧型手機 App 的第二篇短文中確認相關內容。(A) 和 (B) 是短文沒有談到的內容。(C)「keep up to date with information on next year's event by downloading the festival's smartphone application」中談到下載智慧型手機 App 就能知道明年活動的相關最新資訊，由此可知智慧型手機 App 有下次音樂祭的詳細資訊，所以答案是 (C)。(D) 是短文沒有談論到的內容。
換句話說
information on next year's event 明年活動相關的資訊 → details about a subsequent festival 後續音樂祭相關的細節問題

字彙 undergo v. 經歷、進行 subsequent adj. 隨後的

問題 181-185，請參考以下表格和電子郵件。

買賣契約

本合約是指 11 月 5 日 181 丹維爾的 City Street Motors 公司（由 Blaine Ritter 代理）向 Grace Huang 出售二手車，當事者均依照本合約所述協議買賣，除非買賣雙方解除，否則本合約有效。

製造公司與型號：Merriton Motors 公司，Juniper
外部與內部顏色：藍色、灰色
車輛辨識編號：XCN138004832738
販售價：14,000 美元
185 支付方法：■現金 □支票 □信用卡

賣家轉讓了有關車輛事故和維修明細的所有資訊，買方同意依照現況購買車輛，在合約上簽名後，無論發現任何缺陷都不能取消這筆交易。

182-B/C/D 賣家簽字時，將會把汽車銷售正式收據、兩把車鑰匙、近期檢驗紀錄給買方。

賣方代理人簽名＿＿＿＿＿＿＿＿＿＿

買方簽名＿＿＿＿＿＿＿＿＿＿

---

sales contract 買賣合約書 represent v. 出現、代表
used car 中古車 party n. 當事者 outline v. 記述；n. 輪廓
valid adj. 有效的 terminate v. 解除、結束
identification number 辨識號碼 pay in full 支付全額
release v. 轉讓、放開 as is（無論條件、狀態）維持原狀
defect n. 缺陷

收件人：Blaine Ritter
　　　　<blaineritter@citystreetmotors.com>
寄件人：Grace Huang
　　　　<gracehuang@huangdesign.com>

➊

日期：11 月 2 日
主旨：檢視契約

Ritter 先生，

感謝您擬定 Juniper 轎車的合約，我很高興能買到那樣的好車，183-C 我原本的車已經無法修理，所以我才會特別希望能換新車。184 昨天我們談的時候協議 11 月 6 號碰面，但合約上寫的販售日期卻是 11 月 5 號，日期不是該訂正嗎？麻煩您變更一下，並在我抵達之前準備好修正後的文件。

我預計上午 10 點抵達您的分店，我的朋友會讓我在那邊下車，所以您不需要來載我，但謝謝您的提議。185 為了在抵達時就能付款，我會在前往 City Street Motors 公司的途中先去一趟銀行。

謝謝您的幫忙，185 期待 11 月 6 日與您的見面。

Grace Huang 敬上

eager adj. 渴望、急切的　correct v. 訂正　drop off 讓～下車

181 推論題
Blaine Ritter 最可能在哪裡工作？
(A) 汽車經銷商
(B) 租車行
(C) 法律事務所
(D) 車輛零件商店

解析 這是針對關鍵詞 Blaine Ritter 進行推論的題目，在談論到 Blaine Ritter 的第一篇短文中確認相關的內容。第一篇短文「the sale of a used car by City Street Motors of Danville (represented by Blaine Ritter)」中談到 Blaine Ritter 代理丹維爾的 City Street Motors 公司販售中古車，並說明販售中古車的相關條件，由此可推論 Blaine Ritter 在汽車經銷商工作，所以答案是 (A)。

字彙 dealership n. 經銷商　law office 法律事務所
vehicle part 車輛零件

182 Not/True 題型
根據表單來看，賣方沒有提供哪一個東西？
(A) 保險表格
(B) 檢驗結果
(C) 鑰匙組
(D) 支付證明書

解析 這是針對關鍵詞 the seller ~ provide 詢問的 Not/True 題型，在談到賣方提供之物品的第一篇短文中確認相關內容。(A) 是短文沒有談到的內容，因此答案是 (A)。「The seller will provide two keys for the car and recent automobile inspection records ~, along with an official receipt for the sale of the automobile.」中談到將會把汽車銷售正式收據、兩把車鑰匙、近期檢驗紀錄給買方，(B)、(C)、(D) 和短文內容相符。
換句話說
an official receipt for the sale of the automobile 汽車販售正式收據 → Proof of payment 支付證明書

字彙 proof n. 證明（書）

183 Not/True 題型
關於 Huang 女士目前的車有何描述？
(A) 必須噴漆。
(B) 需要新零件。
(C) 無法修理。
(D) 太小。

解析 這是詢問關鍵詞 Ms. Huang's current vehicle 的 Not/True 題型，因此必須從 Huang 女士的信件中確認相關內容。(A) 和 (B) 是短文中沒談論到的內容。(C)「My old car cannot be repaired」中談到 Huang 女士本來的車無法修理，因為和短文內容一致，所以答案是 (C)。(D) 是短文中沒談論到的內容。
換句話說
cannot be repaired 無法修理 → is unfixable 無法修理

字彙 component n. 零件、要素

184 5W1H 問題
Huang 女士對合約有何不滿？
(A) 名字的拼字錯誤。
(B) 遺漏簽名了。
(C) 日期不符。
(D) 價格不正確。

解析 這是詢問 Huang 女士說合約中出現什麼（What）問題的 5W1H 問題，在與關鍵句 problem ~ Ms. Huang have with the contract 相關的電子郵件中確認相關內容。第二篇短文的「we agreed to meet on November 6. But the contract says that the sale date is November 5.」談到 Huang 女士和賣方約在 11 月 6 日見面，但契約上卻寫販售日期是 11 月 5 日，因此答案是 (C)。

字彙 misspell v. 拼字錯誤　incorrect adj. 不符合、不正確的
inaccurate adj. 不正確的、有錯誤的

185 推論題
Huang 女士 11 月 6 日要去銀行最可能的原因是什麼？
(A) 為了去拿支票
(B) 為了去匯款
(C) 為了領錢
(D) 為了申請信用卡

解析 問題關鍵句 Ms. Huang visit a bank on November 6 中詢問 Huang 女士為什麼 11 月 6 日要去銀行，因此要先確認 Huang 女士寫的電子郵件。
線索 1 第二篇短文「I will stop by the bank on the way to City Street Motors so that I'll be prepared to make the payment when I arrive.」和「I look forward to meeting with you on November 6」中談到 Huang 女士為了在 11 月 6 日抵達時能付款，在前往 City Street Motors 公司的途中會先去一趟銀行，不過，Huang 女士沒有談到使用何種方法支付，所以要從表單中確認相關內容。
線索 2 從第一篇短文的「Payment Method: ■ Cash」中可確認 Huang 女士是使用現金支付款項。
綜合兩個線索來看，可知道 Huang 女士之所以 11 月 6 日要去銀行是為了領現金，所以答案是 (C)。

字彙 pick up 接　wire transfer 匯款　withdraw v. 提取
apply for 申請

問題 186-190，請參考以下網頁、電子郵件和訊息。

首頁	建築物	住宅設計	預約拜訪

在 Fairview Estates 發現夢想中的房子吧！

位於美麗的波特蘭的 Fairview Estates 目前正在營業中！

看看我們美麗的房產，186-B 點擊「預約拜訪」擬定造訪日程吧。

189 Fairview Estates 包含兩房、三房、四房的住宅，點擊上面的「住宅設計」觀看我們的樣品屋照片，每個住宅都有廚房、用餐空間、客廳、設有浴缸的兩個浴室。186-A 所有住宅都有室內車庫。189 兩房的住宅車庫可停一輛車，其他房型則有能容納兩臺車的車庫。而且 186-C 社區為了各位與各位家人的安全設置有 24 小時的保全人員。

186-D 每一戶都要繳一年 865 美元的管理費以維持該物業。

property n. 建築物、不動產、財產　discover v. 查出、發現
be open for business 營業中　arrange v. 建立日程
show home 樣品屋　come with 伴隨發生
full bathroom 完整的浴室　garage n. 車庫
complex n. 園區、綜合大樓　security guard 保全人員
loved one 親友　management fee 管理費
maintenance n. 維護、補修　ground n. 區域、地面

收件人：Fairview Estates 公司管理事務
　　　　<inquiries@fairviewest.com>
寄件人：Mona Sawyer <monasawyer@genmail.com>
主旨：拜訪預約
日期：3 月 2 日

187 我收到一份新工作邀約，因此我必須搬離芝加哥現在的家，我的房子剛完成買賣，所以我正在考慮購買新房子，我將於 3 月 8 日抵達，有興趣看看您的物業並參觀樣品房。188 我先生和我有兩個孩子，需要三個房間，但也請帶我們看四房物件，因為我們正考慮把多出來的房間改為家居辦公室。因為我們必須趕快找到房子，希望您能盡速回信。只要回信到這個電子信箱或傳訊息到 555-2833 就行了。

Mona Sawyer 敬上

position n. 工作　look to 希望

寄件人：Andrew Kraft (555-5121)
收件人：Mona Sawyer (555-2833)

時間：3 月 10 日下午 2 點 10 分

關於明天的見面，我想告訴您幾個細節，我想和您約上午 10 點在管理室見面。187 因為您說上午 8 點要去一趟會計事務所，我認為這個時間您應該會很方便，完成文件作業後，我會把您 189 四房新屋的鑰匙和安全密碼給您，190 請一定要把銀行貸款合約也帶來好嗎？謝謝。

administrative office 管理室　go through 經由、檢討
paperwork n. 文件作業　code n. 暗號
loan agreement 貸款合約

---

186 Not/True 題型

關於 Fairview Estates 哪一個是錯誤的？
(A) 每一戶都有停車的室內空間。
(B) 客人可預約看房。
(C) 社區只有晚上會有警衛。
(D) 要求房客支付管理費。

解析　這是針對關鍵詞 Fairview Estates 詢問的 Not/True 題型，因此要從談論到 Fairview Estates 的第一篇短文中確認相關內容。(A)「All homes have indoor garages.」中談到所有住宅都有室內車庫，因此和短文內容相符。(B)「arrange for a tour by clicking on "BOOK VISIT"」中談到點擊「拜訪預約」安排行程，和短文內容一致。(C)「the complex has a 24-hour security guard available」中談到大樓 24 小時都有保全，此一選項和短文內容不符，所以答案是 (C)。(D)「An annual management fee of $865 per home is charged for the maintenance of the grounds.」中談到每一戶每年都要繳 865 美元的管理費維持物業，和短文內容相符。

換句話說
Garages 車庫 → spaces for parking 停車的空間
arrange for a tour 安排造訪日程 → make reservations to view homes 預約看房子
management fee ~ per home is charged 每一戶要支付管理費 → requires tenants to pay for the cost of maintenance 要求房客要支付管理費

字彙　tenant n. 房客　protect v. 守護、保護
cost of maintenance 管理費

187 5W1H 問題

Sawyer 女士為什麼要搬家？
(A) 因為家族人口變多，現在的房子不適合。
(B) 最近獲得會計領域的工作。
(C) 丈夫需要更大的家居辦公室。
(D) 她為芝加哥的房子支付過多的錢。

解析　這是在詢問 Sawyer 女士為什麼（Why）要搬家的 5W1H 問題，因此要從 Sawyer 女士的電子郵件中確認相關內容。
線索 1 第二篇短文「I have been offered a new position and I have to move from my current place here in Chicago.」中談到 Sawyer 女士有新工作，因此必須搬離目前在芝加哥的家，不過文中沒有談到新工作的內容，所以要確認訊息內容。
線索 2 第三篇短文「you[Ms. Sawyer] mentioned you need to stop by your accounting office at 8 A.M.」中可知道 Sawyer 女士必須去一趟會計事務所。
綜合兩個線索來看，Sawyer 女士有新工作且必須去一趟會計事務所，由此可知她的新工作是會計領域，所以答案是 (B)。

字彙　relocate v. 搬動、移動　outgrow v. 因太大而不適合
residence n. 住宅　overpay v. 超額支付

188 5W1H 問題

Sawyer 女士為什麼想看四房樣品屋？
(A) 需要額外的停車空間。
(B) 考慮設置工作空間。
(C) 計劃邀請大批客人。

(D) 想要幫子女準備寬敞的遊戲空間。

解析 這是在詢問 Sawyer 女士為什麼（Why）想參觀四房型的 5W1H 問題，從關鍵詞 Ms. Sawyer 的信件中確認相關內容。在第二篇短文「please show us the four-bedroom unit as well because we are considering turning the extra bedroom into a home office」中談到 Sawyer 女士考慮把多的房間變成居家型辦公室，所以才會要求參觀四房樣品屋，所以答案是 (B)。

換句話說
turning ~ into a home office 變更為居家型辦公室 →
setting up a work space 設置工作空間

字彙 parking spot 停車空間　set up 籌備、建立
work space 工作空間

189 推論題
關於 Sawyer 女士選擇的房子，暗示了什麼？
(A) 包含可停放多輛車的車庫。
(B) 目前有房客在住。
(C) 位於社區的正門旁邊。
(D) 有一個小壁櫥。

解析 先確認和問題關鍵詞 Ms. Sawyer's chosen home 相關的內容。
線索1 第三篇短文的「your[Ms. Sawyer] new four-bedroom home」中談到 Sawyer 女士的新房子有四個房間，但沒有談到關於房子的其他資訊，所以要確認不動產相關網頁中的內容。
線索2 在第一篇短文的「Fairview Estates includes two-, three-, and four-bedroom homes.」和「The two-bedroom units include a single-vehicle space, while the others have garages that can accommodate two cars.」當中談到四個寢室的房型有可容納兩臺車的車庫。
綜合兩個線索來看，可知道 Sawyer 女士選擇的四房房型有可停放多輛車的車庫，所以答案是 (A)。

字彙 multiple adj. 多個、多數的　situate v. 使處於
storage closet 壁櫥

190 5W1H 問題
Kraft 先生提出何種要求？
(A) 簽名的租賃契約。
(B) 初期保證金。
(C) 金融文件影本。
(D) 公寓出入密碼。

解析 這是在詢問 Kraft 先生提出什麼（What）要求的 5W1H 問題，因此要在問題關鍵詞 Kraft 先生寄出的訊息中確認相關內容。在第三篇短文「could you please make sure to bring a copy of your bank loan agreement with you?」中談到 Kraft 先生要求一定要把銀行貸款合約影本一起帶來，所以答案是 (C)。

換句話說
a copy of ~ bank loan agreement 銀行貸款合約影本 →
A financial document copy 金融文件影本

字彙 housing contract 租賃契約書　initial adj. 初期的
access n. 出入、存取；v. 進入

問題 191-195，請參考以下廣告、電子郵件和訂單。

[192] New Leaf 食品店：便宜的天然農產品！

維持少加工基改食品、無農藥的健康飲食或許是很困難的！閱讀標籤上的所有資訊需要花費大量的時間，調查哪些產品是天然的、哪些產品是有機的，則可能很枯燥乏味。好，既然 New Leaf 食品店已經來到金士頓，那個問題就成為過去式了。我們經營一間有全面服務的食品店，最大不同是保證店裡只有 [192] 販售天然有機產品，我們嚴格把關產品，各位可安心從我們商店購買的任何物品對自己和家人都很安全。[191] 請在 www.newleafgrocer.com 查詢每週特選產品與其他優惠！另外，星期一到星期五上午 8 點到下午 8 點，週末上午 11 點到下午 6 點請來 Victoria 街 694 號光臨我們的店吧！

produce n. 農產品　affordable adj.（價格）低廉的、適當的　diet n. 菜單、飲食　low in 少的　process v. 加工　genetically modified 基因改造的　free of 免於　pesticide n. 農藥　time-consuming adj. 耗時的　tedious adj. 枯燥的　full-service adj. 提供全面服務的　rest assured 確信是　special n. 特殊商品；adj. 特別的　offer n. 優惠、提供；v. 提供

收件人：Rob Dawson <robdawson@selectcereals.com>
寄件人：Ariana Septus <arianas@newleafgrocers.com>
主旨：訂購
日期：5 月 2 日
附加檔案：訂單

Dawson 先生，

[193] 在拉斯維加斯的 Eco-Food 博覽會期間，很高興能在貴公司的展位上見到您，您給我的 Select Cereals 公司產品的幾個樣品，我分給同事一起吃了，他們也都很喜歡。[192] 因為 Select Cereals 公司的食品符合 New Leaf 食品店販售之產品的所有標準，我們想讓顧客試試您的穀物，並進行第一次訂購。[194] 我們對附件訂單中要求最大數量的產品有意進行定期配送。往後的配送量都一樣，希望是每個月的最後一週送來，如果您的其他產品也受到顧客喜愛，那我們也有可能會定期訂購。

謝謝您抽出時間，如果需要其他資料請告知一聲。

Ariana Septus 敬啟

colleague n. 同事　test out 測試　place an order 訂購　regular adj. 定期的、定期性　be open to 對～開放

---

[194] SELECT CEREALS 公司
訂單

顧客姓名：Ariana Septus　　電話號碼：(613) 555-2039
[194-195] 公司：New Leaf 食品店　電子郵件：arianas@newleaf-gro cers.com
[195] 支付方法：公司支票　　配送地址：安大略省金士頓，Victoria 街 649 號

➡

194 產品	每一箱單價	194 箱子數量	總額
藍莓麥麩穀片	24.00 美元	2	48.00 美元
蜂蜜燕麥穀片	20.00 美元	3	60.00 美元
水果堅果玉米穀片	24.00 美元	2	48.00 美元
194 葡萄乾綜合穀片	22.00 美元	194 4	88.00 美元

小計：244.00 美元

營業稅：24.40 美元

配送與處理費用：56.00 美元

總訂購額：324.40 美元

＊每箱都裝有五盒穀物，可使用信用卡或銀行轉帳，195 雖然也能使用公司支票支付，必須等貴公司的銀行批准，金額存入我們的帳戶後訂單才會出貨。

contain v. 容納、包含　acceptable adj. 允許的
clear v. 承認　deposit v. 儲備　account n. 帳號

191 5W1H 問題

根據廣告來看，在商店的網站上可看到什麼？
(A) 前往商店的路線
(B) 假日休息的日程表
(C) 特殊促銷商品的細節
(D) 產品成分的目錄

解析　這是詢問在商店的網站上可確認什麼（What）的 5W1H 問題，在廣告中確認相關內容。第一篇短文的「Check out our weekly specials and other offers at www. newleafgrocers.com!」中談到去網站上確認商店的每週特殊商品與優惠，由此可知在商店的網站可確認特殊促銷商品的細節問題，所以答案是 (C)。

字彙　closure n. 停業、關閉　ingredient n. 成分、材料

192 推論題

關於 Select Cereals 有何暗示？
(A) 希望能擴大有機產品的多元性。
(B) 只有專門店有販售其食品。
(C) 每年都會參加拉斯維加斯食品博覽會。
(D) 產品使用天然食材製成。

解析　先確認與關鍵詞 Select Cereals 相關的電子郵件。
線索 1 在第二篇短文的「As food items from Select Cereals meet all the criteria for merchandise sold at New Leaf Grocers」當中談到 Select Cereals 公司的食品全都符合 New Leaf 食品店的食品販售標準，不過卻沒談到 New Leaf 食品店的販售標準，所以要在廣告中確認相關內容。
線索 2 在第一篇短文的「New Leaf Grocers」和「only natural, organic products are sold in our establishment」當中可確認 New Leaf 食品店只販售天然和有機的產品。
綜合兩個線索來看時，可知道 Select Cereals 公司的產品是使用天然的材料，所以答案是 (D)。

字彙　range n. 多樣性、範圍　specialty store 專門店

193 推論題

關於 Dawson 先生，提到了什麼？
(A) 在食品業活動中代表公司。
(B) 送了幾個產品的樣品給同事。
(C) 出差時填寫了購買訂單。
(D) 是 New Leaf 食品店的定期供應商。

解析　這是針對問題關鍵詞 Mr. Dawson 推論的題型，從寄給 Dawson 先生的信件中確認相關內容。在第二篇短文的「I very much enjoyed meeting with you at your company booth during the Eco-Food Fair in Las Vegas.」中談到他很高興在拉斯維加斯的 Eco-Food 博覽會期間能在 Dawson 先生公司的展位上遇見 Dawson 先生，可推論出 Dawson 先生代表公司參加食品業的活動，所以答案是 (A)。

字彙　represent v. 代表　mail v. 寄送；n. 郵件
fill out 填寫　supplier n. 供應商

194 5W1H 問題

Select Cereals 公司會定期配送什麼產品給 New Leaf 食品店？
(A) 藍莓麥麩穀片
(B) 蜂蜜燕麥穀片
(C) 水果堅果玉米穀片
(D) 葡萄乾綜合穀片

解析　問題是在詢問 Select Cereals 公司定期提供哪一種（Which）產品給 New Leaf 食品店，因此要先確認電子郵件中與定期配送相關的內容。
線索 1 第二篇短文的「We[New Leaf Grocers] are interested in regular delivery of the product we requested the greatest amount of on the attached order form.」當中談到「我們對附件訂單中要求最大數量的產品有意進行定期配送」，但因為沒提到最大量的產品是什麼，所以必須確認訂單內容。
線索 2 在第三篇短文的「SELECT CEREALS, Order Form」、「Company: New Leaf Grocers」和「ITEM, Multigrain Cereal with Raisins」、「QUANTITY OF CASES, 4」當中可知道 New Leaf 食品店從 Select Cereals 公司訂購最多的產品是葡萄乾綜合穀片。
綜合兩個線索來看時，由此可知 New Leaf 食品店會定期收到葡萄乾綜合穀片的配送，所以答案是 (D)。

195 推論題

根據訂單來看，關於 New Leaf 食品店可推定出什麼？
(A) 想要的玉米穀物比燕麥穀物更多。
(B) 使用電子郵件寄送收據給顧客。
(C) 下次的訂單不需要運送費。
(D) 款項處理完畢後才會寄出訂購物品。

解析　這是針對問題關鍵詞 New Leaf Grocers 推論的題目，在與 New Leaf 食品店相關的訂單中確認相關內容。第三篇短文的「Company: New Leaf Grocers」、「Payment method: Company Check」當中談到 New Leaf 食品店的支付方式是公司支票，「Payment by company check is also acceptable, but the order will not be shipped until the check has been cleared by your bank and the

money has been deposited in our account.」當中談到
「雖然也能使用公司支票支付，必須等對方銀行批准，
金額存入我們的帳戶後訂單才會出貨」，因此可推論出
必須等 New Leaf 食品店完成付款後訂單才會出貨，所
以答案是 (D)。

換句話說
order will not be shipped until the check has been cleared
~ and the money has been deposited 訂單要等支票獲得批准且
款項入帳後才會出貨 → order will be sent after a payment has
been processed 付款處理完畢後才會寄出貨品

字彙 oat n. 燕麥片　process v. 處理、加工；n. 過程

問題 196-200，請參考以下報導、電子郵件和信件。

政府有意實施減稅方案
Evan Proust 筆
1 月 3 日

196 幾名新南威爾斯州政府官員昨天舉行了會議，並提出新
的稅金優惠方案，他們說如果這項方案獲得批准，196 將能
讓住宅和生產工廠的所有人在太陽能板維修費用方面獲得
免稅優惠。不過，200 沒利用的太陽能板產出能源若被販
售，仍將會持續徵收 12% 的稅金。

197 此一方案在 1 月結束前交由環保局表決，如果獲得批
准，屋主與企業主可在環保局網站申請註冊。

---

incentive n. 優惠、獎勵　hold discussion 議論
propose v. 提議　exempt v. 免除；adj. 豁免的
residential adj. 居住的　solar panel 太陽能板
generate v. 生成、引起　enrollment n. 報名、記載

收件人：Patty Kindale
　　　　＜patkin@eastonmanufacturing.co.au＞
寄件人：Rich Ward
　　　　＜richward@eastonmanufacturing.co.au＞
主旨：新任務
日期：2 月 10 日

Patty，

我寫這封信是關於上週和您討論過的事情，197 我希望您
能就我們每一個使用太陽能板的廠房準備需要的文件，以
申請近期批准的稅金優惠計劃，申請所需要的必備條件會
因設施種類不同而不一樣，請在環保局的網站上再次確認
細節。我很清楚這工作可能很繁雜，但我們盡快註冊此一
方案真的是很重要的一件事，我已經請 Jerry Headley 和
Brianne O'Neil 也一起協助您進行準備。我希望所有申請
文件盡可能在星期五之前準備好，如果時間不夠充裕的
話，請告訴我比較合理的截止日。198 如果這項業務需要額
外的協助，我也會讓我的秘書 Vera Santos 協助。

謝謝。

Rich 敬啟

---

documentation n. 文件　property n. 建築物
double-check v. 複查　potentially adv. 可能地、潛在地
enroll in 註冊　preparation n. 準備、預備
simply adv. 絕對、簡單地　reasonable adj. 合理的、理性的
deadline n. 截止日、最終期限　assistant n. 秘書、助理

---

3 月 28 日

Rich Ward
會計部長
Easton Manufacturing 公司
2774 新南威爾斯州，Blaxland
Grahame 街 44 號

Ward 先生，

此一信函確認您申請政府新實施的太陽能稅收優惠方案已
獲得批准，自 4 月 1 日起，貴公司將獲得各製造設施稅金
優惠的資格。

不過，我們發現貴公司的廠房中有三個產出了由太陽能板
產生的多餘能源，貴公司一直以來都將此販售給在地企
業，此稅金優惠政策在這方面的規定並沒有變更，希望貴
公司能記得這一點。

感謝您參與此一方案，為新南威爾斯州的潔淨與安全的能
源生產有所貢獻。

Fred Dionne 敬上

環保局

---

verify v. 確認、證明　implement v. 執行；n. 工具
excess adj. 超過的　take part in 參加

---

196 5W1H 問題
根據報導指出，昨天官員們做了什麼事？
(A) 針對公家機關制定相關新方針。
(B) 駁回免除太陽能板相關稅金的提議。
(C) 提出為了社區購買太陽能板的協議。
(D) 討論有利於部分不動產所有人的計劃。

解析 這是詢問昨天官員做了什麼（What）事的 5W1H 問
題，因此要從報導中確認相關內容。第一篇短文的
「Several New South Wales government officials
held discussions yesterday and proposed a new tax
incentive program.」中談到幾名新南威爾斯州官員昨天
舉行了會議，並提出新的稅金優惠方案，「this program
will exempt residential building and manufacturing
facility owners from paying taxes on repair costs for
solar panels」則談到這項方案將能讓住宅與生產廠房
所有者在太陽能板維修費用方面可獲得免稅的優惠，由
此可知昨天部分官員在討論嘉惠部分不動產持有者的計
劃，所以答案是 (D)。

字彙 guideline n. 準則　government office 公家機關
reject v. 拒絕、排斥　deal n. 契約、交易、協定

197 推論題
關於稅金優惠方案有何描述？
(A) 1 月時經政府通過了。
(B) 只適用於私人企業。
(C) 吸引了國外製造商來到該地區。
(D) 明年開始可申請。

解析 先確認談論到問題關鍵詞 tax incentive program 的報
導。
線索 1 在第一篇短文的「The program[tax incentive

program] will be voted on by the department of environmental protection before the end of January. Should the program be approved, residence and business owners will be able to apply for enrollment」當中談到此一方案在 1 月結束前會由環保局表決，如果獲得批准，屋主與企業主可在環保局網站申請註冊，但沒談到專案是否已經獲得批准，所以要在電子郵件中確認相關內容。

線索2 第二篇短文的「I'd like you to prepare the documentation we need to apply for the recently approved tax incentive program」中可確認寄件人說想要申請近期批准的稅金優惠方案，必須準備相關的文件。

綜合兩個線索來看時，可知道稅金優惠方案已經在進行申請了，在 1 月結束前由環保局投票表決定案，因此答案是 (A)。

字彙 apply to 適用於　privately adv. 私下地、暗自地　attract v. 吸引

198 5W1H 問題

Ward 先生提出要為 Kindale 女士做什麼事？
(A) 提供專案需要的額外資金。
(B) 指派 Vera Santos 進行某項業務。
(C) 傳送有幫助的資料。
(D) 要求 Jerry Headley 檢查設施。

解析 這是詢問 Ward 先生向 Kindale 女士提出要為她做什麼（What）的 5W1H 問題，在 Ward 先生寫的電子郵件中確認相關內容。在第二篇短文的「And should you [Ms. Kindale] need extra help with this task, I can have my assistant Vera Santos help you out as well.」中談到 Kindale 女士如果需要其他協助，可以讓祕書 Vera Santos 幫忙，所以答案是 (B)。

字彙 assign v. 配定、任命　inspect v. 檢驗、調查

199 目的問題

為何會寫這封信？
(A) 為了告知研究結果
(B) 為了批准建設提案
(C) 為了確認有資格申請方案
(D) 為了核實收到了繳納稅金

解析 這是詢問寫信用意的題目，因此要確認信件的內容。第三篇短文的「This letter serves to verify that your company's applications for the government's newly implemented solar energy tax benefit program have been approved.」當中談到此一信函確認已批准貴公司申請政府新實施的太陽能稅收優惠方案，所以答案是 (C)。

字彙 confirm v. 確認、證實、肯定　eligibility n. 合適（性）、適任

200 推論題

關於 Easton Manufacturing 公司部分廠房，暗示了什麼？
(A) 可能會徵收 12% 的稅金。
(B) 比原先預期需要更多電
(C) 2 月 10 日降低產量了。

(D) 重啟營運前需要整修。

解析 先確認談到問題關鍵句 some of Easton Manufacturing's facilities 的信件。

線索1 在第三篇短文的「I did notice ~ that three of your [Easton Manufacturing] buildings have an excess amount of energy generated by solar panels, which you have been selling to local firms.」當中談到貴公司的廠房有三個產生了由太陽能板產出的多餘能源，且一直以來將其售予在地企業，「Please keep in mind that the tax incentive program's policy regarding this practise has not changed.」中談到稅金優惠政策在這方面的規定並沒有變更，希望貴公司能記得這一點，但沒談到沒有變更的規定是什麼，因此要從報導中確認相關內容。

線索2 在第一篇短文的「a 12-percent tax will continue to be charged for the sale of any unused energy generated by the panels」中可確認把沒使用的太陽能板產出能源拿去販售，將會持續徵收 12% 的稅金。

綜合兩個線索來看時，可知道 Easton Manufacturing 公司把超額生產的能源販售給當地的公司，因此販售未使用的能源會增收 12% 的稅金，所以答案是 (A)。

字彙 be in need of 很需要　electricity n. 電力、電子　anticipate v. 預料　cut back on 減少　renovation n. 裝修、翻新　resume v. 重啟　operation n. 運作、企業

線上學習資源

Test 1 模擬測驗音檔

Test 2 模擬測驗音檔

Test 3 模擬測驗音檔

Test 4 模擬測驗音檔

Test 5 模擬測驗音檔

單字記憶本 PDF + 音檔

聽力訓練筆記 PDF + 音檔

線上學習資源

不方便掃 QR Code？輸入網址也可以！

Test 1 模擬測驗

https://www.suncolor.com.tw/2024Toeic/index7.aspx?id=1

Test 2 模擬測驗

https://www.suncolor.com.tw/2024Toeic/index7.aspx?id=2

Test 3 模擬測驗

https://www.suncolor.com.tw/2024Toeic/index7.aspx?id=3

Test 4 模擬測驗

https://www.suncolor.com.tw/2024Toeic/index7.aspx?id=4

Test 5 模擬測驗

https://www.suncolor.com.tw/2024Toeic/index7.aspx?id=5

單字記憶本

https://www.suncolor.com.tw/2024Toeic/index7.aspx?id=6

聽力訓練筆記

https://www.suncolor.com.tw/2024Toeic/index7.aspx?id=7